Hugh Walpole

Vanessa

Pan Books
in association with Macmillan London

First published 1933 by Macmillan & Company Ltd
This edition published 1971 by Pan Books Ltd,
Cavaye Place, London SW10 9PG
in association with Macmillan London Ltd
4th printing 1978
This book is copyright in all countries which
are signatories to the Berne Convention
ISBN 0 330 02643 7
Printed and bound in Great Britain by
Cox & Wyman Ltd, London, Reading and Fakenham

Vanessa

Everyone said that Benjie was no good by any standards but his own.

At fifteen, Vanessa had Benjie in her blood. She would never betray him . . .

Rich and varied in its scope, with a crowded gallery of unforgettable men and women, this absorbing novel dovetails the lives of successive Herries generations from the triumph of Judith's hundredth birthday in the eighteen-seventies to the tragic disillusionment of the early nineteen-thirties.

Above everything this is a story rich in love and the understanding of love, told with a mastery only equalled by its descriptions of the wild Cumberland countryside where the past was never dead and the spirit of Rogue Herries lived on . . .

'A grand book – full of life, movement, colour and zest' OBSERVER

for Erik Palmstierna
in friendship

A Prefatory Letter

My dear Erik,

I take the greatest pleasure in dedicating this final novel in the Herries series to yourself because during those last years our friendship has been one of the best things I possess.

With that pleasure I must contrast a very real sense of loss. I am, as I write the last lines of *Vanessa*, saying goodbye to work that has been, for the last six years, my constant preoccupation. It cannot interest my readers that Judith, Benjie, Vanessa and the others have appeared to me such real and constant friends, but now, as they vanish down the wind, I feel a true and personal loneliness.

But I should like to thank those readers who have also found them friends, and to urge upon one or two critics that long novels are no new thing, and have been always in the tradition of the English novel.

Yet more boldly I would say that in this present case these four Herries novels are intended to be read as one novel, and I hope that some day there will be a reader who will both live long enough and be idle enough to read them so? But one ambition of mine is realized. Some of those who love and know Cumberland have found in these pages a tribute to that country which has pleased them.

Affectionately,
HUGH WALPOLE

'Therefore, like as May month flowereth and flour-isheth in many gardens, so in like wise let every man of worship flourish his heart in this world, first unto God, and next unto the joy of them that he promised his faith unto; for there was never worshipful man nor worshipful woman, but they loved one better than another: and worship in arms may never be foiled, but first reserve the honour to God, and secondly the quarrel must come of thy lady: and such love I call virtuous love.'

SIR THOMAS MALORY

Contents

Part One
THE RASCAL

Part Two
THE HUSBAND

Part Three
THE LOVER

Part Four
THE GHOST

The Herries Family in *Vanessa*

Judith Paris, *daughter of Rogue Herries*
Adam Paris, *her son*
Margaret, *his wife*
Vanessa, *Adam's daughter*
Sally, *Vanessa's daughter*
Sir Walter Herries, *son of Sir William Herries*
Elizabeth, *his daughter, widow of John Herries*
Benjamin, *her son, m.* Marion Halliday
Tom, *Benjamin's son*
Sir Ellis Herries, *son of Sir William, m.* Vanessa Paris
Lady Herries (Valerie), *his mother*
Dorothy Bellairs, *Jennifer's daughter*
Timothy, *her son, m.* Violet Greenacre
Timothy }
Violet } *Timothy's children*
Veronica *m.* Robert Forster }
Amabel } *Dorothy's daughters*
Jane }
Captain William Herries, *son of Ven Rodney Herries*
Dorothy, *his wife*
Dora, *his sister, m.* Fred Beauchamp
Cynthia, *Dora's daughter, m.* Hon Peile Worcester
Mary Worcester }
Rosalind Worcester } *Cynthia's children*
Garth Herries, *grandson of Pelham Herries*
Sylvia, *his wife*
Amery *his brother, m.* Hilda Coates
Alfred, *Amery's son, m.* Lucy Collison
Maurice }
Clara } *Alfred's children*
Carey Bligh, 5th Lord Rockage
Mary, *his wife*
Maud }
Helen } *their daughters*
Horace Newmark, *son of Phyllis and Stephen Newmark*
Sidney, *his son, m.* Mary Ratcliffe
Gordon }
Ada } *Sidney's children*
Phyllis Newmark, *Horace's sister, m.* Clarence Rochester
Philip Rochester, *her son*
Emily Newmark, *her sister*
Barnabas Newmark, *her brother*

Part One

The Rascal

THE HUNDREDTH BIRTHDAY

AT THE SIGHT of her son Judith's eyes and mouth broke into the loveliest smile that any member of the Herries family, there present, had ever seen. It was Judith Paris' hundredth birthday. The Family was making a Presentation.

Adam bent down and kissed her. Her tiny, trembling hand rested on the velvet collar of his coat then lay against his cheek. Her triumph was complete; her exceeding happiness overflowed so that, laughing though she was, tears rolled down her cheeks.

Afterwards, at the luncheon downstairs, Adam was to make the speech, but when the time came, the one that he made was very feeble. Everyone (except of course Adam's wife, Margaret, and Adam's young daughter, Vanessa) agreed that he was no speaker; the speech of the occasion came, oddly enough, from Amery Herries, of whom no one had expected very much. There were more speeches at the dinner later in the day – Timothy, Barney Newmark, Carey Rockage, Captain Will Herries, all spoke – but it was Amery who was afterwards recalled.

'Damned good speech, d'you remember?' years later one Herries would say to another. 'At old Madame's Hundredth Birthday party up in Cumberland ... Best speech ever I heard in my life.'

Adam was a failure. He never could say anything in public, even long ago in his Chartist days. More than that, he was thinking of his mother, the old lady upstairs, all the time. And more than that again, he couldn't sound the right Herries note. He was only *quarter* Herries anyway, and he simply wasn't able to think of them in the grand historical light that all the family, expectant round the luncheon table, desired.

But Amery could. He thought of them all (including himself) in precisely the grand manner.

All Adam said was:

'I am sure we are all very happy to be here today for my mother's hundredth birthday. You'll forgive me, I know, if I don't say very much. Not very good at expressing my feelings.

Yes – well – I know what you're all feeling. We're all very proud of my mother and we all ought to be. She's like the Queen – nothing can beat her. I don't need to tell you how good she is. Of course I know that better than the rest of you – naturally I would. There's no one like her anywhere. I ask you all to drink her health.'

And so they did – with the greatest enthusiasm. Nevertheless there was a feeling of disappointment, for he had said nothing about the Family – not a word. It was expected of him. After all, even though he *was* illegitimate, his father had been of Herries blood. They knew, they had always known, that Adam Paris failed at anything that he tried. What could you expect of a fellow who had once been a Chartist and approved of these Trades Unions, was always on the wrong side, against Disraeli, in favour of tiresome agitators like Mr Plimsoll? (They disliked any and every agitator. They disapproved of agitation.)

But Amery made everything right again with *his* speech. He didn't look his sixty-five years, so spare of figure and straight in the back; he had not run to seed like poor Garth, who led, it was feared, a most improvident and dissolute life. Amery's speech was short but entirely to the point:

'Only a word. I won't take more than a minute. But I do want to say that my friend Adam is quite right – this *is* a great occasion for all of us! There is not, I venture to say, another family in England with so remarkable a lady at the head of it as Madame whom we are gathered together to honour. It is not only that she has reached her hundredth year – although that is an achievement in itself – but that she has reached it with such vigour, such health, such courage! It is interesting to remember that nearly a hundred and fifty years ago her father, as a young man, rode pack-horse into this district, a stranger and almost you might say homeless. There were, I suppose, members of our family scattered about England at that time, but no one, I fear, had ever heard of any of them. Now, sitting round this table today we have one of England's most famous novelists – spare your blushes, Barney Newmark – the widow of one of England's most prominent financiers – I bow to you, Lady Herries – whose son is following worthily in his father's footsteps – I drink to the City, Ellis – the son of one of England's leading Divines, the gallant Captain here – one of the most active members, I'm told, of the House of Peers – never been there myself, but that's what they tell me, Carey, my son – and one of the loveliest women in the whole of England, Mrs Robert Forster — I bow towards you, Veronica!

'I promised that I would be short, so I will not point out to you how unusual a family ours is. You know it already.' (Loud and happily complacent laughter.) 'We *are* a remarkable family. Why should we not say so? We have done, we are doing something for England. England, glorious England, Mistress of the World as she deserves to be.' (He was going on to say something about foreigners but remembered just in time that Madame's husband had been a Frenchman and that Adam had married a German.) 'So here's to Madame and here's to England and here's to the Herries family! May they all three live, prosper, and help the world along the way that it should go!'

What cheers, what enthusiasm, what excitement! He had said exactly what they were all longing for someone to say — the one thing needed to make the day a perfect success!

Judith's granddaughter, Adam's daughter, little Vanessa Paris, aged fifteen, sat between her mother and father and was so happily excited that she found it difficult to keep still. Some of the ladies thought that it was not quite correct that she should be there. In 1874 the golden rule was that children should be seen (at intervals) and never heard. She was Madame's granddaughter and it was proper that she should have been present at the moving ceremony when the presentation was made to the old lady, but the right thing then was for her mother to send her back to Cat Bells where she lived. Nevertheless Lady Herries agreed with Emily Newmark that the child was tall for her age, was certainly pretty in her blue dress, and behaved with decorum. 'It's only to be hoped,' Lady Herries said with foreboding, 'that indulgence like this won't spoil her. But what can you expect? Her mother's a German. Adam Paris can have no idea of how to bring up a child. I never allowed,' Lady Herries added, 'Ellis any liberties, and no mother could wish for a more perfect son.'

Vanessa, of course, neither knew nor cared what anyone was saying. She trusted the whole world and everything and everyone in it. She loved everybody and especially her mother, her father, her grandmother, Aunt Jane Bellairs, Benjamin, Will Leathwaite (how she wished that he was here and could see all that was going on! She was storing everything up to tell him when she was home again).

From where she sat she could watch everything that Benjamin

did and said. For the rest she was sharply observant. She noticed the large and very hideous yellow brooch that Lady Herries wore on her meagre bosom, the beautiful colour of Aunt Elizabeth's hair (many of the ladies were her aunts, although not strictly so in chronology), the way that fat Garth Herries swallowed his wine and smacked his lips at intervals, the funny way that Aunt Jane (who had just come down from upstairs and reported that Madame was doing *splendidly* – not the *least* tired by all the fuss) made little pellets of her bread, Aunt Amabel's suspicious manner of eating as though she suspected poison in every mouthful, and the shy frightened air of Ellis. (She supposed that *that* was because his mother was watching him!)

Of them all there were two who especially interested her. One was Benjamin, whom she loved with all her heart, and the other was a lady whose name she did not know, whom she had never seen before, who appeared to her the perfection of grace and beauty.

First Benjamin, whom she knew so well that he was like part of herself. She had loved him from the first moment of seeing him when, himself between six and seven, and she somewhere about two, he had made her first sticky and afterward sick with toffee that he had made against orders at the kitchen fire. Her first memory of him was connected with disobedience; so she had known him ever after, always against the law, always doing things of which she shouldn't approve, but she kept sacred to the death every secret confided to her. She would never betray him; she would always love him for ever and ever. It was as simple as that. She knew with that intuitive quickness given to children that her mother did not approve of him. She knew more – that no one approved of him. He lived up at the Fortress with his mother, the lovely Elizabeth, and his grandfather, old brokendown Sir Walter, and it was supposed that Benjamin looked after the estate. In a way, as Vanessa knew, he did. In his own way. He would work like a saint and a hero for a week, really work and with good solid common sense. Then he would have a mad spell, disappear for days to the sorrow and grief of his mama. He told Vanessa that he simply couldn't help it. 'Must breathe fresh air,' he said. He never told anyone where he went. He was already, as Vanessa knew, 'suspect' by the Family. He had been a failure at Rugby: there were stories of scandalous doings in Town. 'He's going to be no good.' 'The makings of a fine Rascal,' and, as always with the Herries family when speaking of someone of whom they disapproved, their voices took on a sort of ceremonial ring, a kind of chanting sound. 'But what can you expect? His grandfather shot himself, and his uncle murdered his father. What an inheritance! And look at his other grandfather! – up at the Fortress – what a life he's led! Nothing better now than an idiot!'

No, poor Benjie has no chance at all, they decide with satisfaction. Nevertheless they could not help but like him – when they were with him. Of course it was different when their backs were turned. But in his company it was difficult not to smile. He was so merry, so gay, always laughing. So generous too. 'No one's enemy but his own,' Barney Newmark, who liked him greatly, said – and poor old Garth Herries, who had been no one's enemy but his own to such an extent that he was a complete wreck and ruin, sighed sadly in reply.

Vanessa was aware of much of this, although no one had ever told her. She was always hot in Benjie's defence, no matter what the charge might be. When someone accused him it was as though she herself were accused; she was conscious at such times of a strange pain in her heart – a feeling of tenderness, sympathy, and apprehension. Now, as she looked across the table at him, she knew that he had no need of her sympathy. He was at his very gayest. He was not large – he would be rather a small man – but his shoulders were broad, his head round, bullet-shaped, his colour red and brown like a healthy pippin, his nose snub, his blue eyes bright and sparkling. If all the Herries were like horses, as someone had said, then Benjie was like a racy little pony, ready for anything and especially mischief. 'He's wild and, I'm sure, wicked. In fact I *know* he's wicked,' Lady Herries said. 'And Ellis doesn't like him at all. But what can you expect with such a family history?' Then dropping her voice and looking into Emily Newmark's eyes with that intimate confidence felt by one upright woman for another: 'Women! Of course – I hear that already . . .'

Nevertheless he was happy, he loved his beautiful mother, he feared no man, he was generous, almost everything – even the tiniest things – gave him pleasure. What if he did find women enchanting, forgot to pay his debts, possessed no sense of class at all so that a tramp was exactly the same to him as a Herries, found it difficult to work at a thing for more than a week at a time, took no thought for the morrow, saw a joke in everything? – there he was, enjoying life to the uttermost, which was more than could be said for some of the other Herries seated round the table.

As to the very beautiful lady whom Vanessa so greatly admired, her name was Rose Ormerod.

After the luncheon Vanessa flung her arms round her father and kissed him.

'Happy, my darling?'

'Oh yes. Oh yes, I've never been so happy—'

'That's right. I didn't make much of a speech, did I, my pet?'

'Oh yes, Papa! It was much better than the other one because you were thinking of Grandmamma.'

'Thank you, darling. So I was. But I'm not good at speeches. That's a fact.' She laid her cheek against his. Then, remembering, straightened up.

'Papa, may I go for a walk with Benjie? He's asked me to.'

Adam hesitated. Then, taking her small white hand between his, he said:

'All right.'

He could trust her with Benjamin. And yet—

She clapped her hands and ran off, crying: 'Yes, Benjie, I can. Papa says I can.' She ran into Ellis Herries and looked up laughing. 'I beg your pardon.' She put her hand for a moment on his sleeve.

His thin anxious face looked down at her.

'My fault, I'm sure. It's – it's a nice day, isn't it?'

'Yes, it is.' She stood there, waiting, but longing to get off to Benjie. It was good manners, though, if a gentleman wished to talk to you, to wait while he did so.

Ellis Herries was tall, thin and pale. She noticed that he had a little brown mole in the middle of his left cheek.

'A very happy party we're having,' he said in his stiff anxious voice. He always spoke as though he were afraid that the words he used would betray him, laugh at him behind his back, as it were.

'Oh, it *is* nice!' She smiled, felt that she had done her duty, and ran off.

When they walked out on to the road they saw that they had but an hour before dark. Frost was sharpening the air. They mounted straight on to the moor and moved swiftly through a moth-grey world where mountains were gigantic and the turf was crisping under their feet. The house stood behind them like a lighted ship. The candles were burning in every room. Vanessa had sometimes to run to keep up with Benjamin, but in any case she ran because she was so happy, deeply excited and enchanted to be alone with him. Soon they slowed down, stood on a hillock and looked over to Scotland.

'There's Criffel,' he said, pointing.

'I can't see it,' Vanessa said.

'No, but it's there all the same.' He took her hand. 'I approve of you in that fine hat. Where did you find the feather?'

'Mama bought the hat in Keswick.'

He stood close to her.

'You are almost as tall as I am, Vanessa. You are going to be very tall.'

'Papa says I am. Will you never be taller, Benjie?'

'No, I hope not. You see, it's very useful to be short.'

'Useful?'

'Yes – if there's a row you can crawl under tables or hide behind a curtain or creep into the clock. I remember once in London—' He stopped.

Vanessa's innocence must be protected.

'Oh, do tell me about London!'

'One day, when you've been there. It wouldn't mean anything to you if you don't know the places.'

They walked on. They were both strong, sturdy, filled with health and excitement.

Benjamin flung out his arms.

'Don't you love this country? But of course you do. We belong to it. There'll never be any other country for either of us. Your father once told me that when he was a boy he had a tutor called Rackstraw who knew more about this country than anyone. He said it was all stones and clouds. One stone wall running up a hill, one sky with the clouds pouring over it, and you're happy. It's so old. There are Romans' bones under your foot. It's so strong – Border fights and Picts and Scots. It's so wide and smells so good. Don't you like the smell of dry bracken, of the trees, of the stream water when you lie flat and drink it? Which hill do you like best?'

'Cat Bells,' said Vanessa promptly.

'Oh, I mean a real hill. Skiddaw has wings, Saddleback's like a shark, Gable is a helmet . . .' He stopped suddenly, put his arms round her and kissed her. 'Oh, Vanessa, I do love you!'

'And I love you,' she said, a little breathless.

'Will you marry me when you grow up?'

'Of course I will,' she said, laughing.

They walked on, more slowly, he keeping his arm around her.

'Well, you'd better not. Everyone disapproves of me.'

'What does that matter?'

Her trust touched him most deeply.

'Would you marry me if your father and mother forbade it?'

That was an awful question. She stopped to consider it.

'Yes,' she said.

'Oh, you darling! But I won't allow you to marry me. Ask anyone. No woman ought to marry me. I couldn't be faithful.'

'You would be,' said Vanessa, 'if we had children.'

'Will you like to have children?' he asked her, wondering what she would say.

'Of course. But you can't help it. God brings you a baby. You wake up in the morning and find it lying there beside you. That must be wonderful. Mama says that God knows just when you want one.'

'So you believe in God?'

Vanessa laughed. 'Why, of course. What a silly question, Benjie! Everybody does.'

'Everybody doesn't—' He pulled up. He must not disturb her.

'Of course everyone does!' she answered indignantly. 'Why, who made everything if God didn't? God's everywhere. Will Leathwaite says that when he has been swearing too much God gives him the rheumatism just to remind him.'

Benjie thought some other topic wiser.

'Well – but if I was in disgrace with everyone, had done something shameful and no one would speak to me, would you still marry me?'

'Of course I would.'

'But if you yourself thought it shameful?'

'I shouldn't think anything *you* did shameful,' she answered.

'If I killed someone as my uncle killed my father?'

She stood, puzzled, staring into the grey cold landscape.

'Yes,' she said, nodding her head. 'I would know why you did it. There would be *some* reason that I should understand.'

He caught her hands in his.

'Will you promise me that whatever happens you will always stand by me?'

'Yes, I promise.'

'Always and for ever?'

'Yes.'

'Whatever I did?'

'Yes.'

'I'll remind you of that one day.' He turned round. 'Now we'll go back to all the cats and monkeys,' he said.

They were both quiet returning. They had to go arm in arm, very close together, because it was growing dark. For a brief while there was a faint orange glow over Skiddaw like the reflection of a distant fire; the air grew with every moment more frosty.

Once as they were nearing the house he said:

'Don't you hate Ellis? I do. *And* his old pig of a mother.'

In the hall, standing for a moment to accustom herself to the lights and splendour after the half-dark, Vanessa found her father. He had been standing there, waiting for her, hearing the voices and laughter all over the house, the distant click of billiard balls, someone singing to the piano sentimental songs like *Drink to me only* and *My hero, my Troubadour,* Elizabeth coming back from the Fortress where she had deposited poor old Walter, quite in pieces. She had put him to bed. He had fallen almost at once to sleep; all he had said, she told Adam, just before he went off to sleep, was: 'Wake me when Uhland comes in.' Very touching, but, as she said, a comfort for him to think that Uhland was still alive. Sometimes, Elizabeth confessed, she thought that he was and she could hear the tap-tap of his lame leg mounting to his tower ... Then along the passage from the kitchen came bursting Barney Newmark and Garth and Timothy, stout, noisy, and triumphant. Why triumphant? Had they been kissing the maids? But the Herries men got like that very easily if things were going well and there were no ghosts about.

In the middle of all this Adam waited anxiously for his little daughter. His wife, Margaret, was sitting in the parlour trying to be on terms with Lady Herries and that fascinating Rose Ormerod from Harrogate (she wasn't beautiful, Adam decided – not to be compared with Elizabeth or Veronica – her nose was a little crooked, she had a faint, a very faint moustache on her upper lip. It was her colour, dark, black, crimson, like a gipsy: and then she was silent – she spoke very rarely, only smiled and used her eyes). Poor Margaret would not be happy in there; he knew how anxious *she* was about Vanessa! When he told her that the child had gone for a walk with Benjamin she gave a little cry of dismay.

'Oh, Adam! You should not have allowed her!'

'Pooh, my dear! Benjamin's safe!'

'No, he isn't! You know he isn't! And Vanessa's growing!'

'She is only fifteen.'

He had calmed her a little, but his own fears had increased. What was he to do about this? He knew that Vanessa loved Benjamin with all the fire, loyalty, ignorance of an adoring child. Benjamin's reputation was bad, very bad. And yet he liked him. He could not help it. He had always had a weakness for sinners . . . But Benjamin and his own child! No, no!

As the darkness strengthened about the house his alarm grew. He was about to get his coat and go after them when in they came, Vanessa glowing with colour, her eyes shining, her body so alive that it could not keep still.

He told her that she was to come up and say goodnight to her grandmother.

'We must not stay for more than a moment. She is in bed and tired, of course, after such a fatiguing day. It's something to be a hundred, you know!'

Vanessa was at once subdued and still. She lived so entirely, at present, in her interest in other people that, in a moment, she became what they wanted her to be. That is if she loved them. She was quite otherwise, it is to be feared, with one or two – Aunt Amabel, for instance, whom she couldn't abide, and Timothy's fiancée, who had aggravated her by talking to her in baby language.

Judith's bedroom seemed now a mysterious place, quite different from the bright sunlit room of the morning, crowded with happy faces, and the old lady sitting so erect in her chair, smiling as they brought her their presents.

The curtains were drawn now, the room dark save for the fire and the dim lamplight beside the bed. That old four-poster with its dark hangings appeared like a little room in itself. Aunt Jane was moving softly about. When Adam and Vanessa appeared in the doorway she put her fingers to her lips.

She went over to the bed, leant over.

'Aunt Judith! Aunt Judith!'

'Yes, my dear,' said a very lively voice. 'What is it?'

'Adam and Vanessa are here to say goodnight.'

'Turn up the lamp.' Judith sat up, put out her hand for her

spectacles, and, her eyes as sharp behind them as a bird's, said: 'That's right. Very kind of you, Adam. Come over here, my dears.'

They crossed the room, and Jane put the crimson armchair for Adam. Vanessa stood close to him, her hand on his shoulder.

The old lady seemed a little breathless. She was wearing a cap as white as snow with the sun on it, and over her shoulders Jane laid a thick white cashmere shawl. Her little face was drawn and lined, waxen in the lamplight. It was her eyes and hands that were alive, and her enchanting, humorous, slightly ironical smile.

'So I'm a hundred at last!' she said with a sigh of satisfaction. 'That's something, Adam, isn't it?'

'Indeed it is, Mother.'

'Yes, and a *very* nice day it's been.'

'You're not tired?'

'Well – a little. Yes, a little tired. My heart' – she put her hand to her breast – 'jumps. There's nothing odd about that though. It's been jumping for a hundred years. It was never so steady as it ought to be.'

Vanessa smiled.

'Have you had a happy day, my darling?' She put her hand out and took Vanessa's. How hot and dry it was, Vanessa thought – burning bones under parchment, and at the touch of it the child had a moment's realization of what it was to be old, to be a hundred years old, to be burnt up with life and all the things that you had seen and done!

'It was nice,' Judith said, 'poor old Walter coming. Very nice. He's sadly broken up, I'm afraid. Sadly aged.' She spoke with tenderness, satisfaction, and triumph. She had beaten Walter at last. She was older than he and yet here she was as lively as you like and he a poor old man who had to be led about, weak in the head, uncertain where he was!

Yet she herself was suddenly weary. She lay back on her pillow, her spectacles falling to the edge of her nose.

'I hope everyone is happy,' she murmured.

'Very happy, Mother dearest,' Adam answered, catching a command from Jane's watchful eye. 'You must go to sleep now. You will be fresh as anything tomorrow.'

'Yes, dear,' Judith murmured.

Vanessa bent forward and kissed her. Then Adam, moved by

the deepest emotion, tears rising to his eyes, kissed her, felt her hand lift for a moment and touch his cheek in the old familiar way.

Before they had stolen from the room she was, it seemed, asleep.

The first Ball of Vanessa's life!

Was Ball too grand a word to give to it? There was for orchestra Mrs Blader from Troutbeck at the piano; Mr Murdy of Keswick, violin; old Mr Bayliss of Keswick, 'cello. There was perhaps in all thirty couples, and the dining-room, cleared, within the hour following dinner, miraculously of its table and chairs, had a perfect floor. It had often been tested. The room looked lovely, Vanessa thought, with the gleaming, glittering candelabra, the candles in their silver candlesticks, the coloured paper streamers slung from corner to corner against the ceiling. It was colours everywhere, dresses – pink, white, blue, orange – billowing and surging as the dancers moved, necks and shoulders bare, jewels sparkling; almost everyone to Vanessa seemed beautiful – even old Lady Herries, although she was absurdly painted and had a neck like a writhing chicken, had diamonds in her hair that must, Vanessa thought, be worth a fortune.

Three of the women were beautiful beyond compare – Elizabeth Herries who was fifty-nine years of age but had the arms and shoulders of a girl; and Veronica, now proudly Mrs Forster, 'a queen of a woman, by Gad,' Will Herries murmured somewhat unwisely to his wife, who was a good woman but no beauty. The third was Ruth Cards, who went shortly after this to live in the wilds of Northumberland and but seldom left them.

At first Vanessa had felt a devastating shyness. At dinner she had been very quiet. She was wearing her first grand evening dress and only she and her mother knew what consultations there had been with Miss Kew of Keswick, how often they had paid visits to Miss Kew's stuffy little room near St John's, how important it had been that it should be *half* grown-up – Miss Kew had been alarmed: girls of fifteen did not go to Balls, but then of course this was a family affair, a little different . . . nevertheless, as Miss Kew confided to her brother, Mrs Paris was a German woman – 'Such things might be well in Germany' just as though she had said Shanghai!

So they had planned between them something very original,

the neck and shoulders bare — 'Miss Vanessa has such beautiful shoulders' — the skirt full, but not *too* full. A pale pink silk and round her slender neck her only piece of jewellery, a necklace of crystal beads that her father had brought her from London.

At dinner she was certain that they must *all* be saying: 'And what is *this* child doing here?' All day she had been so happy that she had not given herself a thought, but at dinner Garth Herries had been on the one side of her and Ellis on the other.

Rose Ormerod was Garth's other companion and very quickly he surrendered to her as apparently all men did. He did not speak to Vanessa once. And Ellis! Well, Ellis was very strange. He stared at her in the oddest way. He spoke to her confusedly as though he were afraid of her. He said: 'I hope you are enjoying yourself,' and then later: 'I do hope, most sincerely, that you are enjoying yourself.' He made her embarrassed. It was he perhaps who made her self-conscious. He looked at her shoulders and hands, and once he said, in a strangled fashion as though food were choking him 'I hope you will give me a dance.' Very bravely she asked him once whether he liked to live in London. 'Oh yes, indeed yes. Very pleasant. Lived there all my life, you know.'

She coloured; she felt that it had been a very silly question; she looked about her to find her father, but he was sitting on the same side of the table as herself.

Then, at first, no one asked her to dance. She sat on a little sofa with her mother, feeling that everyone must be looking at her bare shoulders, not very far, if the truth must be known, from tears. It had been a lovely day, but she had no right to be here. She thought that, in a little while, she would whisper something to her mother and slip away to bed . . .

It was Benjie who came to her rescue. The most beautiful waltz had just begun and he charged down upon them, had her on her feet before she knew, and then they were lost in Paradise.

She was a lovely dancer. She had danced all her life, danced up and down the parlour at Cat Bells while her father whistled the tunes, danced by the Lake in Manesty, danced in the kitchen with Will, had had dancing lessons in Keswick at Mr Kew's (brother to Miss Kew) dancing class. She was a dancer by all the light of her nature.

'That child dances well,' said Lady Herries to Rose Ormerod. 'Very pretty.'

'That child will be a beautiful woman,' said Miss Ormerod. The two were passing them at the moment. Miss Ormerod's intense gaze followed them round the room. In a second of time Vanessa's misery had been changed to timeless, priceless delight. They did not speak. Benjamin also loved dancing. He knew at once whether his partner was worthy of him. Already many a young woman had found herself, after a round or two, sitting to her own surprise on the sofa, and Benjie beside her, charming but static.

'You dance better than anyone else in the room, Vanessa.'

'Oh, do I?' Vanessa whispered. 'Oh, Benjie, do I really?'

He did not tell her that he had said that to many a partner in the past. He knew that he would say it to thousands in the future. But tonight he meant every word of it. When the dance was over and they were sitting on the stairs he confided to him how unhappy she had been at dinner.

'You will often be unhappy again,' he instructed her. 'Everyone is so. Dinners are the devil. You never know whom you will get. It's a game, you see, Vanessa, and the worse ninny you have beside you the better the game is. Flatter them. That's the way. Everyone likes to be flattered. You can't put it on too thick. And do it as though you meant it. Then you'll discover you *do* mean it, for the moment anyway.'

'What do you flatter them about?' she asked.

'Oh, you'll soon discover their weak point. Everyone has them. Ask them first what they like best – games or travelling or adding up sums in a stuffy office as Ellis does. After that, all you've got to do is listen. Nobody wants you to do anything but listen, no men anyway. Women are different. They like you to tell them that they are beautiful or clever. And why shouldn't they? We all get enough of the other thing. Parties are meant to cheer you up and make you feel for a moment that all the things the people who know you best think about you aren't true.'

'Well,' said Vanessa, 'whatever happens now it won't matter. I've had one lovely dance.'

But she need not have been afraid. Soon Amery came to ask her, then Will Herries, then young Richard Cards, then Carey Rockage and, at last, Ellis.

She gave them all places on her flowery programme. She swung round the room in an ecstasy. 'Isn't this lovely?' she murmured to Amery.

Amery, who was anxious about his brother Garth, now rather drunk and quarrelsome in the parlour, answered at first absent-

mindedly, then realized that he was moving with a grace and
charm that he hadn't known for years. 'By Gad,' he thought, 'I'm
more of a dancer than I knew I was,' and wondered whether if he
had been more gay in his past and his brother less gay, it wouldn't
have been better for both of them! 'Poor Sylvia!' he thought,
seeing Garth's wife, painted, raddled, and weary as she bumped
round with Rockage, who was no dancer. 'She's had a rotten
life!' He was suddenly charitable to everyone. This charming
child, light as a fairy – by Jove, she was bewitching! Why had he
known nothing like this? He had married late, and it hadn't
lasted long. There had been others of course – Doris, whom he
had had to keep so long after he was tired of her, and Alice
Mason, who'd smashed all his china one night in a fit of temper,
and the Frenchwoman, Marguerite Calvin, whose father's debts
he had paid. Had he had much in return? No, not very much. As
he felt Vanessa's hand on his arm he sighed. What was the use?
He would be just the same tomorrow.

Vanessa, to her own great amusement, began at once to put
Benjie's advice into practice with all these gentlemen. It worked
like a miracle. Amery talked to her about money, horses, and the
Family. Will Herries talked to her about the Navy, the sea, the
West Indies, Glebeshire, dogs, Polchester, the sea, the Family.
Young Richard (whom she liked greatly) talked about books
(*Middlemarch*, Mrs Browning, Hawley Smart), gardening,
riding, and the Family, and Carey talked about the place in
Wiltshire, the weather, the weather, the weather, the place in
Wiltshire, and the Family. She found that they soon forgot that
they were talking to a child. She found that they all wanted
comforting, consoling, reassuring, and so learnt one very useful
never-to-be-forgotten lesson about Men. She discovered, too
that all of them, except young Richard, felt that in one way or
another an injustice had been done. They hadn't had fair treat-
ment. Someone was to blame. Carey Rockage in especial was like
a blinded bewildered animal whom unseen persecutors were
prodding with pitchforks.

'Oh, I *am* so sorry!' she found herself saying over and over
again.

And Ellis? Ellis was another matter. She had noticed that he
watched her. Often, feeling that someone's eye was upon her, she
saw that it was his. When their dance came it was 'Sir Roger',
and he asked her whether she would mind sitting with him instead. She *did* mind because she loved 'Sir Roger' and something

in her was afraid of a long talk with Ellis, but she followed him meekly out into the hall and to a top corner of the stairs.

Here the sounds of the music were very dim, the house was still, and she thought of her darling grandmother, not far away, deep in sleep. It was as though for a moment something drew her into that bedroom. She stood there, looking at the dim light by the bed.

'Are you asleep, Grandmamma?' she seemed to say.

'Yes, dear. I'm sleeping beautifully,' the answer came. She put her hand on Ellis' thin arm. 'Did you hear anything? Anyone call?'

'No,' he said.

There seemed to her a sound of light steps along the passage above them. Then she was compelled to give all her attention to Ellis. He forced her to do so. She did not know how old he was (he was in fact close on thirty-two), but he seemed to her both very old and very young.

He was unhappy, she was sure, and, like her grandmother, she could not bear that anyone should be unhappy. So, wanting to console him, she felt older than he. He was not exactly plain; he was distinguished in his thin, pale, quiet way; very serious; he scarcely ever smiled. But when he did his smile was rather beautiful. It lit up his thin face and his colourless eyes. It was as though he were pleading to be liked. He wants feeding up, she thought. His eyes were sometimes a little mad.

For a while he could do nothing but stammer out disconnected sentences. Then, following Benjie's advice, she asked him questions, about London, the City, theatres, and what he did in his spare time.

'I haven't any spare time,' he assured her. 'You see, my father had so many affairs in the City, and it all devolves upon me. I like it, you know. The City is a very agreeable place, it is indeed. Yes.' Then he said, staring at her with all his eyes: 'You must come one day, Cousin Vanessa, and stay with my mother and myself in Hill Street.'

'Thank you,' she said. 'I should love to go to London. I have never been to a theatre or a circus, and oh! how I should like to see the Queen!'

'The Queen is very much in retirement,' he said solemnly, as though he kept her in his pocket, 'but the Prince of Wales and the Princess are often to be seen driving.'

Then there was another awkward pause, until he broke out:

'I do hope you will come, Cousin Vanessa. Our house is not very gay, but if you came it would be—' He choked in his throat. 'Will you, please, not forget me? Will you think of me sometimes?'

'Of course I will think of you, Cousin Ellis,' she answered, laughing because she felt, for some strange reason, uncomfortable.

'Will you indeed? That will make me very happy . . . I have not many friends,' he added. 'My own fault of course. I am shy. You may not have guessed it, but I am very shy indeed.'

She certainly *had* guessed it – not only was he shy but he made others who were with him shy too. Then the music, to her relief, began again.

'Oh, we must go!' she cried, jumping up.

'You promise to think of me?' he asked again urgently. 'I shall think of you often – very often indeed.'

When she was with them all again she sat for a while among the ladies and was aware of something that she had never thought of before (she was making so many discoveries tonight!), namely, that this family to which she belonged contained the real benefactors of the human race. Dorothy Bellairs, Veronica, Emily Newmark, even Sylvia Herries – they were all the same! If it were not for them the Poor, the Unprotected, almost everyone in fact who wasn't Herries, would perish. Vanessa had a strange picture of all the cottage women of England seeing through their window the arrival in a carriage and pair of Dorothy, Veronica, Emily, Sylvia. These ladies were armed magnificently against the cold, their hands were in muffs, the high collars of their coats reached to their bonnets. Majestically they moved down the cottage path, John, James, William following behind with basket on arm. Then the cottage woman hastens, straightens her apron, puts the children in their places, arranges grandfather by the fire, hurries to the door.

'Good afternoon, my lady.'

'Oh, good afternoon, Mrs Cottage Woman. How are you this afternoon?' The seat of the chair is dusted, even the cottage clock, the cottage cat, the cottage table are deferential. Glory has descended upon the cottage woman!

Vanessa had never thought of this before. The life that they enjoyed at Cat Bells was so very different; she had never had on every side of her so many Herries women. She had never, never realized that were it not for the Ladies of England the Poorer

Classes would fade away. She had never known that there *were* any Poorer Classes.

Even Veronica! Beautiful, lovely Aunt Veronica!

'Oh, well, I told her ... that if she didn't drink the soup ... *would* give it to her worthless old father ...'

And Rockage's wife: 'They complained about the drains, but Carey explained to them ...'

She turned it all over in her mind while she was dancing with young Richard.

Afterwards, when they were talking, she asked him:

'Are you glad you're partly a Herries?'

'Glad?' he said, turning round and smiling.

'Yes. Is it better being a Herries than being a Jones or Smith?'

(While she spoke she thought: What *is* happening to me? I've never thought of these things before.)

'Well, don'tcherknow,' said Richard slowly, 'there *is* something fine in being one of the oldest families—'

'But *are* we one of the oldest? I mean, aren't the Jones and the Smiths just as old really?'

'I suppose they are. It's being English that counts.'

'Is it better to be English than German or French?'

Richard, who had no notion that Vanessa's mother was a German, answered with no hesitation at all:

'By Gad, yes – I should jolly well think it is.' So that settled it.

As the evening went on she was aware that she had seen but little of Benjamin. She went to look for him and found him in the billiard room dancing solemnly up and down with Barney Newmark, both of them swaying a little as they moved.

Vanessa – quite suddenly a child again – stood hesitating in the doorway, and Benjamin, looking up, saw two Vanessas, both lovely, both darlings, both the beloved of his heart. But he was never so much a gentleman as when he had drunk too much, so he disengaged himself from Barney and gave a courtly bow.

'Sit down, Vanessa, and I will fetch you some lemonade.'

She stood there, bitterly disappointed. She had often seen gentlemen who drank too much, but never Benjamin. She saw that his hair was ruffled, his eyes shining, and that he swayed on his feet, but she knew also that she loved him as dearly as ever, that her impulse was to go to him, smooth his hair, straighten his tie ...

'No, thank you,' she said.

He came up to her and took her hand. He saw that she was frightened.

'Come and we'll dance, Vanessa,' he said.

'I am afraid that this one is engaged,' she answered, looking over his shoulder at Barney Newmark, who was gently singing to himself. She hurried away, leaving Benjamin staring after her.

In the dining-room again she danced once more with Amery and soon she was happy. How could she help it? Everyone was so happy around her. The musicians played like mad, the candles shone like stars, the noise filled the room so that it was like a paper bag on the point of bursting. The waltz was a lovely tune. They began to sing to it. The 'Blue Danube'. Oh! the 'Blue Danube'! How lovely! One was not on earth but swinging, swaying in an azure heaven, limitless, lit with radiance. The wide, full dresses eddied and billowed, the naked shoulders and arms were gleaming, there was that gentle undertone of music rocking, rocking . . .

Wait! What's the matter? The music had stopped! With a surge the room has reasserted itself, the candles have lost their radiance, everyone is silent, standing looking . . .

Vanessa, near to the door, saw that Aunt Jane, white-faced, shaking, Rockage's arm around her, was speaking. Amery turned to the child.

'How sad! How tragic! Madame! . . . dead!' Then realizing that it was Vanessa: 'Your grandmother . . .'

The silence that followed was so strange. Life had fled from the house.

'Yes, in her sleep . . . Jane went up five minutes ago . . . Quite quietly . . . in her sleep . . . They have sent for Doctor Bettany.'

As they stared, conscious, every one of them, of the precariousness of this moment of existence, of the folly of their pretences of safety, thinking at the same time of the figure of the morning, so upright, so grand in her pleasure and happiness, all this only a moment ago, they themselves, perhaps, before the morning . . .

But she was A Hundred! She had reached her Hundred! Nothing could deprive her of that. A great age. Best of all to go quietly in your sleep . . . A wonderful woman!

But beyond the windows the snow has begun to fall. Are there figures there on the frosty road? Old Herries, with the scar on his cheek, upright on his horse as when, so many years ago, he had

ridden up to that same gate to tell his son that his wife had run
away; stout David, young again, riding on the wind to his beloved hills; Georges, waiting now for Judith who had been in
spite of his many infidelities, his only love; Charlie Watson waiting too, after so long an uncomplaining patience; poor Warren
with that one hour of happiness to remember – and for those
silent motionless watchers was there a sudden opening of the
gates, a running out of a little figure, happy, daring, triumphant,
a moment's stare up and down the road, and then a cry?

'Georges! Georges! ... Charlie! Warren! ... Father!'

Vanessa felt an arm around her as Adam drew her away with
him, murmuring:

'Don't cry, my darling. It was the happiest way. Quietly –
without any fuss – while we were all dancing.'

FOUNTAIN AT THE ROADSIDE

WALTER HERRIES died in April 1880.

For the last five years of his life he was unaware of all that was
happening in the world and perfectly happy. His daughter
Elizabeth nursed him with infinite kindness and care and he was
an infant in her hands. The Fortress, during those years, was a
very quiet place. Benjamin, Elizabeth's son, managed the estate,
which was not now large in extent – two farms and a cottage or
two in Lower Ireby were the full extent of it.

He managed it, that is to say, when he was there. For much of
that period he was away; he visited the East, was said to have left
his young mark on Shanghai and to have invaded the sanctities
of Indian temples, to have assisted pirates in the South Seas and
to have been knifed within an inch of his life in Sarawak: it was
whispered even that he had five Chinese wives, numberless
Asiatic concubines. He returned, however, looking very much as
he went – brown, stubby, solid, cheerful, and without a conscience.
'I care for nobody, no, not I, and nobody cares for me' was said,
by all his friends and relations, to be his daily song.

He did, however, care for his mother, and after his third
return in '79 swore that he would settle down and become the
Cumberland squire. He loved Cumberland with passion and he

had a good head on his shoulders, so that, for a while, he was successful. Everyone liked him; for a brief time it seemed that he might be the most popular man in Cumberland. But soon stories were everywhere. He could not, it appeared, see a woman without kissing her, could not tell the truth (was it possible that his acquaintances had no humour?), had no social sense at all, so that he invited farmers' wives to meet Mrs Osmaston and took a shepherd with him to supper at Uldale. He was also, it was said, an atheist and openly defended Bradlaugh. He visited London frequently and never returned thence without a scandal hanging to his tail. It was said that the lowest ground in that city was *his* ground, that he drank, gambled, spent a fortune over horses and cheeked his relations. How many of these stories came from Hill Street, from old Lady Herries and her son Ellis, who both hated him, no one could say, but certain it was that he was himself responsible for many of them because he never denied anything and never admitted anything, cherished no grudges, accused no one and told anyone who asked him that yes, it must be true if everyone said so; he had no morals, he supposed; he would like to have some; they must be useful things, but he simply didn't know where they were to be found.

On the other hand everyone was forced to admit that, as he grew older, he did not look dissipated. His colour was of the healthiest, his body of the toughest, his eyes bright and glowing. When he bathed in the Lake or a mountain stream in the summer with young Osmaston or Timothy Bellairs or Robert Forster it could be seen that his limbs were brown and supple as though he lived for ever in the open air. He was never drunk now as many of his neighbours were; smutty stories never appealed to him in the least, and if girls were the worse for his friendliness nobody knew of it for a fact. It was said that he walked vast distances over the hills and alone. Nobody ever saw him out of spirits or out of temper. He was generous to a fault. With all this nobody really knew him and nobody trusted him. 'He's a rascal,' said the Herries in London, in Bournemouth, in Harrogate, in Manchester, in Carlisle, 'and he'll come to no good.' In fact they longed, many of them, that he *should* come to no good as quickly as possible.

His only friends among his relations were Aunt Jane at Uldale, Adam Paris and his daughter Vanessa, Barney Newmark, and Rose Ormerod at Harrogate, who always said she'd marry him tomorrow if he asked her.

His one saving grace, they all said, was that he loved his mother – loved her, they added, quite selfishly because he left her whenever he pleased and for months she had not a line from him. It was not hard, they added, for him to love his mother, for she was the sweetest and gentlest of ladies and gave him everything that he wanted.

It was also added that he possessed that strange and mysterious quality known as 'charm' – which meant that when you were with him you could not help but like him and that, as soon as his back was turned, you wondered whether he had meant a word that he said.

He happened to be at home when his grandfather died. Walter was sleeping late on a spring afternoon, and his room was bathed in sunshine. Wrapped in a padded crimson dressing-gown, his long white hair falling over his face as he slept, he seemed a bundle of clothes topped by a wig. Then he looked up, blinked at the sunlight, called for his son Uhland, saw him come slowly tap-tapping with his stick across the floor to him, grinned joyfully at the long-expected sight, and died – or, if you prefer it, went from the room, leaning on his son's arm, happy as he had not been for many a day.

That night, when the old man had been decently laid out on the four-poster in the room upstairs, Elizabeth and her son sat in the little parlour off the hall and talked. The evening was very warm and a window was open. The trees faintly rustled; there came the occasional late fluting of a bird; the scent of early spring flowers, dim and cool with the night, hung about the room.

Benjamin sat opposite his mother, his legs stretched wide, and thought how beautiful she still was, how dearly he loved her, how selfish and restless he was, how quiet and unselfish was she! Elizabeth's beauty had always been shy, delicately coloured, fragile. She was a Herries only in her strength of will and a certain opposition to new ideas. She had never cared for ideas but always for persons – and then for very few persons. As she looked across at her son she thought: 'He is all that I have left. I know that he loves me and I know that I have no power over him.' Then she raised her hand ever so slightly as though she were touching someone who bent above her chair. John Herries, her husband, had been dead for more than twenty years to everyone but herself. It was not sentiment nor vague superstition nor longing that made her aware that he was always alive at her side. It was plain fact – and as it was her own concern, her own experience, it was of no importance that others should say that this was absurd, or weak, or against facts. She worried no one else about the matter, not even her son.

Benjamin loved her so dearly that evening, thought she looked so lovely in her full black dress, felt so intensely how lonely she would be, that he was ready to do anything for her – except sacrifice anything that threatened his liberty. Everything threatened his liberty.

'So your long service is over, Mother. How wonderful you were to him! Everyone marvelled at it. I'm terribly proud of you.'

She looked at him, smiled (and with perhaps a touch of affectionate irony):

'And now, Benjie, I suppose you'll go away again?'

'Oh no, Mother. Of course not! Leave you now!'

'Well, perhaps not just now – but soon. Jane is coming to stay later. And Vanessa. Vanessa is coming tomorrow for a week.'

He looked up sharply.

'Vanessa!'

'Yes. You didn't know that she was here this evening? It was quite by chance. She had ridden over to Uldale. She had stayed the night with the Grigsbys. She came up to ask how everyone was. I told her the news, and like the darling she is she said that she would come tomorrow. Adam is away at Kendal, so it suits very well.'

'Oh, I'm glad!' He drummed his heels into the carpet.

'You know, of course, that she loves you?'

'And I love her.'

Elizabeth smiled. 'You say that very easily, Benjie.'

'Well, you know how it is.' He got up and stood in front of the fireplace. 'We've loved one another all our lives. Whatever else happens she always comes first. There's no one in the world to put beside her. But she's too fine for me to marry her. You know she is. No one knows it better than you do.'

He came and sat at her feet, his hand resting on her knee.

'How too fine?'

'You know what everyone says of me; that I'm no good, that I spoil everything I touch – a rascal, a vagabond, all the rest. And it's true, I suppose. I'm no man to marry anyone.'

She stroked his hair gently.

'Is it true what they say?'

'You know me better than anyone else, Mother – or rather you and Vanessa do. I don't think about myself. I take myself as I am. But I know that I can't stick – to anyone or anything. It grows worse as I'm older. I want to do a thing – and I do it!'

'Is there any harm in that – if you don't do bad things?'

'But perhaps I do – things that you call bad. I can't tell. I don't think that I know the difference between right and wrong. Or rather my ideas of right and wrong are different from other people's. I'm too interested in everything to stop and think. I think when it's too late.'

He laughed and looked up into her face.

'I'm a bad lot – but I love you and Vanessa with all my heart.'

'Yes – but not enough to do things for us?'

'Anything you like. Tell me to fetch you something from Peking now and I'll go and get it. But I can't be tied, I can't be told what to do, I can't be preached at by anybody.'

'Perhaps,' Elizabeth said quietly, 'if you married Vanessa that would steady you.'

He shook his head vehemently.

'Vanessa is so good and so fine. She isn't strait-laced. She's wise and tolerant, but she's high-minded. She believes in God, you know, Mother.'

'And don't you?'

'You know that I don't. Not as she does. Not as she does. I may be wrong. I dare say I am. But I *must* be honest. I don't *see* things that way. I'm ignorant. I don't know any more than the next fellow and I want the next fellow to believe as he sees, but I must be allowed to see for myself. I can't *see* God anywhere. The things that people believe are fine for them but nonsense to me. To me as I am now. I've got all my life in front of me and everything to learn. God may be proved to me yet. I hope He will be.'

'Proved!' Elizabeth laid her cheek for a moment against his. 'God can't be proved, Benjie. He must be felt.'

'Yes, I suppose so. That may come to me one day. Meanwhile – a heathen and a vagabond can't marry Vanessa.'

She thought for a little and then said: 'Have you talked of these things to Vanessa?'

'No. I don't want to hurt her.'

'I don't think you would hurt her. She's very wise and very

tolerant. She doesn't want everyone's experience to be hers. Her father isn't religious in her way, but she understands him perfectly. So she may you.'

'Oh, she understands me, as much as she knows of me. But I know things about myself that I'd be ashamed for her to know. I'm not ashamed of *myself*, Mother. I'd like to be different – settled, noble, unselfish. Or would I? I can't tell. I'm not proud of myself, but I'm not *ashamed* of myself either. I'm simply what I am. All the same I don't see why I should burden someone else with the care of me. That at least I can do. Save others from troubling about me.'

'Yes,' said Elizabeth. 'But if someone loves you they want to trouble. They can't help but trouble.'

He flung his arms around her and kissed her.

'Funny I should be your son. The luck's all with me.'

Next day Vanessa came. She was now nearly twenty-one years of age. Her beauty had a quality of surprise in it. She was tall and slender. Her face was young for her age, much younger than her carriage, which was mature and controlled. She moved with such grace that you thought, as you watched her, that she was fully assured. Then when you saw her eyes and mouth, her perpetual gaiety, the sudden change of mood, the constant excitement, her stirred animation, you felt that life had not yet touched her. She was like her father in sweetness of expression but unlike him in her alertness, so that she seemed to miss nothing that went on around her. She was immensely kind, but could be sharp and irritated by slowness and stupidity and most of all by any pomposity or show of self-conceit. That is, except in the case of those whom she loved, when she simply could not criticize. For example, she loved Timothy Bellairs at Uldale and he *was* a trifle pompous.

Her hair was very dark but her colouring rather pale, unless she were excited by something. She blushed very easily, which exasperated her. When she moved she was like a queen, but often when she talked or joined with others in a game or a sport she was childish and impetuous. She was intensely loyal, obstinate, forgiving, so warm-hearted that her father often feared for her, but of late she had been learning many things about human nature. She was no fool where people were concerned.

Her mother had died in the autumn of '77 and since then she had lived with her father and Will on Cat Bells. They had been always devoted friends, she and her father, but now, after losing both his mother and his wife, Adam seemed to turn to Vanessa with an urgency that had something almost desperate about it. He remained always humorous, kindly, a little cynical, half in his fairy stories (he tried his hand at a number of things – books for boys, biographies of Nelson and Walter Raleigh, even two novels, but they were all fairy stories), half in the wild, loose, stormy Cumberland life that was in his blood and bones. Everyone liked him, nobody knew him. Many people laughed at him in an easy generous fashion. Vanessa alone understood him. She under-stood him because she had (although as yet she did not realize it) very much of her grandmother's character. Adam, of course, knew that. He saw his mother in his daughter again and again: her kindness, generosity, sudden flashes of temper and irritation and a constant exasperation at belonging to the Herries family.

'We don't belong, my dear,' he said one day.

'We belong enough,' she answered in a flash of prophetic per-ception, 'to have to fight them for the rest of our lives.'

Another thing. He knew that Vanessa loved Benjamin. It made Adam unhappy whenever he thought of it. He was himself fond of Benjie, but oh! he did not want him to marry Vanessa! Mar-garet's last words had been: 'Adam, you mustn't let Vanessa marry Benjamin', and he had answered: 'She must be free'.

But oh no! oh no! he did not want her to marry Benjamin! They never discussed it. That was their one silence.

Walter was buried in Ireby churchyard and, ironically, not far from the grave of Jennifer Herries, into which he once so long ago had terrified her. At the funeral, besides Elizabeth, Benjie, and Vanessa, there were Adam, Veronica and her husband, Tim-othy and his wife, and dear Aunt Jane. Also a few neighbours.

It was a cold windy day, one of those days when you realize how true it is that Cumberland is composed only of cloud and stone: lovely iridescent stone with green and rosy shadows but rising in pillars of smoke to meet the cloud, and the cloud coming down to settle like blocks and boulders of stone on the soil until, with the wind in your ears, you do not know which is stone and which is cloud. The little church tugged at the wind like a cloud striving to be free, and the clouds rolled in the sky as though some giant hurled rocks at his enemy.

They all stood, blown about, in the little churchyard, and poor old Walter, a capital example of the waste of energy that hatred involves, was dropped into the ground.

That same evening Vanessa and Elizabeth had a talk. Elizabeth had done all she could with the house. Her taste had never been aesthetic and she had dressed the cold bare bones of the place with heavy, very heavy, material. The big bleak rooms she had filled with large sofas, heavy carpets, big chairs, all in the manner of their period, which, if it was not a very beautiful manner, was comfortable.

She had crowds of things partly because everyone she knew did the same, partly because she hoped thus to escape the stoniness, the melancholy, the ghostliness of the place. She could not escape it. The rooms that were empty and shut up – the rooms in the two towers for instance – were heavy with ghosts. Not only she knew it. Everyone in the countryside knew it. Voices and steps were heard. Pale faces looked from behind windows, dogs barked, and parrots screeched. The Fortress, in fact, was not to surrender to a confusion of cornucopias, steel and brass fire-irons, japanned coal boxes, tables covered with beadwork, satin walnut chairs, and wax flowers under glass shades. Nevertheless in the few rooms that she herself inhabited her presence warmed and comforted. There were fires, Cumberland servants who adored her, flowers and books.

But Vanessa, in spite of the flowers, shivered. She had her father's taste, her grandmother's passion for order and arrangement. How, thought Vanessa, can Elizabeth, who is so beautiful, endure this hideous place? She did not realize that Elizabeth could endure anywhere so long as John, her husband, was with her.

Benjamin had gone that evening to see a farmer in Braithwaite. He would not be back until the following afternoon, so the two women had the house to themselves. They sat close together over a roaring fire and tried not to listen to the wind, which found the Fortress the happiest hunting ground it knew. Although Elizabeth was sixty-five and Vanessa only twenty-one they understood one another very well. They believed very much in the same things and they both loved the same man.

That evening, in fact, was a crisis for Vanessa, and in the course of it she set her feet resolutely along the path that was to lead her so very far.

'What are you going to do, Elizabeth, now?' Vanessa asked.

'Do, my dear? Why, go on as before.'

'Won't this house be very lonely for you?'

'I am used to it, you know. I'm an old woman now and like a quiet life.'

'Benjamin will be with you. That's one good thing.'

'Oh no, he won't!' Elizabeth smiled. 'He'll come and go as he's always done.'

'Oh, but he must,' Vanessa answered vigorously. 'He can't leave you all alone here. He has plenty to do, loves the country. He has wandered enough.'

'You know that he has not,' Elizabeth answered. 'He will never have wandered enough. He might settle down if you married him. Otherwise, never.'

She had spoken quietly but, as both women knew, it was a challenge of the deepest import.

There was a long silence, then Vanessa said slowly:

'Benjie has not asked me to marry him.'

'No. That is because he is afraid – afraid of himself. He loves you more than anyone in the world and does not want to make you unhappy.'

'Yes,' Vanessa said at last. 'He might make me unhappy, but I would not mind, I think.' After a pause she went on: 'You see, Elizabeth, I have Benjie in my blood. I have always had. I'm quite shameless about it – to myself, I mean. What is the use of being otherwise? I would rather be miserable with Benjie than happy with anyone else. And perhaps I should not be miserable. I understand him very well.'

She waited, but Elizabeth said nothing.

'We are very alike in some ways. I want my liberty quite as much as he does his. My great-grandmother was a gipsy, my great-grandfather a vagabond, my father illegitimate. And Benjie—' She broke off.

'Thinks he is a vagabond too,' Elizabeth went on, 'because of his father. You needn't fear, Vanessa darling, to talk about it. Here we are in the house that is filled with it. Sometimes I wake in my bed and hear the tap of Uhland's stick on the floor. I was impetuous, too, once, my dear. I ran away and married John. I had courage for anything in those days; but I know now that every impetuous step, every blow in anger, can mean tragedy for the next generation. There is no end to the consequences. They are never done.'

'Perhaps it isn't what we do,' said Vanessa, 'but something in ourselves. A strain that won't let us alone. You know, Elizabeth, that when I go over and stay with Veronica there's so much Herries stolidness and convention that I feel, I'm sure, just as Judith did when she ran away to Paris. That's where I understand Benjie. And sometimes when I'm with Timothy, although I'm very fond of him, I could whip him. I could really. He *won't* see things and is proud of not seeing them. He believes in Gladstone but has never heard of Rossetti.'

'Rossetti, dear?' asked Elizabeth.

'Yes – well, never mind. He writes poetry and paints.'

'Oh yes,' said Elizabeth. 'I'm sure I've heard the name—'

'I expect you have. But that doesn't matter. The point is that I would understand if Benjie wanted to go away by himself. I think it's silly of married people always to be together.'

'And then there's religion,' Elizabeth said. 'Benjie declares that he doesn't believe in God, foolish boy.'

'Many people say they don't believe in God,' Vanessa answered, speaking as though she were sixty and Elizabeth twenty. 'I don't think Father does, not as I do. But if you love someone those things settle themselves. I could never be as Timothy and Violet are, keeping the children in awe of them, never allowing them an idea of their own. Why, they have to come to the dining-room and bow, poor little things, after every meal! And Tim's only three, but I know he's going to be an artist. He's always drawing things. And when I spoke of it to his father the other day he was as shocked as if I'd said Tim was going to be an actor.'

'Well,' said Elizabeth, 'that wouldn't be a nice thing for little Tim to grow up into.'

'I don't know,' said Vanessa. 'There are the Bancrofts anyway. They have luncheon with the Prince of Wales.'

'Come here, dear, and give me a kiss,' Elizabeth said. 'I'd rather have you for a daughter than anyone in the world.'

Then came the last day of April, the day before Vanessa returned to Cat Bells. After dinner that night there was a large full moon. The air was warm and the moonlight filled all the garden with silver dust so that one seemed to walk on white powdery surf, now rising on a wave of quicksilver, then passing into an ebb of luminous grey. The hills were thin like silver tissue. Benjie, governed as ever by his mood, by the food that he had eaten, the wine that he had drunk, thinking Vanessa perfect in her dark dress that below the narrow waist broke out into bows and frills and trimmings, swearing that no neck and arms in all the world were so lovely as hers, seemed to see her as though this were for the first time, a new Vanessa to whom he had but just been introduced, so that under his breath he must murmur: 'This is the loveliest in all the world. All my life I have been waiting for this.'

At first she would not go out with him, as though something warned her. She stood by the fire, laughing, talking about anything, nothing. She had had a letter from Rose Ormerod, who was having a gay time in London.

'No, but you must listen to this, Benjie.'

'I don't want to listen. I don't like her. I can't think why she is your friend.'

'But she likes *you*! In this letter she says: "If you see Benjie give him my love, my *love*, mind." And she means it.'

'Oh, she gives everyone her love – far too many people.'

'She has been having a beautiful visit. Lady Herries gave a dinner party. Very sticky, she says. And she went to the Haymarket Theatre and saw *Money*. A silly old play, she says, but Marion Terry was lovely as Clara Douglas, and Mr Bancroft was Sir Frederick, and Mrs Bancroft, Lady Franklyn, and—'

'What *do* I care who they were? This is the last night of April. Tomorrow is the first of May. It is as warm as summer – silly to have a fire – and the moon is the largest—'

'Oh yes, and she went to Mr Alma-Tadema's studio to see the pictures he's sending to the Academy, and one is called "Fredegonda", and it shows an angry Queen looking out of a window at her husband—'

'Please, Vanessa.'

She looked at him and saw that he was unhappy. She nodded.

'All right. I'll come out.'

She went upstairs to fetch a shawl. Benjie, while he waited, wondered what he was going to do. This was the moment that for years he had determined to avoid. He must not marry Vanessa. He must not marry anyone. At the thought of marriage something within him warned him. But Vanessa – Vanessa ... He shivered. Outside in the garden it was warmer than in the firelit room. The house was always cold, do what you would with it. Vanessa – Vanessa ... Why had he been such a fool as to stay? He had an impulse to go round to the stable, fetch his horse, and ride off. Ride off anywhere – not seeing her again until she was safely married to someone else. But would that end it? All his life, however far away he had been, he had been tied to her, tied by her goodness, her beauty, her love for himself – and by all that was best in him. His best? A very poor thing. He had never thought so humbly of himself as at that moment when she came towards him, saying: 'I'm ready. How lovely the moonlight is!'

They walked into the garden arm in arm. Originally Walter Herries had planned a series of garden walks and a succession of little waterfalls, dropping stage after stage into a lily-covered pond. Now there were the sad ruins of these things, tangled shrubberies, little winding and melancholy paths, the doubtful splash of water and a weedy pool. Over the ruins the moon rode throwing its silver in a conceited largesse, penetrating the uttermost tangle of the trees.

'I have just finished a very amusing book,' said Vanessa, who felt as though the moon were scornfully wishing her a disastrous destiny, like the old witches her great-grandfather had known.

'What is it called?' asked Benjamin, wondering for how long he could resist to kiss Vanessa.

'*Travels with a Donkey.*'

'What a silly name!' The muscle on his arm suddenly jumped at the touch of Vanessa's hand. 'Who wrote it?'

'His name is Stevenson. I have never heard of him before, have you?'

'No. Never.'

'He writes well.' Vanessa almost whispered as they stepped into a pool of moonlight. 'Very precious, as though he'd licked every word on his tongue first before he stuck it down. Oh, look at the moon insulting Blencathra. There! Stand here! You can just see it between the trees.'

Benjie took her in his arms and kissed her with a ferocity that Ouida – a novel by whom Vanessa had recently been enjoying – describes somewhere 'as the lovely tiger's grandeur and the abandoned wildness of the jungle'. Benjie had never kissed Vanessa before save almost as a brother. This was the first time in her life that Vanessa had ever been passionately kissed. She found it entrancing. They stayed for a long while without moving. The shawl fell from Vanessa's shoulders, but she felt no cold. The pressure of Benjie's strong hand on her shoulder was surely the thing that since the day of her birth she had longed for. Her hand touched Benjie's hair as though he were her child. He kissed her eyes, which was another thing that no one had ever done to her before. They separated. He bent down and picked up her shawl.

'This is something,' he said breathlessly, 'that I have been longing to do for years. And now we'll talk if you don't mind.'

They walked hand in hand.

'I am going away tomorrow morning and will not see you again until someone has married you.'

'I can wait,' she answered confidently. 'I will marry you any time.'

'You are not like the modern maiden, are you, Vanessa? If their young man proposes to them they faint with astonishment although they have planned nothing else all their lives.'

'No. Why should I be astonished? I always knew that we would be married one day.'

'We are not going to be married,' Benjie answered, taking his hand from hers and walking by himself. 'I ought not to have kissed you. After tonight we shall not be alone together again until you are safe. I love you as truly as any man ever loved anyone, and that is why we are not going to be married.'

Vanessa laughed and took his hand again.

'I am not a child, Benjie. I know that you are afraid of marriage – and perhaps you would be right if it were anyone else, but we are different. We know one another so well. I shall never marry anyone else.'

'Now listen.' He put his arm around her and drew her close to him. 'You must not try to shake me, Vanessa. Really you must not. You say you know me, but it isn't true. You don't know me. Everyone is right about me. I'm no good by any standards but my own. I should make you terribly unhappy, and that I won't do. No, I will not. I will not. Other women – well, that's their affair. But you – you've got to have a wonderful life, be a queen, have everyone worship you, adore you, have splendid children, a husband whom everyone looks up to . . .'

She interrupted him, laughing.

'But I don't want that kind of husband! I don't want to be a Queen! I don't want to be admired. I want to be free quite as much as you do. You talk as though it were my ambition to be head of the Herries family, live in Hill Street and give parties like old Lady Herries. Of course I *enjoy* parties and it will be fun to go to London one day, but without you I don't want *anything*!'

'Oh Lord! How can I get you to understand? Don't you see, Vanessa, that I'm no good? Really no good. One day I'm this, another day I'm that. If I see a pretty woman I want to kiss her. If I want to gamble I gamble. I'm no sooner in a place than I want to go somewhere else. My mother and yourself are the only two people I love. I have hurt my mother many times already, but you I won't hurt—'

'But, Benjie,' she broke in, 'I don't think you *could* hurt me! I should understand whatever you did.'

'You don't know.' He spoke angrily, breaking again away from her. 'You don't know *anything* about life, Vanessa. You don't know the things I've done, the company I've kept. If I could say to you, "Vanessa, I've sown my wild oats and now I'm going to settle down, go to church on Sunday, read Tennyson with you in the evening—" '

'But, Benjie, how absurd you are! I don't *want* to read Tennyson, and if you don't wish to go to church you needn't! Father never goes to church. And as to the rest, what you have done is no business of mine. I'm sure I'm no saint myself. I know that Timothy and Violet think me often disgraceful and are afraid that I shall harm the children. Look at Grandmother! *She* wasn't a saint although she was one of the finest women who ever lived *and* one of the bravest. And her father! He's a kind of legend for lawlessness and roguery. I think we should suit one another very well. And as to the relations and all they say about you – what do they matter? A stuffy lot! That's what they are!'

He shook his head. 'That's not the point, Vanessa. You may say what you like, but you are good and I'm not – that is by all that anyone means by good. You talk of Judith's father. I expect he was a fine fellow. I often think of him and wish I'd known him. I like that man. I could have been his friend, I know. But the truth is he made everyone unhappy who trusted him. And so shall I. I can't help it. It's something inside me. And I won't make you unhappy. I love you too much. It would be the one sin for me. I don't care about the rest, but *that* I'll avoid, so help me God!'

They had walked down to the weeded pool which lay now, like a foolish white face, dirtied and soiled, at their feet.

Vanessa spoke, but more gravely because she was feeling that her whole future life was to depend on the next ten minutes. What did she see? The man as he was? Perhaps ... But herself in relation to all that he might be? She did not yet know life enough for that.

'Benjie, listen. I am not asking you against your will to marry me. I don't *wan't* you to marry me. We have been friends all our lives and we can go on as we are. But if you want to marry somebody, then it had better be me. I'm sure you will never meet anyone again who knows you so well.' She put her hand again in his. 'Do you remember that time – Grandmother's hundredth birthday – the day she died?'

'Yes, of course I remember.'

'We went for a walk, and I told you that I would never marry anyone but you and that I would wait as long as you liked. I was only a child then. I'm a woman now. But it is the same. It hasn't changed. I don't see how it can. No one can ever be to either of us what we are to one another. As to risks, life's made for them. I'm not afraid.'

She felt his hand tremble as it clutched hers.

'Listen, Vanessa. You *must* listen. If I don't make you understand now you never will. You say you are not afraid of life, but that is because you don't know. How can you? You have been sheltered always. Your father worships you as he ought to. Everyone loves you. You have never been treated unkindly, never had to put up with slights, never made an enemy. You hear people say: "Oh, Benjamin Herries, he's a bad lot, he's a rascal!" But they are only words. You've never seen me *do* the things, *say* the things that they mean. I am at my best – a poor best but still my best – when I'm with you because I love you and I'm not a bad fellow if I'm in a good temper, not bored, able to get away when I want to. We've seen one another at long intervals. We've loved to be together and they have been grand times because we were free. But to *live* with me – that's another thing. I'm no man's good company for long. I've got old Rogue Herries' devil in me, I think. Sometimes I fancy I'm the old Rogue himself come again. And if that's nonsense – and I'm sure I don't know what's nonsense and what isn't in this ridiculous world – at least I'm like him in that I'm my own worst enemy, can see what's right to do and never do it, curse my best friend and all the rest. Oh, mind you, I'm not pitying myself or even condemning myself. I'm not bad as men go. I enjoy every minute of the day unless I've got the toothache or lose money at cards or some woman won't look at me. And even those things are interesting. But I'm not the man for you. You're as far above me as that moon is above this silly-faced pond and, do me justice, I've always known it.'

He had spoken swiftly, the words pouring out, his face serious, mature, almost grim, as though he were resolving that this once in his life at least the honest truth should come from him.

'All that you have said, Benjie, I know,' Vanessa answered. 'I may be a fool as you say, protected from harm and all the rest. But Father has never treated me as a child. We've been companions for years and talked freely about everything. When I stay with Veronica and Robert Forster's drunk, as he is sometimes, I can see some of the things marriage can be. You may be nasty when you're drunk, but not half as nasty as Robert is. Of course I know that marriage isn't all fun. It isn't for anybody. Only I think that you and I would be often happy together if we were married because we know one another so well. We'd be unhappy too, but I don't always want to be happy. That would be dull. When we fought we'd know that we still loved one another. If you left me I'd know that you would come back.'

'No, I might not,' he said in a low voice. 'I might never come back. Loving you as much as I do now, I might still say: "No, I can't stand this". And I'd be off – and perhaps never return.'

'Oh, Benjie, would you?'

They were standing now by the gate that led into the road. The road stretched in front of them, and beyond it the country fell to the valley like a sheet of shadowed snow.

'Oh, would you?' She was thinking. She turned, as though she had resolved a problem, and looked up at him, smiling. 'Then I'd be a grass widow. They say that they have a glorious life.'

Both laughing, they walked out into the road and at once were encompassed by a field of dazzling stars above them, sparkling and dancing as though they knew that tomorrow was the first of May and the beginning of a new summer world.

'You know, Vanessa,' Benjie said, looking over to Skiddaw, 'that I have an odd fancy. It isn't really mine. Some old shepherd told me some tale once. There's Skiddaw Forest where – where my father died. Of course it's often in my thoughts. When you stand below Skiddaw House and look over to Skiddaw you can see sometimes, just before the hill rises, a dark patch that looks like the opening of a cave. It is only a trick of light. There's no cave there, but when I was a boy I often walked there and I used to fancy that it was the opening to a great subterranean hall, a gigantic place, you know, that ran right under the mountain. I told myself tales about it. I fancied that all the men who had loved this place returned there, had great feasts there, jolly splendid affairs, with singing and drinking, everything that was fine.

All of them grand comrades, whoever they were, farmers and shepherds, huntsmen, squires and parsons – any man to whom this piece of country is the best in the world. Perhaps on a night like this there they all are singing and laughing, happy as grigs – old Rogue Herries and my grandfather, my father and my uncle, John Peel and Wordsworth and Southey, little Hartley, "auld Will" Ritson of Wasdale, James Jackson of Whitehaven, Ewan Clark, John Rooke, thousands on thousands more – I used to fancy on a still day that I could hear them laughing and singing. A great hall, you know, Vanessa, where they could wrestle and run, ride their horses, shout their songs, tell their stories ... That's where I'd like to be, Vanessa. I could do without women there. I wouldn't want to roam the world. I'd need no other company—' He broke off. 'Yes, I'd want you, I think. Wherever I was, whatever I'd be doing.'

They turned up the road and stopped at a little water trough where from a rudely carved dolphin's head water trickled into a small basin. The thin drip of the water was the only sound.

'Why don't you say,' he murmured, ' "Benjie, you're a bad lot. We'll meet no more"? It would be better for you.'

'I can't say that,' she answered, leaning close to him, 'because I love you.'

The pause that followed marked both their lives. It had a sanctity, an intimacy that went beyond all their experience. They kissed again, but quietly now, gently meeting in complete oneness.

At last he said:

'Be kind to me, Vanessa. I've tried to do the best. Maybe I'll change. Mother said that loving you might do it for me. Give me a chance.'

He waited, then went on.

'My darling – let us be engaged, here and now, for two years. This is the last day of April 1880. In April 1882, I'll come to you and ask you if you are still of the same mind. If you are – if I can trust myself – we'll be married. If, before then, you think otherwise you shall tell me. And in the two years we will tell nobody, not a word to a soul. I shall be twenty-seven then, and if I'm no good at that age I shall never be any good. Give me that chance.'

Vanessa looked in front of her, then at last turned on him, smiling.

'Yes, if that's what you'd like, Benjie.'

'Not a word to anyone.'

She waited again.

'I have always told Father everything—'

'No. Even your father. I'm on probation. If he knew he might not understand.'

'Very well. Here's my hand on it.'

They held hands, looking one another in the eyes.

'It's a poor bargain for you,' he said. 'Mind, if ever you want to be free of me you have only to tell me—'

'I shall never want to be free,' Vanessa said proudly.

'All the men under Skiddaw heard you say that,' he answered. 'And they think me a poor lot for asking you.'

'Ah, they don't know you as I do,' she answered.

As they walked up to the house she held her head high, feeling the proudest woman in England.

And Benjie, for once in his life, was humble.

HERRIES DRAWING-ROOM

VANESSA paid the first visit of her life to London in the spring of 1882.

Old Lady Herries had, during the last two years, invited her repeatedly to stay in Hill Street, but the trouble had been that her father refused to go with her and Vanessa would not leave him.

Adam was obdurate and Vanessa was obdurate.

'No, my dear, I won't go. I hope never to see London again. I am sixty-six and entitled at last to my own way. London would upset me. I know I'm nothing at all, but London would make me feel less than nothing. I'm quite contented where I am. But of course you must go. It's time that they saw you and fell down before you. It's always been the custom that the family in London should see the Cumberland branch once and again and realize how superior it is. Your grandmother took me up when I was a boy and they all fell flat before her – so they shall before you.'

Vanessa refused. She did not want to go, she did not wish to see London, they would all think her an absurd country cousin and mock at her. With her father at her side she could mock back at them, but alone she would not dare to open her mouth. (None of these were, of course, real reasons. She longed to see London and she was afraid of no one.) He wished her to go because he was afraid that they were growing, as he described it, 'inside one another'.

For the last two years Vanessa had been strange. She was, it seemed, quite content to be alone with her father and, except for visits to Elizabeth at the Fortress and to Uldale, saw nobody. She seemed happy enough, but there were times when she appeared abstracted, lost, far away. Once or twice he wondered whether Benjie Herries had anything to do with this. Benjie had been out of England for most of the two years, deserting, everyone said, his mother most shamefully. Could it be that Vanessa still cared for him. Adam put the thought violently away from him. He had an affection for Benjie, but the fellow was a wanderer, a wastrel, would come, Adam very much feared, to no kind of good. And yet some wildness that there was in Adam attracted him to the man. He might have been, had things gone otherwise, just such himself. And Vanessa had some wildness in her too. Was it that that kept the men of the county away from her? No one doubted that she was better looking than any other girl in the North of England. And she was gentle with them, gave herself no airs. But she was alone. Save for her father, Elizabeth, and little Jane Bellairs at Uldale, she had no friends. Oh yes, and the children at Uldale – she adored *them*, especially young Tim.

But there it was: she had no friends of her own age, had no gaieties, did not appear to wish for any. It was not good for her. She must go to London.

And at last she yielded. He could not tell the reason. A letter came from Lady Herries. She looked across the table at Adam and said: 'Very well, Papa; I'll go.'

Then, when it was all arranged, he did not want her to go. He realized that he would be most damnably lonely. He was sure that, after this visit, she would never be the same again. She was still, in spite of her twenty-three years, very much of a child. She could be surprisingly naïve and impetuous. She seemed at one moment to judge human nature most wisely and then she would trust someone for no reason at all. She reminded him constantly of her grandmother in her simple directness to everyone, her lack of all affectation, her complete ignoring of class differences, her generosity and warmth both of heart and temper. But she was unlike Judith in that she had many reserves and no wish to dominate anybody. In those things she resembled himself. Oh, he would be all right, he supposed. There was plenty to do – his writing, his garden, the hills of which he never wearied; he was still, in spite of his sixty-six years, strong enough to walk over Stye Head into Eskdale and so to the sea, or over Watendlath to Grasmere. He had old Will Leathwaite for company. But he would miss her – miss her damnably. There was no one else he cared for now but Will. He was growing old. He continued to write – he could not help himself – but it was poor, secondary stuff. Not at all what he had meant once to do. Why, Dickens had told him once that he would be the equal of them all. But Dickens was warm-hearted, generous, with his variegated waistcoats and passion for theatricals. A great man: no one like him now. Him and Wordsworth, that arrogant but child-hearted little man whose genius seemed now to cover all the country like a soft sunny cloud, impregnating the air, calling the scent from the flowers, echoed in the birds' call. Dickens and Wordsworth – simple men both of them – while today these Merediths and Swinburnes and Rossettis ... He picked up the *Poems and Ballads* from the table, read a line or two, turned away with a sigh. Very clever. You could not call Wordsworth clever, thank God.

And so she went. It was arranged very easily, because Mrs Osmaston was travelling to London at the same time. Mrs Osmaston was a good serious woman who would bore Vanessa considerably. That would teach her, Adam thought quite fiercely, to leave her old father!

She went: and Adam discovered, not for the first time in his history, the tactful beauties in Will Leathwaite's character. Will had all the Cumbrian gift of showing his affection without mentioning it. He scolded and grumbled and protested as he had always done. In the evening they played backgammon together, and Will invariably won.

'You have the most damnable luck,' Adam swore at him.

'Aye,' said Will, 'I have. And I play nicely too.'

Four days after her departure Adam received a letter, the first that he had ever had from his dear daughter.

'My dearest Papa,' it began.

'A letter from my daughter,' he said to Will, who was sprawling against the doorpost, his hands in his pockets. He was fat now, red in the face and grizzled in the hair. It was in his eyes that you saw his youth, for their blue was as clear, gay, and sparkling as though they were fresh from their Maker.

'Aye,' he said. 'That's grand. Hope she's enjoying herself. Not too much, you know. She's better than anything London can give her.'

Adam, after glancing through, read Will her letter. Will never stirred. His eyes, shining, luminous, and in some fashion rather sardonic, were fixed on his friend – as though he said: 'Yes. She's spreading her wings. You'll find I'm the only stay-by. We're a pair of leftovers. And who cares?'

The letter was:

MY DEAREST PAPA – I don't know how to begin I've so much to tell you. The journey was very long of course, the carriage smelt of escaping gas and oh, it was cold the last part! My feet were frozen. We couldn't see to read but it would not have been so bad had Mrs Osmaston not chattered so! She is *so* contented, *so* fortunate, has so perfect a husband, such *lovely* children (you know little Mary and James Osmaston – not lovely at all!) but the worst is that she loves all the world. Her charity is too general to be personal. We are all God's children in a kind of celestial nursery. Well, I must get on. Here I am two days in Hill Street and I *must* say that I am enjoying it. I find them very kind. Do you know that Lady Herries is seventy-eight? She is immensely proud of it and all our relations are proud of it too. If you live long enough in our family you are always looked up to whatever you may be or do. It is when you are young that you must be careful. She paints of course prodigiously and wears the brightest colours. Bustles have come in again you know, and she likes a sash and a bow at the waist! But I must not mock for she is really kind and wants me to be happy. So does Ellis. He is grave and nervous. He is dreadfully afraid of doing the wrong thing. He is exceedingly wealthy everyone tells me and ought to be married. I am very sorry for him because he does not know how to be careless and happy. Rose Ormerod says that he is always his own Governess and that no sooner does he do a thing than the Governess tells him he should not. Hill Street is a kind of Temple for the family. They come here and worship the god of the clan – a three-faced god, one face Queen Victoria, one face Commerce, and one face the Herries features, high cheek-bones, noble foreheads, and a cold eye. They are very different though. Barney Newmark, old Amery and his son Alfred, Rose and her brother Horace, Emily Newmark. These are the principal ones who come to the house. Captain Will Herries and his wife are in town. Also the Rockages. I think they like me. I amuse them and perhaps shock them. I like Barney the best. He laughs at everyone. The house is very large and very cold, but of course you know it and I should imagine that it has not altered at all in thirty years. Very cold, full of noise from pipes and cisterns, masses of furniture, statues and little fires that burn up the chimney. There is the great Charles, too. Charles is the butler and he is so large that it is always warmer when he is in the room with one. He is very gracious and would be perfect if his eyes were not so glassy.

Just imagine! We have been to the theatre both nights! The first night was *Romeo and Juliet* with Mr Irving and Miss Ellen Terry. Shall I whisper to you, dear Papa, that I was a little disappointed? Mr Irving is better when he is not making love. In the balcony scene he stood behind such a ridiculous little tree that it was difficult not to laugh. When he makes love it is not the *real thing*. He has thought it all out beforehand. Miss Terry is *lovely*. Oh, how beautiful and charming! But she, too, acts better when she is *not* with Mr Irving. With the *Nurse* she is perfection. I liked Mr Terriss as Mercutio but the best of all is Mrs Stirling as the Nurse although propriety makes them cut out all her *best* lines. The scenery is almost too good to be true I think. You admire the moonlight when you ought to be *lost* with the lovers. At least that is what I felt.

Will you be very ashamed of me when I tell you that I enjoyed the second evening more? The piece was *The Manager* at the Court Theatre. This was Barney's party and I think Ellis was a little ashamed at *laughing* at a Farce. But he could not help himself. There is an actress in this piece called Lottie Venne who is *perfect* and Mr Clayton *splendid*! I laughed so much that Rose, who was with us, said Mr Clayton played twice as well as usual!

Of course I have not seen very much of London yet. Rose and I are to have a morning's shopping tomorrow. There is to be a grand party in Hill Street next week and Madame Trebelli of the Opera is to sing. I have ridden in a hansom-cab and found it very exciting.

And now I must go to bed. I have been writing this in my room and I am so cold that there is an icicle on the end of my nose! Do you miss me? I do hope so, but also I hope that you are not lonely. Give Will my love and the children at Uldale if you see them. If I *allow* myself I shall be homesick, but that will never do. Last night I dreamt that you and I walked to Robinson and met five sheep who turned into the five Miss Clewers from Troutbeck! Have you seen Elizabeth? Is her cold quite gone now? I am hoping there will be a letter from you tomorrow – Your very loving daughter,

VANESSA

'That's grand,' said Will and went off to his work.

No one could guess from Vanessa's letter, nor indeed from anything that she herself said or thought, that her arrival in London was the sensation of the year for her relations. Afterwards, among them all, 1882 was remembered as the year 'when Vanessa first came to town'. And this for two reasons. One was the natural astonishment at her beauty, for which they were quite unprepared, although some of them recollected that 'she had been a damned pretty child at old Madame's Hundredth Birthday'.

By chance it happened that the fashion of the moment suited Vanessa: the dresses looped up behind, crossed with fringed draperies rather in the manner of the heavy window curtains of the time, the waists very narrow (and Vanessa had, all her life, a marvellous waist), the top portion of the costume following as closely as possible the lines of the corset, flaring out below the hips in frills and bows and trimmings. The violent colours just then popular also suited her dark hair and soft skin. The dress that she wore at her first Herries party, dark blue with an edging of scarlet, white lace frills at the throat and wrists, was long remembered. She arrived with only a dress or two and they of Keswick make, but Adam had insisted that she must 'dress like a peacock in London' and gave her money to do it with. They were the first grand costumes of her life, and Rose Ormerod saw to it that they were fine. Her beauty staggered them all, the more that she seemed to be perfectly unaware of it. And they saw immediately that here was a family asset.

This raw naïve girl from Cumberland might marry anybody. There was no limit to the possibilities. Old Amery said to his son Alfred (Amery had married late in life a parson's infant fresh from the schoolroom: she presented him with Alfred in '62 and incontinently died) after his first sight of Vanessa in the Hill Street drawing-room: 'That girl will be a Duchess – bet you a "monkey".' These possibilities gave her at once a great importance in their eyes – one more factor in the rise of Herries power!

And here that queer old Lady Herries, known familiarly as 'the witch of Hill Street', comes into the story. No one in London knew anything about that old woman save that she was useful as an entertainer and adored her son. When Will Herries had married her she had been a buxom, silly, empty-headed woman of no character and less common sense. She had given Will a son, and that was the only sensible thing she'd ever been known to do. But as Ellis grew to manhood her love for him created in her a kind of personality. People must always admire in this world any strong, undeviating, unfaltering devotion: for one thing it is rare, for another it appears unselfish although it may have all its roots in selfishness. This example was the more admired because Ellis was, most certainly, not everybody's money. Only was anybody's money, in fact, because he had himself such a profusion of that admirable commodity. They led, those two, in the Hill Street house, a life of extraordinary loneliness. In spite of the dinners, receptions, conversaziones, balls and theatre parties, they had no friends, nor did they communicate, so far as anyone could see, with one another. Old Lady Herries broke into frequent rages with her son and to these he listened with a grave and unaccommodating silence. Abroad she talked of him incessantly, his brilliance in the City, his nobility, his love for his fellow-men. At home she often told him he was stupid, ungrateful, and cold. Her extravagances grew with her age, her paint, gay colours, fantastic screams of laughter. She was a sight with her trimmings, fichus, shawls, her little hats perched high on her old head, her fingers covered with rings, bands and twists of hair, dyed, and interwoven with strands of ribbon and sprays of foliage. It remained, however, that she won respect because it was known that, selfish in everything else, clinging to life like a tigress, she would die for her son at any moment if the call came.

On the night of Vanessa's arrival, when the house was as silent as the moon, Ellis visited his mother in her bedroom. Sitting up in bed she looked the old, shrivelled, lonely, exhausted monkey that she really was. Ellis stood gravely beside her bed and said:

'Well, Mama, it is as I thought. Vanessa is the only woman whom I will ever marry.'

Lady Herries blinked her eyes. For eight years now, ever since the Hundredth Birthday in Cumberland, he had told her this. She did not care for Vanessa; she had thought Adam a country yokel, old Judith a mountebank. Moreover the girl's mother was a German. But if Ellis wanted anything he was to have it. God, she thought – she believed in a God made exactly in the image of herself – must be of the same opinion.

She could not deny that she had been struck by the girl's beauty. She had both the scorn and jealousy of beauty felt by many women who have fought life's battle without that great advantage. But this girl was exceptional. Raw, untrained, straight from the country: nevertheless with care and attention the girl could undoubtedly be turned into something. She had long made it a practice to refuse, at first, any request that Ellis might make of her, because she never lost hope that he might one day become more urgent in his prayers. She knew, in her heart, that this was one of the many hopes that would never be fulfilled.

So now she said: 'Nonsense. The girl's straight from a farm or a dairy or whatever it is. She's got no breeding.'

'She has perfect breeding,' Ellis said, and left her.

Next morning, considering the matter, she determined to make the girl devoted to her. Assuming, as do many old people, that she would live for ever, it was important that when Ellis married his wife they should continue to live in Hill Street. To lose Ellis was, of course, not to be thought of, but Vanessa might influence him. In her grinning, chattering way she did her best to be charming. It was not difficult to win Vanessa's affections if sincerity was there, and Lady Herries was, in this, sincere. Before three days were out the old woman felt that for the first time in her life someone cared for her. For the first time in her life she herself cared for someone other than her son. But truly everything was enchantment to Vanessa. She never saw London again as she saw it in those early days.

Everything about London was a miracle. The first morning she walked out she saw an old crossing-sweeper who stood at the corner of Berkleley Square and Charles Street dressed in an old faded scarlet hunting coat, given him, Barney told her, by Lord Cork, Master of the Buckhounds. That old man, with his broom, in his scarlet coat, seemed to her delighted eyes the very symbol of London, its incongruity, unexpected romance, humanity and pathos. There was an Indian crossing-sweeper, too, who stood with his broom outside the Naval and Military Club. There were the many Punch and Judy shows, the poor, dark, melancholy Italian sellers of cheap statuettes, and the old hurdy-gurdy man with his monkey.

Hyde Park was her chief delight. Lady Herries liked to drive in the afternoon, and so they paraded in a grand victoria, the old woman sitting with a back like a poker, gay as the rainbow, while Simon the coachman, in a multi-coloured livery, in figure like a sealion, drove, as though he were acting in a pageant, his magnificent horses.

But it was all like a pageant, the small phaetons with their high-stepping horses, the pony chaises conveying ladies of fashion, the victorias, the smart buggies driven by men about town, and the quiet-looking little broughams containing, it was supposed, all sorts of mysterious occupants!

This was a fine and warm April, and in the evening, between five and seven, everyone took the air in the Park. It was, it seemed, a world of infinite leisure where no one had anything to do but to see and be seen. On the other hand, there was nothing extravagant or forced in the display. No one, it appeared, wished to stagger anyone else. Everyone's position was too sure and certain. Rotten Row was, in fact, for more sophisticated eyes than Vanessa's, a superb affair.

In every way London was a magnificent show. The omnibuses alone gave it an air, for painted red, or royal blue, or green, they were always handsome and individual, with their strong horses and their swaggering, accomplished drivers who had, with the flick of their whips, the air of conjurers about to produce rabbits out of their greatcoats.

The horses indeed were wonderful, Vanessa thought, never needing the whip, the drivers' cheerful hiss all the encouragement they wanted. They were, she thought, both fiery and gentle, a glorious combination. The doors, the straw on the floor, these things were gone. The omnibuses were now the final word in the modern science of travel. But best of all were the hansom-cabs, the splendid horses driven by the most elegant cabmen who wore glossy hats and had flowers in their button-holes. On the first day that Barney took Vanessa down Piccadilly and Westminster in a hansom-cab, she sat, her hands clasped, her eyes shining, her smart little hat perched on her dark hair, Queen, it seemed to her, of all Fairyland.

Finally London then was a town of constant surprises. You never knew what at any moment would turn up. Every building had life and character of its own, little crooked houses next to big straight ones, sudden little streets – dark, twisted, and eccentric – leading to calm dignified squares, fantastic statues, glittering fountains, shops blazing with splendour, hostelries that had not altered for hundreds of years. Everywhere colour, leisure, and, in this first superficial view, light-hearted happiness.

In that first week she spent her days with Lady Herries (Ellis was in the City all day), Rose Ormerod, and her brother Horace. The power that Rose had over Vanessa from the beginning came from her jollity, her kindness, her humour, her warm-heartedness. Rose had also other qualities which appeared later in their friendship. Horace, her brother, had a job as secretary to some big benevolent society. He was rosy-cheeked, square-shouldered, spoke well of everyone, was the friend of all the world. He was a little naïve. He talked frankly about himself. He was modest.

'I'm nothing exceptional, you know, Vanessa. I don't suppose you think I am. What I say is – why not see the best in everyone? It's easy enough if you try. People have a hard enough time. Why shouldn't we all make it pleasant for one another? I must confess that I find life a good thing.'

He was very jolly, had a hearty laugh, seemed generous and genial to everyone. There was something faintly episcopal about him as though he were in training to be a bishop. Rose was sometimes a little sarcastic about her brother, but then she was sarcastic about everyone.

Vanessa was happy, but underneath this exciting London adventure one consuming thought possessed her. Where was Benjie?

This was April 1882. The time had come when Benjie would demand the conclusion to the vow that they had made by the water dolphin of Ireby. Perhaps because she had seen him so seldom in these two years the thought of him by now completely possessed her. If she had loved him two years ago it was by this time as though he were part of her very flesh. She was neither romantic nor sentimental in her idea of him. She saw him as he was just as she saw herself as she was. Would he come? Where was he? He had written to her, on some dozen occasions, little letters, from Burma, China, India, North America. In these he had not said much, and yet she knew that he needed her, that he was thinking of her as she of him. Would he come? London brought him nearer. When the first sharp excitement of her visit paled a little she began to look for him, in the Park, the streets, the theatre. Often she thought that she saw his small stocky figure, dark face, often fancied that she recognized the quick determined step with which he walked. Would he come, and, if

April passed without him, what would she do? Was he faithless, volatile, careless, as they all said of him? Could she trust that he was faithful at least to her? Would he, oh, would he come? She spoke of him, of course, to no one, not even to Rose.

And then, in the second week of her visit, she began to be embarrassed by Ellis. She liked Ellis. She understood him better than others did. Most of all she was sorry for him. She wanted, as she so often wanted with people, to make him happy. There was something about his spare, grave figure that touched her heart. He was so *alone*. He wanted, she was sure, to be jolly with every-one but did not know how to set about it. She saw in him some-times an eagerness as though he said: 'Now this time I shall be lucky and find touch.' But always his shyness, his fear of a rebuff, checked him. As Lady Herries became more confidential the old lady poured out to Vanessa the truth about Ellis as she saw it, his goodness, kindliness of heart, diffidence. 'He can't chatter away,' Lady Herries said indignantly, 'like Barney Newmark or Horace Ormerod; but he has ten times their brains.'

Vanessa supposed that he had. He must be very clever to remain so silent for so long.

As the days passed she had an odd impression that he was approaching her ever nearer and nearer. He was not in reality; he always sat at a distance from her and when he walked with her seemed deliberately to take care that he should not by accident touch her. And yet she was ever more and more conscious of his body, his high cheekbones, the pale skin pulled tightly over them, his sharp-pointed nose, very Herries, with nostrils open, slightly raw, sensitive; his thin mouth, his high shoulder blades, his spare slim hands, his long legs that seemed always so lonely and deso-late inside his over-official London clothes. He was very tall and walked as though he had a poker down his back. He was dis-tinguished certainly with his top hat, his shining black tie, collar and cuffs almost too starched and gleaming, his pale gloves, his neatly rolled umbrella with its gold top. People looked after him and wondered who he might be, just as once they had wondered about his father. His pale thin face peered out anxiously at the world over his high collar. When he spoke you felt that his words were important although they seldom were so. He had a nervous little cough and often he blinked with his eyes.

One fine spring day he took a holiday from the City and in the company of Horace and Rose and Vanessa walked in the Park.

Very soon Vanessa found herself sitting alone with him while Rose and Horace talked to friends. She was wearing her most beautiful frock, rose and white, the pleated and flounced skirt with tucked panniers over the hips, the bodice cut high in the neck, long and pointed at the waistline. The wide skirt, the modified bustle, the little hat with roses, the different shades of rose in the dress itself, all these things were remembered by her when many times afterwards she recalled that costume as one of the loveliest of her life and the one that she was wearing when Ellis first proposed marriage.

He plunged at once like a man flinging himself with the courage of despair into icy water.

'Vanessa, I must tell you. I can avoid it no longer. I love you with all my soul. Please – please – will you marry me?'

It was then, although his seat was apart from hers, that she felt as if the moment, which for days had been approaching, had arrived. He seemed to have flung his body on to hers; she felt his thin hands at her neck, his bony cheek against hers, she could feel his heart wildly, furiously beating. She looked and saw that he had not moved. He was sitting, staring in front of him at the carriages, the riders, the colours, the sun; his gloved hands were folded on the gold knob of his umbrella.

She wanted then, as never before in her life, to be kind.

'Ellis! Marry you! But I don't want to marry anybody!'

(That was untrue. She wanted, oh, how she wanted, to marry Benjie!)

He had recovered himself a little.

'I know that it must be a shock to you, dear Vanessa. I recognize that. I must give you time. But you must not think that it is any sudden idea of mine. I have had no other thought since I first saw you, years ago, in Cumberland. That time – we were downstairs at Uldale. From that moment I knew that only you of everyone in the world could be my wife.'

She laid her hand for a moment on his knee.

'I am proud that you should think of me like that,' she said slowly, 'but I'm afraid I can't. Ellis, I like you very much, but I don't want to be married – really I don't. I couldn't leave my father. It wouldn't be kind to him now he is all alone.'

(How stupid and stiff her words were! She wanted to be good to him, to say something that would take that wistful, forlorn look from his eyes.)

'Your father could come and live with us.'

'I'm afraid he could never live in London. He is miserable now if he is away from Cumberland.'

'If you could – if you could – love me a little, Vanessa. I would wait. I would be very patient. Perhaps you could love me a little—'

She must be honest.

'No. I don't love you, Ellis. Love is very rare, isn't it? I like you so much—'

'Well, then,' he caught her up eagerly, 'that will perhaps turn into love. If you stay with us a little while. My mother likes you so much. I have never known her like anyone so much before. I can be very patient. I will give you as much time as you like—'

'I am afraid time will not alter it,' she answered gently. 'Friendship and love are so different—'

But he did not seem to hear. He went on eagerly.

'I will give you everything you can want. There's nothing you can ask for that you shan't have. I will never interfere with you. Only let me love you and serve you. I am not a man who has many friends. You have noticed that perhaps. I have been always shy in company, but with you beside me I feel that I could do anything. You are so good, so beautiful—'

Now the little scene was becoming dreadful to her. His intensity, his earnestness shamed her as though she had been caught in some misconduct.

'Ellis, dear. Listen. I don't love you. I'm afraid I never shall. We would be both of us most unhappy. Let us be friends, better and better friends, and you will find someone who *will* love you, who will make you so very happy—'

Words that every lady has used to every disconsolate lover! She knew it. She had not conceived that she could be so stupid. But, it seemed, he had not heard her. Rose and Horace gaily approached them, Horace laughing, greeting all the world as a jolly brother.

'Never mind, Vanessa,' Ellis said quietly. 'I will ask you again. It is a shock, of course. I am afraid that I was very sudden.'

'We do apologize,' cried Rose. 'That was Colonel Norton. I haven't seen him for an age. We were only gone a minute.'

It seemed to Vanessa that they had been an hour away.

When, alone in her room that night, she was dressing for dinner, she most unexpectedly had a fit of crying. She did not often cry, although young ladies thought nothing of it. But now, sitting in front of the glass, twisting her hair into ringlets, she found that

the tears made ridiculous splashes on the pincushion, which was
fat and round like a large white toad with a bright pink eye. She
was crying, she discovered, because that Ellis should love her
made her want Benjie so terribly. Oh, if it had been Benjie who
had said those words in the Park! But it was not. It was Ellis.
Then she found that she was crying because she felt, for the first
time in her life, lonely and needed her father. She seemed to see
him in the glass facing her, his brown beard, his soft rather ironical, rather sleepy eyes, his broad shoulders, rough coat ... She
thought that tomorrow morning, as early as possible, she would
take the train to Cumberland ...

Her tears were quickly dried because she was, she saw in the
glass, so long and lanky. Now Rose might cry very prettily because she was slight and delicate in spite of her dark colour. But
Vanessa was too tall for tears. She stood up in her skirt, all
flounces and frills, raised her arms, threw up her head. Because
Ellis had proposed to her was no reason for tears!

Then she laughed. The day before she had paid a visit with
Rose to one of Rose's friends, a Mrs Pettinger. Mrs Pettinger's
husband was an artist, and their little house in Pimlico had shone
with the new aestheticism. The walls had Morris wallpapers,
everywhere there were Japanese fans, bamboo tables, lilies in tall
thin glasses, Japanese prints. Also two drawings by Mr Whistler
which, privately, Vanessa had thought very beautiful. Privately,
because Rose had confided to her that she found them absurd.

'Why, anyone could do that!' she said. 'I could. Just take your
pencil and draw a few lines up and down. You have to stand a
mile away to see what they're about.'

What made her laugh was the contrast between the room that
she was in now and Mrs Pettinger's house. It seemed sym-
bolically to be the contrast that she felt between her love for
Benjie and Ellis' proposal. Her large cold bedroom had not, she
supposed, been changed in detail for thirty years. Especially did
she notice, as though seeing them for the first time, two armchairs of light oak carved with floral decorations and upholstered
with dark-green velvet having a floral pattern. When you sat
down in one of them it clung to you as though asserting its
righteousness. Then the frame of Tonbridge-ware that contained
a picture of a little girl outside a church made in seaweed, the
Coalport toilet service, the dressing-table and mirror trimmed
with glazed linen and muslin, the mahogany bedstead, the
needlework bell-pulls. Yes, she thought, sitting down on the green

velvet armchair, there were two worlds, as her father had always told her. Sitting there, without moving, staring before her, thinking of her mother, her father, Benjie, all those whom she loved, she moved naturally, simply into another world that had been, all her life, as real to her as the plush chair on which she was sitting. There was no effort, no conscious act of the will. An inner life flowed like a strong stream beneath all external things. This life had its own history, its own progress, its own destiny. She never spoke of it nor tried to explain it. It needed no explanation. Sometimes the two lives met, the two streams flowed together, but whereas the external life had its checks, its alarms, its vanities, and empty disappointments, this inner life flowed steadily, was always there. Yes, two worlds in everything. How to connect them? The Saints, she supposed, were those who had learnt the answer, men and women in whose lives one life always interpenetrated the other. But she, Vanessa, was no saint. She could only, at certain moments, be conscious of an awareness, an illumination, that irradiated everything so that in that brilliant light both things and people had suddenly their proper values.

Sitting on her plush chair she had now such a moment . . .

In the days that followed, Ellis behaved to her exactly as he had always done. It was as though their little conversation in the Park had never been. She obtained increasingly from the Herries family both instruction and amusement. Old Amery greatly amused her with his intimate stories of high places, of the adventures, for example, of King William of the Netherlands, one of whose ladies broke all the crockery in his palace during one of her tempers, of some Italian prince in Paris who disguised himself as an organ-grinder for a whole month that he might station himself outside his lady-love's door, of young Lord So-and-so who, rejected by his mistress, put a large black band on his hat, went to his rooms, and committed suicide by cutting his wrist open with a razor, remembering first to place a slop pail by the chair that there might be no mess. Young Alfred amused her because he would tolerate anyone who promised to be notable. She liked Captain Will with his breezy manner of finding the sea the only possible place, and yet now he never went there. The Rockages were redolent of the country. Carey himself, although he was tidy enough, seemed to carry good Wiltshire mud on his boots, and little Lady Rockage walked as though she were ready to spring on to a horse's back at any moment. She soon knew

them all and liked them all with the single exception of Emily,
Barney's sister, who was pious but not charitable, prudish with
an unpleasant inquisitiveness, and a mischief-maker for the best
of motives.

She found them all most strangely alike in some basic way.
They had no pose, made no attempts to assert themselves, took
everything for granted. For them all, the Herries were the backbone of England, and England was the only country in the world
that mattered at all. It was Barney Newmark, however, who best
explained the family position to her, sitting beside her on the
occasion of the splendid Herries party in Hill Street when Mme
Trebelli sang and Signor Pesto played so enthusiastically the
violin.

Vanessa liked Barney best of them all. Rose, of course, excep-
ted. Barney was now fifty-two, stout, fresh-coloured, and care-
lessly dressed but not untidy. He looked a little Bohemian but not
very; you would not know that he was a writer, said Vanessa.
That was a period when writers *looked* like writers. He took life
very lightly, laughed at everyone and everything, but behind that
was, she thought, a disappointed man. He had published a dozen
novels and lived comfortably on the proceeds. She had read several of them. They were not very good and not very bad. They
were like the books of other authors. But he never spoke of his
novels, laughed scornfully when they were mentioned to him.
She felt, however, that he would like it very much if someone else
praised them. At their first meeting in London she said what she
could. At once he stopped her.

'Dear Vanessa. Thank you very much. And now we need never
mention them again, need we? No friends of mine can read my
novels. That is a sign of their friendship.' Very different, had she
but known it, from the man who once at a prize-fight had
clasped Mortimer Collins by the shoulder!

They sat now in a corner of the big drawing-room and
watched the splendid affair. The room was very crowded. It
looked for the first time alive, for the heavy furniture was gone
and, save for the palms, ferns and flowers packed into the corners,
round the piano, in front of the great marble fireplace, only
human beings filled it. The ladies wore their jewels, their shoulders gleamed under the gaslight, everyone was splendid, dignified,
assured and, it appeared, happy. Vanessa would never have had
courage to penetrate the throng, but almost at once she saw
Barney, who carried her off into a corner, saying: 'Now I shall be

the proudest man here for five minutes, before you are discovered, you know. Soon there will be so many proud men that you won't be able to breathe.'

She was very happy alone with him. She would like to stay thus throughout the evening.

'Tell me who everyone is, Barney dear,' she said.

He pointed out a few. 'That dignified cleric is the Bishop of London. That fine fellow there is Mr Bancroft.'

'And oh, who is that darling old man?'

That darling old man looked like a ship's captain. He had a grey beard, grey hair erect and curly through which he often ran his hands, a florid complexion, clear eyes. He was the finest man in the room.

'That is Mr Madox Brown,' said Barney.

'And that lovely lady?'

'That lovely lady is Mrs Samuel Maguire, and her husband gives her a diamond every morning with her coffee.'

'And that very dark man?'

'That is Isaac Lowenfeld, the financier. He once blacked gentlemen's shoes in Constantinople. Jews are coming in. The Prince of Wales likes them, and why should he not? I like them myself. They have the best hearts, the best brains and the staunchest religion in London.'

She noticed two young men with high white foreheads, long pale hair and a very languishing manner.

'And those?'

'Those are the aesthetes. They look at a lily for breakfast, worship china teacups and lisp in poetry. I don't like 'em myself. They are not my kind. But they have their uses.'

'Everyone is here then? Lady Herries will be pleased.'

'Yes, it is a success because soon the room will be so crowded that no one can move, so noisy that no one will hear anyone else, and so hot that several young ladies will faint.'

She soon found members of the Herries family here and there.

'There is Emily. How nice and healthy Captain Will looks! I think Alfred is over-dressed.'

'Yes, we are all here,' said Barney. 'A great satisfaction to all of us. A fine family. And yet we are not of the first rank. Oh, I don't mean in history. We are, I suppose, as old as any family in England. But we are not, and never shall be, like the Chichesters, the Medleys. Nor like the Beaminsters, the Cecils, the Howards.

Although in fact we *are* a kind of relation of the Howards. But we're not like the new democrats either, people like the Ruddards, the Denisons. All very poor kind of talk this, but it's important, the social history of England, partly because it's history, partly because in another fifty years' time there won't be any social history. There, do you see that little woman in black with that jade pendant – with the hard mouth and the small nose? That's the Duchess of Wrexe. That's her daughter, Adela Beaminster, with her. Well, she walks as though she owned the world, every scrap of it. Contrast her with Lady Herries. Oh, I know *she* isn't a Herries really, but she's acquired *all* the Herries characteristics. The wives of Herries men always do. That's what I mean. We are upper middle class. We belong in the country, small Squires, maiden ladies in places like Bournemouth and Harrogate, houses like Uldale for example. That's where *we* are. For the last hundred years we've been rising or seeming to. Will made a heap of money and Ellis is making more. Then there are the Rockages, a small pocket-nobility. But we are not first class in anything. We write – well, as I do. We are parsons and one of us becomes an Archdeacon. We make money in the City but can't *touch* Lowenfeld. We entertain, but when we bring off a party like this it's a kind of accident. Not that we see ourselves like that. We think there's nobody to touch us, but that's because we have no imagination. That's why we are of real importance in the country. If there's ever a revolution in England it's the Herries and others like them who will save us all. Even as we begin to die out the lower ranks take our places and become just like us. We are filled up from below, but we never *rise* any higher. We have our good points – we are not acquisitive, we are not greedy, we are kind if we are not attacked, generous even; we never lose our heads, we adore our country although we criticize it. We never have to speak foreign languages, we revel in our abominable climate, on the whole we are contented.'

'But?—' asked Vanessa.

'We have one great weakness. We are terrified of anything out of the normal. If we see it we fight and slay it. Unhappily there is a strain of the artist in our family. It breaks out again and again. Then we are shamed, disgraced, humiliated. We have never learnt how to assimilate it. That is why if we breed an artist he is always second-rate. The family is too strong for him. That is why we fight among ourselves and why some of us, if we are courageous enough not to come to terms, are so unhappy. Oh, you needn't look at me, my dear. I *have* come to terms. I couldn't fight it out. That is why I am what I am. I am always hoping that we shall breed an artist who, because he is forced to fight, becomes a *great* artist. Why have the English the finest poets in the world? Because the other members of the family have always done their best to kill them. Why was your grandmother so splendid? Because she never capitulated.'

'Father always says that she declared that she *did* capitulate,' said Vanessa.

'Capitulate? She? Think of her! Capitulate? Not she! If she were in this room tonight she'd blow out the Duchess of Wrexe like a farthing dip!'

'And have you altogether capitulated, Barney?'

'Yes, my dear. Entirely. I'm no good at all. But I tell you who *hasn't* capitulated. That's Benjie!'

At the unexpected sound of his name the lights blurred, the voices faded.

'No,' said Barney, 'but if he doesn't they'll drum him out of the field. You watch them. It will be a fight worth beholding!'

And now the room was crammed indeed. The roar of conversation, like the break of the tide on shingle with here a whisper, here a grating clatter of pebbles, here a resounding hiss, made private talk impossible, so Barney, pleased with his analysis of his relations, stood up and looked about him while Vanessa watched Mr Madox Brown roaring at the Bishop of London, and the lovely Mrs Williamson (who was reputed to bathe in milk every morning) listening kindly to one of the young aesthetes, who twisted and bent like a reed in a gale.

She caught fragments of conversation. 'I heard Trebelli at Sims Reeves' concert in February. No, he couldn't appear, so we had Trebelli and Santley instead. Oh, of course Trebelli's the best contralto in the world. But to tell you the honest truth I enjoyed better Santley's "Vicar of Bray" – irresistible. Quite irresistible . . .'

'Oh, but Bradlaugh! . . .'

'And then, my love, *what* do you think? She went to the pastrycook's round the corner and *herself* fetched a dozen cream buns in a paper bag . . .'

'Yes, but what *I* say is that they could keep Jumbo here perfectly well, doncherknow, if they wanted to – really wanted to. What I mean is, that Jumbo is important for the country, for the *Tourists*, doncherknow – something for them to go to the Zoo and look at. What I mean is, we all feel it *personally* . . .'

'Very *unkind* of *Punch*, I think. Poor Mr Irving – to print his picture and then quote "Romeo! Romeo! Wherefore are *thou* Romeo?" That's too personal in my opinion. All the same he is *not* the young, ardent lover . . .'

'Yes, but what Russell wants is to buy out the Irish landlords and present the holdings to the tenants! Simple! I should think so! If Gladstone would only say what he means . . .'

'And so, darling, Henry said to him, "That lady is intended evidently for a Chinese" – trying to be witty, poor man, and the large man with the teeth whom he'd *never* seen before said furiously, "And why, pray? That lady is my sister." And oh, wasn't Henry clever? He answered at once, "Why, because she has such exquisitely small feet." '

It was Vanessa's first London party, and, standing there, waiting before she should be drawn into the middle of it, she knew, as her grandmother had known on just such another occasion, that something in her responded to this with excitement and eagerness. It was as though, a vagabond and wanderer, peering in through a window at a splendid feast, she exclaimed to herself: 'I can do this as well as anyone. I know all the tricks.' She would never truly belong to it, but it was a part that she could play as well as anyone there. The personal drama had seized her. The drama of London, the Park with the brilliant sunlit figures, the old crossing-sweeper with the scarlet coat, Ellen Terry laughing into the wicked eyes of old Mrs Stirling, Mr Conway rebuking his errant daughter, Gladstone in his high collar thundering at the House, old Lady Herries fixing, with trembling hands, the jewels about her throat, the melancholy wail of the hurdy-gurdy two streets away, the Prince of Wales talking to Mr Lowenfeld, the 'greenery-yallery' young men yearning over a Japanese print, the carts packed with flowers arriving in the early morning at Covent Garden, Gambetta drinking his morning coffee in Paris, and that picturesque brigand Arabi ordering an execution in Egypt, an account that she had read only last week in a paper of a Professor who had invented 'little electric lamps of the Cat Bells garden, watching the thin spidery rain veil the Horace Ormerod's friendliness, and Rose's adventurousness, Barney's kindness, and, behind it all, sitting in the hut at the top of the Cat Bells garden, watching the thin spidery rain veil the Lake in webs of lawn while fragments of blue sky, as bright as speedwells, flashed and vanished and flashed again. Her mind was a jumble of this kind; at the back of the jumble was the deep unceasing preoccupation. Would Benjie come before the month was out? Would he keep his word? Was there nothing that could still this burning ceaseless preoccupation of hers? And, if he cared no longer for her, could she make her life without him? She could! She could! She was not so weak, so helpless! But her throat was dry at the thought! Her hand touched her breast to check the wild beating of her heart.

She was discovered. Rose and Horace discovered her. They led her into the throng and at once her own life was broken into little scattered fragments. She had no life. She was nothing but a laughing, smiling, murmuring adjunct to all the other laughs, smiles, murmurs.

She was introduced to Mr Madox Brown. They sat down together near the piano. At first he said nothing, pushing his strong brown hand through his curly hair, muttering a little, looking as though he wanted to escape. Then something happened. *She* did not know what it was. In actual fact it was his sudden realization of her beauty. He never saw her again, but many times after he would growl:

'One night at one of those damned musical parties I came on a girl ... you never saw anyone so lovely. Quite unconscious of it too.'

He became gentle and most friendly. He told her about his son. 'He died seven years ago. There never *was* anyone so talented. Only nineteen when he died. One day, when he was dying and I sitting at his bedside, he smiled and said I smelt of tobacco. I said, "All right. I'll not smoke again until you're better." I never *shall* smoke again. Never. Paint? Write? He could do anything. And sweet-natured. Oliver was the only genius I've known. No one else. Not *genius*. Genius is something from another world. Nothing to do with this shabby one.'

He asked her where she came from.

She told him, Cumberland.

'Oh yes, Wordsworth and all that.'

Looking at her he said:

'You have beautiful eyes. Forgive an old painter's impertinence, my dear. I always begin with the eyes, you know. Paint the eyes of the central figure first and that gives tone to the picture. I begin at the top left hand of the canvas and go straight down to the bottom. And what do *you* do?'

'I can't paint,' she answered, laughing. 'I can't do anything.'

'You don't need to,' he told her.

They could have become great friends had life arranged it.

Then she was alone with Rose, sitting behind a gigantic pessimistic palm. They were clearing the space about the piano. Trebelli was going to sing. What, she thought, was Rose's power over her? Why was she so fond of her? Rose was like a carnation, set deep in colour, slight, with a wine-dark air. Not beautiful, for her eyes were too large for her small face, her nose a little snub, and her mouth, Vanessa must confess, rather hard. Her eyes laughed, danced, sparkled, but her mouth was always a little cold, a little cruel. If you judged people by their eyes, then Rose was a dear sweet girl, but if by their mouth, then Rose was nothing of the kind. She said once to Vanessa:

'Horace and I are both completely hard and self-seeking!'

'Oh no!' protested Vanessa.

'Oh yes, we are! The only difference between us is that I look at myself in the glass and know *exactly* what I am. Horace looks greedily into other people's faces for his reflection and woe betide you if it isn't a pleasant one.' She added: 'We are both adventurers. We have scarcely a penny to our name. I'm the Becky Sharp in Thackeray's stupid novel except that I'm sometimes sentimental. After I've been sentimental I'm so angry with everyone that I could commit murder. I dare say I shall one day. Probably my husband. First I must get one. I'm twenty-seven, you know.'

She talked a great deal about herself, and this Vanessa found delightful, but Rose's real attraction for her was that she knew life so thoroughly. Girls who were Vanessa's contemporaries knew nothing about life at all. They were not supposed to know and, what was more, they really did not know. Most of them married without the slightest idea of what came next, with the simple result that, for the rest of their days, they were a little melancholy and looked at all men, except clergymen, with a faint distrust. The women on the other hand, like Rose, for whom life (including men) had no secrets, were like gipsies who pitch their caravans at their own risk. The female world looked on them with suspicion, and the male world frequently presumed further than slight acquaintance warranted.

Rose had by this time told Vanessa everything she knew, and Vanessa, because she possessed certain beliefs, fidelities and a strong sense of humour, was not at all shocked. She hoped nevertheless that Rose would be married soon. It would be wiser.

Rose, on her side, loved Vanessa. She might be herself a lost angel – and she was a great deal more lost than Vanessa realized – but she adored a good angel with a sense of humour. She admired passionately in Vanessa all the qualities that she did not herself possess. She was no fool about human nature. She knew quite well that even from her mercenary point of view the virtues pay better in the end than the vices.

So they sat together behind the pessimistic palm and talked about those present. Rose knew something about everyone. She knew just what to tell Vanessa, amusing things but not cruel ones. She kept her cruel ones for other audiences.

Then, touching Vanessa's hand, she said: 'There, I think, is the man I am going to marry.'

'Oh, where?' cried Vanessa. 'Rose, dear, do you mean it,'

'I *think* that I mean it. That man with the eyeglass, the pale whiskers, the beautiful figure.'

Vanessa looked. He was certainly very handsome.

'Oh, who is he?'

'He is Captain Fred Wycherley. He is in the Army and is very rich.'

'Oh, Rose dear, I am so glad! Has he proposed to you? Do you love him very much?'

'No, he has not proposed, but I think within the week he will. I don't love him, of course. It would never do for me to love my husband: it would give him too much power over me. But he is agreeable, amusing. I think we shall understand one another.'

Before they could say any more Trebelli began to sing. She had an extremely powerful voice and sang as though she were commanding a regiment. She was made, it appeared, of brass from head to foot.

After the singing everyone began to move about again and Vanessa was introduced to a number of people. Among them was a stout, round gentleman with fair hair and the face of a very good-natured pig, whose eyes beamed with kindliness. This, she discovered, was Lord John Beaminster, a son of the Duchess of Wrexe. He spoke in jerks, smiling upon her as though he had known her all her life.

'Very hot, these parties,' he said.

'Yes,' she said, copying Barney. 'The hotter they are the more successful they are.'

'Do you care for music?'

'Yes, sometimes.'

'That woman has deafened my eardrum. All the opera women shout. Do you like the opera?'

'I've never been in my life,' said Vanessa. 'I live in the country.'

'Oh, in the country, do you? Wouldn't want to live there. All right for a day or two. What part?'

'Up in Cumberland.'

'Doesn't it rain there?'

'Yes, when it wants to, but nobody minds the rain.'

'I do, unless I'm shooting or hunting, you know.' He smiled as though they had reached the most delightful intimacy. 'Oh, that damned feller's going to play the fiddle.'

It was then that as she looked beyond him towards the door, as though something had compelled her, the miracle of her whole life occurred. Beaminster was saying something to her. The violin began to wail. The shining shoulders of some woman at her side spread, as it appeared, into an infinite distance.

In the doorway, looking about him with a friendly grin, stood Benjie Herries.

She did not move. Beaminster, seeing a friend, said, with a bow: 'Excuse me one moment.'

Then Benjie seemed to drive, like a swimmer breasting the tide, straight towards her. She saw people greet him. She heard (for he was very near to her now) Will Herries exclaim:

'Hullo, Benjie! Where have you come from?'

She did not move until his hand was on her sleeve. She heard him say: 'Come out of this. Outside.'

She went with him down the room. In the passage above the stairs there was no one. From the room within, the violin went on and on like a voice speaking only for them.

She stood up against the wall, staring at him, feeling that at any moment she might cry, unable to speak because her heart beat so fiercely, hammering her body as though it must throw her down. But there was no need to speak, no time for it.

'You thought that I wasn't coming back. Didn't you? You thought that I had forgotten. Quick, Vanessa, tell me – do you love me? Do you love me as much as two years ago? Is there anyone else? If so, where is he? I'll kill him. Quick. Tell me. I have run all the way from Brindisi. If you knew how I've run! Tell me. Tell me. Do you love me? Are you going to marry me? Can I go in there now and tell them all? Quick. Don't waste a moment! Do you love me?'

'Benjie, wait! Of course I do. I thought you'd never come! I've been longing—'

But she did not finish her sentence. He kissed her, patting her shoulder, her arm, laying his cheek against hers. Then he caught her hand in his.

'Now come! At once! We must tell everyone! We mustn't lose a moment!'

He pulled her with him to the door. The voice of the violin came towards them, dancing over the crowd, the flowers, the palms.

Seated by the door was an old lady, blazing with diamonds, listening to the music through an ear-trumpet.

'Excuse me—' said Benjie.

'Hush! hush!' said everyone near the door. The violin rose into a thin, long, vibrating note. Then ceased.

The old lady, turning to a man beside her, said:

'And *now* it ought to be time for supper.' Then, looking up: 'Why, it's Benjamin Herries! I thought you were in China, young man.'

Benjie wrung her hand as though she were the friend of his heart.

'I was, Lady Mullion. I was – only yesterday. Let me introduce you to Miss Vanessa Paris. We are going to be married—'

'Going to be what?' she asked, her round red face ignorantly beaming.

He took the ear-trumpet, and, in a voice loud enough for all the world to hear, shouted: 'We are going to be married.'

'Oh, is that all?' said the old lady. 'I thought there'd been an accident. And now I do *hope* we are going down to supper.'

THE SEASHORE

TIMOTHY BELLAIRS took his wife and family that summer to an old house, Low Dene, in the village of Gosforth, which was situated ten miles from Wastwater and a little more than three miles from Seascale on the coast.

Young Tim, now aged five, had not lately been very well; one cold had followed the other. Sea air would do the children good, and he would have found some place *on* the sea had it not been for Mrs Bellairs, who disliked the sea and all its works. So a compromise was effected.

Low Dene was one of those large, rambling, untidy houses of which at that time the country offered many examples. They were especially suited to the large families that good English parents thought it proper to create. The house was in a hollow under the hill to the right of the village; fields ran to the edge of the big scrambling garden; there was a croquet lawn, a wood, shrubberies, a stream, everything that children desired. The place belonged to a retired Indian colonel whose children were now grown. He had gone with his wife and four daughters to Brighton, where he hoped to marry the daughters and recapture some of his own youth. It was one of those houses which here are furnished and there are not. The drawing-room, some of the bedrooms, were crowded with large and small impedimenta, so crowded that you could scarcely move without disabling a china figure, upsetting an Indian idol, or flinging a wool mat to the floor. On the other hand most of the passages, some of the bed-rooms, the bathroom, had no covering to the bare boards, the wind whistled through the thin faded wallpapers, the piano was altogether out of tune, every fireplace smoked, the gas hissed, the cistern groaned, there was an odd smell of dog in every room, and draughts played in every corner. In spite of these things the house had an air of cosiness and comfort – why, it would be difficult to say. It was, maybe, because a large family had grown up in it and their games, quarrels, intimacies, pleasures had sunk into the brick, permeated the boards of the passages, helped to stain curtains and wallpapers into their faded homely colours.

Timothy, his wife, and children were well pleased. Fell House, Uldale, was the joy and boast of Timothy's heart, but it was pleasant for a while to escape its responsibilities. Timothy was lazy although he disguised the laziness with true English aplomb. As to the children this was the happiest summer of their young lives. Discipline was relaxed; their father condescended to walk with them, there was the Farm at the top of the hill, the fields with the haymaking, the mysterious wood, the sea, and above all Vanessa.

It was Timothy who had invited Vanessa to stay with them. Mrs Bellairs had objected, although in her sleepy, limited fashion she rather liked Vanessa. They had both been deeply shocked – as had Herries up and down the country – when they heard of her engagement to Benjamin Herries. They had thought at first that they would never speak to Vanessa again. But Timothy had as true an affection for her as he had for anyone in the world. In his stout slow body there was little rancour, no spitefulness, temper only with his own children. He was negative in all his emotions except his family pride. He thought that he had the finest house, the finest wife, the finest children in the world, and perhaps, deep in his heart, he loved his children and had an affection for his wife. But it was not the fashion for either husbands or parents to be demonstrative. He was now forty-five years of age, laziness and corpulency made him virtuous, but he had still an eye for a pretty woman, and Vanessa's beauty, although he might not speak of it (for Mrs Bellairs could be a jealous woman), gave him the greatest pleasure to look upon. He would stare and stare at her with something of the same emotion with which he would gaze upon a fine shoulder of mutton freshly come to table. Nevertheless he cared for Vanessa. He would, at a push, do more for her than for anyone.

Discussing the tragic Vanessa–Benjie affair in the large family bed at Uldale, he declared that Vanessa should be invited to come with them to Gosforth. Mrs Bellairs groaned and lamented, but knew that if he had decided on something it was decided. They were both lazy people, but she was lazier than he. His point was that they might influence Vanessa. She had been carried off her feet by the London atmosphere. (He had the greatest contempt for London. He knew that he would not shine if he went there.) Let her spend a week or two with them in the country and they would soon show her her silly mistake.

'And her father?' murmured Mrs Bellairs.

'Let him come too,' said Timothy, who tolerated Adam but scorned him because he did nothing with his time but write books. 'The house is big enough.'

However, Adam refused. He might come over for a day or two.

Timothy, his wife, his sister Jane, now an old maid of forty-two, the children, Mrs Clopton the nurse, Agnes the young maid, Jim Wilson the coachman, Peter the dog, all moved over to Low Dene in the large family chariot.

Vanessa arrived there two days later.

The real reason of Vanessa's visit was that she wished to escape from Benjie, whom she had been seeing almost every day for the last three months.

It was not that she loved Benjie less: it was that she loved him more, and this love had plunged her into a turmoil of problems, excitements, and distresses not only about him but about herself as well.

She had never, until now, known any very close and intimate relation with anyone save her father and mother. Her life had always moved on certain fixed and stable laws. Her own faults and failings, which were many – impetuous feeling, hasty temper, neglect of obvious duties – had all, when tested by a few principles, been clearly faults and failings. There had never been any question about what she *ought* to do. Simply she had been wicked and failed.

But she was as honest as anyone alive, both with herself and everyone else, and, after a week with Benjie, she saw that neither right nor wrong conduct would ever be so clear and simple again.

That she had been carried off her feet by Benjie's return and proposal did not at all blind her to the fact that no one else had. She realized immediately at the first half-hour in the party at Hill Street that no one anywhere was going to approve of the engagement – no, not even Rose. 'She is throwing herself away,' she could hear everyone saying. Benjie's charm and light-heartedness when he was happy affected many when he was with them, and during that final week in London he was very charming indeed, but, returning to Cumberland, she found that even Elizabeth was doubtful. 'It is what I have always wanted,' Elizabeth said. 'And oh, my dear, I do hope he will make you happy!'

And her father? He kissed her and told her that her happiness was dearer to him than anything else on earth. She was a woman now. She knew where her happiness lay.

She simply said: 'I have loved him all my life.' He said no more, but she noticed in him after this a constant anxiety, an extra tenderness, and in herself, a certain reticence that had not been there before. Their relationship was for the first time in their lives a little clouded.

Benjie came up to the Fortress and lived there quietly with his mother. At first he was happy with an exuberance, a generosity to all the world, that showed him at his very best. Everyone noticed the change in him.

'I think,' Elizabeth confided to Vanessa after a week or two, 'that it will be as I hoped. You are going to change him altogether.' He told her again and again how, during those last months abroad, her image, his adoration of her, obsessed him more and more completely. On his journey home his impatience was a fever. At the sight of her at last in that silly drawing-room he nearly died! They must be married immediately. She was quite ready. She did not want to wait. Let them be married tomorrow!

Then it was he, Benjie, who postponed it. One afternoon, walking again in the garden at the Fortress, all the old doubts came forward. He was not good enough for her. Everyone was right. He would make her unhappy. When she knew him better she would hate him. She calmed him. She laughed at him. She told him once again that she had known him all her life, that she was not blind nor ignorant about men, that they must trust one another and take what came. She was so certain of her own deep, unchangeable love that they need have no fear. He asked her, in a kind of despair, why did she love him as she did. Soon against her will she was asking herself that question. What was Benjie's power over her? She loved him because he alone in all the world drew everything out of her: she loved him as a woman, as a mother, as a sister, as a friend and a companion. He was honest, generous, gay, independent, brave. He was also careless, selfish, casual, forgetful, always surrendering to the mood of the moment, hating to be tied. But that he adored her no one could doubt. He knew, his mother knew, even the men and women about the place knew that, with all his faults, this love for Vanessa was true, staunch, unyielding. Had his character been as fine as his love they would be happy for evermore!

The wildness in him was quite untamed. She knew that and reckoned with it, but to watch it working at a distance and to have it in close daily communion with herself were two quite different things.

He could conceal nothing that was in his mind, and soon he attacked what he called her 'childishness'. He attacked her religion. He told her again and again that he did not want her to change in the least and tried to change her. 'You know that there can't be a God, Vanessa. In your heart you must know it. You are a wise woman. You read and think. Well, then, ask yourself. How *can* there be a God and life be as it is? If there is one He ought to be deuced ashamed of Himself, that's all I can say.'

She disliked intensely to talk about her religion. She had never done so with anyone save her mother and Elizabeth. Her father had always respected that reticence. But quietly and with humour she answered Benjie's indignation. 'We go by our experience, I suppose, Benjie dear. God is as real to me as you are. Of course I don't know *why* life is as it is. I am a very ignorant woman, and Mr Darwin's monkeys are beyond my scope. But a hundred thousand monkeys wouldn't alter the truth that I love you, nor would they change my love of God either. Don't worry about it, Benjie. Let us be what we are.'

Then soon there was another thing. She had never known before what physical love was. She had never been close to Benjie so constantly. She had never conceived her own weakness. One fine day they had ridden out to Borrowdale and, sitting in the sun under some trees above Rosthwaite, they had talked. She knew that everyone thought it very disgraceful that they went about together without a chaperon. Even her father had shyly spoken to her of it. She had laughed and said that he need have no fears. But now, quite suddenly, she realized that he was right to be afraid. It was as though she and Benjie were caught up into a hot burning cloud of light. The world turned so that both sound and vision were obliterated. For a fearful dumb blind moment she was almost lost. Then by the grace of God she escaped into sight and sound again.

Next day she said

'Benjie, why should we wait? Let us marry soon.'

But there was her father. She could not endure to leave him. It is true that she would be at the Fortress, not far away, but the thought of his lonely days, his sitting at his table writing, looking up out of window, thinking of her, wanting her, was intolerable. He told her with a smile that he would be quite happy. He had Will, he had his work and garden. She knew that he was doing his best. He did not take her in at all. Then in June he fell ill. He caught a cold, suffered from rheumatism, had to go to bed for a while. When he was better Benjie, who had been wonderful during Adam's sickness, coming constantly to visit him, laughing, cheering him up, reading to him, suffered from all his old scruples again.

'Vanessa, give me up! I'll go away and never come back! I'm not worth all your sacrifice. I'm not worth anyone's sacrifice.'

But he loved her more than ever and he was more charming than ever. He was, during those weeks in July, unselfish, thoughtful, considered her in everything. But they decided that they would wait until the spring. 'You will know then finally, once and for all, whether I am worth it.'

'I know it now,' she said gently. 'Nothing can change.'

But she perceived by now that, beyond any doubt, it was something he knew about himself that stirred all his self-depreciation. That, because he knew himself so well and loved her so dearly, he was determined to do this one decent honest thing – not to ruin her life.

But what was it that he knew about himself? He was not, in his attitude to anyone else, self-depreciatory. Far from it. 'Take me as I am; as I take you,' was his attitude to the world. Only he would not spoil Vanessa's life for her.

'But of course you will not spoil it.'

'You don't know me.'

'I take the risk,' she answered.

By the end of July she felt that she must, for a little while, be at a distance from him. This indecision and hesitation could not go on. It was making them both sensitive, moody, self-conscious. So she went to Gosforth.

When she had been a day there her spirit was quieted, her gaiety returned.

Gosforth itself, small quiet village that it was, contained all the past. In the churchyard there was a cross of red sandstone which represented a figure chained beneath a serpent dropping upon him poison. This was a Christian cross and yet it had on it a heathen symbol. No one could tell its age, but many Vikings, she understood, had been half Christian, half heathen. She liked to think that this had been a Viking cross. Then there was Gosforth Hall near the church, the very house where Bishop Nicolson in the seventeenth century, as a young archdeacon, courted Barbara Copley. Near the Hall was a holy well where there had been once a mediaeval chapel, and half a mile from the Hall was the Dane's Camp, and farther from that again the King's Camp, at Laconby. Many of the old houses in the neighbourhood, like Ponsonby Hall and Sella Park, were packed with history, while not far away was Calder Abbey.

In the middle of all this concentration of Time slept the perfect English countryside. There was often sunshine that August and sweeping shafts of it fell across the cornfields, warming the colours into red gold, falling at the feet of the dark shadows of the woods. It was pastoral everywhere, while on windless days the silence, made more musical by the creaking of a cart, dogs barking, the call of the farmer to his horse, seemed to carry all the summer scents of flowers and corn and trees and pile them about you so that on the hot lawn you need not stir but gather, without motion, everything into your heart.

Yet how strangely even in this country of cornfield, wood and hedgerow still the mountains dominated. At every point, from every rise, Black Combe, thrusting its head like a lazy friendly whale into the sea, held your eye. From Black Combe's top you could hold in your grasp the Isle of Man, the Scottish and Welsh coasts with Snowdon greeting you, while landwards were Lancashire and the Yorkshire Fells.

To the right from a little hill above the house you could salute the Screes and in your mind's eye follow them as they rushed with all their power to bury their foundations deep in the heart of the black lake. Standing on her hill Vanessa would watch the clouds hurrying like smoke to invade the serried tops, then to spill themselves in storm or to break into pavilions snow-white or crimson with fire, or to shred and scatter into strands of gold and crimson. And she liked to sense, as she felt the motionless peace of the cornfields below them, catching the sun and throwing it up to her again, that above those hills the wind was raging and that their shining, slanting surface glistened with hardness, and the stone walls, straight as a sword, ran to the skyline over ground that was rough and peaty and free. All history was in this small patch of ground, and all nature too, shadowed by the triumphant wing of the great Eagle to whose kingly progress History was but a day.

In the house and out of it there were the children. They were sternly disciplined. Mrs Clopton, a tall dark woman with heavy eyebrows and a faint moustache, was a Tartar. She was not unkind, but she thrived on her despair of human nature. She hoped for the best but gloried in her constant disappointment. Her God – she was a deeply religious woman – was the real God of the Israelites, revengeful, on the watch for every blunder, cruel in His punishments. Oddly the children liked her; they were proud of her. She had no need to punish; a look, a word from her was sufficient. Not that they were perfect children. They made their own lives in their world of perpetual discipline. They learnt their Collects on Sunday, said 'Yes, Mama' and 'No, Mama', never spoke when with their elders unless spoken to, but once by themselves, the official eye removed from them, they were free, natural, and often naughty. It was as though they understood the terms under which they lived and made their plans accordingly. Violet was delicate – fair-haired, slender, blue-eyed and was already making her poor health her pleasant advantage.

But Tim was Vanessa's darling. He was fair and slender like Violet, but strong and wiry. She saw that he was an artist born and that nothing would stop him. He drew unconsciously without any deliberate awareness. He noticed the shapes and colours of clouds, the patterns of leaves, the path that the wind made through the corn, a snail's shiny track on the lawn, the purple shadows on the flanks of Black Combe. He was already at odds with Herries common sense.

His father would darken the doorway.

'Tim, what are you doing?'

'Making a picture, Papa.'

'Let me see.'

Then after a pause:

'Now what is this?'

'A ship with pirates, Papa.'

'Pirates! Pirates! What do you know about pirates?'

'Aunt Essie told us, Papa.'

'And you call this a ship?'

'I don't know ships very well and—'

'Well, wait until you do. Wasting your time like this! What have I often told you?'

'Not to waste my time, Papa.'

'Exactly. Now put away that rubbish.'

The children worshipped Vanessa. For half an hour before they went to bed she was allowed to tell them stories. Mrs Clopton listened in stern astonishment. There was nothing of which she disapproved so thoroughly as stories, but, while her needles clicked, she found herself attending: fairy palaces rose above her head, the Crystal Lake was at her feet and a White Horse of incomparable splendour strode the ice-bound hills.

'Time for their bed, Miss Vanessa.'

But, over her solitary supper, she wondered, against her will: 'What did the Princess find behind the secret door? Did the dwarf climb out of the cellar? Why was the Green Necklace the King's most treasured possession?'

Best of all there was the sea. On fine days they drove there in the victoria. The sand stretched in a floor of mother-of-pearl to the line of trembling white. On the horizon the Isle of Man hung between sea and sky. Timothy slept, Mrs Bellairs talked, the

children were busy with their fantasies, Mrs Clopton read her
Bible, Vanessa thought of Benjamin.

On a sunny afternoon, staring dreamily at the incoming
tide, she saw him coming towards her.

At first she was delighted, then she was angry, then delighted
again. She wanted *not* to be pleased! He was for ever breaking his
word. They had agreed that they would not meet for three weeks.
And why had he not written to her to tell her that he was
coming? Or had he perhaps ridden over and tomorrow was returning? Or did he intend? ... The children had seen him and
began to run towards him, then stopped, remembering their
elders. They loved, however, Benjie better than anyone else in the
world – far better indeed. No one, not even Aunt Vanessa nor
Aunt Jane nor any other, could create for them a world and then
live contentedly inside it as Benjie could.

'Uncle Benjie! Uncle Benjie!' Tim cried and woke up his
father. Mrs Bellairs disapproved of Benjamin completely. She
was terrified lest he should contaminate the children. She *said*
this, but in actual fact when he was in her company she always
surrendered to him. Had she been honest with herself she would
have acknowledged that to be so vicious and yet so amiable
touched the adventurous woman in her. Although stout and
forty, completely the British matron, there hid somewhere within
her a girl who longed to see what the other half of the world was
like. This girl was slowly starving to death. Once and again
she received sustenance: Benjie more than any other kept her
alive.

Nevertheless he *was* dangerous to the children with all the
horrible things he had seen and done, the dreadful women he
must know. Moreover, had they not invited Vanessa to stay for
the sole purpose of showing her how shocking, how impossible
Benjie was?

But what were you to do when in a moment he was down on
his knees in the sand helping Tim with his castle, which the
child had already decorated with a pink shell, the green stopper
of a ginger-beer bottle, and a piece of red rag tied to a stick?

And *what* were you to do when, smiling all over his face, sand
on his trousers, waving a child's spade, he came over to you
crying:

'Just think, Violet, I've come all the way from the Fortress on a
bicycle.'

'On a bicycle!' She sat up, settled her bustle, arranged the large yellow brooch neatly on her bosom and stared with what she trusted was a mixture of disapprobation and dignity.

'Now don't look like that, Violet! You know you are glad I have come. One might think I was Cetewayo by your disapproval. I'm not going to poison the children or tell them naughty stories. I *may* tell you a few later on, but to be honest with you I've come to see Vanessa, the lady to whom I'm engaged, and nobody else . . . Yes, I've come on a bicycle! I bought it in Carlisle last week.'

'Where is it?' asked Mrs Bellairs, speaking as though he had brought with him the late-lamented Jumbo from the Zoo.

'It is at my lodging.'

'Your lodging? Then you are going to stay here?'

'For a day or two – as long as Vanessa will put up with me.'

'Well, we can't offer you a bed at Low Dene if that's what you want. There are rooms enough but no servants. I'm sorry, but you should have told us you were coming.'

Benjie laughed. 'But, my dear Violet, why will you not understand? I have not come to see *you*. Of course if you appear sometimes I shall be glad to talk to you and to listen to what you have to say. If you are *very* good I will tell you a story or two about Port Said. But I have not the slightest interest in either yourself or Low Dene just now. I prefer the company of Mrs Halliday and Rosemary Cottage.'

'And *who* is Mrs Halliday?'

'A retired gentlewoman with a beautiful daughter, who, an hour ago, lured me with a card in the window which said that a bedroom was to let on moderate terms. Rosemary Cottage has a sea view, the beautiful daughter was in the parlour tending the plants. Within five minutes terms were arranged, and my bicycle is now occupying all the space in the front hall.'

'Very well. If you are satisfied. But I'm sure you might leave Vanessa alone for a little. You do not mean to say that you've come thirty miles today on that bicycle?'

'No. I stayed last night in Whitehaven and transacted a little piece of business.'

'I see.' She rose with great dignity, patted her bosom, shook her dress so that the frills and ruches settled in their proper places, and said:

'Timothy, it is time we were returning. Come, children. The air is chill.'

But the victoria had to be ordered, and Benjie was able to secure a moment alone with Vanessa.

'Why have you come?' Vanessa asked him. 'Three weeks was our bargain.'

'I know. I could not help it. I had to show you the bicycle.'

'No, but I am angry. Really I am. You should not have come.'

'You haven't written, Vanessa.'

'I have only been here four days.'

'Yes, but *four days*! An intolerable time. But see how tactful I am. I am here at Rosemary Cottage. There is Mrs Halliday's beautiful daughter. I am quite happy, and we need not meet at all.'

'You know that we shall meet.'

'Let the others go in front.' He caught her hand. 'Vanessa. We must stop this nonsense. We must be married immediately. I mean it. I cannot live even four days without you.'

'Tomorrow you will say something quite different. I cannot trust you from one day to another.'

'No, I know. That is why we must be married immediately. Next month. I have told my mother. There is nothing against it.'

'There has never been anything against it,' she answered. 'Only your own indecision.' Then she laughed. 'Oh, Benjie, I am so glad to see you! I have been wanting you every minute I have been here!'

'If,' he said, 'we walk up through those sand-dunes no one can see us.'

Between the sand dunes they kissed as though they had been parted for years.

When he had seen them all drive off in the victoria he walked to his lodging, singing. Everything was settled at last. His own indecision was ended. After all, was he not changed? Did he not adore Vanessa? He knew that he did! How beautiful, how very, very beautiful she had looked in the simple blue dress with the high dark collar, the white frill at the throat, the little gold brooch that he had given her, her hair brushed from her splendid forehead, she kneeling there on the sand watching Tim's castle. No one was so lovely, no one so good and true, no one loved him so dearly! The wildness was gone from his nature. They would settle at the Fortress, soon there would be children, boys like Tim, girls better than Violet; the garden should blossom with the rose, the Fortress should burn with light and heat . . .

He was approaching Rosemary Cottage. It stood by itself, its feet almost in the sand dunes, a small wind-blown desolate garden looking on to the sandy track. As he approached it he ceased to sing. The sun was setting: shadows crept over the sea and a mist veiled the little moon.

Before he entered he hesitated. Something about this place checked his high spirits. Vanessa seemed far away. A little wind, suddenly rising, blew the sand in thin spirals among the strong tufted grass.

In the sitting-room the lamp was already lit and a meal spread on the table – a ham, a dish of stewed fruit, cheese.

Mrs Halliday appeared in the doorway.

'Shall I bring the eggs and tea now?' she asked. She was a spare desolate woman in a black silk dress. He noticed that she had no eyebrows and wore mittens on her hands.

'Thank you,' he said. He pulled off his boots, changing them for slippers, found in his bag a novel by Ouida, pulled out his pipe. She reappeared with the tea and eggs.

'I trust you have no objection to smoking in here?' he asked, looking up at her with a smile.

'Oh, none at all, Mr —' She paused. 'I beg your pardon. I did not catch your name before. Pray forgive me.'

'Oh, certainly. My name is Herries.'

'Thank you. I am a little deaf in one ear.' She waited as though she expected him to speak.

'That tea looks splendid.' He moved to the table. 'I am exceedingly hungry.'

'I am very glad, I am sure.' She waited, then went on. 'I do hope we shall satisfy you. My daughter and I are not accustomed to having lodgers. We have been in this place barely a month.'

'Oh yes?' He cut the bread.

'Yes. We come from Warwickshire. My husband was a gentleman of means. He was carried off with a severe fever six months ago.'

'Oh, I *am* sorry,' said Benjie. 'What brought you, then, to this district?'

'I have a son who has taken a farm in the Buttermere direction. He always was fond of the country, but was of course in very different circumstances when my poor husband was alive.' She paused, gave a dry little cough. 'He passed away with great suddenness. His affairs were sadly involved. He was ruined by one whom he thought his friend.'

'Oh dear, I *am* sorry,' Benjie said. But he had been startled by the extreme vindictiveness of that last sentence. Up to then she had spoken so very quietly.

'Yes, and so after that my daughter and I have had to do what we can ... Thank you, Mr Herries. I hope that you have everything that you need.'

'Oh yes, thank you.'

She left the room. What an extremely quiet woman she was! It was not only that she spoke quietly, the words coming from between her thin lips reluctantly, but her movements were quiet, almost stealthy. She had been in the room before he noticed it. Had he been anyone but Benjie he would have said at once that he did not like her, but his charity was all-embracing, at any rate until he had full and sufficient reason for a stern decision. But as he ate his ham and his eggs he felt uncomfortable. He thought that perhaps tomorrow he would make a move. He had half an impulse to get up and see whether his bicycle was safe in the hall. At any rates it was stuffy in here. The room was too full of things, china dogs, pale yellow daguerreotypes, large sea-shells, little tables covered with plush fastened with bright gilt nails. There was a smell in the room as though the windows had not been opened for a very long time – a smell, was it of seaweed, of stale scent, musty and clinging? Ah well, he was an ancient mariner, he had travelled the world over and known every discomfort. He would not be disturbed by a musty smell and a china dog or two. Nevertheless he disliked intensely a large daguerreotype of a pale severe gentleman in black cloth whose cold eyes followed him wherever he moved. Possibly Mrs Halliday would not object to moving *that* picture in the morning!

There was a knock on the door; he said 'Come in!' and the daughter entered.

'Mother wished me to see whether you needed anything,' she said.

'Not at all,' he answered. 'Everything is excellent, thank you.'

The girl stood against the table looking at him.

She was certainly not beautiful, not even pretty. She was thin like her mother and very fair. Her colour was so pale as to be almost white; her large eyes were blue-grey. She looked at him and smiled faintly. No, she was not pretty but there was something striking about her. It was true that she was thin, but her very fragility seemed to claim your protection.

He smiled back at her.

'Do you like it here?' he asked her.

'No,' she said. 'I do not.' She came nearer to him and laid her hand on the cloth. He noticed at once what a beautiful hand she had, finely formed, with slender fingers. Her hand moved towards the teapot while still she looked at him.

He had a mad impulse to put out his hand towards hers.

He jumped up from the table.

'I shan't want anything else tonight, thank you,' he said, turning his back to her abruptly as he filled his pipe.

The world does not grow less mysterious as it grows older, and it is one of its more striking but less incalculable secrets that human love when it is strong enough defies physical distance. This was not the first time nor the last in their history that Vanessa, as now, riding in the victoria through the dark summer hedges to Low Dene, was quite suddenly aware that Benjie was in danger. Benjie was so often in danger, whether spiritual, mental, or physical, that there must have been many occasions when Vanessa was unaware. There is also the perfectly plausible theory that Victorian women were exceptionally sensible to chills because they wrapped up so much. In any case Vanessa, sitting in the victoria, perfectly happy, feeling that at last she was on a relationship with Benjie that was safe and secure, began to shiver. They were turning into the long straggling Gosforth street. The sky in front of them was a pale translucent green in whose bright waters some trembling silver stars were glittering.

'Why! you are shivering, my dear!' said Mrs Bellairs. 'Wrap this round you! I do trust that you haven't caught a chill!'

Young Tim was sitting beside her, and his hot damp fist was enclosed in her gloved hand. In his fist, as she knew, were several shells and a piece of golden seaweed. She had the obscure and unreasonable fancy that it was through his hot little fist that she caught the sense that Benjie was in danger. How could he be in danger? He had left her only half an hour before to walk, happy and singing, to his lodging. Rosemary Cottage! There *could* be nothing wrong about Rosemary Cottage. Nevertheless they were both of a strange ancestry, she and Benjie. Francis Herries fighting in the frosty air, Mirabell bending over her lover's body on the Carlisle stones, Francis Herries looking at a picture on the wall in a London lodging for the last time, John – his son – calling through the mist in Skiddaw Forest: 'Is anyone there?',

Judith, released at last, running into the road joyfully to greet her friends – these are only moments in a contemporary history where facts are important only as pointers, and where the significance is only externally material, and where Time has no significance at all.

'Thank you, Violet,' said Vanessa, gratefully accepting the Shetland shawl. 'It *is* cold after the sun sets.' At the same moment she had a most incongruous thought – that it was so *like* Timothy and Violet to christen their children with their own names!

She was uneasy all that evening and, next morning, a little talk that she had with Aunt Jane only increased that uneasiness.

It was a blazing summer day and they sat out on the lawn while the children, under the stern eye of Mrs Clopton, knocked the croquet balls about. Vanessa had on her knee a novel by Rhoda Broughton, and Aunt Jane had on hers a novel by Mrs Alexander. Aunt Jane had a dear little face that would soon be covered with wrinkles. Her ringlets, her shawl (even in this warm weather), the spectacles that she used when reading, her little apprehensive starts as though she expected that at any moment a bear would jump out on her from the shrubbery, a round silver biscuit tin from which she would produce suddenly sweet biscuits for the children when Mrs Clopton wasn't looking, her extreme delicacy about other people's feelings, her willing slavery to the wishes of other people, her single-hearted devotion to those whom she loved, none of these attributes concealed from Vanessa the fact that, in spite of her modesty, reserve and deep religious beliefs, she knew a great deal more about life and men and women than did either Timothy or Violet.

Vanessa had not often an opportunity of being alone with her. She was constantly busy on other people's business. Timothy especially was always providing her with occupations. She was, when others were present, very silent, and her brother and sister-in-law would have been amazed had they realized the things that she perceived and pondered. They were certain that she adored them and considered them perfect human beings. In the first of these they were correct or nearly correct (she loved people in her own way, which was not at all theirs), in the second they were altogether wrong.

The little conversation that Vanessa now had with her was punctuated with Mrs Clopton's sharp: 'Now, Master Tim, don't dirty your stockings!' and 'Let your brother have the ball now, Miss Violet', and 'What did I tell you? You must look where you are going.'

From the field above the garden came the voices of the hay-makers.

'Benjie has come to stay in Seascale, Aunt Jane,' said Vanessa.

'Yes, dear, I know. That's very nice for you.'

'And we are going to be married in the autumn.'

Aunt Jane took off her spectacles.

'I'm glad of that too. I think you have been engaged quite long enough.'

'Why do you think that?' Vanessa asked quietly.

'Oh, my dear, I know nothing about marriage of course, but Benjie, I always say, is not at all an ordinary man. I would never expect *you* to marry an ordinary man, Vanessa dear. You have too much of your grandmother in you. But when a man is *not* an ordinary man I always say that it is better that he should be married.'

'Of course Benjie's not an ordinary man. But then nobody is ordinary if you know them well enough.'

'Quite so. That's what Mrs Alexander, whose book I am finding it extremely difficult to read, does not appear to have discovered. All her characters are so *very* ordinary.'

Vanessa hesitated. Then she went on:

'Aunt Jane, I am going to ask you something. You are so very wise. You have known both Benjie and me since we were babies. Why is it, do you think, that when we are together we so often misunderstand one another?'

'That is just what I mean about marriage,' said Jane. 'People always misunderstand one another. But the point about marriage is that if you go on long enough together you arrive at an under-standing. Once you are married you are bound together. I believe all married people find the connexion very irritating for a long while, and if they were not married they would separate. But being married they cannot, and so, at last, the understanding arrives. I put it very badly of course. I am not clever as your grandmother was. But there it is. That's what marriage does.'

'We must not be engaged too long, Benjie and I,' Vanessa said, as though she were speaking to herself. 'There is something dangerous about waiting.'

'There is something dangerous, my dear, about every human relationship. That is God's intention. People would never learn anything if there were not plenty of danger about. That is what your grandmother always said.'

'Oh, how I wish she were still alive!' Vanessa cried. 'She would have helped me. I know nothing about life at all – nothing about Benjie either, I sometimes think, although I've been with him all my life. How can we know anything about men? We are never alone with them; all they do is concealed from us; when they are with us they never tell us the truth.'

'Yes, dear, you are quite right,' said Jane. 'I often think that women today are far too sheltered. Not that I like the girls that your Miss Broughton writes about. That is surely going *too* far. But when your grandmother was a girl, as she often told me, women were far more free. I dare say they will be again one day, but as it is just now they have to spend all their time guessing.'

'Aunt Jane,' Vanessa said, staring at the rising field, the sunlight that soaked the lawn, 'I'm frightened. I feel that one wrong slip and Benjie will be carried away into some place where I can't reach him. I love him so terribly, but I am only *close* to him at moments. He's here. He's gone. And when he is gone I am so helpless . . .'

Jane smiled. 'Don't be frightened, my dear. Trust God. He knows so very much more than we do. Remember always that Benjie has a tragic history behind him, his father, his grandfather . . . You know, don't you, that I was the last person to talk to his father on that dreadful day? He was leading his horse from the stable. Of course I was only a little girl then, but I have always thought that perhaps I could have stopped him if I had known what to do or say, I loved him when I was a child more than I loved anyone, and I have been haunted all my life since by the thought that I failed him. But what I say is,' she went on more cheerfully, 'that if we do right as far as we can it's all we can do. Life's a dangerous thing, my dear, and you can't escape the danger by staying in bed all day or making other people act *for* you. Don't expect things to be easy. Why should they be? God doesn't arrange the universe only for me – nor for you either. To listen to the way the people talk in this novel of Mrs Alexander's you'd think that every time they have a toothache God ought to be ashamed of Himself . . .' She nodded to herself, picked up her book. 'I'm at page one hundred and fifty-three and that's as far as I shall go. I always like to finish a book if I can; when the writer's taken so much trouble it seems only right; but *this* time I simply can't be bothered. Mrs Alexander will never know, so there's no harm done.'

For one reason or another this little talk left Vanessa – who as a rule was sensible enough and level-headed – in a kind of panic. That was the quality that Aunt Jane had, that when she *did* talk she always suggested so much more than she said. Her honesty forbade her to offer false consolations. If people did not inquire what she thought she was too thorough a lady to tell them, but if they *did* ask her they must accept the consequences. Vanessa now had the conviction that Aunt Jane thought her love for Benjie a disaster!

She endured three days of a distress and apprehension altogether new to her experience. For much of this the child that she still was was responsible. These were perhaps the last days of immaturity, those days when persons and events have still the size and colours of nursery hours, moments when we are left alone in a room where the flickering firelight throws gigantic shadows on the wall, when the clock's tick is a menace, and the twig snapping on the windowsill threatens the approach of some dreadful stranger!

She had three days of nightmare – and was transported into Paradise!

Timothy, as befitted a Bellairs, liked society if it was proper enough, and at the houses in the neighbourhood – Muncaster and Ponsonby and others – there was plenty. It was still the fashion, if you went out to dinner, to take a footman with you to assist at the meal; there were elaborate croquet parties and magnificent picnics.

So one fine day Timothy and his wife set off to Muncaster, and Vanessa went with the nurse and children to the sea. They had not been settled on the shore five minutes before Benjie was with them. He and Vanessa started to walk across the long, shining sands.

It was a day of perfect peace. Chroniclers may define that moment as the final peaceful one in English country life – a moment of historic tranquillity when the cornfields lay placid beneath the sun, the hedgerows slept, woods were untrodden, and every village sheltered under its immemorial elm while the villagers slumbered off their beer on the parochial bench. At the final moment, then, before the trumpet of the new world sounded, Benjamin and Vanessa crossed Seascale sands!

She knew at once that he was disturbed. There had been something, then, in her own unrest.

She said at once: 'Benjie, what is it?'

He caught her arm with his hand and pressed her against his

side so that they might walk like one man. She was taller than he. She was wearing a small, rather masculine hat ornamented with blue flowers. She held her parasol high over her head. She was smiling, she was happy. She could feel his hand within her arm against her heart. All her fears were fled.

'There is nothing the matter except that I love you. And that *is* the matter, for we must be married in a month's time. I can wait no longer. I am bad through and through. I am without a redeeming point, but I have told you all that so often that I shall never mention it again.'

'Certainly we will be married in a month's time. Tomorrow if you like! I have been dreadfully unhappy these three days. I can't tell you why, but as I was driving back the other evening I had a sudden fear that something had happened to you. That cottage – what did you call it? Where you are staying. I have been dreaming of it, crawling with spiders and earwigs. I have been thinking that if we are not married at once we never will be married. And Aunt Jane frightened me.'

'What has Aunt Jane been saying?' he asked quickly.

'Oh, nothing – dear Aunt Jane! She loves us both, I know. But she is afraid for us. I know she is. She thinks there is dangerous blood in our veins. She wants to see us *safe*.'

'She's right!' he said fiercely. 'We must be *safe* – or someone will part us, something will happen!'

They were standing at the sea edge, on a floor of mother-of-pearl. The incoming tide drew thin lines of white as with a pencil on the shore and beyond the line the sea heaved without breaking, as gently as a sigh.

'No,' she said. 'I think that *nothing* can part us. I don't mean because we love one another. I can imagine that you might come to hate me or I would be so proud that I would never see you again, but still we would not be parted. It has been like that all our lives.'

Then she added, as though to herself: 'That is my worst fault, my pride.'

He turned and looked at her as though he were seeing her newly.

'What do you mean, Vanessa – your pride?'

'I would endure anything, I think,' she answered, 'or so I feel. I would show what I was suffering to nobody, but it would remain inside me. I could not let it out. I cannot let things go – words that someone said years ago, little things that people have done.

No one knows that I remember them, but I never forget. They do something to me. I hate my pride. I would like to be free as you are, Benjie – every day a new day—'

'No, Vanessa darling,' he broke in. 'Not like me. If there were two of us, both like me, oh, what a time we would have! You are the only one in all the world who influences me! That is why you are to marry me, teach me, change me.'

'I don't think I can teach anyone.' She sighed. 'I don't know why it is, but I would rather leave people alone, leave them as they are. Father is like that too. Mother used to be constantly distressed at how bad people were. Not that she blamed them. She was too kind. But it bewildered her. Right was so right and wrong was so wrong. I have no conscience for other people, I think – not even for you, Benjie.'

He asked her again for the thousandth time: 'Why do you love me, Vanessa? Everyone tells you not to.'

'I love you,' she answered, 'as I shall always love you, because you are part of me, because you are all that I have in the world, because without you I am always lonely, because I am not alive without you. There!' she said, turning round and laughing, looking at him too with infinite tenderness, with a kind of brooding devotion as though she could not look at him enough, could not have him close enough to her. 'Now – are you satisfied?'

For a moment he was silent, then he took her hand and kissed it.

'God helping me,' he said, 'you shall not regret it.' Then, characteristically, added as they turned to walk back: 'Although I don't believe in Him, I expect Him to help me, you see.'

They discussed details. He had written to Elizabeth the night before. They would be married in Ireby church, a very quiet wedding.

'There is only Adam,' Benjie said. 'I hate to think how he will miss you. We will do everything we can. You can go and stay with him whenever you wish, and he shall stay with us.'

'He will be happy if I am,' she answered. 'And he is well now – stronger than for a long while.' But nevertheless she knew leaving him would be terrible. They must think of a plan ... some way ...

As they neared the children two women passed them. Benjie raised his hat.

'Do you know them?' she asked.

'Yes,' he said, laughing. 'That is the enchantress of Rosemary

Cottage. Two enchantresses. Mrs Halliday and her lovely daughter Marion.'

Driving home, with Violet on her lap while Mrs Clopton told her stories of the heathen in Africa and all that was being done to improve their minds, she was thinking in an ecstasy of happiness:

'We are safe! We are safe! In a month we shall be married. Nothing can touch us now.'

In the morning the old postman, bent and twisted like a gnome, brought her a letter. It was from her father.

DEAREST VAN – I am not very well – nothing serious – but I think perhaps you had better come home – Your loving   FATHER

FALL OF THE HOUSE OF ULDALE

ADAM PARIS hovered through the whole of that autumn between life and death. His sickness began, it appeared, with some mysterious poisoning, was followed by pneumonia, and left him with a heart so weak that every excitement, every sudden movement, was a danger.

So he was told not to move, not to suffer excitement. In the early days of January he was permitted to walk a little, supported on Will Leathwaite's stout arm, in the garden. During those months Vanessa scarcely left his side; even Benjamin was almost forgotten by her.

Whatever else Adam might be, he was always a philosopher. By January 1883 he was sixty-seven years of age – sixty-seven was three years from three score and ten. To die at that age was no very terrible misfortune. He did not want to die. He did not want to leave Cumberland, nor Will, nor Vanessa. Every day held some adventure, some charm, some beauty. But he most certainly did not care to linger on an invalid, a trouble and anxiety to everyone about him. He knew that had it not been for his illness Vanessa would now be married, and although he did not wish, had never wished, that Benjamin should marry her, he wanted to see her settled before he went. Moreover, he had now perceived that it was Benjamin and Benjamin alone whom she must have, and he made the best of it.

If anybody could make anything settled and secure out of Benjamin, it was Vanessa. So great an opinion had he of her wisdom, common sense and fidelity that he thought that she might.

During those long trying days of convalescence he kept a Journal – not a very regular one, not a very original one, but he put into it his honest opinions, some of his experience. These were some pages of it:

. . . A long and dangerous illness is an odd enough thing, I find. It is a commonplace that it seems to you, when you are in good health, incredible that you should ever die, and that when you are very ill you do not care a hang whether you die or no. Nature has arranged that very cleverly. But now that I am growing stronger again I find that I want to live for the smallest, most insignificant reasons. I have, for example, a new dog that Benjie gave me the other day, a rough clumsy kind of terrier. I have called him Tux after Rousseau's animal – the one that the Duchess of Luxembourg gave him. I have always liked Prince de Conti and the Luxembourg for their niceness to Rousseau, who must have been, just then, as tiresome and sensitive a creature as God ever made – but the queer thing and the enduring thing about Rousseau is that he had in him something of Everyman. He would have felt, I am sure, just as I did yesterday when Timothy and Violet came up from Uldale to pay me a visit. So very well-meaning, so extremely irritating! However, in one thing I am luckier than he. I have no Thérèse for them to patronize! But I felt just as he did about presents. Timothy gave me a shawl 'to keep my knees warm' as though the whole of the Herries family were presenting me with a medal. However, it is quite natural that he should think me a fool who all his life has wasted his time over nothing! And I had my ambitions once, too, but ambitions when you get to my age are cheap affairs. Would I have been a happier man had I been Gladstone or Dizzy or Dickens? Sour grapes perhaps to say that I would not. It is natural that I should like now to clap my hand on the table and say: 'Yes, I have added *that* to the world's achievements, a law or a poem, a picture or a character.' But my illness has left me altogether indifferent. My dear mother, I suppose, went the wrong way for both of us when she stayed at Uldale instead of escaping the family and going to

Watendlath. She always said that it was the mistake of her life. Had she gone I would have been a farmer, never seen a relation, never lived in London, never married Margaret, never had Vanessa for a daughter. What I would have missed! But I might, I fancy, have been a stronger man, a more determined character, and I would certainly have had more of this country, the sight and smell and sound of it. But I would have been always a dreamer who never pursued his dreams far enough. There can be no man but is dissatisfied with his life when he looks back on it. What a confusion of shreds and patches, of starting first here and then there, of one blind move after another – walking at night along a dark road and thinking every tree a hobgoblin! But I was never much of an adventurer, too easily disheartened, too ready to be an idealist without suffering for my ideals, far too ready to shrink away into myself if I met a rebuff. A failure, I suppose, trying to conceal my failure with a certain cynicism, and yet on the whole what a happy life I have had. I have known three glorious women – my wife, my daughter, and my mother – one or two magnificent men – Dickens, Caesar Kraft, Will, and in my babyhood, Reuben Sunwood. I have been given the perception of beauty in art and in nature and, although my own writing has been less than nothing in its result, I have had, in the pursuit of it, some glorious visions. Best of all, I have never been betrayed by my own failure into thinking man a poor affair. I have never come to thinking human nature a bad blunder, although in my Chartist days I met some poor specimens. Nor, thank God, have I ever suffered a fool gladly, least of all myself.

The whole pageant of life has been, and is, of an extraordinary interest. I can see now clearly enough that Time is nothing, that each and every man is tested with the same tests and rises or falls according to what he learns. Learning is everything. But for what? I have never been sure of any kind of personal immortality. As my mother used to say: 'I don't *feel* it and so I don't *believe* it.' But Margaret was sure and Vanessa is sure and they are both wiser than I. There is a great deal of the pagan in me, as there was in my mother. We inherit that, I suppose. But even with my paganism I wonder that the world should be so beautiful and men often so fine and courageous if there is nothing more than this brief experience. I have touched some grand moments too: my first sight of Margaret in that little room off the Seven Dials, Dickens' hand on my shoulder, the day when I finished my first story, walks with Will, the day when in a kind of panic I ran away from Margaret up Cat Bells here, hours with books, sunrises and sunsets, even yesterday when looking from this window I saw the hills rosy and the Lake a misty blue. Do these mountains of perception mean nothing at all? I don't know, and up to a week or so ago in all those months of illness I certainly did not care. One night in September I was sure I would be dead before morning and everyone else was sure too. I was quite clear-headed and quite indifferent – yes, even to Will and Vanessa. But I remember that I felt intolerably wise, that I thought that I had discovered the secret. Will turned me over in bed that I might lie easier and I muttered: 'Well, *that's* it. Why didn't I discover that before?' But what I had discovered I haven't now the least idea. Nothing is certain except love, love of anything or anybody that takes you beyond yourself. This may be, for all I know, a proof of God. It's as good a one as anything the parsons can give you. 'For what we have received let us be truly thankful . . .'

January 9th, 1883
Benjie came up yesterday afternoon and we had a talk. I never saw a man look so healthy. He is a gipsy for colour and hard as iron. Nothing seems to fatigue him and nothing bores him. What is best about him is that he is an individual. He is like no one else at all: you never know where you have him, or at least I don't. If you think him happy he isn't. Behind his merriment (and I must say I like it when he throws his head back and laughs as a boy laughs) there is a strain of melancholy. That he loves Vanessa there is no mistaking, but I am certain that he has misgivings about their marriage. He is right when he says he can't stick to anything. He is always against the law, whatever the law happens to be, and in that he is, I suppose, like my romantic grandfather and the Frenchman my mother married. He is of their world and so all against the Herries world, which is altogether anti-indi-vidualist. I couldn't help thinking yesterday as I listened to him that that may be the fight the whole earth is slipping into – the type against the individual. All the troubles in our family have come from the individual refusing to conform. Do I want Van-essa to be engaged in that kind of battle? No, indeed I do not. Nor do I want her to marry a type-Herries either. The truth is, I suppose, that I love her so much that I shall never find anyone good enough for her!

Benjie yesterday was in a queer state of indecision. He came, I fancy, that I should make his mind up for him, but about what? He never said. He asked me the absurdest questions all covering something deeper that he never owned up to. Should he go to a Ball at Greystoke? Yes, I said, if he wanted to. Oh, he'd be sick of it in half an hour and do something outrageous. There's some woman and her daughter whom he met in the summer at Seascale have come to live in Keswick. Should he go and call on them? Why, yes, I said, if he liked them. But he didn't like them. Well, then, don't go. They had been friendly to him in Seascale and so on and so on. Vanessa had gone to Uldale, and I could see that he was deeply disappointed and yet was relieved. Nevertheless how charming he can be! I never knew anyone better with Will. He gets behind that man's defences in a moment. He knows by instinct what are Will's reticences. He is on a level with him completely, no patronage and no sycophancy either. His heart is good, but he is so restless and so impulsive that he is in trouble before he knows where he is. He is like a wild man who has never been tamed, and then, in a flash, a perfect courteous gentleman. Can Vanessa tame him? I believe that he fears himself that she cannot, and trembles lest he should do her a wrong. Like him I must, and fear for the future I must too. How I wish that my mother were alive! She would understand him as no other. She was the daughter of one wild man and tamed another – but my mother was unique. There will never be another like her again.

When he was gone I was tired enough and Will helped me to bed. That pain just over my heart returned like an old familiar friend. Odd how a pain, to which you are accustomed, seems in a fashion friendly. I could feel its fingers pinching my flesh, then pressing heavily, constricting the muscles, and as I laboured for breath I could almost hear its voice: 'Now we are together again, you and I. Is not our intimacy pleasant?' I could not altogether own that it was, and yet I could have almost replied: 'Yes, but don't press too hard, old fellow. Spare me what you can.'

And now this morning, this bright frosted January morning, I am well and the pain is forgotten. How quickly the past is over! How dim the pain of five minutes before! Yes, and the pleasure too! I can remember how often on a fine day, walking or sitting lazily in my boat on the Lake, the beauty has been so intense that I have longed to catch it in my fingers, hold it, wrap it up, put it away for safety. And in a moment it is gone. A rosy cloud turns grey, there is a whisper on the water, the shadow envelops the hill and *that* beauty is lost! But the intensity of the realization is caught at least. My friend Jean-Jacques, of whom for some reason I have been thinking much in these last weeks, speaks of that. I haven't the *Confessions* with me but the passage goes a little like this: 'The movement and the counter-movement of the water, the stirrings, rising, falling, gave me pleasure in mere existence. No need to think, to live at that moment was enough! Letting my boat go where it would, I would abandon myself to reverie. I was completely under Thy power, Nature! No wicked men to interpose themselves between us! Yes, all is a perpetual movement on earth. Nothing is constant. Our affections change and alter. Everything is in front or behind. We recall the past to which we are now indifferent or anticipate a future that may never come. Nothing solid for our hearts! But the soul may find a state solid enough on which it may repose with no thought of the past, no fear for the future – and so long as such a state endures he who experiences it may speak of bliss . . .

Once on a day I knew that passage by heart, I think: now it comes to me only in fragments. Poor Rousseau, demon-haunted, finding no spot where his foot might rest. How in those days when the *Confessions* were so actual to me, I hated Voltaire and the vile Grimm and the false Madame d'Epinay!

But after all I suppose that his troubles were of his own making. There would have been no genius had there been no sickness. But I think at my age I hate most in this life the jealousy and rage of men against one another. How trivial and worthless our plottings when we are here for so short a time. How easy, you would say, for Man to tolerate his brother. And yet how I myself detested old Walter, so that I would lie awake and think how I might injure him. And then at the last that poor, weak, crying old man to be fed with a spoon and have his mouth wiped! I swear that if I recover from this I will never be angry again. And yet it has been, I dare say, that I have not been angry enough in life, have not known indignation enough. I have hated injustice, but men are too often like birds in a cage. They would not be there if they could escape, and the cage is not of their own designing. This wandering along on paper has passed an hour – and now for *The Story of an African Farm* that they are all praising. New militant woman eager for her rights! If the world is to be full of them, as I suspect it will be, I shall not be sorry to have gone . . .

FELL HOUSE, ULDALE,
April 3rd, 1883

. . . so three days ago Vanessa and I moved to Fell House for a
week or two. I am a very great deal better, can take a walk by
myself and am not so utterly dependent on Will as I have been –
how patient, tolerant, and sensible he's been no words can say,
but I recognize sufficiently that two moments in my life have
been supremely lucky – one when as a small boy I watched Will
win a race through Keswick, the other when as Victoria returned
crowned from Westminster I tumbled up against Caesar Kraft.
The love of one man for another is an odd thing: it is bare of sex
and yet does in certain moods surpass the love of woman. Maybe
I have never been a sexual man. Looking back now I can see that
it was not virtue kept me free in my youth but a certain fastidi-
ousness that I got, as I got so much else, from my mother. I
sometimes think that had I been the child of a street-woman and,
say, a card-sharper, I could have been something of a writer. But
no matter now. Never was anything of less importance. All the
same, being what I am, I doubt whether any relationship could be
finer than mine with Will. And it has been his fineness, not mine.
Complete unselfishness, unsparing devotion, and a deep, always
by me perceptible, emotion under it all. With all that it has been
always humorous, mixed with plenty of plain speaking. I cannot
see that it has had any falseness in it anywhere. And, although I
have no belief in immortality, it is hard for me, I confess, to
imagine a state when Will and I will not be together and con-
sciously together. Such a relationship as ours goes far beyond the
body and, maybe, survives the body. There is this at least about it
that it makes you think well of your fellow-men. It makes me
wonder sometimes whether any country but England (and sometimes I wonder any county but Cumberland) could produce such
a man as Will. He is altogether Cumbrian in his honesty, reticence, obstinacy. But this of course is nonsense. There are men
like him, I don't doubt, all the world over. My grandfather had
such a one. Quixote found one, Montaigne had one; thank God
the world is full of them.

Well, after this sentiment which no eye will ever see but my
own, here is the other side of the shield. The only other visitor
here but ourselves is Phyllis Newmark's boy, Philip Rochester.
Rochester, whom she married some thirty years ago, has something, I fancy, to do with railways and has amassed a nice fortune. Barney, I know, dislikes him and always calls him a

humbug. As for Master Philip, I have seldom disliked a young man so much. He is thin and willowy, talks in a piping voice about the 'Inevitability of Sin' and that 'Art is the only Moralist'. It happens that in this very week's *Punch* there is a little piece which I shall have great pleasure in showing him. It is apt enough to copy into this Journal:

TO BE SOLD, the whole of the Stock-in-Trade, Appliances, and Inventions of a Successful Aesthete, who is retiring from business. This will include a large stock of faded lilies, dilapidated sunflowers, and shabby peacocks' feathers, several long-haired wigs, a collection of incomprehensible poems, and a number of impossible pictures. Also, a valuable Manuscript Work, entitled *Instruction to Aesthetes*, containing a list of aesthetic catch-words, drawings of aesthetic attiudes, and many choice secrets of the craft. Also, a number of well-used dadoes, sad-coloured draperies, blue and white china, and brass fenders. To shallow-pated young men with no education, who are anxious to embark in a profitable business which requires no capital but impudence, and involves no previous knowledge of anything, this presents an unusual opportunity. No reasonable offer refused. Apply in the first instance to Messrs SUCKLEMORE and SALLOWACK, Solicitors, Chancery Lane.

A trifle sledge-hammer but it has got Mr Philip exactly. I wouldn't mind the young man's effeminacy, his ridiculous clothes, and his languor, were it not that he considers himself the Prince of the World. The scorn that he feels *and* expresses for everyone in his house is nauseating. Everyone but Vanessa, whom he condescends to admire, and talks of 'a perfect du Maurier' and how he wishes that Whistler could paint her. He would apparently make the attempt himself (for he paints the most atrocious daubs) 'had he the time'. Had he the time! When he never gets up before ten, wanders about the house like a misplanted lily, pecks at the piano and studies himself in the looking-glass. His morals would be, I have no doubt, revolting had he any blood in his poor body. He speaks of his 'soul-mates and the tyranny of the marriage laws' and such disgusting nonsense. I should shudder whenever the children approached him, but they, unlike his elders, find him a kind of clown. Amazingly, Timothy and Violet are both rather impressed, and Vanessa, in

her goodness of heart, is kind to him. How my mother would
have dealt with him!

April 8th

It is perhaps my illness, but whatever the reason I cling to this
old house as never before. My mother's presence is everywhere,
but, beyond that, the house itself for ever speaks to me as though
this were the last time it would ever shelter me, as though I were
the last human link it will ever have with all the life that is gone.
And that is true enough. There is no one else alive but myself
who knew it as it was. When I first came here Francis and Jennifer were living, David and Sarah were remembered and had seen
old Rogue Herries himself ride up, looking for his wandering
wife. David, Jennifer, my own mother died under its roof. Violet
has done all she can to ruin it, as the house very well knows. How
easy and pleasant to have left some of it as it was – at least the
little parlour that my mother so dearly loved. I can yet see it as it
was when I was a child – the old spinet with the roses painted on
the lid, the famous music box that was played for me when I was
good, with the King in his amber-coloured coat and the Queen in
her green dress. Then the carpet, upon which I sprawled with
John, that had the pictures of the great Battle, cannons firing
and horses rising on their haunches; the Chinese wallpaper with
pagodas of blue and white, temples, bridges, and flowers. Best of
all the sofa, the stuff of which was decorated with apple trees and
red apples. How well I remember that room and the way the
clock with the gold mandarin would strike the hour, coughing a
little between the strokes.

All gone now and also the things from my mother's bedroom,
the red chairs, the four-poster bed. All gone, all gone, the house
tonight seems to echo around me. And instead so many ugly
things, mahogany wardrobes like coffins set up on end, attempts
here and there to be in the fashion with imitation Morris wallpapers, sham Burne-Jones tapestry in the drawing-room – but
the dining-room how awful with its circular cellarette, the vast
Sheffield soup tureen, the sideboard with its malignant and obscene carved ends, the lacquered knife-tray, the needlework bell-
pulls that Timothy tugs at so furiously when he is impatient, the
sheep-faced mahogany clock – and all these things both Violet
and Timothy think so handsome! Yes, I can hear the old house
groaning through all its brickwork. I am the only one who knows
how deeply ashamed it feels!

April 15th

I must write tonight to banish some of this intolerable melancholy that has seized me. There is a real Cumberland wind wailing about the house, as though it had lost a thousand children. How sharp and strong it must be on the Tops! Almost impossible to keep your feet with the black heavy clouds driving furiously like chariots above you, and all the streams preparing for rain ... I have not been so well these last days and I have an assurance in my breast that my time now is short. I had my evening meal in my room and Vanessa came up to talk to me. I was allowed a fire and by the light of two candles we chatted, comfortably, easily, like the old friends we are. Why was it that I had so dreary a sense that this was to be our last talk? Nonsense, of course, and in the morning, as has happened so often before, feeling well again I shall laugh at my past terrors. But as I sat opposite over the fire I put out my hand to touch her dress as though I were frightened to lose her, and she drew her chair over to mine. She was cheerful and nonsensical as she often is, laughing at Phil Rochester who had been reading her some of his poems, one called 'The Lovers Last Cry' which was, I gathered, especially comical. Benjie is staying in Keswick. She is sure that he has some attraction there and takes it quite calmly. All she said about *that* was:

'When we marry and are together, I'll make him happy, I know.'

And to that *I* said:

'You'll have to beat him once a week. He says so himself.'

How I hate to leave her no one knows but me! She talked about herself, a thing that she very seldom does.

'I find that I'm intolerant, Papa. Intolerant and impatient.'

'Very well,' I said. 'Those are not bad things to be.'

'I was so angry with Timothy tonight that I could have smacked him. He was so extremely self-satisfied. I think all men are except yourself. Why should he talk as though he had *made* England?'

'That's a Herries habit,' I answered.

'Yes, but it's also something masculine. We were talking about Moody and Sankey and the Salvation Army and he said that such things weren't English. Englishmen never show their emotions, he said, and *that's* why England is what it is. What he meant was, "*I* never show my emotions and *that's* why England is what it is." '

'There's something in what he says,' I answered.

'Oh, well, I wanted to scream and beat that hideous Indian gong in the hall. Then he said that *The Story of an African Farm* is a disgusting book and ought to be burnt. When I asked him about it I discovered that he had only read the first chapter. And then after that he was going to say something about Benjie, but Violet stopped him.'

'Altogether a very pleasant meal,' I said.

'But why are we so different, you and I, from Timothy and Violet?'

'Two halves of the whole,' I told her. 'Life isn't complete without both of us.'

I could see that in reality she was deeply dissatisfied with herself. She is maturing, and I am sure that this long uncertain time with Benjie is affecting her seriously, although she is too proud to say anything about it.

She sat close to me, holding my hand, her splendid noble head raised high, looking into the fire.

'Well, I'm a perverse creature,' she said, nodding. 'I seem to have no control over myself at all.'

'But you *have*,' I assured her. 'You see you didn't bang the table and you didn't beat the gong.'

'No, but I can't be rational, the thing that all nice women ought to be. I laugh when I should be serious, I'm angry when there's nothing at all to be angry about. I'm not at all proper in my feelings either. Violet thinks it dreadful to mention the word adultery. She positively said the other day that the Commandments in church made her quite shy. She thinks it dreadful to be seen with a French novel. Oh! I do hope I'm not going to be a prig!'

I laughed at that.

'Why, no, I should say the very opposite.'

'No, but, Papa, virtuous about other people being *not* virtuous! ... In fact I hate myself tonight. Everything is wrong but you.'

She kissed me, laid her cheek against mine, made a fuss of me, told me again and again how she loved me, asked me to forgive her for all the trouble she had been to me. Never was she more sweet, never more my friend and companion. Before she went she turned at the door and blew me a kiss with her hand, laughing and saying: 'And now I'm going to the drawing-room to listen to Timothy telling us out of *The Times* what *he* would do if he were Gladstone.'

Tomorrow we are going for a drive.

This is the end of Adam's Journal. They were the last words that he ever wrote . . .

He lay in bed for a while, rather wide-awake, watching the shadows from the fire leap on the wall, hearing the wind scream about the house, tug at the windowpanes, belabour the trees and hammer the tendrils of the vines against the glass. He thought of the cottage at Cat Bells, how cosy, warm with life and human affections. He had brought there many of his mother's things, her books, some pictures, the account she dictated to Jane of her early days, bound in a fat, green-leather volume, the presentation that they made her on that fatal Hundredth Birthday. Vanessa would have these things and would pass them on, pass them on to her children and Benjie's, and they to theirs, and so it would go on and on, until at length it might be that it would only be through Judith's green book that anyone knew that once a man sold a woman at a Fair or fought for his beloved on Stye Head . . . He was growing sleepy. He laid his head on his breast inside his shirt as though to say goodnight to his heart and request it, as a favour, to keep quiet for an hour or two. He did not want to wake sharply to that grinding pain, that squeezing of the muscles between two inhuman fingers, that beating and struggling for breath . . . He was falling asleep and a stout man was riding on a horse and he a little boy as bare as your hand danced to annoy him and the stout man raised his whip . . .

He awoke. What had roused him he did not know. He sat up, resting on his arm. He was so deeply accustomed now to find himself woken at night by pain that that was his first thought: 'Where is the pain this time? Which part of me is misbehaving?' But there was no pain. His heart beat calmly and his back did not ache. He had no neuralgia across his forehead. The room was intensely dark. Many hours must have passed since he fell asleep, for the fire had been strong. Now there was no glimmer of dying log or fading coal. The wind was roaring like a beating lively voice in the darkness but, listening, he heard something beyond the wind – a small chattering whispering voice. Was there some-one in the room? No, it sounded like several voices, human and yet not human. He raised his head, sniffing. A moment later he was out of bed. Somewhere something was on fire. He opened the door and a belly of smoke blew towards him. He cried out: 'Fire! Fire!' and ran back into the room. It was then that the strange stillness of everything struck him. The house slept like the dead, he heard clocks ticking and somewhere a snore.

He pulled on a dressing-gown, and again, calling out 'Fire! Fire!', ran into the passage. His first thought was of Vanessa. He knew that her room was on the floor above his and, covering his mouth with his arm, turned towards the stairs, but even as he did so the passage to the left leading to the servants' quarters began – as it seemed to his excited imagination – to tremble, and a moment later through the green-baize door there shot a tongue of fire exactly like a vindictive criminal struggling to be free. A second later the flame shot upwards and little tongues began to lick the green baize, and a thin line of light, clear as day, shone between the hinges and the wall. At the same time the smoke rising in the same direction began to roll in thick grey waves, and the voices that it contained grew louder and angrier. What was strange was that the rest of the house, his room, the staircase from the hall, was cold, quiet, aloof, and even as he turned to the stair leading to the other floor he heard the cuckoo-clock that was at the corner of the hall below begin to sound the ridiculous bird's voice: 'Cuckoo! Cuckoo! Cuckoo!'

Still calling out and wondering in a mad irritation why nobody had been aroused by all this commotion, he stumbled up the stairs but, halfway up them, was met by another curling strand of smoke that seemed to issue from the wall on his left. For some reason that smoke bewildered him. It increased very rapidly, seeming to come from below him and to encircle him, to beat about his head, to come even from within himself, from his heart and lungs. He should now have been outside Vanessa's door, but he did not know where he was, for his eyes were blinded and weeping with the bitter and acrid thickness that now began to fill his mouth and heart and lungs.

He knocked his knees against a box or a chair, heard something fall somewhere and, turning his head, saw below him spurts and whirls of flame and a light that had a ferocity in it and a gigantic sense of power. He called out again and thought that some voice answered him, but he spoke against a wall, almost as though some enemy held a cloth over his mouth to deaden his cries. He thought: 'But this is absurd! Where are they all? What are they doing?' Called again and again: 'Vanessa! Vanessa! Wake up! Fire! Fire!' He moved to the right where he thought that her room must be, but now was caught in a perfect fog of smoke. His feet struck some more stairs and he remembered that above this floor were the attics. If he could reach those he could fling open the windows, for even his mad anxiety for Vanessa was countered by his agony for breath. His lungs were choked, he could not see and, although his brain was clear, his limbs refused to obey him. At that same moment pain leapt on to him, pain moving in the centre of the smoke. An iron hand crushed his breast. The fingers pressed and pressed. He fell on to his knees. 'A moment,' he thought. 'This pain will pass and I shall be able to move again.' But it did not. The giant hand turned and turned, so that he could see his poor heart crushed, screwed round and then squeezed until the pain seemed to draw his very eyeballs down into his stomach.

His last conscious thought was of Vanessa. 'Vanessa,' he murmured, 'Vanessa.' He rolled over and lay there, prone, while the eddies of smoke – strong, careless, singing a song – rose, saluted the wind, filling every cranny.

Vanessa had been long in a dreamless sleep when she awoke to the sound of a loud banging on her door. Even as she opened her eyes Violet and Timothy rushed in, behind them a strange glare and everywhere in the air a crackling, murmuring, buzzing frenzy.

She did not need their cry: 'Vanessa! Get up! The whole house is on fire!'

In an instant everything was visible and clear to her. She seemed in that moment of springing out of bed to have time to notice everything – the calm undisturbed paraphernalia of the bedroom, her clothes across the chair, the yellow sofa that she always thought so ugly, the long looking-glass in which were reflected Timothy and Violet, Timothy with a riding coat over his nightshirt, Violet in a bright blue dressing-gown, and behind them that sinister glitter veiled with sudden mists. The air stank of smoke. She heard a dog bark.

Violet pulled at her arm.

'It's terrible! It's terrible!' she continued to cry. 'The whole house is on fire!'

And Timothy, running back, called:

'The children! The children! Get the children!'

But her own thought was at once for her father. She thought of nothing and nobody else. She put on her dressing-gown and slippers with a single gesture and ran out. She saw them flocking down the stairs – Philip, Timothy, Violet, the children. The stairs were still untouched. You seemed from the lower stairs to

plunge into darkness while on the first floor the baize door was a
sheet of flame and all around her the smoke rose like water,
flooding forward, eddying back again. She ran down the first
flight and crossed at once into her father's room. It was empty.
At that same moment she thought that through the crackle of the
fire she heard a cry from above her: 'Vanessa!' She listened, and
even as she did so saw Timothy's head and shoulders above the
lower banister.

'Father!' she cried. 'He is not in his room!'

Timothy shouted back. 'Come down! The whole place is falling down. It's all right – everyone's out. Yes, Adam too. He is on
the lawn!'

She turned back once more into his room, saw the bed disordered, caught – without knowing what she did, obeying some
blind instinct – things from the table, his Journal, a book, his
gold watch; then ran out to meet in full force a towering column
of smoke that rose in front of her like some genie. Gasping, her
hand over her face, she ran forward, was down the stairs,
through the door, and, in an instant, in a wild, chill, blowing
world, the wind screaming above her, voices everywhere, shouts
and cries, some child's wail, the neighing of horses, and faces
white like paste in the blinding light of the fire.

She ran from figure to figure, not recognizing them at all as
persons, for they also seemed to be running, moving in some kind
of dance through the wind.

She called again and again:

'Father! Father! Where are you?' She pulled at some man's
arm: 'My father! Is he here? Have you seen him?' and some
figure that she did not know, someone holding a clock and a
picture, cried, as though in an ecstasy. 'The house! The house!
The roof will be in!'

Then she ran into Leathwaite. He cried before she could speak:
'Miss Vanessa! The master! He's not here!'

They turned together and ran towards the house which was
now all bright with flame and alive in every part, while from its
heart there came a beat like a drum and above it arms of fire
strained up to the ebony sky, starred with the pigeons from the
loft, flying into the light as though splashed with bright water,
then vanishing into darkness.

Will dashed through the door. She would have gone after him
but some man's hand held her, gripping her shoulder. 'You
mustn't go, Miss Vanessa,' someone shouted in her ear as though

she were deaf. 'It's not safe—' and then called, 'Will! Will! Come back! Everyone's out!'

She struggled. 'Let me go! What do you mean? They are not all out. My father is there—'

A moment later Will's face, strangely unreal, appeared at a window. He shouted to them.

'He's not here! I'm in his room!' And then, after looking into the room again: 'I can't go back! The fire's too strong!'

'Jump!' several voices cried, and a woman screamed. He climbed out on to the windowsill, let his legs dangle, caught his arm in something and fell.

And, at once, as things happen in dreams, inconsequent, without reason, Vanessa saw that Benjie was beside her. She heard his voice, as from an infinite distance, explaining that he had come back from Keswick that evening, been roused and at once ridden down. 'Oh, thank God you're safe, Vanessa,' he said, hurried from her as figures do in dreams, was back again, his arm round her, crying, 'It's all right. Will's broken a leg. No one else is harmed. Everyone's safe.'

She tore herself away from him.

'No, no, Benjie! Don't you see? Father's in there! Father's there!'

She ran forward. He pulled her back.

'Don't be mad. No one can live in there! The roof is falling!'

She fought him, she struck his face.

'Let me go! Let me go! We must find him!'

He held her with all his strength, pressing her against him. The ground was covered with people; the horses that they had taken from the stable trampled and neighed. With a great gesture, as though in a frenzy of exultation, the flames flung up their arms, the roof crashed.

The house gave up its life.

WILD NIGHT IN THE HILLS

THERE was at that time in the hills between Derwentwater and Cummock a very lonely farm called Hatchett's Fosse.

To this farm Benjamin Herries rode some three days after Adam Paris' burial at Ireby.

Adam's charred and almost unrecognizable body had been found when at last the fire had died sufficiently for safe search to be made. The red brick walls of Fell House still stood, blackened and scorched but enduring. But these walls were a shell. Nothing else remained. The wind that night had been so ferocious that in any circumstances there could have been small hope of saving the house, but everything had contributed to aggravating the disaster: the ancient fire-engine at Braithwaite broke down on the road. There was nothing at the house itself, no protection of any kind. The horses and animals were saved. No life was lost but Adam's. A little furniture, some pictures, were rescued. That was all. Fell House, Uldale, was no more.

The death of Adam Paris shocked the whole countryside. He had not been widely known. He was held to be a 'shy sort of man' but he was liked. He was said to be kindly, friendly, generous. No one had anything against him. He was old Madame's son, even though he had been born on the wrong side of the blanket, and he wrote books. But more than any of these, he was the father of Vanessa, whose beauty was renowned from Silloth to Kendal. Everyone knew how she had loved him, and there was something deeply real and true in the sympathy that rose now on every side of her. Cumberland people are reputed by those who know them little to be too blunt of tongue for complacent comfort, but any man in trouble will be lucky if he has Cumbrian friends near to him. They have not been masters of their own soil for hundreds of years without learning what courtesy means, and courtesy is not in this part of England another name for heartlessness.

But Vanessa was stricken down in these first days beyond any possibility of help. With Jane Bellairs and Will she went back to Cat Bells and there she stayed, seeing nobody. On the day before the funeral she saw Benjie. He knew at once that she could not just then bear either to see him or talk to him.

She spoke in a low voice, looking beyond him at the door as though she expected someone to come in.

'I don't blame you, Benjie. You did what you thought right, but you should not have held me back.'

'Vanessa, *how* could I have let you go? The roof fell in a moment later. You would have been killed as well as Adam. What good would that have been?'

'I had rather have been killed. To think that he was alone in there! That nobody but myself and Will thought of him!'

He saw that at present there was nothing to be done. He kissed her. She made no movement, no response. She said in a low voice:

'The awful thing is that I heard him calling me. From some other part of the house. But Timothy told me he was out. I will never forgive Timothy and I will never forgive myself.'

When he went home things were no better. His mother had been unwell for some months, and the night of the fire with its tragic consequences was a shock from which it was unlikely that she would recover. The destruction of Fell House was a dreadful thing to her. She had been there so often. John, her husband, had been born there; he had walked out of there to his death. More than that, this appeared to her to be a revenge from the past. Her father had built the Fortress to triumph over Fell House. It had seemed at his death that he was defeated; but he had *not* been defeated. This was the last unexpected triumph of the Fortress, a house that she had always hated and now detested. She seemed to hear her brother Uhland tapping with his stick night and day about the passages. How satisfied he must be! These vindictive people were stronger in death than they had been in life and there was no end to their malevolence. She had loved Adam, and her heart ached now for Vanessa. She was old, alone with ghosts. No one could help her.

Benjie, her son, it seemed, least of all. She had been very patient with his selfishness, but now at last she was exasperated. He seemed to her hard and callous. For once her intuition failed her. She did not know that he was suffering more deeply than she. On the day after Adam's funeral he came into her bedroom and said:

'I can't bear this, Mother. I must go away for a day or two.'

'What can't you bear?' she asked him quietly.

'Vanessa,' he broke out in a kind of storm of indignation, 'thinks that I was responsible for Adam's death.'

She thought that he was indignant with Vanessa, but had she been well and strong she would have known that the indignation was with himself.

'She is suffering from shock,' she answered. 'You must be patient and wait.'

'Wait! Wait!' he burst out. 'For what? Everything is changed, Mother. It will never be the same again.'

The farmer at Hatchett's Fosse was Fred Halliday, the son of the woman with whom Benjie had stayed at Seascale.

Some months back Benjie, riding along Main Street, saw Mrs

Halliday and her daughter Marion looking at him from across
the street. His first impulse had been to move on, but something
had prevented him. He did not like them, he did not wish to see
them again; nevertheless he rode over and spoke to them. They
were to stay in Keswick for a while. Mrs Halliday had notions of
opening a boarding house there. Still with that strange mingling
of attraction and repulsion, he had met them a number of times.
Mrs Halliday was definitely repugnant to him: she whined, she
crept, she was genteel, she was vindictive. The girl spoke little,
had little colour in her voice or movements, but she had some
power over him. He kissed her and hated himself for doing so.
She appeared to expect his distaste; indeed she said to him
once:

'How you dislike me!'

But she did not seem at all to resent this except that, in her
still, motionless way, she resented everything. Her pale skin, thin
anaemic body, quiet, almost stealthy movements, stirred him as
though he were attracted by his own exact opposite. She did not
speak to his mind nor his heart, but his senses. When he touched
her – and always it seemed that it was by her volition and not his
– he felt no tenderness nor affection, but a sensual inquisitiveness
as though something persuaded him to explore further – as
though some sensual secret were hidden there which would,
when discovered, excite and surprise him.

He did not know – and he did not care – whether she liked him
or no. She appeared to like no one, to have no life beside that of
sudden little movements, unexpected advances and withdrawals.
One evening he met her in the dusk walking down the hill behind
St John's Church. He talked to her and then embraced her
passionately. She eagerly returned his embraces. He went home
in a mood of bitter revulsion against himself. He had met her
brother several times in Keswick. Fred Halliday was a big, broad,
red-faced hearty man, quite unlike his mother and sister, who
laughed at everything, drank a good deal, and was friend of all
the world. And yet it was true that nobody in Keswick liked him.
He was not trusted, and it was said that when drunk he was very
quarrelsome and abusive.

Not a very worthy family for Benjie to be friendly with, but
then it was always like that with him. When he was jolly, as at
most times he was, anyone would do to be jolly with. At this
period of his life almost anyone was good enough to pass the time
of day with. Who was he to be a judge? Except for his mother and

Vanessa no one alive mattered. He was proud of not caring. Life was not important and one man resembled another. He loved Vanessa, who was much too good for him, and if women liked to be kissed, why, he liked to kiss them! In spite of his escapades he had never yet got any woman into trouble. His luck in that had held. He would not hurt anyone for the world.

But as he rode out to Hatchett's Fosse he was not sure that he did not want to hurt everybody. Fred Halliday had often invited him to come and see the farm; he had never thought that he would really go. But now anywhere would do, anywhere away from his own unhappiness, his sense that he had lost Vanessa for ever and that he deserved to have lost her.

The morbid side of his character had grown stronger during this past year. Although he loved the place, this Cumberland country always increased the strain of superstition so deeply ingrained in his character. Away from his home he was as other men and could consort with them on equal terms, but at the Fortress and in the country around him he felt sometimes like a man caught in a trap. On the one hand was the small lonely house in Skiddaw Forest where his father had been murdered; on the other – and only a step away – the great cavern beneath Skiddaw where all the spirits of the true men lived and rejoiced for ever. Surely fantastic nonsense as food for a healthy man's brain! But in this Benjie was not healthy, nor are most imaginative men free of certain dreams, omens, and apprehensions. These two contrasted things were for him perhaps only symbols, but they brought with them a conviction that, whenever he returned to this country, he was not his own free master. And yet he must return! He could not keep away from it. He could not remain in it when he was there. And were his instincts altogether wrong? Had he not, in this last year, been twice prevented from marrying Vanessa, once by her father's illness and now by this cursed fire? The Men under Skiddaw would receive him in their company *if* he could reach them, but, like a man in a dream, he was held back. Who could dare to deny that the past was more powerful than the present and that you must fight like the devil or the moment you were born you were done for! That old ancestor of his, Francis Herries, might still have something to say!

All this was, of course, only a part of Benjie's mind. None of the men who knew him as he roamed the world would credit him with *this* kind of imagination! But he was compounded of stiff

incongruities – proud and yet humble, faithful and yet most
unfaithful, wandering but steadfast – and at this time he was still
young with most of his soul-making ahead of him.

So as he rode down Bassenthwaite and on towards Braithwaite
he felt only an urgent need of escape: escape from the senseless
waste of Adam's death, from all the grief that that was causing
(he had an eager sensitiveness to the unhappiness of others);
escape from his mother, whom he knew that he should not be
leaving; but above all escape from Vanessa, whom he loved now
when he was sure that he had lost her, with a deeper sense of
frustration than ever before.

Then he raised his head, looked up at the stormy sky and
swore. 'Well, *this* has settled the business. She is better, far better,
without me. She'll know that at last.'

But even while he said this he felt that they were inseparable,
that however their lives went they would be bound together for
ever – yes, even when he was secure and singing with the Men
under Skiddaw he would be thinking of her!

As he began slowly to climb Whinlatter he felt the wind tugging at him. On the day following the fire the wind had folded its
arms and stolen away as though the purpose of its coming were
accomplished. Then, as is often the case in the late spring, it
sprang up again and rushed about the country in flurries of
excitement, blowing the daffodils silly, making the young leaves
tremble and the young sheep skip, and flashing quivers of light
like turning glass across the streams. The colours were all delicate
– faint shadowed plum, a gold so pale that it was almost white
under cloud, a wet virginal green of the young bracken. And field
after field, up and up the hillsides, was silver-grey.

This afternoon, though, quite another mood was in the air,
spring was forgotten. It happens sometimes here that the hills, as
though an order had been given, suddenly dominate all the scene.
The pastoral fields, the farms, the roads, towns, villages
shrink together into nothingness and the hills step forward,
spread their shoulders, swell their chests out, raise their heads
and begin to march. If you listen you can almost hear the tramp-
ing. It is at such times that you can understand Benjie's fantasy
of his men under the mountain, for it is no fantasy just then. Lie
down on the turf and listen with your ear to the ground and you
can catch the echo of the voices, a rumble of a drinking song and
laughter like the cracking of a drum's skin. At such a moment
when the hills take power there is a sense of menace in the air.

The sky is disturbed with a furious confusion, great sweeps of cloud smoking along with a wind behind them that is personal in its strength. The old pictures of Aeolus blowing the four winds from his mouth is true now. You can see him standing behind the hills, his strong legs spread across the sea, his broad naked shoulders stretched above his vigorous lungs. The wind and the hills act in unison. The hills, that are in actual measurement so slight, take on themselves additional properties that belong to the great mountains of the world. With white mist flanking them and black funnels of cloud eddying above their heads, they seem as powerful as Everest. Their power is menacing. They seem to crowd together in conclave: 'Now shall we step forward and crush out of existence these little fields, cowering hamlets, tiny midgets of humans?' You can watch them as they bend their heads together and twitch their shoulders with the impatience of a group of boys waiting for the word of release. The wind is enchanted with the sport promised. It goes swinging from arm to arm of the hills, crying: 'Now let us go! Now we are off!' and it sweeps whirlwinds of rain now here, now there, making it sting the earth like a hail of small shot, then raising it again in sheets of steel as though all the heavens were letting down their defensive gates. A great game that leads to no ill because the power here is friendly. They have not learnt any deep vindictiveness. This square of earth is kind to the men who settle, for a moment, upon its surface. The Genius here is benevolent.

Such a storm of wind without rain rose about Benjie as he climbed Whinlatter. The water of Bassenthwaite below him that had been a field of grey shadows as he rode beside it was now, when he looked down upon it, trembling with white waves that gleamed with an almost phosphorescent glow under the blackness of Skiddaw. The clouds were so low that when he was at the highest point of the Pass they skirted him on every side, shifting from place to place with long sweeps of spidery grey. It was bitterly cold and he had to lower his head, pulling up the collar of his riding coat.

He knew that with Lorton Fell on his right, before he turned off down to Swinside, his path branched away to the left. The farm was just here somewhere, in a hollow between Grisedale Pike and Hobcarton. He directed his horse across the rough turf, moving very slowly under the sting of the wind. To his right he looked down on to the flat plain that stretched to the Border with fields like squares of a chessboard and trees and houses like dolls'

furniture. The wind raced over this flat country with a shrill
whistling exultation; thin patches of white broke the grey sky
above the sea. It was raining above St Bees.

It would be difficult to find this place, and if the mist came
down, impossible. He might wander here for hours. He cursed
himself for coming, and had an impulse to turn back. In certain
moods this driving wind and cold sharp air would have exalted
him, but not today, for he was sick with his own self-distrust and
disapproval. Nothing grand about him today to answer the grandeur of the elements. Why should he not turn back and wait
patiently for Vanessa to recover? How impulsive he had been to
have taken her present mood as permanent! And how selfish he
had been to ride away from her at the very moment when, in her
heart, she needed him! He half turned his horse's head. He
would go back. Then, as he looked round him, he saw the farm, a
little to his right in the fold of the hill, a bare meagre place with a
few bent trees and a stone wall. The first drops of rain stung his
cheek. He rode on.

When he reached the farm two dogs ran out, wildly barking:
he heard Fred's voice cursing them and then saw the big stout
man filling the doorway.

He gave a shout when he saw who it was.

'Hullo, Herries! What a surprise!'

He came to meet him, his face beaming.

'You've come for the night, I hope?'

'Yes,' said Benjie. 'If you'll have me.'

'Of course I'll have you. Couldn't be better.'

They led the horse round to the stable at the back of the house,
Halliday talking all the time.

'My mother and sister are staying here and some friends of
ours are coming up from Lorton this evening, so you've struck
the right moment. It's going to be a wild night. The wind's
blowing great guns. Come along in and get warm.'

Benjie went in, hung up his hat and coat, passed into an inner
room that seemed half kitchen, half living-room. Sitting beside a
roaring fire were Mrs Halliday and her daughter.

At the moment when he saw them, the large smoke-stained
fireplace, the window that looked out on to a little scrambling
path where a cluster of primroses was hiding, two canaries in a
cage, and a large sheepdog lying in front of the fire with his nose
on his paws, his mood changed. This was jolly, cheerful,
friendly. They were all friends of his. Other friends were coming.

They would make a night of it. He had closed a door, a heavy silent-swinging door like one that guards a cathedral, upon all that other world where his friends were burnt, those whom he loved blamed him and, worst of all, where he blamed himself. Here he loved no one and no one loved him. It was not a world of hurting, haunting intimacies. He would be happy. So, as always when he was happy, he wanted to do things for everybody, drew a chair to the fire and chattered like a boy, threw back his head and roared with laughter, his rather ugly face with friendliness and generosity in all its wrinkles. And the two women quietly answered or asked questions while Fred Halliday leaned his bulk against the kitchen dresser and, with a smile on his face, watched them.

Benjie had all the London gossip: of the success that *Iolanthe* was and the other piece that the German Reeds were running, *The Mountain Heiress*, where Corney Grain was a solicitor and sang a wonderful song called 'Our Mess', and that Goring Thomas' *Esmeralda* at the Lane, where Mr Carl Rosa had a month's opera season, contained, they say, some pretty songs but that Mme Georgina Burns couldn't act for toffee.

Mrs Halliday said that the matter with the London theatre today was that it was too expensive, not comfortable enough, and that most of the plays were silly. In fact, with a few well-chosen words, she demolished the London theatre. And Benjie said, oh, he didn't know. That was a little severe, wasn't it, and that one went to the theatre to be jolly, didn't one, and that he'd go a long way to hear Corney Grain sing 'Our Mess'. Then they discussed the Budget, which had been introduced a week or two before by Mr Childers. Certainly had forestalled the Conservatives, who had been intending to come out as Champions of Economy, but Gladstone knew two of that. Everyone talking of Economy now. Yes, said Mrs Halliday, the great thing was of course to *be* economical, but easier to say than to do. Benjie, nodding his head profoundly, agreed that that *was* the problem!

Then they discussed books, and Benjie said that he did hope that Miss Marion didn't read French novels, and Miss Marion said that she sometimes did and thought them very amusing, much nearer to real life than silly writers like Rhoda Broughton and Ouida. She liked poetry, though. Did Mr Herries read poetry? No, Mr Herries didn't. A writer like Tennyson took such a long time to say what he wanted to. No, Miss Halliday did *not* agree. Poetry could do something that nothing else could do.

Wouldn't Mr Herries agree to that? And, yes, he thought on the whole that he *did* agree to that!

So they talked in the pleasantest fashion and the time flew by while the wind roared outside and the rain that had swept up from the sea beat against the window frames. Fred Halliday had some excellent beer and Benjie drank plenty of it. The fire, the beer, the pleasant easy talk all comforted and reassured him. Yes, the door, with its heavy leather curtain, had swung to; all sounds from the outer world were deadened. Mrs Halliday, he thought, was a more agreeable woman than he supposed. She sat there knitting a stocking most domestically. Her face was grave, but after all, not repellent at all. The glow from the fire softened her rather gaunt features.

Once and again she smiled, baring her teeth with her upper lip, almost as though she were about to whistle.

And as to the girl he felt once more, and increasingly as the beer warmed him, that he would like to touch her. He must be kind to her, poor child, for she could not have much happiness in her life. He began to wonder whether she had not finer feelings, more sensitive tastes than her mother and brother could satisfy. She read French, she liked poetry. Not that she had any pride. No one could be quieter about her accomplishments. Once or twice he caught her looking at him, her pale eyes staring at him, and he felt then a little embarrassment, as though he should be ashamed of his brown face and strong body when she herself was so delicate. At the thought of her delicacy some sensuous nerve in him was touched. She was so slight, so fragile, that in his arms she would be powerless, must submit to anything that he wished. Not that he would hurt her. He would not hurt anybody in the world.

The shrill clock on the mantelpiece struck seven and, a moment later, the door was flung open and Halliday came in, bringing three men with him. These men had taken their coats off in the passage; two of them were youngish, had rough corduroy trousers with long black coats containing deep pockets. One of the two was little and wiry, with bright red hair and a small, shaggy, red beard; the other was broad, strong, very dark with bright, glancing, restless eyes and a close-clipped black moustache. He was a handsome fellow. These two men might be both between thirty and forty in age. The third, as Benjie immediately learned, was the father of these two. He was tall and thin, dressed in a long black coat with wide tails and black trousers. His hair was grey and sparse; he had little eyes and above them a very high domed forehead. He looked something like a schoolmaster.

Halliday introduced them to Benjie. Their name, he discovered, was Endicott; Thomas the elder one, George and Robert the two sons. They all sat down by the fire. Thomas Endicott had rather a shrill piercing voice, small in compass and high-pitched. He spoke with care as though, with difficulty, he had learned how to be cultured. The voices of the two younger men were rough. Robert, the little red-haired fellow, spoke with an effeminate note; he was restless and given to gestures. George's voice was deep but without any Cumbrian accent. They seemed friendly. They knew the two women and were old acquaintances, it appeared, of Halliday. Endicott the elder talked to Benjie, a little pompously and always with that slow carefulness as though he would choose the right word and never on any account drop an 'h'. Oh no, they did not live at Lorton. He himself resided in Whitehaven. Yes, oh yes, his wife and her sister lived with him. This boy George here, oh! he was a rascal, could settle to nothing, had been in the Army for a bit, hadn't he, George? Could put his hand to anything, a fine boxer; oh yes, a splendid footballer if he kept in condition – but a rascal. Wouldn't settle to anything, would he, George? They all laughed, and George smiled at Benjie in friendly fashion, as much as to say: 'I like you. I've taken to you. We shall be friends.'

Oh yes, and Robert was a wanderer too. He would go from place to place selling things, go round Fairs, you know, all over the country. What you would call a pedlar in the old days. Didn't mind what he did any more than George.

Oh, they were a wandering family. That's what his wife always complained of. Yes, an old Border family. Nothing much to boast of a hundred years ago – smugglers and worse, so he heard.

'As a matter of fact, Mr Herries,' he said, 'I have been wanting to meet you. We're almost related in a kind of way. There was a girl in our family years ago married one of your ancestors, well known in the Borrowdale district. Rogue Herries he was called.'

'What!' cried Benjie. 'Rogue Herries! Why!—'

'Aye, there were two brothers, George and Anthony Endicott, mad Tony they called him. Their sister married a man called Starr and these two had a daughter. It was her old Herries married.'

Why, that was Judith's mother! Benjie was indeed amazed;

what with the beer and the warmth of the kitchen everything seemed to him now wonderful and jolly and all that it should be. Here they were, these three nice fellows, and their ancestress was Judith's mother. Judith's mother, Vanessa's great-grandmother – but at that thought the leather-curtained door, that had for a moment swung back, was closed again. No thought of Vanessa. Vanessa was far away.

'Aye,' said Thomas Endicott. 'Funny how small the world is. I've often thought I'd like to meet one of you, although maybe those ancestors of ours are nothing to be proud of.'

'Proud of them!' cried Benjie. 'I should think I am! Francis Herries you're speaking of, was a great man, a grand fighter, and a man of his hands.'

'Aye,' said Thomas Endicott slowly. 'There are plenty of stories of him in Borrowdale. He sold his woman at a Fair once, they tell.'

'And a good thing too!' Benjie cried. 'What do you say, Mrs Halliday? If you're tired of a woman and someone else wants her? Why not sell her? Fair exchange, you know.'

But Mrs Halliday only smiled and went on knitting.

Then they had supper, a very good supper too, ham and beef and chicken, a big apple tart, rum butter and cheese and plenty of cakes. Halliday produced a wine, a good warming Burgundy, and while they ate and chattered and laughed the wind tore at the house as though it would tumble it over. But the house was strong, very old, Halliday told them.

'There was a man murdered here once,' Halliday said. 'In the 'forties it was. His wife and daughter murdered him for his money. Cut his head open with a hatchet and he bled all over this very floor.'

After supper they all helped to clear the table and then they sang songs. There was an old piano there, not strictly in tune but what did that matter? They roared out the songs and banged the piano and laughed and stood with their arms round one another's shoulders.

Soon Benjie knew that he was very merry, very merry indeed. Not drunk; oh no, not drunk at all, but as happy as a grig. He had never had a better evening. What splendid fellows they were, and especially George! His hand rested on George's shoulder. He must see George again, must see George often. This was the kind of evening he enjoyed. Yes, he would like to do something for him, put George in the way of a job if he wanted one. And

George looked at him as though he liked him. He didn't say much, but he smiled and pushed out his chest when he sang and poured beer down his throat.

The ladies said goodnight. It was time for them to retire.

'We shall see you in the morning,' said Mrs Halliday. 'What a wild night it is, to be sure!'

Some time later Benjie thought that he must go to the door for a moment to cool his head. He slipped out, opened the front door, and was almost tumbled off his feet by the wind. The world was raging outside, the rain sweeping through the air in whipping fury. With great difficulty he closed the door again and turned back to see the girl standing there quite close to him. There was a dim reflection of light from the upper floor. The voices of the men singing came raucously from the inner room.

'Why, Marion!' he said.

'I am just going up to bed.'

'It was so hot in there I came out for a breath of air.'

'Yes, I know. I was hot too.'

Her hand was touching his. He caught it, then putting his arms around her, kissed her, She kissed him passionately in return, her lips clinging to his as though they would never leave them. When he held her in his arms, so slight and slender was she that he was afraid of hurting her.

'I'm hurting you,' he whispered.

'I like you to hurt me,' she whispered back, then gently freeing herself, said 'Goodnight' and ran up the stairs.

Oh, well, he shouldn't have done that. But she was so close to him. She was in his arms before he realized it. Kissing a girl – nothing in it. It was natural to kiss a girl. There was something about her ... not that he liked her ... He stood for a moment leaning against the wall in the dark passage, and felt an odd chagrin, an almost desperate loneliness, an impulse to leave the house at once, fetch his horse from the stable and ride home ...

But he went back into the room, joining the chorus with them as he entered it.

Now that the women were gone, gaiety and friendliness rose a note higher. This was what life should be, men together with care thrown out of the window, plenty to drink, a wild night outside, all friends together. They might have known one another all their lives. Father Endicott was not such a school-master as you might suppose. He possessed, in fact, a grand fund of bawdy stories. Very funny they were. That one about the old farmer's wife of Esthwaite and the two simple young men and the lady from London. There was nothing about old Cumberland life that he didn't know, the life that was going now so fast with all the tourists in the summer and the railways everywhere. A pity, a pity! Those were the good old days when Lizzie O'Branton, the witch, jumped out of her coffin at her funeral and rode away on a broomstick, and Mrs Machell of Penrith would drive her ghostly carriage whenever a 'helm' wind was blowing, when the 'need fire' charmed the cattle, when the song was sung at the shearing. Here they broke out all together:

> Heigh O! Heigh O! Heigh O!
> And he that doth this health deny,
> Before his face I him defy.
> He's fit for no good company,
> So let this health go round.

Good fun, too, when they had the public whippings, or the hangings in Carlisle or the witch-drownings.

'Changed times,' said old Endicott sadly. 'All the fine spirit gone.'

But *their* spirit was not gone. It increased with every drop they drank. The table was pushed aside and George and Benjie tried a 'wrastle'. They took off their coats, waistcoats, and shoes and went to it. Solemnly they circled round and round trying for a hold. But Benjie was no very great wrestler and soon George had 'buttocked' him and, throwing him, tumbled over him. They crashed to the floor and then lay there, panting, one on the other. For they were not drunk, oh no, not drunk at all, but it was comfortable there on the floor and Benjie had his arm round George's neck, looked up at the whitewashed ceiling, pulled George's hair, said, laughing, 'I like you, George. We're friends, we are,' and George's hand rested on Benjie's back and he said nothing at all. Old Endicott played a polka on the piano and they danced heavily, clumsily, staggering about the room, and Benjie cried:

'There's a fine place under Skiddaw, George, where we'll go when we're dead and we'll dance and sing for ever and ever.'

'Aye,' said George. 'Aye. That'll be grand.'

In all the merry evening there was only one unpleasant incident, which Benjie could never after properly recall.

He said something to little red-bearded Robert, and Robert took offence. The little man was dancing with rage and screaming out:

'You're a liar, I tell you. A damned bloody liar!'

'Call me a liar?' shouted Benjie.

'Aye, and I will too. Who do you think I am?'

'Why!' cried Benjie. 'I'll tell you who you are. You're a funny little man, that's who you are!'

'I was here in this country before any of you were born. Aye, and I was too, selling laces and silver boxes, visiting the witches in Borrowdale—'

'Shut your mouth, Robert,' cried George. 'Who wants to listen to your lies? Why, man—'

'Lies, are they?' The little man was screaming, dancing up and down until to Benjie's dazzled eyes he seemed a dozen little men with peaked caps on their heads, riding through the kitchen on the wind and rain. But the little man wanted to fight, and the others, roaring with laughter, held his arms and they knocked the lamp over. The room was dark save for the firelight. Oh, but the little man's red beard shone and he was angry! And Benjie embraced him, pulled his beard, gave him a friendly kick on the pants, and he went and sat in a corner by the fireplace, waving his hands and making shadows of rabbits on the wall with his fingers.

Later, Benjie found himself with a candle wandering on his way to bed. Halliday showed him where his room was, a little whitewashed room at the top of the house. Halliday helped him into bed.

And later than that, as he lay looking at the ceiling and smiling, the door opened. The girl stood there, a candle in her hand, wearing a dressing-gown with a wool collar over her nightdress.

He sat up on his elbow and looked at her. She closed the door very softly and came over to him. She smiled and said:

'The wind's died down. Everyone's sleeping.'

He could only stare at her. She took off her dressing-gown and carefully laid it on the chair. Then she blew out the candle, climbed into bed and lay down beside him.

INSIDE THE FORTRESS

IT was early in the wet and stormy weather of that year when Vanessa came to stay with Elizabeth at the Fortress.

Elizabeth had been seriously ill ever since the fire at Fell House in April. No one could say exactly where the trouble was. It was what was known as a 'decline'. She was weak, instantly tired by any exertion; her features now had the delicacy of a thin rose-tinted shell. Her hair was snow-white, her figure still slim and erect, but ghost-like in its fragility. She walked a little from room to room: although she leaned on a stick she was still tall. She was kind and gracious to everyone, but most of her, as Mrs Harwen, the cook-housekeeper, said, was 'otherwhither'.

'It's my opinion,' John Harwen, the handyman about the place and Mrs Harwen's little hostler-like spouse, remarked, 'That the difference between her living and her dead is so slight that you'll not notice it. After she's gone she'll still be here, so to speak.'

'We've enough ghosts in this house already,' said Mrs Harwen.

Benjie had not been home since June. No one knew where he was. No one had heard from him. Elizabeth had through many years practised herself to be patient about these absences, but now it was another matter. For she knew that she had not long to live and she had only one desire in her heart – that Benjie and Vanessa should be married before she went.

She had not seen very much of Vanessa. The girl had stayed first with Timothy in Eskdale, where he had thoughts of buying a house (for he had decided not to rebuild Fell House), then had returned to Cat Bells, where Will and the old cook had looked after her.

In July she visited Elizabeth, who saw at once that here now was a woman of self-command, deep reserves and a very fine courage. Vanessa was cheerful, talked freely about her father, seemed indeed to wish to talk of him, recalling days and moments and words and phrases; saying: 'Papa always felt that' or 'Papa never troubled to be angry – he said it was waste of time.' But his death, Elizabeth saw, had made a fundamental change in Vanessa, had brought out certain qualities that were latent before, and had checked others.

She was not so impetuous: her heart was as warm but it was guarded now against shock.

Just before she went she said:

'And what about Benjie?'

Elizabeth told her that she had not heard, that she had no idea where he was.

'It's a shame!' Vanessa cried indignantly. 'You wanting him—'

'Yes,' said Elizabeth quietly. 'I am not going to live much longer, my dear, and I *must* see him. But no one knows where he is.'

'I think,' said Vanessa lowly, 'that perhaps I am partly to blame. He came to see me – after the fire. I was not myself. I didn't want Benjie or anyone. I wanted to be left alone. So he went away.'

'We'll be independent of him,' said Elizabeth gently.

Then Vanessa asked if she might come and stay. Elizabeth's pale cheek flushed.

'Oh, Vanessa dearest, do you mean it? Will you really come? How happy I shall be!'

Early in September Vanessa came. No one knew what that was to her, the first time that she looked from the long windows of the Fortress down to the valley where, very clearly, in the pale colourless moving air, the walls of Fell House were still standing. She had been dreading this moment from the instant when she made her proposal of a visit to Elizabeth. She had not seen the place since the day of the funeral. But she knew that it had to be faced, that everything had to be faced. She had learnt many things since April and one of them was that the only way to make anything of life was to fit, resolutely, with courage, into the patterns that life, in change after change, presented. To attempt to force life into *your* pattern was to challenge disaster. You must accept *everything* and turn it to good.

So she stood there that morning in her black dress, her hands clenched at her sides, the house silent about her with that dull brooding silence that seemed the Fortress' special property. In the valley the four bare walls stood, the moors climbing above them as though they already recognized that here was a spot that now they would soon reclaim, as, one day, they would reclaim everything.

Tears rolled down Vanessa's cheeks, but she made no sound. For a moment she cried within herself: 'Oh, I cannot endure

this! I *cannot* endure it!' and this was followed by the strong
response: 'I *can* endure it! I can endure anything!'

The hardest thing to bear was that she had not at present
recovered her father for herself. When someone dearly loved
passes away there is a period when everything is blurred. The
personality has broken up into a thousand pieces, something
here, something there, but the radiant heart is absent. Slowly the
friend returns, never – if feeling has been true – to be lost
again.

Elizabeth, watching her, felt at first the girl's deep loneliness.
There they were alike. She, too, was lonely, had been for years,
but that is a lesson that women learn and it is one of the principal
bonds between them. Vanessa was only setting out on a road that
Elizabeth knew by heart, of which she was even proud. At the
same time they were not a gloomy pair. They laughed, drove out
in the landau, had visitors, read together, played piquet and backgammon. Elizabeth's extreme weakness was what Vanessa
needed. She needed, more than she had ever conceived that she
would, someone to care for. It was the strongest need of her
nature and would always be, as it had been her grandmother's.
That was why she wanted Benjie more with every day that
passed. Now that Adam was gone she had nobody else but Benjie.
And, as Elizabeth needed him too, these two, although they
seldom mentioned him, thought of him all the time.

But there were other things growing in Vanessa, as Elizabeth
one day discovered.

A Mrs Marrable from Rosthwaite called. Now the Marrable
family, its colour, personality, and circumstances, would make a
very fit subject of study for anyone interested in English family
life in the eighties. Mr John Marrable had interests in China. He
was now retired, wore a black beard, smoked a kind of Oriental
hookah, and was to be seen for the most part in green-and-red
worsted carpet slippers walking up and down the glass-covered
passage on the outside of his Rosthwaite house. Mrs Marrable
was round, stout, full-bosomed, and her skirt so beflounced and
beribboned that she was all bits and pieces. John Marrable was
severe and extremely self-satisfied. Mrs Marrable very talkative,
serious-minded, but gay with that nervous gaiety peculiar to
wives who expect their husbands to enter at any moment in the
worst of all possible tempers. The Marrables had five children,
four girls and a boy; they lived entirely up to the later car-
icatured notion of Victorian manners in that the four Miss Mar-

rables had been completely sacrificed to their brother Edward, for whom everything had been done. The result of doing everything for Edward was that he had turned out very badly indeed, being sent down from Cambridge for grossly insulting a Proctor and then, while supposedly following his father's Chinese interests in London, mixing in the lowest society and incurring a multitude of debts. Meanwhile the four Miss Marrables, who were not beauties, waited patiently at home for someone to marry them, were bullied by their father and grew ever more plain of feature. One of them, the third in age, Lettice, Vanessa had liked, been kind to; the result of this was that Lettice Marrable worshipped her with a passion that was made up of religion, sexual hunger, and a devastating loneliness. Lettice Marrable's adoration for Vanessa had its consequences.

In any case for the moment here Mrs Marrable was, taking tea with Elizabeth and Vanessa in the drawing-room of the Fortress. She chattered on for a long time in the eager, apprehensive, incoherent manner that was especially hers, and as she talked a large locket jumped about on her stout bosom like a thing imprisoned and mad for freedom.

'Yes, thank you, we have heard from Ned. His present enthusiasm is for Miss Mary Anderson. He goes to see her every evening in *Ingomar*, although every evening is of course the dear fellow's exaggeration. The play is a failure, he tells us, but Miss Anderson is lovelier than ever.'

'Why don't you take the girls up to London, Mrs Marrable, for a jaunt, and go and see her?'

'Take the girls up to London! My dear Miss Paris! With things in China as bad as they are! No. Mr Marrable says we must economize in every possible direction, and we are thinking of cutting down the landau. He tells the girls that we must all make sacrifices and he is quite right. Ned went with some friends to Hurlingham last weekend and seems really to have enjoyed himself, and he actually saw the Duke of Cambridge riding down a side street on a bicycle the other day! I agree with Mr Marrable that our Royal Family should keep up their position. Do not you, Mrs Herries? And Mr Marrable says that with all this odd behaviour of France in China there is no knowing where we shall all be and we look to the Royal Family to keep us all together. Although Ned writes in his letter that the Prince of Wales really *does* encourage some very light-hearted behaviour. Now is it right? What I mean, Miss Paris, is that we all look up to the

Royal Family. What kind of example is he setting our girls? And
that reminds me. They tell me that Miss Nettleship, the daughter
of Doctor Nettleship, is going up to Girton. Now I don't know
what *you* think, Miss Paris, but my opinion is – and Mr Marrable's too – that all these things that girls are wanting to do are
the *greatest* mistake. More than that, they are unwomanly – the
very word that Mr Marrable used this morning.'

'What things?' asked Vanessa, smiling.

Now it happened that that smile which Vanessa had intended
in all friendliness irritated Mrs Marrable. She had had a trying
day. John Marrable had come down to breakfast with a cold and
had been very severe with everyone. She was anxious about Ned's
doings in London, and Mrs Martin of Keswick had asked for her
bill (a thing that nobody in Keswick ever dreamt of doing unless
seized by some sudden insanity). Moreover, neither she nor Mr
Marrable really approved of Vanessa. It was true, of course, that
she was a great beauty, but was she quite nice? It was said of her
that she had some very odd opinions, and unusual she certainly
must be to engage herself to that rascal of a son of Mrs Herries,
who, poor woman, was popular with everyone, partly because she
did no harm and partly because everyone had the luxury of pitying her.

Mrs Marrable did not approve of Vanessa although she could
not deny but that black suited her, she was a very lovely girl, she
was kind to Lettice, and belonged to one of the best families in
Cumberland. This smile, however, hinted at broad views, was
patronizing, and the drive back to Rosthwaite would be very
long. She wished now that she had brought one of the girls to
bear her company . . .

'What things?' cried Mrs Marrable, a little sharply. 'Why, anything that takes a woman away from the home where she belongs.
All this gadding about, doing as men do – it isn't natural and you
know it isn't, Miss Paris.'

'Why isn't it natural?' asked Vanessa. She was suddenly weary
of Mrs Marrable. She wished that she would go. Mrs Marrable's
bright green dress was most unsuited to her figure.

'Why isn't it natural?' Mrs Marrable had a maddening habit of
repeating everything that the last speaker had said. 'Why, my
dear Miss Paris, what did Nature intend women for? Marriage
and the home. Marriage and the home.'

'But if they don't get married?' Vanessa continued, not very
wisely. 'There are more women than men in this country. Many

more. What are they to do? What do they do? Sit at home, twiddle their thumbs, and look out of window for a husband.'

This was unwise of her because it was exactly what the Miss Marrables spent their time in doing, as Mrs Marrable very well knew. She bridled in every limb.

'Well, if they do sit at home it is better in my opinion than that they should unsex themselves. Why, they are actually doctors, some of them! It is *my* opinion, Miss Paris, that that Doctor Garrett Anderson they are always talking about should be put in prison!'

Elizabeth, who was watching Vanessa rather anxiously, saw her straighten her tall body and throw back her head.

'Another cup, Mrs Marrable?'

'Oh no, thank you, Mrs Herries. I positively must be going.'

'Why should she be put in prison?' asked Vanessa.

'Well, really, Miss Paris,' Mrs Marrable said, patting her locket and smiling rather nervously, 'I wonder you can ask such a question! But you, of course, are of the younger generation. We older ones wonder sometimes where the world is going to!'

'No, but, Mrs Marrable,' Vanessa persisted, 'I truly want to know. *Why* should Doctor Garrett Anderson be put in prison?'

This was plainly intended as a challenge and Mrs Marrable took it as such.

'I consider her a wicked woman and a dangerous influence. I read an article about her only the other day. Do you know that she once actually read a paper on "The Limits of Parental Authority"? Do you happen to know, Miss Paris, that she actually supports the fantastic idea that women should have a vote? A vote indeed! If that is not against Nature I don't know what is! And do you know,' and here Mrs Marrable dropped her voice to an awful trembling hush, 'that she took the part of the fallen women in opposing an excellent Act of Parliament demanding their supervision? – yes, and she and her friends positively succeeded in having the Act repealed.'

'If women do not protect fallen women I scarcely see who will. Certainly not men.'

'Protect! Protect! My dear Miss Paris! And you quite a young girl! One naturally dislikes discussing such a matter at all, but people seem to discuss everything nowadays. All I can say is that if you approve this condonation of gross immorality I – I – I'm most surprised!'

'Let that be as it may, Mrs Marrable,' Vanessa said. 'I know a few things also about Doctor Anderson. She is one of the bravest and finest women alive in the world today. In fact, with the exception of Florence Nightingale, there is not a finer. I also could tell you one or two things about her that perhaps you don't know. Have you ever thought of the conditions women lived under when Doctor Anderson was a girl? A married woman was scarcely a human being. She had no rights, no property, nothing. Did you ever read Miss Leigh Smith's *Brief Summary of the Most Important Laws Concerning Women*?'

'No, indeed I have not,' said Mrs Marrable, panting with nervousness and annoyance.

'Well then, you should. It was written long ago and is still excellent reading. Do you know that when Elizabeth Garrett wanted to be a doctor she could not find a physician in England to whom she could be apprenticed? Do you know that she worked all day at the Middlesex Hospital, where there were no antiseptics and anaesthetic was scarcely used? That needed some courage, did it not? Do you know that the whole medical profession tried to stop her, that they got up a memorial against her, that London University when she tried to matriculate was closed to women? Do you know that she had to fight every step of the way and that when at last with Sophia Jex-Blake she started the School of Medicine for Women a howl went up through the whole of England? And all for why? Because, Mrs Marrable, at last women in England have grown tired of sitting still and looking out of the window for husbands! They want to have a life of their own, they want to be independent, as one day, please God, they shall be!'

Elizabeth had never seen Vanessa like this before. Her voice rang across the room as though she challenged the world. With her shoulders back and her eyes flashing she looked as though she would like to crush Mrs Marrable to powder. In fact at that moment she hated that good, kindly, and quite unoffending woman.

Unoffending but not unoffended! She was so deeply offended that she would never forget – never forget and never forgive. She was not, in her life and circumstance, a happy enough woman to forgive. Like all women who have a grievance which they refuse to admit, she made her friends take the blame. Vanessa was to be blamed for ever and ever.

The lady got up to go, smoothing her bosom and arranging her wide and voluminous skirt.

'Thank you, Mrs Herries, for a most delightful afternoon.'

'I am so glad that you came, Mrs Marrable.'

She carried it off. She shook her fingers playfully at Vanessa. 'When you are my age, Miss Paris,' she said, 'you will see the danger of these things.'

'Oh dear,' said Vanessa after her departure. 'How intolerable of me! And how unexpected! It was the very last thing I thought of doing. And in your house too.'

'You were rather vehement,' said Elizabeth. 'I have never seen you like that before.'

'No, but I am afraid you will see me like that again. I have a terrible temper and it flies up before I know that it's there. You are wise, Elizabeth. Tell me what I shall do about it.'

'No. I don't think you lost your temper, dear. You were indignant. That's all. And I agreed with every word that you said.'

Nevertheless, going to bed that night, Vanessa was very unhappy. Something was wrong, and what was wrong was that her spirit was weighed down with an intolerable loneliness. With every day that passed she realized more bitterly the agony of her father's loss. She had been wrong, perhaps, to build her life so entirely around him. It was the caring for him, the watching that he should be happy, the comfort of knowing that they loved one another – these things, gone, left in her utter desolation. Dear Elizabeth . . . but Elizabeth was now almost out of the world and did not need her. Nobody needed her, nobody anywhere.

And at that she faced the other trouble besides her father's loss. She wanted Benjie: she wanted to be married to Benjie, to care for him, understand him, comfort him, make him happy. And Benjie was away, would perhaps never return.

'That's amusing,' she thought as she lay down in bed. 'Here was I railing at Mrs Marrable about women's independence and I myself the least independent woman in the world!'

Two days later a telegram came:

'Arriving tonight. Benjie.'

Elizabeth ran to the door, flung it open, called out 'Vanessa! Vanessa!' and Vanessa came running down the stairs, thinking that Elizabeth was ill.

'Oh, what is it?'

But Elizabeth caught her hand.

'He's coming – tonight. That's all he says. It's sent from Liverpool.'

Vanessa took the telegram.

'Tonight! Oh, Elizabeth, I am so glad! He'll take the train to Carlisle, I shouldn't wonder, and then drive. He says nothing about being met.'

All day preparations were made, roses in his bedroom, Mrs Harwen roasting two ducks, the silver polished, the garden paths brushed, and everything at the end of it as dead around the house as it was at the beginning.

It was four in the afternoon. Tea had been just brought in. The hills beyond the windows lay like dark purple prehistoric animals bathing in a sea of orange mist. You could see them sprawling, burying their snouts, heaving their scaly backs, while below, all about the valley, the mist, like bales of wool, rolled from field to field.

Vanessa, holding Elizabeth close to her, stared at the hills.

'Benjie thinks there are men under Skiddaw,' she said. 'Dead men. A kind of Cumbrian Valhalla.'

But Elizabeth had not heard. She looked exceedingly frail today. Excitement was bad for her heart. She trembled a little, leaning against Vanessa's strong side.

'This house,' she said, 'whatever you do to it, it refuses to live. It was conceived in hatred, my dear. It has always hated everybody and everything just as poor Uhland did. It is this place should have been burnt, not Fell House. Look at this room. Look at the roses! I have put them here, there, everywhere. They are dropping with uneasiness. Nothing good will ever happen in this place. Benjie is bringing some bad news. I know it.'

Vanessa led her back to the sofa.

'Now lie down, Elizabeth darling. I'll bring you your tea. Don't *think* about Benjie until he's here. What bad news *could* there be?'

She was herself triumphant. She felt that she was able to deal with *any* situation that Benjie might offer. Were he in trouble through some foolishness she would stand by him. There was nothing that he could confess, as she had told him years ago, that she would not share with him. And then at last, after all these postponements, they would be married. There was nothing now to prevent it save the old obstacle of Benjie's scruples, which came, as she knew well, because he loved her so much. Now when he saw that her sorrow had only made her the more resolved, he would be as eager as she.

She went about the house, singing. She petted Mrs Harwen, who in any case adored her, went several times to Benjie's room to see that everything was right, put Elizabeth to bed.

'He will be late. He has thirty miles to drive, you know. He shall come up to you the moment he arrives.'

It was after ten when he came. She was standing at her window and saw the lights of the carriage, heard the crunch of the wheels on the road, heard the driver shout 'Whoa!' to his horses, then, with a recognition that drove her heart against her ribs, the well-known timbre of Benjie's voice.

'All right, driver. I'll get someone to help you with the box.'

He came up the path, saw the light in her window, and looked up.

'Hulloa, Vanessa. Is that you?' he called out.

'Yes. I'll come down.'

As their hands clasped she knew that he loved her as dearly as ever. She was so happy that she could have flung her arms around his neck, but all she did was to say, smiling her quiet steady smile:

'Elizabeth has gone to bed. She's longing to see you.'

Old Harwen helped the driver in with the luggage. Benjie took off his coat, nodded to her, and saying, 'I'll see Mother a moment and come down,' he ran up the stairs.

It was something in his voice and look that frightened her. *What* was it? He did not look well, but he would be tired, of course, after his journey. It was not that. As he spoke, he had avoided her eyes.

She went into the dining-room where some supper was laid out for him. She told Mrs Harwen to bring in the soup in ten minutes. Then she stood there under the gas that hissed very faintly above her head and tried to calm her fear.

Something was the matter. Had she not said that nothing that he could tell her would alarm her? Now, face to face with him, she was not sure. She felt herself quite inexperienced. She had thought that she could deal with him, but what did she *really* know about men? Perhaps he was going to tell her that he did not love her any more. No, she knew that it was not that. That first gaze into one another's eyes had told her that they still belonged to one another just as they had always done. What else could it be? Had he done anything disgraceful? She would share that with him, whatever it might be. She moved restlessly about the room, moving the things upon the table, seeing that the bowl of red and yellow roses was in the centre, arranging knives and forks.

Mrs Harwen came in with the soup tureen.

'Yes, Mrs Harwen, I think he'll be down in a minute now.'

'And you'll ring for the meat and vegetables, Miss Vanessa?'

'Yes. He must be hungry.'

'Yes, Miss. It's a couple of ducks – and an apple tart to follow.'

She walked to the window. Why did this house always fill her with apprehension? Her anxiety was needless. He was tired after his journey. After five minutes with her he would be his old self.

The door opened and he came in. He smiled at her, sat down and began to eat: she drew a chair to the table near to him.

'How well you are looking, Vanessa.'

He had not seen her since the week of the fire. They were both conscious of that, she thought. That is why he is uneasy and will not look at me; but her fear increased.

'Where have you been, Benjie, all this time? Are you hungry? Is the toast dry? I told Mrs Harwen not to make it before she heard you arriving.'

'I've come from Liverpool.' He looked at her and smiled, a pathetic smile as though he longed to be friends with her and for some reason must not be. The childishness so often apparent in him – one of his strongest appeals to women because he was quite unconscious of it – caught her heart, making her ache to take him in her arms and comfort him.

He was terribly unhappy: that was certain.

'And where have you been besides Liverpool?'

'Oh, abroad. In June I went to Germany. I thought that I'd like to see Bismarck. Not to speak to him, of course – simply to have a sight of the old man. And I did. He was driving one day in Berlin in an open carriage. It was strange, you know, Vanessa, because when I was a boy at Rugby in 1870 I hated the Prussians – I would have done anything to help the French – nearly ran away to Paris to share in the Siege. But when I saw the old boy riding through Berlin I cheered like the others.'

'What did he look like?'

'Oh, just an old man. But he sat up straight and bowed. Very striking eyes.'

Mrs Harwen came in with the ducks.

'Hulloa! Mrs Harwen! How are you?'

'Very well, thank you, sir, and I hope you're the same?'

'Oh, I'm well enough! Two ducks! I can't eat two ducks!'

'I thought if one wasn't tender you could try the other, sir.'

'Thanks. But I'm not hungry.'

'There's an apple tart to follow, sir.'

'No. Not for me tonight. I'll have it cold tomorrow.'

He carved the duck, ate a little of it, then pushed his plate aside.

'I'm not hungry, Vanessa.'

'Oh, you ought to be after that long journey.'

'No, I'm not . . . Mother's not very well, I'm afraid.'

'No, she has grown much weaker lately. I'm afraid she can't live much longer, Benjie.'

His face seemed to be shadowed. The constraint between them grew deeper with every moment.

'No, I can't eat.' He got up. 'Let's go into the other room. There's something I must say to you.'

He opened the door for her and she went out, crossing the passage, down the stairs, into the little room off the hall that had been poor old Walter's sanctum.

There was a fire there and yet the room was cheerless. They sat down in the old leather armchairs opposite one another.

'Don't you hate this house?' he asked her.

'I don't like it. It is impossible to make it comfortable.'

'Old Walter sees to that,' he answered grimly. There followed an awful pause. At last she could endure it no longer.

'Benjie, what's the matter?'

'Nothing. Oh yes, there is. Of course there is.'

'Well, tell me. Don't be a coward about it.' She hesitated. 'Is it that you don't love me any longer?'

He, too, hesitated. Then he answered, looking her at last straight in the face:

'I love you more than ever.'

A wave of joy, burning with splendid warmth, swept over her. She was, for an instant, submerged by it, blind, deaf, conscious of her joy as though she were alone in space, the beautiful glass-green wave arching above her head.

'I'm glad of that,' she said at last, 'because I also love you more than ever.' She went on: 'Father's death has left me with only you. I have no one else to care for, no one else to care for *me*. When you were away so long I thought I could not endure it — not if it went on much longer. I find that I cannot live without someone to love, and as there is only you, Benjie—'

'Don't!' he broke in with a cry. 'Vanessa, don't!'

He had sprung to his feet. A panic of apprehension caught her. Something terrible had happened. She held the arm of the chair with her hand.

'What is it?'

'It's this. We can't be married. We can never be married.'

She waited for the next word.

'We can't be married because – because' – he turned away from her, staring at the window – 'because I was married last week.'

He had rehearsed this moment to himself all day, and for many days past. He had not known what he would do, nor what she would do either. He had thought of everything – every possibility but one.

He had not thought that, after what seemed to him an age of silence, she would murmur:

'Oh, poor Benjie. Oh, what a dreadful thing!'

She had thought first of himself. She had guessed instantly that he was in some bad, inescapable tangle. He could have fallen at her feet and kissed her hands for her perception.

'We should have married last year,' she said. 'That would have saved both of us.'

He turned and looked at her with a deep sombre gaze as though he were fixing her for ever in his mind, just as she was, now that he had lost her. Then he knelt down, at her feet, bowed his head: she held his hand. Neither of them spoke for a long time.

He got up and sat in the chair again.

'I must tell you about it,' he said. 'You must know everything.'

'Yes, tell me,' she answered.

'After the fire when I came to see you, you were upset. I thought that you blamed me for your father's death. I'm so ready to be blamed. I'm blamed so often. But I don't care. I don't care perhaps enough – unless it is you who blame me. So I rode off in a temper. You remember that in Seascale last year I stayed in rooms with a widow and her daughter?'

Vanessa, looking at him with eyes that were so unhappy but so resolutely determined not to flinch that he could not face them, nodded.

'Yes, I remember. I saw them walking one day on the beach.'

'Yes. Well – a mother and daughter called Halliday – I didn't like them – not either of them. I was thinking only of you, Vanessa, that summer – you were obsessing me. Nevertheless I kissed the girl, disliked her more than ever, and kissed her again.'

He flashed a look at her, then dropped his glance and went on, looking at the floor.

'You and I would have been married, of course, that autumn, had it not been for Adam's illness. Fate. Call it what you like. Perhaps really the best thing. In any case the widow and her daughter came to live in Keswick.'

'Tell me,' Vanessa said, 'what she looks like. I saw her only for a moment at Seascale. Is she beautiful? *What* is she?'

'No, she is not. She is not beautiful, she is not clever. My eyes have been open from the first. She held me like one of one's pet cheap temptations – those you are always ashamed of, never resist, never confess to anyone . . . I must be fair to her, Vanessa. Whatever happens I must be fair. But you will see in a moment what she is like.'

Vanessa drew a deep, trembling breath. Her hands were folded in her lap. Benjie stared at them as though hypnotized, noticing how white they were against the black dress. He thought that he could tell the rest of the story better were he holding her hand, but he did not move.

'Yes, I must be fair to her. She knew that she had some attraction for me. She was, I think, determined from the very beginning that I should marry her, but really because, I am afraid, she loved – loves – me.'

'Yes,' said Vanessa.

'Thinking of you always, loving you more every day, yet I went to see the two of them in Keswick. I must speak of something difficult, Vanessa. It is this. The more I saw you the more I loved you – and with my body as well as the rest of me. I have always wanted my body to have power. I have liked to see it travelling about the world, getting experience, eating, drinking, strong, vigorous. I have always thought that most people do not give their bodies all the chances. Well, that spring you were occupied with Adam, of course, and I would leave you, restless and unsatisfied. Both of us were, I think. But I was doubly unsatisfied – because I wanted you so badly and because I was so unworthy of you.'

She murmured: 'That has been where the mistake was.'

'Oh, don't misunderstand me, Vanessa. I don't go about the world thinking I am unworthy of people. Of nobody else. Only you. But the one thing I must not do, I tell myself, is to spoil your life. I mustn't. I mustn't, I tell myself – and then – I do ...

'So I went to see them. Then a day or two after the fire I rode out to Halliday's farm – the brother, you know. I stayed there the night. I drank too much. The girl slept with me.'

He waited. There was a mouse scratching somewhere. They both raised their heads together, and Vanessa thought, as she had often done before, that she heard one of the dogs that Uhland used to keep in his room howling from the Tower. Somewhere a dog *was* howling, and at that moment she realized a hatred for that girl such as she had never felt before for anyone.

'Next day,' Benjie went on, 'I came back to the Fortress. I stayed for a while, then I went off with Halliday and two of his friends called Endicott shooting. I met the girl again. She was quiet, most respectable, as though now she had got what she wanted. I am sure her mother knew. I think her brother knew too. I was extremely unhappy. I wanted to come to you and ask that we might be married at once, but I was ashamed and afraid – you are the only human being I have ever been afraid of, Vanessa. I went abroad to Germany.

'When I came back the girl, her mother, and brother were in London. The girl came to see me and told me that she was going to have a child – my child, she said. I don't know whether that was the truth or no. That was a month ago. Will you believe me, Vanessa, when I tell you that I loved you during all this time more than ever?'

'Yes,' said Vanessa. 'I believe you.'

'The girl said that of course now I would marry her. The mother said the same. The brother the same. I was not frightened of them in the least. I have never been afraid of anyone or anything except your despising me or doing you harm. But also, in spite of all that I have done, I have never got a woman into trouble. I tell you that I didn't know, I don't know now, whether I was responsible in this case. I want to be fair to her in every way, but I cannot be certain of her virtue. They were all three quite friendly and quite frank. The girl said that she had always loved me, always meant to marry me. The brother said that of course it would not be pleasant for my mother if she knew of this. I agreed with that. Ill as she was it would probably kill her. But I think that my mind was entirely on you. Although I loved you so dearly I might do this again. I have never had any trust in myself. It is only myself that I blame, but from my birth, as I have always told you, there has been some strain in me that I could never trust, as there was in my father, my grandfather. And I have always been honest with you. I would have had to tell you of this, and when you knew that this was to be my child – would you marry me? Would you, Vanessa? Would you have married me knowing this?'

He waited with passionate eagerness for her answer, leaning forward, looking into her face.

At last she said:

'No. Perhaps I would not.'

He nodded his head. 'I thought not. "This ends it," I thought. All this struggle about you that I have had for years. You will be free. Perhaps you will hate me and so be clear of me, then after a while you will marry somebody splendid. One day, long after, you will acknowledge that I was right. That's what I thought. So I married her – last week in Liverpool.'

A long, long silence followed.

At last Vanessa said:

'Do you care for her? Are you fond of her in any way at all?'

'No – not in any way at all.'

Then she said:

'Thank you for telling me so honestly.' And then again, after another pause: 'This will be terrible for Elizabeth.'

'Yes,' he answered.

She got up and went over to him and laid her hand against his cheek.

'You must do all you can for her.'

He caught her hand fiercely; kissed it again and again.

'What are we to do? I can't live without seeing you.'

She shook her head.

'No. Of course we must not meet. That would be too difficult for both of us.'

She bent down and kissed him.

'How foolish we both have been, Benjie dear.' She held him close to her like a mother her son. At that moment, with his head against her breast, she realized with the utmost clarity the desolation of her loneliness. She kissed him again, then drew herself from his grasp.

'Goodnight, Benjie darling. I'll go back to Cat Bells in the morning. You won't write or anything, will you? It will be much better.'

'I'll do anything you say.'

At the door she turned back.

'I don't know whether it's right. Very wrong perhaps. But although we mustn't meet or write, if you're in trouble – real, serious trouble – you must tell me.'

'I'll tell you,' he said.

Then she went out.

THE DUCHESS OF WREXE'S BALL

ONE day in November 1884 Barney Newmark went in to drink a cup of tea with his sister, Phyllis Rochester, in her pleasant little house in Eaton Place.

He chose this afternoon because he knew that his brother-in-law, Clarence Rochester, was at Brighton. He did not like Clarence at all – he thought him a humbug. And Clarence did not like Barney – he thought him an obscene, conceited libertine. Phyllis, who cared deeply for Barney and had grown accustomed to Clarence, kept the balance between them.

Phyllis, who was now a buxom woman of sixty-three (all the Newmarks of this generation were stout), loved her comforts and adored her eccentric son Philip. So long as she had plenty of the little cakes, jams, and preserved fruits that she preferred and so long as Philip lived with her in Eaton Place she had no alarms. She had a charming complexion, and Clarence was away as often as not. Her one fear had been lest Philip should marry. But now it did not seem likely. Philip did not like women.

Barney today was in an excellent temper. He had that morning finished his novel, a novel in which Newmarket, Boulogne, and Scottish shooting parties were his principal backgrounds, where everything was very light and careless and the principal scene was a baccarat-cheating scandal. Like the majority of novelists he enjoyed, for a day or two following a novel's conclusion, an extraordinary sense of freedom and light-heartedness. Unlike most novelists these happy days were not followed by an intense gloom. He knew the thing was of no value at all. He told everybody so. He wrote to make money. He was none of your Mere-diths, Zolas, or Shorthouses. He couldn't write a novel like – what was its name? – that *John Inglesant* to save his life. Nor did he want to. So long as a fellow or two got his novel from a library he was perfectly satisfied – and so were his publishers.

Between the brother and sister sitting together having tea in the pleasant little drawing-room there was a strong resemblance. They were both stout, jolly, and easily amused. Barney was the best of fellows when alone with his sister. They were both glad that Clarence was at Brighton. The room was very warm, heavily curtained, and crammed with knick-knacks. There were china dogs, china shepherds and shepherdesses, china mandarins. There was even a large china copy of a Chinese temple with little bells that tinkled when there was a draught, and of this Phyllis was inordinately proud. There were photographs everywhere. Four photographs of Mary Anderson, two of Ellen Terry, three of Mr Terriss, photographs of Ellis and Garth and Emily Newmark (very forbidding) and Barney (riding a horse) and Vanessa and Carey Rockage. There were numberless little tables, all heavily loaded, a great many little chairs and a basket near the fire in which a fat pug called Charles was now wheezing. The two round tea tables were covered with cakes, pastries, muffins, piles of buttered toast.

'Good Heavens, Phil,' Barney cried, 'how many people are you expecting?'

'Nobody except you.'

'Why all the food?'

'Oh, I like to have plenty to eat. And Philip may come in.'

'Oh, may he? And what is he doing today?'

'He has gone to an Art Exhibition with Samuel Roscoe.'

'Oh, has he?'

To change the subject – which might be an unpleasant one – Phyllis asked:

'And what's the news?'

'I finished my novel this morning.'

'Oh, did you? What is it called?'

'*Neck or Nothing.*'

'What a clever title! I don't know how you think of all these things.'

'No, nor do I. I have been helping John Beaminster to choose a horse.'

'Oh, have you?' Phyllis was greatly interested. The Beaminsters were always exciting. 'Did he tell you anything about his mother?'

'No. What should he tell me?'

'Oh, I don't know, but I do think it is so extraordinary her being shut up in that Portland Place house all these years. Do

you remember when she came to that party that Ellis gave a year
or two ago?'

'Of course I remember.'

'Well, they say she hadn't been out of doors for years before
that. Then for a week or two she was seen everywhere. Then she
went back again and has shut herself up ever since.'

'That was the party,' said Barney slowly, 'when Benjie suddenly appeared. Do you remember? And that night he was engaged to Vanessa.'

Phyllis, shaking her head, choosing with great care the richest
of several little cakes, answered indignantly:

'Oh, don't mention Benjie to me! I have finished with him for
ever and so has everybody! I consider him a murderer!'

'Oh, come now,' said Barney, smiling.

'Well, isn't he? He killed his mother by throwing Vanessa over
and marrying that horrible woman.'

'You don't know that she's horrible. You've never seen her.'

'No, but other people have. Alfred was up that way with a
friend the other day and thought he'd call. They had the most
dreadful visit. Benjie would do nothing but swear, and the house
was a pig sty and the baby howling. Alfred said that the woman
was awful! As thin as a pole and cross-eyed.'

'Oh no, not that!' said Barney, laughing.

'Well, there was something odd about her eyes, Alfred said.
And she hardly spoke a word.'

'I like Benjie,' Barney said. 'I always have and I always will.
There was something behind that business we don't know.'

'Nothing to Benjie's credit, you can be sure,' said Phyllis.
'Poor Vanessa. So beautiful and buried up there. She's only been
to London once since it happened. She stayed with Rose for a
week, you remember, and I never saw anyone more lovely. Very
nice she was too. Philip was in a passion over her.'

'You needn't pity Vanessa,' said Barney sharply. 'She needs no
one's pity.'

'Oh no, of course not!' Here again seemed a dangerous subject,
so Phyllis, finding safety in general affairs, asked:

'And what do they say about General Gordon?'

'There is little news since Stewart's murder. Wolseley is
moving up the Nile.'

'Do you think Gladstone has made a mistake?'

'Possibly. He'll hear of it if he has.'

'Some people say that Gordon is mad.'

'Mad people do most of the things in this world. That, my dear Phil, is what our family will never learn.'

'I sometimes think Emily is mad. What do you think she came in here raging about yesterday?'

'I *never* think about Emily.'

'She wants to close the Alhambra and have all the women who go there put in prison.'

'Emily will be improperly assaulted one day by a Salvation Army worker. Then she will learn something.'

The maid opened the door and said: 'Miss Ormerod and Mr Ormerod.'

Rose and Horace came in and were eagerly welcomed.

Rose looked charming indeed, in one of the Scottish plaid costumes that were then most fashionable, and her hat tilted over her hair arranged in a bun was so small as to be almost invisible. 'Where,' thought Phyllis, 'does she get the money to buy her clothes from?'

Horace, red-faced, amiable and enthusiastic, was like a successful clergyman on holiday. His vibrating enthusiasm made Barney very cynical. 'I always believe well of human nature,' Barney said, 'until Horace Ormerod comes along.'

Horace rubbed his hands together, beamed, pushed his spectacles (he had been wearing spectacles for a year or two) back on to his short nose and cried: 'Well, this is splendid indeed! Rose and I were walking in the Park and I said to her, "We'll take a hansom and see if Phil has some tea for us!" Splendid day! Fresh and bright! I never felt better in my life!'

Barney said: 'I'm glad of that, Horace. We need cheering, with so many of our fellows without employment and the City in a scare and Egypt in a muddle!'

'Nonsense! Nonsense! You *will* look on the black side of things! I have it on the best of authority that the City is doing very well indeed. And as to Egypt, you trust Gladstone. He did the right thing in sending Gordon. You can take it from me!'

'I don't take it from you!' said Barney. 'How do you know?'

'What I always say,' said Horace, 'is that you can trust Old England. She always does the right thing in the end. I hate this pessimism. It's men like you, Barney, who do all the harm. But of course you're a novelist, live in your imagination and that sort of thing.'

'Now, Horace,' Rose interrupted, 'don't be tiresome. Barney

knows more about everything than you do. But I know something that *he* doesn't know!'

They were eager for information.

'Vanessa arrived at Hill Street this morning for a long visit!'

'No!' cried Barney. 'Vanessa! How splendid!'

'Yes. I saw Alfred in the Park, and *he* had seen Ellis in the City. Our dear Vanessa is with us again, and it shan't be our fault if she doesn't stay for months.'

Phyllis nodded.

'Ellis will be glad,' she said.

'And Ellis' ma will be glad,' Rose went on. 'And I have come in only for a moment because I am going to Hill Street to see her.'

An hour later Rose was in Hill Street.

'I will tell Miss Paris,' the butler said, leaving her alone in the big cold drawing-room.

Old Lady Herries was now eighty years of age and spent most of her time in bed where, rumour had it, she arranged her pearls, rubies and diamonds on the counterpane, played games with them and counted them over and over again. But because she was in bed and Ellis for most of the day in the City, the house was more like a mortuary than a living-place. The drawing-room was decorated in mustard yellow, the curtains had heavy folds of it, the chairs and sofas were wrapped in it. On the mantelpiece was a clock of yellow-and-white marble. The marble statues that had been there ever since Will Herries first bought the house glimmered whitely under the gas. Rose shivered.

'*What* a house! But now that Vanessa has come they will entertain again. Now that Benjie is out of the way they will think there is hope for Ellis. Is there? Vanessa is lonely enough, poor darling, to try anything, and she has always had a kind of maternal feeling for Ellis.'

Ellis came in.

Rose did not dislike Ellis. She thought him absurd and pathetic. She was also blind neither to his baronetcy nor to his wealth. At one time she had thought that she might herself marry him, but her clear common sense soon showed her that she did not attract him in the least.

'He has no eyes for anyone but Vanessa.'

Now when he came in she was compelled to admit that he looked distinguished, and not really his forty-two years. Or rather he might be any age. His body was slim and erect. His closely fitting black clothes and high sharp-pointed collar gave him distinction. He was Sir Ellis Herries, Bart, all right and a ridiculous physical copy of his father. A very hideous painting of his father hung on the left side of the fireplace. Yes, ludicrously alike, but the real Ellis, Rose (who was no poor judge of character) well knew, was nervous, highly strung, sensitive, unbalanced as his father had never been.

But now as she shook hands Rose liked him, for today he was radiant with happiness. When Ellis was happy you were touched because his hold on his joy seemed so precarious. He was like a man who, to his own surprise, looks to be, for once, winning a game. In the end he will in all probability lose it, but this unusual, unexpected chance gains you to his side.

'I came in only for a moment,' Rose said. 'Alfred told me that Vanessa had arrived. I couldn't wait to see her.'

'Vanessa,' said Ellis, speaking in his precise careful voice, 'is, I am happy to say, under our roof again. She will be delighted to see you.'

'But this is splendid. None of us knew that she was coming.'

'No. *We* did not know until last week. She has been staying with Carey in Wiltshire.'

'How is she looking?'

'Oh, very well. Very well indeed. But here she is. Vanessa, my dear, here is Rose to see you.'

They flung themselves into one another's arms while Ellis stood benevolently by, stroking his chin and smiling.

'But, *dear* Rose! How sweet of you to come so soon!'

'Well, of course! But why not a line to anyone that you were coming?'

'I truly did not know, did I, Ellis? You see Carey and May quite suddenly were invited to Panshanger and they thought they should go. They wanted me to stay on until they returned, but – well, I fancied a little London gaiety.'

They sat down on the sofa together.

'And now, young ladies,' said Ellis in his best paternal fashion, 'I shall leave you. I am sure you have a great deal to talk over. Dinner at seven, Vanessa.'

'Oh Lord!' Rose cried, looking at her watch. 'And it is six now.'

'No, no,' said Vanessa eagerly. 'Come up with me when I dress. It is so *lovely* to see you. And are you not engaged yet to

Captain What's-his-name and what other gentlemen are there and have you seen dear Barney? How is Horace? How, in fact, are all the Herries?'

They noticed at once changes in one another, as was natural after a year's separation. The difference that Vanessa saw in Rose was the same difference that her grandmother had once noticed in this same room years ago in Sylvia Herries – a slight, oh, so very slight, fading of the natural bloom, a heightening of the artificial colour, a little hardening of the voice, the eye a trifle more anxious. The Scottish plaid was extremely pretty, with its red and grey, and the little hat was a beauty – very expensive clothes. Rose looked altogether very expensive. Upon what in reality did she and her brother live?

And Rose saw at once that Vanessa was a girl no longer. She was even for a moment or two afraid of her. Had she lost her? But very soon she realized the thing that she would realize again so often – that once Vanessa was your friend it was not easy to lose her.

Vanessa's dress was dove-grey, her dark hair brushed back from her forehead. Her hand caught Rose's and held it.

'Rose, I want to have *fun*! I want to see people, plenty and plenty. I want to go to the theatre. There is Mary Anderson as Juliet, isn't there? and Mr Wilson Barrett as Hamlet, and Gilbert and Sullivan and Mrs John Wood. I've been studying the papers. Lady Herries has asked May and Carey to come and stay so that May can chaperon me. They are coming from Pans-hanger the day after tomorrow. I want to see everybody and do everything.'

'And everyone wants to see you. You are much the most beautiful woman in London. Mrs Langtry is nothing at all in comparison.'

Vanessa smiled, very happy.

'I want to be beautiful just for a week or two – after that I don't care in the least. I want everyone to think me lovely, to say, "Oh, who is *that* lovely girl?" In fact, Rose dear, I want some encouragement. I've been fighting things by myself – without any help from anyone.'

'I know, dear, I know,' Rose said, stroking her hand. There was something feverish, she thought, in Vanessa's tone, something unlike her natural restraint.

'Yes, Timothy and Violet have been very good to me. I stayed there for months in the house they've bought in Eskdale. Lovely.

Not far from the sea, with the mountains behind them. But of course I couldn't *talk* to them. And there was another thing—'

She broke off, then, holding Rose's hand more tightly, went on:

'This is something I want to say and then we will never mention it again. About Benjie. I know that everyone is against him, that they think he treated me badly, that he made a wretched mess of everything, which is what they have always hoped for. Now, Rose dear, I want you to make them understand – *all* of them – that I will not hear one word against Benjie. That I will never speak again to anyone who attacks him when I'm there. Barney is the only one I'll talk to about him. Barney is his friend, I know. Will you make them all understand that?'

'Of course,' Rose hesitated. 'Vanessa, what is it? What happened? What made him do it?'

'No, Rose, I can't tell even you. It's his affair. We don't meet. We don't write. But I understand what he did. I'm his friend, and not one word shall be said against him in my presence.'

Rose felt her hand tremble, she saw that her eyes were misty. She put her arms round her and kissed her.

'And now, Rose darling,' said Vanessa cheerfully, 'tell me about yourself? How are you? When are you to be married? That hat and costume are lovely!'

'Yes, very nice,' said Rose. 'But not paid for, my dear. Never mind me. Horace and I live in a little house in Shepherd Market. Well, to tell you the truth they are four rooms over a grocer's. We got them cheap from old Lady Martindale, who lost her money at cards and had to decamp at a moment's notice. They are the very best address and are cosy even if they are small. For the rest I have debts, and gentlemen who admire me and ladies who don't, just like any other lady – and I shall marry the first decent man who proposes to me, whoever he is.'

'And Horace?'

'Oh, Horace is getting along fast on the simple plan of refusing to know anyone save those who will be useful to him. He smiles on everyone and has a genius for not seeing those he doesn't want to see. And now, dear, let us go to your room. I am longing to know what you are going to wear.'

So they went upstairs.

Vanessa dined alone with Ellis and Miss Mabel Fortescue, the

lady who now 'ran' the Hill Street house. Miss Fortescue reminded Vanessa at once of Miss Murdstone, and she herself
would have felt not unlike David Copperfield had she not
quickly seen that the situation was serious and she must rather be
Betsey Trotwood. So from the very beginning she was firm with
Miss Fortescue. Really remarkable, her resemblance to Miss
Murdstone. She had the stiff poker back, the dark complexion
and black hair, the heavy eyebrows that nearly met over a large
nose, and Vanessa was certain that in her bedroom were the 'two
uncompromising hard black boxes, with her initials on the lids in
hard brass nails'.

Ellis thought the world of her – 'Most efficient woman, Vanessa. Excellently behaved. Knows just how to treat my mother.'
Then waking in the early morning hours to hear the London
sparrows cheep beyond the window, Vanessa discovered two
other things.

'Miss Fortescue hated me at sight. And hopes to marry
Ellis.'

The dinner was a very agreeable one: Ellis was so happy and
when he was happy he was childlike. Vanessa knew, too, that he
was happy because she was there, and it was so long since she had
been cared for in this way. Timothy and Violet took her for
granted. Aunt Jane loved her but thought her still ten years old.
So also Will Leathwaite. Carey and May were fond of her, but
liked their dogs and horses still better. She was, she discovered,
hungering for affection, and placing her foot in London had as it
were set all her world alight. That afternoon, going for a walk,
the window of a florist in Piccadilly had been ablaze with chrysanthemums; down Bond Street into Piccadilly had come the
carriages, shining in the November sun, the coachmen stout and
splendid, the horses sleek, the harness glittering, and from a distance, through the walls of the houses, the echo of a barrel-organ,
heard as it always should be, a street or two away. She had
thrown up her head and sniffed the air, sharp and horsy and
honeyed with the sun. London! She adored London! She could
manage without Cumberland, clouded with unhappy memories,
for a while. Then against this background there was first Rose,
who loved her, and now Ellis, who loved her too. Ellis was im-
proved. He was intelligent. He talked about Gladstone and
Gordon, about the 'New Radicalism' that was interesting itself in
the conditions of housing and the happiness of the poorer classes,
about the Trades Unions, about the abolishing of the Income

Tax, about the provisions of the Electric Lighting Act, about the Redistribution Bill, about all these serious things, sensibly, with inside knowledge. His tact with her was extraordinary, for he was not by nature a tactful man. He studied her without appearing to. He was affectionate, but with the affection of a brother. She knew of course that he loved her, but he did not embarrass her with any implied emotion.

After dinner she went upstairs to visit Lady Herries. She saw at once a great change in her. Some of the stories they told about her were true, for she was sitting up in bed and on a white shawl on her lap were rings, bracelets, and necklaces. She played with them like a child, holding them up to the light, rubbing them with her fingers, laying one against the other.

Nevertheless she appeared quite sensible. She was enchanted to see Vanessa.

Her great pleasure was to talk about people. Staying in her room as she did, she brought the world around her, speculating, gathering stories, chuckling over scandals and foibles.

'You will find London very much changed, my dear. Money is the only thing, getting it and losing it. If you have money you can go anywhere. That is why London is much more amusing and not nearly so remarkable as it used to be.'

She talked about the family.

'Alfred, Amery's boy, will make a fortune. He's in with all the Jews. His nose gets sharper every day. Dora, old Rodney's daughter, has such a pretty child, Cynthia. Dora married Freddie Beauchamp. Do you remember him? A thin man with a long nose. They live in London now, and Cynthia will marry well. Very well, I shouldn't wonder. Then Barney has made quite a name for himself – amusing books he writes – but he has some very odd friends. However, that doesn't matter if he's a success. Then Phyllis' boy, Philip – you remember him? – a little affected but very clever. He's quite a friend of Mr Oscar Wilde. I'm glad Carey and May are coming. Their two girls, Maud and Helen, are *very* plain, poor things, but of course they have never done anything but ride horses, so what can you expect? They will improve as they grow older.'

She chattered on, moving the jewels about on the white shawl, sometimes talking to herself:

'Now *that* won't do! If Carey and May come on Friday I must put off Miss Blades. She comes and reads to me, my dear. A very nice woman with the funniest stories about everyone ... I will

not have that fish three days running. I must tell Miss Fortescue.'

Then quite unexpectedly she fell asleep, letting her head, with
its tousled white hair, fall on the pillow, opening her mouth and
snoring.

Vanessa soon discovered that she was to be a gathering point
for all the family. They had been longing for something of the
kind. Hill Street sprang to life, and Ellis was rejuvenated. May
Rockage was a simple creature whose heart was in the country
with her horses, her dogs, and her two girls. But she had a hearty
power of enjoyment and, although she dressed badly, laughed
like a man and was extremely innocent of the world, she became
very quickly an excellent companion for Vanessa.

Vanessa threw herself into the family interests. Soon she knew
all their secrets, their fears, their ambitions, and their odd little
ways.

First of all there was Rose, who, she declared to Vanessa, was
going 'the primrose path'. She had two or three gentlemen
friends, a Captain Rackrent, horsy and raffish, a Mr March-
banks, who was some sort of a publisher and encouraged young
men to write as much like the French as possible, and a Mr Easy,
who was like a Jew but said he was not one, Assyrian, purple-
bearded and, Rose said, very rich. He had something to do with
the Theatre. Rose said that he proposed marriage to her every
week – and she added, 'One day when the bailiffs are drinking
beer in the parlour – the awful thing will happen – I shall marry
him.'

Cynthia, Rodney's granddaughter, was the prettiest, most
fairylike creature. She at once fell down at Vanessa's feet and
worshipped. Her hair was spun gold, her eyes the tenderest blue,
her little figure exquisite; wearing a tiny hat perched on a golden
bun, her dress gathered into loops behind her, her bosom clearly
defined, she was something to make men tremble. She was sweet
and tender and loving but, Vanessa thought, quite ruthlessly determined to make the best marriage possible. All the girls were
sweet, tender, and loving, and all the girls were determined to be
well married. 'You would think,' said Rose, 'to listen to these
infants talk that they didn't know what men were made of. But
they *do* know. They know very well indeed.'

Barney's set were writers, painters, horsy men, theatrical men,
and men about town. All these men – including Barney – had
feminine friends who were never obtruded. Once Vanessa, going

with Rose unexpectedly to Barney's rooms, found an elegant creature seated on his sofa, mending his stockings. She was delightful, and most maternal to Barney. Her name was Miss Montefiore, an actress 'resting between engagements'.

Then Vanessa was forced, against her will, to see something of Emily Newmark. Vanessa did not like Emily, but had to confess that she did good in the world. She was for ever 'rescuing' people, 'unfortunate women', drunkards, young pickpockets and foreigners – Chinamen, Negroes, lost and strayed Scandinavians. Her only interest in people was that they could be 'rescued'. She lectured Vanessa, patronized her, and was sometimes unexpectedly human, bursting into tears and saying that she was 'misjudged'.

Old Amery, tottering and bewildered, thought only of his son Alfred. That sharp young man was always adding up figures and subtracting them again. He came to Ellis once a week with schemes. Ellis said that many of these were clever. Alfred would get on.

A very odd world, too, was that of young Philip, Phyllis' boy. The young men, Philip's friends, looked and were ridiculous, but they lived up to their gospel. They wrote little stories, painted little pictures, and treated all the Arts as their own especial property. They arrived from Oxford in increasing numbers. They lisped, they languished. They thought Mr Whistler, Mr Wilde, French poets, and the art of Japan all 'too utterly beautiful'.

In short the Herries were everywhere. Into every corner of London life they drove their strong determined wedge of common sense. Even Philip, with his absurdities, had common sense. England was now at the top of the world, was at a stage of material success and triumph that exactly suited the Herries character. No member of the family ever boasted or wondered or explained. They simply went everywhere, into the Beaminster house in Portland Place, into the theatres and restaurants, into the churches and lecture halls, into the Kensington drawing-rooms, into the City, into the slums and did their good work. No Herries was at the *top* of anything. No Herries (with the exception of Ellis) accumulated great wealth, cared for property, dominated politics or the Arts or the Church or the Army. They simply were everywhere and influenced everything.

Vanessa, however, soon discerned that her arrival was for all of them a dramatic event. At certain times in their history a combination of circumstances produced an Event to which all the family, gladly and joyfully, reacted. Their hatred of the eccentric, the queer, the abnormal made them respond ecstatically to anything that allowed them to display that hatred. It had been so in the old days of the Rogue, in the quarrels about the famous Fan, in the dreadful scandal of Uhland, and now it was so in the affairs of Benjamin, Vanessa, and Ellis. Benjie was their rogue, their scapegoat. Vanessa was, at this moment, their heroine. What had happened in the North about her engagement? No one knew. Would she marry Ellis and become not only the most beautiful but also one of the richest women in London? Why had she come to Hill Street if not to marry Ellis? Her presence made that winter one of the most exciting in their lives.

And Vanessa let herself go. She was there to forget all the past. She must make a world for herself in which she could be independent – never, never would she depend on anyone again. She went everywhere, to balls and theatres and Hurlingham and concerts and immensely long, elaborate dinner parties.

She and May travelled down to Brighton in the ten o'clock Pullman, lunched at Mutton's, where Barney and Alfred joined them, watched the dowagers in the carriages, the girls in the dog-carts, the invalids in the both-chairs, the babies in the goat-chaises, men on bicycles. They went on the electric railways in Madeira Road, visited the Aquarium, listened to the band in the Bird-cage and had dinner at a fine hotel. A glorious day! Brighton in November, sunshine, sea air. What an enchanting world!

Vanessa went to the House and heard Mr Gladstone speak on the Maamstrasna Murders question, and when Mr O'Connor rose and called the speech 'the lamest, weakest and most halting I have ever heard', and young Mr Stanhope shouted out, 'That's what the ferret said when the lion roared', she could have clapped her hands in her delight because that was exactly what *she* thought!

She went of course to *Romeo and Juliet* at the Lyceum and thought Mary Anderson so lovely that she never troubled about the acting. She saw Mrs John Wood in *Young Mrs Winthrop* and laughed herself into tears. When Mrs Wood meets her husband, from whom she has been divorced, they do nothing but wink! Oh, *what* a wink! In fact all London went to see this not very good little play because of Mrs Wood's wink.

She was sad when Henry Fawcett died, thrilled by what Mr Ruskin had to say to his friends at Oxford, read William Black's *Judith Shakespeare*, wanted to go to a Spiritualist meeting but could find no one to accompany her, gazed at Mrs Langtry at a party, ate oysters and pheasant, drove so often in hansoms that she thought nothing at all about it, and enjoyed Mr Corney Grain in the German Reeds' entertainment. 'Nothing,' as Emily Newmark said to her severely, 'nothing but a life of idle pleasure.'

In that winter Vanessa caught a sense of London that she was never after to lose, its smells and odours, flowers and horses and fogs, its incongruities, its shabbiness, as for instance when you passed, on the way into the Underground, the faded photographs, smirking from the wall, of old burlesque actresses, Planché's ghost hovering around them, or when in some of the smaller theatres the smell of beer, the dim rose coverings of the stalls, the dirty globes of gas, the white spots of plaster between the flaking gilt, the past, mournful, pathetic, strangled the struggling present. But everywhere and in every case London was homely – homely in the clack-clack of the horses, in the scattered rumbling of the omnibuses, in the barrel-organs and the German bands, in the sudden flashing splendour of the Guard riding up St James's from the Palace, in the gentlemen's servants taking the air, in the elegant dandies of the Row, in the melancholy street-singers, the lingering notes of the church bells, in the fogs that, yellow and sulky, crept from street to street, in the comfortable laziness of afternoon tea, in the high collar of Mr Gladstone, the radiance of the Jersey Lily, the dignity and humanity of the Prince, and, above all, in that stout little regal figure, never forgotten, sitting somewhere behind the walls of plain-faced Buckingham Palace or bird-haunted Windsor, receiving an Indian prince, being sharp with Mr Gladstone or smiling at her grandchildren. All this was London and London was all this.

One further thing that winter dominated the Town: the thought of Gordon. This great victory of common sense, this triumph of plain reality – was it threatened by that figure, fanatical, heroic, and alone, fearlessly erect among his enemies? Could it be – and it was a question forced again and again upon the Herries through all their history– that common sense was not enough, that there were other things, dangerous, mysterious things of the spirit that could spring upon you and defeat you did you too long disregard them? Is there another world with which we have refused to reckon?

After the disaster of Abu Hamed there was silence. On the day that Herbert Stewart started across the desert there was a message: 'Khartoum all right. 14.12.84. C. G. Gordon.'

After that, silence again.

On the 22nd of January, the day on which London learned of the battle of Abu Klea, Ellis proposed to Vanessa the second time.

They were about to go up to bed. The candles with their heavy silver snuffers stood there waiting. May Rockage had said good-night and started up the stairs, the great drawing-room with its yellow hangings stayed patiently for their departure. Ellis touched Vanessa's arm.

'Vanessa – one moment.'

She turned to him, smiling, then knew at once what he was going to say. He was very nervous, he put his hand to his throat, looked at her with a beseeching smile.

'I have been good, have I not? You have been happy during these weeks here?'

'Very happy, Ellis.'

'Your presence here has been a joy to all of us. My mother has been a different being, and I – I must tell you – I have never been so happy in all my life before.'

'I'm very glad. You have been wonderfully good to me.'

'How could one help being? But I cannot wait any longer. I must ask you once more. It is a long time, is it not, since the last occasion in the Park. Vanessa, will you marry me?'

Before she could answer he went on with a trembling eager passion that touched her and made her long to be kind to him.

'Listen. I implore you not to answer before you have thought it over. I know how much older I am. I know that you do not love me. But you like me. You are friendly, aren't you? I can feel that you are friendly.'

'Of course I am friendly, Ellis. And more than that. But—'

'Well, then, that's all I ask. Indeed it is. I ask nothing more. If you will marry me everything shall be as you wish. I know that money makes no appeal to you, but perhaps power – the power to do good, to help others, to put wrong things right – may mean a little. You are so good, you have so wonderful a character, that you *should* be able to influence your generation. I will help you to do that – under your guidance. And we are friends. We have known one another for a long time and surely can now trust one another completely. Think it over, Vanessa. Do not answer me now. Please, please not now. But think of it . . . Goodnight.'

And before she could speak he was gone

In her room that night she did indeed think of it. Ellis, during these two months, had been so kind, so unselfish and so wise –

they had been such good friends – he had talked about so many things with so much understanding – that she had come to care for him as once would have appeared impossible. She did not love him. But with the impetuous certainty both of her youth and past events she was sure that love was over for her, would never return. Or, rather, she loved as she had always done. Benjie was as truly now in her heart as he had always been. But she must never think of him, neither now nor in any possible future time. So love being over was this not perhaps the next best thing?

Men had in these London weeks gathered round her. Two had proposed to her, and in the very moments of their proposal she had realized that the very thought of any man but Benjie in *that* world of romantic passion was fantastically unreal. Well, this was not romantic passion. But Ellis was the only one save Rose who belonged to her childhood and youth. She had known him so long that he was part of all that early life. And he wanted to be cared for, and *she* wanted, now more than anything else in the world, to bestow her care on someone.

Was it also not true that she could do good in the world with the power that his money would give her? She was still very young in many things and believed that to do good to your fellows was not so very difficult. She did not want to make them better, only to make them happy. Was this not, perhaps, her duty? She knelt down and prayed, passing as she always did into a world of comfort and security. God was more real to her than Ellis, more real to her than Benjie ... But tonight she heard no reassuring voice. She rose from her knees in a struggle of bewilderment, for, coming she knew not whence, a wildness that sometimes seized her, descended on her. She did not want to be here. Her spirit was caught away into a fantastic air of wind and rain, of streams running wildly, of clouds tearing at the turf, of the sea tossing at the foot of the hill. Her blood was not tamed. Cold January night though it was, she threw up her window and, beyond the reddened haze of the gigantic town, she saw Skiddaw's dividing lines, the serried edge of Blencathra, and within the rhythm of a solitary hansom's clatter was the whisper of the running water against the shining boulder and the bark of the dog beyond the sloping hill. She thought of Judith. She thought of her father. She thought of Will Leathwaite's slow smile.

She closed the window. No. Oh no, she *could* not marry Ellis!

*   *   *

A few days later came the invitation to the Duchess of Wrexe's Ball, February 18th.

This Ball had been talked of all through the winter. Very very seldom was there a big function at the Portland Place house, but when they *did* have a show – well, it *was* a show! The old Duchess must have some reason for this event. Perhaps her eldest son Richard was at last to marry. Or maybe John – or Adela. But the Duchess herself of course would not appear. Somewhere hidden in the dark confines of the Portland Place house, unseen by all save a few intimates who played cards with her, her physician and the family, she plotted and planned. This Ball was to be a protest, some people said, against the new world that she detested, the Jewish financiers, the American heiresses come to search for titled husbands, the South Americans, the Theatre, and the rest. The Ball would be exceedingly exclusive. The Prince and Princess would be present.

It was very quickly an interesting question as to who among the Herries had been invited. Quite a number – Ellis, Vanessa, Carey, May, Barney, little Cynthia and her mother. It was characteristic of the family that so soon as it was known that there would be several of them there, everyone was satisfied. There was no individual jealousy. Granted that the Herries were sufficiently represented, that was all that was necessary. There was no flavour of snobbery either. It was important that members of the family should be present because it would be for the general good of English Society. Anything anywhere was better for having a mixture of Herries in it. Barney was invited because of his friendship with Johnnie Beaminster. Little Cynthia had achieved quite a friendship with Lady Adela. Moreover, the Herries were the type of English of which the Duchess approved – not Upper Ten, of course, but good sound English stock with practically no foreign mixture. The snobbery, in fact, was *English*, not *Herries*. Barney commented on this. 'The English will always be snobs because they care about caste. But it's a fine sort of snobbery as the world is at present. Keeps the right people at the top. One day when the whole world is democratic and cares more for doing things than being them, it will all seem most ridiculous. Then England will become a third-rate Power and everyone will be happier than they've been for centuries.'

They were having an artistic hour at the Winter Exhibition of the Royal Society of Painters in Water Colours, Vanessa and Barney, Horace and Rose. Very delightful, Vanessa thought the pictures. Mr Birket Foster's grand 'West Highlands' made her feel quite sick for home, and Sir John Gilbert's 'Retreat' was splendid. Mr Watson's 'Bathers' Pool' was enchanting, and Du Maurier's 'Last Look at Whitby' so very clever. But best of all Mr Goodwin's 'Strayed Sheep', so homely and English with its cawing rooks and gentle colours.

'Oh, Horace, *do* look at the pictures! What have we come here for!'

But Horace's thoughts were on England.

'Really, Barney! England a third-rate Power! What about our Empire?' Everyone was beginning to beat on the word Empire as though it were the family gong.

'Our Empire! Who says it's ours? It's ours for the moment. One day it will be off on its own.'

'Politics are *so* tiresome,' said Rose. 'Doesn't that man over there look like the Claimant? He's been appearing at a music hall. Yes, dear, I think the pictures are sweetly pretty.' She wandered off, her arm through Vanessa's. 'Vanessa darling, do you think Ellis would lend me fifty pounds if I were to ask him?'

'Oh, Rose, I shouldn't. Can't you get it in any other way?'

'Not without being under painful obligations. Oh, do look at Horace watching the door so that if anyone useful comes in he can snatch at them!'

'Rose, dear, are you in a fix?'

'Yes, I am – about ten fixes.'

'Perhaps I can help. How much do you truly need?'

'About twelve hundred pounds. But twenty would help.'

'I think I can manage that.'

'Oh, you are good to me!' Rose was charming when she was grateful. She looked so pretty, so young, so sincere. She *was* sincere. She loved to be grateful – but to the right people.

Vanessa, thinking about this and other things, discovered that the family had come to regard her as Ellis' private conscience. When anyone wanted anything of Ellis, an opinion, an invitation, a tip from the City, Vanessa was the oracle. She could do with him, they said, anything that she liked. She knew that she could.

Then a little incident occurred. One afternoon when he had just returned from the City and they were discussing the evening plans, Ellis cut his hand. He was sharpening a pencil, the knife slipped. It was a bad gash, blood flowed, he turned ashen. She rang the bell for Buller, the butler, and helped Ellis to a chair,

staunching the blood with his handkerchief, which soon was
soaked. Very white, he leaned back against her, her arm around
him. She thought that he would faint. Smiling very wanly he
kissed her cheek. She did not move. His slender body in her arm,
his confident reliance on her, his touching submission, made her
feel as though he were her child. As she waited for Buller to come
she thought that when Ellis depended on her for comfort she
could do anything for him. At that moment she loved him. He
said something, and she bent forward to catch his words. Her
cheek touched his.

'I think I am going to faint.'

'Buller will be here in a moment.'

Her arm tightened about him. She just heard him sigh.

'Oh, Vanessa, how I love you!'

Then Buller came in, advancing as he always did like a
churchwarden to whom the morning's money offerings had
proved disappointing.

'Sir Ellis has cut his hand badly. Get brandy, Buller, and
something to bandage it with.'

She sat there, with Ellis in her arms. Miss Fortescue appeared
in the doorway, then hurried forward.

'Oh, Sir Ellis, what *have* you done?'

'Only a slight cut, Miss Fortescue. Buller has gone for some
brandy.'

Miss Fortescue looked at them darkly.

'How that woman does hate me!' Vanessa thought.

As January drew to a close and February began there were only
two topics in the London world: General Gordon and the Beaminster Ball. About the first it was said on the one side that an
awful mistake had been made, on the other that exactly the right
thing had been done. About the Ball it was said that it would be
the grandest ever given.

On the 24th of January the steamers started up the Nile on an
advance on Khartoum; on February 6th it was known that
Khartoum had fallen and the relief force had been too late.
Meanwhile, having satisfied himself that Khartoum was
wholly in the Mahdi's hands, Sir Charles Wilson had turned his
steamers and gone downstream. Then for ten days England remained in suspense. On the 16th of February a telegram was
published from Wolseley saying that Gordon had been killed.

Vanessa came down to breakfast on that morning to find family prayer over and Ellis-standing with *The Times* shaking in his hand.

'A crime!' he cried, with an odd shrill voice that she had never heard before. 'The most monstrous crime! Gladstone will never be forgiven for this! Never! Never! Never!'

She thought for a moment that she had to do with a madman. His pale eyes were shining, his hands jerking the newspaper as though they would tear it. They were alone, for Carey and May had not yet come down and Miss Fortescue had meals in her own fierce fastnesses.

'What is it? What has happened?'

'Gordon has been murdered! We have basely deserted him. Left the bravest Saint and Hero to go to his death alone! England will be shamed before all the world!'

'Gordon murdered! Gordon killed!'

'Yes, yes; there is the telegram!'

It seemed in thousands of homes that morning as though a veil of darkness fell over the world. Nothing could be clearer, simpler than that splendid figure, selfless, a missionary thinking only of his God, fearless; it was told of him how he had gone through all the campaign in China, his only weapon a cane, of how he had thought always of everyone but himself in the Sudan. It seemed now that the blackest treachery, the meanest political chicanery had betrayed him. There were other colours in the real picture, and it says something for the accused that, through all those weeks of almost insane vituperation, they never attempted to dim the saintliness, the courage, the selflessness. But Gordon's death was, perhaps, the first warning cloud on a horizon that had been now for a whole decade stainlessly blue.

That terrible news had also its private personal repercussions.

Ellis dropped the paper to the floor, sat down by the table, then, speaking now quietly, said:

'I feel as though I had myself betrayed him. Why do we all wait and trust to a kind of luck? Why are we all so cowardly? Vanessa, I am bitterly ashamed.'

His hand trembled against the tablecloth.

'I never thought that it would happen,' he said. 'I was afraid sometimes, but Gladstone was so sure. We have come to think that Gladstone always has God in his pocket. That they have intimate talks together and Gladstone tells God what to do. Well, this time God has not listened.'

Ellis was always best when he forgot himself. He had a kind of almost fanatical pure-mindedness at such times. Then something robbed him of his self-consciousness, his fears, his absurd egotisms. He would now have thrown his money, his physical cowardice, his fear of offending public opinion, even his Herries blood out of the window could he, by doing so, have saved Gordon. He had a kind of grandeur.

He and Vanessa were very close at that moment. He took her hand.

'Oh, Vanessa!' he sighed. 'You and I – if only together we could help it to be a better world!'

Then Carey and May came in and the world was at once a more mundane place. After breakfast Vanessa went upstairs to find old Lady Herries in tears.

'Oh, poor General Gordon! All alone! Such a good man! Those savages! And Gladstone worse than any of them!'

Then as though she realized that Ellis downstairs must be very unhappy, her last word to Vanessa was:

'Be kind to Ellis, won't you, my dear?'

We quickly forget. Two days later, although Gordon's death was the only topic, the tragedy had become impersonal. No one any longer thought it was possible to have died at his side. Not even perhaps quite desirable. What *was* desirable was to have Mr Gladstone's head on a charger.

Vanessa went to the Beaminster Ball in a turmoil of varying emotions. There was, of course, her dress, the loveliest that she had ever had. It was a white dress, with a red rose fastened at the narrow waist its only ornament. The bodice fitted very tightly to the figure. She wore long white gloves and carried a beautiful white fan of ostrich feathers, a present from Lady Herries. Her only ornament was a diamond brooch, bequeathed her by Judith, fastened on her right shoulder. The effect of her dark hair and all this cloud of dazzling whiteness was very splendid, but, Ellis thought as he glanced at her, it was the softness of her eyes, the charm and kindliness of her eagerness, her youth, her excitement, her happiness that made her so brilliant, so unlike anyone else. For tonight she *was* happy. She could have taken all London into her arms and embraced it. Her mind was set on the future, the life that she would make for herself, the friendliness of all the world. She was aware of her beauty and delighted that she was beautiful. She had never *believed* that a dress could be so marvellous a fit! She would see the Prince and Princess! How good and kind of Ellis to give her all this happiness! She let her gloved hand rest on Ellis' coat as the carriage rolled on through the lighted streets and she heard men calling as though it were for her that they were crying some message. She sat very straight, her head forward, taking all this life into her heart and intending to give it out again with all the fullness of which she was capable. Benjie was never out of her mind, but tonight he was in the back of her consciousness. One day she would be with him again, quietly, confidently, his friend. Perhaps after all it had been for the best. This was the safer way.

They halted. They were in a stream of carriages that stretched down Portland Place. Then on either side of the red carpet was a crowd of sightseers whom a large policeman kept in order. Vanessa and May passed up the steps, into the hall. Looking up for a moment before she turned to the right to the cloakroom Vanessa saw a line of footmen in red coats and velvet knee-breeches on either side of the great staircase. Dimly she heard the echoes of the band.

As she arranged her hair before the looking-glass she heard May's whisper: 'Oh, you do look lovely, Vanessa darling!'

Ellis and Carey were waiting for them and slowly they mounted the staircase. At the top Adela Beaminster, blazing in diamonds, received them.

'Lord and Lady Rockage!'

'Sir Ellis Herries!'

'Miss Vanessa Paris!'

They passed on into the ballroom. It was one of the famous rooms in London with its white walls and gold ceiling, and on the white walls were hanging the Lelys, the Van Dycks, the other famous Beaminster portraits. The far end of the great room where the band played was banked with masses of white flowers. Although so many people were standing about there was plenty of dancing space. The roar of voices rolled in waves from wall to wall.

She stood at first with May, extremely happy, quite contented to watch. Decorations were worn, the dresses of the women were superb. How ridiculous of her to have been proud of her own! She had never seen in one place so many beautiful women. The air sparkled with diamonds. A tall thin woman near her was wearing a tiara that focused all the light to itself, that made, in truth, her plain pale face shadowed like a mask. Vanessa unfolded her fan and stood, waving it slowly, smiling as though she could never have enough of this lovely scene.

She was not, however, to be left alone for long. Soon one man came up to her and then another. During these months in London she had made many friends and was in fact very much better known than she had any idea of. A Captain Verrier, who had been sending her flowers, who had taken her and May on one occasion to Hurlingham, asked her to dance. She adored to waltz – surely there was no experience in life so perfect! He talked to her, but she answered him only in monosyllables. When the music stopped and they had moved into a long narrow room beyond the ballroom and sat down, he said to her:

'I don't think you heard a word I said when we were dancing.'

'No. I love dancing so much, it seems a pity to talk.'

'I'm sorry, because I said some very amusing things.'

'You can tell them me now, Captain Verrier.'

'You know, to look at you, Miss Paris, one would imagine that you had never been to a Ball before.'

'I never have – a Ball like this. When will the Prince and Princess come?'

'Oh, later on. About midnight, I expect.'

'And is the Duchess sitting in her room upstairs all this time?'

'Yes. Like a field-marshal. And her generals deliver dispatches.'

'I saw her once. She came to a party in Hill Street.'

'Yes. She went out for a little while some years ago. But she soon went in again. She found that her importance was lessened as soon as she became visible.'

Then he began to make love to her. Laughing, she stopped him.

'Are you asking me to marry you?'

He was embarrassed.

'Well, no, not exactly. You see—'

'I should make a very bad mistress, I am afraid. I can imagine nothing more uncomfortable.'

'Oh no. You misunderstand me. I only meant—'

'I like you very much, and I am very glad we are friends.'

'You are not offended?'

'Oh dear, no. Why should I be? Only why don't you marry? There are so many nice girls who are longing to be married—'

'Well, you see, I haven't a penny. Only my pay—'

They discussed his affairs, and Vanessa was very maternal.

After that she was dancing all the time. She found everyone delightful. Some tried to make love to her, some confided their troubles to her, some laughed and behaved like schoolboys, some were extremely pompous, one asked her to go to India with him.

'India!' she cried. 'What should I do in India?'

He was not sure, except that she would make him very happy.

Then something occurred which, on looking back afterwards, affected, she found, strongly her later behaviour that night. Barney appeared and with him a charming, shy young man.

'Vanessa,' Barney said, 'here is a cousin of yours. An unknown cousin. Be kind to him.'

The boy, who looked about nineteen, was slender and tall with fair hair and bright, ingenuous blue eyes.

'I'm not a good dancer,' he said, blushing furiously. 'Shall we sit this out? I think that you will be more comfortable that way.'

She discovered that his name was Adrian Cards and that he was at New College, Oxford. He was a younger brother of the Ruth and Richard Cards who had, years ago, been present at Judith's Hundredth Birthday. He was a great-nephew of Jennifer Cards, Benjie's grandmother.

At first he was very shy, but no one could be shy for long with Vanessa. He began to pour out his heart. He had many enthusiasms. Literature. No, he did not like the Aesthetes much. They still read Swinburne, but were not he and Tennyson a little – well, pontifical? The earlier Browning, but not these 'Inn Albums' and things. Pater, yes. The *Renaissance* was wonderful. He had met Pater. A Society called 'The Passionate Pilgrims' had invited him, and there he had sat, cross-legged, looking rather like a Chinaman. He had seen Matthew Arnold and often Jowett. You could see Miss Rhoda Broughton out walking. But he was all, she discovered, for philanthropy! Toynbee Hall, W. T. Stead. They had started a Mission in Bethnal Green that he visited. Oh, Miss Paris, he did hope that she would not think him a prig. He was not that. He rowed in his College boat. He didn't like saints, he did not wish to improve people's *souls* – no, but their *bodies*! Oh, Miss Paris! Did she *know* of the distress and unemployment? Did she realize that last month four thousand men came to the Mayor in Birmingham and asked for work, that they were starving and could scarcely stand? Had she heard of the Industrial Remuneration Conference, of all the things that

the Trades Unions were doing? There was a Mr Bernard Shaw
who had read a brilliant paper, and Mr John Burns had warned
them all of what England would be in another thirty years! He
was burning with it all, words poured from him, while the splendour and almost fantastic pageantry of the evening passed back-
wards and forwards in front of them.

Then he checked himself with a most charming smile.

'You have been so sympathetic! I am ashamed of my
preaching. But you are staying with Cousin Ellis, are you not? I
can't help thinking of all he might do with his money if he liked!
Can't you influence him, Miss Paris?'

'Don't call me Miss Paris,' she said. 'We are cousins, you
know. My name is Vanessa.'

'Oh, thank you. And *my* name is Adrian.'

'Yes, Barney told me.'

'Cannot you influence him? The things he could do! If only
you could persuade him just once to go to Bethnal Green.'

She told him that she had very little influence with anyone.

'Someone as beautiful as you are must have influence! Oh, I
beg your pardon! Have I been impertinent?' He broke off and
then with the same eagerness he asked her about Cumberland. He
had never been there. Ruth had told him how lovely it was! She
often spoke of Madame. What a marvellous old lady she must
have been! And how sad that the house at Uldale had been burnt
down!

'Oh, your father—' He was always rushing in and then out
again!

'No, I like to talk of my father. He was the best man who ever
lived!' She began to tell him things about Adam and Cat Bells
and Uldale. She told him about Hesket and Caldbeck, of John
Peel and the Herdwick sheep and the best-cured hams in the
world. They had there the largest water-wheel and the smallest
parish in England. Of the grand old farmers and their splendid
ploughing, of an old lady she knew who had eighteen children
and was ninety today, of how if you asked an old ploughman,
strong as the horse he was leading, how old he was, he'd say 'Ah's
nobbut eighty!' of how they would sing 'Old Towler' under the
fellside, of Tom Pearson, the wrestler, who could dance a better
step-dance than any woman, of the 'Ivinson' grey tweed, the
strongest in the world – and, as she talked, all Skiddaw broke into
the London house, clouds came down over the gold ceiling, and
the bleating of the sheep was louder than the band!

She had missed a dance with someone or other. She rose and held out her hand.

'You'll come and see me, Adrian? Come tomorrow to Hill Street, tea time.'

'Yes, I will,' he said fervently.

But when she was dancing again she knew that something had happened to her. The wildness was upon her again, but now it was full of fear and warning. She must not return to Cumberland! She must make her life in another fashion. Where Benjie was, danger lay. That boy was right. It was being shown to her clearly that, at the side of Ellis she should help the world. The two of them together – what could they not do? Ellis had told her that he was waiting for her to help him. Already in these weeks in London they had grown close together. At the thought of all they could do for the world her cheeks burned, her heart beat high.

She had been living without any thought of all the unhappiness, the poverty! The things that Ellis and she might do together! ...

There was a pause. Everyone moved to the right and left. The Prince and Princess had arrived.

They walked up the room, bowing and smiling, stopping once and again to speak to a friend, while the women curtsied and the band blared. It was a glorious moment. He looked so kindly and she so beautiful. England was safe for ever and ever: the peoples of the world were bowing. A hero had died for his country in the Sudan. Here and there were a ruffian or two to be taught their place and duty! The Beaminster portraits smiled down their loyalty and patriotism, the jewels blazed, England lay like a cloak at the royal feet, and the Empire did obeisance.

'Oh! to do something splendid!' Vanessa's heart cried.

It was Ellis who took her in to supper. He was quiet, stealing glances at her once and again. She seemed to be carried high on some wave of exaltation. She looked at him so kindly that when they moved away and sat down together in a distant corner where from the hall below they could hear them summoning the carriages, he said, now for the third time:

'Vanessa, will you marry me?'

She, staring beyond him into an imagined world, nodded her head, saying:

'Yes, Ellis dear – if you want me.'

Part Two

The Husband

JUBILEE

EARLY IN JUNE of the great year 1887 Ellis and Vanessa went one evening to hear Albani in *Lucia* and, waiting in the portico of the Opera House, were caught by a breeze that, in spite of the warm evening, made Ellis its victim.

In the following days he paid no attention to his chill, sternly from morn to eve pursuing his City adventures. On the eighteenth of June there was a grand party in Hill Street, a Jubilee party, with Royalty and Colonel Cody. Next day Ellis was threatened with pneumonia. On the morning of the supreme Tuesday he was as hopelessly a prisoner as any poor wretch in Vine Street.

It was a tragedy. Ellis and Vanessa had seats in the Abbey; for months Ellis had looked forward and, in his odd way, half child, half man of importance, he had come to feel (as perhaps many other Herries were feeling) that the Jubilee was created only that he should sit with the loveliest woman in London and give his approbation to his Queen's Thanksgiving.

He lay there, his cheeks mottled, his nose sharp and white, his thin body stretched like a corpse, his eyes rheumy with cold and bitter disappointment. Vanessa refused to go to the Abbey without him. She would watch the Procession from Piccadilly with Rose and Barney and young Adrian. When she came in to say goodbye she felt so vividly his own bitterness that she cried: 'Ellis, I won't go. I'll stay here with you. Rose will tell me all about it, and besides the heat is fearful or will be soon. Ellis, I'll stay.'

He longed to agree that she should. He would not miss it so grievously if she also missed it, and the thought that she had given this up for him would be a salve to that intolerable unceasing doubt, the doubt that she loved him.

But he was not so selfish; no, no, he was not so selfish. So, in a voice thick with cold, drawing the bedclothes close to his chin, he murmured: 'Absurd! How absurd you are, my darling! You had better not kiss me. Go and enjoy yourself!'

He knew that when she was gone he would repeat to himself again and again: 'She offered to stay. One word from me and she would have stayed.'

How beautiful she was! He watched her hungrily. Her dress
with its full bustle, rose-coloured, fitted her tall graceful body
with exquisite symmetry. No woman in London wore clothes as
Vanessa did; the little hat, perched on her dark hair, was
wreathed with rosebuds. The parasol that she carried was rose.
Two roses, dark and rich like the summer weather, were at her
waist. She was a Queen, he thought. Had we gone to the Abbey
she would have been lovelier than any other woman there. 'The
beautiful Lady Herries . . .' and he would have been with her, the
proudest man in England.

'Give me some more of those drops, dear, before you go.'

She thought the big bare room chill and stuffy. Beyond the
window the sun blazed on the street; very faintly from the far
distance came the sound of a band. She could see a flag gently
moving in the morning breeze from an opposite house. She was
all impatience to be gone. She might be a grand lady now who
must never forget her dignity, but for nothing at all she would
dance down Hill Street waving her parasol. How terrible had he
said: 'Yes, dear. Remain!' How terrible not to see the kings and
the princes, not to hear the blare of the bands, not to see the
colour and the excited happy faces of the people, not to wave to
the Queen! She was so sorry for his disappointment that tears
filled her eyes as she smoothed his thin hair with her hand,
straightened the bedclothes, laid the books and *The Times* close
to him! How old he looked when he was ill! How old and how at
the same time like an ugly disappointed little boy! How near and
how intimate to him she was, and how far away and separate!
How kind and tender she wished to be to him! And how her very
heart contracted in her breast when he made love to her! How
grateful for all his kindness, how deeply irritated, against her
will, by his unceasing care of her!

She sat in the chair beside his bed, holding his hot dry hand.

'You will take care not to be in the sun.'

'Oh yes, there is a large awning over our stand.'

He was moved by a sudden spasm of irritation and kicked up
his knees beneath the bedclothes.

'It is too bad. It is really too bad. To happen just now! In
another week I could have gone!'

'I know, I know, dear. Oh, why did we go to that silly Opera?
. . . Ellis, let me stay! I'll go with Rose this evening and see the
illuminations . . . After all it is going to be so hot, most
uncomfortable, I expect, and a procession is always so quickly
over . . .'

He sighed. How wonderful if it had been she who was ill and he had been given the opportunity of sacrificing himself! At once he was ashamed of such a thought. His love for Vanessa prompted him to strange wicked desires. He who would give her anything in the world, to wish anything so wicked! He choked, coughed, drank a little water, smiled with wan bravery.

'What you must think me! As though I could be so selfish! Enjoy yourself, my dearest, and tell me about it . . .'

He picked up Walter Besant's novel, laid it pathetically on the bedclothes. 'I shall count the minutes until your return.'

Afterwards in the sun and splendour she felt as though she had escaped, by a miracle, from prison.

Early though it was, the streets were thronged and the stands already crowded, but she had only to slip down Berkeley Square and in at a back door, be conducted by an extremely polite young footman through a drawing-room and so out to the stand where Rose already was.

When she settled herself and looked about her she uttered a cry of childlike delight. The sky was an unbroken blue, the full green of the trees of the Green Park was soft and deep and luminous like a sunlit cloud. From her seat she could watch the hovering flutter of the flags, the massed colour of clothes, the splashes of scarlet that broke the pearl-grey of the London stone. All this colour was translated by the sunlight into something trembling and unsubstantial as though lit by some unseen fire. There was a brooding silence scored like a sheet of music with the clatter of a horse's hoofs, the echo of distant band music rising and falling on the slight morning breeze. Above the buildings flags drifted against the blue as though under the impulse of some secret rhythm. The front of the stand was banked with flowers.

She sat there, her gloved hands clasped, her lips parted, her eyes shining. At that moment, if she had been ordered, she would have died for her country, for the Queen, for any cause that needed her. For a very little thing she would have burst into tears.

Rose, who looked very exotic with her dark colour, her red dress, was as deeply excited as Vanessa.

'This is all very foolish,' she said. 'By this afternoon I shall be ashamed of myself. No matter, I like being ashamed of myself.'

Rose read from her programme:

Her Majesty will be accompanied on horseback by the

following Princes placed in the order of their relationship to Her Majesty:

Grandsons and Grandsons-in-Law of Her Majesty

HIH the Grand Duke Serge of Russia

HRH the Prince Henry of Prussia, GCB

His Highness the Hereditary Prince of Saxe-Meiningen

HRH the Prince Albert Victor of Wales, KG

HRH the Prince George of Wales, KG

His Highness the Prince Christian Victor of Schleswig-Holstein

HRH the Prince William of Prussia, KG

HRH the Hereditary Grand Duke of Hesse

His Serene Highness the Prince Louis of Battenberg, KCB

Sons-in-Law of Her Majesty

HRH the Prince Christian of Schleswig-Holstein, KG

His Imperial and Royal Highness the Crown Prince of Germany, KG

HRH the Grand Duke of Hesse, KG

Sons of Her Majesty

HRH the Duke of Connaught and Strathearn, KG

HRH The Prince of Wales, KG

HRH the Duke of Edinburgh, KG

She talked without ceasing, waving her hands, half rising from her seat, turning to look for friends. Did Vanessa know that people were paying twenty-five pounds for a good place? That nearly three hundred books of gold leaf had been used for decorating the State Coach, that there was still living a survivor of George III's Jubilee, an old lady in Gloucestershire, that the Pope is so pleased at the Jubilee that he wants England to reestablish relations with the Vatican, that so much gas was to be used in the illuminations, that? . . .

She said:

'Oh, Vanessa, I am so happy!'

She caught Vanessa's hand, then drew away again whispering:

'No, I won't spoil your fun. Don't listen to me. It isn't true. I'm too excited to know what I am saying.'

Vanessa turned to her.

'Rose, what has happened? What have you done?'

'Nothing. Nothing. I didn't mean what I said.' Then abruptly again she broke out:

'You know that Horace is engaged?'

'No. When? To whom?'

'A few nights ago – at the Ball at the Reform Club. A Miss Lindsay. A nice little girl. With money of course. And he will treat her abominably.'

'You'll be alone, Rose. You won't like that even though Horace isn't the most—'

'No. Yes. Well, perhaps.'

'Rose, you are going to do something foolish. What is it? Tell me. I insist on your telling me.'

Their lives had been bound together. Ever since that day of Judith's Hundredth Birthday when Vanessa, looking across the luncheon table, had seen her, wanted her for a friend, loved her, there had been a bond which Rose's recklessness, her risks and mistakes and gradual descent from safety into danger, had only strengthened.

'Vanessa, you will always love me, always, always, whatever I do?'

So also Benjie had claimed. She had fulfilled her promise. She laid her hand on Rose's arm.

'Rose, don't do anything without telling me. You must not. It is not fair to me. We have been friends so long and have helped one another so often. Promise me! Promise me!'

'Look! There is someone riding up the street. He is seeing that everything is clear. Doesn't he look grand with his feathers?'

'Rose, tell me. What are you doing? Not Fred Wycherley? You told me—'

'Vanessa, darling – it is all right. Really it is. I was excited. I'm always doing something silly. Look! how the stands are filling up! Why don't Barney and Adrian come? They are missing everything—'

'But it isn't Wycherley? Promise me that it isn't Wycherley – with his wife and those two children—'

'No, of course it isn't Fred. Oh, do look at that woman in that bonnet! There, to the right! Did you ever *see* such a thing?'

At that moment Barney and Adrian Cards arrived.

Adrian, who, young as he was, was now in the Foreign Office, who wrote articles for the magazines on religion, economics, French poetry, who loved Vanessa with such open devotion that

everyone thought it charming, sat on one side of her, Barney,
who was now very stout, on the other.

'Here we are!' said Barney. 'I have just seen Timothy and
Violet and their offspring.' (Timothy had brought his family
with him permanently to London.)

'I have also seen Phyllis and Rochester struggling for breath in
Northumberland Avenue, Amery, son Alfred, and the new plain
wife nestling under the lions in Trafalgar Square, so I have not
done so badly by the family. How is poor Ellis?'

'Oh, Barney,' said Vanessa, 'he was crying with disappointment. He had been *so* looking forward—'

'Yes. It's a shame. Poor Ellis.' But he was not thinking of poor
Ellis as he leant his fat body forward and drank in delightedly
the scene, except perhaps, without any unkindness, to relish his
own fun the more because Ellis' catastrophe made him realize
that he too might have caught a cold and been prevented. He
pushed out his chest, stretched his stout arms a little, wondered
how little Daisy McPhail (the present lady of his apartments)
was getting on somewhere along the Mall (he had loved her now
for three months and still found her good company), considered
(as all novelists consider) whether he would be able to describe
this heat, colour, movement, expectation on paper, looked at
Vanessa and marvelled yet once again at her beauty ('But this life
with Ellis is telling on her, and I don't wonder'); leaned yet
farther forward to gaze down Piccadilly and saw, a little to the
right, only a row or two away, Benjamin Herries.

'By Heaven—'

'What is it?' Rose asked – and he could feel that she was trembling with some agitation deeper than any Jubilee warranted.

'Nothing.' He had pulled himself in. 'Only that everything is
so jolly. *What* a day! Doesn't that old lady have luck with her
weather?' (*Was* it Benjie? Yes, certainly. He had half turned. He
had seen then.) Barney suddenly was assured that Benjie had
seen Vanessa from the moment of her first entry. The little man,
square-backed, brown as a berry, in some fashion independent,
alone like a hill-man who had come down to study for a moment, the people of the plain, sat erect, his chin resting on the
handle of his stick, the most significant thing about him his
living, questing, eager eyes.

'A bandit!' Barney thought. 'For tuppence he'd hold a gun at
the lot of us!'

Benjie half turned again and gave Barney a nod, slight,
humorous, secret.

'His eye never leaves Vanessa. But Vanessa must not see him. Lucky that Ellis is locked away in Hill Street!'

And again, like any novelist, he considered that here was a situation, old and hackneyed though it might be, that would make a chapter or two: Benjie, Ellis, Vanessa – all of them so much more real than anything that Barney could do on paper. And he summed up for judgement the half-written efforts of his present work, *Julia Paddock* . . . Poor thing, how she wilted and died before the sharp indifference of actual life!

'Look here, Adrian, change places with me, will you? I'm a bit deaf in this right ear. Creeping senility, you know.'

They changed places, Adrian seated now between Vanessa and Rose. Barney's broad body would, with decent luck, hide Benjie from Vanessa.

Young Adrian talked of the People's Palace which Besant's *All Sorts and Conditions of Men* had started as popular philanthropy. Vanessa was on a Committee. Mr Besant had come to tea in Hill Street. A nice, booming, self-confident, bustling kind of man.

'Oh, don't let's think of committees!' cried Vanessa. 'This is so much nicer. I'm not very good at committees, Adrian. My thoughts wander.'

He was only twenty-two years of age, and Vanessa was the love of his whole life. He had the imagination of the abnormal, but with it the common sense and balance of the normal. He was, in fact, closer to Will and Ellis and Timothy and old Pomfret than to Francis and John and Adam. He would never commit suicide nor dream his life away. His philanthropy, idealism, poetry, would be practical, definite things. He was the straight, normal Herries at its best. So, looking at Vanessa, he worshipped her without any thought of contact. She was the greatest lady he would ever know, the kindest, the loveliest. And how glorious to be beside her today when she was like a child in her pleasure! He had seen her of late so often as the hostess sitting at the end of her table at those endless dinner parties in Hill Street, curtsying to Royalty, talking to Ambassadors, moving down the room with all eyes upon her . . . Now, for an hour, she was close to him, friend with friend. Not that she was ever affected or grand. The world in which for two years now she had moved had not touched her, but, as he had often noticed, when Ellis was not there, she was free, spontaneous, self-forgetful . . .

'Oh! they are coming!' she cried. 'They are coming! I can hear the bands!'

Distant music broke across the heat and light as though somewhere a door had opened. All individuality was lost; colours,
blue, crimson, green, hung like painted cloths about an empty
room, for here in the sunlight there was a bare space which only
one figure could fill. The empty room waited for that entrance;
the door would be opened and soon, for the briefest instant, a
small stout old lady would be borne forward, would stay for a
moment, looking about her while the colour, the music, the sunlight made a canopy over her; then, with a little bow, she would
retire and all would be ended. A bell would ring, a trumpet blare,
the door would close.

A kind of sanctification fell upon those people. They turned,
their eyes straining down that long pathway between the banks of
colour, a pathway so oddly bare. There was a fear of a last instant's frustration. Would a thunderbolt fall, the final trumpets
for Judgement sound, and so – after the agonized anticipation –
that royal carriage with the little bowing figure never appear?
The sky, the trees, the flags, the splashes of crimson, all a painted
prepared pattern for that instant of completion that even yet
might not occur. Vanessa, looking upwards for a moment, saw
three birds, dark and remote, slowly fly across the blue. At the
sight of the first advancing soldier, glittering in the sun, his black
horse moving with dignified austerity, she turned to Barney and
whispered:

'My father met my mother for the first time on the Queen's
Coronation Day.'

She wanted to evoke Adam. She wanted him there with his
kind, sleepy smile and that touch of his hand on her arm ...
Then she forgot everything but the Procession. Thicker and
thicker they came. The pathway that had been so bare sparkled
now with silver and gold. She was drawn down into a medley of
colours, sounds, and, pressing close upon her, that clear clop-
clop of the horses' hoofs like the ringing of little hammers on
stone. Men were detached from the river of movement; a figure,
the back straight as a board, the thighs stiff, one gauntleted hand
raised, would become real against fantasy. You believed suddenly
that it breathed, it touched its bearded cheek with its gauntlet:
the rider and the horse stood out above the flood as though the
trumpets had summoned it. The three Kings were in closed carriages – very disappointing of them. The cheering increased.
Now, glittering with gold, an open carriage could be seen, and
then, in an instant, the air broke into cheering, the caparisoned

horses, the outriders, the scarlet and the gold swung into being before the green clouded trees. The Queen, her parasol raised, in a dress of black and white, passed by. One horseman, in a silver helmet and shining cuirass, seemed her especial guardian – the Crown Prince of Germany. The door closed.

'Oh!' said Vanessa. 'How lovely that was!'

The soldiers were still marching, the drums and trumpets sounding, but the ordinary real world had assumed its place again. She heard someone behind her say: 'The twenty-sixth, remember. I'll have the carriage and we'll go straight down.'

She sat there watching for a while, happy, tranquil, remembering things to tell Ellis, suddenly thinking of Will Leathwaite in the cottage on Cat Bells. He would be going out that evening to see the bonfires and he would think of her as he always did when anything of interest happened.

'Didn't you love that, Rose? Didn't you think her splendid?'

But Rose was gone. How strange!

'Adrian, did you see Rose go?'

'Yes, she slipped away just after the Queen passed. She didn't want to disturb you.'

'Oh, I wanted to tell her—' Vanessa looked back to see whether she might yet catch her. People were rising, moving about, already many seats were empty.

Then, turning to the right, looking over Barney's head, she saw Benjie.

He was staring at her, standing up in his place. They looked at one another. He raised his hat, bowed, gave her one more long stare; then, turning his back, climbed up the wooden benches and disappeared.

She had invited Barney and Adrian to luncheon and they returned to the house with her, but, before she joined them, before she went in to see Ellis, she stood, without moving, in the middle of the floor of her bedroom, gazing in front of her. She had but a moment. Ellis, in the next room, knew that she had returned but, with the sunlight streaming about her, still wearing her hat and gloves, she stayed there, lost.

Benjie! She had not seen him for close on four years, but in that momentary glance it had been as it had always been. They had not separated. They *could* not separate. Marriage altered nothing, distance altered nothing; she must confess to herself what indeed she had never denied – that Benjie and herself could not be parted. He had looked as he always looked. His London clothes, his tall hat and dark coat could not change him, his apartness, his humorous defiance, his challenge to the world. He had been, apparently, alone. Had he been aware of her for a long while? Had he intended to speak to her? Was he staying in London? Was he here permanently, perhaps with his wife and boy? Or had he parted from his wife? Or was he on his way abroad? How strange that out of all the thousands who had watched the Procession they two should have been so close together. He could not have known where she would sit. Or had he perhaps met Barney the day before and asked him? Would he call at Hill Street or would he keep his part of their bargain? During these four years he had never written to her, nor sent a message. As she took off her hat and slowly drew off her gloves she knew that she would at that moment give everything – name, reputation, happiness – for one word with him.

Her body shivered. She knelt down for an instant beside her bed, pressing her hands against her eyes. Oh, how she wished that she had not seen him! Oh, how glad, how glad she was that she had! The sunlight fell hot upon her head like a caress. She bathed her face and hands and went through into Ellis' room.

Ellis lay there, his long hands with their prominent knuckles on the counterpane, and he looked at her steadily, following her with his eyes as she moved as a painted portrait does.

She came to the bed, sat down, took his hand and began to tell him all about everything. 'The colour, Ellis! You can't imagine it! The trees of the Park made everything so much brighter, and then the splashes of scarlet and the grey buildings and all the flowers. We had beautiful places, better than the Abbey. We could see both ways down Piccadilly and had a view of the Queen's carriage for ever so long. Rose was there. She was rather restless. I do hope she isn't getting into trouble again. And Barney and Adrian. Barney is really disgracefully fat. He said he'd seen Timothy and Violet and Amery and his son.'

'Did you see anyone else you knew?'

She realized at once that Ellis was hostile, that something had happened here in her absence. *Had* Benjie called? Had he written? Had Barney been up to see Ellis already and told him? Oh, but he would not! That was not Barney's way. Had someone else seen Benjie about London and told Ellis? Since their marriage Ellis had never uttered Benjie's name . . .

She answered quickly:

'No one to speak to. We left before the Procession was over to escape the crowd. And we did. The Square was quite empty. Not a soul about. But the crush in the streets was dreadful, and what the heat must have been . . .'

He interrupted in that small cold voice always used by him when he was offended (he was very proud of it: he thought it was calculated to strike terror into any heart).

'Some letters came for you while you were away.'

So that was it! There was a letter for her in some hand that he suspected. She had noticed of late that he looked at the writing on the envelopes of her letters with an eager curiosity which he always thought that he hid.

'Miss Fortescue brought them in,' he went on. 'She thought that you were still here.'

('She *knew* that I was *not* here,' Vanessa thought indignantly.)

The letters were in a little pile on a table near the door. She went across, picked them up, then turned and smiled at Ellis. 'Well,' she said, 'what has disturbed you, Ellis? Something has made you unhappy.'

He said at once, his voice shaking:

'One of those letters is from Benjamin Herries.'

(Was it so? Then he had written to tell her that he was coming to London? He had written to make an appointment?)

She looked quickly. There was no letter from Benjie. One, in a man's hand, was from Keswick, but, as she knew at once, it was from a Doctor Harris there who had written asking if she would subscribe to some sports to be held in August at Threlkeld. She did not dare even glimpse at her own fierce disappointment. She was *not* disappointed. It was *much* better that Benjie should not write, should never write, never see her, never speak to her . . .

She came quietly to the bedside and gave Ellis the letter.

'There is nothing from Benjie. This, I suppose, is the letter you meant. Read it.'

He looked quickly at the letters, then pushed them towards her.

'No, no. Of course I will not read them. I am very ashamed. Please, please forgive me. If you knew how I have been suffering!'

'It has done your cold good anyway,' she thought, 'having something else to think about.'

Her anger and indignation, of which she was always afraid

because they were so strong when they were aroused, stirred in her eyes. She did not ask herself whether her disappointment assisted her anger.

'Please read them, Ellis, if you want to. I have no secrets from you whatever.' (Had she not?)

He looked up at her abjectly, a look that she detested, in human beings, in animals, in anyone or anything that should have pride.

'Please, please forgive me. The handwriting was like. I thought that he might be coming to London for the Jubilee. I have been lying here all these hours longing for you . . . You are so beautiful today . . . I love you so terribly. I cannot grow used to it. I used to think that in time it would become part of life, ordinary, but it does not. It is stronger every day because it is never satisfied. It is not your fault. But you don't love me. You never loved me.'

That was just. That was true. At once she felt tender towards him because of that injustice. He was like a small son who had asked for a present that she could not give him, and so she put her arms around him and comforted him. She sat down beside him and took his hand again.

'Ellis, dear, we all care for one another in different ways. That is everybody's trouble. I think perhaps I am not passionate in the way you mean. Many women are not. But we are such splendid friends. More every day. Let us be thankful for that. And don't begin to suspect things. Let's trust one another. If we do not we shall torture one another. We have been married for over two years and have trusted one another perfectly. Ask me always if anything makes you uneasy; suspicion in marriage is horrible. It's worthy of neither of us.'

He moved towards her, put his thin arms round her, laid his head on her breast.

'Love me! Love me! Love me!'

She tried to comfort him; her relief when at last he moved away made her feel ashamed. Today something new had entered their married life, something not quite new. Rather a forgotten acquaintance who unexpectedly arrives and says that now, from henceforth, he will live in the house.

She kissed him and stood up.

'I must go down to Barney and Adrian. They are waiting for luncheon. I will come up afterwards.'

He lay staring at the door long after she had left the room.

*   *   *

And even then this day was not done with her. When Adrian and Barney were gone she went upstairs again and read Besant's novel aloud until Ellis slept. Then she went down to the drawing-room. She had done what she could with it. There was a portrait of her by Whistler in a white dress standing against a dull gold wallpaper, holding a fan. She had not filled the room with odds and ends as many of her friends liked to do. It had now a silver-grey wallpaper, there were many flowers about, there was a deep purple Persian carpet, but the place was not alive. It would never live, it would never be home to her. The two tall windows were open – a pale blue light shadowed the houses. The sky was pale with the evening heat. There was holiday everywhere, shouts and cries, distant bands, and the flags moving lazily in the gentle summer breeze. There was that scent of burning that a very hot day in London leaves behind it, and the odour of flowers, roses, carnations, and the dry dusty fragrance of geranium leaves. She turned back into the long dusky room that was like a cool deserted cave. She walked up and down, knowing that life, after two years of comparative quiescence, had in a moment taken another turn. Everything from this hour was different. Tonight there was to be a family dinner party. Ellis had insisted that his illness should make no change. Rose and Horace, Phyllis, Clarence Rochester and Philip, Barney, Amery and his son and new daughter-in-law, Timothy and Violet and Aunt Jane, Carey and May Rockage, pretty Cynthia, Rodney's granddaughter, and her husband Peile Worcester, Adrian ... they were all coming. No one but the Family. What an odd mixed lot they were, and yet how alike – even the wives of other stock. They moved forward in one body, not to the outer world important and yet affecting the world by their quiet insistence on normality, confidence, the domestic virtues, patriotism, deep suspicion of the foreigner, belief in the Church, Tennyson, the Houses of Parliament, the Royal Family (with reservations about the Prince of Wales, Barney's mistresses, Rose's reputation, Jews – unless they were very rich – and one or two things more).

They had been very kindly to Vanessa. Old Lady Herries before she died last year had said: 'My dear, never fight the family. I know you often want to, but it isn't worth it. They always win in the end.'

But did they? Had not Judith defeated them, and Uhland and even her own father? The battle continued. She had not, herself, surrendered. And Benjie? Oh, *where* was he? Was he quite close to her somewhere in London? She had the maddest impulse to go to Barney's rooms in Duke Street. He would know, she was sure. She went to the door, opened it, and listened. The house was as still as the inside of a drum. Only the beating of her heart seemed to thud down the passages. Then there was something else. Someone was coming up the stairs.

She went back into the drawing-room with the wildest thought that it might be Benjie. What would she do? How could she defend both herself and him? She stood, one hand pressed to her breast, staring at the door. But, when it opened, it was Finch, the new butler, a man she did not like because she was sure that he was in league with Miss Fortescue, a fat red-faced man with sandy hair.

He had a note on the salver.

'A letter for you, my lady. A boy has just left it. He said that he was told that there was no answer.'

She saw at once that it was in Rose's hand, and as soon as Finch was gone, opened it, reading it there where she stood.

> DEAREST – I could not tell you this morning. I went to the Procession with a wild hope that something would occur, that I should break a leg or be strangled by the crowd. Nothing *did* occur, so by the time that you get this I shall be on my way to France with Fred. Insane. I know it. I think that we both of us know it. But I would not care if it were not for you. But you said that you would love me whatever I did. Remember – your love is all that I shall have in a year's time.
>
> ROSE

The note fell from her hand to the ground. She bent down and picked it up. A foreboding, dusky and cold like the room, crept to her side and touched her hand.

THE FLITTING

BENJIE HERRIES, a week or two after Jubilee Day, walked up the hill on a lovely summer evening towards the Fortress. He had been playing cricket with the young men of Ireby village. On his shoulder he was carrying his son Tom, aged three years, and

beside him was Bob Rantwood, a famous poacher, drunkard and
ne'er-do-well, one of Benjie's best friends. A sunny haze covered
all the world. In the village there had been much motion, the
long wagon drawn by its splendid team of horses, the chatter at
the little inn with its coloured prints, its gay pictures of hunters
and horses, and a grand flower-and-fruit piece that was the land-
lord's especial joy, left there by some travellers to pay a debt more
than a hundred years ago, the flagged passage, and beyond the
bottle-green windows the clear blue of the summer sky. Mrs
Enderby's shop with the liquorice, bull's-eyes, bootlaces and a
portrait of the Prince of Wales, the long fields rising to the grey
hills, the deep oaks, the bleatings of sheep, the brilliant leaves of
the copper beech, the scent of clover and bean blossom.

He was at peace and not at peace; he had enjoyed the game, the
comradeship (for they liked him), the taste and sound of Cumbrian air and soil, but Rantwood unsettled him. He had poached
with him many a time, knew all about salmon and trout poach-
ing, the 'draughting' and 'poling'. Lovely nights he had had with
Rantwood draughting a river, or, by himself, guiding his poles,
knowing exactly where there is a spile or a crook. The thrill, in
mild weather, to find a spot where the fish are spawning, or on a
dark night to see the dawn steal over the fan-shaped hill, to hear
the moorhen plunge! Or, draughting with Rantwood, trailing the
net slowly down the river, stoning the water to frighten the
salmon into the net – or best of all on a moonlight night, when an
old coat had been soaked with paraffin, the thrill of the moment
when this improvised torch is lit and the men with him, sticks in
hand, plunge into the water . . .

Rantwood, like most poachers, was a discontented, cursing,
but most amiable fellow. Nothing was ever right with him. He
would swear at the game laws by the hour together, 'gloweran'
aboot' like a madman, and then he would laugh, throw his thick
arms around, and call Benjie, for whom he had warm friendship
but no reverence, 'thoo girt daft cauf, thoo'.

He was always restless, always wanting to be somewhere where
he was not – and so was Benjie. But Benjie knew what was now
the matter with him. He should not have gone to London, should
not have seen Vanessa . . .

Three days he had stayed there. He had not especially enjoyed
his visit although he had done all the things that would, he
thought, amuse him. He had visited Earl's Court and seen
'Buffalo Bill' Cody's Wild West Show, had travelled on the

Underground Railway and been stifled by the sulphur and smoke from the engine, the fumes from the oil lamp, the reeking pipes of his fellow-travellers. He had visited the Gaiety Bar and talked to the magnificent ladies who served him, had spent several hours in the Argyle Music Hall, admired the Chairman who with such militant authority banged the table with his gavel, and wondered at the amount of liquor he could consume.

He had wandered the streets and like any country yokel stared at the illuminations, had watched London Society display its elegance in Hyde Park, had been pleased with the superb procession of curricles, landaus, victorias, the powdered footmen, the silk stockings, the yellow plush; had found a beautiful lady at the Alhambra, gone with her to her room in Portland Street, but once there, after half an hour's most elegant conversation, had politely left her. He had been, in fact, the loneliest of men. That seat from which he had viewed the Procession (a pretty penny he had paid for it!) had been his ruin. He had gone to London on a sudden impulse, resolving to visit no member of the family. It had been the cruellest fate (the kind of check to his virtue that fate was for ever dealing out to him) that Vanessa should be sitting there almost at his side! For two hours he had watched her. Every detail of her dress, every movement had been absorbed by him. It was not her loveliness that had struck him to the heart, but his intimacy with her so that he knew instantly, at the first sight of her, that nothing was altered, that his four years' exile from her had hindered nothing.

He had made no attempt to speak to her. Weak, irresolute as he was, he would keep his word – at least, for a little longer. But he returned to Cumberland a haunted man.

He shifted young Tom a little, liking to feel the warmth of those small confident fingers against his neck. A funny freak of chance that Tom should have in him some kindred blood with the second wife of Vanessa's great-grandfather. After Vanessa he loved Tom – the only two in the world whom he loved.

'All the family have cleared out of the country,' he said aloud, following his thoughts. 'I'm the last here. We were all over the County a while ago.'

'Aye,' said Rantwood, who was pursuing his own thoughts. Would Herries ask him in for a drink? He had a thirst all right. But Mrs Herries – she didn't like him. Nor he her – whimsey-whumsey kind of female.

'My great-great-grandfather rode into Keswick one night from

Doncaster. That's how it all started. We were all over the place once. Oh, I've told you before. And now we're all away again.' He looked over the hedge down the valley where the summer evening breathed tranquilly under a stainless sky. Around them the insects were humming and on the other side of the hedge a brook sang beneath the willows. Voices cried through the stillness with a dying fall. As though he spoke aloud: 'I am walking up this hill and soon I will be gone. I have done my best. I have kept my vow, but soon I shall be wandering again. I can neither be free of this country nor settle in it, and when I am away I shall remember just such an evening as this, the meadow falling into dusk, and all the names that I love – Blencathra, Uldale (almost all the bricks of the house are gone now: soon there will be nothing but the turf and the sheep cropping it), Bassenthwaite, Ireby – beautiful names like the words of a vow, a vow that I have kept but can keep no longer. I hate this house I am coming to. I have always hated it. I hate this woman in the house. I have always hated her, and one day soon I shall take young Tom and we will walk away and never come back. The last Herries . . . but the place will be always in my bones. I shall never tread on such turf again nor drink such running water nor see such lithe walls running into the sky nor hear such friendly voices. But I have lived long enough away from Vanessa, and although I never speak to her again I must see her once between one day and another day.'

'That was a good catch I made to get Will Davidson,' he said aloud.

'Aye,' said Rantwood. 'Thoo can play at cricket a' reet.'

'Well, goodnight to you, Bob.' He turned in at the gate.

'I mun slacken my thirst wi' watter,' Rantwood thought discontentedly, starting down the hill.

Inside the house even on this summer evening it was damp. They had come down to live only in three rooms and the kitchen. An old woman, Mrs Cumming, was the present successor to all the in-and-out females who had done service in that place. The room at the top of the first stair-flight that had once been the drawing-room with the fine gilt chairs, the naked goddesses, the rosy cupids on the ceiling, was now the general living-room. All that remained of Walter's splendours was the long mirror with the gilded frame, and reflected in this Benjie now stood with his little son. His shirt wide open showed his brown chest, his neck firmly set, his head like a hard apple, the twinkling kindly eyes alive and eager, his small restless body upon which clothes seemed always an excrescence, Benjamin Herries, rogue, good fellow, a 'deep' chap, a good-for-nothing, the kindest man in the county, the suddenest-tempered, 'a man all by himself', a jolly man, a man of his word, a man you couldn't trust, a gentleman, a vagabond, a wise man, a fool — just as your personal experience happened to be.

And his small son stood beside him, like his father because he had the brown colour and the sparkling eyes, a child always laughing, filled already with secret plans and plays of his own, never wanting company, never afraid, never asking anyone to help him.

The mirror also reflected the room, which was a scramble and a confusion, littered with fishing rods, guns, a woman's dress, a child's playthings, a table with the remains of a meal, and a sofa with a hole in it.

'Vanessa,' said Benjie, looking into the mirror.

Later, to the light of a smoking lamp, Mr and Mrs Herries enjoyed their evening meal together, old Mrs Cumming clattering in on her clogs bringing the beef and gooseberry pudding, banging them down on the table, going out with a toss of the head because she and Mrs Herries had but now crossed swords in the kitchen.

Mrs Herries was the thinnest woman in all Cumberland and her face was of a faintly green pallor. But she was the same reserved passive woman she had ever been. In years she was still a girl, but her features were of that ageless cast belonging to women who have matured when very young and live on their passions. Benjie was always kind to her; that he hated her was not her fault. He knew that she had been many times unfaithful to him, but she was no more personal to him than her pale reflection in the mirror might be. It was amazing to him that they had stayed together in this horrible house for three years, but his vow had kept him, he supposed. He had shown Vanessa that he could be faithful. This woman had at least done that for him; so he was kind to her, smiled across the table at her and told her he had made thirty runs in the cricket game. He ate his beef, seeing that the long gilt mirror was loose on its nail and swayed ever so slightly, so that the room rocked too a little. The two high windows were open and the place was suffused with the summer evening heat, with the odour of the roses that rioted about the garden. A moon, tip-tilted on the edge of one small cloud lit from within like cotton wool around a lantern, drunkenly grinned through the window.

'Mrs Cumming can't cook meat, that's one thing certain,' he said, smiling at his wife.

'No, she can't,' the late Miss Halliday agreed. 'But we never get a decent servant here.'

'We pay them plenty,' said Benjie, who from land, from money left him by Elizabeth, was not so badly off.

'They won't come here. They are afraid of you.'

'What! that I'll go to bed with them? You know that I've been faithful to you since our wedding day.'

(He had, marvel of marvels! Or no – to put it better, he had been faithful to Vanessa.)

'That doesn't interest me,' Mrs Herries said. 'You know you're free to do what you like. Oh, it isn't you. They would know how to deal with you if you started anything. No, it's the house.'

'Ghosts?' said Benjie.

'What you like to call them. Mrs Cumming was talking about it tonight – steps up and down the passage, a dog whining. You've heard the dog yourself up there in the Tower. Someone tapping with a stick. And that woman in black wandering about the garden.'

'Do you believe in spirits, then?' he asked her.

'Spirits!' she answered impatiently. 'These gooseberries aren't half cooked. Well, what are you to think? Those friends of my brother's, *your* friends, those Endicott men, they've seen things time and again. But there's something queer about this house.'

'Yes, from the moment the first stone was laid. My grandfather spoilt it with his obstinacy. If you see a thing isn't going to turn out well you should give it up. No good going on if the signs are against you.'

She sat leaning forward, her sharp-peaked chin resting on her hands. He noticed that she was regarding him with great attention tonight. He felt that something was in the wind.

'Ghosts!' He smiled. 'I saw one in London the other day – a beauty. She was tall like a lily, carried herself like a queen, she was dressed like a rose and a had dark, dark hair. It makes you think of a ghost like that when you see a room in the mess this is in. Why don't you tidy things a bit, Marion; keep things in order more?'

'Ah! What's the use? You're never in, and nothing would ever stay neat in this house. Three years I've had of it—'

'You're a strange woman.' They regarded one another in friendly fashion. 'You've never had any liking for the boy, and he's a fine little chap too. It has meant nothing to you, being a mother.'

'No, nothing at all,' she answered. 'Women mean nothing to me, no, nor children. But men – ah! that's another story! And you, Benjie, more than any. I want to be in your arms as badly as ever I did the first time I saw you. But what's the use? Why you've stayed with me all this time I can't imagine ... Well, I must wash the dishes. I won't have that sneak of a woman in the house after tonight. She goes tomorrow.'

'Why, what has she been doing?'

She was standing up, her hands on her hips, staring at him as though she would never see him again.

'I like you like that with your shirt open. You're brown all over like a foreigner. Where did you get that skin from?'

'Who knows where one gets anything from? That's the mystery. Where we come from, who made us what we are, what we make ourselves into, where we are going to. And we've lived three years together, Marion, and are as far apart as ever we were.'

'Yes,' she said. 'It's all the body, what it looks like, what its clothes are. I'm not your beautiful ghost like a rose, tall as a lily. But see the rose's nose crooked and give her a black eye, and where's your love for her then?'

'I'm not so sure,' said Benjie. 'I'm not so sure.'

'But I am! It's only because you've a brown skin and are strong and haven't an ugly mark on your body that I'm in love with you. But what's the use? You don't care for me and never did. And you're the only man I've never tired of. Most men are the same after you've known them once.'

She said all this in a quiet, dispassionate voice. Was it because of her own unresting physical passion that he had once on a day been caught by her? Maybe. But that didn't matter now. It was not her fault. A pity that she didn't care about young Tom, though. That might have been something of a bond between them.

'Well, I mustn't stay talking here. That woman's stealing the spoons, I wouldn't wonder.' She went out, carrying the beef with her.

He wandered out into the garden.

Moonlight on a summer's night is a most impermanent thing. Everything is new born, but only for a moment, and when the silvery world rises it is like a dream that, even while you are enchanted, you know that you must not trust. The flowers on such a night are ghosts that at a touch will vanish away, and water, shining under the moon, belongs to no earthly stream. This garden had never yielded to any man's will. Flowers had died when you cared for them and waxed abundant when you neglected them. The moonlight poured out now from under the trees like a flood that, at the beckoning of a cloud, would be withdrawn. Only the trees stood firm, waiting the moment when they would advance, cover the ground, swallow the house and resume their kingdom. Man had never been wanted here, especially man filled with the spirit of obstinacy, revenge, and pride.

Was there some dark figure moving under the trees? He stood there watching. It was easy to imagine, with all that you had heard, that a tall woman in black, now in moonlight, now in grey shadow, moved, hesitated, moved again. He walked forward, the plants crowding about him; then he turned to the stone steps that ran to the higher ground at the side of the house. He had always disliked these steps. His mother had told him that for some reason they had always frightened her. Uhland had tap-tapped down them with his stick, Walter's drunken friends had sprawled against them and fallen from top to bottom like the helpless fools that they were. Now they were washed white in the moonlight and you could see the tufts of grass like black bunches of fingers pressing up between the broken flagstones. Here, standing halfway up, he was exactly under Uhland's stair and he could fancy that behind that dark window Uhland was standing and behind him perhaps old Rogue Herries. The two of them watching the third in that sequence. He stretched his arms. He whistled a tune. He might be of their family, but he was not of their destinies. He was fit and well and strong; he had a son and he loved a woman, he had friends and a hundred miles of country that he would not exchange, with its clouds and stones, for all the sunny kingdoms of the world. He looked down on that moonlit garden. He could hear the water falling from one pool to another. An owl hooted. *Was* not that a woman who moved from tree to tree? He whistled his tune, kicked the loose stones from under his foot and went in to see that his child was comfortably sleeping on this hot night.

Tom slept in a corner of his own bedroom, a room in Uhland's Tower, once used by Walter as a guest room. It was sparsely furnished, his bed, Tom's small one, a large tin bath, a dressing-table, his hunting prints and the faded painting of the old Elizabethan Herries that had once hung in Borrowdale. A fierce, frowning old boy with no nonsense about him! The carpet had holes, the cupboard where Benjie kept his clothes creaked with every wind, but tonight it was transformed with the moonlight and the scent of the roses. Although the window was open the room was very hot, and the child had thrown off the bedclothes and lay, his nightshirt ruffled to his chest, his little legs drawn up, one fist – clutching a small wooden horse – still clenched.

Benjie stood there, looking at him. This was his son, and not a bad son either. Pity he had that Halliday blood which was no good at all in his veins, but Benjie flattered himself that his own Herries blood could beat the Halliday mixture. Vanessa had as yet no child. That anaemic husband of hers would never give her one – and, perhaps, one day Tom would know her and love her and get his idea of women from her.

Poor Benjie sighed. He was really ashamed of himself for having a son at all. He was no sort of father for a boy to have, and he knew already what a man, who is no great hero and has done a shameful thing or two in his time, can feel when a small boy thinks him perfect. 'Well, he won't think me perfect long, and I can teach him to shoot and ride and not be afraid of anyone . . . Still, he ought to have some sort of mother to care for him.'

Then he undressed. He could not find a nightshirt so he slept naked, curling up his legs as his child had done. Father and son slept side by side and the clouds came up over the moon, drenching the room with darkness.

Tom always woke very early and came into his father's bed. He would lie, his small head against his father's chest, looking at the trees beyond the window, waiting until his father should wake. He talked to his horse, named Caesar, telling him about the things that they would do that day, bacon for breakfast, a visit to the village, and, if very lucky, a ride to Bassenthwaite. He didn't *promise* Caesar these delights. He had learnt already that it did not do to expect *anything*, that one was left alone when one least expected it, or worst of all, handed over to Mrs Cumming with her constant: 'Now don't be a worrit' or 'Keep quiet, do'. He was accustomed to being without his father for days at a time and, although his mother was never unkind to him, he knew quite well that she did not care for him. Only once had she been really angry with him, and that was when, coming into a room unexpectedly, he had seen her sitting on a fat man's knee. She had slapped him severely although he did not know what wrong he had done, and then the fat man had given him sixpence. The only fear that he had was that, when his father went away, he would never come back again. He discussed this often with Caesar, and Caesar reassured him. *Of course* his father would come back. But when he was in bed with his father he clutched him very tightly, his arm on his breast or his neck. That comforted him greatly.

At last the grand moment arrived when his father opened his eyes, grinned, yawned, stretched his arms, played a game or two. Then he watched his father splash in the tin bath, after which he was himself plunged into the same. His father helped him with his clothes, fastening his buttons, brushing his hair, and tying his boots. This was a lovely morning, as fresh as a bird's wing, and between the trees you could see Blencathra's shoulder resting against the faint early summer blue. His father whistled and sang, which showed that he was happy this morning; then, hand in hand, they went down to breakfast together.

The big untidy room was bright with sunshine, but there was no breakfast; no cloth was on the table, and, although it was by now half past eight, no sign nor sound of Mrs Herries.

Then Mrs Cumming came clopping in, carrying a plate of bacon in one hand and a dented silver coffee pot in the other.

'Where's Mrs Herries?' asked Benjie.

Mrs Herries is gone,' said Mrs Cumming, her eyes staring with a fat, half-sleepy curiosity.

'Gone?'

'Aye. Mr Ewart's trap come and fetch her seven this morning. She told me they was driving into Carlisle and she left me a letter.'

She felt in the pocket of her cotton dress and produced it; she gave him a stare and went out.

He held the letter in his hand, but, before he opened it, settled Tom in his place, cut the bread, gave him some bacon and poured out the coffee. Tom wriggled until he was comfortable, set Caesar up on the table in front of his place and set to.

The letter was as follows:

DEAR BENJAMIN – I have gone away with Charlie Ewart and shall never return. He has been pressing me for a long time. I'd have told you last night, but what's the use? There's nothing to be said. You don't want me, you never have after the first night or two. I did a wrong thing in the first place to

force you to it as I did, but Mother pressed me and I was in
love with you. I wonder we've stayed together as long as we
have and I must say you've always been very patient, your
nature being what it is. We haven't had what you could really
call a cross word all these years. All the same we haven't been
happy, either of us. I wish I could have felt more for the boy.
I'm sure I've tried, but it isn't in my nature. I wasn't meant to
have children and if I can help it shan't ever have another.

You'll be much better without me; I haven't a gift for keeping things straight and tidy. What Charlie Ewart sees in me I
can't think, and I don't suppose we shall be together long
although he says different. You can divorce me if you want to
but I don't want any money from you and I'll never be married
again. Well, goodbye, Benjie. One thing I'm glad of, that I
shan't have to live in the Fortress any more. It's a place would
make a cat sick – Your sincere friend,

MARION

Benjie read the letter through three times, then he gave his son
some more bacon. 'Well, that settles it,' he said aloud. As though
the sunshine penetrated his heart he felt a great joy and gladness.
He was free again; he had been set free. He had kept his vow and
now, without any act on his part, he was liberated. Charlie
Ewart! That thin, shanky, lop-eared farmer! Poor Marion! He
was so sorry for her that had she at that moment appeared in the
doorway he would, in spite of his disappointment at her return,
have been kind and considerate. But, thank Heaven, there was no
need to be kind and considerate any more!

He went into the passage and called Mrs Cumming.

'Mrs Cumming, Mrs Herries has gone to London. I am going
also and I want you to order Sam Bender round with the trap in
an hour's time. I'll catch the train from Carlisle. I'm taking the
boy with me. I don't know when I'll be back, but I'll write from
London.'

So that was the end of the Fortress. He would sell the damned
place and be done with it for ever. He would be in London and
Vanessa would be in London. He had done what he could, and it
was not his fault that now he was free to go where he would.

Poor Marion! Charlie Ewart! Well, well . . .

He went to his room and packed a few things, Tom going hand
in hand with him everywhere. He dressed Tom in his best suit
and his grey summer jacket.

'We are going to London,' he said. 'You, I and Caesar.'

While he was sitting waiting for the trap, he talked to his son. 'We're going away, Tom, and I don't expect we'll ever live in this house again. Years and years ago a man rode into this country with his son and went to live in a little house the other side of Keswick. He had a brother living in Keswick too. And as the years went by his son had a wife, and they went and lived in a house down in the valley there which was burnt in a fire later on. There were many of our family in the country, but, one by one, they died and went away until you and I are the only ones left. And now we're going away too. But that's not the end of it. You and I have got this country in our blood. You don't know what that means now, but you will one day. Everything you ever do will be affected by this country, and however far you travel you'll never find any other country so beautiful nor any other that's in your bones as this one is. You'll come back to it. Be sure of that. But I hope you won't come back to this house, because it was built in a bad temper and hasn't been any good to anybody.'

Tom seemed to understand. 'The funny thing is,' thought Benjie, 'that one remembers after the things that one was told although one was too young at the time. I remember things that Adam told me about birds and wrestling. Very rum that.'

'You've got to be a better man than I've been, Tom,' he added. 'And I hope you'll stay in one place sometimes. You never learn anything if you're always moving. But you'll be all right so long as you're never afraid of anyone. There's nothing to be afraid of really.'

It wasn't like him to preach, but the warm sun was comforting and he felt so happy and cheerful that he had to be talking to someone.

They took a last look at the place together, the Cumberland stone, the overgrown garden, the two cross-faced towers. A dog was whining somewhere and little flakes of plaster fell from the ceiling of the living-room.

Then Sam Bender came with his trap and took them both away.

VIOLET BELLAIRS IS PREVENTED

WHEN Timothy Bellairs and Violet his wife had been established in London a year or so they became the centre of social exchange for the London members of the Herries family.

Hill Street was of course the Temple: all the splendour and
sanctification were in Hill Street. Only Vanessa of all the Herries
entertained the Prince and Princess to tea (although it was said
that the Prince *had* paid pretty little Cynthia a visit at her pretty
little house in Charles Street); only Vanessa invited Archbishop
Benson to luncheon; only Vanessa was on friendly personal
terms with Mr Chamberlain.

During these years Hill Street was the Temple. But neither
Ellis nor Vanessa cared for gossip. At least Vanessa enjoyed it but
appeared to consider some things spiteful when they were only
amusing. Now Violet Bellairs was quite different from this. A
Cumberland country cousin, she had become very speedily a
most entertaining London hostess. She was not, of course, very
clever: you could laugh at her to her face and she seldom perceived it. She had no talent for the Arts, thought Oscar Wilde an
actor, and supposed that *Robert Elsmere* was written by a clergyman, and had only just heard of young Mr Kipling. But it was
not for the Arts that any Herries went to Onslow Square. They
went, quite frankly, to hear about the other Herries. You could
always tell when any scandal was afoot because Violet, her stout
body enclosed within the brightest colours, her red face beaming,
her hat elegant with a stuffed bird, her eager, friendly voice with
its 'Well, how are you? Haven't seen you for an age!' was to be
seen everywhere – at Charles Street, in Barney's bachelor rooms
in Duke Street, in Phyllis' overcrowded drawing-room, even in
the cold and gloomy place in Kensington where old Emily Newmark held her prayer meetings.

Violet was always in the best of spirits, kind and friendly to
everyone, leaving a trail of scandal behind her. She *did* enjoy a
gossip, she freely confessed, and liking, quite naturally, to be the
centre of any company, if she had no thrilling tale to tell she
invented one. Her husband, who was fat and sleepy, spent his
days in the Conservative Club and his evenings at Jimmie's or the
Alhambra or where you please. He was no trouble to her at all.

Violet, like so many women who married Herries men, became
more Herries than the Herries. She was patriotic, strictly moral
and all for the law. Nevertheless any human failing made her
happy because she was never censorious, but treated a 'mishap' as
a town crier treats a lost dog – rang her bell, felt kindly towards
the dog but hoped that it would not be found before the whole
town had had time to observe that it was lost. Her best women
friends among the Herries were old Phyllis Rochester, Cynthia

Worcester, Alfred's wife (Amery's daughter-in-law) and (again oddly enough) old Emily Newmark.

She had, of course, many many friends quite outside the Herries circle, but they were not of quite the same importance to her. As she often said: 'Our family holds together. There's not another family like it in England for that.'

It happened that, early in September 1889, Violet was very busy. It had not been a dull summer, for first there had been Mrs Maybrick (dreadful woman: why was she not hung?), and then those terrible Dock Strikers who, week after week, poor abandoned creatures, went about demanding their Rights, starving and altogether behaving disgracefully. It was not, however, either Mrs Maybrick or the Strikers who gave her so agreeable a week or two at the beginning of this September. It was a real Herries sensation – *what* was happening in Hill Street?

Two years earlier, a week or two after the Jubilee, the question had been – what *will* happen in Hill Street? for Benjamin Herries had come to Town, leading his son by the hand, and one of those family crises so greatly beloved by the Herries promised to be on the way. Then, to everyone's surprise – to the surprise of old Garth, old Amery, young Alfred, heavy Emily, dear little Cynthia, even the stout Barney himself – *nothing* occurred. Benjie called on none of them. He spent an evening or two with Barney; he never went *near* Hill Street. So far as anyone could tell, he neither wrote to Vanessa nor spoke to her. Everything had been the more dramatic in that summer of 1887 because of the dreadful (but rather delightful) Rose scandal. She had escaped to Paris with Captain Fred Wycherley, leaving Mrs Wycherley, poor thing, and two young children in London. ('Did you expect him to take them with him?' Barney asked ironically.) More than that, she met Carey Rockage in the Rue de Rivoli one September day and laughed and joked with him as though nothing had occurred.

Carey was in a fine way because May, his wife, and Maud, his elder daughter, were at a hotel not two streets distant. How fearful if Rose should suggest that she should call! But Rose (who was looking both young and pretty, Carey thought) suggested nothing of the kind.

'I know you have May and Maud with you, Carey. You were at the Opéra-Comique last night. If you are making a domestic parade one day and meet Fred and myself, we shall expect to be cut, you know. So don't worry. Only, if out on a little bit of

evening fun on your own, Carey, remember that Fred has his
spies everywhere. He'll give you a tip or two as to the best places if
you ask him! He's the kindest of creatures!' She went off, laughing, swinging her bustle. Poor Rose. She had been always a coarse
woman. Horace, her brother, married last autumn and it was
understood that he did not wish Rose's name to be mentioned.
Simply because of the awkwardness that it caused to others.
Looking more like a Bishop than ever, he let it be understood that
he was devoted to Rose. 'Which of us is above reproach?'
he inquired of Barney. 'What I mean, old fellow, is that charity is
the finest of the virtues. For my part I look at the good qualities
in my fellow-men. Who am I to judge? And Rose has loved Fred
Wycherley for years.'

Nevertheless it could not be expected that Miss Ada Lindsay
that was, a plain pale-faced girl, twenty-one years of age to
Horace's thirty when he married her, coming as she did straight
from a wealthy but Christian family in Kensington, would care
to hear such things mentioned. What Ada herself thought of it
nobody knew because she seldom spoke. No one knew what her
thoughts were about anything – including Horace.

However, the really interesting side to Rose's disgrace was that
it was well known in all Herries circles that there was a deep
difference of opinion concerning it in Hill Street. Ellis was disgusted. Vanessa would not listen to a word against Rose. Cynthia
Worcester was known to be devoted to Vanessa, to worship her in
fact, but even she confessed that if Vanessa was going to 'bite her
nose off like that all about nothing' she would think twice about
visiting Hill Street again. All that she had said was that Rose had
got at last what she wanted, and Vanessa had turned on her,
scolded her in front of Ellis as though she were ten years old.

It was plain then that Vanessa's own views on morals were a
little queer. Had they not always been queer? After all, had not
Judith Paris been her grandmother, Rogue Herries her great-
grandfather? Had not her own father been illegitimate and her
mother a German? No one meant any of this unkindly. Vanessa
was so beautiful, so generous and socially so resplendent that one
could forgive her almost anything; nevertheless she belonged to
the quarter from which the dangerous winds were for ever blowing, those winds that had for centuries disturbed the peace and
order of the right-living, right-thinking Herries.

Benjie, however, was a disappointment. He did nothing spectacular. Nobody saw him. They said that his wife in Cumberland

had run away from him after he had beaten her to jelly, that he drank like a fish and consorted with abandoned women. But these things were but rumour and Barney stoutly denied all of them. In the winter of '87 he left London for what destination no one knew.

It was in the spring of '88 that everyone began to say that things were not well in Hill Street. On the surface everything was very well indeed. Vanessa went everywhere and Ellis was often at her side, looking as proud as a peacock. Everyone *loved* Vanessa; how could you help it, so kind and generous and simple-hearted as she was? Nevertheless she made few friendships. Cynthia complained that 'there was always a barrier', but old Phyllis Rochester said that Cynthia was 'socially jealous'. Did Vanessa give herself airs? Surely not. She was the same to everyone, knew no social distinctions, and had been seen one day by Emily Newmark sitting on the top of a bus and chatting to the driver. Her only close friend was young Adrian Cards. She certainly spoilt that young man, who, because he was in the Foreign Office, looked after a Boys' Club in the East End and wrote for Mr Henley, thought himself quite out of the ordinary. *Of course* no one suggested that Vanessa was in love with him, but it was agreed that he visited Hill Street a great deal more often than Ellis cared for, and he helped Vanessa with her many charities.

Ellis was, in fact, the mystery. What went on behind that cold reserved official manner of his? He loved Vanessa madly: ever *more* madly as the time went on. He behaved to her in public with a really exaggerated courtesy and deference, but it began to be said that in private he was impossibly jealous. How do these things become known? Miss Fortescue (who, as everyone was aware, did not like Vanessa) told a thing or two, and there was that occasion when Alfred and his wife were lunching at Hill Street. Ellis had left the table abruptly and had not appeared again. Very odd. They all shook their heads over it. Then, in the late spring of '89, Benjie Herries once more reappeared in London. He lived in two rooms in Soho Square with his little boy. Poor little boy! That was the first thing that everyone said. Benjie did not now conceal himself as he had done on the earlier occasion. He paid calls on everyone – including Vanessa – and aroused the greatest interest. They all surrendered to his charm while he was *with* them. He looked peculiar, wearing clothes of a rough tweed, sometimes the new knickerbockers, but for the most part loose baggy trousers. His tie was generally a deep red in colour and enclosed in a gold ring, and this colour with his dark skin gave him the nickname of 'the little gipsy'. They told one another, however, with a rather reluctant satisfaction, that you could never mistake him for anything but a gentleman. He was always at his ease, laughed like a boy, was worshipped by any Herries children who happened to be about. He made no effort to win the affections of his relations: they could take him or leave him, and for a while they certainly took him. After June there was an exodus from London: Cynthia and her husband went to Ostend; Timothy and his family to Eastbourne; Alfred and his wife to Brighton.

Old Emily of course remained, and it was from her one must suppose that the story spread – the story that one night at the Alhambra, Benjie was engaged in a disgraceful scuffle, knocked a man down and spent the night in a police station. There *had* been a scuffle, that was certain, but Barney said that it had been extremely creditable to Benjie. Some drunken ruffian had insulted the lady in Benjie's company and Benjie had knocked him down. But what was Benjie doing at the Alhambra with a lady and what sort of a lady was she?

Then in August came the great news that Benjie had paid a call at Hill Street and been forbidden the house for evermore by Ellis. This was from Miss Fortescue.

Well, now, what do you think of that? Somebody said that Ellis had slapped Benjie's face, someone else that Vanessa had had to rush in between the two men and separate them. No one knew what had happened because nobody was present. Ellis and Vanessa left town to pay a series of visits. They stayed with the Rockages in Wiltshire, and with Horace Newmark – Barney's brother – now an old man of seventy in his grand house near Manchester.

It was reported that Vanessa was serene and happy, but that Ellis was 'queer'. What do you mean by queer? Well, May Rockage was bound to confess that she didn't like the look in Ellis' eye. He seemed unhappy if Vanessa left him even for a moment. Pathetic to see how he adored her, and Vanessa looked after him as though he were her son, but he was restless and Carey confessed that 'he didn't seem normal', the most alarming thing that any one Herries could say about another. All the old family scandals were revived, the misbehaviour of the ancient Rogue, the old quarrel at Christabel's ball, the suicide of Francis, and of course the dreadful affair of poor John and the crazy Uhland. Was the family never to be allowed to sit down quietly by its fireside and enjoy its domesticity, serve the country and worship its Maker? What was this crazy spirit that refused to leave them alone? Benjie was as bad as the old Rogue, and the sooner he left the country for good the better.

Early in September most of the Herries were back in London again; Vanessa was at Hill Street, Amery and Alfred in Tavistock Square, Timothy and Violet in Onslow Square, and Emily remained in Tutton Street, South Kensington.

So one fine September afternoon Violet thought that she would go and see what everyone was thinking. She took her son, young Timothy, aged now twelve, with her. Timothy was a beautiful boy; she refused to cut his hair, which fell in gold ringlets to his broad white collar. For parties or calls he was dressed in a black velvet suit. He was the pride of his mother's heart. It is sad to have to record that at this period of his life he detested his mother. He was not allowed to go to school, but shared his sister's governess. He was washed and dressed and brushed morning, noon and evening. He loathed his long hair, his velvet suit, the comments of his mother's friends; he was mocked at and shouted after by little street boys; he cried himself to sleep at nights because of their insults. The only thing in the world for which he cared was to draw and paint; this he must do in secret because his father, whom he rarely saw, laughed at such nonsense and his mother showed his drawings to her friends. He had to drive in an open carriage in the Park with his mama, he had to sit on a chair in ladies' drawing-rooms and be commented on as though he were something in a circus. His settled resolve was to run away as soon as the proper moment occurred. Barney Newmark was his only friend. Barney had said to Timothy: 'What the devil do you dress the poor child up like that for? It's cruelty to children, poor little beggar,' and Violet, hearing of this, never forgave him.

On this particular afternoon in Cynthia Worcester's drawing-room, he was not altogether out of place. Two young poets were present, a lady dressed in blue velvet and peacock's feathers, and Mr Oscar Wilde. Mr Wilde was very kind to him, sat beside him in a corner and told him a story about a young Prince who ran away from his father's kingdom and became a bell ringer in a church with a wonderfully high tower. One day when the Prince was ringing the bells, a swallow flew into the tower and rested on his shoulder. The swallow had damaged its wing, so the Prince took it back with him to the cottage where he was living . . .

At this point the ladies demanded that Mr Wilde should entertain them, so the tall heavy man with the grave eyes and the
beautiful voice had reluctantly to leave young Tim, who never
afterwards forgot him.

Two more men and a girl came in. There was a great chatter.
Violet admired Cynthia's looks but she must say she couldn't
admire the way that she did her drawing-room with the pale
grey wallpaper, some flowers in a white vase, a Japanese screen,
one little table with some odd-looking thin books upon it –
nothing else. No photographs! No cosy coverings to her room,
no fans pinned to the wall, or shelves with cups and saucers and
large blue plates. However, Cynthia *loved* a good talk and was
just jealous enough of Vanessa to enjoy a story or two. You could
not find two types more exactly opposite than Cynthia – so small
and fair, with such very light-blue eyes – and Vanessa – tall,
dark, 'one of Du Maurier's women', or as Horace Ormerod liked
to say impressively, ' "A daughter of the gods divinely fair" – fair
in the sense of beautiful, you know.' So that there was just
enough difference between the two for Cynthia not to object to a
little scandal . . . no harm, only to ask where Benjie was, had
anyone seen him, did Cynthia know what Ellis, when he was
staying down in Wiltshire? . . .

So that Violet was pleased when the two young men and the
girl came in, because now it would be perfectly easy to have a
little chat with Cynthia without disturbing the others. Smiling
happily upon everyone as though she would say, 'Now I know
I'm a large woman and when I move it is a little upsetting, but I
like you all immensely and you must none of you be disturbed,'
she drew her chair closer to Cynthia's.

'Cynthia darling – what *beautiful* teacups! Where did you find
them? Everything you have is always so lovely. Listen, dear.' She
dropped her voice. '*Have* you heard what Benjie has been doing?
They tell me that Ellis . . .'

But something was wrong. For once Cynthia did not appear to
be attending.

She said: 'Yes, Violet dear, how interesting!' but her sharp
blue eyes were fastened on the heavy frock-coated man with the
pale jowl, the friendly smile, the heavily lidded eyes, who, standing in front of the fireplace, talked with a self-confidence that
awed Violet although privately she thought it a little vulgar.

One of the young men said something with a titter about the

Queen. All the patriotic Herries in Violet (acquired by marriage) was affronted. Smiling very brightly she said:

'The Queen! Surely we must be proud to *have* such a Queen. Young man, you are disloyal.' (Shaking her finger at him playfully.)

'Violet is really dreadful when she's coy,' thought Cynthia, and for the first time (because she was not interested in children) wondered whether it was not rather a shame that poor child on the sofa (to whom one of ladies was now talking) should be dressed as a doll.

Mr Wilde said: 'The Queen? Do you know, madam, what Thackeray once wrote about our Queen?'

'No,' said Violet, 'Something fine, I'm sure.'

'Very fine,' said Mr Wilde, looking at her with so kindly an expression that she wondered whether she would not invite him to luncheon. 'He wrote, as nearly as I recollect, something like this: "I salute the sovereign; the good mother; the accomplished lady; the enlightened friend of art." '

'How very fine – and how true!' said Violet.

'Not true at all, madam. The Queen has not been a good mother, she is not accomplished, and she has not been a friend to art in any fashion whatever.'

Everyone laughed. Violet felt most uncomfortable.

'We owe to her in fact the present interest in the Arts. An Englishman is only an artist when those in authority despise the Arts.'

'What about Queen Elizabeth?' said Cynthia, laughing.

'Do you imagine that Elizabeth was an artist or cared for the Arts? She wanted to be entertained and made love to, and because the Arts then were part of a man's daily life, to tempt a man to make love to you was to rouse the artist in him. The Arts today can only exist by separating themselves from daily life. That is why the real artists today are never successful lovers, live from hand to mouth and wander the streets. Very different from the life of our Queen.'

'You are forgetting Mr Kipling,' said Violet, who had been persuaded only a week or two ago to read *Soldiers Three*.

'Mr Kipling believes in the Empire,' said Mr Wilde, smiling.

'Do we not all believe in the Empire?' asked Violet, pleased that she was holding her own in this very intellectual conversation.

'Do you know what Tennyson wrote for the Jubilee?'

'A very splendid poem, I remember,' said Violet.

'He wrote:

> *'Fifty years of ever-broadening Commerce!*
> *Fifty years of ever-brightening Science!*
> *Fifty years of ever-widening Empire!'*

Everyone laughed, but Violet did not see that there was anything to laugh at. Uncomfortable without knowing why, she waited a minute or two and then attempted Cynthia again:

'Do tell me, Cynthia darling. Have you been to Hill Street since they came back from the country? How did you think Vanessa was looking?'

'No, I haven't seen Vanessa for weeks.'

'It seems that Ellis has been behaving so very strangely – not sleeping, they say, and absurdly jealous. Phyllis had a letter from May Rockage . . .'

Everyone was laughing. The young man with the flowing black tie on the sofa had been drawing a picture for Timothy, and here was Timothy actually himself drawing something!

'It's a ship! It's a ship!' he cried excitedly.

One of the other young men jumped up and began to recite dramatically:

> *'Spirit of Beauty! Tarry still awhile.*
> *They are not dead, thine ancient votaries,*
> *Some few there are to whom thy radiant smile*
> *Is better than a thousand victories,*
> *Though all the nobly slain of Waterloo*
>
> *Rise up in wrath against them! Tarry still, there are a few*
> *Who for thy sake would give their manlihood*
> *And consecrate their being. I at least*
> *Have done so, made thy lips my daily food,*
> *And in thy temples found a goodlier feast*
> *Than this starved age can give me, spite of all*
> *Its new-found creeds so sceptical and so dogmatical.'*

'A very good poem,' said Mr Wilde, 'whoever wrote it. Its fault is that it contains a philosophy. Poetry has nothing to do with philosophy, but only with feeling.'

'You had a philosophy when you wrote it, Oscar,' said one of the young men.

'Yes, and got rid of it by writing about it. Any philosophy is foolish if you look it in the face. Christ hid His face, you remember, to cover the foolishness of His disciples. And that is why He loved John, because John had no philosophy – only feeling.'

'What very bad taste,' Violet thought, 'to talk about Christ in that ordinary fashion.'

Nevertheless it was now that she was disturbed by an odd sensation. There was something in this room that deprived her of her desire for gossip. It was not that she thought the Arts import-ant; the young men looked most unhealthy, and Mr Wilde's complexion was anything but hearty. Nor was she ashamed of wishing to talk about the family, but there was something here before which personalities seemed unimportant. She felt frus-trated, prevented. Even Cynthia, whom she knew so well, was different. The things of which these men talked were not in Violet's mind beautiful, and yet beauty was in the air. Perhaps after all her drawing-room in Onslow Square was a little over-crowded. The flowers in the white vase were a pretty colour . . .

It was almost as though someone had laid a hand on her mouth. She was most uncomfortable and thought at the first opportunity she would make an excuse and go.

One of the young men had, it seemed, but just returned from Paris and had seen there a performance of *Othello*.

'The absurdity about *Othello*,' Cynthia said, 'is that he should be upset so easily by so trivial a matter. A magnificent general, the strongest man in the State, and a little strawberry-spotted handkerchief—'

'You are wrong, dear lady,' said Mr Wilde. 'The tragedy of *Othello* is not Desdemona. She is only one element in his down-fall. We know, when he appears before the Senate, that he is poised above an abyss. He knows, we know, the Senate knows, that this new command is his last chance. He would have been recalled from Cyprus and Cassio given his place had there been no wife, no jealousy, no murder. Before the play begins he has reached the moment that comes to every man when the journey downhill has started. I have always seen Othello played as though he were a king of men in the majesty of purple triumph, with the trumpets sounding about him. That is wrong; he has the bitter knowledge that the glory is already in the past. It is of the past that he speaks to Desdemona, not the future. He comes to

the Senate, leading Desdemona by the hand, and despair is
already seated in his eyes. Great success demands great failure.'
He laughed, smiling at them all. 'I am already preparing for the
day when I shall know St Helena, and perhaps Calvary. I hope I
shall not complain, because the only artist who can count himself
fortunate is he who has learnt the value of great failure. When
Othello pierced his breast with his sword and remembered
Aleppo his soul cried triumphantly: "Now my experience is
complete. I thank the Gods!" For Othello was undoubtedly a
great artist.'

'You are making him out to be as self-conscious as yourself,
Oscar,' said one of the young men.

'Not to be self-conscious is not to be conscious at all,' Mr
Wilde answered.

'And not to be conscious at all – well, that is to be "Ruskin".'

Everyone laughed, although again Violet saw nothing funny
in the remark. Mr Ruskin, whose name was constantly in the paper,
was most certainly of a greater importance than Mr Wilde. To be
important was, apparently, with these young men, to be mocked
at. The Queen, Lord Tennyson, Mr Kipling, Thackeray, Mr
Ruskin ... it was some comfort to her to recollect that she
admired them all. She wanted to remain and she wanted to go.
Something stirred in her. The house in Onslow Square,
Timothy, the general trend and colour of her daily life – she was
suddenly dissatisfied with them all. Family gossip, for a moment,
seemed stupid and worthless.

But this was absurd. She resented her disloyalty to herself. She
got up to go.

'Do tell me, Mr Wilde,' she said, 'one or two interesting new
poets to read.'

He regarded her with so kindly a glance that once again she
wondered whether she would not invite him to luncheon.

'I am afraid there *are* no new poets,' he answered her. 'But
then there never have been. The best poets are old from the
beginning. Mr Dowson there is a poet, and a very old one indeed,
although he only left Oxford a year or so ago.' He indicated one
of the young men on the sofa.

'I will remember.' She nodded graciously to the young man.
'Come, Timothy. Well, Cynthia, it has been most delightful. You
must come to luncheon one day soon, dear, and perhaps you will
bring Mr Wilde with you.'

But in the carriage she was indignant. Whatever had possessed her to be affected by two or three young men who were so irreverent and common? And how stupid of her to have determined to have a word or two with Cynthia. It was a lovely afternoon; she would drive to Kensington and see old Emily, who always loved a gossip and was certain to know the latest thing about Vanessa and Ellis.

Timothy was silent as he always was when exposed in public. But he was not unhappy. He thought longingly of the large heavy man who had begun to tell him a story and the other pale-faced man who had drawn things for him, who had not laughed at his own drawing of a ship but on the contrary had liked it so well that he had shown it to his friend.

The weather brought out the bicycles. What Timothy longed for more than any of the world's treasures was a bicycle. As a very small infant at Uldale he had seen Mr Rander, the clergyman from Ireby, ride a penny-farthing, and that glorious entrancing vehicle with its high front wheel and tiny back wheel had seemed to him the height of possible adventure. Now first Mr Stanley and then Mr Dunlop had provided safety and reasonableness. Everyone was beginning to bicycle. Timothy, sitting stiffly opposite his mama wishing that his hands were as large as umbrellas that they might cover his velvet suit, thought of the kind gentleman who had told him a story, and then with longing eyes looked out on the driver of the omnibus, yet more fervently on the driver of the hansom, but most passionately of all upon the bicyclist. It was the bicycle that must be – not, he hoped, so far distantly – his engine of escape!

'Now here we are at Miss Newmark's,' said Violet to her little son, speaking with some severity. She was still uncomfortable, still felt the touch of an unknown hand upon her mouth . . .

Here at any rate there would be no hindrance to a nice heart-to-heart gossip. But, as always when she was ill at ease, she was severe with her children, and now she spoke impatiently to Timothy and told Hunter, the coachman, that she might be a long time, she might not, she did not know, she could not tell, all this in the severe irritable voice that the Herries always use when they are nervous.

She had no need to be nervous as she stood, holding Timothy's hand outside the gloomy plague-stricken door of Miss Newmark's Kensington home. She had been here so very often before and called the door 'plague-stricken' because the paint had faded and blistered until the surface represented a chart for one of the more

sinister Oriental diseases. Above the door was a top hat made of
iron and painted a faded green. The lower part of the house had
once belonged to a hatter. Violet had often noticed how, when
she called upon Emily on a sunny day, there was always a gloomy
sky in Emily's street. Very odd – as though the houses in Emily's
street were mountains! It was the same today. Just as Parker,
Emily's viperish maid, opened the door, the first drop of rain fell.
Parker had been with Emily for twenty years and hated and
despised all her fellow human beings without any exception
whatever, save only her mistress. She could not be said to love her
mistress, because she was part of her, bone of her bone and flesh
of her flesh, and both Parker and Emily were above any kind of
personal vanity. But Parker was of importance at this moment in
the Herries family affairs because she was on speaking terms with
Miss Fortescue from Hill Street. Miss Fortescue, who as a child
had lived in a family of Second Adventists, visited Emily frequently and had many a chat with Parker before she left the
house. These little social contacts have made history before
now.

Violet and Timothy climbed the steep dark stairs and heard
the thunder roll beyond the walls.

'I said it was going to thunder,' said Violet. All the way up the
staircase Timothy gazed with a terrified eye at the series of pictures from the Bible decorating the wall. He hated to come to this
house for many reasons, but chiefly because of these pictures,
which represented all the more dreadful scenes in Old Tes-
tament history – the murder of Abel, the destruction of the Cities
of the Plain, the Flood, the Serpent in the Wilderness, the
Plagues of the Egyptians. He wanted to hurry past, but his
mother held him always tightly by the hand; her movements
were slow and solemn. He wanted not to look, but was compelled.
There was in one picture a fat snake with a flicking tongue,
which writhed its coils around a shrieking woman and her
child. That snake was remembered by Timothy all his life
long.

'Mrs Bellairs and Master Bellairs, Miss Newmark.' So Parker
always announced them in tones of the deepest dissatisfaction.
She called her mistress 'Miss Newmark' on every occasion. They
both preferred it.

In spite of the gloomy and uncertain light of the drawing-
room, Violet saw at once that there were other visitors. Emily,
now a large and heavy woman with hair of steely grey, a slight

grey moustache on her upper lip, dressed always in black and having the oddest resemblance at times both in voice and features to her very different brother Barney, came forward and greeted them.

'Miss Pope. Mr Pope. Mrs Glass,' she said, introducing a pale young woman, a young man and a stout round lady wearing an old-fashioned bonnet, a very large bustle and a cashmere shawl.

On all ordinary occasions when Violet paid Emily a visit the same procedure was followed: first Timothy was put into a corner of a sofa and given a large illustrated Bible to look at and then the two ladies drew up to the fire (or the window if it were summer) and gossiped away the fortunes and happiness of every Herries in England. But today things were different. The lady in the shawl, Mrs Glass, said almost at once to Timothy: 'Oh, the pretty dear! Come and talk to me, my dear, and tell me where you got your lovely curls from.'

The room was littered with properties, sacred and reminiscent: Bibles, huge sea-shells, family albums, and volumes of poetry of a pious nature. These things gave the room the homely comfort which it needed. But today there was no homely comfort. Although the curtains were drawn and the gas lit, the thunderstorm could very distinctly be heard.

'I'll ring for some fresh tea,' said Emily.

'Oh no,' said Violet. 'I have had some tea with Cynthia' – then wished that she had not mentioned Cynthia, because Emily disapproved of her even more than she did of Vanessa. But today the mention of Cynthia roused no response. Emily seemed absent-minded. The three visitors were talking together, making a fuss of Timothy, who was struggling with a vast fragment of ancient and desiccated seed-cake.

Violet sighed, then patted Emily's knee.

'Well, how are you, my dear? I thought that I must just drive round and see how you were. For one thing Phillis has had a letter from May Rockage that would, I was certain, interest you. Vanessa and Ellis have been staying with them, you know, and it seems from what May says that Ellis's jealousy is becoming *quite* abnormal. She says that if Vanessa leaves the room for a single moment he begins—'

'There you are, Miss Pope!' Emily suddenly interrupted. 'Just what you said! A thunderstorm! Now isn't that strange after Mr Euclid's sermon last Sunday evening? Did he not foretell this very thing? God will thunder forth from His Heavens that we may be warned of the Wrath to come! Those were his very words. Violet, I've told you again and again that you should go to St Hilary's of a Sunday. Yes, and bring your husband with you. It would do him a world of good . . . Listen to that thunder! God speaking to us if ever He did and yet we will not listen . . . I beg your pardon, Violet . . . What were you saying about May Rockage?'

But here the pale young woman, Miss Pope, interrupted. She had, Violet thought, a *hysterical* face, for set like little fires in that pallor were her large burning eyes. She had a quiet, rather pleasing voice; her long, thin hands were clasped together as she spoke, and her body trembled slightly.

'Miss Newmark, you must come next time with my brother and myself. Really you must! You cannot imagine how affecting it was! The dock directors are monstrous. They could not behave as they do had they seen some of the sights that Edward and I see every day. They refuse to agree to the payment of sixpence an hour. Sixpence an hour! They would give a dog more! Dr Liddon's fund for the women and children is being wonderfully supported and that shows what the public feeling is! You should go down to the docks, Miss Newmark! They are empty. The Corn Exchange and the Coal Exchange are practically empty. You should have heard how Mr Burns and Mr Tillett were cheered last week, by big City men themselves. I cannot sleep, Miss Newmark, thinking of the women and children – the starving children—'

Violet thought that she was about to cry, and oh! how uncomfortable that would be!

Emily said: 'God is working for them. The day will come when these wicked oppressors will be punished as they deserve.' Her voice was gentle. She was touched as Violet had never seen her before. Really, with the thunder outside and this emotion inside, the atmosphere of the room was quite embarrassing, but soon the three on the sofa with Timothy began to talk eagerly together once more.

'Have you seen Vanessa since she returned, Emily?' Violet asked.

'No, my dear.'

'I do hope that everything is all right in Hill Street. You know that Benjie is in London again . . .'

'We should go through the streets,' Emily cried, 'with Christ at our head and *force* the world to listen. I suggest, Miss Pope, that you go and see Mr Euclid and suggest something of the kind to him. I know that you would find him sympathetic. We don't ask God's help enough. That's what *I* think! We try with our own feeble hands to build up His kingdom. We can do nothing of ourselves.'

'You are right, Miss Newmark,' said the young man in a voice unexpectedly deep and manly. He got up. 'Would you mind – should we not offer up a prayer now to Almighty God and ask Him to help these poor brothers and sisters of ours? Where two or three are gathered together . . .'

He went down on his knees, almost upsetting the table as he did so. The three ladies did the same and Violet was also compelled to do so, although she felt extremely awkward.

'O Lord!' said Mr Pope, 'we Thy humble servants gathered by chance together speak to Thee with one voice for our unhappy brothers and sisters. We have sinned in our selfishness. We have not asked for Thy guidance. Show us, dear Lord, in Thine own good time how these, our suffering brothers and sisters, may be rightly helped and taken out of their undeserved misery, and open the hearts of the wicked taskmasters that they may incline towards mercy and know that without Thee the temple that they build rests on sand. Show us what to do, O Lord, and give us strength so that without fear we may go forward in Thy good work to Thy glory, world without end, Amen.'

'Amen,' said everyone.

Then Emily repeated the Lord's Prayer.

When they rose from their knees they showed no shyness at all, but began eagerly to talk together.

For the second time that afternoon Violet felt that a hand had been laid on her mouth.

There was nothing to do but go.

'Come, Timothy! . . . Well, Emily,' she broke in upon their talk, 'we must be on our way. Do let me know in what way I can help. I had no idea that the poor people were suffering so. It does seem too bad indeed.'

She embraced Emily, bowed to the others and departed.

In the carriage again, as she turned towards home, she felt vexed and uneasy. There had been something very queer abroad this afternoon. Now, as they drove through the streets, the lamps seemed to blow in the breeze that had sprung up, everyone was moving swiftly as though bent on some secret mission. Her mind hung about Vanessa. Vanessa was in great trouble. She was sure of it. It was as though the lights, the passers-by, the air of the September evening thickening as though with a film of thin smoke about the roofs and chimneys – all these formed a clouded mirror in whose glass she saw pictures shaping. Real trouble. Not something at a distant remove, about which it would be amusing to gossip. Her heart was moved, she could not tell why. She made Timothy sit beside her, wrapping the carriage rug round him, then put her arm about him drawing him closer to her. She would go and see Vanessa tomorrow . . .

Vanessa was in trouble. And then these poor people at the Docks . . .

'How much is there in your money box, Timothy?'

'I don't know, Mama. About three shillings, I think.'

'Wouldn't it be nice to give it to those poor women who can't give their children enough to eat?'

'Yes, Mama.'

But he thought: 'Now it will be longer than ever to buy the bicycle.'

'We must be kind to everyone,' said his mother, kissing him.

A JOURNAL AND SOME LETTERS

BARNEY NEWMARK kept for many years a Journal. In 1896 he squeezed out of it what he felt to be some of the more interesting passages and made a volume of reminiscences which failed to attract much attention,[1] but for the purposes of a family chronicle some extracts from the original diaries are of interest. It was their misfortune, from the ordinary reader's point of view, that they dealt with private persons rather than public, family incidents rather than general affairs. He had always kept them for his own amusement and in that at least he had the advantage of some of his contemporaries.

February 4th, 1890

. . . I could not conceive what he wanted me there for. I came to the house, I'll confess, in spite of my advanced years, rather like a naughty schoolboy ordered to the headmaster's study. He has of

---

[1] *Some Memories*, by Barnabus Newmark. Hatcher and Thorburn, 1896.

course never liked me. That is in fact putting it mildly. I date his positive antagonism from that evening long ago when he went with me and young Benjie on an evening out, went reluctant and returned disgusted. With the years his dislike has grown to a kind of horror. I stand for everything that he most abominates – a writer of cheap novels, irreligious, a lover of horses and women, a gambler, a drunkard. That I have been none of these things very desperately has given him only the greater displeasure. Had I gone to the dogs he could have pitied me. As it is I have kept my head just sufficiently above water to be still a danger. Vanessa's persistent loyalty to me has only aggravated the trouble. This is the first time that he has asked to see me for at least twenty years. The odd thing is that I have always rather liked him. He has an integrity that I can admire. Then I understand so well his desire to win affection and his inability to do so, his shyness, his rectitude of conduct, his honesty. But is not his rectitude at last threatened? After yesterday I am inclined to think so.

I arrived at Hill Street punctually at four o'clock. Orders had been given that I was to be taken straight to his private Cave and I was conveyed up dark stairs and along sombre passages as though I were either a criminal or a spy – both, perhaps.

He was not there when I arrived and I had time to look about me in what is surely one of the gloomiest little rooms in London – bookcases filled with those dreary volumes of Journals and Papers marked with little white paper labels, a bald bust of some dead Roman, a large stern writing-table with silver writing things and an immaculate blotter, a grim, grizzling little fire and two leather armchairs. Poor Ellis! Many is the time, I am sure, that he has paced that little room, wondering why things are wrong when he is himself so right, shrinking from a world that he would give his soul to placate, lonely and bewildered, suspicious and uneasy.

I was not there very long. He came in, said: 'Well, Barney, how are you?' asked me to sit down, seated himself opposite me, and then, tapping his fingers together, looked all round and about him with a kind of distressed dismay on his features that was both pathetic and funny.

We hung about for a long time without coming to the point. He said that it was a long while since we had met, that it was a pity, that he understood that Allsopp's brewery was in difficulties, that the shortage of gold made separate bank reserves very difficult, that it was high time the Treasury dealt with the

Coinage question, and so on and so on. He asked me whether I
was writing anything just now in that tone in which people who
despise novels speak to novelists – as you might inquire of a
coiner whether he has been doing well lately.

I made some suitable reply and then silence fell. I had no
intention of helping him out. It was his affair, not mine.

Then suddenly it came:

Would I use my influence to persuade Benjie Herries to leave
England?

So that was it? I stared and said nothing. He was extremely
uncomfortable. He got up and began to walk the room. I must
understand that he had nothing against the fellow. He disliked
him, of course. He would be perfectly frank with me. He had
always disliked him. He dare say that he was well enough from
his own point of view, but I would have to admit that he had
never been a credit to the family – very much the opposite in fact.
His life, quite frankly, had been something of a scandal. That
was Benjie's private affair. The last thing that Ellis wanted to do
was to interfere with anyone's private life, but his continued
residence here in London was distressing to many of us, and he,
Ellis, as head of the family in London, had felt for a considerable
time that something ought to be done. He wished me to understand that he brought no kind of personal charge and he hoped
that I would regard this conversation as most strictly
confidential. I broke in there that of course he understood that I
was Benjie's friend. I also asked him did he wish me to tell Benjie
that he had spoken to me?

To which he answered in great distress, Oh no! of course not!
The last thing that he wanted was any quarrel with Benjie. It was
unfortunate, most unfortunate, that some time ago he had been
compelled to ask Benjie not to pay any more visits in Hill Street.
He regretted it, regretted it greatly, but on his last visit he had
been so outrageous in some of his views and had behaved most
insultingly to Miss Fortescue – 'My wife's lady housekeeper,' he
added, poor dear, as though he didn't know that *I* know exactly
all that Miss Fortescue is and how thoroughly Vanessa has
always detested her.

But really, he went on, the point was simply this. He did not
wish to detain me. He knew that I was an extremely busy man.
Did I think that I could persuade Benjie that a residence abroad
would be more suitable, more suitable in every way ... more
suitable in every way? ... While he was speaking my mind ran

over past family history. How odd this perpetual desire in our family for one member to rid himself of another! Old Francis the Rogue and his brother, Jennifer and Christabel, Walter and Jennifer, John and Uhland – as though it is a law with us that one half of us shall always aggravate the other to madness! Yes, to madness! As I watched Ellis, with his pale face, long restless hands, pacing up and down the room, it seemed to me that there was a kind of insanity, born of brooding unhappiness and perhaps jealousy – born anyway of a tormented unsatisfied love – not so far away!

I replied, quietly enough, that I certainly could not ask Benjie to leave the country. I could not agree with him that Benjie was a scandal. He was sometimes in London, sometimes abroad; he had his own friends, lived his own life. I could not see that he did harm to anyone.

At that Ellis became more agitated. Oh, indeed! And what had I to say to his fight at the Alhambra and a night in Vine Street? What had I to say to ... Here, with a great effort, he pulled himself up. He must repeat that he had no charges against Benjie. It was only for his own good, for his own good and the general good ... Did I think— Here he paused, seemed to be greatly agitated. Did I think that a sum of money? ... He was prepared to offer ...

At that I rose from my stiff leather chair.

'Look here Ellis,' I said. 'This goes no further of course. It ends here. But you don't know what you're saying. You send for me and suggest to me that I should bribe a friend of mine for no reason whatever to leave the country, go into exile. He has a son, you know, a fine little boy. Frankly I shall forget that we ever had this conversation. It is not worthy of you.'

I went to the door. He followed me and looked at me for a moment with such malevolence that it was a new Ellis, one I had never seen before.

'Oh, of course,' he said. 'You are his friend. I might have known ... *Good* afternoon'

And that was all. I was out of the house almost as soon as I was in it. As I walked away I thought that I had never known a queerer business. How could he have supposed for a moment that I would have listened to anything of the kind? And to what a pitch of brooding and suspicion he must have come to send for *me*, whom he has always so greatly disliked! At first I was so angry that I felt like turning back and punching his head. Then

the pathos of the man himself came to me. And after that real
fear and anxiety for Vanessa. I have known for some while that
things are not going well with her, but she keeps up so brave a
front that none of us can tell what is really happening to her. Is
she meeting Benjie? Does Ellis know of something hidden from
the rest of us? Of one thing I am sure – that she will be honest
and straightforward in all her dealings; but all last night the
thought of her enclosed behind those walls with Ellis for her
companion and Fortescue in attendance – well, frankly it spoilt
my evening. But I have put everything concerned with this little
incident down here exactly as it occurred. The facts may be
useful one day. I am Benjie's friend, Vanessa's friend, even – who
knows? – Ellis' friend. A nuisance for an old, selfish, comfort-
loving bachelor who hates to be disturbed. All day today I have
been tempted to go and see Vanessa. But no. It is better that I
avoid Hill Street for a time. The nuisance is that tonight when I
should have been getting on with my novel I haven't been able to
think of a thing. Quite impossible to get Vanessa and Ellis out of
my head!

*From Vanessa Herries to Rose Ormerod at
27 Rue Montaigne, Paris*

September 6th, 1890

My dearest Rose – I have the whole evening to myself –
Ellis has gone out to some meeting and I have done what I love
better than anything else in the world, gone to bed, had some
supper on a tray and now can write you a long letter without fear
of any interruption.

After you left on Wednesday I was very unhappy. We had so
short a time together and said so little although we both wanted
to say so much. I was unhappy too because I knew that you were.
You could not disguise it from me. All your brave talk about
your loving to be alone and Fred's having been so generous in his
settlement and your finding it such a relief to have done with
men for ever – none of it deceived me in the least. The very fact
that we had to meet as furtively as we did in Miss Mercer's rooms
speaks volumes! You and I furtive! Doesn't that of itself show
that there is something very wrong? Why not have come to Hill
Street? Ellis would not have eaten you. You never used to be
afraid of anyone. And although you pretended that it was for *my*

sake. Well, I can deal with Ellis, you know. I haven't lived with
him all these years for nothing! It struck me suddenly tonight
with a kind of terror that for the first time in all our married life I
have, in this one week, concealed two things from him – one my
meeting with you, the other, well, I will tell you of the other in a
moment.

But now, Rose, listen. Let me tell you here sitting alone in my
room, loving you very dearly, something that I could not when
we were together. The association with Fred Wycherley has been
dreadfully bad for you. You know it better than I. I was shocked
at the change and more shocked still at your own consciousness
of it. You saw also a change in me. Yes, it is true. I know now this
about life – that, far more than I had ever supposed, we affect one
another. To live with another is to have to fight for your own
integrity morning and night. I suppose if you love someone
enough you lose your own integrity and find another much finer.
But if you don't ... You know, Rose, when leaning on that
hideous mantelpiece at Miss Mercer's you looked over your
shoulder and said: 'Vanessa, men don't mind what they turn
their women into', I knew and you knew where you have got to in
these last years. Rose darling, oh darling darling Rose, let this life
go. Leave Paris. Settle somewhere in England where it isn't too
dull. You have some money, you have intelligence enough not to
need the kind of life Fred gave you. I suppose you don't hunger
for Cumberland all day and every day as I do, but why not try it
for a while? Try Eskdale or Coniston or Ullswater for a month or
two. They are lovely in the autumn. The Cumbrians are kindly
uninquisitive folk. Why not bring that Mlle Mathieu with you
whom you like? I don't know. Making plans for others is never
any good, but if you were to tell me that I was to have a week on
Cat Bells beginning tomorrow, I think I'd just go crazy with joy!
But Ellis is frightened of Cumberland. He thinks I'll go wild
there, leave him for a gipsy or something. Yes, after all these
years of my good proper social behaviour he still fears it. More
now than ever. Which brings me to the other thing. I nearly told
you on Wednesday. I tell you now because you are the only one I
can tell. I won't even say that it's a secret. If Ellis asks me
tomorrow morning: 'Have you seen Benjie Herries?' I shall say
yes and tell him all (or almost all) about it. But if he doesn't ask
me ...

This is all it is, my grand secret. Since 1887 I have seen Benjie
a few times and spoken with him, but never by arrangement. I

saw him at the Jubilee Procession. I saw him once at the Theatre. On neither occasion did we exchange a word. Last week on a lovely afternoon I had been visiting Cynthia. I sent the carriage back and walked in the Park. I was wandering down one of the paths, thinking how old I was getting (I am thirty-one, you know), frightened as old married ladies will be at the way that life was passing, when I looked up and there was Benjie with his little boy walking straight into me! Well, what were we to do? We couldn't, all things considered, just pass one another with a stiff bow! I had never seen his little boy. But in any case we could not stop to reason. We have been friends since we were babies. He belongs to all my life, all of it that I love the most passionately. We – oh well, why explain anything to you? There we were and both of us so happy at meeting that we could only look at one another, without words. It was, as it always is when we are together, as though we had never parted. We sat down on a bench, the little boy beside me. We had then the happiest hour of our lives. We did not mind who saw us. People were passing all the time. If Ellis had come by, I would not have cared. What was there to be ashamed of? Even Ellis must admit that all this time we have done our duty, never tried to see one another, never written. We love one another of course. We have always loved one another. I have no doubt that if we had married as we meant to, we would have been very unhappy, but happiness and unhappiness have nothing to do with love. If Ellis asks me – as he will one day – do you love Benjie, of course I will say yes. I will never lie to him or to anyone. We thought of none of this, not of Ellis nor the family nor anyone at all but ourselves. He told me about his life, that he was lonely, that Tom his boy – who is six now – is going soon to a little day school in Bloomsbury; I told him a little about Hill Street – not everything. But we didn't talk very much as I remember. We were simply so happy to be together again. Then we walked a little way and parted. We made an arrangement to meet in Barney's rooms. He was to be there and I was to come as though by accident. But in the evening when I was home again I knew that it would not do. I wrote him a letter saying that we must not meet again and I know that I was right. Nothing stands still. At every meeting it would be harder to part and what would the end of it be? But, Rose – never forget it – Benjie has been wonderful during these years. With his character and nature to keep away as he has done, to help me by keeping away – no man has ever done anything finer.

Well, there it is. So we go on, the three of us, doing our best. The queer thing is that since that meeting, Ellis, although he can't possibly know of it, has been increasingly uneasy and suspicious. He isn't well, is working too hard and has dreadful headaches. Then there is Miss Fortescue, who hates me, of course, and would do me harm if she could. Poor Ellis – if only he would be content with what we have. All these years we have been friends. When he is happy we are *such* good friends and life goes so calmly, but lately I have been afraid. He behaved so strangely last year in Wiltshire that everyone noticed it. His love frightens me often and is becoming every week less tranquil. Can I manage all this? Of course I can. I have never been beaten by anything yet, but marriage isn't easy when it's dramatic – or perhaps it is I who hate scenes. *How* I hate them! Their childishness and extravagance ...

Rose, darling, goodnight. Come away from Paris. Come home. I saw Horace yesterday and his silent wife. He was *very* cheerful and bright and breezy – Your most loving

VANESSA

*Part of a letter from Mrs Timothy Bellairs to Miss Lavinia New-
mark, Constance Court, near Manchester.*

June 25th, 1891

... I do hope that your father is better. Of course at his age one must expect a day in bed now and again. Timothy has been complaining of lumbago and I insisted on his staying in bed last week. As you may imagine, no one has been talking of anything but the Baccarat Case. Poor Sir William! I am quite *sure* that he did not intend cheating and I really think that some of them showed great vindictiveness. Mrs Lycett Green is quite a friend of May Rockage you know, and Timothy has often met Lord Coventry at his Club. Of course the Prince's appearance in the witness box was *the* sensation and everyone thinks that he came out of it very well and that it was most unnecessary of *The Times* to say what it did! It is all a great pity and very bad for the working classes, who are inclined in any case to be troublesome just now. Timothy says that that man Burns is a danger to the country and ought to be in gaol. I suppose you haven't heard of poor Vanessa's illness. So unlike her to be ill and nobody *quite* knows what the matter has been. They say all sorts of things, but I refuse to listen to gossip, especially of the family variety ...

Barney Newmark's Journal.

February 18th, 1892

I haven't entered anything in this Journal for weeks, but yesterday afternoon deserves a record. Stephen Bertrand, the novelist,
came in most unexpectedly to see me. And then who should enter
directly after but dear Horace Ormerod? It was really entertaining to see them together. Horace I knew had come for some
purpose. He would never waste his time on me unless he wanted
something. Bertrand had met him once or twice before and was
pleased to see him again, as well he might be, for no human alive
could better satisfy his passion for innocent copy! I could see
Bertrand's round, obese little body hurrying home that he might
not waste a moment before putting Horace's self-revelations into
his notebook! And how Horace gratified him! He was nervous a
little, I suppose, of Bertrand's cold penetrating eye and talked
therefore twice as much as ordinary! His healthy rosy face
beamed with complacency; his honest, clean, and incipiently
stout person vibrated with energy. His friendly eyes shone behind
their glasses. With jolly deprecation he told us how good he
found life to be, how easy it was to be generous, how simple to see
the best in everyone! 'Have you seen Valentine lately?' Bertrand
asked rather cruelly. Valentine at the time of the success two or
three years back had been a great friend of Horace, who liked to
be intimate with one of the most promising poets of the day. *Then*
one thought that he would be John Lane's proudest boast, that
Dowson, Lionel Johnson and the rest were not in the race compared with him! But alas, the bottle and the ladies have been too
much for poor Valentine! No one is a greater adept than Horace
at dropping a failure gracefully! There were, I swear, tears
behind his glasses as he cried:

'Poor Valentine! I wish I could do something for him. He's his
own worst enemy, I fear. I did have a word with him some six
months ago, but he has become oddly embittered, poor fellow.'

This was joy indeed to Bertrand, who most skilfully led poor
Horace on until I could not bear it any longer and had to interfere. When Bertrand was gone Horace said complacently:

'Nice fellow, Bertrand. I must invite him to lunch at the Club.
He seems to know everybody and that last novel of his had quite a
success, hadn't it?'

I told him that it had.

'What was it called?'

I told him.

'I must remember and read it before he comes to luncheon. You novelists are all so sensitive!'

Funnily enough, on reflection, I felt a strong resemblance between Bertrand and Horace, although I must confess that I like Bertrand the better of the two. Both are equally complacent, Horace because he is a fool and Bertrand because he is pleased with his gifts, with his penetration into human motives, with his cold, clear eye, with his horror of sentiment. But both are sentimentalists, Bertrand perhaps the greater of the two. Bertrand cannot understand that he is disliked (as I fear that he is) and attributes it to the fear of his fellow human beings for the naked truth. Bertrand is the kindest of men and Horace one of the unkindest, yet Bertrand is held to be cruel and Horace, although a fool, good-natured. Bertrand means no unfriendliness when he puts his acquaintances into his books. Indeed he thinks they are lucky fellows to be used for so fine a work of art! 'The artist,' he says, 'thinks only of his art', and forgets that his friends, and still more his friends' friends, think only of their reputations. And this is odd because Bertrand himself thinks a great deal of his own reputation. But I like Bertrand and give him free leave to make any use of me that he pleases!

But now to the point, Horace's point. Violet Bellairs and Horace have become great friends of late. They have many things in common. Violet, it seems, often appeals to Horace for help in her troubles. Here is the latest! Young Timothy (a very decent kid who will be an artist one day) has, it appears, been indulging a secret friendship with Tom, Benjie's boy! Where they first met, or how, I don't know. It has been a complete and most dreadful surprise to Timothy's poor mother! Tim is fourteen and Tom under eight, so you would not suppose that Tim was in great danger! But Tom is already – according to Horace (who by the way has never set eyes on the child) – a young ruffian and a moral danger to any companion. This letter was discovered by Violet Bellairs in the pocket of one of her young son's jackets. Horace left it with me and I copy it here verbatim, spelling and all:

DEAR TOM – Mother is going out tomorrow afternoon and it's a harfholiday. The old cat is in bed with inflewensa so i can meat you the same place – Your loving

TIM

I at once inquired of Horace whether 'the old cat' was Tim's

mother, but it seems not. She is apparently Violet's governess, and
I at once said that Violet deserved all she got if she wouldn't send
Tim to a decent school like any other boy. 'Oh, well,' said
Horace, who never defends his friends whole-heartedly unless
everyone around him is doing the same, 'Violet thinks Tim's
delicate.'

'She only thinks he's delicate because she's tried to make him
so,' I burst out, 'with his curls and all. The kid's a fighter and
with a will of his own. He'll be a grand artist one day. But what's
the matter anyway if Tim does make a friend of young Tom?'

Oh, then Horace broke out, forgetting all his natural caution.
Benjie was a danger to everyone. They were all coming to feel it.
I, poor fool, was the only one left to stand by him. He was
contaminating the family reputation. Ellis had done with him
long ago. Alfred hated him. Cynthia wouldn't have him in the
house, and now, through his nasty little boy, Benjie was per-
verting Violet's child. Only I and of course Vanessa ... and
everyone knew that Vanessa was in love with him even though
she *didn't* see him ...

At that I did gloriously what I haven't done for years. I lost my
temper. I lost it so that I took Horace by his fat shoulders and
shook him so that his glasses rolled on his fat nose. All my long
dislike of Horace was at last expressed. I called him every name I
could think of, obscene words that Horace's soul would shudder
at; I told him what I thought of him, that he was false, syco-
phantic, mean, treacherous. (Only one side of Horace after all,
for he is not a whit worse than the rest of us, only naïver.) I told
him that I was Benjie's friend and that Benjie was worth all the
family put together (which Benjie isn't, of course), I told him
that he was not fit to breathe in Vanessa's presence and that if I
ever heard him utter a word against Vanessa again I'd murder
him. I'm sure he thought that I would. I never saw a man look
more frightened. So I threw him out of the room, washed my
face and hands and laughed a little. But it is truly no laughing
matter. The thing grows. It is instinctive. Benjie is some wild
half-human animal to them and Vanessa *does* love him. And
Ellis' brain begins to turn. Well, God help them all, say I, and
myself no less than the rest. But how the troubles in this world
come from chatter! Fools like Horace and Violet! – and perhaps
ruin to nobler men because there are parrots on the trees. Could
we but keep silent for a little while and let men work out their
own salvation without comment. Too much ever to hope for!

A letter from Benjamin Herries to Vanessa Herries.

TOLEDO, Spain, *April 6th, 1893*

Vanessa, will you ever see this? For the first time I am breaking my vow and now I shall continue to break it, for my endurance has been tested too sharply. This goes to Barney. I have told him to let you have it. I expect no answer but I am hungering for one – only one line to tell me that you understand the sort of fate that follows me, a ridiculous fate that I cannot escape and shall no longer try to, by God! This last time was too much! As though it wasn't enough that Cynthia should be there, but Alfred and his wife as well! I had not drunk a drop that evening. You may believe it, Vanessa. I have never lied to you yet. I came into the place as sober as a church. The woman who was with me was a poor thing I used to know, hadn't seen for years, found that afternoon longing for a meal in a decent restaurant, quietly, with a friend. Well, the Café Riche is decent enough, isn't it? We were having our meal as quietly as two churchwardens all sober in our corner. I saw Cynthia come in with a man. Then a little later Alfred and his wife. We had nearly finished when Fanny Church (the girl with me) caught my arm, begged me to pay my bill and go. There was a man at the other side of the room of whom she was terrified. She had been his mistress once, it seemed, and he had treated her damnably – a heavy man with a black beard. Before I could do anything he had seen us and come to our table. He paid no attention to me, but, smiling at Fanny, said he was glad to see her again and where had she been all this time and wouldn't she tell him where she was living? She was trembling all over, poor girl, looking at me to protect her, and I, very quietly and most politely, asked him to go. He asked me who the devil I was and did I know that I was interfering with his friends, his *very* old friends. Then he put his hand on her arm. What could I do then but knock him down? Wouldn't any man have done the same? He was a big man and he fell heavily and a table went over. Of course there was a row. I waited quietly, told him that I would pay for the damage, left my card and went out with Fanny. That was all. But quite enough of course. Cynthia and Alfred had all the evidence they wanted.

But the *second* public row, Vanessa! After all these years of discipline. Was there ever anyone born more unlucky? Well, this is the end. I can do no more. I was never made for this hypocrisy

nor were *you* made for that life in Hill Street. Tom is at a good
school, that's one comfort, and I am finished for ever with
London and that farce of civilization and the damned family and
their chatter and my trying to be what I'm not. I'm finished for
ever with everything but loving you. I shall write sometimes and
tell you how I love you, for I am a boy no longer. If you do not
answer me it will make no difference. I cannot believe any longer
that you are happy, for I know that you are not. I shall always let
you hear where I am, one way or another, and one day, if it is all
too much for you, come to me. In this black town I am at peace
again. The walls go sheer down to the plain. As I look from my
window I can see the gipsies moving off along the narrow street,
and in the Cathedral it is so cool and dark that you can stay there
by the hour and hear no man's chatter. I have a room in an inn;
my room is high up. Everything is grand here, the gold in the
Cathedral, the wind against the wall, the sound of water falling
as it does in Cumberland. One thing already makes me think of
you. In a little church at the end of my street there is a picture
painted years ago, they say – *pictor ignotus* – of a Black Centaur
pawing the ground, his head up, while over the hill there goes a
Procession carrying the Host. I don't know its meaning, bringing
Christ to the Heathen or some such thing, but the Centaur is
noble. His head is up, he is ready for what may come, and he
made me think of you because of that dream you used to tell me
of – the horse that strikes the mountain with his hooves, springing from the water. I *will* not be dismayed, Vanessa! That little
London is behind me. I have only Tom and you in the world, but
you know and *I* know that as long as life lasts we will go on
finding the meaning of it, loving one another although we never
meet again, not fearing anything, not despising life until we
know that it is worthless, which it is not and never will be. I have
tried hard all these years to do as you say. *You* know how I have
tried – but I will be tied down no longer. They think, Cynthia
and Alfred and Ellis and the rest, that life is a cow to be milked –
but it is rather the Centaur on to whose back I will leap. One day
you will ride with me. When you see Barney tell him to write to
me once a week about Tom. That's a good school, they say, and I
liked the man when I saw him. There's someone playing music in
the inn room and I'm going down.

You won't despise me I know, or believe anything they say.
You are part of me and the law is we must *not* despise ourselves.
Give my love to dear Violet and Timothy and Barney's sweet

sister Emily. Oh God! but I'm glad I'm done with London! —
Your loving, loving

BENJIE

A letter from Vanessa Herries to Barney Newmark in Rome.

March 13th, 1894

MY DEAR BARNEY — The moment I received your telegram
I went down to the school. Fortunately Ellis was away on a visit
to old Horace for three days. I went down, taking Lettice Marrable with me. You don't know who she is, do you? She is a girl
from Cumberland whom I have brought to Hill Street as my
secretary — a kind of counter to Miss Fortescue. She is an odd
girl, would like to dress like a man, has all this new craze for
tennis, breeches, women's freedom — all a result of the frightful
way she has been kept down all her life at home. However, you
won't want me to waste your time with *her* except that she is the
most loyal, faithful, attached creature who ever lived and a great
comfort to me. We went by train to Salisbury and drove over to
the school. The headmaster, Mr Collins, was exceedingly kind. I
took the greatest fancy to him, his wild black beard, his black eyes
so lively behind his glasses, and his evident friendship and loyalty to Benjie. He took me to the Infirmary where Tom was. He
has been very ill, but is much better. He lay there as white as
paper, but he has Benjie's smile, hasn't he? I had only ever met
him once before — in the Park a long time ago — but he remembered me and told me about the book the nurse was reading to
him — a Talbot Baines Reed — and he was greatly amused by
Lettice's hard straw hat and the sort of golfing suit she wears! He
likes funny things, Mr Collins says. He asked me had I seen Tim,
Violet's boy? He showed me a letter Tim had written him in
secret. Awkward for me, wasn't it? He was too white-faced for
me to say it was wrong for himself and Tim to write to one
another. I said nothing. In fact, dear Barney, *all* my ideas of the
difference between right and wrong are fast vanishing! Which
brings me to this. You must send me Benjie's address, tell me
where he is. I had a letter last year from Toledo. I did not answer
it. I have not written a line to him since he left England, although
you know how I have wanted to! But I can keep it up no longer. I
must send him word about Tom, right or wrong. He worships his
father of course. He said to me over and over again: 'When is he

coming? He hasn't been here for a long time!' For the Easter
holiday he is going, as you know, to the Quintires again at Longbridge Deveril. He says it is nice there, they are kind to him,
pleasant girls who tell him stories. They write them themselves,
he says, which seems to him marvellous. They have a magazine
among themselves and oh! Tom said, wouldn't they be lucky if
they could get Tim to draw pictures for it! He is a warm-hearted
little boy. I wished, coming back in the train, that I had one like
that of my own. Lettice slipped some money under his pillow. I
saw her do it, and it's good of her because she hasn't a penny!
But he's all right, Barney, and I like that master. For myself what
shall I tell you? Nothing. You're in Rome and London is far
away. We have been to *Charley's Aunt* and *The Second Mrs
Tanqueray*. We have had a party. Cynthia has had a party. I have
had a letter from Will Leathwaite, from Cat Bells. Barney, Cat
Bells! Cat Bells! Cat Bells! . . . No more of that. Shall I tell you
about clothes? Sleeves are very wide, waists narrower than ever.
Skirts are long and trailing. My arm aches with holding mine up.
Everybody is wanting to be rich. If you are rich enough you can
go anywhere. Alfred gets richer every day. But this is not what
you want in Rome. I have read a beautiful book by a man called
Yeats, *The Celtic Twilight*. Have you heard of him? But of
course you have. Ibsen is the fashion. Ellis – but I will not weary
you with my silly troubles. Am I happy? No, Barney, I am not. Is
anyone happy? Possibly no one. Are we all being gay and merry?
Very gay and merry indeed. Send me Benjie's address – Your
loving

VANESSA

Extracts from Barney Newmark's Journal.
April and May 1895

COPLEY BECK, DUDDON VALLEY.

. . . This letter. What am I to do about it? Ellis has not spoken to
me for years, thinks I am altogether on Benjie's side and must
know that Benjie is in England. I showed him the letter at once
and asked him what I should do. It is a number of days old,
forwarded with some bills and papers from Duke Street – and we
have been walking from Seascale to Boot, from Boot here – that's
two days. Vanessa is probably in Cumberland by now. She gives a
Keswick hotel as an address. But Benjie swears that she can have
no idea that he is even in England, much less that he is walking

up here with me. But is Ellis likely to believe that? Can I prevent them meeting, do I even want to? I put it to Benjie on his conscience. 'My conscience says that I am to see her,' he answered, and his silly brown face lit up with such happiness at the thought that I would be a thief robbing a blind man to prevent him. Why should I stop their half-hour? She has the Marrable she-male with her, she tells me, and she is surely enough for anyone as guard! Ellis need never know – *will* never know! Benjie is even now, as I write, standing out on the sward, looking at the lambs, the water jumping the rocks of Harter Fell in a thundercloud and the sun striking like a sword on the fresh green of the larch. He is standing there kicking stones with his foot, giving little leaps. For a small man, he is a packet of vitality, but it is happiness that makes him leap! To see her, out of the blue, without arrangement on his part ... by divine accident! He will go over to the little hotel at Dungeon Ghyll for a day. Vanessa and the Marrable girl can stay the night there or drive over from Ambleside. Could anything be more discreet? And I'm tired of Ellis. He has been considerably rude to me for years and he is making Vanessa unhappy. That's enough for me ...

... Benjie and I have been talking for hours about the Wilde affair. Benjie sees her tomorrow and can think of nothing else, so I talk to divert him. But poor Oscar! What a muddle of vanity, British hypocrisy, snobbery and false judgement. As to the crime itself I say nothing. It has not, thank God, been one of my temptations, but as I have always yielded to every temptation I *have* had, if that had been one of them I might have yielded to it. How do I know? Anyway it is more mental than criminal, I suspect. But this I do know: that Oscar is always at his best with very simple childish people. He is himself a child with his vanity, heartlessness, kindness, generosities and self-confidence. I always disliked him when he was showing off, but put him with children or stupid kindly men or warm-hearted impulsive women and he is lovable indeed. Men like Whistler or Charles Brookfield or Carson really terrify him at heart, as children are frightened when, sent for by unwise parents to show off to their elders, they suddenly see the cold eye of a guest speculatively fixed upon them.

This remains at least, that never even in hypocritical England has there been such a revolting show of hypocrisy as this – and it will put Art and Letters in England back for twenty years ...

*　　　*　　　*

... Well, we are back again, and Benjie is out walking in the rain and dark by himself. I have had a happy afternoon walking for two and a half hours with the Marrable girl. We landed at last, after climbing Wrynose, back at Blea Tarn and sat there patiently. I never saw it more beautiful with the trees coming down black as thunder to the very edge, Wordsworth's 'Solitary's' cottage white in the sun and the sky pale yellow behind the Pikes. I was interested too, for she told me enough about Ellis to fill a volume. Vanessa's patience with him must be a marvellous thing, and even Lettice Marrable who hates him, pities him too. It must be a weird household now with the monstrous Fortescue, Ellis half mad with a vague torturing jealousy that has no facts at all to justify it, and this odd, masculine country girl who worships Vanessa. 'I would *die* for her!' she cries, looking into the green water of the Tarn.

'Now would you?' I ask her cynically. 'Easily said.' Then look at her and feel that she really would!

What will be the end of it?

Of what Vanessa and Benjie said to one another I know nothing. I asked nothing. I was told nothing. Vanessa is better than ever. She is surely the grand lady. To see her walk across a room is a benefit to humanity. But she is a child too. When she saw Benjie there she simply laughed, took his arm and walked off with him. I don't think I ever before realized so sharply that, behind all this present fuss and bother, there is the fact that they have been friends all their lives long. That makes a difference, of course.

I said: 'Miss Marrable, shall we take a stroll?' And so we did. *What* a plain girl! But I can't help liking her.

Part of a letter from Violet Bellairs to Cynthia Worcester.

September 9th, 1896

... We have been with the Rockages a week now. I can't say that it's a comfortable house – horses and dogs morning and night, and Carey is so far behind with *The Times* – which he intends to read every night but goes to sleep over – that he is still discussing the Jameson Raid. It has been the hottest summer ever known here and the children feel it. Timothy is being very difficult. Carey agrees with me that this painting nonsense must be knocked out of him! I never knew anyone talk so much about *Cricket* as Carey does. It's Ranjitsinhji for every meal, or whether Cambridge or Oxford bowled balls that *weren't* balls in the University Match! Men are too strange and I've simply given up trying to understand them. Timothy *will* read this nasty new paper the *Daily Mail*. I think it's the *halfpenny* that appeals to him. He always *loves* to get something for nothing. I hear that Benjie Herries is in Africa and has married a Negress. Thank heaven that friendship between his boy and Timothy was nipped in the bud. Did you ever know anything so horrible as the baby-farming murder? I hear that the Dyer woman actually ...

From Master Tom Herries to Timothy Bellairs.

LONGBRIDGE, DEVERIL

September, 9th, 1896

DEAR TIM — I will bicycle over on Tuesday and be *just inside* the farm gate by Locker Wood at half past three — Your loving

T.

ELLIS IN PRISON

ON that warm evening in July 1897 Timothy Bellairs senior left Ellis soon after dinner and went home. He was going to bed; he had a touch of lumbago and would catch it in time.

'He looks a lot more than his sixty years,' Ellis thought with some satisfaction. And he did. He had grown terribly stout. It would have been better for his health had he stayed in Cumberland.

The house was still as the tomb after Timothy's departure — and why was it never really warm even on these summer evenings? Or was it Ellis who was never warm? After seeing Timothy off, he stood in the hall listening to the silence. Vanessa was at the theatre with the Worcesters, and he had promised her to go to bed early because all day he had had one of his terrible headaches. It was she who had suggested that he should invite old Timothy to have dinner with him, because Timothy was no trouble but

would chatter on and on about anything or nothing. So he had
done; about the Jubilee, very different from the '87 affair – not
many people in the streets and the Queen so feeble, poor old lady,
that it had almost killed her; all the same, *what* a country England was! The Review at Spithead made you feel that: no other
country could touch us for a Navy! Still, the country hadn't the
style it used to have with cohorts of young men on bicycles and
these halfpenny papers. Fine poem, Kipling's 'Recessional'. (He
recited some of it as though Ellis had never heard it before!)
Made you feel proud to be a Briton *and* a Herries! He could
remember when he was a boy in Cumberland ... And Salisbury
had said that Africa was created to be the plague of the Foreign
Office. Some truth there! They had better watch President
Krüger. (He spoke with scorn of Krüger as though the Herries
family had decided in conclave that Krüger was a rat and ought
to be stamped on.) Well, we are getting on, getting on ... Sixty
last birthday, and yet it seemed only yesterday when old Madame
– Judith Paris – had threatened him with the cane she always
carried, for stealing gooseberries out of the Uldale garden. Pity
that place was burned down! Fine place. And there was something about Cumberland which ... But Ellis did not like to hear
about Cumberland, and changed the conversation. Well, he must
be getting home. This damnable lumbago ... Driving with Violet
yesterday in the Park. Did Ellis know that Alfred had bought one
of these motor-cars, and only last year, wasn't it, they had
changed the law about a man walking in front with a red flag?
Pity in his opinion they *had* changed the law. How were you to
protect the public with these things charging all over the place?
However, they would never do away with the carriage, thank
Heaven. Sensible people would always prefer the horse to those
stinking, screaming engines that nobody could control. Well,
well, it was a changing world and time he went home. Violet
wasn't quite the woman she had been. A bit puffy in the chest and
they were not quite happy about Timothy, who was at Cambridge
now and not settling down as he should. Always wanting to go to
Paris and paint! Ridiculous notion for a gentleman's son.

Well, well, goodnight to you, Ellis. Give my love to Vanessa.
Still the handsomest woman in London ...

Why was the house so silent? When would Vanessa be back
from the theatre? It was of no use to go to bed. He never slept
until she came to say goodnight to him, and she knew that, and
was good about returning early. Good? Was Vanessa good? As

usual, so soon as he began to think of her his heart thumped in
his thin bony breast, and that other man, taller than he, with the
handkerchief wrapped round his head, stole out of the wall and
stood beside him. *Why* was the house so silent? The servants
must be moving about somewhere. Miss Fortescue must be in her
room. He climbed the stairs to his study, the other figure keeping
pace with him. The room was cold. The bust of Cicero watched
him with its blind lidless eyes. Could you watch anyone if you
were blind? Why, most certainly. His shadow with the handkerchief bound about its head was blind and yet, with ceaseless
preoccupation, it watched him.

He began to pace the room as now so many, many times a day
he paced it. The distance that he must cover was not of great
extent *and* how well he knew it! So far to the writing-table where
he would pause and arrange and arrange, rearrange, arrange again the silver
writing things. Then, half turn, four paces to the wall where
there hung an excellent engraving of that fine picture, 'Christ
Leaving the Praetorium'. Christ, so gentle, so kindly, His hands
bound in front of Him, the crowd pressing forward, the stout
muscle-swelling guards restraining them. One guard Ellis had
come to know well, a broad, cheerful, helmeted fellow looking
over his shoulder at Ellis and, Ellis thought, in some friendly way
warning him. Warning him of what? Well, and then, half turn
again and down the room until you reached the door. This door,
which was painted an ugly light brown, had for a handle a round
cold white knob. Ellis always touched this knob, grasped it
indeed with his warm fingers, for its chill indifferent hardness
comforted him; it stilled his beating heart. He thought of it sometimes when he was in the City or the Park or at the Play. That
cold white knob, so gloriously indifferent! What did *it* care
whether he were torn with jealousy, whether Vanessa loved him?
... But of course Vanessa did not love him. That was the first
fact. He stopped, as a thousand times he had stopped in the
middle of that floor, and marshalled the facts that, when seen
in an ordinary row, would make him a sensible clear-headed
man.

It only needed that they should be properly marshalled, and he
saw them like little children (cretins perhaps) with large round
white heads like the doorknob, all sitting in a line, their white
fleshy hands folded, waiting to be marshalled.

Bald-headed Fact One. Vanessa did not love him, had never
loved him, would never love him.

Bald-headed Fact Two. He loved Vanessa with a burning, devouring fire. (It was literally that. In a cavity behind his ribs this fire was burning. He could see the flames leap and fall and leap again.)

Bald-headed Fact Three. He was jealous without reason. Jealousy. Dreadful. Like catching a disease that turned your bones to water. Intermittent. It was most devilish in this – that it left you for five, ten minutes, so that, within that space, you saw quite clearly and wondered how you ever could *be* jealous. See! See! No reason. Vanessa has never been faithless to you. She is honest, is fond of you, has been very, very good to you for more than a dozen years. And then, the more savage for its brief absence, the jealousy returns, just distorting everything so that the wallpaper is tinged with green and the cat moves to its platter of milk with private purpose in its eyes.

Bald-headed Fact Four. That he is no longer any good in the City. That his business powers have left him. That young Alfred who has come into the Firm is already taking his place. He must see to this. He is losing money.

Bald-headed Fact Five. His body. That he cannot sleep. That he has headaches. That he is suspicious of everyone. That he is drinking. That his body is hot at one moment and cold the next. That he sleeps with Vanessa when she does not wish it, which is what no gentleman should do. That the Family – Violet and Cynthia and Alfred and Emily and the effeminate Philip – are watching him just as he is watching them and everyone else. Cat and Mouse. Mouse and Cat.

Bald-headed Fact Six. That he thinks much about the past. His father who wanted him to love him, but he could not; his poor old mother; his shyness and awkwardness and longing to be liked; the first moment when, on old Madame's Hundredth Birthday, he had seen Vanessa. Shadows, shadows of the Past. That Cumberland which he hated and feared. Always trying to lure him back to it again so that it might set its fingers about his throat and hold him there while the mocking rain poured down on his upturned face and the stone walls crowded him in and the clouds came lower and lower ... All the ghosts of the Past. Old Herries, poor Francis who shot himself, John who was murdered, mad Uhland.

Bald-headed Fact Seven. That this beastly, threatening world had as its representative that brown, ragamuffin, dissolute gipsy whom Vanessa loved. Had always loved. They had been children together.

Bald-headed Fact Eight. That when all the Facts were seated quietly in the row he would see how unreal they were, would see that he was Sir Ellis Herries, third Baronet, a wealthy decent citizen of Queen Victoria, much honoured by his friends, thought well of in the City, possessing the handsomest woman in London for his wife, the kindest, the truest, most popular. There was, he would see, no reason at all for agitation. All was well. He had reason to be happy. He must go about and show people that he meant them well, that he was a likeable good man, that the hospitality for which his house was famous was practised because he wished them well, because he liked them and wished them well ...

Someone was in the room. He started as though a gun had been let off in his ear. Oh! it was Miss Fortescue.

'I beg your pardon, Sir Ellis. I thought you had gone to bed. I came to put these papers ready for you in the morning.'

Miss Fortescue was now, in appearance, completely the sinister remorseless figure of one of Mr Wilkie Collins' savage women. She was hard, black (hair, eyes, eyebrows), efficient, and humourless. Nevertheless, she was no villainess. She was sentimental, read with passion and admiration the novels of Ouida, Miss Braddon, and that comparatively new writer Mr Hall Caine. She was lonely and romantic and had, from the first moment of seeing him, decided that Ellis also was lonely and romantic. She was not in love with him; she had loved, so many times, so many heroes in fiction that no man in everyday life could satisfy her. But she had from the first considered her master as her child, to be protected, guarded, aided. Vanessa's beauty had always irritated her. She thought her kindliness a posture, for she was convinced that she had married Ellis for his money while in secret she had loved another – which was quite in agreement with her reading. She also by temperament distrusted Vanessa's general friendliness, her high spirits, her generosities. This was not a world in which women could let themselves go. There was danger, as her novels told her, on every side. She kept her romanticism and sentiment for her reading and for one or two human beings – Ellis, her ancient mother who lived at Canterbury, and an ailing brother. It had, however, taken many years for her dislike and distrust of Vanessa to grow into hatred – that true and unalterable hatred that can come to any human being who has never known passion nor independence nor compliments. In daily life she was an excellent practical woman. She gave no joy to the house in Hill Street but she managed it perfectly. Vanessa always admitted that all the burdens were taken from her shoulders. She added that she would willingly sweep the floors and make the beds were Miss Fortescue removed. She had never asked for her removal because, as the years advanced, it became more and more evident that Ellis would be a lost man without her.

She stood now, her black dress sweeping the floor in iron folds, the high puffs of her sleeves made, it seemed, of steel.

Her pale cheeks might, had she been another woman, have betrayed her excitement. The moment for which, during many long, unjust, weary years, she had been waiting, had arrived.

He had paused in his walk and seemed to be listening. Then he realized her.

'I thought you had gone to bed,' he said.

'Yes, Sir Ellis. I am just going. But there is one thing—'

'Yes?' he said, more at ease and comfortable now that the silence was broken and that the tall figure with the handkerchief on its head had slipped into the wall again. He sat down in one of the armchairs, picking up aimlessly a Society paper that was lying there. He opened it, turning over the pages, looking at the illustrations. There was a supplement illustrating the Spithead Review.

She stood near to him, her hands folded.

'You have often told me,' she said, 'that if there was anything that I thought you ought to know, I should tell you.'

'Certainly,' he answered. 'Yes, Miss Fortescue.'

'Something has come to my ears that I think you should know.' This was like a scene in one of Miss Braddon's novels. She recognized every step and movement. She was (a luxury seldom allowed her) herself a figure in one of her beloved stories. At the same time this was real life. The room was real; the persons concerned were real. She was the sort of woman who might poison an acquaintance, with no malice at all, simply that she might justify her own reading. Neverthless there was malice, true revenge for beauty, wealth, power, that she had never enjoyed.

'I learnt today from an unquestioned source that a little more than two years ago Lady Herries spent a whole day, practically alone, with Mr Benjamin Herries in Cumberland. Probably she has already told you of this; if she has not, I think it right that you should know. It is exactly information of this kind that you have said to me that you *wish* to know.'

He asked her: 'Where did you learn this, Miss Fortescue?'

'A sister of Miss Marrable's is in London. She told Miss Emily Newmark, who this afternoon told me. Both Lady Herries and Mr Herries, who are of course well known in the district, were seen in a compromising position at a hotel called the Dungeon Ghyll Hotel.'

He was shaking from head to foot, but all that Miss Fortescue saw was that his hand trembled against the paper and his foot tapped the floor.

'It is a long while ago.'

'Yes; but it can be completely substantiated by reliable witnesses if you wish it.'

Incredible that, loving Vanessa as he did, he should not have sprung from his chair and banished Miss Fortescue from the house for ever, but at her first word he had moved from the world where things are as they are, to the world, long familiar to him, where men are seen as shadows and a mist-like smoke reveals only monsters of distrust.

'Where and when do you say this occurred?'

'Just over two years ago. At a hotel called the Dungeon Ghyll Hotel in Cumberland.'

He waited a long time; then he said:

'It is of no importance. Lady Herries, I think, spoke to me about it.' He looked at her. 'You misunderstood me if you thought that I wished to hear such things. I know that you always wish to help me, but I have complete confidence in Lady Herries.'

She cleared her throat, a small, dry, mechanical sound.

'I thought it my duty; I cannot bear to see you deceived. Whatever I do, I do out of loyalty to you. You are the only interest that I have and you have taken me on many occasions into your confidence.'

'Yes, yes,' he said. 'But I do not wish you to speak of Lady Herries to me. That is not your province.'

'I understand,' she answered. 'If I have done wrong, please forgive me. I considered the matter and thought that it was better that you should hear of it from me than from someone – someone less loyal.'

He took the paper and began to read.

'Goodnight,' she said, and went.

He read very seriously with knitted brows the Society paper. He read every word.

The sight of London divested of its boards and bunting was too distressing to my aesthetic soul, so I came down to Medmenham Abbey Hotel for a few days' perfect rest, where the flags are not scarlet and blue but violet and purple, and where they rest not against crimson cotton, but on a tender background of green leaves. It is quite beautiful down here, the only drawback to its complete charm being its distance from the railway station. I have a passion for flying from my fellow-creatures, so that they can flee after me; but when it is a question of a four-mile drive after an hour's journey with a change of trains at Bourne End, their pursuing ardour seems to cool. However, Mr Playfair, whose marriage was such a blow to me last year, and who is living in the neighbourhood to write a book, offers to supply the social deficiences of my existence, and Florrie's husband has comforted me with the loan of his punt, which looks absolutely beautiful with new blue and white cushions, so I expect I shall get on very well, and by my calm acquiescence in my solitary state excite the suspicions of my unworthy family. I have seen only two dresses worthy of the name since I came here, and they were both my own; one of light drab homespun with a mauve batiste shirt, with a turn-down linen collar and a black necktie, which does duty with a white linen skirt, crowned with a pale-green mushroom-shaped hat, trimmed with a mass of shaded green wings. Now I must go out and see if I can get Mr Playfair to agree with me as to the charms of this latter.'

Of all of this he read every word; he read it all twice over, murmuring aloud some of the sentences: 'A tender background of green leaves' ... 'I have a passion for flying from my fellow-creatures' ... 'Mr Playfair, whose marriage was such a blow to me' ... 'Florrie's husband has comforted me' ... 'The suspicions of my unworthy family' ... 'A pale-green mushroom-shaped hat' ... 'A mass of shaded green wings' ... 'If I can get Mr Playfair to agree with me'.

'Mr Playfair, Mr Playfair, Mr Playfair,' he repeated, looking at the shaded eyes of Cicero. Although he read the whole of this passage with such intensity and although some of the sentences from it were to remain with him for the rest of his life, he was not, at the moment, in the least aware of anything that he had been reading. He put the paper down, got his hat, and went out.

*   *   *

It was after ten o'clock, and the streets were quiet. Berkeley Square was very still, the leaves of the trees rustling faintly in an evening breeze, the clop-clop of a hansom's horse sounding once and again from Piccadilly. At this hour London streets and houses take on themselves a listening, watching air. They resume their own proper purposeful life which has been disguised during the day by the rushing torrent of human beings; with their lighted windows they watch the traffic of the world that moves without sound, their chimneys and doorways re-establish communication one with another. Like cats they can see in the dark.

Ellis walked, his tall body bent, his head with its high black hat a little forward, his hands clasped behind his back. He passed into the light of Piccadilly, then back again into thin-shadowed streets. His companion walked with him. It is the condition of the disease of jealousy that love, self-pity and hatred move forward together. The victim can be cured, in a moment, by a word, only to be the more diseased by another. He moves always in double form, for while he sees clearly his own madness he at the same time embraces it with eager conviction. He cries out for relief from his torture and at the same time refuses to allow himself to be relieved. Every word, every sound is a significant portent, and yet he is aware how insignificant these words can, in the final truth, prove themselves.

He accepts greedily evidence that he knows to be no evidence at all.

With Ellis this was the climax to years of unsatisfied desire – a climax, the night, the trees, the houses, the lighted windows, thundered into his ears, and yet he knew also that the facts were in themselves almost nothing. Two years ago. In all the time since then Vanessa had been kind, honest, attentive. If, at any moment, he had spoken to her of the letter, he had scarcely mentioned knew that she would at once have replied: 'Yes – in Cumberland on such a day.' Thousands upon thousands of times in these twelve years he had longed to ask her this question and yet never once had he dared to do so. Since the day of the '87 Jubilee, when he had spoken to her of the letter, he had scarcely mentioned Herries, but in blind, secret, surreptitious ways he had spied upon her. That had been disgraceful. It had been disgraceful that he had permitted Miss Fortescue to speak to him tonight, but it is a symptom of jealousy that the noblest of men may commit disgraceful acts as a chaste woman will utter obscenities in delirium.

And Ellis was not the noblest of men. He had, all his life, been lonely, mistrustful, caught in a web that he could not break.

This remained: Vanessa had spent a day with Herries and had not told him. She had spent one day – why not others? She had deceived him in this. Then she had decieved him often. But she had not deceived him because he had not asked her. She had not lied. She had, he knew, never lied to him – but is it not a lie when a woman sees her lover in secret? Was Herries her lover? It was at that agonizing moment, a moment that had visited him often before but never with such tyranny as now, that he looked about him and saw that the starlit sky, the houses, the deserted street, were coloured a faint green. 'A tender background of green leaves.' 'A pale-green mushroom-shaped hat.' 'A mass of shaded green wings.' This faint green light trembled like the mist of a cloud of greenflies, touching the steps before dark walls, the white posters of the evening papers outside the closed and barred newspaper shop, the bent figure of an old woman in a battered straw hat picking something from the gutter, the light of a gas lamp.

A hansom clattered past. A bell from some church sounded the hour. Trembling with a terrible chilling heat, Ellis turned homewards.

He was half undressed when he heard Vanessa come in. As though he were a man with a thousand ears he had been listening ever since he entered his room for those sounds. His door was just ajar. He knew what he would hear. The closing of the hall door, the soft voice of the butler, Vanessa's softer one, a little pause. Then 'Goodnight', the butler's 'Goodnight, my lady', then the sweep of her long dress as she climbed the stairs. Then the opening of her own door, its shutting.

After that he undressed feverishly, but was extremely careful to fold his clothes, to place his studs in their silver box, to brush his scanty hair. Over his nightdress he drew on his dark grey dressing-gown, went into the passage, listened, then knocked.

She knew of course his knock. He heard her say: 'Come in.'

She was sitting in front of her mirror, a white wrap over her shoulders, brushing her long dark hair which fell to her waist. As he came in she looked at him over her shoulder, smiling.

'I thought you would be asleep. I came in as quietly as I could.'

He stood by the door staring at her; seeing her in the lamplight

with that dark flood of hair, the white wrap over the loose white
robe, her smile so friendly and simple, he felt so furious a storm
of jealousy sweep over him that he lowered his eyes as though, in
actuality, he had been overwhelmed by a tremendous arching
wave of blinding deafening water.

At last he moved across the room and sat in a chair near the
bed. She continued to brush her hair, talking happily. 'We went
to *The Prisoner of Zenda* after all. Peile had seen it before, but as
he never remembers anything *that* didn't matter. It was new to
the rest of us. George Alexander and Fay Davis, you know. Miss
Davis is handsome, but *what* a stick of a part, and Alexander
never can forget the clothes he's wearing. The house was full, but
of course it was only revived last week. I saw Johnny Beaminster
and, oh yes, Alice Parlington. You remember – you danced with
her at the Devonshire Ball. She was Isabella of Spain or something. Well, she asked about you and wants us to go to dinner one
night . . .'

She moved into her dressing-room. For a long while he sat
there, staring in front of him. She returned and got into bed,
giving him a light kiss on his forehead as she passed him.

'What sort of an evening have you had? Was old Timothy a
terrible bore? I thought of you when Alexander was an hour or
more kissing Flavia's hand. I was most dreadfully bored, but
comforted myself with thinking that you were equally bored at
home. Cynthia looked so pretty, but I am sure she is harming
herself with her tiny waist. It is smaller every time I see her. And
the smaller her waist grows the more intellectual she becomes.
Ibsen is her only wear. Elizabeth Robins and Janet Achurch her
only actresses. So was so horrified when she found that I hadn't
read *Esther Waters* that I thought she'd fall out of the box, and
yet she puts up with Peile Worcester who can hardly spell his
own name. She loves him, I really believe . . .' She stopped. She
was aware that he had not spoken since he had entered the room.
She sat up, resting her head on her hand.

'What is it, Ellis? Aren't you well? Is your head still bad?'
She put out her hand and touched his forehead.
'Why, you're in a fever. Let me—'
'No,' he said. 'Don't do anything. I want to speak to you.'

She saw then that he was trembling from head to foot and, as
always when someone near her was suffering, she forgot everything save that distress. She got out of bed, put on the white wrap
and went towards the door.

'You're ill. You're shaking all over. Wait, while I—'

He looked across the room at her.

'No, please. There's something I must say. Go back to bed.'

She did so. She knew that something had occurred while she was at the theatre. She had now for so many years been prepared for some crisis that never arrived. How many times there had been a preface like this: Ellis in misery, dumb with some hidden trouble, beginning to speak, turning away like a child afraid, and because he was always a child to her she always comforted him, not asking what his trouble was, but consoling him. Men seemed to her completely inarticulate in any real distress – her father, Benjie, Ellis, they were all the same. They could not speak when they had something important to say, and when there was nothing they chattered interminably. She had been tired, wearied with her day, the gossip, the heat of the theatre, but now she forgot herself, wondering only, as she had wondered so often before, what she could do to soothe him.

Then he said, not looking at her:

'I heard this evening that two years ago you were alone in Cumberland with Herries – alone for a whole day, seen in a compromising position.'

So *that* was it! Two years ago. Ridiculous. A compromising position. That angered her. She drew back into the bed like a child who has been hurt.

'It is quite true that I was with Benjie in Cumberland one afternoon two years ago. The "compromising position" part of it is insulting. You remember, I went to Cumberland for a week. I had no idea that Benjie was there, of course. When we found that we were so near, we met. If you had asked me I would have told you.'

'Then you admit it?'

'Admit what?'

'That you met him secretly, spent the day with him alone, and told me nothing afterwards.'

'I met him certainly. We were alone for part of the time. I would have told you had you asked me.'

She looked at him, forgetting very quickly her own anger because the fuss was about so little, was so unimportant. Once sure of that, her earlier sensation swept back – that here was something small, childlike, suffering, and that she must comfort him. She moved nearer to him. She put out her hand and let it rest very gently on his shoulder.

'Ellis dear, there is no mystery, no adultery, nothing sensational. Miss Fortescue, I suppose, told you – tonight while I was at the theatre. The "compromising position" could be only hers. Now listen, Ellis. I have seen Benjie perhaps half a dozen times since our marriage – and we have been married over twelve years – so that's not bad, is it? I have spoken to him twice alone, once in the Park, once in Cumberland. I gave no promise not to speak to him. If you had ever asked me I would have told you. You must remember that Benjie and I have been friends all our lives. I know that some of the family don't like him, that you don't like him, but when you have known someone always – you see them differently.'

She had broken off abruptly, the tone of her voice had changed, her hand had withdrawn from his shoulder, because suddenly in the middle of a sentence she saw that he, not hearing what she was saying to him, was staring at her and that his stare was crazy. Two people living together with some ill-adjustment often find that they go with slow measured steps for a long period and that then quite suddenly, and for no apparent cause, as though someone caught them in the small of their backs and jerked them forward, they are hurled into a precipitous and often catastrophic descent. It is only afterwards, on looking back, that they can see that this sudden jerk forward had the beginning of its impetus in those very first slow steps.

It was so with Vanessa now. She looked at Ellis and saw a grotesque. Under the shade of the lamp a man with a high domed forehead and a lean peaked nose was sitting. This man wore a grey dressing-gown and a nightdress that was open at the neck so that two protruding bones, pink in the lamplight, gave him a hen's neck. His bare ankles, too, were pink and sharply boned. This thin bony man with his long body looped together in the chair had two eyes that looked at Vanessa but did not see her, looked beyond her at the room but did not see that either, saw something that frightened and angered them, something that no one else saw. This separate and apart vision – which is what the sane man means when he calls his brother insane – gave the figure in the chair an aspect of loneliness, isolation. Put this man in a crowded theatre and he would be quite alone, put him in a solitary cell and he would have company.

Vanessa saw life very simply. She had some of the good sense and quiet of her father, some of the good sense and love of action of her grandmother. She was entirely sane about all things. That

she was also a poet, because of the country blood in her veins,
affected not at all her relations with her fellows. She had lived
with Ellis for more than twelve years and had needed all her
patience, sanity, humour, and common sense. Any woman, living
with a man who loves her, whom she herself does not love, needs
all these things, day by day and week by week. But she had learnt
that you can care for a man without loving him and obtain
satisfaction of your need — so she cared for Ellis. But behind her
care there had grown and grown the fear that one day the situation would be too difficult for her. As she always herself said,
she hated scenes, melodramas, floods of tears, self-pityings,
shrieks, and beatings of the breast. She did not know how to
behave in such a world. Her father and mother had been quiet
people and she was a quiet person, although as with her grandmother there was a wild passionate life at the core of her nature.
She had also a strong sense of the ridiculous both in herself and
in others.

But now, looking at Ellis, she had no sense of the ridiculous.
There was something here both real and terrible. Instinctively, as
she always did in a crisis, she thought of her father. 'Help me
through this,' she said, as she had done when she was a little
child on Cat Bells.

She suspected that Ellis was going to scream.

'He will rouse the whole house.' She even remembered that
Miss Fortescue would not yet be asleep and that her room was
not far away. However, Ellis did not scream. He said very
quietly:

'You are a liar. Herries has been your lover for years.'

(Even as he said it he knew that it was not true. A very quiet
little animal squatting inside his head observed rather wearily:
'*That* you know is not true.')

'Ellis, let us talk sense.' Vanessa held her hands tightly together
under the bedclothes. 'You are fifty-four. I shall soon be thirty-
eight. We have lived together for years and you know that I have
never lied to you, not in the smallest, most unimportant matter. I
have never been Benjie's lover nor anyone's lover. You must trust
me as I trust you, otherwise we must separate.'

He leant forward towards her: her impulse was to shrink back,
but courage in this dangerous moment for which, she felt now,
she had for years been preparing, was of more importance than
any other quality. So she sat up, put out her hand and picked up
the white silk wrap from the chair on the other side of the bed;

then with it warmly around her, her hair falling darkly about her, leaning forward, her hands clasped on her raised knees, she said, very quietly:

'Ellis, listen. We are too old not to be sensible about this. We matter too much to one another to have scenes. Besides, I hate scenes. You mustn't be unhappy and there is no reason—'

'No reason!' he broke in. His thin hand shot forward and caught her upraised knee. 'No reason when you have made me unhappy for years – not loving me, pretending, taking people in, but not me. Do you hear? – never me! Do you hear? Do you hear? I've had enough of it. You drive me mad with your unkindness! You – your lover . . .'

All drama verges on the ridiculous, and especially English drama. Vanessa had once, years ago, in the Park, felt Ellis' physical contact although he had not touched her. When her protective affection was aroused Ellis' body was there for her to comfort. But when he was angry or sexually passionate she hated his touch. One hand had closed about her knee, the other was on her breast; his face was close to hers, his body stretching up to the bed. If this scene was ludicrous she was too angry to notice it.

'You are hurting me,' she said.

He threw himself on the bed, his body convulsed, trembling, thrusting against hers. He tore open her nightdress; with his knees on the bed, his arms around her body, his hands bruising her, he pushed her down into the bed. Then his hands moved to her neck: panting, murmuring unintelligible words, he twisted her head round into the pillow. His hysteria gave him great strength; she began to wonder, in a quite detached way, whether he would kill her, and she had no power at all to resist. She tried to conserve her strength, for his hands now were so tightly about her neck that she could not breathe except in little gasps of pain. A black cloud, scattered with spots of intense light, pushed against her vision.

She thought: 'This is absurd', and anger, fear of death, pain were all mingled in the dark wavering cloud.

The pressure of his hands relaxed. His body, without moving, lay heavily on hers. He was crying. She listened, as it seemed for a long time, to his sobs. At last, very wearily, she turned. He slowly raised himself, slipped off the bed. She lifted herself painfully and saw that he was kneeling on the floor, his head bowed, hidden in the bed, his body shaken with sobs.

For a long while there was no other sound in the room. At last
she rose, went into the dressing-room, bathed her face and hands,
stood there for a while wondering what she would do. When she
came back he was still there, his body bent low, his face buried in
his hands, crying.

She touched his shoulder.

'You will catch cold, Ellis.' She took her white cloak and
wrapped it round him, but as her hands came into contact with
his body he trembled. She went back into bed and waited for him
to recover.

THE GREAT TIMOTHY SCANDAL

'Yes, that is the cruel moment, when you really begin to feel
old,' said Barney, nodding his head and settling his fat body
more comfortably in his chair. 'I am sixty-eight, you know, Vanessa, in this year of grace eighteen hundred and ninety-eight –
close on seventy – and I had no sense of age at all until last week
when Nevinson took me to a Fabian Reception. There we were
all walking about, already in the New Century, and every maca-
roon was a hard little Fact and every cup of tea an admonition
not to be silly. Well, I like to be silly. In the coming century no
one is going to be silly. It will be motor-cars, telephones, and all
our food will be in little pills. If it weren't for things like the
Klondike madness and the German Emperor and Sarah Grand
I should know that the Fairy-Tale World was gone for ever. I've
lived all my life in it, you know – charming world where everything had a meaning, when we believed in Faith, Hope, and
Charity, assisted by Watts, when we really meant to be good even
if we were not, when our children said "Sir" and "Ma'am",
when we thought the Albert Memorial lovely, and were certain
that it was our duty to convert every unhappy Black Man to
trousers and the worship of our Sovereign. Why, in the coming
century I wouldn't wonder if we don't believe in the Empire any
more! I wouldn't be surprised if even adultery becomes a
scientific fact rather than a moral crime. But I liked the old
world. It was *my* world. My silly novels amused it (or a small
fragment of it). I could lead my own life without interference so
long as I didn't shock anyone in public, I could eat and drink as

much as I liked. I remember, Vanessa, when I was a lad, going to the fight between Sayers and Heenan, the last great fight in England it was. It was just an adventure then, but I can see now that it was the end of an epoch. Epochs are always ending, I suppose; it doesn't matter unless you're seventy. Well, I've had a good life. I can grow as fat as I like. Nobody cares any more.'

'I care,' said Vanessa, smiling across the table at him. They were having tea alone together in Hill Street.

'While I'm getting fatter you're getting thinner.'

'Am I? I'm thirty-nine this year, you know.'

He looked at her intently. He loved her very dearly, more now than any other woman in the world.

'You haven't been very merry lately, Vanessa,' he said. 'I haven't heard you laugh as you used to do for a long time.'

'I'm not very merry,' she answered, getting up and walking about the room, her long black-and-white dress trailing behind her. She turned round, came over to him and stood beside him.

'Barney – what are the family saying?'

'The family?'

'Yes – Violet, Cynthia, Alfred – all of them.'

'Saying about what?'

'Us – Ellis. This house.'

He didn't answer at first, then he said slowly:

'Nothing much.'

'Oh! They are! In the last few months they've been closing in – nearer and nearer. For one thing Miss Fortescue's going must have been enough to start them—' She drew a chair close to him and sat down.'

'I can't keep quiet any longer. Something must be done. I've never been beaten by anything before, and I said that *this* shouldn't beat me either. Two other bad things have happened to me in my life – once when my father died, once when Benjie and I – oh, well, that's past history. Each time I held my head up and said: "I can manage this" – and manage it I did. My married life hasn't been easy, you know, but there have always been all kinds of little things to help it along. Life, I'm sure, isn't *meant* to be too tragic and I've had great consolation in feeling that I was dressing up – *pretending* to be a grand hostess, you know. Grandmother had a devil of pride inside her and so have I had, and all the time that I was longing to run away to Cumberland and be my real self I have felt as though she and father knew about this game that I was playing and wanted me to do my best

at it. Then there's been Ellis. I did him a terrible injustice in
marrying him when I didn't love him. The only thing I could do
in return was to be kind to him, protect him, be his friend . . . I'm
not boasting, Barney, but I truly have played the game all these
years. Now I can play it no longer. I'm beaten.'

Barney took her hand in his.

'What's happened, my dear?'

'Last July Ellis and I had a dreadful scene. Miss Fortescue
told him one evening that I had been alone with Benjie two years
before in Cumberland. You know – that day at Dungeon Ghyll.
In itself that was nothing, but Ellis had been wretchedly jealous
long before, as you know. This was the climax. I was in bed and
he almost strangled me – a ridiculous scene, and it ended in his
crying all night, imploring me to forgive him, going to sleep at
last in my arms. For weeks after that he was abject. He dismissed
Miss Fortescue, as you know, and for a time I thought that I
could manage him. That was July. This is February. I know now
that I'll never be able to manage him again.'

She paused. Barney felt her hand tremble in his.

'What is it?' he asked.

'Ellis is mad. He has been mad for months. Oh, only at times.
We have parties here, he goes to the City. So far as I know no one
except Lettice Marrable suspects anything. The servants may. I
don't know . . . You can't think, Barney, how pitiful it is! If I
could help him neither you nor anyone else should know anything, but I can't help him. It is I who aggravate him. I would
give him anything, anything he asks if it would help him.
Nothing can help him. I don't know whether to go or stay. But
one day it will be too much for me and I shall go. The worst of it
is that now, although I am so sorry for him, I don't feel even
kind. If I had loved him I would stay with him for ever, but the
dreadful thing now . . . the dreadful thing . . .' She turned her
head. 'I hate him. I fear him. I have never been afraid of anyone
or anything, but now the very sound of his step . . .'

She began to cry. Barney had never seen her cry before.

'I am middle-aged. I have loved one man all my life with my
whole heart and he has loved me. Why should I lose everything?
What have I done?'

Very quickly she recovered herself. She walked to the window
and he waited. When she returned she was quite calm again.

'Listen, Barney. You are to say nothing of this to anybody.
Only . . . if it gets too difficult . . . I shall ask you to help me. It

may be better soon. He has been quite normal for the last month. Very quiet. Very submissive. Poor Ellis! Listen! He's coming ... I know his step now, even when I don't hear it.'

Ellis came in. But he was not alone: on either side of him walked a lady, and Barney remembered afterwards with amusement that the first sight that he had of his two relations, Miss Vera Trent and Miss Winifred Trent, was this entry, guarding and protecting Ellis.

For they were, it seemed, distant cousins. Ellis, quietly and with much courtesy, explained it. 'Henry Cards – he had a wife back in the eighteenth century, Lucilla. I can remember, dear Miss Trent, my father speaking of her. My father was born in 1770 – it seems odd, doesn't it? – and Lucilla died about 1780, I think. She painted very charming watercolours. I shouldn't wonder if there are not one or two still about somewhere. Henry and Lucilla had two sons. One of them, Prosper, was Jennifer's father, my dear Vanessa. Well, Prosper married a Miss Amelia Trent, and our two cousins descend from her younger brother. Now what does that make you to us, Miss Trent? About second cousin twice removed, does it not? Still, there's always a strong family feeling, a very strong family feeling ...'

Everyone laughed. The butler brought in fresh tea. Who were these two ladies? Vanessa had the sense that they had been in this house all their lives and had known Ellis for ever. However, it appeared not. They had never visited Hill Street. Their carriage had driven up just as Ellis had arrived from the City. They had met on the doorstep. Oh! they must apologize, but the fact is that they had lived all their lives in Bournemouth. Such a charming place, and a hundred years ago there was nothing at all but the sea waves, the sand, a tree or two! Yes, they loved Bournemouth. Vanessa interrupted. That was where Jennifer's father and mother had lived, was it not? Yes, indeed, Doctor Trent of those days had been a close friend of Mr and Mrs Cards. Mrs Cards had been *so* proud of Bournemouth, so proud that she used to speak and write of the town as a fashionable watering-place when it was really only a house or two. Doctor Trent and Mr and Mrs Cards had been among its earliest inhabitants. Oh yes, they remembered all about the beautiful Jennifer! At one time it was thought that she would become the Duchess of Wrexe. She was actually engaged to the Duke for a brief while, they believed ...

They chattered on, most happily. They were both tall and elderly women and remarkably alike. They were slim and had

soft grey hair under their large black hats. They wore black
feather boas, black silk dresses very long in the skirts; each lady
had a big bunch of imitation Parma violets pinned to her breast
and wore a very thin gold chain. Their faces resembled those of
placid, extremely kindly sheep, but behind the mildness, Vanessa decided, there was a strong and possibly relentless determination. It certainly appeared that they had made complete
appropriation of Ellis. They sat one on either side of him and,
although they smiled at Vanessa and listened with deference to
Barney, it was Ellis whom they admired. Their voices were soft
with that comforting murmur that belongs to a distant mowing
machine on a summer day. They took off their gloves; each wore
two or three rings, thickly studded with diamonds, on the
fingers. They were alike in almost every particular; the only
difference perhaps being that Miss Vera was a little the more
severe and determined of the two, Miss Winifred the softer and
more melting. They were greatly interested in all the Herries
relations – Alfred and his wife, Horace and *his* wife, Emily,
Phyllis' son Philip, old Horace in Manchester, the Rockages in
Wiltshire and their girls Maud and Helen, Cynthia and Peile
Worcester. They seemed to have the fullest information about all
of them. Vanessa noticed that they made no mention of Benjie or
Rose and that they shook their heads over Timothy at Cambridge. Yesterday, it appeared, they had paid a call on Violet.
With all their comments and questions they were kind and
hushed. They behaved, Vanessa thought, as though they were
nurses in a sickroom.

Barney watched all this in amazement. He found that he could
not tear himself away. How dramatic a transition! A moment
before Vanessa had been telling him the most awful things,
speaking, he could not doubt, with the most absolute sincerity,
and now here they were all drinking tea together, these two old
maids like two cows in a field, and Ellis, calm, benign, dignified,
smiling and courteous! Had Vanessa been imagining her terrors?
No, he knew her too well. She was the least hysterical of women.
He would not wonder but that the tears that she had just now
shed were the first since her childhood. As he saw her now so
quiet and so lovely in her black-and-white dress, laughing, looking after the two old women as though they were her first care in
the world, smiling up at Ellis, her broad unruffled brow, her large
dark eyes that had never lost the frankness, the eagerness of her
earlier simplicity, her dignity as hostess, her natural friendliness
as one human being with another, he thought: 'Well, I'm

damned if she can't manage this. It's not so bad as she said.'

When he got up to go, Ellis most courteously went all the way downstairs with him, bending his long neck to hear what Barney had to say, rather as an Ambassador listens with the utmost attention to a diplomatic visior.

'Hullo! That's a new clock you've got!' Barney said, at the turn of the stairs. It was a long thin clock of gilded red Chinese lacquer.

'Yes,' said Ellis. 'Vanessa saw it somewhere and liked it.'

'Of course he hates me,' Barney thought. 'We both know that. Still, he's behaving very well.'

Finally, in the street, he shook his head. Ellis was not mad. He, Barney, knew a madman when he saw one!

When the ladies were gone Vanessa praised them. Ellis walked about the room and praised them too. How quiet, intelligent, and well-behaved! He had feared that the women in England were lost, with their clubs, their passion for 'this Bridge', their bicycle riding, their indecent novels, their conceit. He understood that there were in London alone thirty clubs for ladies. What did ladies want with clubs? What—

He stopped, went to a table and fidgeted with a small silver box, a paper knife, a book. He picked up the book, put it down.

'Vanessa, I did not care for that hat you were wearing yesterday.'

The room was rather dimly lit, the fire low. Her nerves had been shaken by her little talk with Barney, and as she got up and went across to him she felt an impulse, so strong that she wondered whether she would be able to conquer it, to tell him that she could endure this no longer, that she must leave the house, London, all the life that had, so ridiculously, been built up around her ... leave the house, at once, without a moment's delay ...

'What hat?' she asked.

'The one you were wearing yesterday. The one with the – green birds' wings.' He seemed to have difficulty in speaking the last words.

She was standing close to him. Her agitation fell from her because his eyes were so weary that she was suddenly filled with pity.

'Oh, Ellis, you're tired. Go and lie down until dinner. Or stay here. I'll read to you.'

'No. But you understand, Vanessa? Please don't wear that hat again.'

She laughed and was frightened. His hand was shaking against the dark stuff of his trousers.

'It's quite new. Yesterday was the first time I had worn it. I thought you would like it.'

'Then you must change its colour. You know that ... green ... I don't like it as a colour.'

She tried to speak easily. 'Certainly. You shall never see the hat again.'

He put his hand out and touched her forehead. All her strength was needed not to move away, so she came closer to him.

'How cool your forehead is! Mine is always burning.'

She put her hand through his arm and drew him to the sofa. She helped him to lie down, arranging the cushions, but he said, as though he were half asleep: 'No, sit here – close to me.'

She sat down and he laid his head on her lap. He closed his eyes. The creeping whisper of the fire, the steady determined tick of the large gold clock on the mantelpiece filled the long, shadowy room. She sat there without moving. Her childhood – the friendly figures of her father, Will Leathwaite, Elizabeth, Aunt Jane, her grandmother – the places, the Cat Bells garden with the little sturdy wood, the stream, the line of the hill above the cottage, lovely days at Uldale, the seashore at Seascale, the purple shadows of Skiddaw, sunlit brilliant clouds of snow on Blencathra, the main street of Keswick, someone riding by on a horse, the scarlet coach from Kendal, the friendliness, the small gardens of daffodils and primulas, the grey steeple of St John's above the green fields running to the Lake's edge, the hillsides flaming with bracken, the Herdwicks moving their thick sturdy bodies slowly in front of the shepherd ... her father, her father waving his hand to her from his writing-table as she passed along the garden path, her father with his soft lazy eyes, his loving ironical glance, his hand resting on Will's shoulder ...

Tears stole down her cheek. Without moving, yet she felt that she was hastening, against her will, down a dark path away from everything in life that was loving and good into a house dark and chill, with doors that would be locked behind her. How dearly she loved life! How hard she had tried to do what was right, and now she was nearly forty, frightened like a small child, and lonely! ... She had never known that it was possible for anyone to be as lonely as she was. What was she to do?

And Benjie? She had, in these hard minutes, kept him away

from her, but now, heart and mind opened, too weak any longer
to resist, she threw out her arms, he came running, running to
her. She clasped him to her, felt his face pressed close to hers, his
heart beat against her breast.

The Chinese clock on the stairs struck. The gold clock followed it. For an hour she had not moved and Ellis, pallid as a
dead man, lay with his head on her lap.

Then the Great Timothy Scandal sprang upon her. It was an
excellent moment for a family excitement. There was but little in
May 1898 for anyone to discuss. A small coal strike, a war between the United States and Spain, the death of poor old Mr
Gladstone, the Dreyfus case, the low spirits of the Liberal Party.
In none of these things did the Herries take a very extravagant
interest. Cynthia redecorated her little house and gave an evening
party for the Ibsen enthusiasts, Alfred introduced everywhere an
astonishingly uncouth South African who was said to be worth
millions, Emily discovered a Prophet from Shoreditch. The Season began and huge evening receptions rolled from house to house.
The West End was populated with coachmen, footmen and men
with grave diplomatic countenances hired for the evening. Every
kind of carriage and every kind of horse glittered and shone. The
window boxes blazed with geraniums. The Opera sparkled with
diamonds. There was so much money that everyone despised it
and would do anything, invite anybody, go anywhere, to obtain
more. Morals were as loose as usual and manners beginning to
crumble. Woman was no longer subservient to Man, and the
Empire was at its apogee.

The Herries took all this for granted as every other English
family was taking it for granted. The Herries concluded that
everything would last for ever just as it was. Emily's Prophet said
uncomfortable things, and Cynthia, Violet, Mrs Alfred, went to a
meeting to hear him. They found him very sweet with his deep
black eyes and flowing black hair. Melba sang at the Opera. Also
at one of Vanessa's parties. A man called Conrad published a
book called *Tales of Unrest,* but no member of the Herries family
read it. Several ladies and gentlemen rode in electric cabs. Violet
wore an evening dress with a high collar encircled with four rows
of pearls. Lettice Marrable was seen bicycling in a pair of knickerbockers. For some while, however, inside this dazzling world
the Herries circle had been moving quietly. There had been no
family sensation. Something strange was happening in Hill Street

although Vanessa appeared as usual and Ellis was stiff, courtly, and boring as usual. Rose, it was said, was drinking herself to death in Paris. Nothing had been heard of Benjie. One topic of interest was the career of the two Miss Trents, who went everywhere and were constantly at Hill Street. That, however, was not a scandal – far from it. Two quieter, gentler ladies could not be found anywhere.

The Great Timothy Scandal, then, burst brilliantly and, small though its cause, it brought in its sequence changes to many people. It struck Vanessa on a sunny May day when, coming back after a drive in the Park with Cynthia, when they had both been very gay and talked much nonsense, Lettice Marrable threw the news at the quiet tea-table. Cynthia always regarded Miss Marrable as a kind of aboriginal savage: her little hard hats, her manlike tunic, short skirt, her brusque masculine tone and quite extraordinary masculine attitudes, her public smoking of cigarettes, her abilities at tennis and golf, her passionate desire that women should sit in Parliament, all these things filled Cynthia with a wondering amaze. She was never weary of looking at her, although she did not care to be seen with her in public.

Lettice Marrable now came in and said:

'Timothy Bellairs has run away to Paris with Tom, Benjie Herries' boy. Violet has just heard. Timothy had a letter written from Paris. Violet is in a terrible way and says that Tom has perverted Timothy or some word like that. Timothy senior has left for Paris. If he sees Benjie he is going to shoot him. They are all talking at Violet's now. I've just come from there. Horace and the Miss Trents and Carey Rockage ... Benjie Herries is to be horsewhipped whenever he's found. Oh, you never saw anything so funny in your life as Horace threatening to whip Benjie – *when* he finds him! And the real joke is that Tom is only fourteen. He must have run away from school up to town and met Tim here. Anyway they are both safe in Paris.'

Cynthia said: 'I wish I was.'

Vanessa said: 'But it is ridiculous of Violet to blame anyone but herself. Tim has wanted to be a painter since he was a baby. It is nothing to do with Benjie at all.'

After that with every hour the affair grew. It seemed that Benjie *was* in Paris and that the two boys stayed with him. Then came news of a meeting between old Timothy and Benjie. Old Timothy gave it him, it was generally understood, 'hot and strong'. What really happened no one knew because no third person was present: it was difficult, however, for the Herries to believe that Timothy gave anyone anything 'hot and strong'. He was sixty-one, suffered from his heart, was as fat as a barrel. Moreover he was amiably minded.

It appeared that Benjie's attitude was that, as regarded his own boy, if he wanted to leave school and see the world, he should do so. Benjie was the same at his age. As for Timothy, he was twenty-one and ought to know his own mind. As a matter of fact he always *had* known his own mind, and it was only the stupid conventionality of his parents that held him back. It was said that at this point old Timothy called Benjie 'a damned blackguard' and that Benjie did not resent the insult as any gentleman would have done, but offered Timothy a cigarette. It was further said that the interview between Timothy and his son was extremely painful. Young Timothy declared that now that he was in Paris he was going to stay there and that Tom Herries had had nothing whatever to do with it. They had been friends all their lives, he and Tom; Tom hated his school and wanted to be with his father. By this time it was generally admitted that Benjie was the Devil. He had always been the Devil. It was time the family were rid of him.

Would Benjie come to London and face his accusers? It was understood that, with a shrug of his shoulders, he said that of course he would come to London, although he had no idea what he was to be accused of.

He came to London.

A meeting, as famous in its own small way as Christabel's Ball or Walter's historic visit to the Christmas party at Uldale, took place on the second of June at the Rockland Club between these gentlemen: Carey Rockage, Timothy Bellairs, Alfred Herries, Horace Ormerod, Barney Newmark and Benjamin Herries, Esquire.

The best evidence of what actually occurred is to be found in Barney's Journal (the Journals are all in the family archives at Centor Park, bound in faded red leather, behind glass, in the library. Judith Paris' book and the earlier eighteenth-century papers are in the same bookshelf, equally protected and equally unread).

DUKE STREET, W. *June 2nd, 1898*
I will try to put down as briefly as possible what occurred today at Rockland's, a matter purely of family interest but important

perhaps one day to young Tim and to Tom.

I met Benjie at the Criterion for lunch. I hadn't seen him for a
considerable time, but there he was, just the same as ever, brown
with health, cocky as a robin – very like a robin. He has just that
bright, roguish, adventurous, don't-care-a-damn kind of eye
and, although he's stocky, his lack of height (always a sore point
with him) gives him a birdlike appearance. He looked, I'll
confess, a bit odd because he wasn't wearing a hat; he had a
soft nondescript collar with his usual dark red tie in its gold ring,
and his clothes were a sort of wine-coloured tweed. He is always
scrupulously clean, though. Benjie's careless but at the same time
spruce, and his brown cheeks, bright eyes, stiff close-cropped
wiry hair, hands that look as hard as iron, taut, springy body – all
these, with the very kindly wrinkles about his eyes and his extremely engaging smile, prejudice you in his favour if you're an
ordinary man on two legs and not a hypocrite like Horace or a
prig like Ellis.

Anyway there he was, saying 'Hullo, Barney!' just as though
we'd met yesterday, and walking into the big room at the Criterion as though he owned the place and at the same time found
it very absurd.

As usual he ate very little. He didn't talk much either. He
couldn't understand what they wanted to see him about. 'I'm not
a boy, you know. I'm forty-three. I haven't harmed the family so
far as I can see. They seem to think that I've lured Tim to Paris
and that I may ruin his body and soul – using young Tom as a
decoy. Damnable nonsense! Tim's a fine painter. I don't know
much about it, but he's started away at Lucien's, which is, I
believe, one of the best of those places, and old Lucien himself
thinks highly of him. Tim's crazy about these men I don't understand – Gauguin, Van Gogh, Cézanne – but I'm ready to tell him
he's right. How do you and I know? We may have taste but we
don't care enough really to know. You can only know about Art
if you happen both to love it and have a trained taste. Anyway,
there he is and Tom's learning languages. He's got a passion for
them and his great idea is to train for a War Correspondent.
"What'll you do if there's never a war again?" I asked him. "Oh,
there'll always be one somewhere," he said, and I expect he's
right. He can put things down on paper pretty smartly for his
age. Well, there they are, a decent pair of kids. What's the
trouble? *I* had nothing to do with it. What do they want *me* to
do?'

'As I understand it,' I answered, 'they want you to tell Tim to return to his parents. They think you've got some unholy influence over him.'

'Unholy be damned!' said Benjie. 'I've never had the smallest influence over anyone.'

'If you refuse they'll expel you with bell, book, and candle.'

'Expel me from what?'

'The family circle.'

'A fat lot *I* care!'

So after luncheon we went along. Rockland's is, I have always thought, the stupidest and slowest Club in London. It is just right for elderly Herries like Timothy and Carey Rockage and old Horace when he comes down from Manchester. It is small and dingy, and the room where they waited for us smelt of whisky and stale cigar-smoke. The windows looked as though they hadn't been cleaned for months. Timothy and Carey belong to grander Clubs of course, and when they want to show off they go to them, but for a real family bust-up Rockland's is the place. They were all waiting for us in an upstairs card room which we had to ourselves. When we came in it struck me at once how large physically we were compared with Benjie and how physically unfit. Carey, Timothy, Horace and myself are all stout men and Alfred is pasty. Benjie could have taken the lot of us on and thrown us all out of window! However, he was not in the least aggressive. He smiled at everyone as though he loved them and if no one smiled back that was not *his* fault! Oddly enough as I looked round the room I felt, although I'd come there of course as Benjie's friend and supporter, an acute sympathy with all of them. I understood exactly how they felt. With the exception of Horace they are all decent men, and in my opinion the decent normal Herries man is about as decent as any Englishman anywhere. He is brave, loyal, patriotic, God-fearing, good to his women and generous to all men. Simply he hasn't any imagination. A little imagination and they would understand that Benjie's type is permanent. You can't get rid of it by cursing and abusing it. You've got somehow to make terms with it. Put it in gaol, exile it, and it will always return. When men like Carey and old Timothy have learnt how to assimilate men like Benjie, the Herries family will rule the world – until then it will be always second-rate. But, of course, that assimilation will never occur. So there will be always tales to tell, poets formed out of rebellion, and wars between nations. But I understood how they felt about

Benjie. You could see, as they looked at his country clothes and his round head with its sharp little eyes and his sturdy little legs, that he was the personification of disorder to them! And they were right.

Old Timothy, as the principal sufferer, took charge, and, standing in front of the fireplace, with his legs spread, he outlined the case. Unfortunately he was both lengthy and pompous. He said the same thing over and over again. What it came to was that he wanted his son back, that Benjie had tempted him to Paris and must therefore bring him back to London again. There was nothing personal in this. He spoke as though Benjie were the kind of man with whom he could not possibly *have* any personal relations.

When Timothy had finished at last, Benjie answered quietly that he had *not* tempted young Tim to Paris, that Tim was of age, and that, although of course it was a pity that he and his father did not agree, it was nevertheless the boy's own affair. 'In fact,' said Benjie, beaming round on all of them, 'I cannot see what I have to do with it or why you have asked me to meet you here.'

At that everyone wanted to speak at once. It was interesting to me to see the strong likeness that springs up between the men of our family when we are together. Alfred with his sharp nose that is always a little shiny, his high cheekbones and short black curly hair can hardly be said to resemble short-armed, short-legged, paunchy Carey who is the perfect Country Gentleman, or Timothy who is a kind of hundred-times-cleaned-scrubbed-and-brushed pillowcase, or myself who am just fat, careless and, alas, now purple-veined about the nostrils. And yet alike we all are, alike we always have been. Is it our English beef and cabbage that has made us so? Or our politics? Or the Battle of Hastings, 1066? Or insular security?

There in any case we all were, leaning forward like one man wanting to tell Benjie what we thought of him. Carey, who always speaks as though the thick Wiltshire soil had through the years crept up and swallowed his tonsils, had his word. He spoke as an English peer who has the crops, the family, and the British reputation among foreigners all to protect at once.

'Why we have asked you here,' he said, 'is because we feel, rightly or wrongly, that you are responsible for Timothy's boy's behaviour. The lad has caused his mother and father much pain. He has carried on a clandestine correspondence with your boy, it seems, for a long time past and of that we feel that you must have been – ah – cognizant.' (Here I caricature old Carey's style a bit.) '*Therefore*, therefore we have asked you to meet us. We are representing here today the family in London. I need not emphasize to you the grief that this has caused the lad's mother, nor the necessity we all feel that her boy – her only boy – should be restored to her. The lad is a good lad – fundamentally a good lad – and we feel that he must have been under some most unfortunate influence to persuade him—'

'Rot!' Benjie broke in. 'Never was greater nonsense. Tim's been pleading since he was in that unfortunate velvet suit that his mother always made him wear, to be allowed to be a painter. There isn't one of us here who understands anything about Art, including Barney, even if he does write novels. Why the devil,' he went on, suddenly attacking Timothy, 'couldn't you have let the boy try his hand? It's none of my business or was none until I was dragged into it like this, but no one is responsible for Tim's running off to Paris except his parents – and that's the truth!'

This was from every point of view a most unfortunate speech, and after it there was no hope at all of saving anybody's bacon. I had tried to advise Benjie at luncheon that he must go slow, placate the old boys, show them that he meant them no harm. But it was of course hopeless from the start. The very sight of their London clothes, the air they had not only of owning the Rockland (to which they were thoroughly welcome) but the whole of England, annoyed him, exasperated him. However, it might not have been so bad had it not been for his allusion to Art. Now none of them – not Timothy, nor Carey, nor Alfred, nor Horace – cared a damn about pictures, but they hated to be told that they knew nothing about them. Carey said to me long afterwards: 'It was the arrogance of it, you know – telling us we don't know a picture when we see one! Why, damn it, a picture is a picture, isn't it? A feller has eyes, hasn't he?'

When Benjie had finished Carey rapped out:

'Are you going to bring young Tim back to London or not?'

'Certainly not,' said Benjie.

Horace broke in:

'Oh, but, Benjie, I'm sure that Carey misunderstands you! What you mean to say is that you will do all you can in the circumstances—'

Benjie jumped to his feet.

'I mean nothing of the sort!' (He really loathed Horace.) 'I

consider it a piece of damnedest impertinence, all of you sitting
round here as though you were in judgement on me. I only came
to show you that I didn't care a damn for any of you! You can
all go to hell for all I care!'

Both Carey and Alfred, who were hot-tempered, jumped to
their feet and I thought for a moment that there would be a bit of
a fight. Alfred is tall and wiry; Carey, although his arms are so
short, has shoulders like a coal-heaver and-is strong for his sixty-
odd years. Benjie stood there, almost touching them, waiting for
anything that might come. Horace was nervously pushing at his
glasses in a way that he has when he is frightened (Rose used to
imitate this very well), Timothy threw out his stomach as a sort
of vanguard of protection.

But this was where I came in. I took Benjie by the arm and led
him out of the group.

'We're not in the Klondike,' I remarked (or something equally
cheap). 'Benjie doesn't see that he has any responsibility for
Tim's being in Paris and I don't see that he has either. Feeling no
responsibility, he doesn't see that he can do anything about it.
And that's the end of it.'

I could see them looking at us and classing us together. All
writers are queer to men like Carey and Timothy, and at that
time, with the Wilde trial still fresh in their minds, queerer than
queer. It was perhaps some feeling about the Wilde business that
made them the more intolerant of Benjie although they all knew
that Benjie was normal enough. The fact remains that the Wilde
trial made many people in England think, for a long time, that all
writers, painters, musicians, were freaks and dangerous freaks.
So there we were, the 'little gipsy', the rogue of the family, and
the loose-living, novel-writing eccentric. We were damned
together.

'That's not the end of it,' said Carey at last. 'We don't want to
be unfair, Benjie, but the fact is that we've had about enough of
you. For years now you've been upsetting everyone. Even as a
boy you were a family scandal. You've been mixed up in two
public brawls already and now there's this business. It is the
feeling of all of us that we wish to have nothing more to do with
you. And if you're a gentleman we trust you'll respect our feeling.'

Then it was I who figured in the scene. I lost my temper.
Never mind what I said. It's of no importance. But as I once told
Horace what I thought of him, so now I told Timothy, Carey,

and Alfred. I enjoyed myself for at least five minutes.

When, scant of breath (for I'm nearly seventy and my heart is not as good as it was), I had ended, it was Benjie who drew me away.

He smiled at them all. 'Goodbye, friends and relations,' he said. 'I shan't bother any of you again.' (He liked a little theatrically at times. It stirred his sense of colour.)

So, his arm through mine, we went out together.

VANESSA IN PRISON

HYSTERIA is the only word for the emotional state in which the Herries family now indulged. It is little exaggeration to say that as London once saw Jack the Ripper behind every area step, so now the Herries saw Benjie.

In 1898 and 1899, as afterwards in 1913 and 1914, London itself became hysterical. A mad craze for wealth and pleasure, an extravagance of display, a fantastic exhibitionism of non-morality raged everywhere. Diamonds and politics from Africa, an international plutocracy from the Holy Land, a pride and arrogance and self-confidence, a recklessness of materialism, the beginning of the breaking down of all barriers of caste and exclusive traditions: these things marked these years, the last defiant 'Ta-ra-ra-boom-de-ay' before the drums beat in the figures and the problems of the new world.

The Kaiser waved his theatrical arm in Potsdam, old Krüger sat in his kitchen reading his Bible, in London jumping signs for the first time illuminated the night sky and frightened the horses, *The Belle of New York* and *The Gay Lord Quex* shocked the religious, vast audiences swallowed gladly the wild tales of de Rougemont; Kipling frightened two hemispheres by threatening to die of pneumonia; the cry was everywhere, 'Let 'em all come!'

In the week of the Rockland meeting young Timothy caught pneumonia in Paris, nearly died of it and refused to see either his father or mother when they hurried over to him. But Violet saw Benjie. She could not deny that he was quiet and courteous. He was eager that she should see her son: it was Timothy who refused to allow her to enter his room. She returned to London like an insane woman. It was perhaps that she felt in her heart that she had herself been to blame in the first place. She was an old woman. She was a tiresome woman. Her passion for chatter had grown into a garrulousness that bored the world; her grievances were so many that she was herself confused by their number. She said that 'everything had begun' on an awful day when old Emily Newmark had prayed over her and Oscar Wilde had laughed at her. Violet – her daughter – married in 1897 a Colonel Caldecott. The house in Onslow Square was the stiller and emptier for old Violet's ceaseless chatter.

Bore though everyone found her, it became the accepted fact that Benjie had stolen her son from her and ruined her life. Respectable people like the Rockages and the Worcesters and the Alfred Herries were, in sober fact, terrified of what Benjie might do next. The Worcesters and the Alfreds now had young children – Cynthia had two girls, Alfred a boy and a girl; who knew but that Benjie might kidnap them and hold them for ransom?

He was seen in London and the whole Herries world shuddered. The situation was developed by the part that Adrian Cards played in it. He went everywhere – and he was now a man of importance in the London world, an Under-Secretary and a writer of witty articles ('Very malicious', Alfred and Horace thought him) – saying that Benjie Herries was the best of fellows and that his relations were ridiculous people. The Herries – the Worcesters, Alfred, Violet and old Timothy, the Rockages – felt that everywhere Adrian went they were mocked. They knew of course the reason of his championship of Benjie. It was, as they assured everyone, because of his passion for Vanessa. He went with Vanessa everywhere. She was, at last, after years of good behaviour, forgetting her position, her duty to Ellis. All that wildness that *must* be in her blood when you remember her grandmother and great-grandfather, was at last coming out. It was true that Ellis must be very trying. But could she not remember what she owed to her position? There, too, Benjie's influence could be traced. After the scene at the Rockland Club, Benjie was banished from all decent male society, and yet Vanessa was known to have said that all the Herries men, except Barney, had behaved like fools in that affair.

It was true, Vanessa was at last angry. For thirteen years she had behaved, both in public and in private, as she ought to behave. Now she was beginning not to care whether she behaved or no. For she was increasingly unhappy, frightened and indignant. She was moving swiftly, with a crazy husband at her side, no close woman friend except Lettice Marrable in the world, a sense of deep injustice burning within her, to a climax.

The two ladies, Miss Vera and Miss Winifred Trent, helped to precipitate it. 'What is reality? This mirror is real because I can touch the silver tracing on the woodwork of the frame, but I stand, looking into it, brushing my hair, and Ellis is suddenly standing behind me. Ellis is not real. Then is the mirror not real any longer? Ellis is listening behind the door? I open it and the carpet on the stairs is real, the ticking from the Chinese clock is real, but is there not the sudden sharp click of a closing door, the very crack of the finger of unreality? And through all this I am a woman who longs to love and be loved in return. I am nearing forty and my life is more than half gone. I have no children, no one — since my father died — to whom I might freely give my whole heart. Only Benjie and Rose — both disgraced, both exiles ... Is that, then, at last *my* reality, my hunger for love, my *hunger*, my *hunger* ... in a woman who is nearly forty surely *that* cannot be real? ... The Miss Trents have called. As they call now every day.'

'Dear Vanessa. We drove round to see how you and dear Ellis are. *How* is Ellis? Is his headache better?'

'Yes,' says Vanessa. 'Tonight we are going to *The Canary*. They say that it is a most amusing play.'

They look at her, inspect her with their large, soft and yet most resolute gaze. Everyone is watching her just as Ellis never ceases to watch her.

'If I don't get out of this I shall go mad, just as Ellis is ...'

Yet, with all this, she could not prevent herself from enjoying to the full any fun that came her way. She went out and about with Adrian, Barney, Cynthia. She had plenty of the great world, for the Duchess of Devonshire was less formidable with her than with any other woman in London, she watched Lady Londonderry's passion for power with all the more sympathy because she had never herself known the passion, and she helped Lady de Grey turn the Opera from a shabby squalling business into a splendid tiaraed pageant. Of all the grand ladies Lady Dorothy Nevill was to her taste the most delightful; she never tired of her daintiness, her humour, her anecdotes, her resolute vulgarities, and her eager curiosity about human nature. No one who came to Hill Street thought that there was anything but peace and plenty there. Only the Family knew and the Family didn't say. It was the business of the Family to inform the world in general that anything Herries was right. Vanessa was the Family public pride and of the utmost importance to them all.

Adrian was Lady Dorothy Nevill's especial pet, and he and Vanessa went together very often to the house in Charles Street.

'You're not in love with the young man, are you, my dear?' she asked.

'Not the least little bit,' said Vanessa, laughing.

'Not that it matters,' said Lady Dorothy, tossing her little head with its marvellous auburn wig, shaking her many beads and necklets and amulets. 'You're not like these modern girls with all their paintin' and powderin'. How men can kiss them *I* can't understand. What Dizzy if *he* were alive . . .'

Vanessa had friends everywhere, girls in shops, young men from the East End in whom Adrian was interested, writers famous like Henry James and Kipling, obscure like young Mr Smith who brought her the tattered manuscript of his novel to read or Mr Brown who had written an Epic on the Armada, actresses and actors like Irving, Ellen Terry, Forbes-Robertson and young men who walked on at the Lyceum. All were alike to her. She had no pose, no arrogances, no prejudices. So life whirled on the outside while within steadily the drama grew more intolerable.

Insanity is of all things the most pathetic, the most piteous, the most intangible. Everyone *within* the house knew that Ellis was insane. The servants nodded their heads together and watched him as children watch a strange and unaccountable animal. They developed a kind of pride in him. They marvelled that towards the outside world he was 'always all right'. Seriously, with an almost magisterial dignity, saying very little, listening to his guests with a sort of absorbed gravity (he was not listening; he was watching the figures *behind* the figures), he played his part. With Finch the butler, Mrs Martin the cook, the two men-servants, the housemaids, Lettice Marrable, he was the master of the house, betraying himself to them only by the twitching of his fingers, the way in which he would look over their shoulders, the sudden impatient 'Very well, very well' or a sharp 'Is that door closed? I can hear someone moving upstairs.'

The servants had for both their master and mistress a new and rather touching kindliness. They were very well treated, were paid excellent wages. Vanessa they adored. (Even Finch, who, after Miss Fortescue's departure, robbed right and left, drank the best wine and so had a real friendliness to his employers.) They were kind, did their duties, but they waited ... Something would happen soon ... They might all be murdered in their beds ... This made them feel privileged.

Vanessa herself wondered, often enough, whether there were not two Ellises. He was very often, when alone with her, so quiet and rational that it was almost as though the old friendly days were back again. When he slept beside her he moaned in his sleep and she drew him to her, stroked his forehead, felt as though she were protecting him against an evil demon. Yet, with this, she suffered an appalling fear of him that, do what she would, always increased. Perhaps one night he would kill her. She was always prepared for that. She would not, she thought, mind very greatly. Oddly, pity and fear went hand in hand together. She, too, waited for the next step ...

Then one day in June 1898 she received a letter saying that Will Leathwaite was dead.

She had just come in from a drive and stood in the hall, the letter in her hand. It was from Mrs Newson, who had looked after the cottage and Will for some years – a very decent woman. It simply said that Will had been ailing for some time past, hadn't cared for his food, complained of his legs. Mrs Newson had gone to Grange to see a friend and, returning about seven of the evening, found Will dying in his chair by the fire.

'I thought you'd like to know, my lady, that it was your father's name he kept saying before he died, over and over. I don't rightly think he was ever the same man after your father died. But he was tranquil up to the last, and a finer-looking man not to be found anywhere I always said. And no trouble at all, not to no one.'

She stood there, lost in the past. Will was gone: now everyone was gone. She remembered her father's description of Will winning the race at Keswick years and years ago, how he pounded up the hill to the Druids' Circle, and young Adam, himself only a boy, riding in front of Will's father on the family mare, yelled encouragement. And then how Will had come up to Adam one Christmas Day and asked if he did not want a servant. Will's love for Adam had been the best that one human being can find for another: its character was paternal, protective, selfless, and also gay, simple, unsycophantic, man to man, brother to brother. It had been perhaps the finest thing in her father's life, Vanessa thought, looking back. Was there not always antagonism in every sex relation? But in this perfect charity, honesty, and – above all, best of all – equality . . .

There was no Past when you experienced a love like this, for Adam and Will would go on for ever, for ever racing up the Keswick hill, for ever meeting, the snow sun-glittering at their feet, the blue smoke rising in the silent air, for ever one waiting the other's return, for ever that exchange of glance, sure and trustful, for ever that touch of hand on hand . . . In all this changing, bewildering, unstable world the one sure and certain proof that there is something eternal in man's soul; that, once in a lifetime, one touches, deep in the heart, evidence of immortality.

The letter fell to the ground: she heard the Chinese lacquered clock strike the half-hour with its sententious solemn purr. The clock's voice resembled Horace's. Will's death increased her loneliness. She had not seen him for so long a time and yet he had been behind her – they two together thinking of Adam.

She picked up the letter and saw that Ellis was standing near to her and looking at her. Why did she never hear his step these days?

'Oh, Ellis!' she cried. 'Will Leathwaite is dead!'

Ridiculously, tears stole down her cheek behind her veil.

'Will Leathwaite?' he asked.

'Yes. Father's servant. You've seen him – a big fair-haired man with blue eyes.'

She had trained herself never to mention anything in connexion with Cumberland, but at this moment she was thinking of Will, not of Ellis.

He nodded, looked at her without speaking, and walked upstairs.

A few days later a very unaccountable thing occurred. He came to her in her room where she was reading, and timidly, as though he were asking a favour, said:

'Vanessa, let us go to Cumberland for a week – to your cottage on Derwentwater.'

He stood in front of her, very tall, very pale and rigid, as though she had ordered him in front of her to be scolded.

'To Cumberland?' She was so deeply astonished that she dropped the book. 'But, Ellis, you hate Cumberland!'

'No – who told you that?'

'Nobody, of course. Only yourself.'

'When have I said that I hated Cumberland?'

'Not *hated*. But disliked it. The rain – and you don't like the North—'

'Who told you that I hated Cumberland?'

She got up and walked away. His eyes frightened her. He bent down and picked up the book. 'Why do they bind books in green? It is such an ugly colour.' Then, in rather a shrill voice: 'I don't hate Cumberland. Of course not. It will be very agreeable. I need a holiday.'

She came back to him, smiling.

'That *is* good of you, Ellis. Of course I shall love to go.'

And they went. On the evening of her arrival she could not believe that she was there. In the living-room there were all her father's things just as they had always been. His books – the little blue volumes of the *Iliad* and the *Odyssey* – the tattered shilling parts of *Pickwick,* the *English Poets, Sir Charles Grandison* and *Tristram Shandy,* Barney's novels, *Dandy Grimmett* and the rest.

And all the old beloved things, part of her very life: the two cornucopias, Zobel's sand picture, 'The Saddle Horse', the old watercolour, 'The Lady of the House', the Baxter print 'Dippers and Nest', the Peepshow of the Central Hall at the Great Exhibition, above all, the spinet from Uldale with the roses painted on the lid, and the music box with the King in his amber coat and the Queen in her green dress.

As she stood at the window, with all these beloved things around her, she held her hands tightly together lest she should show her emotion. The last evening light touched the hills: Skiddaw's twin peaks lay like islands in a clear cold silver above bars of fleecy cloud, and the ridge of Blencathra was black against the whitewashed sky. Between the trees the water of the Lake, struck by the trail of a tiny boat, fell into darker and darker shadow. The wood pigeons murmured from the wood. Some ghostly sheep wandered, just as they had so often done, slowly up the road. This was her home. How foolish she had been to be so long an exile from it! And as she watched, the years fell away from her. Twenty of those years were suddenly gone. She raised her arms above her head and, smiling, saw herself, another very different woman, moving slowly up the staircase of some grand house, hearing the names called, the distant band – Lady Herries, a middle-aged woman with a dull, stiff husband, still beautiful but soon not to be very interesting, to be nothing more than a London hostess who knew everyone, whom everyone knew, who mattered to no one, to whom no one mattered. Her body seemed to her young again; she would hear her father call her name, Benjie would be riding over from Uldale, all life was before her ... All life before her? She shivered. It was behind her. She was in prison with Ellis.

But in the following days she could not keep down her joy. She had come home. What is it that makes in a certain square of ground every blade of grass, every hovering uncertain cloud, every note in a bird's song one's own? She had heard often enough, in London, scorn of this country, its rain, its ponds, its little hills, old Wordsworth and his daffodils, Coleridge and his opium, reading parties from Cambridge. She had had often to hold herself back from a ridiculous personal protest as though the scoffers had insulted herself. She had wondered why Lettice and Timothy and Violet, who had lived so long here, had had no personal feeling. She had heard Timothy thank his stars that he had done with the 'beastly climate'. She had asked Lettice whether she did not want to go back. 'Go back? All the unhappiest part of my life was there. I never want to see the place again.' She knew for herself that if her childhood had been one long misery still she must return ... and return ...

There was something deeper here, some inheritance that was mingled with all the truest, most importunate things in life. Her love of this place was her key to the connexion between the two worlds. 'Only connect ...' 'Only connect ...' The whole problem for man and for woman was here. They move as in a game of blind-man's-buff from figure to figure turned, twisted, bewildered. Guess rightly and the light floods in ...

As she stood at the window, the world beyond it sinking into darkness, she knew with sudden certainty that to find the key of connexion was man's only business on this earth. All else was folly beside it. And the key for her, as it had been for her father, her grandmother, her great-grandfather, was here – like a pot of gold hidden in this square of ground. For Benjie too perhaps? She had, in that instant, one of those illuminating flashes of revelation that once and again are granted the Hoodman Blind. God the Invisible and man exploring; she smiled as she thought of the ironies of Barney or Benjie or Rose if she told them of her naïveté.

'I looked out of the window as the world grew dark and knew that there are two worlds, that they are linked together, and that it is God's purpose that we should find the connexion. All beauty is for that. I must have courage, honesty, and I must rid myself of my Blind Man's Hood, my egotism ... I must test life by no experience but my own. For you, dear Barney, God is an exploded superstition. That is *your* experience. You are right to hold honestly by it. But for myself, standing at this window, I have another guide. Credit my honesty and I will credit yours. Let us be tolerant to one another.'

As she turned back into the lighted room she had a moment of almost blinding happiness. Her troubles faded. What matter if she were close on forty, if she loved Benjie whom she could never be with any more? What was her fear of Ellis? All the values of life were for a moment altered. She had courage for anything.

She needed that courage in the days that followed.

They were sitting quietly after supper, she reading a novel, he a newspaper. He said, still looking at his paper:

'Vanessa, when we return to London, I shall wish you to see a doctor.'

'A doctor?'

'Yes,' he said, leaning forward and laying his long bony hands on his knees. 'I have been long coming to the conclusion that you are not well. I came up here with you that I might observe you a little. In London it is so difficult. So many people to interfere. We do not see enough of one another. My suspicions – my suspicions,' he repeated the word softly, 'are quite confirmed.'

'What suspicions? I am perfectly well, Ellis dear.'

'Ah, so you think,' he went on quietly. 'That, I fear, is part of the disease.'

'Disease?' she broke in. Her heart was hammering. She looked quickly about among the old familiar things in the room to reassure herself. 'Why, I was never better in my life, and especially since I have come up here.'

'There, there. You mustn't get excited. Excitement is bad for both of us. I have said nothing until I could be certain. I did not wish to alarm you. I have myself for some while been none too well, but now I am quite recovered – quite recovered,' he repeated, nodding his head. 'But now that I have mentioned it, you can speak to me without fear. There is no one listening. At least I think not.' He got up, went very cautiously to the door and listened, then to the windows, pulling back the curtains for a moment. He walked on tiptoe.

'Listen, Vanessa. For a long time we have not been happy. Oh,

I know that it has not been altogether your fault. For a time I was accompanied everywhere by someone. Very unagreeable and difficult to account for, but now that he is gone again – and I took care not to bother you with his intrusion – I realize that your care of me during these last years, in addition to all your social duties, has been too much for your strength, your mental strength. And then it is hereditary, no doubt. Your grandmother ... You will need great quiet in the future, and an able doctor – perhaps retirement into the country to some soothing place ...'
He stopped to listen. 'You heard nothing? The city is so noisy and restless. Always something moving.'

She picked up her book. Her hands were trembling, but she answered quietly:

'There is nothing the matter with me, Ellis.' Forcing herself, she looked up at him and smiled. 'We have both been tired a little by London. That is why this week in the country was such a good idea.'

He bent down, patted her shoulder, kissed her forehead.

'There, there. You must not disturb yourself. I will see to it.' He straightened himself and tiptoed to the door. He listened, looking anxiously into the wall. 'And now I think I will go up to bed. Don't worry. Worry is bad for you. Quiet, quiet. We must all have quiet.'

She lay awake for hours that night, wondering what she should do. In the large bed that they shared he slept the peace of the insane just. He breathed like a child, never stirring. She beat herself into common sense. Panic was so near that, all the night through, she kept it off only by using her utmost strength. She could run away, leave him never to return, but that would mean defeat and cowardice. If she left him it would not be long before he would be put somewhere, in some awful, silent house, faced with dark silent windows, inhabited by poor sufferers like himself. She must not go until the last test of endurance had been reached. But this new twist of his brain was so awful that she refused to face it. If he, mad though he was, thought *her* mad, might not others also think so? Had the strain of these last years been too much for her? Had there been something hysterically unreal in her manner? In the darkness of the room she saw the Misses Trent, in their large black hats, their trailing gowns, standing close together watching her. 'Yes,' she heard one of them say to Ellis. 'You are right. Vanessa has been behaving very strangely ...' But then her common sense returned. She had never been more sane in her life than she was now. She could deal with this as she had dealt with everything that preceded it. She turned on her side and slept.

Then, after one happy hour, she realized to the full the danger that she was in. That day, the seventeenth of June 1898, was stamped, in its tiniest detail, on her memory for ever.

In the afternoon she drove to Rosthwaite. A lady, Mrs Merriman, who lived in Borrowdale, gave a party for some of the children from Grange, Rosthwaite, Seatoller, and invited Vanessa. They all knew her here. She was one of themselves and had it not been for her silent, pale-faced, alarming husband they would have asked her everywhere. They hoped, now that she had returned to her real home, that she would often come and, although they did not say so, without her husband. They knew that she was a grand lady in London, but Cumberland people take things naturally. Everyone is on a level, and if anyone behaves grandly they look foolish and are to be pitied. Vanessa of course did not behave grandly at all. No one could be more simple, and on this afternoon in Rosthwaite she sat on the floor and allowed the babies to climb all over her, played musical chairs with breathless excitement and then, to the cracked piano, sang songs for them and afterwards played for them to dance. Mrs Merriman, who was thin and pale, had an invalid husband and more children than she wanted, had been inclined to be jealous at first of this woman with her lovely clothes, her beauty, her life in the great world. 'She has everything. How unfair it is.' But soon she was not sure that she had everything. There was something, she told her husband, pathetic about Vanessa. 'She played with the children as though she could not bear to let them go. She told me that coming back here was heaven to her. She went to the window and looked out at the hill like a starving woman. "Well, why don't you come here more often, Lady Herries?" I asked her. "After all, it's your home. We are all delighted to have you here." "Oh, how I wish I could!" she said. I wouldn't wonder if she's not happy with her husband. I'm sure I shouldn't be. He really frightened me, he was so stiff and solemn. I never saw a woman carry herself so beautifully, and such lovely dark hair as she's got and such a kind expression. But I'm certain she's not happy. Lovely dark hair with not a grey thread, although she can't be far off forty. No airs at all, although the Prince and Princess often come to her house, I believe. You know, Philip, I felt like a mother to her. There's something makes me feel that she needs someone to love her. Oh, I know you'll call me romantic. But I can't help it. She's the most beautiful woman I've ever seen and simply sweet with the children. You could tell her anything, I'm sure.'

When the children were having tea Vanessa slipped out, crossed the road, the bridge, and looked at the solid, comfortable little Victorian house with its sloping lawn, its trim garden, the house built on the very spot where her great-grandfather had once lived. She stood there, listening to the running water, feeling the afternoon sun on her face, wondering where that old wild man now was. He, too, had stood here, looking at the hills, feeling the sun on his face, waiting for his wife to return. It had been wild then: the bare rock, the tumbling water, the valley beyond uncouth and deserted. The sun had shone on his purple coat and silver braid. She felt intimately close to him. Once again time was not. Was it fancy that a hand rested on her shoulder, comforting her? Of course it was fancy.

Here was the trim garden and on the lawn two garden chairs, a small mowing machine, a watering pot. An old bent gardener was clipping the roses. Two bicyclists passed down the road, and then a scarlet coach filled with tourists. But, after the coach was gone, silence tumbled back again, the hills, clear and defined in the sunshine, cut the cloudless sky. The gardener pushed the mowing machine, and the soft dreamy whirr filled the world with summer peace. As she turned to the bridge she whispered 'Goodbye'. Was it fancy that a figure in a purple coat watched her go?

'And now, children, we must all thank Lady Herries for helping to make our afternoon such a pleasant one.'

They all thanked her in shrill treble voices. They ran into the road to see the splendid lady in her rose-coloured coat get into the carriage, and one baby cried because it was not allowed to go with her. She kissed Mrs Merriman.

'Come back soon,' Mrs Merriman said.

'Yes, I will,' said Vanessa.

Ellis locked the door. Vanessa looked up from her book at the sound of the turning key. Why had he locked the door? She had thought that he had gone up to bed. The little clock with the painted moon and stars (as a baby she had been lifted again and again to count them) pointed to quarter to eleven.

Mrs Newson and her husband slept on the far side of the

cottage. They would hear nothing. She continued to read. This was a very clever book of short stores; it was written by a woman who must be simply too clever to do any of the ordinary things that ordinary women did. The stories were in the manner that was becoming popular; they had no beginning. One story called 'The Haystack' started with this sentence: 'Oh, but dripping is so cheap ... and it's really not bad when you get used to it.' Nor had they any conclusion. 'The Haystack' ended: 'Yes, but half a crown – that was altogether too much for such a second-rate article.' They were depressing stories. London in the rain, hateful boarding houses, shabby men making love, the British Museum Reading Room, someone wringing a chicken's neck outside the kitchen window. They were very feminist. Men figured as poor creatures, mean, faithless, and greedy. But oh! what cleverness! What observation! Nothing escaped this lady's eye; the yellow stain on the tablecloth where mustard had been spilled at the last meal, the tear in the cheap umbrella, the shabby feather in the outworn hat ... Vanessa knew, as she read, that one thing that was the matter with herself was that she was not clever at all. Neither clever nor witty. She could not remember that she had ever said a brilliant thing in her life. Rose, Cynthia, Lady Dorothy Nevill – what clever things they were always saying! 'I'm a bore,' thought Vanessa. 'The woman who wrote this book wouldn't endure me for five minutes.'

But why had he locked the door? He came and sat down opposite to her. The clothes that he was wearing, a dark brown cloth intended for the country, did not suit him nor did they look like country clothes. Wherever he might be, he wore always the deep sharp collar that belonged to the Gladstone caricatures, and that did not suit him either because his throat was so thin, his Adam's apple so large. She noticed tonight for the first time that the back of his pale long hand was freckled.

He sighed, then said:

'It was not kind of you, Vanessa, to have me watched all this afternoon.'

She looked at him steadily, determining that tonight at least she would not be afraid. They were returning to London tomorrow and then something must be done. For her own safety, for his, something must be done.

'What *do* you mean, Ellis? No one was watching you.'

'Ah, come, Vanessa. Why lie to me? I don't blame you, not at all. I know that you are not yourself. But it is wrong of you to

embarrass me. And such an unpleasant man. I stood here for half
an hour while he watched me outside the window. He never
moved until I came myself to the window; then he vanished into
that green bush beyond the flowerbed. Then when I returned to
the fireplace, pretending not to notice him, he came to the
window again. A long thin man in a green coat. I fancied that I
had seen him before.'

She got up and came over to him, seeming very tall in that
small room.

'Ellis dear, let's go to bed. You know that I haven't had you
watched. Why should I? Now come to bed.'

'Oh, I'm not vexed, my dear. Not at all vexed. I said to myself,
"If he hadn't got that green coat I really should not mind. He
could watch me as long as he pleased. But I dislike green as a
colour and his eyes were most unpleasant." When I went out into
the garden he was gone. Then he came back again. He pressed his
face to the windowpane. All the same you would dislike it if I
had *you* watched, you know. You wouldn't like it at all. In fact,
lately, I've had it in my mind because, being as you are, it isn't
safe for you to go about alone.' He sighed, deeply, deeply as
though in dreadful distress. 'The truth is that we are neither of
us well. Life has been a failure for both of us. It is better for us to
end it.'

She looked about the room to reassure herself with the old
homely comfort of the familiar things – the spinet, the books, the
music box, the pictures. She walked to the window, then from
the far side of the table said: 'Ellis, give me that key. You have
locked the door. Give me that key.'

'No, my dear, certainly not. Because you had me watched this
afternoon is reason enough. We have not been happy for a long
time; indeed I have never been happy. I cannot remember a time
when I was happy. Nor are you happy. So here, very quietly,
while there is no one about, is a very good opportunity to finish
all this tiresome business. I feel it my duty. I have hesitated for
some time, but now my duty is quite clear.'

He fumbled in his inside coat pocket and brought from it a
large kitchen knife with a thick brown handle.

'You will feel nothing,' he said smiling. 'It will be no more
than a cut on the finger. And then I will follow you. I can't
possibly express to you how agreeable it will be to be tired no
longer, to have no more headaches. For both of us it will be a
relief, I am sure—'

He held the knife in one hand and stroked its edge, very gently, with the other. The little clock struck eleven.

'This is the silliest scene,' she thought, 'I have ever been in. So unreal that all the things in the room have become unreal too.' She thought also: 'But this ends everything. At last, thank Heaven, this ends everything.'

'I have thought it all out,' he said. 'Sit in that chair, Vanessa. Close your eyes. You'll feel nothing at all.' He was very close to her now, but she did not move.

'Ellis, give me the key. Put down that knife. Go to bed. You are behaving like a baby. Put that knife down on that table.'

'Perhaps I will,' he said, looking at her very cunningly. 'Perhaps I will not. But it won't matter, because nothing you can say will alter my decision. And how absurd of you not to do as I wish! But you have never done as I wish. A pale-green mushroom hat that you are always wearing. You know that I dislike it. And yet day after day you persist in wearing it.' He murmured: 'A mass of shaded green wings. A mass of shaded green wings. That's what Mr Playfair said.'

He threw out his hand and caught her arm.

'Come to the chair, Vanessa. Come to the chair. That is the easiest way.'

He looked up at her like a beseeching child. His eyes were filled with tears.

'Dear Vanessa. How I love you! How unhappy we are!'

His arm encircled her body ... His head fell forward and rested on her breast. The knife tumbled to the floor. She led him back to the armchair, he submitting like a child.

'Please, Ellis, give me the key,' she said.

Tears pouring down his cheeks, he fumbled for the key, found it, gave it her.

'Another time,' he sobbed. 'Perhaps another time will be better. I meant it for the best ...' Then, as she moved away, he caught her hand: 'Don't leave me. Don't leave me. I am afraid of being alone.'

She knelt down beside him, comforting him as she had done so often before. But, in her heart, she knew that this was for the last time.

ESCAPE INTO DANGER

THEY had to leave very early next morning to catch the train for London. Vanessa, who had not slept at all, stood at the lawn's edge and found that the world was rolling in rosy smoke. It would be a hot day. The smoke lifted from the Lake even as she looked, as someone lifts the covers from a bed: the Lake shivered, trembling, at the touch of the sun that itself also dared as yet only to breathe upon the water, but to breathe like God, strongly, confidently (in spite of so very many disappointments) and with the very tenderness of love. The colour flew upwards from the hills and broke into petals of rose against the sky that would soon be drenched with sun. All the hills waited – Cat Bells, Robinson, Gable, Scafell, the Langdales, Helvellyn, Blencathra – they all waited for their illumination high, high above these madmen who today are one thing and tomorrow another.

This would be a horrible journey – and so it was.

'Perhaps,' said Ellis, when they were halfway down England, 'you would like my *Times*?' He spoke to a stout fellow in a suit of loud checks who had been, ever since Penrith, staggered by Vanessa's beauty. For she wore a small toque, a spotted veil, her rose-coloured coat; behind the veil, the man in the checks was, with beating heart, assured, breathed the only woman for whom all his life he had been searching. He had money, he had rude health, a kind wife and a mistress in Carlisle, but he had not, he had never, never had, the Beauty for which he longed.

'Thank you, sir. Very kind of you. Hooley's bankruptcy means the end of the cycling boom. Mark my word.'

The fields rushed up to the window and all the houses bobbed and curtsied in the sun. Vanessa sat there, her clever book of stories on her lap, and fought down her terrors. She had not slept, and Ellis, who now looked like a Prime Minister, a director of a railway company or the real author of *Robert Elsmere*, had last night wished to cut her throat with a knife with a brown handle. He had, as usual, wept leaning against her breast. He would never weep against her breast again, for her duty there was ended. Once she had loved him as a mother her child, then she had pitied him because he was sick, now she was a weary, angry woman resolved on escape. Next week they were giving a Ball in

Hill Street, a very grand Ball indeed, and that should be the last. That should be the end, for her, of Ellis, Hill Street, London ... One need not, one must not, be stuck so deep in a quagmire of ludicrous danger ... ludicrous kitchen knives, Ellis' tears and tiptoe to the window, Ellis' man in the green bush beyond the window, Ellis' moaning in his sleep, poor Ellis ... 'To find some life that is neither false nor dangerous ...' Letting her head fall, she slept at last, dreaming that the babies in Rosthwaite pulled her with eager hands up the hill to the water falling with such cool certainty down the face of the rock. Standing waiting for her there was Benjie.

At Hill Street was a letter for her from Rose. Next day she went to see her. Rose was living in two very small dingy rooms off Baker Street. She met Vanessa defiantly, as though to say: 'I know you will find me changed and you can say, if you wish, that you never want to see me again.' Yes, Rose *was* changed. Her cheeks were painted, the puffed shoulders of her dress absurdly exaggerated, her waist too small for any comfort, her eyes un-happy. Her room was untidy, clothes thrown about, a dusty piano open with a bright green hat ornamented with a bird of paradise plume flung down on the keys.

A strange thought struck Vanessa. 'This is the world into which, very shortly, I may be moving.'

But oh! it was wonderful to be loved again! She could not believe that she had endured all these years without it! She was like a woman starved as, sitting with Rose on the shabby hole-and-corner sofa, she heard what Rose chose to tell her (a sort of fairy story in which every gentleman was kind, money sprang from the carpet, and life was one long victory).

At the end of it Vanessa said:

'I'm glad you're so happy.'

And Rose said:

'Life's hell. Don't believe a word I've said, Vanessa.'

They discovered very quickly that life just then was bad for both of them. Vanessa did not tell Rose that Ellis had wanted to cut her throat with a kitchen knife, but she *did* give her to under-stand that the end of Hill Street had arrived at last and that Rose must be prepared ...

There came in upon them without a word of warning the most dreadful man – Major Featherstone-Haigh. The Major was short, purple in the face, smelt of brandy, called Vanessa 'My dear' and looked at Rose as though he owned her – which, at that moment, he probably did.

Vanessa went back to Hill Street. She went back to Hill Street to find Miss Vera and Miss Winifred Trent waiting for her in the drawing-room. Standing in her room, before she went down to them, she knew a moment of fear worse than any that had preceded it. She stood, motionless, her head up as though she were listening. Then with quick nervous movements she took off her white soft-feathered toque, her veil, her long gloves. She listened again. It was a hot thundery day and her windows were wide open. A hansom clop-clopped down Hill Street; she looked out and saw a man crying his flowers which blazed in a cloud of colour on his barrow – roses, carnations, lilies. Below the windows of the houses the window boxes shone with bright blue, with scarlet, with flaunting yellows. At the end of the street was a barrel-organ that played again and again an old air from *Trovatore*. Light, colour, music: but inside the house it was cold and dark as it always was. Her dress was white and black, the shoulders very puffed, the waist very small. She looked at herself in the long silver mirror. She seemed to herself hideous, her pale face beneath the dark hair, her long white neck, her full bosom; her height was ridiculous. She hated the way that she carried her head, stiff, pompous, 'as though I were for ever at the top of the stairs, receiving. Thank Heaven, it is ended. In a week or two, in one way or another, it will be over. I will never receive anyone any more. Death, perhaps.' It did not seem impossible, for there was Ellis loose about the house, and the house so still, and those two old women in their long trailing black waiting for her in the drawing-room.

At that moment, looking at herself in the mirror with disgust as at someone for whom everything was over, someone moving in a crazy house cold as the grave, a lunatic its master, she had almost, for the first time, lost all her courage. Rose lost, Benjie somewhere wandering, no one else . . . Then also she remembered her grandmother, that small indomitable woman with the white hair and ivory cane who lived to be a hundred, who had faced everything because she knew how to be indifferent to life whilst adoring it. 'She did – so can I.' She went down to the two ladies.

'Ah, dear Vanessa, how nice to see you again. And how are you?'

'Very well indeed, thank you.'

They both kissed her, and as they did so it was as though they were graciously inviting her to stay for an hour or so in her own drawing-room. They were extremely quiet. When they moved, their long black dresses scarcely rustled. They appeared also to have a secret understanding. They had moreover the power to make you feel that you could not take a step without their permission. Finch brought in the tea, and it seemed likely for a moment that Miss Vera Trent would instruct him where the table should be placed. Their voices were what Barney once called 'boneless'.

'We have already seen dear Ellis,' said Miss Winifred.

'He says that his holiday has done him good,' said Miss Vera.

'But we advised him to be careful during these hot weeks in London,' said Miss Winifred. 'The worst thing possible for his headaches. How is he, do you think, Vanessa?'

'Oh, very well,' said Vanessa brightly. 'We had such lovely weather in Cumberland.'

'You did?' said Miss Winifred. 'Now isn't that delightful? Cumberland when it is *fine* must be indeed charming.'

'And for you – to return to your old home again – how delightful!' said Miss Vera. 'There is no place quite the same as one's childhood's home.'

'And what have you been doing?' asked Vanessa. 'What are the family scandals? Whom have you seen?'

'Oh, we lead quiet lives, you know,' said Miss Winifred. 'We had tea one day with dear Cynthia. May and her girls were in London for a week. And poor Violet – not at all well, I fear, and now that both children—' She broke off. The Misses Trent were nothing if not tactful, and, after all, Vanessa most strangely defended that horrible man who had lured poor Violet's boy—

They both looked at her together, a strange look, a look full of some knowledge that at present they would keep to themselves. Miss Vera said, smiling, raising her hand on which her diamond rings sparkled, to help herself to a little cake: 'And what is this that Ellis tells us, dear Vanessa, about your own health? Rather a sad report, I fear.'

'My health?' said Vanessa. 'Why, it was never better.'

Miss Vera shook her finger. 'Now that is not at all what dear Ellis tells us. He insists that you see a doctor. Altogether over-fatigued, he says, and I am sure that I don't wonder with all that you do. And then this great Ball next week to which Winifred

and I are so greatly looking forward. But after it Ellis thinks that
a quiet time in the country—'

Her anger rose. She was suddenly aware that she hated these
two women as she had never hated anyone in her life before. 'I
think that I am the best judge of that,' she said quietly. 'I am
perfectly well.'

The door opened and she saw that Ellis had come in. The two
ladies rose and moved to either side of him. He greeted them with
a grave smile.

Surely, they must be aware of his strangeness, his eyes are
never still nor do they see the things at which they are looking,
and he walks now like a cat with padded feet . . .

All three looked at her. Then Ellis said:

'A little tea, my dear. Thundery weather.'

They all sat down.

One more move needed to complete the preparation. Next day
meeting Barney at Cynthia's he put in her hand a note. It was
from Benjie.

18 HALF MOON STREET.

DEAR VANESSA – I am here and shall be so for some weeks.
If I may not see you I may at least be happy because I am
near you.

B.

The last Ball ever given by Vanessa and Ellis in Hill Street was
a brilliant success. Vanessa, in a dress of white satin and with
diamonds in her hair, stood at the top of the stairs. She saw, as
though it were a mechanical toy wound up for her amusement,
the figures appear around the bend of the staircase – one two, one
two, one two – the ladies' heads erect, bosoms thrust forward,
trains draped over their arms, jewels glittering, a scent of powder
and roses and the heat of the London June evening . . .

'Lord and Lady Danesborough.'

'Sir James and Lady Ford.'

'Mr Forbes-Robertson.'

'Lady Carteris.'

'Lord John Beaminster.'

'Lady Adela Beaminster.'

'Miss Rachel Beaminster.'

'Mr Timothy Herries.'

'Miss Vera Trent.'
'Miss Winifred Trent.'
'Lady Dorothy Nevill.'
'Sir Henry and Miss Nevill and Lady Wade.'
'Madame Sarah Bernhardt.'
'Mr and Mrs Peile Worcester.'
'Lord Clancarty.'
'Mr Henry James.'
'Mr Edmund Gosse.'
'Mr and Mrs Colvin.'
'Lady Sarah Meux.'
'Monsieur Felix Brun.'
'Mr Yale Ross.'
'Lady Carloes.'
'Mr Robert Hichens.'
'Sir Roderick Seddon.'
'The Honourable Lionel Talmache.'
'Mr Adrian Cards.'
'Lady Lettice Forjambe.'
'Mr and Mrs Humphrey Ward.'
'Sir Peter and Lady Thornby.'
'Miss Mary Thornby.'
'Lady Eustace.'
'Miss Pamela Eustace.'
'Mrs Clifford.'
'Mr Barnabas Newmark.'
'Lord and Lady Rockage.'
'Miss Veasey.'
'Mr and Mrs Ormerod.'
'Lady Cynthia Lamb.'
'Mr and Mrs Frederick Macmillan.'
'Mrs Grant Bingham.'
'Mr Herbert Beerbohm Tree.'
'Mr Pendle Smith.'
'Mrs Langtry.'
'General Fortescue and Mrs Fortescue.'
'Mr Max Beerbohm.'
'Miss Carlyon.'
'Mr Ross.'
'Mr Tumer.'
'Mrs Fortescue Brown.'
'Mr Brookfield.'

'Mrs Craigie.'

'Mr Charles Wyndham.'

She deflected: 'It must be midnight. The actors and acresses are arriving.' She glanced back and saw that the long room was now filled to overflowing with dancers.

'Mr Bertrand.'

'Lady Garvice.'

'Miss Garvice.'

'Mr Galleon.'

'Lady Torring.'

'Mr and Mrs Frost.'

Barney, a little later, found himself in a corner with Bertrand the novelist.

'I suppose,' Bertrand said, 'you think I'm here to pour scorn on my fellow-creatures.'

'No, not especially,' said Barney. 'Any more than anyone else.'

'As a matter of fact,' said Bertrand, 'I love my fellow-creatures. I think we are all absurd, of course. And tonight I feel something sinister in the air.'

'Sinister?' asked Barney.

'Yes. I can't explain it except that I think London *is* sinister just now. Have you read Hichens' *Londoners*, or don't you read your fellow-novelists?'

'Not very often,' said Barney.

'Neither do I. But Hichens' book is clever madness – too long, but not really exaggerated. We are all mad.' He looked around him. 'Do you see that little man over there talking to Mrs Langtry?' He pointed to a small, very dapper gentleman, with bright observant eyes, who was talking with exceeding animation and a good deal of un-English gesticulation.

'That is Felix Brun. He lives only for the social history of Europe. He knows all the moves, the undercurrents, the plots, and plotters. Whenever he appears in London, you can be sure that there is a change coming. I met him a week or two ago at the Rede Gallery where he had come to look at Ross' portrait of the old Duchess of Wrexe – a very fine painting, by the way. He was very interesting. Like myself, he has no illusions.'

'You must have been a fine gloomy pair,' Barney said, laughing.

'Oh, not gloomy at all. Why be gloomy? It has been dull, this long sleepy prosperity. Brun agrees with me that things are breaking up.'

'What things?' Barney asked. He was looking at Ellis, who,

standing near to him, alone, had in his eyes so fixed a gaze, and in his pose so odd an air of waiting for someone, that he interested Barney.

'What things?' repeated Bertrand. 'Oh, all this. The conviction that we are the finest people in the world, superior to everything and everybody. The conviction that we rule the world and it is right that we should. Brun says that England's day as ruler of the world is over.'

'That must give you great satisfaction.'

'No – why should it? We do some things very well, but we have no taste, no subtlety, no sensitiveness to what other people are feeling, and our Imperial ambitions are revolting. I am going to live in France.'

Beaminster brought up to Vanessa a very beautiful girl.

'This is my niece Rachel, Vanessa. You were at her Ball the other day. She has not been out long enough yet to be blasé. She thinks you are the most wonderful woman in London.'

Vanessa looked with great pleasure at the girl in front of her. Miss Rachel Beaminster, granddaughter of the old Duchess of Wrexe. Vanessa had gone in May to a very grand Ball in Portland Place given for this child's coming-out. The girl was tall and thin, with dark hair and beautiful eyes, a little gauche and a little foreign. Her mother had been a Russian actress, and the old Duchess had, Vanessa was told, never forgiven her son for his *mésalliance*. But the importance of this meeting for Vanessa was that this girl might be herself – herself twenty years ago.

'I do hope you're enjoying yourself.'

'Oh yes, Lady Herries. It's a lovely Ball.'

'Plenty of partners?'

The girl smiled and became at once transformed; her happiness took away that little awkwardness and you felt pleasure, excitement, anticipation beat through her body.

'Plenty. I could dance all night.'

'I have known your uncle a long time. He is one of my oldest friends.'

'Oh, Uncle John? Isn't he a dear? I should have been terrified of everything had it not been for him.'

Yes, and she might be, Vanessa thought, with that awful old grandmother and stiff, forbidding Adela for an aunt and prim, pompous Richard for an uncle!

'It's so wonderful,' Rachel said, 'seeing Sarah Bernhardt. Uncle John is taking me next week to one of her plays at the Lyric. She looks kinder, more simple—'

'Would you like to meet her?' asked Vanessa.

'Oh yes! Can I? You see, my mother was an actress—'

'Come along and I'll introduce you. Tell her about your mother.'

They went across to where the great woman was listening, with eyes half closed, to M. Brun.

Vanessa presented the girl and was pleased to see with what ease and simplicity the child behaved. She turned and, for a moment before she was caught again, watched the room, swinging under the lights to the rhythm and symmetry of the waltzes. The music softly beat into her ears: 'The last time – the last time – the last time . . .'

What if there should be a scene? What if Ellis should commit some awful indiscretion? He was looking strange tonight. Surely others had noticed it besides herself. She talked, she laughed, she walked with uplifted head. Many said afterwards that she had never seemed more splendid than at this Ball, more easily the mistress of her world. 'And for her age still such a beauty,' said little Brun. 'What is she? Nearly forty? She must be.' He remarked to Bertrand: 'An interesting family, these Herries. So typically English and yet with a strain of something—'

'And we'll have fires out of the Grand Duke's Wood,' quoted Bertrand.

'Fires out of the wood?'

'Yes – a quotation from one of the other Herries – the mad ones, you know.'

'Ah, there have been mad ones then?'

'Oh, plenty. There are several scandals at the moment.'

'Ah,' said Brun. 'That's what makes you English so interesting. You are madder than any other people and yet so conventional. Impossible to understand, you turn and rend your madmen while they are alive and yet are so proud of them after they are dead.'

'That,' said Bertrand, who was suddenly bored with little Brun (he tired of people very quickly – of himself also), 'is why we are so conceited. We have so much common sense that when our poets have written their poetry we kill them. Except Wordsworth and Tennyson of course. But they were mad very young and got over it.'

After that Bertrand sat by himself for a while and collected notes for his notebook. He watched Madame Bernhardt act and Henry James unravel sentences of benignity from his beard, Mrs

Langtry raise her lovely arm, bishops grow genial, politicians indiscreet and all the most beautiful girls in London manoeuvre for husbands. Then he noticed his host, who listened at first with grave intensity to a stout lady in a bright green dress, and then, when she left him, stood as though bewildered, staring about him.

'By Jove, the old boy's trembling from head to foot,' he said to himself. 'He'll have a fit or something.'

Ellis backed to the wall. He straightened himself against it. Then Bertrand saw that he felt the wall with the palm of his hand; he moved his hand up and down against the surface, and in his eyes was the most unhappy gaze that Bertrand had ever seen in a human countenance. Then Bertrand saw that two tall elderly ladies came up to him, stood on either side of him, talking to him. With his hand through the arm of one of them, Ellis moved away. Bertrand wrote in his notebook that night:

'But the strangest thing this evening was the terror of my host. A very commonplace dull man, you would say, but the dullest of us may become interesting when, lost in the bush, he hears the tom-toms of the approaching cannibals.'

The Ball reached its apogee. There was a superb and nearly riotous set of Lancers. Everyone had had supper. The summer morning was breaking beyond the windows. The carriages drove away. Finch, downstairs, entertained the footmen and the maids with his splendid imitations of the more important guests.

Vanessa, reaching her room at last, locked the door. A few minutes later there was a knock. She stood motionless, listening. The knock was several times repeated. Then silence.

As the small brown silver-faced clock that she had brought with her from Cat Bells struck eleven, she awoke. She had told them not to call her; now she rang the bell, looked at her letters, the newspaper, drank her coffee. Through and behind it all was a sense of crisis. And yet why? She had given last night one of the most successful Balls of the season; no hitch, no misadventure. And today there was no reason why anything should happen. Something *soon* must be done, but immediately, today . . .

The sun poured into the room. The paper told her that there was a new successful play at the Court – *His Excellency the Governor* – and that her friend, Irene Vanbrugh, one of the women whom for her generous spirit, unaffected good nature and cheerful courage she liked best in London, had made a great success in it. She read of a hat that sounded a miracle of loveliness:

> *A daring little toque of turquoise straw, jet pins with very big heads, white wings and a black velvet rosette in front.* She also read: *The Louis Seize bow is almost ubiquitous. We meet it on hats, it is a charming head-dress for evening wear, it occurs in almost every embroidery, every appliqué of lace, it airs itself in the lace curtains, on our walls, everywhere.*

'There shall be no Louis Seize bows on *my* walls,' she thought, half asleep, and then remembered, with the sharpness of a knife cutting through tissue paper, an unexpected little incident of the evening before. Just after she had come up from supper Ellis appeared at her elbow and with him a stout roughly bearded man. All that Ellis had said was that this was a friend of his, a Doctor Playfair. She had talked with the man for five minutes. What had they discussed? Bernhardt's season at the Lyric, the Spanish-American War, Gladstone's funeral, Cecil Rhodes – anything, nothing? He had seemed a well-informed, pleasant enough man. As soon as his back was turned she had forgotten him. She had not thought of him again until now when, suddenly, she seemed to see him in the room here with her – his untidy brown beard speckled with grey, his white waistcoat that fitted ill over his paunch, his heavy bowed shoulders, but, above all, his thick glasses behind which his large grey eyes had stared at her without blinking. How he had stared! She had not at the time thought of it, for, by now, she was accustomed that people should stare at her. But how he had stared! She fancied now that there had been some especial emphasis in Ellis' introduction . . .

She must get away! Oh! at once! at once! Somewhere, anywhere. Was she perhaps nervously overstrung? This trembling, this beating of the heart . . . Had people been thinking her ill and not cared to tell her? *Was* her mind affected by this last horrible year? She jumped out of bed, went to the mirror. Nothing ailed her. She was in the full vigorous possession of her brain, her will, her heart. She had never been more conscious of true bodily strength, of real and absolute sanity. She had been imagining the doctor . . . There had been nothing intended, nothing sinister – but with Ellis now from minute to minute you never knew . . . you never knew . . .

She had luncheon alone and afterwards drove to the Rede Art Gallery in Bond Street, where she had arranged to meet Barney. They had agreed that they must see Yale Ross' portrait of the Duchess of Wrexe. He was waiting for her inside the Gallery and she thought to herself: 'What a nice wide-awake amusing face he has for an old man of nearly seventy! How pleasant it is always to see him! What a friend he has always been to both Benjie and myself!'

They went together and looked at the portrait. It was certainly brilliant. The old woman sat, leaning a little forward, holding a black ebony cane, in a high carved chair. The most striking thing in her pose was the way in which her dry claw-like fingers clutched her cane. Her dress was black and the only colour against it was the dull green of a jade pendant. The colour of her face was almost dead white and the skin was drawn so tightly over the veins that a sigh, a breath, you felt, would snap it. She looked indomitable, remorseless, proud, nor was there a shadow of humour in her mouth (which was cruel) and her eyes (which were cold). On either side of the chair were two green and white dragons, grotesques with large flat feet and open mouths. A tapestry of dull figured gold filled the background.

'Theatrical, brilliant, and most uncomplimentary,' Vanessa said.

'She wouldn't think so,' said Barney. 'I'm told she's delighted with the picture. And she *is* theatrical – her life, I mean. She shuts herself up in Portland Place so that she may be a figure. If she went out and about she would be simply an old and tiresome woman who had outlived her time. As it is people think that she pulls all the strings.'

Vanessa thought of the young girl, Rachel, to whom she had spoken last night.

'That girl has character,' she said. 'It would be a tussle between the two of them if they fought.'

They found a quiet corner. The little room with its cool light, its gleaming pictures, its silence, was most refreshing.

'Now tell me, Barney, quite honestly, have you noticed anything strange in me lately?'

'No. Nothing. Of course not. I never saw you more beautiful, more completely mistress of yourself, than last night. Everyone said the same.'

'Thank you, my dear. And now listen.'

Vanessa told him everything; of the journey to Cumberland,

the incident of the knife, Ellis' remarks about her health, the two old women in the house, the few minutes with the doctor. Barney was horrified.

'At least that settles it. Something must be done at once – at once.'

'Yes, but what? I cannot – no, I cannot – endure another week of this. And it is not right for Ellis either. We are not safe and he is not safe.'

Barney stared in front of him. 'This is dreadful. I knew that things were bad, but not like this.'

'How much does anyone else know?'

'Well, we – the family – have realized that something was wrong with Ellis for a long time. But only vaguely. I have only known what you told me and others have guessed a little perhaps, but so long as everything was all right on the surface they have accepted it. They don't *want*, you see, that there should be anything public. There have been enough Herries scandals.'

Vanessa went on:

'And it is all my fault. The sin was my marrying Ellis in the first place when it was Benjie whom I loved. I thought of myself rather than Ellis. But there was this strain, perhaps, in him from the beginning ... I can't *deal* with it, Barney. My courage is gone, and I thought once that I had enough for anything. But how can I leave him like this, defenceless, without anybody, in that awful world of his own? If you saw how unhappy he sometimes looks, the way that he cries, the *bitterness* of his weeping! How lonely one must be!'

She trembled and put one gloved hand on Barney's knee to steady herself.

'Oh, Barney, *what* am I to do?'

'Wait,' Barney said. 'Let's be sensible about this. Under the cold eyes of the old Duchess. What would *she* do? Lock Ellis up in a Portland Place cellar and feed him on bread and water. No my dear, I'm not laughing. This is serious enough for anything, but forgive me if I'm thinking about you first. You have to be protected, you know. Let's be practical. Ellis is dangerous, poor chap. And there are the two old women. And that doctor last night.'

She asked him, dropping her voice:

'Can they do anything? I mean if they really tried to get me away into the country. Oh, I don't mean murder me. But shut me up, isolate me?'

'Oh no – not while Benjie and I are about. That is only a crazy idea of Ellis'. He honestly believes it, I shouldn't wonder. He may have persuaded the two old ladies that at least you are tired, overstrung. But you *must* leave him – for the time, anyway.'

'And precipitate everything,' she went on quickly. 'If I go and refuse to return there will be no question about Ellis – everyone will know.'

'Will they? I wonder. You will be blamed of course.' He looked at her. 'Vanessa, will you mind blame, criticism? You have had very little in your life, haven't you? Everyone has loved you. It will be different. You won't be the splendid Lady Herries any more ...'

'Oh, that! That is nothing. But there *is* something else ...'

Some people had come into the Gallery. She lowered her voice.

'I don't think, Barney, that I can go on any longer without seeing Benjie. I've had thirteen years of it, you know. I love him as deeply as ever I did – more deeply, I think. He is alone, has been for years. I know that it is wrong. I've no illusions about that at all. I'm very old-fashioned about God, my friends tell me, but of this I'm sure – that to live with Benjie would be a sin and that somewhere, sometime, I should suffer and rightly suffer. If I sinned it would be deliberately, one thing against another. But I think *now* that perhaps to sin and be punished is better than to live and die without loving anyone.'

When Vanessa talked like this she seemed to Barney so touchingly childish that he wanted to pat her hand and say: 'There! There! my dear. I'll go with you and tell them it wasn't your fault. I'll see that you're not punished.' Sin! Good Heavens! *What* a word! And the things that *he* had done, the fine times he had had, and here he was nearing seventy and as hale and hearty ...

'Well, that may be, my dear – or it may not be. Sin seems to me a vague word. If you're right and there's some old tyrant waiting to see you slip and punish you, why, then I'd defy him and tell him to do his worst. Let's be practical. Go off with Benjie, well and good. But there are two things to consider. One is the social part of it. Probably that seems unimportant to you, but it isn't so nice in practice. Men and women can be very nasty when they see someone enjoying a freedom they haven't themselves the courage for.'

'Yes,' said Vanessa, and thought of Rose.

'And there's another thing. What about Benjie? How old is he now? Forty something, isn't he? You aren't either of you very young any longer. Benjie's a rover. He *is* a bit of the gipsy they call him. He loves you, I know. That has been the finest, by far the finest, thing in his life. I think if you've courage enough you can bring it off. But you'll need all the courage you've got.'

She stood up, pulling down her veil, standing there in her pale dress of grey and silver, for a moment, as desolate and lonely as he'd ever seen her.

'I know,' she said. 'I'm in a muddle, aren't I? Father always used to say that I was a careless little fool – not those words, you know, but that's what it amounted to. And yet for so long I've been so careful – so absurdly careful.'

As they went out she said:

'I wish we hadn't talked under the eyes of that dreadful old woman, Barney.'

As they went down the stairs Barney caught her hand.

'Remember, Vanessa, that I'm here whenever you want me. Always, whatever you decide.'

'Yes,' she said, smiling back at him. 'You, Benjie, Rose, Adrian, Lettice. Five. In the whole world. Well, I suppose there are many people would be grateful for so many.' She added, as she got into her carriage: 'And I *am* grateful! You're a friend worth having, Barney.'

They dined alone, very late, she and Ellis, and at once she saw that the crisis was upon her. Ellis had some plan that was not to wait long for its explanation. Living with him, as she had done in these last years, she had learnt something of the strange country in which he was now lodging. She knew that his brain always moved along a single path, or rather the paths lay side by side like railway tracks and he might jump at any second from one to another, but that he was conscious *only* of the one that he was, at that moment, treading. Tonight she was very close to him; she could see clearly the character of the world in which he moved, its grey uncertain darkness so that you went stumbling, hitting your shins against sharp edges like razors, or of a sudden putting your hand on a cold soft substance, a gelatinous mass on whose surface spiders wove webs. And then at such contacts you screamed. What could you do other, alone as you were, wrapped in darkness, driving forward but with no knowledge of your destination?

She understood, too, how bewildering were the sudden flares of light – like the up-blazing in some works when, conducted around by the manager, he explains the moving of some minute wheel – both of you lit by the glare of Hell. That was Ellis' world, and these flares of hot flaming light were all he had to guide him. They might be a hat with a mass of green wings, the name of Playfair, a man looking through the window, the swinging of a mirror for no cause, the whistle of a train, a book read late at night when the house is silent – these and such as these were all he had to light his path. But pursue his path he must, and would with an absorbed intensity. One track – one purpose. The burning molten substances flares to heaven, and the track and purpose are changed – changed but as intensely pursued.

She knew tonight that some intention completely absorbed him and that that intention concerned herself. Because she knew this she had a kind of prevision of what was coming. At least she was quite certain that this very evening would see the finish of all her business here. She even knew, as she smiled at Finch and said: 'No, no more asparagus, thank you, Finch', that this was the last time that she would sit at this table, the last time at least for many a day ... One might return. She speculated about that. To what did one not return? The same tests were repeated again and again. She felt that there was neither time nor space tonight but that together she, her father, grandmother, great-grandfather, Will Leathwaite, Rose, Benjie's wife, anyone you please, all in the same moment stood up to be tested while the Eagle flew across the sun ...

Just before she rose from the table to lead the way up to the drawing-room, she had the hallucination, staring at the wallpaper under the candlelight, that it would be for ever thus – she and Ellis facing one another over the broken fruit skins and half-emptied glasses, her father swinging her to and fro above the grass of the Cat Bells lawn, old David falling at the news of the Bastille, older Herries standing at his door waiting for his wife, Rose and Major Featherstone-Haigh, all the Herries, nay, all the world transfixed into immobility while God cries from His judgement seat: 'Now!' The candles blew in the wind, a picture swung very, very slightly on its cord, and it was Ellis, not God, who said 'Now!'

'Now, Vanessa, we will go upstairs. There is something I must tell you.'

So highly pitched was her sensibility that when they were alone together in the drawing-room and the door closed behind them, she felt like an animal entrapped. There was, in fact, good reasonable common sense here, for you could not one evening allow your husband to attempt to cut your throat without, after that, finding other evenings with him rather dangerous. The door was not, this time, locked. Finch and the young footman were within calling distance. She had always hated this room. She had done what she could with it, taken down the yellow hangings, allowed Whistler to paint her portrait, spread rugs, bought roses, carnations, lilies – but Whistlers, rugs, roses, carnations, lilies could not prevent that this room was still the yellow drawing-room that, even though only last night it had swung with a maze of happy figures under the crystal candelabra, was dead like a mausoleum and cold as Hell must be for those who love the warmth.

He made her sit down beside him on the sofa. He patted her hand and his hand was warm and dry.

'Are you tired, Vanessa?' He spoke to her with infinite consideration.

'Not in the least.'

'Not after last night's festivities?'

'No. I slept until eleven.'

'What have you done today?'

'Oh, nothing very much. I went to the Rede Gallery to see Ross' portrait of the old Duchess that everyone is talking of.'

'Did anyone go with you?'

'Yes. Barney.'

'Ah ... Barney ... Everyone agrees that last night's was a most successful Ball.'

'I think it was. Really Finch and the servants did excellently. Finch may have his faults, but he knows his business.'

'Did you notice last night,' Ellis asked her, 'how those who were not invited came and laughed at us? It disturbed me greatly, but I said nothing to anybody. They gathered in groups. I was afraid at one time there would be trouble.'

'No one came who was not invited.'

'Oh yes. You are quite wrong. There were many there who had no right to be present. I thought at one time that I would have them driven out of the house. But that would have made a scene. Neither of us wished for that. Everything must be done quietly.'

She moved a little away. She looked at the clock. It was five minutes to ten. The servants would go to bed early tonight.

'Well,' he went on cheerfully, patting his knee with his hand, 'we must be thankful that all went off well. It is the last Ball that we shall give for a long time, because tomorrow I am going to send you into the country.'

'And where are you sending me?' she asked, smiling.

'There is a Doctor Playfair. At least I call him that. I am not sure at the moment whether that is his right name. He has a place – in Gloucestershire, I think. But I have it all written down. I am sure that it is Gloucestershire.'

She began to speak.

'But why—'

He put up his hand. 'Now, Vanessa, please. I have one of my headaches tonight – spiders in the brain, you know. That is exactly what Doctor Playfair said when I told him about my headaches. "Like spiders in the brain?" he asked. "Exactly," I replied, "and behind the eyes." He understood as though it had been his own experience, and when I spoke to him this morning about you – he had had five minutes' conversation with you last night—'

'I remember,' said Vanessa. 'A large heavy man with spectacles and an untidy beard.'

'Exactly. Doctor Playfair. He called to see me this morning. At this house in Gloucestershire – I *think* he said Gloucestershire – you will find every comfort. It is very quiet there. There are woods. Only the other patients—'

Vanessa laughed. 'This is all nonsense, of course, about my wanting a rest. But even if it were not, do you really suppose, Ellis, that I would leave you all alone here?'

'Ah, that is what I had intended to tell you. I shall *not* be alone. Vera and Winifred will for the future live here. This will be their home.'

So *that* was it! At the same instant as she realized with a flash of discovery that her responsibility was ended – and *how* strange *that* revelation was, liberating her, she suddenly saw, from years of bondage – a horror of being caught seized her. Those two old women! Did she not act immediately she would never escape. How they would hold her she did not know, but hold her they would! So many things came to her at the same instant and with these a new view of Ellis as though he had become twice as dangerous and twice as far removed. Through all the insanity of this last year she had thought at least that he needed her; now, with that spoken sentence, she saw that he did not need her.

Those two old women had taken her place ... But there were three against her now instead of one.

'Vera and Winifred? To make this their home? But that's preposterous. You are joking, Ellis. You—'

'It is arranged,' he answered, smiling and patting his knee. 'Very satisfactory. You will rest in the country and they will see that I am comfortable while you are away. I shall shut up part of the house. I am very tired of parties and I shall see no one – only Doctor Playfair and one or two old friends. The house will be thoroughly cleaned, swept from top to bottom. The windows need cleaning. They have grown darker every day.'

He came very close to her. He put his hand on her forehead.

'See how hot your forehead is! You have been ill for a long, long time. That is why I have myself been so very uneasy. Doctor Playfair agrees that what you need is quiet. And what *I* need is quiet. We will have shutters on the windows and someone will see to the doors. They have been far too noisy.'

He got up. 'Tomorrow afternoon,' he said, 'you shall go down to Gloucestershire.' He stood, looking down at her.

'Poor dear, poor dear!' He kissed her forehead. 'Go to bed now. Rest is what you want. I shall be in my room for a while. I have most important work – very important work indeed.'

When he was gone she sat there thinking. Her first impulse was for immediate flight. But where? Rose. Yes, Rose. Then she thought: 'No. This will be cowardice. And besides this may be all Ellis' imagination. How do I know that this absurd idea about Winifred and Vera is not invented by him? And this ridiculous notion about my going into the country. Of course he cannot *make* me go. I must talk to him again. Just now I said nothing. I must talk to Barney. Perhaps *he* will see Ellis. In any case I can't leave him like this without knowing the truth, the facts ...'

Then she thought of Benjie. She was in a turmoil of weariness, fear, indignation. The appalling element in it was her own isolation, and she saw now that, for months, she had been becoming more isolated; everything had been closing in upon her, shutting her off.

It came to her like a cry. She would see Benjie. About her future now she was reckless. She had done her utmost, she had fought battle after battle, and now she would fight no more. The thought that half an hour from now she might be with Benjie, have, at last, after all this long waiting, his love again ... simply to see him, to hear his voice, to escape from this fantasy of the last years so easily ... the room swam before her eyes.

She ran up to her room, found a hat and cloak, waited on the landing, listening, reached the hall in safety (no sound in all the house but the ticking of the clocks), opened the door and, at the end of Hill Street, found a hansom. She gave the man the number in Half Moon Street. Benjie would, in all probability, be out. Would she wait in his rooms for him? The old stock situation of the Society melodrama ... As the hansom turned into Half Moon Street, which was only a minute's distance from Hill Street, she tried to think what she would do, but she could not. She was ringing the bell before she came to any decision. A grave elderly manservant opened the door.

'Is Mr Herries at home?' she asked.

He did not seem in the least surprised to see her.

'If you will come in a moment, madam, I will see. What name, madam?'

'Lady Herries.'

'Very good, my lady, if you would not mind waiting.'

He disappeared around the corner of the stairs. Almost at once he appeared again, saying:

'Yes, Mr Herries is in. Will you come up, please?'

Benjie was at the door of his room. She went in and he followed her, closing the door behind him. He stared at her as though a cloud of angels had floated down to him from the ceiling.

'Vanessa!'

'Yes. This is just like a play, isn't it?' She was trembling but was determined that he should not see it. At the very sight of him she was so happy that she could only smile, stare back at him, then, with fumbling hands, take off her hat.

'Here,' he said. 'Take this chair. It is the only comfortable one. Oh, my God, Vanessa! If you knew how many times I've sat here imagining just this: saying to myself, "And now the bell will ring and Humphries will come to the door and he will say 'Lady Herries', and I ..."'

'That's in the play too.' She steadied her hands, holding them tightly together. 'But there is nothing dramatic in this, Benjie. I have come only for five minutes. But that isn't true either. It *is* dramatic, I suppose. You must give me advice. Tell me what to do.'

He sat down in the chair on the other side of the fireplace, his small body balanced forward, staring and staring and staring.

She saw that he was looking splendid, as brown and hard as a russet apple, spare, taut, not changed. Oh, not changed in the least these twenty years!

'I shouldn't have done this, I suppose,' she went on. 'At least — I don't know. There's no *shouldn't* any more. The fact is, quite simply, that Ellis is proposing to send me away to a private asylum in the country tomorrow ... It has been tonight a situation that I couldn't face by myself any longer. You know about Ellis? You have heard something?'

'My God!' Benjie shouted, springing up. 'Send *you* away? Send you to an asylum?'

'Yes. Quietly, Benjie dear. We have got to be sensible about this. The fact is that Ellis has been out of his mind for the last year or more. Twice he has tried to kill me, and still I held on. It has been miserable, tragic ... I don't want to talk about that part of it. That is past. But I must do something now, now, at once. You know Winifred and Vera Trent?'

Benjie nodded.

'They have taken charge of him. I think they intended to from the first. Oh, I don't mean that it is they who have planned to get me out of the house. I don't think they had the least idea of it. That is only Ellis' crazy notion. But it has come to this — that tonight, an hour ago, Ellis told me that they were from now on to live in the house, I was to be sent into the country, most of the house to be shut up. I don't know how much is Ellis' fantasy, how much is truth, but I *did* know, as he went on talking, that I could stand no more. I have been alone in this thing too long. And so — I came to see you.'

'Oh, Vanessa!' he sighed. 'At last!'

She nodded, smiling.

'Yes — at last. I have wasted my whole life. I can't go on without you any longer.'

He came over to her, knelt down beside her and took her hand. He sat on the floor, resting his head against her, her hand pulsing against his. They stayed for a long time quietly, without speaking, feeling as at every long-separated meeting they had always done — that there had never been any parting.

Then he became practical. He asked her every sort of question and she told him everything. For the first time in all these many years she poured everything from her heart, her unresting love for himself, her increasing loneliness, the friendship that she and Ellis had had for the first few years, the influence of Miss For-

tescue, Ellis' headaches, the day of the Jubilee when he had first
made her uneasy, the night when he had attacked her, and then
detail after detail to the last Cumberland visit.

'But now – even now – I would not go were it not for those two
old women. How I hate them! Oh, Benjie, how I hate them! But
it isn't that; it is that my responsibility is over.'

He nodded.

'You have always been dreadfully conscientious, Vanessa. And
now you are coming to me – for ever and ever and ever, amen.'

'Yes. I talked to Barney about it this afternoon.'

'And what did *he* say?'

'He pointed out that the world would be shocked, Violet would
close her doors to me, I should no more be asked to Grosset.'

'Yes, that's true. And shall you mind?'

'I don't know – a little, perhaps. What I *do* know is that I am
doing wrong. I shall suffer for it in one way or another. I suppose
that, without realizing it, I have been thinking of this for a long
time. I am not a fool about it. I know the delight – and I know
the punishment.'

'Punishment!' he cried. 'There will be no punishment! We
shall be happy for ever!'

She smiled, shaking her head.

'Of course nobody is happy for ever.' She put her hand under
his chin, turning his face up towards hers. 'Benjie, are you *sure*
you want me? Are you certain? I'm middle-aged, you know.
You're middle-aged too, but for a man it is quite different. Are
you *sure* that you want me – still – after all this time?'

'Sure? Sure? Why, Vanessa, I love you more than I did twenty
years ago. Loving you has been the only good thing in me – that,
and caring for Tom. Are *you* sure,' he went on, 'that *you* want
me? I'm not much, you know, Vanessa. Apart from you I'm
nothing at all. With you I may still do something.'

'Yes, I'm sure,' she said quietly.

'It is true, too, what Barney said. We shall be cut, you know.
Wherever we live someone will be unkind. And as to the relations! Yet another scandal in the Herries history!'

'Oh yes.' She nodded her head. 'I understand just how things
will be.' (Again, for a flashing instant, she thought of Rose.) 'I
understand everything, I think,' she went on. 'I'm not a child
now. I have seen how things go. Often and often I have been
tempted to come to you. You must have known that! But I was
wrong when I married Ellis, and his needing me – or my thinking

that he did — kept me there. And then,' she added after a moment, 'to fly in the face of God. I know those are only words to you, but it is true reality to me. But if I can make you happy — isn't that something? You see, I've never made anyone happy since my father died. No one. Isn't that awful? If I had made *myself* happy it would have been a little, but not even that. Until tonight. Until now. Now I am so happy that there *must* be something right in it somewhere. Don't you think so?'

'I don't know about God. I think that's a tall word. But here and now we are going to do the best we can by one another. Until your God separates us we'll stay together just as years ago we meant to do.'

After a while they discussed the immediate plan.

'Tonight I'm returning to Hill Street,' Vanessa said. 'I must see Ellis once more and know what is fact and what isn't. I can't leave him until I know.'

'Then I am coming back with you,' Benjie said.

'To Hill Street?'

'Certainly. I must see that you are safe. If Ellis has gone to bed and is asleep, well and good. What time is it? Nearly twelve. He ought to be asleep. If he is not, I will talk to him. Don't be frightened. There shall be none of my famous fights. But I don't leave you until you are safe.'

She agreed. She wished now to hide nothing. If Ellis in reality intended to carry out his crazy plan it was right that she should be no longer alone. And she felt a feverish impatience that this absurd business should be settled once and for all. And she could not face Ellis alone again that night.

They walked round to Hill Street. In that clear air they heard Big Ben strike midnight as she opened the door with her key. They went up to the drawing-room. Ellis was standing there in front of the big marble fireplace.

Benjie spoke at once.

'I beg your pardon, Ellis, for coming at this impossible hour. Vanessa came round to me tonight to tell me that you intended to send her into the country tomorrow — to some doctor's. Well, Vanessa and I are very old friends, you know. We have obeyed your wishes all these years and kept apart, but when Vanessa told me this we thought it better that we should both see you. We can talk about it tomorrow if you prefer, but in that case Vanessa will go to a hotel for the night.'

Vanessa said: 'Ellis, after our talk tonight I couldn't stay here alone. For both our sakes—'

But Ellis, without moving and very quietly, waved his hand at the door.

'Would you mind,' he said to Benjie, 'coming farther into the room? They may be listening outside.'

Benjie came forward.

'Thank you.' Ellis looked at him very severely. 'I thought I told you that you were never to enter my house again?'

'Yes,' said Benjie. 'You did, and I wouldn't have come had it not been for Vanessa. Frankly, Ellis, she's frightened. You shouldn't have talked that nonsense about sending her into the country.'

'That is perfectly correct,' said Ellis. 'She is going to Doctor Playfair's.'

'Well – she is not,' said Benjie. 'Nothing of the kind. You must see, Ellis, that she can't live with you any longer after this. I didn't want her to come back here tonight at all, but she said she must know whether you *meant* what you said. It seems that you do.'

Vanessa had been standing, her hand up to the white cloak with the high white collar that she was wearing. She had been looking into Ellis' face, trying to find there some appeal to herself for help, some kindliness. If at that moment he had turned and gone to her, blindly asking her, as he used to do, that she should help him, she would, even now, have stayed . . .

But he did not seem in the least unusual. There was no sign of madness in him anywhere, and after that one sentence to Benjie about the door there was, in this scene, *no* queerness. There was no *queerness*, but there was hatred.

'You see, Ellis,' Vanessa said, 'I have realized that you don't need me any more. We haven't been happy together for a long time, have we? And as you don't need me we had better separate.'

'That is our affair,' he said. 'We can settle that tomorrow. If you were well, Vanessa, I'd have something to say to you for bringing this dirty ruffian here. As it is, Herries, get out and keep out.'

'Come on, Vanessa,' Benjie said. 'Let's go.'

She took a step forward to Ellis.

'Ellis. Don't you see how impossible it is?—'

He moved forward to her. Benjie stepped between them, then, taking her arm, he drew her away.

With quick steps Ellis followed them. He passed them as though he did not see them and ran down the stairs. In the hall he turned.

In a high, shrill, convulsed voice he cried:

'Get out, both of you! Get out! Get out!'

At the same moment the Chinese clock struck the half-hour. Benjie, halfway down the stairs, put his hand on Vanessa's shoulder. They waited. He did not know what Ellis would do. But the scene ended very quietly. Ellis did not move. Vanessa and Benjie walked out of the house.

They found a hansom in Piccadilly.

'And now where?' Benjie asked.

'I'll go to Rose,' Vanessa answered.

She was trembling and he put his arm round her, holding her close to him. Benjie gave the address to the cabman.

Part Three

The Lover

HAPPINESS IN RAVENGLASS

One fine September afternoon of that momentous year 1899, Mrs Runcing of Olive Bank, Ravenglass, came to tea with Mrs Jocelyn of Sea View Cottage. It was a most beautiful day, and the sun caressed the sea, the sea caressed the shore, and the birds rising in little flocks from the island hovered against the quivering sky like blown petals, silver-grey, and as the wing turned, of glittering metal. The cry of the gulls made the lazy sky lazier.

The two ladies sat at the window of Sea View Cottage and drank their tea.

'I'm using this room,' Mrs Jocelyn explained, 'because of my lodgers. I'm not sure that I don't like it quite as well as the other.'

A lady and gentleman rode past on a tandem bicycle. The gentleman rang his bell.

'What's that, dear?' an odd, croaking, half-strangled voice asked from within the room.

'Only a bicycle, Mother.'

On the farther side of the fireplace, almost hidden with shawls, was old Mrs Burgess, Mrs Jocelyn's mother. Mrs Burgess was ninety-two and, except that she was never warm, was a wonder for her age. She was as lively and spiteful and selfish and scandal-mongering as though she had been a young thing of twenty. There was nothing that happened from Barrow to Whitehaven in which she did not take an interest, and most especially, of course, in anything that had to do with love and – most particularly – illicit love. She was a Puritan and had all the eager questing spirit of the Puritan. Her curiosity it was that had kept her alive and would, it seemed, keep her alive for evermore.

Her daughter, Hester Jocelyn, was in every way her opposite: a little, warm-blooded, impetuous, charitable, kind-hearted woman whose husband had, ten years earlier, run away with an actress to South America. She had not loved him very much, but her loneliness was often worst at three in the morning when she could not sleep – quite terrible, yet she was cheerful, busy, charitable and infinitely patient with her horrid old mother. Something of a heroine perhaps.

Mrs Runcing, her visitor, was nothing of a heroine: a long bony woman with three daughters whom she would sell her eyes to marry. She threw them at the men of the district as you throw darts at a dartboard. As with so many women of their time, they had been trained to nothing, taught nothing. Their father thought them too tiresome for words, their mother hated them because no one would have them and yet loved them because they were hers. The poor Miss Runcings!

'Things look bad in South Africa,' said Mrs Runcing. 'Henry says we shall have war for certain. It's all the fault of that wicked old Krüger. And so you like your lodgers, Hetty dear?' She laid rum butter thickly on her bread. She was a greedy woman.

'Like them!' said Mrs Jocelyn. 'I should think so! No one could help it. Mr Herries is as gay a gentleman as you'd find anywhere, always singing and laughing. No trouble at all. But Mrs Herries is my favourite. She's a *lovely* lady – so kind and thoughtful, and so friendly. It's nice to see a married pair so happy – and not young either. I've never had visitors I've taken to so.'

There was a pause. Mrs Jocelyn looked up.

'What is it, Cecilia? You've something on your mind.'

Mrs Runcing paused yet longer, then, dropping her voice, said: 'Hetty, there's something you ought to know.'

Mrs Jocelyn moved uneasily. She knew well this opening of her friend's and always it meant no good.

'Know? What ought I to know?'

'It's just like you, Hetty. The last in the place to be aware of what everyone is saying.'

'*What* is everyone saying?'

'About Mrs Herries. She isn't Mrs Herries at all. She's Lady Herries – and she and Mr Herries are no more married than ... than you and I are!'

'Cecilia, what *are* you saying?' Mrs Jocelyn got up from the window. 'Now I won't have it! You've always got some story about someone, Cecilia. It's too bad. It's a shame.'

'Oh, is it! Always got some story, have I? That's a nice thing to say to an old friend. I'm telling you out of kindness. It's been the talk here for days and you ought to know it.'

There was an excited movement of the shawls from the back of the room.

'I'm sure Mr and Mrs Herries are married. I don't care what anyone says.'

'Well, you're wrong for once. Mrs Herries is Lady Herries, wife of Sir Ellis Herries in London. She ran away from him last year, with this Mr Herries.'

'What's that you are saying, Cecilia?' the old lady from the fireplace croaked. 'Not married, you say? Not married? Well, I never! Well, I never did! Not married!'

'Of course they're not married. The affair made a sensation last year in London. And more than that, they've been lovers for years and years. Everybody knows them. The Herries are Cumberland people or, anyway, they've been in Cumberland for centuries. There was an old Mr Herries lived here in Ravenglass years ago, they say, and this Mr Herries has a house near Bassenthwaite Lake. Lady Herries was brought up on Derwentwater. She was a great lady in London for years. I call it a piece of downright impertinence for them to come back to this part of the country where everyone knows them. Disgusting, I call it. But they say there's been one scandal after another in that family. Years and years ago there was a Mr Herries who was a holy terror, and some fifty years back one of the Herries murdered another one somewhere by Keswick. It's a disgrace their coming to Ravenglass. They should be ashamed to show their faces!'

Mrs Runcing had not intended to be so violent, but, as often before, when denouncing the vices of others her own virtues grew in colour and strength. As others went down she herself went up, and the higher she went the better she felt.

Little Mrs Jocelyn had turned very pale. At last she said:

'I don't care whether they're married or not. They shall stay here as long as they like!'

'Hetty!' Here was a thing for a decent Christian woman to say!

'I don't care! I mean it!'

'Think of what people will say!'

And there was a croak from the fireplace: 'Not married ... in this house!'

Then, beyond the half-open window, they heard a step on the gravel path. Both women turned and looked. Vanessa was coming up from the sea.

'All I know,' said Mrs Jocelyn, almost sobbing with emotion, 'is that that's the finest lady I've ever met. She's welcome to this roof as long as she wishes.'

Vanessa was walking, her head back to the sea breeze, her dress blown against her legs. Her face was warm with colour. She had grown a little stouter in this last year, her bosom fuller, and, carrying herself thus strongly, she moved like a woman who was happy, free and self-confident.

This seemed to Mrs Runcing, whose own bosom, do what she would, was never what it ought to be, insulting.

'You'd think she had nothing to be ashamed of,' she said.

'Neither she has,' answered Mrs Jocelyn indignantly. 'They're happy, aren't they? And that's more than most people manage to be. I expect her husband was horrible.'

Mrs Runcing set her lips. 'You'll be sorry, Hetty,' she said. 'Encouraging immorality. You'll see how people will talk . . .'

Meanwhile Vanessa had gone into the little sitting-room on the other side of the passage, taken off her straw hat, and sat down by the window to wait for Benjie. He had gone fishing. In an hour's time he would return, they would sit reading, talking, the veils of light would fall over the sea, the stars would come out, the cries of the birds would die away; after supper they would take a last walk, then, tired and happy, return, light the lamp, play chess, go up the crooked staircase to bed.

She sat there, dreaming.

More than a year had passed and still God had not let loose His thunderbolts. She had known a period of perfect unrestrained happiness. She looked back, first to the time at Eastbourne, then to the months in France, then to the wonderful glorious experience of coming home to Cumberland. What troubles had there been? In Eastbourne she had been cut by Mrs Harbin, a friend of Violet's. Alfred and his wife had met her in the hotel lounge and that had been a little uncomfortable. On the other hand Adrian, at one time, Rose at another, Barney at another, had stayed with them. The news from London had at first been a little distressing. The talk had been, she understood, terrific. The sympathy had gone, universally, to Ellis. Winifred and Vera Trent had gone to live in Hill Street and, so far as Vanessa could discover, Ellis had been quite tranquil, had enjoyed the sympathy and had allowed it generally to be understood that he was able to bear his misfortunes like a gentleman. Often – and this was perhaps her severest trouble – she asked herself whether she had imagined all that queerness. But no: the scene in Cumberland, the frenzies and tears in Hill Street had been real enough, but how much of it had been histrionic, an attempt on Ellis' side to catch her sympathy, a passion for melodrama?

Strangely the question of Ellis' insanity was no longer the main one. She knew now, in the light of these last months, that for years she had been living in prison. It was only now that she understood how solemn, how unhumorous, how dreary that Hill Street life had been, what a *dreary* creature she herself had become! Everything in it had been false, the social fuss, the hours that she had spent with people for whom she did not care, the shamness of her interests. She thought of the balls, the receptions, the silly games, the sillier country houses and race meetings and baccarat; her weak good nature, her amiability, her own stupidity, she told herself, had kept her there long, long after she should have left it.

And Benjie? She smiled as she lay back in her chair looking at the long dune like the back of a whale over whose brown surface little waves broke in edges of white and silver. Benjie was not perfect. She had never supposed that he would be. There had been the night at Eastbourne when she had entered their bedroom to discover him kissing the chambermaid. Twice, once at Eastbourne, once in Paris, he had left her for two days without warning. Sometimes he was out of temper, sometimes (but very seldom) he was drunk. He knew some very queer people, although he was scrupulous about the company he introduced her to. Once he had declared that he must go immediately to Italy to meet a man in Siena. Tom, who, although he was only still a boy, had much wisdom, had settled that little business. Tom, by good fortune, thought Vanessa the most wonderful woman in the world.

Vanessa, on her side, was not always perfect. Far from it. She was impatient, suffered fools badly (and some of Benjie's friends were very foolish), sometimes nagged Benjie, sometimes (as she well knew) bored him with her naïveté, her religion, her obstinacy. But they had been saved, both of them, by their splendid comradeship. Because they had been friends all their lives long that business of compromise, so difficult in the first year of marriage, had been quite natural for both of them. They loved for every kind of reason, but chiefly because they knew one another so well, and admired and laughed at, for the most part, the same things. The wildness in Benjie Vanessa understood because, in her own way, she had the same wildness. They must both be free. They stayed together only because they loved one another. The troubles that they had were on the surface because the base of their relationship was firm, unshakeable. They were honest, but not so honest that they were for ever challenging weaknesses. *Of course* they were weak, mistaken, faulty in this way or that. They took these things for granted. Because Benjie kissed the chambermaid it did not mean that he did not love Vanessa. He loved *only* Vanessa. He had loved Vanessa only, all his life long.

But the best of their relationship was its gaiety. Vanessa found that she had not been gay for thirteen years but now, like a language once learnt and long unpractised, living with the natives again, back it returned.

Love, if it is to be worth anything, must be honest, trusting, humorous, protective, far-seeing. With them both it was all these things.

And under its influence Vanessa grew and developed. It had been her danger always that because of her great simplicity of nature she would become tiresome company. Her mother and father had both been very simple people and it was possible that they had bored a good many persons. Vanessa, in her London years, had learnt superficial variety – that is, she had been trained to adapt herself to a great many different characters – but her lack of subtlety sometimes revealed her. Bertrand, the novelist, whose eye was so sharp that its rather fishy, sleepy indifference often deceived the innocent, said that the only women who were interesting were the good ones who wanted to be bad, that no women were so dull as the bad women who wanted to be good. The bad ones who were content to be bad were, he said, amusing companions, but they were all the same – know one and you knew all.

Now Vanessa had, in London, been a good woman determined to be unprejudiced and open-minded. She defended Rose because she loved her, but also a little to show that she was above censorship. She had never *really* known the kind of life that a woman like Rose was leading. Her father, Barney, her husband, Lettice Marrable – from none of these did she get the real sense of it. But after a year with Benjie she knew. They talked together like two schoolboys without any reticences whatever. She was now *truly* aware of the humour, the generosity, the comradeship, the dirty untidy tragedy of the 'vicious' world. She knew that it was *not* vicious – simply a place inhabited by the uncontrolled, the needy, the weak, the greedy and, above all, the lonely. That the very last thing that it called for was superior patronage, and that those who lived in it did not wish, for the most part, for any sympathy from anybody.

So Vanessa grew wise. She learnt now to be patient, tolerant

and unpriggish. This continuous love that burnt steadily from
hour to hour, from day to day, warmed her heart so that it was
impossible *not* to be generous. It is only the disappointed,
starved, and robbed who are jealous and unfair.

Waiting now for Benjie she had on her lap and read from time
to time Judith's old green-bound book. She had rescued it from
her father's room at Uldale on the night of the fire. Judith, in her
old age, had dictated it to Aunt Jane, and in Aunt Jane's clear
spidery hand it was as fresh as though written last week. There
was a piece about Ravenglass.

It seemed that, in the spring of 1737, Judith's father, Rogue
Herries, had ridden over with his son David to spend a night or
two with his brother Harcourt Herries, an old bachelor who had
lived for many years in Ravenglass.

'David used to tell us,' Judith's book said, 'of that visit to
Ravenglass as one of the striking incidents in his life because of
the quarrel that he had with his father there. He would describe
to us the ride over Stye Head on horseback, how gloomy his
father was on that ride, suffering from one of his "demons", how
they came into Ravenglass in the evening, clattering over the
cobbles, smelling the sea, and hearing the gulls. Then there was
Uncle Harcourt, who was a very precise old bachelor and
wouldn't have a woman in his house, and he wore, David remembered, a wonderful ring on his finger with a green stone, and
a rose-coloured skirted coat. After supper Uncle Harcourt talked
of the London of Queen Anne, where he had been as a boy, of the
Sacheverell Riots, of the Thames barge the *Folly*, and the coffee
houses, and of how he had seen Mrs Rogers as Berenice.

'Uncle Harcourt was a fervent Jacobite and gave the toast of
"The King over the water", breaking his wine glass after it, and
he recited to them Pope's *Elegy to the Memory of an Unfortunate Lady*. Then David's father lost his temper, took David
out to sea and ordered him to strip for a beating as a punishment
for some fancied misdemeanour. David refused and said that he
was no longer a child, and that was the beginning of a new
relationship between them. This,' Judith went on, 'was one of
David's favourite stories and, as a little girl, while I listened I
could see it all as vividly as though I had been there – the
London of Queen Anne, and the little bachelor declaiming Pope,
and David and his father standing by the sea.'

'And here I am,' thought Vanessa, 'in this same place as
though time never had been. Little Uncle Harcourt might walk

in at this door any moment. I knew Judith so well and she lived
in the same house with the man whose uncle saw the Sacheverell
Riots. In London now they have the telephone and there are
these new "moving pictures" and Alfred Herries has a motor-car.
Time does not separate any of us, but rather our stupidities,
selfishness, and fears. Judith, if she were here, would scold me
for moralizing. She always hated it. But, on the other hand, she
would be glad that I am happy and would altogether approve of
my running away from Ellis . . .'

She heard the hall door open and close, a quick step, and
Benjie had come in. 'They say that when you live with anyone
their features become so familiar that you can't see them any
more. Well, I can see Benjie all right, his bright eyes with the
humorous crows' feet at the corners, his brown hands, the part of
his forehead that grows white above the brown just below his
hair; I know how his arms fasten about me and how strong is his
kiss on my lips. It is all as new as though it had never happened
until now, and my heart beats at the sound of his step as though
now for the first time he was about to tell me that he loved me.'

He went up and washed. Mrs Jocelyn brought in the supper,
and after they had eaten they sat close together by the window.

'I've been reading Judith's book, Benjie,' Vanessa said. 'The
part about Ravenglass. It seemed as though time hadn't passed at
all and little Harcourt Herries might be walking in on us with his
green ring and rose-coloured coat. My great-grandfather was
born in William III's reign, and Alfred has a motor-car. So soon
as I am back in this part of the country time doesn't exist. We
none of us die here—'

'Take a step,' Benjie said lazily, 'and you are at Gosforth;
another, and it's Ennerdale. Then over the hill to Buttermere,
Honister, Borrowdale. Yes, we're back in our own country,
Vanessa. Bold of us, perhaps. The old boatman wasn't so friendly
today. He knows we're living in sin.'

She did not answer. They had been living in sin for a year and
she was not yet aware of it. Was it now, when she had returned to
her own people, that she *would* be aware?

'I've had a letter from that man Alington. He advises me to go
in for those Australian mines – at once, without losing a minute.
Shall I?'

She looked at him quietly. 'No, I don't think so.' Everyone was
speculating. The fever in London had spread everywhere, and
Gold Mines glittered on every doorstep. 'You promised me, you

know. We don't know enough about it. We have enough. We don't want to be rich, either of us.'

'Don't we?' She saw that he was restless. 'I'm not sure that I don't. I've never been rich. I wouldn't mind the sensation.'

She put out her hand and caught his.

'You're restless – what is it?'

'It's South Africa for one thing. It looks bad – or good if you like. A war would be fun. We haven't had one for ages. Tom would go as a war correspondent if he weren't so young.'

'Well, *you're* too old to go. That's one comfort.'

'Oh no, I'm not,' he answered quickly.

'You're forty-four.'

'What's that? No age at all. And I'm as fit as a fiddle.'

'Let's not talk of it.' She stilled her fear. 'I'm so happy. Don't spoil it.'

'If there *was* a war,' he said, 'it would be only for a week or two. I'd be back in no time – with a VC probably and all the Family greeting me like a hero.'

He drew his chair closer to her and leant his head on her shoulder.

'Vanessa, you're not tired of me yet?'

'No, I'm not tired of you.'

'How happy we've been and are!' He sighed. 'Why can't every-one find love like this? It seems so simple when you get it. I suppose that somewhere there's the right person for everyone – one for each – but they don't meet. Do you find there's some-thing a little pathetic in two people of our age loving one another so? We ought to be young – we ought to be twenty – as we might have been had I not been such a fool. And I'm still a fool, Vanessa. It may break out any time.'

She laid her hand against his cheek.

'We used to say long ago that nothing could separate us. Nothing has. Nothing can now.'

'Yes – death,' he answered.

'You know that I don't think so.'

'Without our bodies? Shall we love still? You without your hair, your eyes, without the warm touch of your hand against my cheek? When I can see you smile no longer nor the way that you put your hand up to your hair, nor hear your voice. And I! I'll be a poor ghost, Vanessa—'

'What of your Valhalla under the hill, the men singing?'

'Ah, you won't be there! And I'll be such a wild ghost, flying

from Top to Top, haunting old women down the chimney, stealing the butter from the dairy, pinching the young women. I love
you for every conceivable reason, Vanessa, but without your
body I shouldn't know you. I'd be as restless as I used to be. I'd
never find you. I'd go searching from ghost to ghost ... And
you'd be so good. You'd be in favour in Heaven, one of the
guardian angels. They'd have no use for me, I'm afraid, and
whatever job they set me to do I'd do it wrong.'

She kissed him.

'I'd find you. Wherever you went I'd go too.'

'Are you sure,' he asked her, 'that you never miss London? Not
Ellis, of course, nor Hill Street – but all your friends and the
good times you had with all the nobs. Don't you *mind* being a
disgrace and something to make virtuous ladies shudder over?'

'I've never been so happy in all my life,' she said, her voice
very low. 'I seem to have reached middle age quite emptily – as
though I'd been born yesterday. There was my childhood – that
was happy. And now there's this. Nothing between.'

'And now there's this,' he repeated contentedly.

They were aware that the door opened. They both turned
together, thinking that it was Mrs Jocelyn who had come to say
goodnight. The lamp was burning dimly and in the half-light
they saw the oddest figure in the doorway. It was old Mrs
Burgess, wrapped in a multitude of shawls, leaning on her stick;
she stood there, her old brown wrinkled face pushed forward like
the head of a tortoise. She stared at them, they could see, as
though she could never satisfy her curiosity. Then she vanished.

'What did *she* want?' Benjie asked. He got up and went to the
door. 'What cheek! To come in without knocking—'

'She's half crazy, poor old thing,' Vanessa said. 'Mrs Jocelyn
says that she ought to be in her bed, but they can't keep her
there.'

'What did she want? She looked at us as though she'd never
seen us before.'

They played their game of chess and went up to bed. Long
after Benjie was asleep in Vanessa's arms she lay there awake. He
slept like a child, his hand on her breast. She lay there, forcing
herself resolutely, quite calmly, to a new courage. Instinct, light
words lightly spoken, some shadow like the finger of a cloud on a
sunlit hill, told her that it would be needed.

She was right. It *was* needed. Next day Benjie had moved into

his savage state. That was how she always put it to herself. It was
as though he reverted into some old wild existence where the
rules, objects, dangers, joys of life were all quite different from
this one. He seemed physically to change. He could not stay in
the same spot from one tick of the clock to another. He moved
about the room as though he were unclothed, his brown finely
muscled body moving naked through tall grass, his eyes shiningly
alert for the enemy. As often as not he did not hear what you said
to him, he snapped back replies, he suddenly started walking
down the road saying that he did not know when he would
return.

The happy thing was that Vanessa understood this transformed state to perfection. She was aware of it often in herself
but, being a woman and therefore having all her eggs in one
basket (which was Benjie), Benjie could satisfy her wildest
longings. She could not satisfy Benjie's. Nor did she try. When
this restlessness came on him she let him go free.

But now there was more serious trouble. His words about
South Africa had clutched her heart. Was there going to be war?
If so, then Benjie would be off ... Nothing could keep him ...
He would revel in it. He would be killed, perhaps. People were
killed in wars ...

Today was the eighteenth of September, and it seemed that, on
the sixteenth, the Transvaal had replied to the British proposals
of starting the argument all over again by proposing to revert to a
joint Commission. There was something sinister in the tone
underlying the Boer phrases.

What was it all about? For a long while she had not taken it
with any seriousness. It was all due, it seemed, to Krüger's fear
of Rand dominion of his country. It all went back to the old
Gold Rushes into the Rand. Rather naturally, Vanessa considered, Krüger thought that to give franchise to the Rand
population must entirely alter Boer rule. He was honest, perhaps,
in wishing to keep the Transvaal an agricultural country. On the
other hand, the British Government must protect its subjects.
But ought those subjects to be in that country at all? Didn't it
look as though a small, resolute, independent people were to be
bullied and affronted by a big Power when all that the little
people wanted was freedom to live as they wished on their own
soil? On the other hand, *could* Great Britain allow her own sons
to be persecuted, ill-treated, mishandled, and say nothing?

It seemed, Vanessa thought with a sigh, one of those questions that had so clearly two sides to it. And the Boers were thick-headed, obstinate, stupid, hypocritical perhaps ... On the other hand, it *was* their country! Or wasn't it? She soon, however, abandoned the wider, more public question for the private personal one. If there was a war, Benjie would go ... If Benjie went ... She pulled herself to her full height, clasping her hands behind her head, staring in front of her. The stiffest job of her whole life was approaching her.

Then a very absurd thing occurred. Coming into the house one morning she encountered old Mrs Burgess, who was shuffling along in flat slippers, trailing shawls about her and making that odd wheezy noise peculiarly her own. She saw Vanessa and, thrusting her old head forward, hissed some word. Then, with yellow convulsive hands, drawing her shawls tightly about her, she slip-slopped into her fastness.

Vanessa did not know what the word was, but it was evidently intended to express moral horror and indignation. She asked Mrs Jocelyn to come and speak to her. She told her of it. She liked Mrs Jocelyn extremely.

'Sit down, Mrs Jocelyn,' Vanessa said. 'Let's sit together by the window.' They sat down. 'Now I'm not wrong, am I, in supposing that your mother has learnt that Mr Herries and I are not married?'

Mrs Jocelyn nervously rubbed her hands together.

'No, Mrs Herries. That's correct.'

'I should have told you before. I'm not Mrs Herries. I'm Lady Herries. I left my husband last year.'

'Oh yes ...' said Mrs Jocelyn nervously.

'I should have told you. I did not mean to conceal anything. I would have told you at once if you had asked me, but I really did not feel that it was anyone's business but our own. Now I suppose you would like us to go. I quite understand and I do hope you'll forgive us for putting you into this unpleasant position. We have been so happy here and you have been so very good to us.'

Mrs Jocelyn was a sentimental and emotional little woman. Her eyes glittered with tears as she looked out of the window. Many things made her cry: the music of a band in the street, reading of a deed of heroism in the newspaper, details of a wedding, the more moving portions of almost any novel. But although she was emotional, she had the strength (and sometimes the obstinacy) of Mr Krüger himself.

'Oh no, Lady Herries,' she said. 'Please don't think of going. A friend told us, a week or so ago. It appears that you and Mr Herries are well known in Cumberland and Westmorland. You come from these parts, do you not? So of course the people here have talked about you. But please pay no attention. Mother is a very old lady and not always accountable. It doesn't matter at all. Really it doesn't.'

Vanessa smiled.

'Thank you, Mrs Jocelyn, for saying that. We'll never forget it. But of course we mustn't stay here. It would be wrong for us to make it awkward for you in any way.'

'It doesn't make it awkward,' said Mrs Jocelyn with tremendous energy. 'I hope you won't think it impertinent, but my knowing you, Lady Herries, has been the nicest thing that has ever happened to me. I don't know, of course, what reasons you had for leaving your husband, but I'm sure they were very good ones. There were times in the past when I quite easily might have left Mr Jocelyn, although now that he isn't here I wouldn't like to say anything against him. I'm sorry, of course, that you and Mr Herries can't be married, but as you can't you can't, and that's all there is to it.'

Vanessa was very much moved.

'I'm afraid that isn't all there is to it,' she said. 'I have done something that is wrong. I did it knowing that it was wrong, and the fact that we are both happy doesn't make it any more right. But I did it deliberately and I will take what comes. All the same it's not fair that anyone else should be involved, especially anyone as kind and good as you are.'

'I'm neither kind nor good,' Mrs Jocelyn replied. 'I'm often most unkind to my mother, I'm afraid. And as to being good, I'm too old now, I suppose, to be anything else very much, but when I was younger there were times when I would have run away from Mr Jocelyn most gladly if there had been anyone to run away with.'

She got up and added, smiling rather timidly:

'I've not had many friends and my life hasn't been very exciting, but when I *have* a friend – well, there it is. If you were to go away I should be very unhappy. And don't mind Mother. I'll see that she doesn't worry you.'

Vanessa went with her to the door and kissed her.

'Then we'll stay,' she said.

*   *   *

On October 9th the Boers delivered their ultimatum. For three weeks after this neither Benjie nor Vanessa spoke of the only subject in their minds.

Under the eyes of a watchful and gossiping Ravenglass they spent quiet days, bicycling to Wastwater and Black Combe, seeing the shadows turn the flanks of the Screes to purple and the bracken flame in Eskdale. Then Vanessa had a letter from Adrian.

DEAREST VANESSA – How are things going with you? Here we talk nothing but the War. General opinion is that it will be over before Christmas and everyone – except your humble servant – is turning himself into a soldier as quickly as possible that he may see something of the fun before it is finished. I am not so sure. It seems to me that we are already everywhere on the defensive. I lie low and say nothing, for the general feeling is that it is all a great lark – a sort of polo game in which even the poorest may join. I listened to Chamberlain defending the Government for three long hours and what he *did* say was all right – but how about all the things he didn't?

What is certain is that we are now beholding the end of the Victorian Era. Do you remember young Violet complaining to you and me once how, when the maid was busy elsewhere, she must sit indoors all a fine afternoon because she must not go out alone? Haven't you, at your own Balls, seen the chaperons sitting in weary rows hour after hour? I prophesy that you will never see those chaperons again and that Alfred's girl will, in another fifteen years or so, be smoking a cigarette as she enjoys her luncheon alone at the Criterion.

The Family, by the way, is amusing. They take the War of course as their own affair. Krüger is a kind of Benjie who has insulted them all personally. It is 'Our War' – Horace especially is full of club-martial ardour. Carey is going out in some capacity or another although he's sixty-three or so. Also Peile Worcester and – would you believe it? – Philip is being sent out by some paper. I am generally despised because I say that the Government must be carried on and if *I* go who will remain?

And Benjie? What is he going to do? If he goes, don't worry. Benjie will always survive things like wars. They were made for him, not he for them. Write and tell me . . .

*   *   *

Then Benjie had a letter from Paris. Tom, young though he was, had hitched himself on to some French newspaper man and was already on the sea. Tim had thrown over his painting and come home to enlist.

'You see,' Benjie said, staring at her as though he were taking her image into his very heart. 'I've got to go.'

'Yes,' said Vanessa, smiling. 'Of course you have.'

Their last night in Ravenglass they did not sleep. They lay in one another's arms while the rain lashed the windows and the wind screamed along the sea. A bird, in the early morning, beat its wings against the pane.

'You mustn't be lonely,' Benjie said over and over again. 'I shall be back almost before I've gone. I shall think of you all the time. You mustn't be lonely. You mustn't be lonely.'

As the light wove grey webs upon the wall he said, stroking her cheek:

'When I loved you a year ago, Vanessa, I didn't know what love was. This year has taught me.'

'And I love you,' she answered simply, 'more every day. I thought it couldn't grow; I didn't know . . . I didn't believe . . .'

She began to cry – a ridiculous thing, she thought, a woman of forty crying. But this once when there was no one to see . . . He kissed her tears. He had lain so often in her arms like a boy. Now he held her like a man and she was a child.

They were both very merry that morning. She would not come with him to London. She saw him drive off in the old cab; she waved her hand, laughing, while all Ravenglass watched from behind its windows.

Then she walked, her head bent to the wind, and did not return till it was dark.

THE KOPJE

SHE went back to Cat Bells.

Was not that perhaps a piece of impertinence? Everyone in the neighbourhood thought so. But she was not at all disturbed by the thoughts of her neighbours. She said to Mrs Newson on the evening of her arrival:

'You know, Mrs Newson, that I've left my husband.'

'Yes – so I've heard, my lady.'

'And since that time Mr Benjamin Herries and I have lived as man and wife. He has gone out to South Africa.'

'Yes, my lady. I hope he'll come back safe.'

'So do I,' said Vanessa, smiling. 'But I want you to tell me if you and your husband would rather get some other position. I shall be glad to help you until you are suited.'

Mrs Newson, who was a stout short woman with red cheeks and grey hair, paused. Then slowly delivered her mind.

'It's like this, my lady. It wouldn't be fair to say that me and Robert haven't talked this over. We have. We don't think it right in general for a woman to live with a man she's not married to. I wouldn't do it myself, nor would Robert. But you see, you're different. Folks can say what they like, but you're our own, so to speak. The last thing Will Leathwaite said to me while he was sensible enough to say anything was you was a grand lady and I wasn't to forget it. In Cumberland we're slow but sure, and me and Robert think you must have had good reasons for what you done, and there's no place can be to us what this cottage is after being here so long, so we'll be staying if it's all the same to you, my lady.'

After a week she could not have been more private, she thought, had she lived in a nunnery. No one came to see her; she went to see no one. She walked, read, followed with passionate interest every detail of the war. Gradually the peace of that place stole about her and enfolded her. Her father, her mother, Will, seemed to keep her company. The fell that rose above the roof of the cottage was burnished with the dying bracken; the herons sailed majestically against the sky. The little field circled with its toy-like trees on the slope above Lodore caught the morning light with such confident tranquillity that its curve, like the bowl of a cup, filled, emptied, filled again as though obeying happily its commander.

She bicycled over to the Fortress and looked down into the Uldale valley. There was a church there now and sheep were grazing where Fell House had been. The Fortress, she heard, was let to a Mr Swanwick. Children were playing in the garden, a bicycle leant against the door, two dogs ran to the gate and barked at her.

She thought day and night of Benjie. His earlier training as one of the much-bemocked Volunteers years before helped him now and he had sailed for South Africa early in November. She took a hurried journey to London, stayed there with him for two nights, seeing no one else but Barney, and returned to Cumberland. Then, some weeks later, she received her first letter.

MY DARLING – This must be only a short note. I shall soon have a chance, I hope, of a long letter. The worst part of the voyage was its monotony. From the moment we left London we were shut off from all news. To be without news for a fortnight at a time like this – you can imagine what hell it is! We thought we'd learn something at Madeira. Not a word. We were all inoculated against enteric and I to my shame took it badly. We had cinematograph men on board, but I don't myself think *that* will ever come to much! The machinery is so cumbrous that if they want to take anything that moves it is gone before their machines are ready. Then at last we sighted a sail and were so close that, when they put a board up with some news on it, we could read it easily. What they told us was: 'Three battles. Boers defeated' – and then didn't we cheer? After that no more news till we sighted Robben Island. *Then* there was news all right! . . . But you will know it all by this time and much more.

What else can I tell you but that I love you, love you, my darling? I carry you with me. You are never absent from me for a single moment, your courage, your goodness, your loyalty to a poor old devil whom no one has a good word for. But haven't they? The world has changed, Vanessa. Everyone is to me like a brother. No member of the Herries family here to tell the world what I really am – all damned good fellows – and, old though I am, I'm as lively as the youngest and will make you proud of me before I'm done. So cheer up, my sweetest, and believe in me as you have always done. Tomorrow, I believe, we are off again – whither I don't know. I'm as impatient as a flea on a hot plate. Impatient also for your first letter. Tell me *everything* – how the stream runs down through the garden, what you do every hour of the day, are the Newsons good to you? Have you had a look at the Fortress?

They are calling me. I must go – Your loving and devoted and eternally faithful

B.

A fortnight passed and there was another letter, a long one. Part of it was as follows:

... It was a bit of a battle. How can I make you see it?
Looking back I can see a green hill, kopje, almost blood colour,
and then grass-green veldt. The trains stopped and poured
khaki into the veldt. Funny to see the confused mass, then
order forming out of it, then the line of tiny dots, then a
thicker line, more and more lines, then a mass of khaki. First
the dots were at the base, almost lost in the brown of the hill,
then altogether lost, then suddenly against the skyline. Away on
the right the Imperial Light Horse. Then our guns thudded,
and thud came the answer. Then the shells. Thin whirr,
screaming cry. Ball after ball of white smoke struck the
kopje, then little balloons of shrapnel from our guns; then the
guns pealing faster and faster. Just as our own order to move
came, down crashed the rain. You never saw anything like it,
Vanessa. It drove through macintoshes like blotting paper. The
earth underfoot melted while you looked at it into mud and the
mud turned to water. Everything was blotted out in the cloud
of swirling water, but the guns thundered and doggedly we
pushed ahead.

Soon we were in it – my first battle, you know. What did I
feel? I can't tell you – except that the ridges we must conquer
seemed endless. Up one there was another! I wasn't afraid.
The bugles and the pipes stirred your blood. And then I was
caught into the noise. Officers shouting, swearing, cursing; all
of us stumbling, falling, jumping, killing – and then, like a
maniac's desired dream there at our feet the Boer camp and the
Boers galloping out of it!

As I started down the hill, though, something struck me.
Don't be frightened It turned out to be nothing – a slight
scratch – but my face was buried in mud, all the world seemed
to crash over my head and when at last I raised myself and
wiped the mud from my eyes I seemed to be transfixed by a
small kopje not far off. It stared at me, I at it. Brown-red in
colour, it was shaped like a pig with horns. It seemed to move,
to wriggle as though it wanted to scratch its back. I was
dazed of course, and didn't rightly know for a moment where
I was, but I thought it moved towards me, wagging its ears.
Then the scene cleared. I stood up. I was all right and ran
down the hill ...

Afterwards it was cold and drizzling. Some of the prisoners
joined us and we were all most friendly. Decent chaps the
Boers really – fine fellows with their beards and corduroys,

with a grand dignity, some of them. There's been a lot of
looting and you see men with the weirdest clothes. And you
should watch the guns scatter at a shell. See the legs of the
horses leap! You never imagined such nimbleness ...

And who do you think has turned up? George Endicott, a
friend of my wife's brother. A wild chap but I always liked
him and now here he is in my own regiment. Small world,
isn't it? Young Tom's shut up in Mafeking. Carey Rockage is
in Ladysmith. Are you well, my darling, and keeping up your
spirits? You seem to be always with me. Last night I talked to
you ...

She held on, but the strain began to tell. The loneliness of her
days and nights frightened her. She became restless. She wanted
to be doing something, something for the war, something,
through others, for Benjie.

After the Black Week, the 10th–16th of December: Stormberg,
Magersfontein, Tugela River, the feeling of the whole country
changed. What was this that had happened to England? While
the rest of the world looked on, jeering, hostile, longing for our
humiliation – here was the most shameful time for us since the
Indian Mutiny. Lord Roberts was appointed to the chief command, and Kitchener of Khartoum was to go with him. The
appointment roused a storm of new energy. The gay, light-
hearted jesting was over. This was a job that the country must
settle. The colonies offered new contingents, a great call went out
for yeomanry, and the new infantry volunteers flamed into being.
The City of London would raise and equip a regiment entirely at
its own expense. Everywhere there were new khaki uniforms.
From all parts of the country, shipyard men, squires' sons,
farmers' sons, artisans, and clerks poured into the new forces.
Nothing spectacular any more. Had they but known it, that
Black Week killed spectacular warfare for ever. Nothing to catch
the eye was tolerated. Scarlet fled, never to return to the
battlefield. A new patience, a fresh endurance, no more the reckless charge, but 'the infinitely painful crawl through the long,
long day'.

For Vanessa those first months in the new year became an
agony. She heard now from Benjie at the longest intervals. This
country, for the first time in her life, failed her. The old beloved
names – Skiddaw and Scafell, the running Derwent, the ridge of
Blencathra, the slow ripple of the quiet Lake meant nothing. The

valleys held no peace and the running water no music.

Her ostracism now terribly distressed her. It was a time when she wanted to have part and lot with all her fellow-beings, but on Cat Bells she was like a prisoner. Her loneliness became a horror; she could not sleep. She walked restlessly, tried to read and could not. She grew thin and pale. The Newsons heard her talking to herself, and once Mrs Newson found her crying, her head in her hands.

'Don't cry, my lady. It will be all right. 'Twill be over soon, they all say.'

Then at the beginning of April she had a brief letter from Benjie that frightened her. He had been ill in hospital; he was better, but things moved slowly. It would be all right, of course, but the Boers were obstinate fellows and Tom in Mafeking made it anxious work ... But he was all right ... She wasn't to worry ... That letter was too much for her. She came to London.

She went to a little hotel called 'The Clarence', off Baker Street. A lady in the train told her of it and she thought: 'How funny! I have never stayed by myself in a hotel before!' As soon as she was in the hansom driving to the hotel she was happy. She was nearer to Benjie; she was in touch with human beings again. She had not minded at all when Mrs Hope of Portinscale cut her in the Keswick street, when Mrs Merriman, who had before been so kind to her in Rosthwaite, gave her a sharp little bow and hurried down the Borrowdale Road. No, no, she had not minded ... She had been prepared for it. She had taken it gaily. Nevertheless, how different these things were without Benjie! Loneliness had returned, not the old spiritual loneliness of the life at Hill Street, but physical, material loneliness, hearing no voice, touching no hand, receiving no kiss. Now she was in the middle of life again. She noticed how many motors there were now; all the traffic was speedier and pedestrians were speedier too. One good thing – these new motor-cars would soon kill that London plague, the cab tout who had run at the side of your hansom pestering to serve you. She had a rich grand sense, after the silence of those Cumberland months, of plunging into a roaring new world ready to welcome her. Well, the Family would not be ready to welcome her. But she need not see them – only Barney and Adrian and Rose. And perhaps Cynthia – she had not, in the old days, been so violently shocked! It would be pleasant to have tea with Cynthia again in her pretty room, to hear the gossip, to ask about the theatres and to catch, even though from a distance, the tone and colour of that world to which she had once belonged! She sat upright in her hansom staring through the glass in front of her like a young girl free for the first time!

'The Clarence' was odd enough. A very large lady, her hair puffed out over elaborate pads, her shoulders very high, her waist almost invisible beneath her swelling bosom, her costume sweeping the floor, received Vanessa in an affected manner and directed a minute and rather shabby pageboy to show her to her room. This was dingy, with a view of chimney pots, a large portrait of Queen Victoria and a general gurgling of water pipes to give it character and life. The hotel smelt of fog and dead geraniums. At the head of the stairs was a large tank in which goldfish were swimming. The walls were everywhere very thin. As Vanessa changed her dress she heard from the next room a protesting voice:

'But, Mama, why not?'

'Because Mother thinks it better not, dear.'

'But Mama—'

'Now, Cecily. Mother knows best. He is not a young man who can possibly mean anything seriously. He has not a penny besides his Army pay.'

'But, Mama—'

The intimacy of this conversation terrified Vanessa, and when next afternoon Adrian came to visit her, and they sat in a room crowded with palms and dimmed by windows with blue and red glass, Vanessa told him that this was the most virtuous hotel in London. No indiscretion could be committed without everyone in the hotel being aware of it.

She was gay, merry, full of eagerness to enter life again.

'I must get something to do, Adrian. It was dreadful in Cumberland. I simply moped. I must work, help, tire myself to death until Benjie returns.'

She was aware of a certain awkwardness in Adrian. She remembered unexpectedly that evening, years ago, when Adrian had been led up to her at the Ball, his eagerness, his vitality, his impulsive determination to help the world. He was as kind, as affectionate as ever, but he was now a Government servant, the *Herries* Government servant. His clothes were exquisite, his manner that of one who had to carry a good many public burdens on his shoulders. Was he writing anything? No, he had little time he was afraid. H. D. Traill's death had distressed him greatly; he had given him a good deal of reviewing in *Literature*. Had she read Fleury's *Louis XV Intime*? A most interesting work with a very striking portrait of La Pompadour. And Dr Barry's *Arden Massiter*, quite good as novels go. A little over-written. And a very amusing little book, *Lambkin's Remains*. The writer signed himself H. B. He was the author of *The Bad Child's Book of Beasts*. 'You remember, Vanessa.'

But Vanessa, alas, did not remember. She had never heard of Dr Barry and was not sure whether she had met Mr Traill or no.

'Perhaps he came to one of our parties.'

Oh no, Traill never went to parties. But Vanessa was trembling for news.

'Adrian, tell me about Hill Street.'

Adrian's pale, still very youthful countenance coloured.

'Oh, no one goes there now. Winifred and Vera keep Ellis quite a prisoner. He likes it, I believe. He's queer, of course. They say he makes paper boats and has toy engines. He doesn't go to the City any more. Alfred has everything in his hands. But they say Ellis is quite happy.'

Did Vanessa imagine it or was there a new note in Adrian's voice? Was he a little, a very little, superior? Why did he seem to patronize? Vanessa's imagination. And then he must hate this hotel.

'It's a horrid hotel, isn't it?' she said.

'Yes. Beastly. But you want it quiet, don't you? I mean – you don't want to run up against any of the family.'

'Oh no – except Barney, of course.'

'Dear old Barney – he's getting pretty aged. He plays bridge all his evenings.'

'Bridge?'

'Why, of course!' Adrian expressed surprise. 'Where *have* you been? Don't they play it in Cumberland? London's crazy about it – has been for ages.'

There was a pause. Mrs Mont, the proprietress, came into the room and looked around. It was odd to see her balance her enormous bosom on two such very small feet! She patted her great head of hair and stared at the pair of them.

'Has she already heard about me?' Vanessa wondered.

'Oh yes – and do tell me about the others. Carey's shut up in Ladysmith, Benjie told me. And Cynthia's husband – he's in Natal, isn't he? Adrian! – Cynthia – how does she feel about me? Do you think I could go and see her? Would she mind? She used to be very broad-minded . . .'

There was an awkward pause. Adrian coughed, stroking the side of his nose in a manner common to many of the Herries men.

At last he spoke: 'Look here, Vanessa. There's something I ought to say. You're such a sport, you're so wise, I know you'll understand perfectly. But the whole family has taken this awfully badly. They can't get over it. You see – they admired you so much and they were so proud of Hill Street. And then – if it had been anyone but Benjie, whom they've disapproved of for years! And then there have been so many family scandals! It didn't matter so much perhaps years ago when they weren't anyone particularly, but now they are respected everywhere. Alfred's a great man in the City, and Cynthia thinks herself Queen of London. She does really. You'd be amused if you saw her. Already she's bringing her two girls up most awfully carefully. They're nice little girls too. She wants them to marry Dukes. What I mean is – there's me and there's Barney – but the others – well, I'm afraid you mustn't expect them to change. They won't. They are more respectable than you've any idea of. They can't endure Benjie and they think you – they think you were unkind to Ellis.'

'I see,' said Vanessa quietly. 'Thank you for telling me, Adrian.'

'Oh, that's all right. I say, isn't there rather a queer smell in here? It may be my fancy.'

He got up.

'Well, I must be off. Got some work to do. You tell me, Vanessa, if there's anything I can do. We'll go out one night. We'll do a play. The one at the St James's isn't bad – *The Man of Forty*. Alexander and Fay Davis.'

'Thank you, Adrian.' She stood looking at him with a wise and rather maternal smile. She could not resist saying: 'You won't be ashamed to be seen out with me, will you, Adrian?'

He blushed, looking like a boy of eighteen.

'My God, no! Why, what do you think, Vanessa? *I* haven't any prejudices. I'll be proud!'

But, a little later, sitting in her bedroom and listening to the gurgles of the water pipes, she was not so sure.

Then, next day, when old Barney came to see her, she learnt more about the Family. Barney was seventy, stout, rather untidy. There were pouches under the eyes, his cheeks were puffed out, giving him a childish pouting expression, but the eyes themselves were full of sparkle, humour, kindliness, and his grey hair, though it was untidy, was strong and wiry. He had a paunch, but he walked on his thick legs sturdily, his back straight, his head up, and always that slightly mocking boy-out-for-a-lark expression at his mouth's corners as though he found life more of a joke than ever. And yet you could, if you knew the Family, tell that he was old Emily's brother and pompous, long-buried Newmark's son. He found life a joke indeed because there had been originally enough of the solemn Herries there for him to see how ridiculous it could be.

Sitting again in the room with the palms and the coloured glass, this teatime was very different from the one of yesterday. Vanessa was one of Barney's *real* devotions. As he saw her now, seated very quietly, a middle-aged woman whose hair was turning grey, in this shabby hotel, and thought how barely two years ago he had seen her with her white satin and diamonds leading the cotillion in the Hill Street drawing-room, satin and diamonds seemed to him very vulgar things. But did she mind this shabby hotel, he wondered? Was she still satisfied with her bargain?

'Adrian came to tea yesterday,' she told him. 'I thought him a little – well, a little superior. Has he become so, or is it only with me because I'm a black sheep now, or did I imagine it?'

'Oh, Adrian's a little more Herries than he was – that's all. The Foreign Office might have been invented by our family – it's so exactly what we most approve of.'

He looked at her anxiously, rather as though he were her father.

'You're happy, Vanessa?'

'Well, I'm rather lonely, Barney, at the moment. I miss Benjie, you see – and I want work, something to do. Can you find me something? I must be busy.'

'Yes, I think I can find something. There's a Mrs Cundlip who's a friend of mine. She has a working party. They make things for the soldiers three afternoons a week. She and her friends live very quietly in Kensington. They don't gossip and they are nice kind women. I think you'd like it.'

'Oh, Barney, thank you! You *are* a dear!'

He was touched by her gratitude. Poor Vanessa, she *must* have been lonely! He told her more of the Family. Cynthia was now the star. Worcester was doing very well in South Africa. He was to join Roberts' staff. May Rockage was in London, doing war work, and desperately trying to find husbands for her girls.

Horace was rather chastened. His silent wife had developed into a grim woman who frightened him. Alfred's two children were nice little things. Richard Cards – Adrian's older brother – was now living in London. He had married rather late and had two children. Barney gave very much the same account of Hill Street as Adrian had done. No one saw Ellis and it was generally known that he was eccentric. Barney did not tell Vanessa the general opinion that her flight had turned Ellis' brain. Winifred and Vera Trent never left him. And that was that. Vanessa understood quite clearly that the Family would have nothing to do with her . . .

In another day or two she went to call on Mrs Cundlip, found her a kindly simple woman with a son at the Front and a plain energetic daughter with a passion for the clergy.

Whether Mrs Cundlip and her friend knew Vanessa's story or no, they gave no sign of interest in it. Indeed they seemed never to gossip and had, as a group, a curiously impersonal air as thought they were part of the quiet Kensington scene like the trees in the Gardens, the nurses with their perambulators, the solid policeman at the gates, the decorous shoppers in the High Street. Vanessa found them a comfort. She worked in the gentle Kensington drawing-room hung with watercolours of Switzerland and Italy and thought of Benjie and tried to be happy. As the days passed she found that increasingly she was afraid of a chance encounter with one of the Family. She remained in her unpleasant hotel because it was so safe. None of them would ever come there. When she shopped or went to the theatre her apprehension was always alive. It would hurt her, she knew now, to be cut by Cynthia or May. *Would* May cut her? – that kind, simple countrywoman in whose house she had so often stayed? But May had her girls now to think of. Old Violet Bellairs was very ill and never left her bed. The younger Violet who had married a Colonel belonged, Vanessa heard, to a very fast set (in revenge for her constricted youth) who played bridge all day and all night. And Lettice Marrable? Lettice was secretary now to a branch in Manchester of Women's Suffrage. She wrote very lovingly to Vanessa and said that she would come to see her as soon as she had time to visit London. She was very busy and talked in her letter about The Cause as though there were but one in all the world.

So there they all were.

Then one sunny afternoon early in May, Vanessa tumbled almost into Horace's arms in the Army and Navy Stores. There was no way of avoiding it! There was Horace, red-faced, stout, benignant behind his glasses, buying soap. He stepped back unexpectedly, almost trod on Vanessa, said, 'I beg your pardon' with his customary episcopal courtesy and saw who it was. His plump cheeks were scarlet.

'Vanessa!' he said.

'How are you, Horace?' she replied, holding out her hand and smiling.

They shook hands and she noticed that at once he moved with her a little out of earshot.

'I'm so glad to see you, Horace. You're looking very well.'

'Yes, I'm very well, thanks.'

'I can see you're busy. So am I.'

She smiled at him very gaily. Oh yes, it *was* pleasant to see one of the Family even though it were only Horace, with his high white forehead, large spectacles and protruding chin! For the first time in her life she *liked* Horace.

'Oh yes – indeed yes ... very busy ...' he stuttered, looking nervously about him. No one was near him, no one was looking at him. He coughed. 'Very agreeable to see you, Vanessa. Are you long in London?'

'Yes, for some time, I think.' She looked him straight between the glasses. 'Benjie is in South Africa, you know.'

'Oh yes, indeed. I had heard ...' (Why wasn't he a Bishop? Not that she had anything against Bishops. Often the noblest of men, but Horace's benevolence needed an apron.)

Now that he was assured that no one was observing them he was more at his ease. He began to talk with some of his old eager but, in some odd way, calculated friendliness. He spoke of the nobility of our men at the Front, of Britain's showing the world, of everyone doing what they could, of human nature being at its best in times of stress. He became more practical, revealing himself, as he had always liked to do, at the very centre of affairs. He had just been lunching with a most interesting man – name of Yerkes – the projector of the new electric Underground. He confidently prophesied that we should all be living at least fifty miles out of London owing to electrified trains – we should think nothing of it, nothing of it at all; said what a nuisance half-sovereigns were – he had nearly given one just now as a tip instead of a sixpence; that all the best horses had gone to South Africa, so that the omnibuses were sadly suffering. He talked as though he were delivering an address to a gathering of charity children, Vanessa thought, but he meant to be kindly. It had always been Horace's trouble that he meant so well, but had weaknesses, insincerities, tempers and absent-mindedness like the rest of us. Then he saw some ladies approaching and, raising his hat, hurried away.

'The gentleman has forgotten his soap,' the shopman said.

'He will come back for it, I'm sure,' said Vanessa.

She was very tired. It would have been nice of Horace if he had invited her to take a cup of tea. But certainly that was too much to expect. Her arm ached. She was suffering from what was known as 'skirt wrist'.

A night or two later she had a horrible dream. She dreamt that she was on a vast green plain, bounded by hills spotted with small black patches. She had lost her way and then saw coming towards her the kopje that Benjie had mentioned in one of his first letters. It was coloured red, as Benjie had said, and shaped like a pig. It came wriggling after her, flapping large naked red ears. It covered the ground with extraordinary speed. She began to run but made no advance. It came nearer and nearer; she could smell its fetid breath and see, on its back, tufts of hair. The thing rolled in its movement. It had no face, only the flapping ears. 'This is my punishment,' she thought in her despair. 'I knew that I could not escape it.' She screamed for Benjie and woke.

After that night she seemed always to be tired. The loneliness that she had felt in Cumberland returned. Both Adrian and Barney were kind, but they were busy people; the ladies in Kensington were most pleasant, but they did not invite her to their houses; she grew no nearer in intimacy to any of them, nor did she wish to. After that dream she was haunted with fear for Benjie. It was a fortnight now since she had heard from him, and his last letter had seemed to her dispirited, disappointed. With increasing unrest she looked every day at the casualties in the newspaper. She told herself that she must be calm and brave, that thousands of other women were suffering as she was, but it became soon impossible for her to be impersonal. There seemed to be no one in the world but Benjie. It was not only that he might be killed, but that his restlessness, his passion for liberty, must be fed my this adventure, that the longer he was away from her the easier it would be for him to remain away.

She suffered as all women do who love a man but are tied to him by no official bond. She had no hold on him at all but his love for her, and he might love other women as he loved her. When he was there she knew that he loved her, but now she was tortured by the very indefiniteness of their relationship, although at its heart it was anything but indefinite.

Then, on the eighteenth of May, sitting in her bedroom, reading, she heard a timid knock on the door.

'Come in!' she said.

The blowsy good-natured chambermaid, Kate by name, put her head in through the door.

'Excuse me, mum,' she said, 'but I thought you'd like to know. They're saying as Mafeking's been relieved!'

'Oh no!' Vanessa cried, jumping up.

'Yes, mum. Ain't it grand? Relieved yesterday, they say!'

Her first thought was for Tom. How delighted Benjie would be! And then that it would mean that the war would be soon ended, very soon perhaps. And, after that, that now England could hold her head up again, the long period of doubt and failure was over. She was so happy that, in a moment, all her troubles seemed to be ended. Everyone would be happy! Everyone *was* happy!

At dinner in the hotel that evening even the old waiter in his dirty dicky could scarcely carry the plates for joy. Two old ladies who had never before spoken to her said: 'Isn't it excellent? *Such* good news! We are so glad!' as though it had all been done for their especial benefit.

At the table next to hers a schoolgirl with her mother was in a state of almost frenzied excitement. She had, it seemed, been allowed to come down to dinner in celebration of the great event. She was a plain little girl, wearing the hideous khaki-coloured dress then considered patriotic for schoolgirls. She was talking of some elder girl who was allowed to wear a red, white, and blue costume, with a regimental clasp in front. The 'thing' at school was to pin on to yourself many penny buttons decorated with the heads of generals, and one girl was the envy of all the others because she had found somewhere a regular saucer with the picture of Baden-Powell and went everywhere with this pinned to her chest.

As Vanessa listened she thought, 'I'd like to have a little girl of my own. Would it be unfair to her that Benjie and I are not married? Father was illegitimate and never minded. Is it worse for a girl? Would *I* have minded? Nothing that Father had done would have seemed to me wrong.' Soon she would be too old to have children. She had missed that as she had missed other things. But she had not missed love ... Benjie would soon be back now, and Tom. She would love Tom with all her heart, be a splendid friend to him and, in her old age, stand by him, help his wife when he married. For Tom was unusual like all the other unusual Herries – wild at the heart, wanting often to be free of everyone; hard men for a woman to understand were these Herries!

She would go out and share in everybody's happiness. In Baker Street she boarded an omnibus, but when they reached Oxford Circus they could go no farther. She climbed down and plunged into pandemonium. She stayed for a while in a shop door and let the crowd surge past her. First, looking upwards it was as though the sky itself had gone mad. From nowhere out of nothing (for there had been little warning) the façades had created their illumination. Electric light was still rare and, at its greatest peak of grandeur, could not have rivalled the magic of those gas jets. Their wonder was that they were swayed by those little winds that came and went, running in blue-and-gold ripples like water against the grey surface, seeming for a moment to be blown out and then, with a sense of mischievous laughter, bursting into life again, as though by their own happy agency they had relighted themselves. They ran in waves of trembling light, hesitated, vanished and, with new energy, ran again. The sky was alive with beauty.

Beneath it what a world – as though a new race inhabited the earth! Men in evening dress, hats on the back of their heads, cocked sideways, evening capes flying, danced arm in arm with the ladies of the East End. These women who were to go down in history, dressed in black satin, wore great hats crowned with ostrich plumes; and so they danced, their fine bosoms swelling, the flounces of their long dresses swinging from their tiny waists, petticoats whitely revealed and vanishing. Their own gentlemen for that night at least were in 'high dress' with mother-of-pearl on their flat caps, trousers tight to the knee, flapping round the ankles. They changed hats with their Donahs, moving in the 'double-shuffle in an ecstasy of joy. The East End came West that night, and the West was glad.

And the noise! Everyone was shouting, singing, turning rattles, blowing the coiled paper springs, screaming down pink-and-white tuppenny trumpets gay with silvery angels' hair. You were 'killing Kruger with your mouth'. You were singing 'Duke's

son, cook's son, son of a belted Earl'. You were shouting *'W'ere*
did you get that 'at?', 'Wot price old Krüger!', 'Git yer 'air cut!'
You were singing:

> *Hark! I hear the bugle calling,*
> *And I can no longer stay.*
> *Goodbye, Dolly, I must leave you.*
> *Goodbye, Dolly Gray!*

That night the British Army was worshipped. It was to be
worshipped again, but in another sterner spirit, when tuppenny
trumpets and mother-of-pearl could not meet a far more menacing enemy.

The soldier and the sailor were the heroes, and the 'Little
Englander' was the villain of the piece. Close to Vanessa a girl,
waving her arms, screamed: 'Down with Lloyd George!' and
behold his image was flung deep under the dancing shoes of that
multitude. And there is a god in a monocle, with an orchid in his
buttonhole – 'Three cheers for Joe!' 'Not for Joseph!' 'Good old
Joe!' Labour? One man named Keir Hardie has boldly walked
into the House with a cloth cap on his head. So much for
Labour. Squeakers and ticklers and corncrakes have, that evening, little consciousness of a new world that very soon will be
demanding very different instruments . . .

Vanessa for a while was safe in her doorway, but soon the
crowd was wilder. Hansoms appearing from the very bowels of
the earth discharged young men in evening dress; something
other than tea is the draught of the Town; here there is a fight
between a cabman and a fare, there a policeman has seized some
gesticulating figure, raised him above the crowd, then, as though
abandoning the hopeless charge, dropped him back into the
crowd again.

Vanessa has been swung from her doorstep. It is best to go with
the crowd. Someone has linked arms with her and she is swayed
down Regent Street, all the shouts, songs, cries seeming to catch a
sudden rhythm so that it is as though the very sky itself were
singing. At the edge of Piccadilly Circus the surge forward is
arrested and you see a rising, falling pattern of life – not individual life now but something made up of the windy, swaying
lights, tumbling bursts of sound, the very buildings swinging, it
seemed, in the uncertain glare.

A woman grasped her arm: with her other hand she wielded a

toy trumpet, her straw hat at the back of her padded hair. Vanessa turned and looked. It was Rose.

'Hooray! Hooray!' she cried, waving the trumpet. 'Hooray for Joe! Hooray—' She said confidently to Vanessa: 'Come on, dear! Let's give him a cheer!'

'Rose,' Vanessa said, bending her body sideways to avoid the pressure of a stout perspiring gentleman with a tickler. 'Don't you know me?'

Rose stared. 'Vanessa!' She threw her arms around her, scratching the back of her neck with her trumpet. Her straw hat, falling, disappeared. 'Oh, Vanessa – my darling! my darling!'

Vanessa realized that Rose had been too splendidly celebrating victory. At the moment she could realize nothing further, for the impulse of the crowd swept them both off their feet. It appeared not unlikely that there and then they would find death in one another's arms, bells clanging in their ears, somewhere the trumpets of a distant band, the smell of sweating bodies, broadcloth, patchouli, against their nostrils and, against the sky, grey walls like rocks on whose surfaces flickered in the wind the jets of blue, green, red, thrown up from the tossing dark pool at their feet. It was then confusion. The fountain of the Circus stood out above the singing waters. Heads rose and fell like despairing drowning mariners. Fastened firmly in the midst was the rock of a towering hansom up whose side figures were climbing. Beyond that again an effigy with a tangled beard, a battered high hat, jerked as though in agony against the lights – Krüger moving to his bonfire.

Then the waters parted. Waves of human beings slumped like falling walls. The effigy was moving forward, followed by a great cheering procession, men waving their hats, women screaming, and under the confusion – above it, outside and within it – the steady pulse of *The Soldiers of the Queen*, into whose tune at last all the scattered sounds and voices were gathered.

Driven back at the corner of Shaftesbury Avenue, Vanessa suddenly discovered that, a wide porch of a restaurant protecting her, she was free. Miraculously, still holding to her arm was Rose.

'Oh, where is he?' Rose cried. 'The Captain! The Captain gone! He swore he wouldn't leave me. Oh, Vanessa, I'm lost – I don't know where he lives. He's got my little green bag, my little bag . . .'

They stood in the shelter of the porch against the wall, shoulder to shoulder. Rose cried out as though she were demented. A lock of false hair had detached itself from the disordered pile and tickled her mouth. There was a small scratch on her cheek from which blood was trickling. Altogether a battered Rose.

She looked at Vanessa, and as she looked her wildness fell from her.

'Oh, Vanessa, I've drunk too much. Take me home. I don't care if I never see the Captain again.'

Very slowly they moved up Shaftesbury Avenue; then, turning at the first opening, found themselves in a little dark street, deserted, melancholy, shutting off like a curtain the lights, the singing, the press of the surging crowd.

'Where's your hat, dear?' Vanessa asked. She took out her handkerchief and wiped Rose's cheek. Rose began to cry.

'Oh, you must think me dreadful. Fancy your meeting me like this after all this time. But it was all the Captain's fault, and my bag had all my money in it.'

Vanessa, her hand through Rose's arm, led her from little street to little street. Near Oxford Street they found a hansom.

'Now, Rose, where are you living?'

Rose stared. 'I don't know ... Oh yes, Three Orcutt Street. That's where I was living three days ago, before I met the Captain.'

'Well – is that where you want to go?'

'Yes. You'll come with me, Vanessa? I'm not drunk really. I only had a drop in the Captain's room.'

In the hansom Rose leant her head against Vanessa's bosom and sobbed.

'Mafeking! Mafeking! I wish to God I had never heard of Mafeking or the Captain either.' In a grim little street they stopped at a grim little house.

'No. Don't come in. My room isn't very grand.' She was quite sober now, looking like a dishevelled child afraid of a scolding. 'But you'll come and see me tomorrow? Or I'll come and see *you*. May I?'

Vanessa told her the address of the hotel. Once more Rose flung her arms about her neck and passionately kissed her.

'It all feels different, meeting you. Like old times.' She wiped her eyes. 'I've lost my hat. I don't know what Mrs Blaker will think if she sees me. She doesn't think much of me anyway. Goodnight, darling.'

Later up to Vanessa's bedroom came the shouts and cries of a city madly rejoicing. Some kind of a triumph. A passionate impulse of compassion caught her heart, compassion for the world, for Rose, for all lonely and misguided creatures. The kopje could not frighten her now.

Indeed, indeed it could not. Two weeks later there was a telegram forwarded from Cumberland. Benjie had lost an arm and was being sent home at once.

She sat, with the telegram in her hand, staring in front of her. She was so happy that she could scarcely breathe lest the telegram should prove unreal. Then she knelt down by her bed and thanked God.

YOUNG TOM IN NEWLANDS

YOUNG Tom Herries, sitting one summer evening on a slope below Dale Head, the peak which closes the Newlands Valley, watched the sky. It had for some while fascinated him and distracted him from the second volume of Hardy's *The Woodlanders*, which lay on the turf beside him. He was always known as Young Tom, but even in years he was not so young any longer, for he was now seventeen years of age, but in character, in a subtle intuition of motive and feeling, in self-command, he had never been young. In looks he was something like his father, dark, short and thick with a round hard head and short wiry hair. He had also some of his father's geniality and all of his warmth of heart.

But he was different from him altogether in his self-control, in his patience, in his consideration for others. His early flight to Paris with Timothy, the free life there spent always in the company of his elders, his experiences in South Africa, his acquaintance with all the ways of humankind, bad, good, sensual, virtuous, foolish, wise, had helped him to come to terms with real life long before the common time. But, with this, there was something young in him that made folk, the country people, the townspeople, all who knew him, speak of him as Young Tom. He *was* young in this: that unlike his father he took all his responsibilities with extreme seriousness. His principal responsibilty was to his father and to Vanessa. He loved them both, but he knew his father too well to think him in any way wonderful. He felt to his father as he would to a younger brother whose faults he knew by heart but whom he loved and guarded the more for those faults, but Vanessa he worshipped.

He had been living with them now in this little house in the Vale of Newlands for six months, and the longer he lived with them the deeper did his devotion to Vanessa grow. He was thinking of her now as he lay on his back, his arms behind his head, looking at the sky. She seemed to him of another kind altogether from any women he had ever known, and he had known some very strange ones. Her love for him, which she had felt since she had visited him a little boy ill at school, made her more natural with him, perhaps, than she was with anyone else. They were very often alone together and then she talked to him as though she were a girl of his own age. She poured out all her heart to him: she told him more than she had ever told Benjie. She told him everything: of her childhood, her love for her father, her life in London with Ellis, her love for Tom's father – and they discussed, for hours together, Benjie's character, his sweetness, irresponsibility, restlessness, honesty, infidelities. When Benjie was drunk (rare occasions but unfortunate) Tom managed him to a marvel. When Benjie disappeared, Tom reassured Vanessa until he appeared again. Tom sometimes rated his father as though their positions were reversed. Benjie never resented it. He was as proud of his son as he could be. Tom himself, of course, was far from perfect. He was obstinate and sometimes sulked. He was given to fits of melancholy that he inherited from his own Herries strain, and then he would go away by himself and brood. There were many causes for these, but the chief of them was that he had always meant, since he was a tiny boy, to be a great writer and he thought now that he would never be even a good one. His early devotion to Timothy had been stirred the more by his saying to himself that Tim would be a great painter and he would be a great writer. Now Tim was, if not a great painter, a very good one. He was in Paris selling his pictures. He was known everywhere as a promising and unusual artist. But Tom, although he was a fair journalist, was no more. He talked to Vanessa again and again about this; he showed her his attempts. She was too honest and knew the value that he put on her honesty too well to encourage him.

'What is it,' he said to her in despair, 'that I can't get?'

'It is something, I suppose, that doesn't come by asking for it,

Never mind, Tom. You began so young. You're only seventeen now! There are so many writers. You will do something better in another way.'

Now, thinking of *The Woodlanders,* he felt a sort of rage against fate. Yes, he was only seventeen – there was plenty of time – and yet he did not lie to himself. *This* thing would never be his. And *what* was it? Hardy, Tom thought, was a peasant, he had scarcely moved from his countryside: he already knew far more about the wide world than Hardy could know. Hardy often made his characters talk in stilted, unnatural sentences; his books were filled with ridiculous coincidences – but here in these pages was life, the life that so many polished sophisticated writers missed altogether. Tom looked at the scene around him and his spirits fell into quiet.

For the last fortnight there had been perfect weather in Cumberland. By day the sun had shone, veiled with mist sufficient to give hill and water their rightful size. It was a late year and so the larch still stood in patterns of green flame against the smoky shadows of yew and fir, the stems of the young bracken were pellucid as are the throats of pale-green glasses. And with the sunny mist, over the green flats, up the stony sides of the fells, above the glittering chattering runnels of water, there was now thin shadow, nów a breadth of light, all warm, kindly, beneficent; as a generous man's hand strokes his dog's shoulder, so God bent down from His cloud and caressed His world.

Tom, lying on his back, wondered that now the sky could be so quiet and so pure when so often he had watched clouds battling in armies for supremacy, seen one fierce cloud-captain drag another by his hair, watched the surge upward, from the hinder-parts of the Tops, of whirling frenzied clouds, angrily purple, and the thick grey sullen banks of storm mount and spread until all the world was covered with them and rain fell in spears of steel upon the earth. Now the sky was pale like the inside of a pearl shell; light was translucent and softer than down. Cat Bells and Dale Head, Robinson and Maiden Moor were bathed in a peace that seemed eternal, and towards the dip where Lobstone Band hid its rocky tors, a carpet of purple shadow hung above the little fields that welcomed the evening.

Near him Herdwick sheep were browsing – the bravest little sheep in England and the most adaptable. Their wool may be harsh, but so faithful in spirit are they that all their lives they will not move far from the place where they were born, not because

they are unenterprising, but because here for generations their
ancestors have been and here, like proper Cumbrians, their heart
is set. So, with the old forest trees, the fir, the oak, the birch, with
the stones and boulders that they can, if they will, so closely
resemble, with the running water and the flying clouds, they obey
the law.

Soon the stars would come out, breaking the green of the evening sky, and a young crescent moon would rise, and all night
long the light would last, paler than ivory, quieter than sleep.
The air was scented with the newly cut hay from a field nearby,
with the first honeysuckle, with the summer heat drawn from
grass and fern. Birds winged slowly, making the silence vocal.
The line of the hills grew with every moment sharper as the
shining sky paled.

Tom's thoughts turned to his own future. This had been a fine
holiday, but it could not last for ever. He loved this country as he
loved none other, but soon he must go back into the world again.
He had for so long now been a man – ever since he was fourteen –
that he had not a boy's light indifferennce of waiting until life
should begin for him. He had been kicked about in Paris, he had
endured a historic siege like the other men with him, and time
would not wait. For six months, too, he had been ostracized. No
one came to see them at Cold Fell. His mother's cottage was only
ten minutes away over the hill. It was let to a painter and his
family, but that long slow slope of Cat Bells cut the three of them
from the world as though they were on a separate planet. Sometimes, when he rode into Keswick, he was looked at almost as
though he had a deformity. He minded in spite of himself. What
did it matter that his father and Vanessa were not married? They
would be married if only that crazy old lunatic in London would
die. They loved one another more faithfully than many a married
pair, and, stroking the back of *The Woodlanders* with his hand,
he thought to himself that the writer of that book would understand if he were here and would come to see them and be their
friend. There was something terribly wrong with the world
when people as good as his father and Vanessa could be exiled
simply because some old clergyman had not blessed them. He
knew, though, that it all went further than this, that people
thought it impertinent of his father to come back and live with
his woman here in the very spot where they were so well known,
and that there had been scandals before, old scandals of a hundred and fifty years ago that everyone in these valleys knew,

scandals that had lost nothing in constant telling.

His young heart was passionately in sympathy with all the outlaws. It was enough for someone to be in disgrace for Tom to be on his side, so long as the outlaw was not cruel nor mean nor a coward. At his age it seemed very easy for the world to be wrong and for all the good men to be outlaws. And he was, like his father, a born champion of lost causes.

He heard voices and, sitting up, saw his father coming towards him and with him a large rough untidy-looking man. Benjie, when he saw his son, waved his one arm and, as they came up, introduced his companion.

'Tom, this is Mr George Endicott, an old friend of mine.' Then, reaching his hand up to the big man's shoulder, he said: 'George, this is my boy, Tom. I don't think you've seen him before. Tom, Endicott was with me in Africa. This boy, you know, George, was all through the Mafeking siege.'

The man, Tom thought, was one of the strongest and wildest he had ever seen. He looked like part of the countryside, belonging to the stones and bracken like the Herdwick sheep.

He wore no hat, his face was of a brick-red colour, and his shirt was wide open, showing a brown chest with a pelt of black hair. His body was solid like a stone, but he moved lightly on his feet, making no sound. He had only nodded at Tom and then passed straight up the fell, swinging his arms.

'Tom, look here. I'm glad I saw you. When you go down tell them I shan't be back tonight.'

'When will you be back?'

'Oh, tomorrow likely. Endicott has come over from Whitehaven. We're going for a tramp.'

Benjie looked shamefaced. He knew that Tom knew that he had gone from the house without telling Vanessa.

'All right,' Tom said shortly, and without another word, picking up his book, he started down the hill. He hated it when his father was ashamed, when Vanessa was disappointed, when rough ill-looking men from God-knows-where took his father off to drink and fool with girls and not to return for days perhaps. His father was fine, his father was the best man he knew – but why must he make Vanessa unhappy?

Cold Fell had changed not at all in the last hundred years, with its whitewashed front, its narrow passages and low-ceilinged rooms, the rough cobbling before the door, the slope down the hill where the hens were and the broad fields that crossed the stream and the valley, the cows now clustered for the cool under a large oak, the sheep browsing on the fell slope. Great sweeping shadows of gold covered the valley, and the sun, low now above the hill, struck through the thick leafage of the oak. The river, shrunk though it was now, could be heard very clearly chattering over its stones, so still was the air.

Vanessa was standing in the doorway when Tom came up.

'Have you seen your father, Tom?'

'Yes.' Tom put his arm round her and kissed her. He did not kiss anyone easily, but he liked to kiss Vanessa – her skin was so cool and so firm. Her hair was greying but her cheek had a girl's freshness. 'Yes. He's away for the night.'

She said nothing but went in.

Later they had their supper in the porch. An old woman called Mrs Williams came every day and 'did' for them. But Benjie and Vanessa cooked, and they, all three of them, did the house, looked after the piece of garden at the back. Tom went into Keswick for the shopping. For six months Vanessa had scarcely stirred from the valley. She looked now like a woman who had always lived in the country, her hair very simply brushed back, parted in the middle, leaving her fine brow clear and broad. She wore a plain blue cotton dress, shorter by a great deal than the prevailing fashion. Her waist was not pinched nor were her shoulders puffed. She looked her age, but her body had strengthened. With her height, her broad shoulders, her firm big breasts, she was a woman who would be noticed anywhere, and all her life she had carried herself superbly.

They had cold chicken and Cumberland ham, a salad, a cold apple tart, and a cheese. A fine supper on a summer evening with the murmur of the river coming up to them and the air as sweet as honey.

Vanessa, leaning her arms on the table, looked out to the valley.

'You know, Tom, I think Benjie might have told me.'

'He was afraid to. He had a man with him.'

'A man? – what man?'

'His name was Enderby, or Enderley – something like that.'

'Endicott. George Endicott. I know him. He is an old friend of Benjie's. He met him first when he met your mother. He was a friend of your uncle's.'

'What kind of man is he?'

'Oh, all right, I dare say. Rough, wild, always on the tramp.'

'Father said he was with him in Africa.'

'I wouldn't mind,' she went on, after a pause, 'if only he'd tell me when he's going, but he slips out of the house as though he were ashamed.'

'He *is* ashamed,' said Tom.

'The trouble is that each time I say to myself: "Perhaps this time he won't come back." Judith, my grandmother, used to talk to me sometimes when I was a girl about *her* married life. She's often told me that her husband – he was a Frenchman – would go off just like that, only he would be away for months. The difference was, though, that Judith was married. I'm not. I've no hold on your father except that we love one another. That's the only hold any woman ought to want, but women are funny. I've never known a woman, Tom, who was really sure of a man. Men belong to a different world, and you can't be sure, from minute to minute, that they won't have a new idea in their head. Women are too serious about everything. They can't take things lightly. It isn't that I doubt your father. We've loved one another all our lives – but I've nothing else now. I've put all my eggs in one basket.'

'You've got me,' Tom said proudly.

'Yes. You're very faithful. You'll make a splendid husband one day.'

Tom saw that she was struggling not to be unhappy; he saw how deeply disappointed she was and, with an intuition wonderful for a boy, knew that she was dreading the long lonely summer night. He wanted terribly to help her.

'I know what it is in Father,' he said. 'It isn't anything to do with you and me. He wants to be free sometimes. He told me once that there's bad blood in us. My great-uncle killed my grandfather in Skiddaw Forest and my great-grandfather killed himself. You know all that. And I think sometimes it all comes over my father – a kind of superstition about the past. Of course the past can't do anything to you *really*, can it? But you have to fight it sometimes perhaps. So he goes away and fights and then comes back to you again. That's *how* I explain it!' he ended.

She got up and kissed him.

'The truth is, Tom dear, that I've never been a very sensible woman. I haven't enough humour. If I could only see how funny things are it would be a lot easier. When the Queen died I was unhappy for weeks. Why should I have been? I'd never known her, but I couldn't get used to her not being there. It's always been the same if I've loved anyone. You take life lightly, Tom, and people easily. It's the only way.'

'I'm rather serious-minded too, I expect,' said Tom. 'Tim's always said so. Tim used to say that I ought to have been an old nurse with families of other people's children to look after.' He laughed. 'Don't you worry. Father will be back tomorrow.' He got up and patted her on the shoulder, then moved about taking the plates and dishes into the house.

Vanessa sat there, her chin propped on her hands, staring in front of her.

Three days passed and Benjie had not returned, nor had any word come from him. This was the longest time that he had ever been away from Vanessa since her flight from Hill Street. The hours were quiet, stealthy, and packed with a secret significance. She did not know that time could be so long, and on the third day she found herself walking down the valley towards the hills, standing and looking about her, starting with an agitated excitement at the figure of a shepherd, thinking that stones were men and that every sound in the air was Benjie's voice. Tom's care of her, which he tried to make unconcerned and indifferent, irritated her. She came back to the house on the afternoon of the fourth day, driven by absurd fear. Benjie had been planning this for months past; he was weary of her and had not the courage to tell her so. Some woman somewhere had entrapped him and, as he had always been faithless, so now he proved it to her for ever. She was intensely humiliated. 'I have never been able to hold anyone to myself; there is something in me charmless, dull, wearying; everything that I touch falls away from me.' She was even haunted by the dazzling, dominating figure of her grandmother who, with her head up, stamping her ivory cane, could rule the world if she wished, but she, Vanessa, who had had beauty and all the world to charm, had been able to hold no one. Women between thirty and forty often know an especial terror and apprehension, for youth has gone; if they have had children they are being abandoned by them, men are searching for younger faces, and old age, that demands more wisdom for the subduing of its terrors from women than from men, already leers, like a cocksure arrogant old man, over the fence. Women have greater courage wherewith to meet spiritual loneliness than men have, but their capacity for spiritual experience is also greater.

She came back to the house, its floors flooded with the June sun as though to taunt her, and said passionately to Tom: 'He is never coming back. I can make my mind up to it.'

Tom said something. She turned on him furiously with one of her old tempers. 'What do you know about it? You are only a boy!'

Then she burst out of the house again and walked swiftly away from the hills. She was in a mood for anything. That old, scared, irrational Herries blood for ever mixing in the personal Herries history beat now in her brain. Why not end it? Her life had been a failure from beginning to end. Her father had died when she might have saved him, she had married a man without loving him and he had gone crazy from it, she had risked everything for another Herries who was notorious for his instability and lightness. But even now, in this passion of fear and unhappiness, she would not blame Benjie. No, it was herself – her dullness and heaviness of spirit. 'Why have I not managed life better? What is lacking, has always been lacking in me?' She came to the little church and, scarcely knowing that she did so, finding the door open, entered.

She had often, in the last six months, visited this little place and had grown to love it. Behind its wall, guarded by its trees, hills mounting to every side of it and one of the loveliest small rivers in England at its back, quiet, restrained and confident, it held something in its heart greater than change or fashion. Everything was simple, the whitewashed walls, the altar, the pews, the birds that nestled in its roof, the scents that filled it from the summer fields, and the unceasing rhythm of the river.

Very unhappy, Vanessa knelt and prayed: 'God, in this quiet place, help me to find my courage again. I knew, when I did wrong, that I would suffer, but if it be possible allow me not to suffer without anyone to help me. It is not right that I should ask You anything, for I have not yet repented of the wrong that I did. I know that You ask me to be honest, and so I say that if there was that wrong to do again I would do it again. I feel that I acted against a law and against my conscience, but I did it deliberately. God, don't take Benjie away from me. Let me care for him and watch over him and share his life later when we will need somebody. If You are my Father as, in this quiet place, I feel You to be, do as my own father would have done, and let me be good to someone I love. Don't take Benjie from me. I know him better than anyone else does. I can care for him more than anyone else can. Let me be punished in any other way, but not by

losing Benjie. You have placed this church here that we should
make our requests in it. This is my only prayer – let me keep
Benjie . . .'

She found that she was saying aloud, her hands clenched, her
eyes staring at the little altar on which was a glass bowl filled with
red and white roses: 'Don't take Benjie away from me! Don't
take Benjie away from me!'

The strain of her intensity snapped. She rose from her knees
and sat on the hard bench. She heard a bird singing, the water
swinging by, and the voice of a shepherd as he crossed the grass
by the church wall, talking to another.

'Well, goodnight.'

'Goodnight.'

She knew the man by his voice and with that familiarity all the
outer world swung in. She heard Barney in London saying:
'Why, no, Vanessa dear, if it makes you happy to believe in such
things . . .'

She saw the Prince and Princess entering in procession into
the Hill Street drawing-room . . . She was in a theatre and Bernhardt was speaking . . . Then, someone saying: 'God? Oh, God
died long ago. Didn't you know?'

But the church filled with light. She heard the sheep with their
gentle sleepy rustle pass beyond the wall. A fragrance of flowers
and new-mown hay seemed to be carried, by the sweet, persistent
note of the bird, into the church again. She knew with a sudden
delighted conviction that for herself at least this presence was
true. Some wise power entered into her and, falling on her knees
again and hiding her face in her hands, she was pervaded,
through and through, with intimate kindliness. That intimacy!
To be lonely no more! 'Only connect . . .' The connexion was
there, her hands were held, her bent head blessed. Time was lost.
The bird continued its song as the shadows came down upon the
mountains.

When she came into the house again Tom was there in the
passage.

'It's all right,' he said (a little shyly, for she had been angry
when she went away). 'Father's back. He's upstairs and he's awfully tired, for he's walked miles.'

She went up into the low-ceilinged bedroom and there was
Benjie, lying, stripped to his trousers, on the bed, his arms behind
his head. He grinned but didn't move. She saw the stump of his

arm where the flesh had been joined in a sharp red line, the deep brown of his bare chest, taut and spare as a boy's, his hair tumbled over his forehead, his impudent ashamed grin, and she was drowned in a wave of triumphant happiness. But she must not show it. She must be calm, sarcastically humorous as a wise woman would be, indifferent as though whether he went or came meant little to her. So she stood where she was and looked at him.

'So you're back?'

'Yes.' Then as she still didn't move, with his bright eyes fastened on her face he said: 'Haven't you a kiss for me?'

'No, I haven't. Why did you go off without telling me?'

'Oh, I don't know. That man Endicott came over from White-haven. He wanted a walk.'

'I see. You never thought, I suppose, how anxious Tom and I would be.'

'Why should you be anxious? You knew I'd come back.'

'Four days is a long time without a word from you.' She gave him one long look, then turned to the door. 'I suppose I'd better get you something to eat. You'll be hungry.'

'Yes — famished.' He looked at her, smiling. He put out his arm. 'Here, Vanessa. Come here. Don't be so cross with me. I haven't seen you for four days.'

'I'm not cross.' She came over to the bed and stood there. He put his bare arm round her waist, then drew her down. She knelt by the bed and they embraced. Then she rested her head on his body, he stroking her hair.

'Benjie, it wasn't kind . . . four whole days . . . I was in a panic. Tom and I are all alone here. Nobody comes, and if you're away the days drag. I've been watching the hills all day.'

He turned on his side, drew her on to the bed, put his hand inside her cotton dress that it might rest on her heart. Her hand stroked his back, rejoicing in the strong muscles, the smooth skin warm and fresh like the summer evening. Through the open window she could hear the bird singing and the running water as she had done in the church. He settled himself comfortably against her.

'Now I'll tell you all about it. Quite truthfully. George End-icott turned up and as soon as I saw him I wanted to go off. He wasn't here more than a minute. You were in the back of the house. I said "Hullo, George," and he said, "Hullo." I asked him where he had come from and he said "Whitehaven". I asked him whether he wanted a walk and he said "Yes" and there we were. I *had* to go off when I saw him, Vanessa. I *had* to. I'd have told you, only I knew you'd want to know *where* I was going and how long I'd be, and I didn't know where and I didn't know how long.'

'I wouldn't,' she murmured. (But she knew that she would.)

'Then we went up the Fell and saw young Tom and I told him. It was pretty late by then, but we got on to Robinson and then at dusk on Honister. It isn't dusk, you know – there's a white light in the sky. There was a new moon, too. We found a cave on the other side of Honister. Endicott said that in the old days, years ago, his great-grandfather used the cave when they were smuggling. They were bad lots, you know – as bad as they make'em. When we came to the cave there were two others there – a man and a girl. The girl had red hair and was pretty in a way. They didn't say much, but they were cooking a hare and they let us share their meal.

'Then we all curled up and went to sleep and I was as happy, Vanessa, as I've ever been in my life. I didn't care for you or Tom or anybody or anything. It was just like that – I'm telling you honestly. I was free and the air was fine and warm. I'd drunk their whisky and eaten their meat and beyond the cave there was the misty moonlight over the hills. I was a free man and I didn't want ever to be tied again. Well, I went to sleep and, after a time, I woke to find the girl had come over and was lying close to me, right up against me she was, with her arm around me. There she lay all night. I didn't do a thing to her. I didn't even kiss her. I'm telling you honestly, mind. I'd tell you just the same if there'd been anything, I'm not being virtuous about it. I might have done a lot of things but I just didn't. In the morning we set off again, the four of us. We were together the next three days. We went down into Eskdale, then over to Coniston, on to Helvellyn, along the Saddleback. This morning we separated, and here I am. It was grand, I tell you, Vanessa – lovely days and fine nights, not saying much, any of us. George wanted me to come back to Whitehaven and stay with him a bit, but by this morning you'd all come over me again, Vanessa. I *had* to see you. I didn't feel free any longer. I didn't *want* to be free. So I kissed the red-haired girl for the first time, gave George a kick, and here I am. I know I did wrong not to tell you, but if I'd told you I wouldn't have had such a good time somehow. You've got to forgive me and believe me too. I've never told you a lie yet.'

She sat up on the bed, her arm around him. This was something of a crisis between them and she wanted to say what was best and wisest.

'Yes, Benjie, that's all right. I know you must be free. Haven't I always said so?'

'Yes, you've always *said* so,' he answered, laughing and stroking her cheek.

'Have I prevented you? Have I ever stopped you?' she asked.

'Don't be so serious, darling. Take it lightly. I've only been for a walk – and here I am.'

'That's easy to say,' she answered. 'Does no man *ever* understand these things? Every time you go off I can't be sure you'll ever come back again. Oh yes, I feel safe enough now – now that you are here and close to me – but when you are gone I say to myself, why should he come back? I've no hold on him. He may be tired of me, hiding it from me.'

'Tired of you? I love you more than I ever did. Why, Vanessa, I've loved you all my life! How could I *not* come back? I'll always return—'

'Ah yes, you think so!' she answered quickly. 'But I've seen you change your mind so often about so many things! If I were younger, gayer! But sometimes I seem to myself so dull, so heavy! Women are faithful if they're given a chance – it's the thing they like best to be! But men – when they've got what they want, they want something else. Then,' she went on, 'it's lonely when you're away. For six months here we've seen nobody. When you're with me I don't *want* to see anyone, but when you're away every minute is an hour. It wouldn't be if I knew you'd be back at such and such a time. But when you haven't said a word—'

He sat up. 'Look here, Vanessa. Let's have a child! Then you wouldn't doubt any more—'

'Oh no ,' she answered slowly. 'That would be wrong—'

'Why wrong? Your father didn't mind because he was illegitimate.'

'I think he did. It made a difference to his life.'

'If only Ellis would die!' He beat the bed with his hand. 'Now don't be hypocritical about that, Vanessa. You know it would be much better if he should die. He's old, he's crazy. Life can't be any fun for him.'

But he was afraid of alluding to Ellis. A shadow crept into her eyes. He hated that she should think of the past.

'Look, Vanessa! I have to go off sometimes. Sometimes I'm restless beyond bearing. I think of my father, my mad uncle, my grandfather. There are days when I hate myself, my ancestry, all the past and the present together. Then you can't help me – nobody can. But never doubt that you're the love of my whole life, Vanessa. If ever any man in the world loved anyone, I love you! Why, even now I couldn't be away three days from you without running back! But there's this country, every fell-side, every stream, every stone wall, is in my blood! Why, you know that as well as I! Wasn't it crazy of us to come back here where everyone knows us and all our family history? But could we help it? Of course not! No man escapes the past, nor the fields where he was as a boy if that poison is in his blood. With some of us it is, with some of us it isn't. What do Timothy or Violet or Ellis care for this country? That's why they'll never understand us nor why we do what we do! We are the gipsies, with the smell of the ground always in our nostrils. That's our history, mixed up with the country, with Cumberland, with England.'

He stretched himself and yawned.

'Lord! I'm a poet! And I'm famished too! I could eat a whole sheep!'

He held her tightly in his arm, kissing her again and again.

'Darling, don't be sad, don't be too serious. I'm yours for ever and ever. You're the one thing I'll never leave. You and this country here. And I'll be good next time – I'll tell you before I go. And I didn't make love to the red-haired girl. Remember that! Vanessa, sweetheart, darling sweetheart, don't you *know* that you've got me for ever and ever? Have you no sense? Can't you *tell* a thing like that?'

A little later, going down to prepare the food, she found Tom making, very seriously, an omelette.

'Father's frightfully hungry,' he said. Then he saw how happy she was. He sighed as though a great burden were lifted from him. She kissed him.

'I'm sorry I was angry this afternoon,' she said. Then, as she began to make the meal, she added: 'I'm afraid, Tom dear, that we both take life too seriously.'

An hour later, in front of the cottage, the moon, cherry-tinted in a white sky, rising above the hill, they had the best meal of their lives.

STORM COMING UP

'TIME, of course,' said Mr Benbow who was, during September, taking the work of the Vicar of Newlands, 'does not exist. There *is* no time.' He was, he had always been, of a mathematical mind, but he did not know, as he said this, raising his glass of beer and looking at the charming sun through its smoky depths, the strange things that his simple sentence provoked.

Here, in the September sunshine, sitting with Benjie and Vanessa outside their white house (he was a man who cared nothing for social conventions), he killed history. There was no past. Upon this square of ground, over which the Eagle was magnificently sailing, even as he spoke, across the spine of hill that rose in front of them, Francis Herries, his small son tight against his breast, rode over the wild land, not pastured now, sweeping in unchecked confusion down Borrowdale to the small house under the moon, with its shining suits of armour. 'Take me to the Fair with you,' Mrs Press cried. 'No, I will not,' he answered, while Margaret his wife lay sick in the room above.

Keswick waited basking in the sun while the coach rolled in from Kendal, and old Pomfret, a little drunken, looked out of his study window. At the same moment David, at Uldale, heard of the fall of the Bastille and cursed his son, Jennifer walked tapping with her slippers up the road to the Fortress, and Judith's boy, naked by the Tarn, mocked the big man on the white horse. In his London rooms Francis, David's son, sick of life, blew his brains out while young Tom Macaulay talked with old Rogers in Hatchard's bookshop. Judith saw the big woman count the lumps of sugar in the Paris café, and young Will raced up to the Druids' Circle while Adam cheered him on. 'It's war then,' said Judith, nodding her bonnet at Walter, and, even as she spoke, the flames leapt upon Uldale and her son fell fighting the choking fumes. The carriages moved slowly at Will's funeral, and Sayers with a broken arm faced unflinchingly the blinded Heenan.

'Thank you very much, Miss Martineau,' said Judith, shouting down the ear-trumpet, one eye on the tea tent, and John called through the mists of Skiddaw for his enemy. 'Yes, it's too late,' said Benjie, bowing his head; 'I'm married already,' and Vanessa turned, in the long drawing-room, thinking that she

heard Ellis' step on the stair. The Chinese clock strikes, and old
Emily has offered up a prayer while young Tom, his hand for a
moment on Vanessa's shoulder, says: 'He'll be back soon. He'll be
back soon, Vanessa.'

Behind these figures, mingling with them, giving them their
meaning and sharing in their destinies, fog swallows up Carlisle
to hide Prince Charlie's men, Keswick receives Mr Gray and the
young gentlemen from Cambridge who hope to have a word with
Mr Southey while on their reading party, the Reform Bill rides
in with a cheering mob behind it, trees fall, the roads are bound
with stone walls, figures from here, there, everywhere, buy lead
pencils, picnic on Skiddaw, whose green slopes young Mr Keats
and sturdy Sir Walter find adventurous. A Macclesfield paper
advertises for workers: 'Wanted, between 4,000 and 5,000
persons between the ages of 7 and 21 years.' Thick bellies of
smoke veil the Midland sky. Disraeli sees the war of the two
nations; Mr Joseph Hebergam, aged seventeen, works from five
in the morning until eight at night with a break of thirty minutes
at noon. 'Bravo! Bravo!' cry Will and Horace and the Vicar of
Little Rodney-on-the-Marsh, 'England rules the world', while a
man or two, with pens in their hands – Shelley, Carlyle, Dickens,
Ruskin, Morris – speak of 'a Golgotha of souls and bodies buried
alive'. The Herries are rising, the lights of London grow brighter,
the fields of middle England are lost in smoke, slowly, slowly
men are pushing up from under ground, are meeting, are band-
ing together, demanding their share, pulling down the Park railings, putting up bright little red houses, chasing the Squire's wife
out of the cottages, pushing into Westminster Hall, driving the
South African millionaires out of Park Lane, running here, running there, from coast to coast with their children behind them,
dancing on Primrose Hill, standing in rows of shiny black as, at
last, the old Queen passes . . .

And still on that square of ground, over which the Eagle is
hovering, nothing has changed. The coach rolls in to Keswick
square, the shepherd searches the mist under Helvellyn for his
wandering sheep, the sun falls from Seatoller on to the silent blue
of Buttermere and, under Gable, the Tarn sleeps like a rusted
shield.

'There is no time,' said Mr Benbow. 'Time is an anachronism.
At this moment Caesar falls on the steps of the Capitol and
David challenges his giant enemy.'

*   *   *

At this moment, too, Cynthia Worcester brought her two little girls on a visit to Cumberland. Strange how the Herries were drawn back, again and again, to this patch of ground. But in Cynthia's case it was perhaps Vanessa rather than Cumberland that drew her. Cynnthia had never set an eye on Vanessa since the flight from Hill Street. She had not seen her but had stepped into her place – or very nearly. Peile Worcester was not, of course, as rich as Ellis; they could not, in their house in Charles Street, entertain as Vanessa had done in Hill Street. On the other hand, they were cleverer than Vanessa. Vanessa had not been clever – kind, gentle, generous, most beautiful to look upon, but *not*, oh, most certainly not clever.

Cynthia was as pretty as a rosebud (a flower to which she had been often compared) and *also* as clever as a monkey. She had always been *inside* the Arts as Vanessa had never attempted to be. Indeed, so far was Cynthia now inside that her set embalmed her like a fly in amber. But everyone came to her afternoons, her evenings – Mr Bernard Shaw, the Sidney Webbs and Mr H. G. Wells; while on the other side there were the aesthetes, Mr Sidnney Colvin at the Museum, young Mr Binyon, a wild young man who had sailed before the mast and swept the floor in a bar, Mr Masefield, and, above all, the Homer, the Milton (who knew, perhaps the Shakespeare of our day?), honey-voiced Mr Stephen Phillips. The politicians came too – Cynthia had no Party politics: Sir Henry Campbell-Bannerman dined at her table as well as Mr Balfour. Even the new Labour candidate for Barnard Castle, Mr Arthur Henderson, came to tea ...

Cynthia had taken Vanessa's place. She was the social head of the family now, and the younger generation, Alfred's children, Maurice and Clara, Carey's girls, cousins from Manchester and cousins from Bournemouth, Philip and his odd effeminate friends, young Violet and her stupid husband – they recognized it and submitted to it.

Nevertheless (as is always the case in every family history) some things were not quite right. Cynthia was not as happy as she ought to be. She possessed just enough imagination to wish her position a little different. *Her* struggle between Prose and Poetry was, of course, all on the side of Prose. There was never any doubt as to which party she belonged to. Of the world of Judith, of Rose, of Vanessa she would never even glimpse the borders: nevertheless the world where she was was not quite good enough. Peile Worcester was not quite good enough, their

income was not quite good enough, their two lovely obedient
little girls were not quite good enough. In fact, in this September
of 1903, Cynthia was supremely discontented, her rosebud
mouth curled down at the ends; she, one afternoon, startled Mr
Phillips almost out of his life by saying that today she really
didn't want to listen to *Marpessa,* and she lost her temper altogether with Horace when he informed her that 'in his own
small way he grew with every increasing year more and more of
an optimist'. She could not *abide* Horace, she decided, with his
high domed forehead, his mild eyes naked of eyebrows, his plump
rosy cheeks, and his way of being able to help anyone in the world
out of any trouble so long as he personally got the glory of it.

After her rudeness to Horace (for which she was sincerely
sorry, for she was a kind-hearted little thing) she took herself in
hand. What was the matter with her? Two things. One, her husband. The other, that she longed to see Vanessa again. She must
get away from Peile for a while and she must see Vanessa, if only
for a moment. With a start of surprise, staring into her mirror,
she discovered that, in all probability, she cared for and admired
Vanessa more than anyone else in the world. Vanessa had of
course done a dreadful thing. Had she run away with anyone but
Benjie Herries! Nevertheless Cynthia, feeling as she did at the
moment about Peile, thought that running away from one's husband was not so extraordinary a business. Only it was a thing that
a Herries must never do, because the eyes of the world were on
the Herries family, they stood for domesticity, patriotism, and
virtuous common sense. That was why Vanessa's affair had been
so truly awful!

The matter with Peile was that he never changed. He was
exactly the same as he had been when she married him, *exactly*
the same, and all the things for which she had loved him then
were precisely the things that exasperated her now!

He had not changed in looks; he was as good-looking as ever.
He did not appear a day older (how she wished he did!) with
his crinkly fair hair, his fair short moustache, his splendid figure,
his immaculate clothes. He was an English Gentleman *in excelsis.*
He had today precisely the same complaints against the English
middle classes that he had had when he married her. *Then* they
had seemed to her charming, and she had agreed with every one
of them, for the Herries belonged to the Upper Middle Classes
and thought therefore that almost everything that the Middle
Middle Classes did was a pity. Peile's complaints and sarcasms

now were just what they had always been but were more, far
more, vehemently expressed, because he was older now and had
all the Englishman's touching faith that the older you grew the
more important your opinions were.

At this particular moment there were a number of things that
made the Middle Middle Classes especially offensive to Peile.
Business was bad. The country had not yet recovered from the
effects of that stupid mismanaged war. How ironical to remember the cheering crowds lining the street as the CIVs marched
past, or the shocking vulgar manifestations of Mafeking night!
Then there was the Whitaker-Wright affair that had been dragging on for years, and only in March had the Public Prosecutor
seen fit to prosecute. There was Chamberlain's absurd loan of
thirty-five million pounds to South Africa. *There* was a nice
burden for the Upper Middle Class (on whom now *all* the taxes
were falling!) to pay! There were the unemployed walking about
the streets with their collecting boxes. There was Brodrick's ridiculous 'Phantom Army Corps' of which young Winston
Churchill so rightly made fun. There was this demand on the
part of the Lower Middle Classes for cheap food – and they were
getting it too, mostly in tins, of course, but nevertheless eating
lobster and asparagus, peas and apricots, as though these things
were their right instead of a luxury. There was the horrible 'Art
and Craft' furniture with which the Lower Middle Classes were
encumbering their homes, dreadful cheap confusions of memories of William Morris and vulgar German *Kunst*. A typist
whom Alfred had engaged actually owned a mechanical piano-
player, bought of course on hire-purchase. There was this new
passion on the part of the Lower Middle Classes for learning
things, for buying cheap books about atheism and how to put a
bicycle together. There were their odd forms of entertainment
and exercise – walking races to Brighton. There had been the
other day a race to Brighton for waitresses! There was a sudden
craze for swimming the Channel, and schools for quite inferior
children were mad about hockey teams, just like the school attended by his own girls. There was this crazy ugly music by
Richard Strauss that had not a tune in it, and this vulgar new
halfpenny paper, the *Daily Mirror*, for women. There was the
sordid excitement over the Moat Farm Murder, and there was
this fearful increase in motor vehicles, so that a law was to be
passed ordering them to be numbered and some 'test of efficiency'
for the driver . . .

It was not that Peile was a snob. He did not think himself
better than anyone else, or only so very, very little better, but
anyone could see that this new power in the Lower Middle
Classes, their crazy desire for the best of things and intolerable
fashion of making themselves heard through the daily Press,
through Leagues and Unions and meetings and speeches was
doing old England no good, was in fact fast dragging her down
from her grand position as Mistress of the World. Something
must be done about it, and the Upper Middle Classes were the
people to do it: it was their right and their duty. Peile did not
know *what* everyone was about! The country going to wrack and
ruin and nobody cared. What was Alfred doing, and old Barney
and older Horace in Manchester? Why, simply nothing at all!

It was after Cynthia had endured months and months of this
at every meal and for an hour or so every night in the quiet of the
matrimonial chamber that she decided to take the girls for a
holiday to Cumberland.

She simply told Peile one evening and, next morning, departed.

Arrived in Keswick, she looked for rooms, preferring these to a
hotel, and found them – most charming ones – on the right side
of the road that ran down to the lake. She spent half an hour
putting the rooms' things away into a cupboard – trays from
India, china figures from Manchester, bead mats, two large
coloured portraits and three huge sea-shells. Mrs Colbourne the
landlady was a little astonished, but there was something about
Cynthia, so tiny but so charming, with such lovely hair, such
lovely eyes, and a manner that had just the right mixture of
kindliness and authority. Mrs Colbourne, who was a widow and
came from near Liverpool (had she been a Cumbrian she would
not have been so quickly melted), surrendered to Cynthia entirely, giving the governess special food (for she had a delicate
stomach), sitting up one night when Rosalind had a cough that
might become pneumonia (you never can tell), and hiring a pony
trap from her friend Mr Lewthwaite at especial terms for Cynthia's especial use. In those few days she used it in fact a great
deal. She became a familiar sight in Keswick, sitting up driving,
her little back like a ramrod, and a veil concealing her lovely
features. The citizens of Keswick are not very easily impressed –
they have too many visitors – but the Hon Mrs Peile Worcester,
driving her pony cart, her two lovely little girls sitting as stiff as

Royalty behind with their governess, Miss King, was a sight that they did not for a while forget.

Then, after four extremely happy days, there came a peremptory letter from Peile. He was not well. He had been in bed all day. He had a temperature. The doctor thought that it might be serious. He demanded her instant return.

She did not return instantly, however. She waited a day. She went with her two little girls and called on Vanessa. The pony trap arrived at the church. There they all three dismounted and walked across the meadows to the white house. Having tea by the house door were Vanessa, Benjie, and Tom. At first Cynthia thought it was the farmer and his wife. It was one of those lovely September days when, above the turning bracken, the sun lies in happy content from shoulder to shoulder of the hills and all the little streams flash with light. Perhaps one small cloud, dark as a mulberry, hangs motionless like a hawk above the glittering valley and, for a moment, the sun slips behind its shelter. Then at that instant all is sombre – the hill, the streams, the little running walls, as though a vast curving wing from the protecting Eagle shadowed the world. Then the sun is free of the cloud, and light leaps up from the heart of the soil.

It was such a day, but very warm: Benjie was in his shirt sleeves, the sleeve of his one arm rolled up; his neck was bare. He was wearing corduroy riding breeches, and Vanessa in a sun bonnet had a cotton dress – white scattered with blue flowers.

After another look Cynthia saw that it was indeed Vanessa: she ran forward with a little cry. The two women embraced.

Two days after her return to London, Cynthia wrote to May Rockage. This is part of the letter:

... But of course I wasn't going to miss Vanessa, the very thing I'd come up there for. So we drove over, the girls and I, to the funny little valley where they live. Peile was very annoyed when he heard that I took the girls. Very annoyed indeed, especially as he has a sore throat and thinks himself on the point of death. (He's better tonight. Nothing but a bad cold. Aren't husbands absurd?) But the girls enjoyed themselves. They went off quite alone with Benjie's boy, Tom. He's nineteen now, Vanessa told me, and *most* serious as though he was eighty. But of course he had all that time in Paris and South Africa, which makes him more grown-up. Anyway I knew the children were quite safe with him. I think both of

them have fallen in love with him. They've talked of nothing
else since. Benjie was nice. I should say Vanessa's calmed him
down. Of course he *looks* rough. He might have been a tramp
or gipsy or anything, and he's brown as a berry. But he's
always a gentleman even if he hasn't always behaved like
one.

But, May dear, here's the great news. Vanessa is going to
have a baby. Any time. It might have come while we were there
having tea! She doesn't attempt to conceal it. Really I was
rather afraid what the girls would think, but they're too young,
thank Heaven, to know anything about it. Miss King is *excellent* at answering awkward questions. When I went up with
Vanessa to her room (*such* a small room, with whitewashed
walls and smelling of hay), she told me that they hadn't meant
to have one – a baby I mean – but there it is, and of course it
will be illegitimate, which is a pity. Isn't it funny how we *can't*
keep illegitimacy out of the family, and yet I'm sure most of us
are as proper as can be? When I was with Vanessa I couldn't
help feeling I'd made a mistake and it would have been much
better to have run away in a caravan with a gipsy instead of all
these silly London parties. Benjie and Vanessa seemed so *very*
happy. But of course as soon as I was in London again I knew
it would never have done. I'd *never* be happy in a caravan
roasting hedgehogs and telling people's fortunes. But what *is*
there about Vanessa? Of course she's still beautiful even as she
is and dressed like a cottage woman with a sun bonnet. But her
features are lovely, so *noble* without being a bit superior. She
has the grandest eyes, the finest forehead, the kindest mouth of
any woman I've ever seen. I've always adored her, even though
I *was* a little jealous of her in London. She's just as quiet as she
always was. She sits there, her hands on her lap, and you feel
you could tell her anything. She isn't clever of course – I mean
she never *says* anything that's clever – but you can trust her
absolutely, which you can't do with many women. She asked
about Ellis, but I couldn't tell her much except that he's quite
happy looked after by those two awful old women. I asked her
whether she were happy and she said she was. I think she is –
part of the time. But I caught her looking at Benjie as though
she expected him to go off at any moment. Not that she lets
him see that. She's too wise. She knows that men want to *feel*
they're free even though they're not really. I asked her whether
she were anxious about the baby. She's forty-four you know

and it's her first. But she said no. She said she didn't mind
dying so long as Benjie was there. But I don't know *what* he'd
do without her. He may be wild and all the rest, but if any man
ever loved a woman Benjie loves Vanessa. And it was all so
quiet there, with the sun on the fields and the sheep grazing
and the noise of running water. If Maud and Helen are
coming up next week to town do let me know. Peile says . . .

'A storm's coming up,' said Benjie, looking back towards Ke-
skadale and Buttermere Hause. The sky was a stainless blue, but
over Whiteless Pike little shreds of cloud like tags of cotton wool
floated and gathered. A low whispering wind stirred the dying
bracken.

'I'm coming with you,' Vanessa said. As she said it she thought:
'Now this is foolish of me. This is what I determined not to do –
not to force myself on him. He doesn't want me. He will be so
much happier by himself. And yet I'm determined. What is it? Is
it the child? I can't bear these days to let him out of my sight.'

'Better not,' Benjie said. 'There's a storm coming. And I'm out
for a long walk – Hindscarth, Robinson, over Red Pike to Ennerdale. You'll never do it, Van, as you are. It wouldn't be
safe.'

How well she knew him when he thought that someone was
laying a hand on him to constrain him – herself, anyone – like a
hare who, with ears pricked, hears the hunter treading the long
grass. But she was determined. All her cautious ways of dealing
with him were gone. She could not *endure* a whole day and night
just now without him. If she had asked him to stay he would
have stayed – but reluctantly, behaving all day as though she had
tethered him with a rope to a stone! How well she knew him! As
though it were herself who was resenting it.

'I can't help it,' she said, smiling, her head up, her hands on
her broad hips. 'I must come, Benjie. It will be all right. Wenlock
says that it won't be yet. I never felt better in my life.'

He looked at her and she knew what he was thinking: 'This big
broad woman stands over me like a gaoler. Why did I tie myself
up? Can't even go off for a walk by myself!'

And yet, all these months, since they had known that there was
to be a child, he had been exquisitely tender for her, taking every
trouble, thinking of her, watching over her as he never would
have done for anyone five years ago. Oh! he had grown. Living
with her, loving her, had taught him something. Had taught *her*

something too – should have taught her not to worry him, to let him go off free! But he ought not to want to go for a night and a day now, when, in spite of what the doctor had said, he knew that the child *might* be born . . . and she alone with Tom in the house. The child *might* be born . . . it was mad of her to insist that she must go with him. And yet she *did* insist.

'I'm coming,' she said obstinately.

'Look here.' He did not look at her, but slanted his eyes, bright, lively, shining in his brown face, away from her, looking at the walls of the house, the sheep cropping, the wind stirring in the bracken. 'Look here, I've told you. There's a storm coming. I must have a walk. I've been cooped up for weeks. ('Oh no, you haven't,' Vanessa thought. 'Last week you were away for two nights.') I'll be back tomorrow morning. It's madness for you to think of coming. Look here. Walk to the end of the lane with me. Then come back.'

'No, I'm coming,' she answered obstinately. She went in to get some things. As she was collecting them she thought: 'What is making me do this? And why, at moments like this, do we almost hate one another? I would give him anything, anything in the world. I would die for him. It wouldn't be hard at all. But now the more he wants me not to come with him the more I'm coming. And when it's like this it seems as though we had always been fighting one another, all our lives long. And yet soon – when we are agreed again – it will seem as though we had never had a fight in our lives worth mentioning.'

When she came down in her short skirt and with her stick and rucksack she looked in at the lower room to say goodbye to Tom. He was seated at the table, his square arm firmly planted, his honest determined eyes bent on a book. He sprang up.

'Why, where are you going?'

'I'm going with Benjie for a walk.'

The look came into his eyes that she knew so well – of fear and love and motherly anxiety.

'Oh, but you shouldn't! Not now. What's father doing to let you?—'

She smiled the old ironical mischievous smile that she had had as a child, a smile just like Adam's.

'He doesn't want me to. He's very cross about it, in fact.'

'Well, of course he is. Oh, Van, you mustn't.'

She caught him to her and kissed him.

'Dear Tom! You're going to have an awful life – always upsetting yourself about other people.'

She went outside. Benjie never said a word, but he was as sulky as a scolded schoolboy. They set off. She waved to Tom who was watching at the window, who would be, she knew, anxious and miserable all day.

'I don't care,' she thought defiantly. 'They're only men. They haven't the least idea what a woman wants. It will be good for me, this exercise. I never felt better in my life.' She walked, her head up, striding, a smile on her lips, and Benjie stepped along at her side, whistling, kicking pebbles. Only as they crossed the beck and she jumped from a stone to the bank he said:

'You're a fool, Van, you know. But on your own head be it.' Then he seemed better. He could never be sulky for long. Any little thing interrupted his mood. 'Look, Van! Look at that hawk! Like a stone on the sky! Ah! it's dropped – a fieldmouse, I expect. Here. Take my hand. This fence is a bit steep.'

Then all was well again; they were as close together as though they were one body, moving through the air, treading the turf so lightly, brushing the bracken as they began to climb. She looked back on the little stream before they left it. It played lingeringly about its gleaming stones as though loath to leave them, and the stones, too, seemed to cling to the water, stopping it, having excited murmurous chats with it, then, as though trying a last strategy, exercising in a tiny dance with flurries of silver lines and circles. All about the stream the scene was 'calm as a resting wheel' and the air so clean that trees and hill lines seemed stamped on the atmosphere like a seal on blue paper. The September day was exceptionally warm, but everywhere was the finger of decay, the leaves gold and dun and then of a sudden brightly green as though defiant of approaching death. At a cottage above the right bank of the stream a woman called to a shepherd striding uphill, two dogs at his heel: 'Well, anudder time . . .' Her voice rang out in the still air like a cry.

'Oh, how happy I am!' Vanessa thought, 'and ten minutes back I was nervous, uncertain, anxious. I only want Benjie to be happy and then everything in me is tranquil.' She remembered, as they pressed past a big boulder and began to tread the turf and to feel the wind, touched with the salt of the sea, in their faces, her London life. How dead and gone that seemed! But Cynthia's visit had stirred her strangely. She had accepted her ostracism almost gladly – she had suffered so little – but she had been moved, deeply moved that Cynthia had brought her children. Yes, and had allowed Tom to take them off across the valley. Tom had thought little Mary the most beautiful creature he had

ever beheld. He had spoken of her again and again. He was to go
shortly to London. He was to be given a trial on the *Standard*
newspaper, a job that dear old Barney had found for him. How
would the Family receive him? Peile and Alfred and Horace . . .
Would May and Carey invite him to Wiltshire? After all, it was
not *his* fault, poor boy, that his father had disgraced himself!
And Society was more tolerant now. Every kind of queer person
was admitted. When she had married Ellis the conventions had
been rigid, as though you belonged to a Regiment, and any social
or moral offence was as bad as desertion. She did not care for
herself – *her* case was socially hopeless and would be more so after
the birth of a child – but she *did* want Tom to have a good
time!

Benjie took her arm to help her up a steep place. At his touch
warmth poured through her body. It was always so. She had
had, in her life, so little experience, but she had always heard
that, when passion was gone, the best that a married pair could
hope for was a kind of compromising friendship. But still, after
all these years, Benjie's body was lovely to her. She would lie
awake at night, while he slept, her hand on his thigh, and know
that his vigour, his warmth, the freshness of his skin, the strength
of his bones was unique for her and always would be. Now she
understood fidelity – spiritual fidelity. Yes, that she had always
understood, but when it was aided by the body how undefeated it
must be! She understood now the tragedy of the marriage in
which physical things were disharmonized. Easy for others to
argue that it must be endured, but the touch, the kiss, the stroke
of the hand, the meeting of the cheek against cheek, the personal
flavour of the flesh, how much of spiritual contact went with
these physical things – they were the very gateway of the spirit!

So, on the brow of the hill, she said that they would sit down
for a moment and they did so. He put his arm around her and
she drew his head to her breast. She felt almost a faintness of
ecstasy here in this high air, with the smell of bracken and short
stiff grass and the sea wind. Far below them she saw a little figure
of a man leading his horse, and she thought of him, the year
going past him, rousing his horses, driving his plough through
flint and marl, the peewit wheeling above him, kestrels soaring,
his eyes always so patient, so wise about so many things, walking
as his forefathers had done in all the old ways. The child leapt in
her womb and, with that lovely sense of new life, her eyes grew
bright with comfort and she smiled.

They moved on again. She asked Benjie:

'I suppose now you think you know me better than anyone else in the world?'

'Yes, I think I do.'

'Yes, now. Father knew me; Rose – poor Rose – knew me ... Don't you know me so well, Benjie, that it's dull?'

'Dull?'

'Yes. I never can surprise you any more. You always know what I'm going to do.'

'I know you as though you were part of myself – the better part. You *are* part of myself. You always have been.'

'A part you often want to be rid of.'

'No, not often. Sometimes. Every man is like that.' He stopped and looked at her. 'Sure you're all right? Not tired?'

'Splendid. I could walk a hundred miles.'

'You know, when you said you were coming with me I hated you for a moment. I could have run off and never come back. That's what I felt like.'

'Yes, I knew you did.'

'Aren't you wise? You resent nothing. You forgive everything.'

'Yes,' she said, laughing. 'I'm placid – like a cow.'

'No. Oh no!' He struck his stick against a stone. 'You've a fearful temper. You can be so angry that the air quivers. But you never resent. You forgive and pass on. Every day you're finer.'

'Am I? That's because I love you.'

'Yes, and I love *you*! I love you! I love you! I love you!' he called. 'Do you hear the echo? It comes from that rift of rock.' Then, looking about him, sniffing the air, he went on: 'I was right about the storm, Van. It's coming. Do you see those clouds?'

Over Newlands a fleet of small, ragged clouds were slowly gathering, as though with purpose, as though marshalled. The sun shone brightly, but the air was colder and the wind now was busy along the ground, whistling in an undertone.

She didn't care about the storm. It would be nothing. She took her last look at the valley, so small but packed with history. In the time of Elizabeth, the German company had worked the mines in Newlands: there had been the Goldscope lead mines worked at the beginning of the nineteenth century. At Stair there had been the woollen mills – all that energy and human life, lovemaking and childbearing, foreign tongues, and Elizabeth's sharp eye fixed on her profits – and now the little valley bathed in silence, the small farms, the enclosed fields, the hawks and kestrels, the shepherd calling his dogs, the farmer ploughing the stiff field . . .

'Benjie, this is the only place in the world for us! The only spot . . . and for my father, my grandmother, her father . . .'

'Yes,' he answered. 'I can't tear away from it. Try as I may I can't. Everything passes – on the surface everything passes. But underneath, Van, you land on the rock, you give a cry of delight, you defend yourself against attack, and then, in a moment, you're gone to join the others under Skiddaw perhaps. We *seem* to change but we don't.'

She stopped, leaning on her stick.

'Yes, God gives you your moment of experience – to overcome fear.'

'Oh, you and your God!' he said, laughing. 'Hasn't science taught you anything yet, Vanessa?'

'Science I don't know . . .'

He looked at her curiously. 'Then God does exist for you, Van? Just as I do?'

'Yes, if one's brave enough to believe in Him,' she said shyly. 'It needs courage like everything else. We never talk about Him, Benjie. Why? Because I'm afraid that you'll laugh, and *you're* afraid – what are you afraid of? Of looking too far. What does everyone say? That Huxley and Darwin have settled the whole question, so why argue? And they leave it like that because it's easier, because it's dangerous to look any further. I shouldn't have the courage if I were not driven to it, but I think God has tormented me all my life. Tormented isn't the right word perhaps. Moved restlessly in and around me. *You* say that that is superstition. *I* say that there's no other choice for me. I *have* to be aware that you are there; I know your step, your voice, your frown. So I'm aware that God is there. I didn't ask for it. I'm not better or worse than you or anyone else because of it. It's simply a fact.'

She had not for a very long time discussed such things with him. He knew that she prayed, that much of the tranquillity that was always increasing in her came from some inner experience, the only thing that she did not share with him. Once he had been jealous of it, angry with her because of it. Now he loved her so much that he only wanted her to be happy. Perhaps? . . . Who knows? . . .

'It's a great thing to conquer fear,' he said. 'Anyone who does that is a kind of god.'

Even as he spoke the storm broke on them. Benjie knew the dangers of this piece of country. Robinson and Hindscarth had rough faces with much scree, and the ghylls into Buttermere had loose and falling rock with water suddenly, and sodden turf on the fell-side. A nasty ground for mist. But, at the moment, he could think of nothing but the wind which, quite suddenly, leapt from the ground, rushed forward from the hillside and tore up the valley. The clouds boiled from behind the hill, and the sun was obscured. The moss, heather, bracken that had been so brightly lit lost all colour.

'Are you all right?' he shouted to Vanessa.

'Yes, yes, I'm all right,' she answered.

Could they reach the bend of the hill they would have shelter. The storm was so furious that it could not last, he thought, but how strange was this sudden roaring of waters! The rain had begun to fall in slanting whips of steel, but the becks and mountain rivulets had not had time to absorb it; yet in his ears it was as though all the thundering waters of the world had been unloosed! It was as though a spirit with inky hair strode the fell and passed, blowing a great horn summoning his army! They could see the rain sweeping from the farthest horizon in curtains of gauze, blowing, bending, but never breaking.

'Turn your back to it!' he cried to Vanessa. 'Get your breath! There'll be a rock soon that we can shelter against.'

She turned, her skirts blown against her legs, her hair in her eyes and, at that same moment, with a little gasp of pain, felt a strong hand clutch her vitals, squeeze them, let them go. She bent her head. The stab of pain passed. She hurried, pressing through the storm so swiftly that Benjie cried:

'Come on! That's the spirit! We'll find shelter beyond the brow.'

They were both soaked through their coats, but a sort of ecstasy seized Benjie. This was what he loved, all the hills bared by the wind, all the streams exulting because they would be strong and vehement again, rain and wind at their full power and the sky black with cloud. If Vanessa were not beaten by it! But there she was, her head up, striding forward, striking the earth with her stick! He ran, he jumped the stones, he sang! Then, through the rain, the mist surged forward. It rose, broke to show dark fell and shining rock, closed again with fingers on your eyes, lifted from the ground a little to reveal the short grass tugging to escape the soil . . .

Vanessa was gone . . . He shouted.

'Van! Van! Vanessa! Where are you?'

The mist broke and he saw one jet-black cloud, and towards it everything, fell and gleaming stone and line of hill, seemed to strain.

He saw Vanessa standing, her hand to her heart. He caught up with her.

'Are you all right?'

Her face was grey in that half-light, but as she answered him the mist came down again, hiding her.

But she was glad that he could not see her, for she was about to die. She knew it as certainly as though the tall figure, grey-cloaked with grave assured eyes, stood in the mist, his curving silver-gleaming scythe in his hand. Her knees bent, her head was bowed on her breast. So appalling was the pain that death held no terrors, nor her loneliness. Strange that her one thought about death for years had been that Benjie must be with her when it came. And now it was here, and she hoped that Benjie would not see her, but would pass on, striking his iron-tipped stick on the stone, and she would drop there where she was and die, alone, hidden in mist . . . She did not want anyone to see her die.

So fearful was the pain that she could not keep back a moan, and then another. But only her own heart heard. The wind screamed in her ear, and the mist, wet like a thin soaked towel, pressed on her eyes and nose and mouth. Dimly through her pain she thought how silly it had been that, only ten minutes before, she had been talking so confidently about God. God was not here. She was animal, only fighting for endurance and to die without cowardice . . .

Then the pain was so fierce that she thought of nothing, neither the storm nor any company. She knelt on the sodden turf, her head back, her teeth set, hands clenched. She fancied that, from a great distance, she heard Benjie calling, and a sudden warming thought as though it were the very last that she would have in this world came to her of his sweetness, jollity, kindliness. Nothing in this world mattered so much as kindliness . . . that men should be kind to one another because they suffered, one and all, and life was short . . .

The pain passed. It withdrew as though a figure that had been bending over her had moved away.

She looked up and saw that the mist had broken, leaving a round cup like a room suddenly revealed, a room furnished with a gleaming rock like a ship's stern. The pain was gone: she would not die yet. The child should be born. Not rain nor wind should defeat her, and she rose from her knees and breasted the wind, moving forward. The mist cleared still further and she saw Benjie moving back to her.

'It's all right,' he shouted. 'There's a farm here just on the bend. Where the trees are.'

She took his arm.

'Isn't the wind strong? It almost beat me to my knees.'

He had noticed nothing, and she now brought all her resources to the business of meeting the pain again when it returned. For return it would. She could hear it afar off as though faintly the thin warning of a distant horn.

When they came to the trees they were rocking and groaning like mad things. The mist was shredded now, blowing in crazy tears and tatters over a landscape that was all fell scattered with stone and rock. The scene was immemorial and had changed in nothing since, maybe, Roman trumpets had echoed there from distance to distance.

It was a little white farmhouse, very simple, with a small beck rushing furiously at its side, the whole world filled with wind and rain. Benjie knocked on the door, two dogs barked, then a woman opened it and looked out. The wind rushed in and they followed it, coming into a clean and bright kitchen. It was low-roofed; there were legs of cured mutton and hams hanging from the smoky rafters. On a shelf nearby there were pots and jars, little yellow cheeses, dried herbs. By the ingle there was an old white-haired man, another younger man with broad shoulders and a bull-neck standing up, the woman who had opened the door, and a pretty girl in a blue gown busy at the table.

They were very cordial and friendly, made Vanessa and Benjie come to the fire to dry themselves. Yes, they had a spare room for the night if the storm kept on. The old man was loquacious; he had light blue eyes like flowers.

'Aye,' he said. 'We're verra oot o't warld – seven mile fra a shop, eight mile fra a church – an' hard roads.'

He was proud of their isolation. The housewife asked them if they were hungry. Benjie said indeed he was. She began to be busy cooking eggs and Cumberland ham.

Vanessa sat there, her knees close together, looking into the fire, waiting for the next pain to come. She wondered how soon she might go up to bed, take her things off: Benjie had noticed nothing. He was exceedingly happy, had taken off his boots and stockings, coat and waistcoat, and sat there, smiling at them all. He told them how he had lost his arm in Africa in the war. The old man had a long story to tell about sheep – 'terrible wark' sometimes. The young man had a newspaper a week old. 'A newspaper! Aye – we mun gang a lang ways to get yan o' thame here.' Benjie laughed and chattered, loving the sound of the storm beyond the house, the smell of the frying eggs and ham. His twinkling eyes rested on the girl. *What* a pretty girl! Dark, slim, and a cheeky upturned nose such as he preferred. He smiled at her and she shyly smiled back again . . .

Later Vanessa said: 'Benjie, I am tired. I think I'll go to bed.'

'Supper's nearly ready. You must be starved. I know I am.'

'I'm not hungry,' she answered. 'I think I'll go up.'

She stood, her hand pressed to her side. He looked at her anxiously but she smiled back at him. The girl went up with her to show her the room.

The storm died down. Benjie had his supper, the woman and girl waiting on him. It was now, in a place like this with simple, friendly people, that he felt at his best. In his shirt and trousers he sat there, eating, drinking big cups of tea, laughing, telling them about South Africa and other parts of the world where he had been. Once and again he smiled at the girl and she glanced back at him, their eyes meeting, holding one another, parting quickly. The storm had died away and beyond the kitchen window a flood of primrose light laced with the tree branches spread above the bare fell.

'Hurray! The storm is over!' Benjie said.

The girl had gone. He could hear her moving on the floor above. He got up.

'I'll go and see how my wife is,' he said. But, even as he spoke, the wind came again, raging in a fury about the house, banging at the house door, rattling the windows. All the trees screamed and the colour ebbed from the sky, leaving it white.

'That was sudden,' he said, turning round. 'I thought it had died.'

He saw a scurry of leaves blow against the pane and flatten. Some stayed pressed against the window.

' 'Twill be a wild neet,' the old man said calmly.

Benjie climbed the crooked stairs that smelt of mice and white-wash. At the top was the girl just coming down. There was a ghostly light from the passage window. He caught the girl with his arm and she surrendered to him at once, pressing closely against him as though she were hungry to be loved, which indeed she was. He held her tight, kissing her eyes, her cheeks, her mouth. Then, behind the pleasure and strength and warm happiness that wrapped him in, he heard a deep breath as of someone close at his elbow. Looking past the girl he saw Vanessa at the doorway. Her hair fell about her shoulders and she had caught a patchwork quilt around her; the colours were bizarre – blue, crimson, orange, green – and above it her eyes, fixed as though fastened on some desperate resolution, stared at him. She said something, but the wind was shaking the window. All the house seemed to be quivering. The girl was as though she had never been, and as he reached Vanessa's side he said:

'Vanessa, it was nothing . . . Vanessa darling . . .'

She looked at him, tried to smile, but her mouth shook. He heard her murmur, 'I'm very ill . . . Tell the woman to come . . .'

So, as nearly ninety years ago Judith Paris, her grandmother, had borne an illegitimate child in the heart of storm and confusion, did Vanessa now.

Sally, daughter of Benjamin Herries and Vanessa Herries, was born at eleven-thirty on the night of September 21st, 1903, at Randle Farm in Cumberland.

PERFECT LOVE

VANESSA sat on the slope of the hill behind the white farm watching for Tom's coming.

Sally, now nearly three years of age, sprawled beside her. Vanessa had a book on her lap but she was not reading. It was a cold sunny May afternoon. The scene was so still that it was like a painted canvas – or a bowl with flowers, for the hills circled her in but flowers were everywhere – crab blossom, speedwell blue as a jewel, anemones. In the garden behind the farm the primroses were still in yellow clumps, violets, celandines, and pansies. Soon the blue hyacinths would be full-blown. But the bowl that held the flowers was harsh with the tang of winter. The higher hills were thinly powdered with snow and the rocks so black that they glittered in the May sun like steel, and the little coppice beyond the stream yet seemed to tremble as though it could not be sure that winter was truly over.

Sally was not a pretty child but she, too, was a flower. She was small, spare, taut. Her hair had a red shadow in its brown, and she was always pale, but not with the pallor of ill-health. She was the strongest child. Nothing ever ailed her. When she cried it was from ill-temper. She had a most determined will, hated to be frustrated, knew her own way and intention always. But she never sulked, loved where she loved, hated where she hated, stood no nonsense, refused to be either flattered or petted and thought her mother the beginning and end of all things.

The love of this baby for her mother was astonishing. It had been so from the very beginning, and Vanessa, sitting there in the sun, felt a supreme content. Three human beings loved her – Benjie, Tom and Sally. They would not love her for ever perhaps. Benjie still moved towards her and then away from her again. Tom, although he was the most faithful of men, had his own life now and much of it she could not share. Sally would grow up and leave her. But at this moment, in this pellucid air, happy in this bowl of flowers, she thanked God for all that He had given her.

'Am I still frightened?' she asked herself. For, since her childhood, she had had to battle with fear. She had, all her life, given her heart to someone of whom she could not be certain and that was perhaps the reason that she loved him so dearly. Would the time ever come when she would be *certain* of Benjie? He was fifty-one now, she nearing forty-seven, but the old alarms returned, day after day, as they had always done. When he went would he return?

Nevertheless in the years since Sally's birth she had known greater happiness than ever before. They had been shut off from all the world; the friends they had made had been farmers, shepherds, wandering men. They had had almost no communication with London. An occasional letter from old Barney, Adrian, once from Cynthia. Benjie had been twice abroad, once to Italy, once to Spain, but had not stayed in London on either occasion. Anything that they knew of the outer life was from Tom. When he came he told them all the news, journalistic, social, family. He was happy on his newspaper; the family were kind to him, and he was deeply, hopelessly in love with Mary, Cynthia's girl, who was still only a child but, Tom said (he confessed only to Vanessa), the love of his life . . .

Time had passed with incredible swiftness. They were forgotten, Vanessa said, not only by the world but by time as well.
They were contented.

But for how long would this endure? Still she never woke of a
morning without wondering whether before night Benjie would
not leave her. He loved her – of course he loved her – but the
restlessness was there in his blood as it had ever been. One day he
would go, and he would be lured farther and farther, always
intending to return, never returning ... What she had suffered
during his two adventures out of England no one would ever
know. She had, by now, trained herself to the complete hiding of
her fear. She gave him no sign ...

Somewhere a dog barked and at the same moment she saw that
a trap had drawn up at the gate behind the church. Someone
climbed out. It was Tom.

'Sally! Sally!' she cried. 'It's Tom!' She was as excited as a
child.

Sally screamed: 'Tom! Tom! Tom!'

She picked Sally up and ran down the slope to the farm.

They hurried along the green sward, she carrying the child in
the crook of her arm. She waved with the other hand. Tom
waved back. A moment later they were all together.

Tom was short and sturdy. He had Adam's figure before he
became stout and he had Adam's quietness and certainty. You
knew always exactly where you were with him. Some people
would think him dull as they had thought Adam. Other people
found that he was to be trusted beyond most men and that, once
his loyalty and affection were engaged, nothing could cause them
to waver again. A dull quality, loyalty, and an unimaginative!
But valuable to some people who believe in knowing where they
are.

He was not dull to Vanessa. For one thing he loved her, as he
showed with every look, every movement. For another he was
their herald from the outer world. As they sat that evening round
the table he had a thousand things to tell them. He had taken
Adrian to one of these wrestling matches, now so popular. There
had been a dinner party at Cynthia's. He had met Edmund
Gosse, who had told funny stories about George Eliot.

'I haven't the least notion who Edmund Gosse is, darling,'
Vanessa said.

Barney had been ill with rheumatism. But the most sensational
piece of news was that Maud and Helen, Carey's girls, had

become desperate Suffragettes. Really desperate. They wanted to break into the Houses of Parliament. They had marched in a procession carrying banners. Their mother was dreadfully distressed.

About journalism there were many exciting things. It was rumoured that Harmsworth, now Lord Northcliffe, intended to purchase *The Times*. Everything in Fleet Street was changing. Men were dismissed from their jobs at a moment's notice. No one was safe any longer.

'Oh, it's nice here!' he said at last. 'It's so quiet. There's such a good smell.'

'How long have you got?' Benjie asked.

'A fortnight.' He wanted to walk. He wanted to go over to Haweswater and spend two days in Eskdale.

'I'll go with you,' said Benjie.

'Oh, that will be grand!' Tom said.

But Vanessa was sure that he wanted to go alone. There was something not quite intimate between himself and his father – something a little uneasy.

And that night as Benjie was undressing he said to Vanessa:

'Tom doesn't want me with him.'

He was pulling off his shirt, a little awkwardly with his one arm. His face flushed, his hair tousled, looking at her over the top of his shirt before he dragged it over his head, he seemed to her suddenly pathetic a little, and her love went out to him with an unexpected fierce rush of emotion. She was sitting before the glass brushing her hair. She turned, the brush in her hand. He, standing bare to the waist, looked back at her. They exchanged a long deep gaze. The room was lit with candles that blew in the breeze from the open window, and their shadows were gigantic on the white wall.

They stayed, transfixed, looking at one another. Then at last, with a deep breath as though he were experiencing some extraordinary new emotion, he came over to her. He put his hand on her shoulder, then moved it to her neck and so held her, her gaze still upon him. Her eyes filled with tears; her heart was hammering. It was as though he had never made love to her before, as though at last he were about to say to her the words for which she had so long been aching.

He knelt down and enfolded her with his arm, his head on her breast. With light gentle fingers she stroked his hair, staring in front of her, all the room dimmed because her eyes were dim. A ridiculous clock that had a note, Benjie always said, like an angry parrot, told the hour, but the sound was an infinite distance away. What had happened? What was then this tumultuous fiery rush of joy at her heart?

'What is it?' she said at last. 'Benjie – darling – tell me. Are you unhappy about Tom?'

He did not answer. He held her only the more tightly. At last he said:

'It's like this, Van ... It's as though I had never seen you before.'

He got up and stood there, looking at her.

'You'll catch cold with the window open.'

But he did not move; only stood there staring at her.

'Isn't it odd, Van? I'm falling in love with you all over again.'

She finished brushing her hair, although it was difficult because her hands trembled. She slipped on her nightdress and got into bed.

He always wore at night an open shirt that came no farther than the knees. For a moment he was naked and, looking at him in the candlelight, she thought how wonderfully he had preserved his body. For a man of past fifty he had an astonishing spareness and hardness. No fat. Nothing slack. And, as always, he looked as though he never wore clothes, as though his flesh were always exposed to the wind and sun. He stretched himself like an animal, raised his arm above his head, swelled out his brown chest. But he never took his bright, blue, fearless eyes from her face. She had never seen such eyes in any other man. They were so childlike, honest, dependable. But he was not a child and he was not dependable ...

She expected that her own emotion would recede. It had been but a moment, born perhaps of her maternal longing over him because he was disappointed in Tom. But the emotion did not recede. She clasped her hands under the bedclothes and tried to beat down her joy. Like many another woman she was afraid of it lest it should lead her to expect too much and bring soon some disappointment that would be almost unbearably bitter – that she would remember afterwards, when the joy was forgotten.

'I mustn't love him too much,' she told herself, as so many, many times she had told herself before. He blew out the candles and lay down beside her. She knew at once by his touch on her breast that tonight he was very gentle. He scarcely touched her

and yet she was thrilled by his proximity as she had never been
before. They kissed and it was a kiss far deeper than passion.
They did not stir, only their two hearts beating the one against
the other, but this kiss was different from any other that they had
ever exchanged. It was radiant with awe and wonder and reverence at something quite beyond and outside themselves.

At last he said: 'What has happened, Van? I have never loved
anyone as I do you tonight.' His hand found hers and now they
lay, very quietly, side by side, hand in hand. She turned on her
side, laying her cheek against his.

'How still it is! Only the running water!'

He stroked her arm with his hand, very gently, as though he
were afraid lest he should hurt her.

'Van, this is heaven. I have never loved you before as I do
tonight.'

'Nor I you, Benjie.'

'We'll never forget this.'

'No. Never, never.'

'I seem to understand at this moment what life ought to be.'
She sighed with a deep, yearning happiness. 'I'm not afraid any
more. I don't care now what happens. We have never been
together like this before . . .'

'No. Never. I wonder why . . .'

They turned to meet one another in a passionate embrace.

And, with the morning, nothing was changed. She knew immediately that he was still moving in this new relationship. She
saw that Tom was at once aware of it and that he came in an
instant more closely to his father. Benjie was quiet. In ordinary
he conveyed a sense of restlessness, of wanting to move from the
place where he was to some other place. But this morning, after
they had breakfasted, he stood in front of the farm looking at the
green field, the hills, the flowers, as though he had never seen
them before.

'Come for a stroll,' he said to Vanessa, and they went. But, as
they walked, they scarcely spoke. They went side by side, and for
Vanessa it was as though they were not walking but rather were
held, in some burning cloud, alone, away from man and time and
destiny. What had happened? Was it not impossible that at their
age, after they had lived so long together, known one another so
intimately, there could be a new relationship between them?
Friendship, comradeship, yes; but a new emotion, a new passion?
Surely it was impossible?

Only at the end of this walk, before they went into the house, he turned to her and said again:

'Vanessa, what has happened to us? Are we in love for the first time?'

Day followed day, week followed week; the summer passed and autumn was smoke and flame, smoke of the clouds, flame of the bracken. With November the rains fell. There was clouded light over the dales and the wind currents were as vexed and troubled as the twists and turns of a stream. A black whirlwind of cloud would rush across the tops, discharging its waters as though from a gigantic tub impatiently overset by a celestial housemaid: you would wake to a morning of universal dark; the very fire burnt dimly and the rain fell with the tramp of armies; or the wet mists would blow from Robinson, from Cat Bells, thin and airy, carrying with them all the scene, a bare hillside lit by a sudden splash of shining rock, a herd of sheep stalwart under the chill stone walls, houses of stone raised into air by the web of vapour. Or it would rain quite solemnly like a clergyman of the old school preaching into eternity, or a writer of stories for whom two hundred years are but as a day, and then nothing lovelier in the world could be seen than that quick break before dusk when a pulse of gold beats through the dark and the sun creeps from under the blanket of cloud and everything is lit with radiance for a short breathless while. In these valleys and hills rain is as beautiful as fair weather and more various, and it is rain always broken by sudden breathtaking surprises. Only in this weather and perhaps only in this country can you see what the ebon flank of a cloud may be above a misty hill, or how purple – richer than grape-bloom – can cover a fell after tempest, or the white shadow, whiter than ivory and thin like glass, that strokes the field under a pale young stormy moon.

Men who write of these things are always defeated by them, so rare and strange is their beauty, but in their hearts an eternal homesickness is created so that they are never either safe or happy again in any land where it is dry and the sun is for ever shining.

Throughout the summer, the autumn, the winter, this miracle remained for Benjie and Vanessa. Many writers for hundreds of years have written about first love, and some writers (but not so very many) have spoken of the happiness of married comradeship. But life is never settled nor arranged, nor does it behave as it ought, by the laws of the written word, to do. Many men and women would behave nobly were they given the perfect conditions and circumstances, but there is always toothache, a broken promise, a jealousy, an unreasonable desire. Only once in a lifetime perhaps a Beethoven Symphony arrives punctually and, in a lighted room, two friends forget that there is such a tyranny as Time. And, even then, sentiment may steal the prize.

Vanessa and Benjie had good fortune. Not by their own desire, and, in any case, they did not know where to look for it. It came to them and they knew what perfect love can be.

During this winter they were never parted. Their happiness was too deep and soundless for them to fear it. For Vanessa it was as though God kept them in continual company. Her ideas of God were, of course, very simple; she felt His radiance as though she moved from morning to night in sunlight. For Benjie it was simpler still. He wanted to be near Vanessa; he did not know why she irritated him no more, why he was restless no longer. He did not search for reasons. He only knew that body, soul, and spirit, he was complete.

One starlit night after Christmas they climbed the hill and sat down together. The sky was quite clear. It was as though they were wrapped in stardust. A little way above them the snow began. It was bitterly cold, but he wrapped his large shepherd's cloak around both of them and, because there was no wind, they took no hurt.

'It would not be bad, Van,' he said, 'if we were to die now, both of us together.'

Then, as she did not answer, he went on: 'That is what all lovers have always said. But *young* lovers. Lovers in their first ecstasy. We are very *old* lovers.'

'I don't feel old,' she answered at last. 'When shall we begin to feel old?'

'Oh, I suppose – with sickness, separation . . .'

'We will never be separated now,' she said quickly.

He held her to him, under the cloak, more closely.

'I don't trust life even now. I think you're the only thing in the whole world I trust. There never was anyone so trustworthy as you are.'

She laughed. 'Yes, that's why I'm dull – for everyone except you and Tom.'

'No. You're not dull. They didn't think you dull in London. But you're shy. You can't show people what you are. You're courageous enough about *things*. You'd stand up to anything.

But you're human beings. Only in these last three months have even I known what you are.'

'For the first time since my father died,' she said. 'I'm not afraid.'

Five weeks later the letter came.

It came, as catastrophic letters often come, with an almost maidenly quietness. Vanessa opened it, looking over the table to Benjie, and laughing at something that he had just said. This was the letter:

HILL STREET, LONDON, W.
February 8th, 1907

DEAR VANESSA — You will, I am sure, be extremely surprised to receive a letter from me — surprised and not altogether pleased, I fear, but Vera and I have, for some weeks now, discussed the matter and have at last decided that this letter must be written. The matter is quite simply this. For some while now — ever since last summer in fact — Ellis has been seriously ailing. He has not, of course, been strong mentally for a very long time past. That you know. But his bodily conditions have been surprisingly good: he has eaten and slept well, and, within his own mental world, has really lived with content under our care. We have done our best. It has not always been easy, but of that I wish here to say nothing. Last summer we took Ellis to Harrogate as perhaps you heard at the time. We found a small and comfortable house where we could enjoy privacy and where, at the same time, my sister (whose rheumatism has for some time been trying) and Ellis could receive medical attention.

It was during our stay in Harrogate that the change took place. He has long been given, as you must have heard, to childish pursuits. He enjoys playing with dolls, soldiers, and trains. We have always, under excellent Doctor Lancaster's advice, humoured him in this and one day in Harrogate Vera bought him a doll to give him pleasure. So soon as he saw it it reminded him of you. I must tell you that he had not, so far as my sister and I were aware, once mentioned your name during all these years. But on this occasion, on Vera's presenting him with the doll, he said at once: 'Why, this is Vanessa come back again!' At first he seemed extremely happy at his fancy, but my sister and I noticed that from this moment he began to be less well. His headaches, which you will perhaps remember, returned. His temperature was often above normal. He was restless. Many of the things that had amused him seemed to amuse him no longer. He is of course, not young any more – sixty-four years of age – and his recurrent fever made us anxious. Whatever you may feel about my sister and myself you must remember, Vanessa, that we have both for a very long time now been most deeply and sincerely attached to your husband. Throughout this last winter he has been most unwell and now for several weeks has not left his bed. Doctor Lancaster says that it is difficult to say that there is anything organically wrong, but he fears that he has not long to live. We feel, Vera and I, that if this is indeed so, we must do everything to make the last months of his life happy. We are two childless women and in these years at Hill Street we have come to feel for Ellis as though he were our son. I hope you will forgive my saying this, but the whole situation is – and has always been – so very strange!

And now to come to the point of this letter (it has not been an easy one to write). It is that, continually, during these last weeks Ellis has begged for your return. He has, it seems, a clear memory of the events that led up to your departure, but his mental decay has wiped from his recollection all bitterness and anger. He is as gentle and submissive as the child that so often he seems to be. 'I want Vanessa!' he cries and, again and again: 'When is Vanessa coming? Why does Vanessa not come?'

In these circumstances my sister and I feel it right that you should know how things stand. It is not easy for us to take this step. We cannot pretend that we approved, or now approve, of the action that you took. But it is not for us to judge and we can only assure you that if you return to Hill Street for the few remaining weeks of Ellis' life (Doctor Lancaster tells us that it cannot be much more) you will hear no single word of reproach from us and we will regard you as the mistress of this house in every way. Your place just now, Vanessa, is with your husband, whatever the past has been. You have it in your power to give him this last happiness. We feel that we would never forgive ourselves if we did not acquaint you with the facts – Yours sincerely,

WINIFRED TRENT

Vanessa read the letter. Benjie, watching her from the other side of the table, saw at once that something of the uttermost seriousness had occurred.

'What is it?' he asked, coming across to her.

She gave him the letter. He read it slowly, sometimes repeating some of the words aloud.

'But this is monstrous!' he said at last. His face was flushed with anger, and also with the beginning of a terrible fear.

She sat down, staring in front of her, then held out her hand for the letter and read it through again.

'Yes,' she said. 'I have always known that the punishment would come. It *had* to come – to make things just.'

'Now – look, Van.' He sat down beside her. 'You are not to consider this for a moment; what the old witch suggests, I mean. Go to London. I'll come with you. Go to Hill Street. Pay him a visit. We'll stay in London if you like and you shall go often and see him – anything else is preposterous.'

She shook her head.

'He wants me back. I never would have left him if he had wanted me. But he didn't. Now he does. He's dying.'

Benjie with an effort to be calm – one of the hardest things he had attempted for many a day (for this *was* preposterous; this was a plot, Hill Street all madmen and witches) – put his hand on hers, which was trembling, and summoned all his wisdom:

'Listen, Van. He doesn't want you. He can't. He doesn't know what he wants. It's some plot to get you back there again. The two old women are tired of their job, I shouldn't wonder. They think it would be a fine thing for you to take it on again. He *can't* want you with his dolls and his trains.'

'No. I don't like Vera and Winifred – but they're honest. They have no imagination and no humour, but they're honest and they've been angels to Ellis. When I wrote to Vera three years ago – you remember – to ask her to persuade Ellis to divorce me, her letter wasn't kind but it was honest and plucky. I don't like them, but there are no lies in this letter.'

She turned round and stared at him. She looked, he thought, quite suddenly an ageing woman. Her confidence and happiness had left her.

'This is awful,' she said at last. 'Terrible. The worst thing that could happen. To go back to that house, that life ... to leave you. Oh!' she cried, her hand on her breast. 'I don't think I can! I don't think I can!'

'Of course you can't – and, I tell you, there's no need to. We'll go to London. We'll see Ellis ...'

But she shook her head. She had recovered her courage.

'Of course I must go – and you know it, Benjie. There can be no other way. What would I feel now if, after that letter, I didn't go? How could I go on living with you as we have been living? Oh, I knew it was too good to last! Something *had* to happen . . . these last six months – we've had a new life – and it was too fine, too wonderful to be allowed much of. It's unfair, it's unfair. That one mistake I made so long ago, to be punished for it so many times!' Then she cried out in a kind of agony: 'That house, Benjie! I can't *stand* that house!'

Then he was really frightened and because he was frightened he was angry. He got up roughly, knocking his chair over.

'Look here Van – if you leave me now because two crazy old women write a letter – if you leave me after all that has happened to us these last months – you'll lose me. I can't keep up without you now. I'm not young any more. I could have done without you once, perhaps, but not now . . . You owe me more than you owe Ellis.'

'No, I don't,' she interrupted. 'I ruined Ellis' life. I've made you happy, I made him unhappy.'

'It was his own fault. He made you marry him.' (He did not remember that it had been *his* fault.)

'No, he did not. I need not have married him . . .' Then she turned and caught his arm. 'Benjie, there's Sally! There's Sally!'

'You see,' he cried triumphantly. 'You see how impossible it is. Of course you can't leave Sally. She's your child, isn't she?'

'No . . . No . . . Of course, I would have to have Sally with me. I would insist on that. I would make my terms—'

Then he swore at her. 'Damn you, Vanessa, am *I* nothing? What about me? You think of your crazy husband, you think of your baby. But I'm to be left out of it. Anything can happen to me—' He was not going to plead for himself. He looked at her and saw that her mind was made up. This was the law: Vanessa's character being what it was, this was fate.

He saw that and saw, also, for himself a future so intolerable that he closed his eyes and bowed his head.

Then they drew together and clung together, without a word. Both knew that in this there was no alternative.

TIMOTHY BELLAIRS PAYS SOME VISITS

OLD Barney Newmark died quite suddenly in his sleep in the autumn of 1909. The Family were sorry because they had approved of Barney's fame as a novelist. It was not, perhaps, very great and he belonged to a very different generation from the present. The obituaries were kind; he had been a genial fellow, always in London, friendly and cheerful with everyone. He was spoken of as the 'Hawley Smart of his period'. The *Referee* wrote: 'Mr Newmark could write of horses and pretty women with a grace and humour that exceeded any of his contemporaries.' But the paragraph that pleased the Family was one in *The Daily Telegraph*: 'Mr Newmark, whose loss was so widely deplored last week, was of course a member of the famous Herries family, so well known in so many directions. Lord Rockage, who owns in Wiltshire one of the finest houses in England, is a member of it; Mr Alfred Herries, the well-known financier, another; Mr Timothy Bellairs, whose picture "Mme Rochambert" created a sensation in last year's Salon, another. The Hon Mrs Peile Worcester, whose parties in Charles Street have long been famous, is a member of the family, and another member, Mr Horace Newmark, who died not so long ago, was known for many years as "the Monarch of Manchester". The Herries family is very well known in the North of England, most especially in Cumberland and the Border country. One of the most remarkable women of an earlier generation in the North was Madame Paris, also a member of the famous family. She has become almost a legend in Cumberland and Westmorland, I believe. Mr Newmark's delightful friendly, easy, and merry novels belonged to a time when the art of fiction was scarcely as seriously considered as it is today. This has been a sad year for English letters, mourning as we do both Meredith and Swinburne. Mr Newmark would have been the first to deprecate any comparison between two such giants and his own agreeable novels. Nevertheless he will be missed and for a long time to come.'

This was very pleasant. It had been for the Herries family a year of definite accomplishment. They had lived down the mis-adventures of the South African War and the disgrace of Vanessa's elopement (both events, in their view, of equal family importance). The Edwardian period, with its gracious (if materially minded) monarch, its common sense, its proper appreciation of money, its fostering of the upper middle class (even though the lower orders *were* behaving immodestly), its enthusiasm for Empire, its general applause for the solider English virtues, exactly suited the Herries: wildness, immorality, gambling, these things, when they appeared, became almost at once socially rationalized. The Family had no objection to immorality when it was photographed at a weekend house party during the shooting season. Private behaviour was no matter so long as it appeared publicly decent, and this was not hypocrisy on the Herries' part. It was simply that they cared for England, guarded her reputation most zealously. And this was natural, for England was Herries and Herries were England . . .

At last they could sit back for a moment and see that all was well. Family feuds (ridiculous, all about nothing – a fan, a green vase, a house on a hill) were things of the past. One possible scandal, the unspeakable Rose – poor Horace Ormerod's sister – had, luckily, been hidden by the grime of mean streets. Vanessa was living once again most properly with her husband; even Barney's death was not so bad a thing, for he had outlived his reputation and had been inclined at times to say oddly sarcastic things about the Family.

England had never seemed more secure, more prosperous, more certain of the grandeur of her great destiny – and as England was, so were the Herries.

It happened that Timothy Bellairs, the painter, came over to London for Barney's funeral. The old boy had been good to him in times past. Barney and Benjie (and of course young Tom) were the only members of the Family for whom he cared. He had lived so long in Paris that he did not feel Herries any longer. Or did he? He came over to London to find out.

He was a tall thin man with very light blue eyes and hair the colour of pale corn. He wore a small pointed beard. He had a way of watching you while you talked, of agreeing with you but causing you to wonder whether he did not think you a terrible fool. His voice was gentle and he had a charming smile. He appeared detached and impersonal. He had in fact only two passions – one was for painting, the other for one or two individuals. He was capable of iron fidelity. Benjie and Tom were two of his devotions, although he had not seen either of them for a very long time. Another was a stout and extremely cynical lady who shared his bed and board in Paris.

Attending Barney's funeral he observed the Family.

Vanessa was there. He had not seen her for many years but, knowing her story and of her return to Ellis nearly three years ago, he watched her with especial interest. Her grey hair under the black hat, the pale face beneath the veil – these gave her a greater appearance of age than he had expected. But her carriage (he watched her as, attended by a little thin woman, she walked up the aisle to her seat) was very fine. She was a big woman, full-breasted, large-shouldered and, he thought, as he saw her before she turned into her seat, apart from everyone else there. 'She has learnt how to play her role.'

Tom was with him and whispered some names. That was Horace, that stout fellow in glasses, with plump cheeks, the full Herries chin and an air of self-conscious benevolence. 'Barney hated him,' Tom whispered. Cynthia swept up, Peile Worcester in atendance. Very smart, Timothy thought, with her beauti-fully fitting black and Parma violets – not thinking about Barney, though.

An extremely thin tall gentleman, wearing pince-nez, his black clothes rigid as though cut from wood, 'very Herries' in feature, moved to his seat as though he were taking his place as chairman of a board meeting.

'That's Alfred.'

A fat cheerful gentleman and a very fat cheerful lady hurried up the aisle, showering benevolence on all around them. 'Sidney and Mary – Horace's son from Manchester.'

Then old Carey Rockage, bent with rheumatism, May thin and short-sighted, with the two suffragette daughters who strode forward looking about them with an air of resentment.

Timothy's sister, who had married a Colonel and lived in Sur-biton, was not present. Vanessa was by far the most interesting person in that church to Timothy. He thought of Barney.

'Good old boy. He had a fine life. Did what he wanted, en-joyed every moment of it.' When he remembered Barney's mis-tresses it amused him that the Family should come, in such numbers, to pay him the last compliments. 'They wouldn't do the same for Benjie,' he thought, feeling the touch of Tom's shoulder against his. But Barney, in some clever fashion of his own, had never openly outraged the conventions. No member of the Family had ever been brought face to face with his mistresses,

while in poor Benjie's case every rebellion had been as open as it
could be! And then, just as the service was about to start, Benjie
walked up the aisle. He walked slowly, his brown face and bright
blue eyes unconcerned, the empty sleeve of his jacket pinned to
his breast. He was wearing a loose dark suit – so far he had
submitted to convention – but he looked, as he always looked in
public, apart, as though he were of another country, an exile and
a rebellious one. 'He looks more than that,' Tim thought. 'He
looks worn and strained. He's too thin.'

Had he seen Tom and Timothy he would undoubtedly have
stopped and sat with them, but, his head up, seeing nobody, he
walked straight ahead. 'He said he wasn't coming,' Tom whispered.

He passed the seat where Vanessa was. Some instinct seemed to
tell him. He stopped for a moment, then turned and found a
place on the other side of the aisle beside stout Sidney and Mary
Newmark. It amused Timothy to observe the startled and frightened look that they gave him.

So old Barney Newmark, accorded by the Family full
honours, joined (perhaps thankfully) the Rogue and David,
Judith and young John, and was, beyond question, glad of their
company.

Timothy had not as yet paid Benjie a proper visit. Tom, who
shared lodgings with his father in Tite Street, told Tim that
Benjie was in one of his bad moods.

'He'll tell you all about it when you go. He's very unhappy –
but he'll tell you. Only you'd better wait till he chooses his day.'

Meanwhile Timothy was painting Mary Worcester's picture.
He had seen, at once, that this was a thing that he had to do. She
was the loveliest child he had ever beheld. She was going to be a
real beauty. The modelling of her face was exquisite, her colour
perfect, everything delicate, gentle, dark hair, dark eyes, already a
sense of poise and movement. But, he decided very quickly, she
was stupid and dull. Her voice was lovely in tone, soft and res-
onant, but she had nothing to say. Her eyes were large and full;
she had a way of using them so that they rested on you as though
they found you enchanting. But she did not find you enchanting.
She was not thinking about you at all. She was only sixteen and
had been kept, at home, closely guarded, but even then Timothy
thought, she surely had *some* ideas about something! It seemed
that she had not.

Her mother, whose little figure was still perfect but was betrayed by her too bony neck and eyes that were older than her complexion allowed for, said about her beautiful daughter that: 'You've no idea how intelligent that child is! Now Rosalind says just what's in her head and nine times out of ten it's nonsense, as I tell her – but *Mary*! No one knows what that child's thinking!'

Cynthia also unburdened herself to Timothy about Vanessa:

'Of course it's awful for her. We all realize that. She came back nearly three years ago thinking that Ellis had only a week or two to live. And now there he is quite strong and hearty! Of course he's mad as a hatter, but quite nice and gentle, I believe. He's simply Vanessa's slave, poor thing. And isn't it odd! Vera and Winifred Trent used to hate her, but since Vera died last year Winifred adores her. I must say Vanessa always had the power of making people fond of her. I always have loved her in spite of what she did. What is it about Vanessa? Perhaps you'll find out, Timothy. Because she's really dull and has no sense of humour at all. I must say she's very sporting. Right or wrong, Benjie's the love of her life and there they both are, eating their hearts out. Between you and me I wonder Benjie doesn't creep into Hill Street and poison Ellis. What's the good of his living? He's quite hopeless mentally, you know. Of course Vanessa's got Sally with her. She insisted on that. Her little girl and Benjie's. It always seems funny to me when Ellis, poor thing, has always been so proper and moral, that Vanessa's illegitimate child should be in his house under his roof. And I believe he's passionately fond of the child. Altogether very queer. Vanessa doesn't go out into society at all, but she likes people to go and see her. I go sometimes although Peile doesn't much like my doing it and I confess the place gives me the shudders.'

'Does she see Benjie?' Timothy asked.

'Oh yes, sometimes. There's nothing improper of course. The fact is, Timothy, they are the only example I know anywhere of real love. It's gone on all their lives and they're as much in love as ever they were. She's quite tamed Benjie. He used to be as wild as anything. It's a bit hard on him, isn't it? Separated from his child, too, but I believe he thinks it the right thing for Vanessa to do. They're an odd pair altogether.'

It happened that on the afternoon following the funeral Cynthia was giving a small children's party. For a brief while Timothy observed the ceremony; not for long – he detested children

unless they were paintable. He was extremely sharp at catching
character from face, voice, and movement. He had a number of
young Herries under his eye (the coming upholders of the
Herries tradition) and quickly decided that only one of them was
beautiful (Mary Worcester of course) and only one charming –
little Sally, Vanessa's daughter. He wondered for a moment that
'a little bastard' should be allowed in among all the true-born offspring, but decided that this was the Herries way of showing
Vanessa that they had forgiven her.

The Herries children were: first Mary and Rosalind Worcester
(Mary a gracious and lovely hostess; Rosalind clutching her
friend little Ada Newmark – Horace's grandchild, the daughter
of stout Sidney and stout Mary – and going off with her into a
corner); the aforesaid Ada and her brother Gordon; Maurice and
Clara, Alfred's children, plain, with good manners, but wanting
the best for themselves. Mary, Rosalind, Ada, Gordon, Maurice
and Clara: little ordinary Herries, all that they should be. It was
amusing, he thought, as he watched, to notice the way in which
these Herries children took command of the other children who
were not Herries. Took command quite confidently, without arrogance or tiresome conceit, but quite as though it must be. And
yet, with the notable exception of Mary, they were not very
beautiful nor certainly were they brilliant. The Herries, he
reflected, were never first class unless they were mad. 'I am not
first class because I am not mad. Benjie, although he has never
done anything with his life except love Vanessa, has something
first class about him. A first-class passion for something outside
oneself can make one first class. I have a passion for my Art. Why
am I not first class? Because there is just enough Herries in me to
prevent my escape from myself.'

Then he saw little Sally and went and talked to her. She was
an odd-looking child, small with straight uncurling brown hair
and a pale face. But she was all alive. She sat on a sofa and her
eyes were everywhere, eager, merry, and very intelligent. She did
not join in anything until she was invited, but she suffered from
no self-consciousness. Little coloured balloons were handed
round (they were to be blown across a tablecloth). Clara, Alfred's
child, preferred the colour of Sally's balloon to her own and said
so. Sally at once gave her hers, but Tim thought that she, at the
same time, looked at her with a little baby irony as much as to
say: 'You're like that, are you, even at your age' – a very elderly
look for a child of six. 'But then,' thought Timothy, 'it will be

odd if she isn't queer, born as she was and brought up in Hill Street.'

Next day he went and visited Benjie. London was very interesting to him. It was so long since he had stayed here. This was a great year for mechanical progress. The virtue of single planes advanced in a sudden leap the history of flying. In July, Blériot had crossed the Channel. In October there was a flying week at Blackpool and Mr Farman surprised everyone by flying for half an hour in wild and gusty weather.

But the great change in London was the advance of motor-cabs. Hitherto motoring had been mainly for the well-to-do. Now it was discovered that cabs could be made both cheaply and strongly. The new cabs, fitted with taximeters, were comfortable, safe, and the old uncertainty of the proper fare for the tiresome and truculent old cabby was gone. Only a little while before, motors had been the property of the rich: now, quite suddenly, they were everywhere. The whole aspect of the London streets was changed. It signified perhaps the final advent to assured power and importance of the middle classes.

Timothy felt this most emphatically during his evening expeditions about the town. He went everywhere: to the White City, to a first night at Wyndham's, or the Haymarket, or the St James's, to a dinner at the Savage Club, to the National Sporting Club, to the London Sketch Club, to a Sunday night at the New Lyric, and everywhere it was the same – the English Middle Class was now triumphant, subservient to nothing and nobody. The reign of the Autocrats in England was over. Sargent painted his Jew millionaires, Wells and Bennett invigorated the novel with their portraits of lower middle-class life. The word 'respectable' had no longer any especial significance in English life. The ordinary man ruled England and he was determined to find pleasure where he could and hold to it. The ordinary man ruled England, and Herries were the ordinary man.

He found Benjie in three rooms of the upper part of a house in Tite Street, Chelsea. When he came in, Benjie was walking up and down. He was wearing an old grey jacket, grey flannel trousers, and a faded red tie. Tim was struck, more than ever, by his spareness, the fierceness of his blue eyes. He noticed that his hair was turning grey at the temples. He looked as though he had been lost in the desert and rescued in the nick of time. After half an hour's talk Tim felt that Benjie would, on the whole, have preferred that the rescue had not take place.

The room was very bare, but it had a broad bright window filled with scurrying clouds and a cold blue sky. Very shortly it would be dark. In the window was a long deal table with Vanessa's photograph (a very old one), a book which Tim picked up and found to be Hudson's *Purple Land,* some writing paper, a pen, and a long truculent-looking ruler. On the walls there was nothing save over the fireplace two grinning masks made of some dark wood. There were two shabby armchairs.

Tim knew Benjie well. In the very old days when he had gone over to Paris with Tom, Benjie had been his saviour. He had protected him against the Family. Tim, who was faithful, would stick to Benjie always because of that, were there no other reason. But there *were* other reasons, plenty of them. He liked Benjie because he was honest, generous, courageous, and his own worst enemy. Benjie had one charming quality, and a very rare one it is. He always, whatever his own personal melodramas, wanted to hear about the adventures of his friends. This was not from self-conscious duty nor from a desire to be kind. He was truly interested.

So Timothy told him – about Mlle Thérèse, his stout but charming mistress, about his new flat, about the portrait he was painting of the two little girls of the Minister of Finance, about his picking up a charming Berthe Morisot for almost nothing, of English writers whom he had met in Paris – Somerset Maugham and Arnold Bennett ('both interested in painting – very odd'), about this and that.

'And you?' he asked at last.

'Oh – I?' Benjie sat on the deal table, swinging his legs. 'I go on – as you see.'

Tim was aware, at that moment, just as a rather slatternly white-haired woman brought in the tea, that he was encountering some experience so deep and poignant that he was frightened of it. He was frightened of very little; he was certainly not frightened of Benjie. But there was something here that belonged to that rarest of all worlds – the world of absolute and positive experience. 'Because,' he thought, 'we all live one skin deep at the most. We do not, most of us, know that we can go deeper.'

So to ease things he himself talked.

'I've been observing the Family. I haven't seen it, you know, for a long time. Coming along very nicely, I should say. It ostracized me once and now it welcomes me because I'm a moderate success. I'm not exactly prejudiced in its favour. But we've settled down. All the quarrels are over. All the same there are a few rebels left, but they're not so grand as they used to be.' Then he said an incautious thing. 'But I tell you what, Benjie – your daughter's going to be a rebel. You should have seen her with the rest of them. It persists, the divine strain. How I wish I had more of it!'

Benjie jumped to the floor.

'You've seen Sally – where? when?'

'Oh, yesterday – at a children's party at Cynthia's.'

'Did you talk to her? She's remarkable, isn't she? Unusual?'

'Yes, I talked to her a little. I loathe children's parties, you know. Certainly she's unusual. I was saying so.'

'I see her, you know.' Benjie came and sat down close to him, bending eagerly forward. 'Quite often. In fact I can see her as often as I like so long as I never go to the house. Odd situation, isn't it?'

'Very,' said Timothy, terribly touched by his friend's emotion, thinking, too of the old Benjie who had been a wandering kind of rascal with no very constant attachment.

'Have you been to see Vanessa, Tim?'

'No, not yet. Do you think she would like to see me?'

'Of course she would. And you must go soon. Then come and tell me about it.'

'Tell you about it?'

'Yes. Vanessa and I meet sometimes. Not too often or it would be unbearable. But I never enter the house of course. And I don't ask her about the house. When we are together in fact we don't talk very much. Talking seems to waste the time. The only one who told me much about what it was like inside was old Barney. And now he's gone. Adrian goes there, but Adrian's a prig. The rest of the family don't see much of me, you know.'

'I see,' said Timothy. 'Of course I'll go if she won't think it impertinent.'

'Oh no, she'll love it. Especially if you tell her you've been here. You'll have to repeat every word of our conversation, you know.'

Tim said slowly: 'It's all damned hard on you.'

Benjie answered quickly: 'It's far worse for her. You see, the bad part of it is that we were having such a marvellous time just before he wanted her. And we thought it was only for a month or two. Now it's been close on three years, and God knows how much longer!'

'Well, if you want my opinion,' Timothy broke out, 'I think

the whole thing's preposterous! There are you, two people in the prime of life, loving one another, and on the other side Ellis who's too mad to know whether she's there or no.'

'You're wrong,' Benjie said quietly. 'Know? Why, she's his very life! He worships her. If she left him it would be like leaving a helpless child, and worse than that, because she married him. She only left him because he *didn't* want her. No, there's no other way – until Ellis dies. She would never be happy for a moment if she came away. Not that she's happy as it is, but she's got Sally.'

'And you?' Tim asked.

'Oh, I? Don't mind about me. Don't think I'm being noble either. I'm not. I curse like hell. I'd hate him if – if he were normal. As it is one can't hate anyone in the affair, more's the pity. Oh, I'm all right. I go abroad sometimes. There's Tom here for company and he's so kind that I could kill him. I'm working at a job too. I go to a travel agency every day and advise people about foreign parts. Sometimes I go wild for a day or two. I've got some awful friends, you know. But I'm never wild for long nor away for long. I come slinking back because Vanessa's here.'

'I'm glad you love her so much,' Tim said. 'Anyone's in luck to have the chance of the real thing.'

'Love her?' He threw his head back. 'Did you ever know our real story, Tim? No. Well, I'm not going to bore you with it. But we loved one another from childhood. We meant to marry. First her father died – was burnt in the fire at Uldale. That stopped it. Then – imagine it! – I married someone else! Fantastic? Not at all. My cursed imbecility that has made me do the wrong thing at the wrong time all my life. But listen. However wild I've been, however caught she's been – caught in a trap, because that's what her marriage to Ellis was – we've never ceased to love one another for a single moment. At the very instant of making love to another woman I've always known it was only Vanessa I loved. And the best time we ever had was just before we parted. And now we'll never be free of one another – I doubt if death can part us. And yet when I say that, how ridiculous, how sentimental! Hasn't every lover always said the same? But we are such *old* lovers! It goes far beyond the body – beyond – into what? Is it simply association, all that we have been through together? Vanessa isn't very clever. She isn't any longer very beautiful. But she's *lovely*, Tim. She never falters, she never lets you down, she has a childish pleasure in tiny things, she's generous, loyal, and although she thinks she's a coward, she never flinches at anything. And yet it's only a little for her character that I love her. One doesn't love people for their character, does one? Or only a little. Why? Why? Why are Vanessa and I bound together? Is she right, do you think? Is there a spiritual life that outlasts the bodily? Will Vanessa and I go on together, never apart, loving one another? ... Sometimes when I sit alone in here at night, hearing the mouse in the wall and seeing those masks grin, knowing that she's there and I here – such a little distance – I begin to believe that I can pull her spirit in here with me, her body there in Hill Street. I could swear that she comes in, sits with her head against my knee as she used to do in Cumberland – is this mad, Tim, do you think? Am I going queer a bit? Do I *look* queer?'

'No, Benjie, not in the least. Only it's bad for both of you, I should think, separated like this and yet so near to one another. Lord! I wish I loved someone like that, though! Or do I? It's a terrible strain. One can't work if one's always wanting someone ...'

He waited a while, then he said abruptly:

'Do you ever read history, Benjie?'

'History? No. Oh, I've read Macaulay and a bit of Froude—'

'You *should* read history. There's nothing so interesting. History or biography. A nation or a family or an individual – it's all the same. The point is that men's values are all wrong. The things that they *think* are happening aren't happening at all. Do you remember Tolstoi's *Anna Karénina* and the racecourse scene? Everyone *thought* that the racing was the important thing. It wasn't in the least. It was the struggle in the hearts of Anna and Karénin and Vronsky. Yes, and in thousands of other souls that day. Little temptations to meanness, lusts, sacrifices. Small tests, tests as small as a pin – but soul histories are the only histories. Write an account of a family or a county and find out where the crises of the human spirit lie. See how it meets all the tests, is beaten, is victorious, encounters its two chief enemies, greed and fear, is encouraged to extend into something wider, grander, nobler than itself. Shakespeare knew that that was the only kind of history. What are the stories of his six great kings but soul histories? What does he care for national history? It is Richard in his tent, Henry praying before the battle, the old king dying in Westminster ... I'm not religious, you know. I can't swear to heaven. I don't know whether there are pearly gates. And I'm not given to preaching. But I do know that you've got the only thing that matters, Benjie. You can feed your soul with an unselfish passion. You're not starving it. You should see old Monet painting. He's like an eagle beating his wings for joy that he's free, gross, fat old man that he is! To escape beyond oneself! To lose one's soul because one's beyond fear, and so to save it. That's the history of the endeavour of every man and woman born on this earth. The only thing that gives us grandeur, fleas on a cinder as we are!'

Benjie smiled.

'I've never heard you talk like that before.'

'No. I'm growing old. I've faced up to the fact that I shall never be the painter I hoped to be, never meet the woman I hoped to meet. We all do. I'm just of the age. I hold my tongue. I haven't talked like this for an age. The French are a cynical people, you know. All the same it's a marvel to me that men can refuse so obstinately to think of the only things that really matter. We'll suffer for it. We're bound to. Well, I must go.'

He raised his long thin body, pulled at his pale corn-coloured beard, stretched his arms and yawned.

'You're going to see Vanessa, aren't you?'

'Yes – tomorrow.'

'And you'll come and see me again?'

'I'll come and see you again.'

When he was gone Benjie sat down and wrote to Vanessa.

Next day Tim went to Hill Street. An old butler with face like a muffin, plump, boneless, without shape, received him and led him upstairs. In the long drawing-room Vanessa was entertaining Mary Newmark, wife of Sidney, old Horace's son. Mary Newmark was fat in a bright, cheerful way. She wore a dress of shining blue and she had a large hat with blue feathers. Under the hat her face, like a gigantic strawberry, beamed on the world. Beside her Vanessa, who was dressed in black, looked very quiet. But Tim was surprised. He had expected her to be grave and a little ceremonious. Not at all. She was extremely human. He could see that she was bored with Mary Newmark, who quite clearly had no idea of it. Mary was one of those women who, without any arrogance, feel that their presence is a benefit to all concerned. She was also convinced that any statement, any opinion on her part, was of the first importance.

Tim saw that Vanessa was surprised to see him and greatly

pleased. Mary Newmark was flustered a little; artists were to her strange creatures: moreover Timothy lived in Paris. She was plainly determined to be kind to him whatever he might have done.

'No, don't send for more tea,' he said. 'This is splendid. If it's stewed I like it stewed.'

'I was telling Vanessa,' Mary Newmark began, 'that Sidney and I disapprove totally of the Suffragettes.'

'Why?' asked Timothy.

'The proper place for women is the home. I don't want a vote. What would I do with one?'

As Timothy was about to speak she shook a finger at him.

'Now, Mr Bellairs, I know you're an artist and have, I'm sure, all sorts of queer ideas. But if women don't look after their homes, who will?'

'Perhaps the men will,' said Timothy.

'Men!' said Mary Newmark gaily. 'Would you like to know what I think about men?'

'Very much,' said Timothy.

'Men are children. Nothing but children. They never grow up. Once learn that about a man and you never have any more trouble.'

'Well, then, isn't it wrong if men are only children that they should have all the say in governing the country? If women are so much wiser—'

'Ah, that's just it,' said Mary Newmark with complete self-confidence. 'Women *are* much cleverer, but their proper place is behind the scenes, influencing the men. Sidney doesn't know it, but there's not a thought in his head that doesn't come from me.' She beamed on the world. 'I've no use at all for all this modern nonsense, nor has Sidney. Modern books, modern pictures, modern women – I don't mean anything personal, Mr Bellairs. I'm sure you paint very nice pictures – very pleasant, I'm sure, but what was good enough for my mother is good enough for me. What modern writers have we to compare with Charles Dickens? Answer me that now.'

'It would be a great pity, wouldn't it,' said Timothy, 'if we had Dickens over and over again? One Dickens, yes – but a hundred Dickenses!'

'Well, I don't know, I'm sure. I've certainly read *David Copperfield* over and over – my favourite bits, you know. Sidney reads aloud to me in the evenings in Manchester.'

The door opened and Sally came in. She stood for a moment, hesitating and smiling. Then she came forward.

'Say how do you do to Mrs Newmark, darling.'

'How do you do?' said Sally.

'And to Mr Bellairs. You met him the other day, you know.'

'How do you do?' said Sally, grinning.

Mary Newmark drew Sally forward and spoke to her in the voice she considered suitable to children, a voice she also used for little dogs.

'Well, darling? And what have you been doing today?'

'I've done my lessons and I've been for a walk.'

'That's a good little girl. And where did you go for a walk?'

'I went in Kensington Gardens.'

'And what did you see there?'

'Oh, nothing particular.'

Mrs Newmark pinched her cheek, a thing that she considered children adored.

'And what lessons have you done today?'

This was frightful. Vanessa intervened.

'At present she has lessons with me. I'm not a very good teacher, I'm afraid.'

There was silence. Sally was looking at Mrs Newmark with a smile that in some undefined way she felt to be sarcastic. A strange child, with her peaked face and dark brown hair. She was suddenly uncomfortable. The house was so very silent and the painter not very friendly. Moreover, there was Ellis somewhere and at any moment he might break in. How unpleasant that would be! Whenever she was uncomfortable she moved on. She moved on now.

'I'm afraid I must be going, Vanessa dear. It *has* been delightful. You must come and see us before we go back to Manchester. Goodbye, Mr Bellairs. Don't become *too* modern in your painting!' She kissed Sally and sailed away. Halfway down the stairs she stopped a moment to listen whether she could hear Ellis moving about. There was no sound anywhere.

After she had gone they all three sat on the sofa together. Timothy had at once noticed that there was a strong and deep alliance between the mother and the child. When Sally moved and spoke it was as though Vanessa moved and spoke with her. Now Sally sat beside her mother; they sat hand in hand. They made no allusion at all to Mrs Newmark. Their feelings about her were identical. They were all three very happy and confidential together.

'Now, darling, you must go to bed.'

Sally got up from the sofa. She sighed.

'Don't you wish you hadn't to go to bed?' she asked Timothy.

'I love my bed,' he answered. 'It's the best place there is.'

She looked at him sharply to see whether he were speaking the truth. She decided that he was.

'When I'm older I shall go to bed only once a week – every Friday.'

'Why Friday?'

'Because Saturday's a nice day and Thursday's a nice day, but Friday's horrid.'

She lifted her face to be kissed.

'I'll come up and see you, darling,' Vanessa said.

She walked away rather sadly. At the door she looked back and smiled.

Vanessa looked at the door for a moment after it closed. Then she turned back.

'It was extraordinarily nice of you to come and see me.'

There was something young about her, Timothy thought, and eager. She was not dull as he had half expected to find her. She had lived, he knew, for years in lonely country but she was not dowdy. Her wide clear forehead, her grey hair parted in the middle, the severity of her black dress, her breadth and height, gave her massiveness, but he had an unexpected conviction that she was younger than he, years and years younger.

'It's very strange,' Vanessa said, 'but I've never set eyes on you since you were a small boy. I can see you now sitting up in an open carriage dressed like little Lord Fauntleroy and hating it.'

'Yes, I did hate it. And I'm afraid I hated my mother too for making a show of me.'

'No – but when you were such wonderful friends with Tom and Benjie ... it's absurd that we should never have met! You were with Benjie yesterday!' she added quickly.

'Yes. How did you know?'

'I had a letter from him this morning, telling me about your visit. He writes and tells me if anything especially nice has happened. How was he? How was he looking?'

'Rather thin, I thought. No spare flesh.'

'No. I saw him last a fortnight ago. I wish he'd eat more. He doesn't look after himself.'

And then, in front of him, her face in a moment aged. She was sitting quietly, her hands folded on her lap, but he felt that

behind her serenity she was enduring to the limit of everything:
one burden more and she would break. He was a man who found
life in general amusing and absurd rather than dramatic, but he
was very sharply aware of the drama now being played in front
of him – this long chill room, the house beyond it where Ellis was
playing at soldiers or nursing a doll, Benjie in Tite Street, and all
the Family moving like figures in a wavering tapestry as a frame
to the scene. Vanessa, he thought, must be fifty or more and yet
he had, at that moment, as urgent a longing to help her to escape
as though she were a lovely girl of twenty!

'Benjie tells me,' she went on, 'that he talked about me – about
us. Do – do you think— Do you think that it is all getting to be
more than he can stand? I mean – oughtn't I perhaps to *make*
him go away, to insist on it? Perhaps, away from me, he would
find someone—'

'There's nothing you can do. He will never be able to go away.
He will never find someone else.'

'I don't want him to go away, you know.' She smiled again. 'I
think I'd die if he did. Oh, don't fancy that I'm pitying myself. I
have him and Tom – and Sally of course. Don't you like
Sally?'

'I do indeed. She's very unusual.'

'Yes, she is, isn't she? And – I'm telling you everything because
you have been Benjie's friend so long and of course that makes
you mine. Ellis . . . I have grown fond of him. No one could help
it. He needs me, and he is so docile and so affectionate. So
different from what he was. But of course it's not a good house
for Sally to grow up in. It's not healthy here, although she's too
young to understand things and behaves to Ellis as though he
were her brother. I thought at first that I would keep them apart,
but Sally made that impossible. She goes to him quite naturally,
never seems to think it strange that an old man of sixty-six
should play with dolls and soldiers. Perhaps she knows more
than we think. Children may be much wiser than we suppose.'

'You are all, it seems to me,' said Timothy, 'behaving very
finely.'

'Oh no, we're not! I don't see how we could behave other-
wise. And I myself am not fine at all. Often I long for Ellis to die.
Sometimes I feel that I *cannot* keep away from Benjie any longer.
You see, we thought that it would only be for a month or two.
Already it has been nearly three years . . .' She hesitated, looking
down at her lap. 'The hardest part of it has been that in Cum-

berland, just before we separated, Benjie and I were happier than ever before.'

'I know. Benjie told me.'

'Oh, did he tell you? I'm so very glad.' She went on: 'You must think this all very sentimental, Timothy. Two old people like Benjie and me both pouring out our hearts to you.'

'Only false things are sentimental,' Timothy said. 'And this isn't false, Vanessa. Your grandmother, Judith Paris, wouldn't have thought so. I gather that she was anything but sentimental.'

'No – she wouldn't have thought it false. I so often think of her and sometimes feel as if she were here helping us both. I still have a tiny tea-set she gave me when I was a little girl, and it seems only yesterday that I climbed on to her bed and kissed her.'

There was a pause. He got up to go.

'I must be moving on. I'm so glad that we have met, and if there is anything I can do, Vanessa, I always will. You can count on me. I've got every weakness except infidelity.'

'Yes; Benjie always says that you are one of the most faithful people in the world.'

Before he went he said, rather shyly:

'Look here! Don't let this be too much of a strain on you. One can only stand so much, you know. Oughtn't you to go out more?'

'Go out?'

'Yes, be gay a little – go to theatres and see the sights.'

'Oh, I do go out. And I've had so much of that in the past. But it's all right. I'm perfectly happy.'

With that brave challenge in her ears he left the house, but for several days he could not get her out of his mind.

When he had gone, Vanessa went up to say goodnight to Sally. She was in bed waiting. Vanessa sat on the bed and Sally lay within her arm, very contentedly, her eyes smiling.

'Mummy, Mrs Newmark *is* a funny lady!' (It was like Sally to have the surname quite clearly and accurately.)

'In what way funny, darling?'

'She thinks children silly. They aren't, are they?'

'Sometimes.'

'Well, not like *that,* anyway.'

Soon she was asleep.

Then Vanessa went to Ellis. The upper part of the house had

now been made into a suite for him. He had a sitting-room, bedroom and bathroom of his own. The sitting-room was large, with high windows looking out on to chimney pots and sky. On the table was a large bowl with chrysanthemums (he loved flowers). Near the flowers was a big wooden fort with guns and soldiers. In one armchair an elaborate doll, dressed in blue silk, was lolling.

Ellis himself was sitting, when she came in, very busy with one of those puzzles the point of which is that little black balls should roll into little silver holes. He was bending over this, shaking it, holding it very still, shaking it again. He looked very old. His thin hair was white now, his shoulders very bent. He had the almost waxen cleanliness of a patient who is constantly washed and brushed by others.

'Oh, Vanessa!' he cried, when he saw her. 'I'm so glad you've come. I've been trying to do this for ever so long. As soon as one's in another rolls out.'

She sat down beside him and took the puzzle. He watched her as she manipulated it, with the eager attention of a dog who is waiting for you to throw a ball.

Soon all the little black balls were in the little silver holes. He clapped his hands.

'Oh, that's lovely! Now shake it! Now I'll see if I can do it!' She sat there quietly beside him.

He put the puzzle down.

'I'm very hungry,' he said.

'Your dinner will be coming very soon, dear,'

'What do you think it will be?'

'I don't know. Something nice.'

'Marmalade pudding?'

'Perhaps.'

'Oh, I hope so.' He sighed, laying his head against his hand. She put her arm around him.

'Did you have a nice drive?' she asked him.

'We saw some soldiers.'

'Was there a band?'

'No. There wasn't a band. I wish we could have a band – here in this room. Wouldn't it make a fine noise?' He sighed again. 'My head aches.'

'It's the weather, Ellis dear. It's been very close all day. My head's been aching all day.'

'Has it?' He put his hand up and stroked her forehead and

then her cheek. He loved to do that. At first she had shrunk from it. His hand was dry and hot and his fingernails very white, like a dead man's nails. But now it moved her strangely when he made any demonstration. And once, years and years ago, he had wanted to kill her! How queer!

With the abrupt restlessness that was characteristic of him he got up and fetched the doll from the chair.

'I've dressed and undressed her three times today,' he said. 'She doesn't seem to mind.' He gave her to Vanessa. 'Will you play for me tonight, Vanessa?'

In the corner of the room was a small piano. Vanessa did not play very well – only old and simple things, old songs, hymns tunes, waltzes. He loved her to play. He could sit for hours watching her.

'Yes, of course, dear. I'll come up when I've had my dinner.'

He was delighted.

'Oh, how nice! Play the one with mice in the can.'

'Yes, I'll play that one.'

'And the one with armies marching.'

'Yes, dear.'

She put her arm around him and he lay back against her with his eyes closed.

After a while Winifred Trent came in. She was very thin and her pale long face was covered with wrinkles.

'I think dinner is ready, Vanessa. I'll stay with Ellis while he has his.'

A gong sounded from below. Winifred Trent said every evening this same sentence.

'Thank you, Winifred.' Vanessa got up. She kissed Ellis and went downstairs.

The dining-room seemed very large and empty. Rodd, the butler with a face like a muffin, waited on her.

'Sole, my lady?'

'Thank you, Rodd.'

She sat staring in front of her. Suddenly she smiled. Benjie had enjoyed Timothy's visit. He would be happier today.

'Brussels sprouts, my lady?'

'Thank you, Rodd.'

After Ellis was in bed she would write to Benjie and tell him about Timothy's visit.

WHITE WITH SWANS

ONE night early in 1912, Vanessa woke and was assured that she was about to die. She was conscious of no especial pain, only a scantness of breath and a general faintness. Dimly, as though she were many miles away, she realized that the early morning light, very cold and thin, laid ghostly shadows on the floor. She heard a sparrow twitter.

But so certain was she that the end had come that she felt that she must write something to Benjie, saying goodbye, telling him to be good to Sally ... but she found that she had no wish to make the slightest movement. She lay there, her eyes fixed on the ceiling upon whose dark surface some strange light, thin and bright like a lustre bowl, seemed to hover. Her brain was quite clear. For months past she had known that her energy was leaving her as water trickles from a cistern. Until less than three years ago (she could fix the time exactly, for the change had come when Timothy Bellairs, the painter, had paid her a visit and, turning to her, had said: 'Don't let this be too much of a strain on you') her resistance had been equal to the struggle. But after that day (she remembered that when Timothy had gone she had been up and said goodnight to Sally, had visited Ellis and dined downstairs alone, and Rodd had said 'Brussels sprouts, my lady') something had snapped. Her nobility had gone, she supposed. Lying now, about to pass away altogether from this silly business, she could summarize the past clearly and without sentiment. Her nobility had gone. She no longer, after that day, wanted to play her part. What she wanted was for Ellis to die and then, for herself, that she should go to Benjie and never again, for one single moment, night or day, leave him.

She seemed after this (it was as though she were now speaking to God Himself, for life was over and He would understand) to be without scruples and yet to be tied with scruples. She was now quite shameless and, in intention, had already left Ellis and was somewhere safe in Cumberland with Benjie, but in fact of course she did nothing of the kind.

For three more years she did as she had already done; nursed Ellis, played her part, ached (oh God, how her heart had ached!) for Benjie, and there it was. But whereas in the first three years she had acted as she did because she thought it right, in the second three she acted as she did because she had to. She could not leave Ellis because he was so helpless, but her heart became a strange confusion of disgust and misery and longing and sheer exhausted weariness.

The effort was becoming always more frightful, and not only for herself but also for Benjie. For one whole year he went abroad. They wrote and met when he was in London. They poured their very souls into their letters. But the longing became too great. He returned, thin as a stick, new lines of age and perhaps of bitterness in his face. During this last year they met more and more often, but always as though, at the very moment of meeting, they must part. As for Ellis, nothing ailed him, and Vanessa was his very life. Then Winifred Trent died. Six months ago a chill had carried her off. Before she died she said to Vanessa: 'You've been wonderful,' and Vanessa, although she had grown to be fond of Winifred Trent, had a terrible impulse to tell Winifred Trent a number of coarse truths . . .

After that strength had ebbed from her. She woke weary; she went to bed too tired to sleep. And Ellis grew stronger and stronger in the body. He liked her to play to him on the little piano by the hour. Well, now she was going to die and the whole thing would be over. She thought of Benjie and Sally and Tom, and summoned them to her side.

To Benjie she said: 'My darling, my beloved, this can't separate . . .'

To Tom: 'Thank you for looking after me, Tom dear. Mary Worcester isn't worth it . . .'

And to Sally: 'Don't forget me. Have a good life, darling . . .'

Then it seemed to her that her heart ceased to beat. She thought of God as very near to her. She clasped her hands and began the Lord's Prayer . . .

A moment later apparently Janet, the maid, came in, carrying the tea, drawing the blinds. So she had not died!

She lay there, drank her tea.

'What kind of day is it, Janet?'

'Nice and bright, my lady.'

Then Janet said:

'You don't look very well this morning, my lady. Have your breakfast in bed. Do now.'

(Janet had from the first, two years ago, been very friendly, maternal, and comforting.)

'Oh no, Janet. I must get up. I didn't sleep very well.'

'What a shame! I should stay the morning in bed, my lady.'

And she did. She was surprised at herself. Sally came in to say goodbye to her before departing to her school in Kensington. She had her luncheon with Ellis in his room.

But, after this, the obsession remained with her that she had not long to live.

One evening she was gay: that is, she went with Cynthia, Philip Rochester and Horace Ormerod to the first night of a new play. It was Tuesday, March 5th – Cynthia's birthday – and they had a very charming dinner first at Claridge's. Cynthia was very coy about her age, Horace hearty and hopeful, and Philip – who painted his face so cleverly that you wouldn't notice it unless you were a woman – was most witty at the expense of all his nearest and dearest.

'But I thought you liked Humphrey Bell!' Cynthia said, when Philip had just intimated that Humphrey cheated at cards and beat his mistresses.

'Oh, so I do! I *adore* Humphrey! He's a perfect pet! I know he wouldn't mind a *word* I've been saying!'

'Well, I'm not so sure,' observed Cynthia.

How very old, Vanessa thought, Philip was! He was all Dowsonish and Wildeish. And how long ago was that buried age with its glittering surface and tinkling music box echoes! The time when she had been a hostess and driven in the Park, had tea with Mrs Langtry in that extraordinarily cosy drawing-room, breathing that lovely lady's good-nature and kindness of heart. It had been a cosy, good-natured time – yes, and an enterprising one too! Now – what was the matter? – everyone was restless, uneasy; nothing seemed secure. She herself felt shabby, an old owl not used to the light. She sat in the back of the box with Horace, feeling a little faint, longing for Cumberland and Benjie and the Newlands farm . . .

The play seemed to answer some of her questions. It was called *Milestones* and was by Arnold Bennett and Edward Knoblock. The little Royalty Theatre contained that night many celebrated persons. The customary first-night remark was made that if a bomb were dropped on the theatre . . . In fact, all the customary first-night remarks were made. Mr Knoblock was discerned sitting in a box with his sister. Famous persons were observed, commented upon. But it was not, as it happened, a first night quite like other first nights. It was, in itself, a Milestone. This passing of time, this blindness of each generation to the significant things, the battle between the helpless imaginative and the confident unimaginative.

'Why, these are Herries!' Vanessa thought. 'These are our very selves!'

And then Haidée Wright's brilliant passionate Aunt was simply Judith Paris come to life. She seemed to Vanessa to be living there on the stage in front of her. She was eternal, immortal, as Judith was. That little figure, her voice trembling with her vitality and courage, dominated not only the theatre but the world beyond it. 'So Judith still dominates us all.' In the last Act an actress made a great success. She was extremely beautiful, and Vanessa, who had never seen her before, searched her programme. Her name was Gladys Cooper. There was something in her self-confidence and scorn of sentiment that spoke of the future. 'Will Sally be like that? Not so beautiful of course, but brave, scornful of anything that seems to her unreal?' Everyone in the theatre that night was thinking a little as Vanessa. How time passes and we don't know it! We are at the mercy of forces greater than ourselves. What if these forces grow stronger than we? What if we become their slaves? A wind of insecurity blew through the theatre that night. The actors seemed like figures in a Morality.

In the second interval, Cynthia and Philip went out to greet some friends. In the back of the box, Vanessa and Horace talked. Vanessa had never liked Horace before, but tonight he touched her sympathy. His wife had died in the preceding year. He said that he was very lonely. This big heavy man with the protruding chin, the shining forehead, the gleaming glasses, was suddenly a small and very unprotected schoolboy.

'I suppose it's my own fault,' he said. 'I'm sure I've always done my best, looked on the bright side, been cheerful very often when I really didn't feel it, but people don't want you to be cheerful and kind and jolly. They like you much better if you're sour and cynical. The fact is, I know it, people get bored with me. There was a woman once, Vanessa, whom I loved to distraction. I'd have done anything for her. For a month or so it was like heaven – it was really. I thought she loved me passionately. One weekend she went to Eastbourne and wrote me two of the most wonderful letters. Beautiful they were. And then, one night, she was to dine with me in my flat. I was all ready and waiting. I'd ordered the most beautiful little dinner. But instead of coming herself she sent a letter – a short, curt note saying that she was afraid she couldn't see me any more. She was very sorry. She had thought about it and decided that it wasn't right her seeing me and so on. But I knew that *that* wasn't the reason. It was simply that she was bored with me. And yet I'd always done my best.'

'You'd spoilt her, I expect,' said Vanessa.

'No. I'd done what any other man would have done. She found me a bore. Yes, it's very strange. People like you if you're cruel and malicious. I've never been cruel in my life to anyone.'

'Would you mind, Horace,' Vanessa said, 'getting me a glass of water? I feel rather faint.'

When he returned with one he had something he wanted to say. It was about Rose. He had seen Rose that very afternoon.

'Oh, Rose!' Vanessa exclaimed. 'Quick, Horace, tell me! I have written to her and had no answer. Once a letter from Madrid, a short one, telling me nothing.'

'I've seen her from time to time,' Horace said. 'Of course it's been very painful. But she was always determined that you shouldn't see her. It's been the one thing that she resolved. She was ashamed . . .'

'Oh no,' Vanessa cried. 'She shouldn't have been. I'm her friend. Quick, Horace, they're coming back. Where is she now? Is she in London?'

'Yes, that's why I told you. She's very ill. She's going to have a serious operation. This is her address. I've written it down.'

(Poor old Horace. Not such a bad fellow – or at any rate not so bad in old age and loneliness, much more bearable in misfortune.)

Cynthia and Philip came into the box. Vanessa had the address. She thought, as the curtain went up – 'They've forgiven me. They consider me respectable again. But Rose they have pushed down and down . . .'

On the following afternoon she found her way to the street in Bloomsbury. It was a fine March day with gay light clouds hurrying like ballerinas across the chimney pots. The pigeons fluttered on the steps of the Museum, and there was a sniff of spring in the air.

Rose's room was at the very top of the thin grey house and, halfway up, Vanessa felt once more her faintness, had to pause while the stairs slowly rose and fell and a grimy window bent anxiously towards her. At last she was there. She knocked on the door and went in. Rose was sitting, a shawl over her shoulders, before a grumbling, sulky fire. The room was stuffy and had the smell of a not very clean blanket.

'Oh! Vanessa!' Rose cried out.

Vanessa bent down and they embraced as though they would never let one another go. Rose cried a little, wiping her eyes with a rather soiled handkerchief. Then she brightened. She was fearfully thin and her complexion was a pale and dry yellow. She was wearing a shabby blue skirt and faded silver slippers. She held Vanessa's hand.

'At last I told Horace that you might come and see me. I wouldn't hear of it before. But my number's up at last and I had to have one last glimpse of you before I met St Peter.'

'I've tried to see you—'

'Yes, I know. I've been abroad. Here, let's have a look at you!'

She took Vanessa by the shoulder and held her off so that she might see her.

'This bloody gas! It isn't very gay, is it? But we don't run to electric light here yet. Well, my dear, you don't look any too grand yourself, if I may say so. You're a fine big woman, of course – always were. But you look as though you hadn't had any sleep for a month.'

'I haven't been sleeping very well, but never mind me. What about yourself? What's the matter, Rose darling?'

'Oh, the wages of sin. As a matter of fact it's cancer and that's the plain truth. Old Furry-Face the doctor says, "Only a little internal trouble. We'll have you right in no time." But *I* know. You can't cheat me. I'm starving to death and I'm sick of it. Horace has been a brick, though. He's paying for the nursing home, insists on it although I tell him any old ditch will do to die in.'

'But, Rose, you're wrong. I'm sure you are! After all, they know—'

'Wrong my foot! You can't kid me. Now look here, my dear, now you *are* here! I want to know everything. How *are* you? How's Benjie? How much longer are you going on in this ridiculous way?'

Vanessa told her something of her life, ending up: 'You see, we thought that it wouldn't be so long. It's been five years.'

'And Benjie and you eating your hearts out! Well, I think it's a bit of sentimental tosh! Giving yourself up heart, soul and body to someone who'd be just as happy with any nurse—'

'No,' Vanessa said. 'You're wrong there. I might have left him,

perhaps, if he hadn't needed me. Because it hasn't been fair on
Benjie. But he *does* need me. Every year it has been more impossible to leave him.'

'And now you're killing yourself! Oh, I know! It's draining all
the strength out of you. I can see it. And here we are, the two of
us! You've done the virtuous thing. I've done the other! Not
much to choose . . .'

They talked about old times. Rose never let Vanessa's hand go.
Her clutch was hot and feverish.

'You needn't be afraid, Vanessa. It's all over. There's no
drunken Major coming in. Even my taste for drink has gone. I
was in Madrid three years. Yes, a Professor kept me – a very nice
little man he was, with a curly black beard and a wife he couldn't
stand the sight of. I was fond of him. I truly was. That's a funny
thing. In spite of the life I've led I haven't got tired of wanting to
be fond of men – really fond of them, mend their clothes, put
their buttons on, that sort of thing. Then I get tired of them.
Domestic one minute, restless the next. But virtue's got nothing
to do with it. I've never felt more virtuous than when I've been
doing my worst . . . There was a young fellow from College once
went off with me. Pretty well broke his mother's heart, too. We
went on a trip to Scotland. We stopped at Keswick. I wanted to
have a look at it, and there it was, same as ever – St John's spire
and the square with the clock. We went down to the Lake the
night we arrived and I can hear the water lapping against the
jetty now. And Friar's Crag. We went on to Friar's Crag and
the boy talked about Ruskin. Well, you never saw a more virtuous
pair than we were that trip, reading Shelley and wondering
whether there was a God and picking flowers . . . and I suppose I
never did a wickeder thing than taking that young man away.
Funny, isn't it? This morality! Very vexed question, if you ask
me!'

After a while she asked Vanessa:

'Why do you love Benjie so, Vanessa? I've never loved anyone
like that. You're the only one I've loved all my life long and
you're a woman. Why do you love him so?'

'Oh, I don't know,' said Vanessa. 'He's everything I want in a
man. You should ask rather why he loves me. I often tell him he
should have a gay, lively woman, witty, and quick to see things.
There's *one* reason I love him, I think. I can see his jokes. It used
to be terrible in the old days in Hill Street when I didn't see a
joke and had to pretend I did. But Benjie and I find one another

amusing. We're comic to one another. That's a good reason for
love.'

They fell into silence. Vanessa thought that Rose had fallen
asleep. At last it was time for her to go.

'Rose darling – are you looked after here? Is there anyone to
care for you?'

'Oh yes, it isn't so bad. The woman's quite decent. And I'm
going to the nursing home tomorrow. You'll come and see me
there, won't you?'

Vanessa promised. She looked back at the door and saw Rose's
eyes – hungry, shining, feverish – fixed upon her. She went
slowly away.

She visited Rose every day in the nursing home. A week later
Rose had her operation and three days after that she died. She
was worn out, the doctor said. Injudicious living in the past ...
yes ... sad ... but, as a matter of fact, there would have been no
hope. She could not have recovered.

Vanessa was happy for her sake. That was the way that she
would have wished it.

Meanwhile the Family watched Vanessa with curiosity. She
went round paying visits on everybody exactly as though she
were going away somewhere.

Cynthia and May Rockage (who was in London just then) and
stout Mary Newmark, putting their heads together, decided that
she was going off with Benjie again. She was gay, light-hearted
and extraordinarily kind. She said some odd things. She said to
Cynthia: 'I can't get that play *Milestones* out of my head. Do you
remember the girl in the last Act saying, "Please remember that
we're in the year 1912"? Isn't it funny to think that for Sally, one
day, 1912 will be as old-fashioned as 1812? Doesn't it make you
feel queer?'

'Not in the least,' said Cynthia.

'Oh, well, then – doesn't it seem odd to you that my grandmother probably said, "Please remember that we're in the year
1812"?'

'Not in the least. Your grandmother lived to be a hundred.'

'Oh, I know. That isn't what I mean. What I mean is that
people are more important than time. What I mean is that my
father, who was a darling, once said in his garden on Cat Bells:
"Look, Vanessa! There's the squirrel again!" That, my relationship to him, our love for one another, all of it comes back as I

think of that sentence: it isn't dead, it isn't gone. He's alive because we loved one another. 1812, 1912 doesn't mean anything at
all. What we think is life is nothing – the secret life has quite
another history. Am I being very stupid?'

'No, dear,' said Cynthia, who was only half listening, because
there were some new and extremely beautiful photographs of her
daughter Mary that she was examining. 'You're being very clever
– too clever for me I'm afraid.'

('One half of our family will *never* understand what the other
half is after – never, never, never!' Vanessa thought.)

'Aren't these good?' said Cynthia. 'I don't want to be the fond
mother, but really Mary is going to be a beauty.'

'Yes, she is,' said Vanessa eagerly, glad that Cynthia was happy
and at the same time wishing, in spite of herself, that Sally was
taller and had a brighter complexion.

'Do you think, Cynthia, that there is something true in what
the old man said at the end of *Milestones*?'

'What did he say, dear?' asked Cynthia, holding one of the
photographs at an odd angle and smiling at it.

'Don't you remember? He said women of today aren't what
they used to be. They're hard. They've none of the old charm.
They're unsexed. Are Sally and Mary going to be hard? They *are*
different from us. I've noticed it. Sally isn't afraid of anything
and she doesn't like to show her feelings. She's rather like a boy
sometimes. Won't it be dreadful if all the women are like men
and all the men—'

'Like Philip,' Cynthia concluded. 'Why do you think so much
about the future, Vanessa? The present is so very agreeable. Peile
hasn't been in a bad temper for weeks. Everything is so comfortable and settled.'

'Settled? Do you think so?' said Vanessa.

Later, the Family recalled the strangeness of Vanessa during
these weeks. They had, perhaps, none of them ever really known
her. She became again rather beautiful. Her pallor suited her
grey hair, and her eyes were still lovely, soft, gentle, and generous. No, they had none of them really known her. There was
something wild in the middle of her gentleness. You might call
her timid because she disliked quarrelling, high words. Yet she
had a temper, she could be most courageous. She had been, by all
Herries standards, grossly immoral, living for years with a man
to whom she was not married, and yet she was religious as none
of them were. She had succeeded in holding a man's devotion for

a whole lifetime, and a most difficult man too. And yet she was not a woman of the type, you would suppose, for Benjie. For five years she had performed a task that was, they all admitted, an exceedingly hard one. They admired her now although they had once criticized her so severely. But she was outside them all – a stranger in the end. 'There have been always odd ones in the family,' Mary Newmark said complacently. 'As Sidney says, "We're different from ordinary families." '

Vanessa meanwhile paid a visit to her doctor.

'Is there anything wrong with me? I'd like to know.'

He examined her.

'You have been under a great strain. You're very tired. Can't you go abroad for a while and have a proper rest?'

'No,' said Vanessa. 'I can't, I'm afraid.'

'Well, you aren't looking after yourself properly—'

'Is anything organically wrong?'

'No. You're nearly fifty-three, though, and should take care of yourself. A chill or an extra strain – any little thing – might be serious.'

She smiled. They were very old friends.

'Thank you. I'll try and take care.'

Then the day came (she had known that it was coming) when she could not leave Benjie. They had been having tea in his room as they did about once a fortnight. ('How old we're getting!' she said to Benjie once. 'No one thinks it immoral for us to be alone any more.') She got up to go. She could not. She stared at him helplessly.

'What is it?' he asked, getting up and coming to her.

'Oh, I don't know!' She tried to smile, but her mouth trembled. 'Suppose that this should be the last time!'

'What do you mean – the last time?'

'It's always been like that lately – harder to part.' She drew away from him. 'Oh, I was forgetting! I brought you something.'

She went to the deal table and picked something up. 'I thought I'd like you to have this.'

'What is it? You're always giving me things.'

She undid the paper wrapper.

'This is Judith's book. You know, the one we used to read out of in Cumberland.' She held it up, with its faded green cover. 'I thought I'd like *you* to have it now.'

'Why? But you are so fond of it!'

'Yes – but if anything happened ... You know, Benjie, I've always thought it such a pity that someone shouldn't publish it; it's so lively and amusing.'

'People aren't interested. We aren't a very remarkable family.'

'Aren't we?' said Vanessa. 'I think we are.'

He kissed her. 'All right. I'll look after it for you. Write your name in it – your name and mine.'

She went to the table and sat down. She wrote: 'For Benjie with love from Vanessa Herries and Judith Paris. March 29th, 1912.'

'I feel as though she were in the room with us now.'

He laughed. He was standing behind her, his hand on her shoulder.

'Ghosts! What a child you are, Van! Once we're gone we're gone!'

He felt her shiver.

'What's the matter?' he asked. 'Are you cold?'

'No.' She turned round, looked up into his face, her hands on his chest. 'Don't say that, Benjie. I can't endure to think that death – physical death – can separate us. After all – who knows? – it may be only after that that we're really together. When two people have loved one another so long and so truly as we have, isn't it absurd to think that a little thing – a cold, a stumble in the street, oh! anything – can separate us for ever?'

'Well,' he said, looking down at her with great tenderness, 'life is absurd, my darling – absurd, meaningless, cruel.'

She lowered her eyes. He felt her tremble again.

'Perhaps I'm wrong,' he said, putting his arm round her, holding her to him. 'I don't know any more than the next fellow. It's ridiculous to dogmatize. But if there's a God and He's kept us apart for five years as a cat tortures a mouse, why, then I say as many a man has said before me—'

He stopped. She was crying. He knelt down beside her.

'Oh, my darling, don't cry! After all, we've got one another. We've had years of one another. That's something. And this can't go on for ever. It mustn't. It shan't. It gets harder every day. It's killing both of us ... Darling, look up! Think of the happy times! Think of the night in Newlands when Tom arrived from London! And even now – the hours we have, the way our love grows stronger and stronger ...'

He knelt, holding her, while she sobbed against his shoulder. He caught some words.

'I'm so tired . . . I love you so much . . .'

She rose, wiping her eyes. 'There! At my age! Wait. I'll wash my face in your bedroom!'

While she was gone he stood there in perplexity. Tonight he could not endure that she should leave him and return to that house, to that dark house, that insane house . . .

This could not go on as it was. They had both endured it too long. He must think of some way.

She came back smiling, but he saw that she was dreadfully weary.

'Come with me to the King's Road until I get a cab.'

At the door they embraced, clinging to one another with an almost dreadful desperation.

'I wish I'd seen Tom,' she said. 'Say goodbye to him for me.'

'Of course. But you'll be seeing him next week.'

'Oh yes. It was so good of him to take Sally out the other day. She *did* enjoy it so!'

They went down the long stairs hand in hand. He walked beside her with the defiant boyish adventurous air that was so especially his, his hat cocked a little to the side, his empty sleeve, a flower in his coat.

In the King's Road they saw a cab, but she said:

'Let's walk a little farther. There'll be another.' The only thing that she said was: 'What do you think? Carey and May are going to America in April. Adventurous for old things like them, isn't it? They're going in this wonderful new ship, the *Titanic*.'

'We'll go to America one day!' he said.

In Sloane Square she found a cab and got in. He stood looking after it until it turned the corner.

It was a quiet, still evening with little clouds of peach blossom floating serenely across a gentle sky. The traffic moved as in a dream and she stopped the cab by the Ritz (she wanted to go to Hatchard's bookshop), got out and walked. Influenced as she always was by the world about her, all humankind seemed, in this evening hush, to be amiable and friendly. She thought of the Family, that they had all been good to her after their lights, Cynthia and Mary and May and Alfred, Horace and Adrian; two old bachelor brothers, George and Stephen Cards, who, having come to live in London, had been especially good to her, leaving flowers at Hill Street and inviting her to their funny little dinners. All the feuds were over. Into what kind of world would Sally, Mary and Rosalind and Maurice grow up? The Family had risen now above the old jealousies and causeless rivalries. She felt that she herself had done her part in the mysterious weaving of God's shuttle by her return to Ellis. Her love and Benjie's had not been wasted. Nothing was wasted, no goodness, no kindness, no little unheeded courtesy.

She lost, for a moment, under that peach-blossom sky, consciousness of her own small personal history and so was happy. But she was tired. She sat down on one of Mr Hatchard's chairs as they fastened up for her a book, *Carnival*, by some new young man. Adrian had told her that she must certainly read it. Then, as she went out into the street again, she was conscious of a small, stabbing pain in her side. As she was aware of it she knew also a sudden mysterious foreboding as though someone had whispered in her ear: 'This is what you have been waiting for. You will need now all your courage.' She put her hand to her side as though to reassure herself.

At home again she went up to Sally's room and found her sitting at her table biting her pencil over arithmetic. She sprawled over the table, the perfect schoolgirl in her dark blue dress, ink on her cheek and her hair ruffled, drumming her heels on the floor.

'I'm no good at sums, darling,' Vanessa said, sitting down beside her and loving her with a passionate desire to draw her into her arms and never let her go again. But she knew well that Sally did not care for demonstrations.

'Oh, that's all right, Mummy,' Sally said. 'I'll do the beastly things. It's in our blood, I expect, not to be good at sums.' Then she added casually: 'I'm playing for the First at Hockey on Saturday.'

Vanessa knew that this had been, during the last two months, Sally's besetting ambition, but she only said:

'Oh, are you, darling? I'm so glad.'

'Yes.' Sally pushed the book away and looked at her mother. 'You *do* look sweet! Who gave you the violets?'

'Your father.'

'Good.' She thought a moment. Then she went on: 'Mummy, ought I to mind about being illegitimate?'

'Why, dear?'

'Well, Mabel Staines said today that she wouldn't be illegitimate for anything, and that her mother wanted to ask me to tea but wouldn't when Mabel told her.'

'I shouldn't worry about it, Sally dear,' Vanessa said.

'Oh, *I* don't worry!' Sally said cheerfully. 'I told her that her mother could keep her old tea. I rather like being illegitimate. I'm different from the other girls.'

'Do most of the girls know?' asked Vanessa.

'I don't think so. They're all quite decent anyway.' Then she looked at her mother again. 'Mummy, you're tired. You want some tea. I'll get some.'

'No, dear, thank you. I've had some.'

Then Sally did what was rare with her. She threw her arms round Vanessa's neck and hugged her. She rubbed her cheek against her mother's.

'I'll look after you when you're older, and you're the only one I *will* look after.'

'Will you, darling?'

'Yes, you shall have everything you want. I'll make money for you and keep you.'

'What'll you make money with?'

'Oh, I don't know – be a secretary or a market gardener or something.'

'Perhaps you'll marry?'

'Indeed I shan't. I think boys and men are awful. All except Tom and Daddy and Ellis.' Then she dropped her voice confidentially. 'Ellis came in here crying a little while ago. He'd broken a green vase they put flowers in. I told him not to worry.'

(Extraordinary, Vanessa thought, how Sally takes everything for granted!)

'I must go up to him.'

Sally gave her a long and very wet kiss.

'Darling Mummy, I do love you so!' she murmured.

'And I love you,' Vanessa said.

She went up to Ellis and found him, quite contented, playing cards. There was a very simple Patience that Vanessa had taught him. As he played he murmured to himself. 'That's the Red Queen. Now where's the next one. What comes after nine, Vanessa?' he asked as she came in.

'Ten,' she said.

'No, the other way.'

'Eight comes before nine.

'Eight. Eight. Eight,' he said.

He had grown, in the last few weeks, to look very old. His face was wizened, very wrinkled. He looked like a pathetic old monkey.

'Play the piano,' he said, smiling at her.

She sat down at the piano, and as she played 'Annie Laurie' and 'Drink to me only' she felt the pain at her side like a knife. He came and stood beside her, humming out the tune. Then he drew a chair and sat there, all huddled up, nursing his knees.

He was like a little gnome, and with his dead white fingernails he tapped on his knee.

Soon she stopped.

'I'm tired tonight,' she said.

'Yes, I'm tired too,' he said and laid his head on her lap. She stroked his white hair as he liked her to do. Poor Ellis! Would it not be kinder? . . . Then, at the thought which sometimes came to her like a messenger falsely tempting her, she put her arms round his thin body and held him close to her.

But she was too weary to go on. She kissed him and left him, he looking after her with his pathetic wondering eyes.

She went to bed. She was brought some food, but could not eat it. When, at last, to her great relief, she was left alone, she propped her pillows up and wrote a letter to Benjie. Then she lay down to sleep. She could not sleep. Out of a cave of darkness where a dragon slumbered, she moved (carefully lest she should rouse the dragon). She thought that she would read, and she opened a book that was on the little table. It was a volume of Rossetti's poems and, to pain now stabbing her with every breath, she read some verses:

> Although the lattice had dropped loose
>   There was no wind; the heat
> Being so at rest that Amelotte
> Heard far beneath the plunge and float
> Of a hound swimming in the moat.
>
> Some minutes since, two rooks had toiled
>   Home to the nests that crowned
> Ancestral ash-trees. Through the glare
> Beating again, they seemed to tear
> With that thick caw the woof o' the air.
>
> But else, 'twas at the dead of noon
>   Absolute silence: all
> From the raised bridge and guarded sconce
> To green-clad places of pleasaunce
> Where the long lake was white with swans.

She let the book fall and lay back that she might struggle the better with her painful breathing. What was the matter with her? She was ill. She felt the heat rising, as in dry dusty wafts from the desert, through her body, and this heat seemed to be mingled with the clear, sharp picture in the poem that she had just been reading. She herself leant out from some high window on a day of fierce heat and in the general stillness she could hear the sudden cool splash of the hound, and then the caw of the rooks tearing the still air, and then, turning her weary head, she saw the lake, like a mirror in a green wall, and over its glassy green-reflected light the swans, whiter than sunny snow, floated. Ah, this heat and this coldness! This stillness behind whose surface heat beat like a drum! And the swans became horses, great white horses struggling through the lake that now was black; out of the icy water the horses struggled up on to the flank of the frozen hills and their hoofs rang against the ice! As the splendid white horses drew breath with pain, so she fought for hers. Everything moved and shifted. She was a child running across the Cat Bells lawn to greet her father, the house was burning, flames rose mountain-high, as high as Skiddaw, and she was burning too.

But Benjie came and caught her up with his one arm and they rode on the white horse over Skiddaw, Blencathra, over Helvellyn and the Pikes, sailed above Scafell and so out to sea, to the magical island on the horizon, and below them all Wastwater was a lake set in a green wall, and the white swans, with a grand remote dignity, floated on its surface . . .

At some moment, she could not tell when, she saw the crumpled face of Rodd, the butler, bending over her.

'No, Rodd,' she whispered from an infinite distance. 'I'm not very well. I don't think I'll get up today.'

Rodd went upstairs to see the nurse who tended Ellis. She was a big bony woman with a serious kindly face. She had a faint moustache and grey eyes that were both practical and gentle. Her name was Milligan.

'Nurse, her ladyship is very unwell. I don't like the look of her at all.'

The nurse went down. Vanessa recognized her and smiled at her.

'I'm not very well,' she said. 'I have a bad pain in my side. I don't think I'll get up, if you don't mind.'

'It's pneumonia,' Milligan said to Rodd. 'I'll get Doctor Lancaster at once.'

Doctor Lancaster came. Vanessa was very ill.

Later in the morning Rodd telephoned to Cynthia. Cynthia had, a moment before, been telephoning about bridge and she was annoyed because she could not, that afternoon, secure the four that she wanted. It was stupid of Anne Fellowes to bother, on that afternoon of all afternoons, about her old husband just because he had only been home from China a week. 'When he's been home another fortnight she won't bother,' she thought. She put down the receiver and wondered whom she should ask. The bell rang.

'Well,' she said, in that little voice exactly like ice knocking against a glass, a voice that was warning enough to anyone who was sensitive. 'Oh, is that you, Rodd?' she said.

'Yes, madam,' said Rodd, who was not at all sensitive. 'It's her ladyship, madam. She's very ill. Pneumonia, Doctor Lancaster said. We were wondering whether you could come to Hill Street.'

Half an hour later she was in Hill Street. As she came into the room she heard a strange sound of recurrent short breaths, something inhuman and cruel. Vanessa did not recognize her, but murmured: 'The white swans. Benjie! Benjie! Look at the swans!'

On the following morning Benjie was roused, at about half past seven, from a deep sleep by the ringing of the telephone. When he went to it he heard to his surprise Cynthia's voice:

'Benjie, is that you?'

'Yes,' he said, shivering a little in his pyjamas.

'I'm at Hill Street. I think you'd better come as soon as possible.'

'Hill Street?' he repeated, bewildered.

'Yes. It's Vanessa. She's terribly ill. Double pneumonia.'

'I'll come at once,' he answered quietly.

He was aware that Tom was in the room.

'Father's what is it?'

'It's Vanessa. She's very ill. Double pneumonia.'

'Oh no! Oh no!' Tom cried.

'Yes. I must go at once.'

He felt nothing except that he must get to Vanessa. He must get to Vanessa and save her.

He found a cab, rang in a frenzy the bell, rushed into the house and up the stairs. On the first landing he saw Cynthia.

'Oh, Benjie!' she cried and stopped. Then, the tears streaming down her face, she said: 'Vanessa's dead!'

He did not see her. He stood in the long drawing-room like a man lost, his eyes wandering from wall to wall. He was not thinking at all.

He felt a touch on his arm and, turning, saw at his side an old, wizened, bent, and wrinkle-faced man who looked up at him with questioning eyes. Moving from some infinite cold distance he came close to this strange figure. Then, with no shock of surprise, he realized that it was Ellis. From this same room Ellis had once driven him out. Now he said, in a trembling voice:

'Where is Vanessa?'

Benjie led him to the sofa and the old man sat down beside him, close to him, shivering a little.

'Vanessa's all right,' he said.

'No. But why isn't she here? Why hasn't she come upstairs? I want her to play the piano.'

He put his arm round the old man. 'We must both be patient,' he said.

'Yes, I'll be patient,' Ellis said and sat there, staring in front of him, waiting ...

Afterwards Cynthia gave him a letter.

'It is for you, Benjie. Vanessa had written on the envelope that it was to be given to you after she was gone.' Cynthia, who had loved Vanessa, looked at him as though she would like to achieve with him some new and affectionate relation, but she discovered at once that she did not know him at all, that he looked 'foreign', and that he scarcely saw her. He took the letter and walked out of the house.

He read it in his own room.

MY DARLING – I'm writing this in bed. Perhaps you will never read it, but I am writing because I feel unwell tonight and for weeks now have had a foreboding that I might die without seeing you. This is probably nothing except my being very tired, as I have been now for a long time. But in any case it is like talking to you, and is better than that in some ways because I can say some things that I might be shy to say to your face, well though I know you – or perhaps because I do know you so well.

What I want most to say is that if I were to die very suddenly and you not see me, you are never to feel afterwards that our love has been wasted. It has been the most wonderful and glorious thing in both our lives, hasn't it? It has been everything to me, not only because of our love, but because it has shown me that there is something in life far deeper than anything physical or material. I have sometimes thought that the separation of these last years has been the best thing that could have happened, because we have been separated and yet in every important way have been closer together than ever we were. I have wished so often that I could have been a different kind of woman for you – I suppose every woman wishes that for the man she loves. I would have liked to be brilliant, witty, the kind of woman clever men describe in their books. I have been unfortunate, I sometimes think, because I have been a woman between two periods. Forty years ago women knew what they were supposed to be and do. In fact there was no choice for most of them. In times to come when Sally is grown up, women, I expect, will be free, equal with men, afraid of nothing. I have not, I'm sure, made a success of my life, and yet I feel that I have, because I won and *kept* your love, and Sally and Tom love me too. I won't say anything about religion, because I know that it bores you, but think sometimes of me that I had no more doubt that God exists than I have of your love for me. People nowadays seem to think that anyone who believes in God is a hypocrite, *trying* to believe because it is more comfortable, but it *isn't* so. There are many people who are not stupid nor false who feel God close to them quite as practically as they feel the people they know close to them. I express this very badly and I don't want you to think I am influencing you – only when I am gone remember that this was the greatest *true* fact in my life. Perhaps you will come to feel one day that there may be some other life that goes on side by side with, or rather *inside*, the physical one I feel that just now everyone is bewildered, unhappy and restless. It wasn't always so, I am sure. People will understand God one day perhaps in a new fashion when they have been unsatisfied and restless long enough.

But I didn't mean this letter to be a sermon. I only meant to thank you, again and again, for loving me so much and so long. Don't be sad if I go. Perhaps I shall be more with you than I have been. Who knows? Do you really think that our love, after all it has been through, can be killed by physical death? I am sure that it cannot. Think often of all the happy times we have had, especially in Newlands. That is our country. That is where I will always be closest to you. It has been our country for nearly two hundred years and perhaps before that. Every stone and tree there is a witness that life is worth living, however hard it is, beautiful and terrible and comic and disappointing and rewarding. Go and climb Robinson or stand by the Watendlath Tarn and think of Judith and remember old Herries in Borrowdale. I *know* that nothing is lost, that everything lives, that there is no death, whatever people say.

You will care for Sally, won't you? She is very high-spirited and determined, and I sometimes think that she is the first *fearless* Herries, the first one to rise above all the jealousy and fear and greediness that there has been so long. Perhaps the world that is coming will be full of Sallies! And give Tom all the love that you can. He will miss me, I think, more than anyone. He has such a warm heart and all his happiness is bound up in other people. Forgive me for all the times that you have thought me sentimental and stupid and slow to see things. But I know you have and will. Remember that our love isn't ended, that it will never end, that nothing can destroy it now – Your most loving and devoted

VANESSA

If you have a chance, see poor Ellis sometimes.

Part Four

The Ghost

KALEIDOSCOPE

I

THE FLAME

THREE WEEKS AFTER the outbreak of war several of the
Herries family dined at Alfred's fine house in Drummond
Street.

It was a kind of farewell dinner, because Tom, Maurice –
Alfred's son – and Gordon – the son of Sidney and Mary Newmark – would be shortly departing for the Front. There were
present Alfred himself, Benjie (who, in two days' time, was leaving for Russia), Tom, Mary Worcester (now twenty-one years of
age and a frantic beauty), Rosalind (her sister), Maurice and
Clara (Alfred's children), Gordon and Ada, with Sidney and
Mary Newmark (their parents) – and Sally, who was not quite
eleven, but was allowed to stay up on this one occasion because it
might be a long time before she had dinner with Benjie and Tom
again.

There were twelve of the family in all.

Dinner was finished. Tom, Maurice and Gordon, looking very
young and innocent in uniform, were sipping Alfred's brandy
with the quiet air of practised connoisseurs.

Alfred got up to make a speech. The Herries family had always
been rather fond of making speeches. Alfred especially enjoyed it.
He was a practised hand at making speeches in the City and prov-
ing in his cold, restrained voice that everything was absolutely
for the best so long as he and his fellow-directors were in charge.

Tonight, however, his voice was not quite cold, not quite restrained. His long nose and thin horse-like face looked down at
them with a kind of anxious tenderness, and he looked especially
at Maurice, his son, whose face was round and rosy, whose tastes
were for the Arts rather than figures, who was unlike him in
everything.

And he was doing for the first time in his life, perhaps, an
artistic thing. He held in one long, bony hand a thin, beautifully
chased silver candlestick. Up its slender stem ran a pattern of
leaves and branches.

'I'm not going to make a long speech,' he said. 'But I must say something. Here we all are as a family, all together, wishing one another well. It hasn't always been so, you may remember. At one time, in the days of our grandfathers and grandmothers, there was some trouble, as I dare say you know. But now we are all united, a symbol, I like to think, of England itself – all united to fight the greatest enemy the world has ever known – Prussian militarism. Whatever else you may say about our family, no one can deny that, on the whole, we have always stood for England's best interests. One of our ancestors helped to defend Carlisle against Prince Charlie and the Scots. Benjie here lost an arm in South Africa, and in countless other ways we have backed our country. And now we are doing it again. She has never needed us as she needs us now, but because we believe she is in the right we are giving all we have, our sons, our money, our lives. Ahem! yes ... well ... It was Maurice's idea that we should do some little thing tonight that we should all remember when we are separated later on, and that when we remember it we should remember one another ... Yes ... I have, left me by my father, a pair of old candlesticks. They belonged, I believe, to an ancestor of ours, Harcourt Herries, who lived in Cumberland in the eighteenth century, and before him to an old Elizabethan Herries who had something to do with the mines in Keswick. Well, that's past history and this is present history, and it was Maurice's idea that we should link up past and present, that we should pass this candle round, each one of us standing up in his or her turn, holding the lighted candle and wishing the rest of us good luck.

'Well ... ahem ... that's all, I think. Except that Sally here, the youngest, shall be the one to light it.'

It was done as he said. Sally – standing on a chair because she was so small – lit it and round it went. The electric light was switched out and round the little flame went, very clear and bright and steady. Everyone wished everyone else good luck.

It was a frosty, sparkling morning and the guns were still. Two hours after midnight there had been a fearful bombardment. On and on went that shattering malignant thunder. Then it ended. There was a perfect cloud of silence everywhere over the desolate country. Tom was ordered to see how the land, now remorselessly altered, might look. New mounds, new pits. Four or five of the raiders lay stretched out, abandoned and desolate; one a stout officer with a snub nose and part of his face gone, another a dark squat-shaped boy who lay, his head on his arm, his wide dark eyes staring at the sky. The raid had been well planned. Tom returned. The light was strengthening, but the air was thin like stretched paper and most bitterly cold. He looked out over a land that might have been trampled by dinosaurs. The country was quite deserted save for one or two snipers at the sap-head. No sound anywhere, but he knew that all about him thousands of men were concealed. Desolation and silence . . .

He went into his dug-out and began a letter to Sally.

DARLING LITTLE SALLY – I've got half an hour to myself and everything's as quiet as the top of Cat Bells. They raided us last night and for an hour or two there was a terrible din. We lost some men, I'm afraid. It's a cold and frosty morning, which is heaps better than the mud and rain. I'm all right, feeling very well in fact. Do you remember the dinner at Alfred's when you lit the candle, and do you remember his saying that we were proud, as proper, right-minded Herries, of defending the world against Prussian Militarism? I suppose we were right at the time to feel like that, and it's still nice to think of that lighted candle going round the table, isn't it? But how long ago that all seems now, and how our point of view has altered!

I haven't had any sleep for twenty-fours hours, but last time I *did* sleep I dreamt of Vanessa. It was scarcely like a dream. She seemed to be sitting beside me holding my hand and wearing the clothes she used to wear in Newlands – just as I would wake sometimes in the morning and find her sitting on my bed. Doesn't she seem *peaceful* now in all this trouble? Do you remember how calm she used to be when something went wrong, and the way she smiled? . . .

He broke off and stared in front of him, smiling at the thought of Vanessa. Then he went on:

The thing I hate most here is being sent out to reconnoitre positions and getting lost. It's awful. Perhaps it's raining, and through the mist you see lights trembling on the horizon, or you think you do. Then, out of nowhere, someone says, as though they were fearfully angry, 'Get down!' and you find yourself in a barrage. Then you run for your life, the wet clay clinging to your legs like hands. Then you're lost again – in darkness. You go up and you go down, not knowing what is hill and what isn't. Perhaps some rifles suddenly open on you. You run and crouch, and slip and crouch and run – always lost, always alone and dirty and cold, like a nightmare after we'd eaten too much as kids.

How are you? Are you doing well at school? Remember there are the three of us – you and I and Father – or four with Vanessa. Never forget Vanessa, darling, will you? Of course I know you won't. Have you heard from Father in Russia? I haven't for ages. Have you seen Mary? Did you ask her to write to me? She promised to but she hasn't yet. *Don't forget this.* It's very important. Do you write to Father regularly? You must, even though he seems so far away. I think he's in Galicia somewhere. Isn't this funny? It's lying on the table beside me. Someone left it:

PLEASE!

Will you help your lad at the Front and all other lads, in a very simple way, and will you give your friends the chance to help as well?

Do it Thus!

Fill in THIS POSTCARD with your name and address, and post it back to us. We will then send you a number of bookmarkers . . .

Bookmarkers! You don't know how funny that sounds here. And lads! Don't you hate the word 'lads'?

Well, darling, keep up your spirits and behave just as though everything were all right. I'm fine myself and perhaps I'll get a spot of leave soon. Don't forget to write to Father and don't forget to ask Mary to write to me. Tell me what she was wearing when you saw her last. That's important – Your most loving brother,

TOM

The candle, stuck in a bottle with a collar of grease, flared up. The flame was bright, pure, steady, of gold.

'There's a flame!' cried Benjie.

The Retreat had begun and with the rest of the Otriad he had been flung into the little town of O—. It was a place of dust, whirling clouds of dust, dust in your eyes and mouth and nose. This dust was blown by the wind and behind the thin spirals of it a hot sun blazed. Everywhere there was the Russian soldier, the

Russian soldier apathetic like a cow but humorous and touching also. He was everywhere, in the streets, on the dirty staircases, crowding the tumbled untidy rooms; the Russian soldier and the dust.

'I never want to see either of them again,' thought Benjie.

But he had cried out at the sudden flame. It was evening and, after the dust storms and the hot malignant sun, the pale blue of the sky and the cool air were friendly. The members of the Otriad were lying or walking or sitting in the half-ruined building into which Molozov, their chief, had turned them. Benjie found this place intolerable. It was a long room with a naked gleaming floor and an apparently endless succession of looking-glasses. This gleaming empty reflection was broken with an infernal clatter through the open window of horses, soldiers and carts that rattled on the cobbles. There was a smell everywhere of dust and dung.

He went to see if he could be of any use with the wounded. Going out originally in August 1914 with two journalists who were friends of his, he kicked his heels in Moscow for some weary months and at last only found adventure by joining, after a week or two in a Moscow hospital, a Red Cross unit attached to the Ninth Army. They had been sent to Galicia and, after some apparent victories, had begun a retreat. He would never forget the moment of that change of fortune. He and several soldiers had gone, under the charge of a rather feckless Englishman called Trenchard, to the forest to bury the dead. This was not his own Otriad. He had come over with two of his own unit to pay this Otriad a visit. It had been pleasant to find another Englishman here, although no two men could have been found more different than Benjie with his short thick figure, his off-hand but commanding independent personality, and this untidy, seemingly foolish Englishman who would wander about singing *Early One Morning* in a cracked voice or, quite unexpectedly, looking so wretched that you thought he would burst into tears. Benjie was told that he had been engaged to a pretty, charming nurse in his Otriad who had thrown him over.

Benjie was to return that same evening to his own Otriad. But he did not. Under the trees of the forest he was looking at a dead man – a man who had been dead some three weeks perhaps. This man was all right until you came to his face. His strong blue-grey trousers were in splendid condition and he had good stout boots. Out of the top of one boot a tin spoon protruded. But he had no

face, only a grinning skull, and in and out of the mouth and eye
sockets little black creatures like ants were crawling. It was all
very peaceful there. The sanitars began to dig a grave. Some
quietly smoked cigarettes. Then a sanitar observed that the bursting of the shrapnel that had been dim and distant all day now
sounded much closer. That was the beginning of the Retreat . . .

But it was at the town of O— that he saw the sudden flame. He
had been for nearly a week now with this Otriad that was not his
own. He had begun to know them all – Molozov, the stocky
square-shouldered Chief who would say over and over again:
'There's no method . . . no system . . . nothing at all . . . By God,
there's a pretty girl!' Nikitin, a doctor who had a charming intellectual face; a surgeon, Alexei Petrovitch Semyonov, a strik-
ing-looking fellow, very thickset and muscular with a strange
square-cut beard of so fair a colour that in some lights it seemed
almost white. A man of very strong personality and great self-
confidence. There was the pretty Sister, Marie Ivanovna, and the
feckless untidy Englishman, Trenchard. He made friends with
them and liked them, but they were nevertheless all shadows on a
screen to him who had his constant, secret preoccupations.

He found work to do in the vast room at O—. This was a
strange place. It had been the theatre of the town. It was lit now
with candles stuck into bottles, and in this dim and wavering
light the doctors did their work. The busy silence was broken
with patient plaintive cries of '*Oh, Steritza! Oh, Steritza!*' or
'*Borjé moi! Borjé moi!*' and then the sharp official questions,
'What regiment? What division? Shrapnel or bullet?'

And across the stage at the back of the room was still hanging,
wavering in the draught, the painted backcloth of some old play.
This amused Benjie by its incongruity, for there was a picture of
a market-place in a town all very gaily painted, and down the
marble stairs flower-girls with legs like bolsters came merrily
tripping while soldiers in scarlet and blue drank with their girls
at little tables.

Meanwhile the real soldiers cried out in their agony 'Oh! Oh!
Oh! . . . *Oh! Borjé moi . . . Borjé moi!*' as Nikitin and Semyonov probed for bullets under the uncertain flame of the
candles, and a soldier in delirium sang a song about gathering the corn, in a shrill broken voice.

The dominating square-bearded man, Semyonov, had stopped
his work for a moment and stood, his arms folded, looking on,
beside Benjie.

'You seem to stand this pretty well,' he said. 'If it isn't impertinent – how old are you?'

'Just gone sixty,' said Benjie.

'Yes. You look fit. Lose your arm in this War?'

'No. In the Boer War.'

'Bad luck.'

'Oh, I'm used to it.'

'What do you think of us – the Russians, I mean?' Semyonov asked.

'Oh, you're plucky – marvellous. I never saw such courage. But you're a bit muddled high up, aren't you?'

'Yes. Hopeless. Everyone's robbing and cheating and spying and betraying. It's a mess of a war altogether. When do you think it will end?'

'Never, I should think,' said Benjie.

'I agree. Why don't you people do something on the other Front?'

'We're doing our best, I believe,' said Benjie.

'I believe you are. But they're beginning to be impatient over here.' He turned angrily, and Benjie thought he had never seen a more determined aggressive profile. 'There's that bloody fellow-countryman of yours messing things up again. Never saw a more useless fellow in my life.'

'Oh, you mean Trenchard,' Benjie said.

'Yes. I wish to God he'd get back to his own country.'

It was then that a candle, close at Benjie's elbow, flared. It was low down in its socket. In the spurt of light Benjie thought that he saw Vanessa. She stood quietly there, smiling at Trenchard, who was nervously bandaging the knee of a large patient-eyed soldier. She smiled at him, then turned her eyes to Benjie's. They drank in one another's happiness. Oh! how glad he was to see her again! But she was not there. Only the flame, bright, pure, steady.

And Sally, seeing it, said to Mary Worcester: 'Look, Mary! That light in the sky!'

Sally and Mary were looking out from behind the blinds in Cynthia's house in Eaton Place. Cynthia had taken the house six months ago. It was small, compact, could be worked with four servants. Everyone must make sacrifices now.

Ellis had died two months after Vanessa. He had been lost, bewildered; he had cried a great deal and would sit for hours, his knees hunched up, staring like an old sick monkey at the closed piano. They had found him there one morning huddled up in the chair dead. So had passed away the son of Will's old age and great hopes.

After his death Sally had gone to live with her father and Tom, and then, when war broke out, Cynthia had taken her. Although she was now, at the beginning of 1916, over twelve years of ago, she did not grow. She did not herself mind.

'I'm like my great-grandmother. She didn't grow, but nobody cared.'

She never worried in the least about her own personal appearance, as, in fact, her great-grandmother had done. How many, many times Judith Paris had wished that her legs were longer, but Sally Herries didn't care a damn!

She was, Mary thought, regrettably tomboyish. She didn't care how she looked, how she sat, what clothes she wore. She might be made to look rather striking with her brown hair and pale face. She said she simply could not bother. She was, at her present stage, direct and honest to a terrible degree. Loyal and warm-hearted, if she liked anyone. Unfortunately she did not like Mary nor did Mary like her. Mary considered that Sally was envious of her great beauty and, further, that she was jealous of her because her adored Tom thought Mary a queen and a goddess.

In the first of these there was no truth at all. Sally *did* think Mary the most beautiful woman in the world. She also thought her the coldest and most selfish, and for this reason she re-sented Tom's quite hopeless passion. For Mary would never dream of marrying a poor journalist like Tom. She was extremely ambitious. On the other hand, she was neither so cold nor so hard-hearted as Sally supposed her. The true basic reason for Sally's dislike of Mary, however, was that Mary had no feeling about Vanessa. Vanessa was the principal abiding fact in Sally's life. There never had been, there never would be again, anyone like Sally's mother. Sally was neither sentimental nor gushing, but deep in her nature lived intense emotion. All this, as yet, was given to the memory of her mother. She adored Tom, she liked her father, but they also were part of Vanessa.

Now, for Mary, when someone was dead someone was dead. Moreover, she had not seen Vanessa very often and remembered her only as a large rather calm lady with a broad white forehead and grey hair parted in an old-fashioned way. Also Vanessa had lived with a man not her husband and of this Sally was the result. Mary was conventional. She liked people to do the proper things. So why *should* she be passionate about Vanessa? Twice she had spoken rather slightingly to Sally about her mother – only in a joke of course, but Mary's sense of humour was not very delicate. She was neither witty nor quick-witted. Like other beautiful women, her beauty was all she needed.

But, ironically, she had, if she had known it, something of the beauty that Vanessa had had as a young woman. She was tall, dark, full-breasted. She had been told that she carried herself like a queen and never forgot it. It was her tragedy, perhaps, that she was moving into an age when carrying yourself like a queen would be no longer an asset.

Sally knelt on a chair beside Mary and stared, from behind the blind, at a dark and dead London. No light showed anywhere. Only on the horizon there had flashed a sudden finger of light.

'A flame in the sky!' Sally cried.

'It's a searchlight,' said Mary.

Rosalind, a plain-faced, good-natured girl, was seated at the table within the room, knitting. They had all been knitting, making chest-protectors. The Ladies' Committee for which they worked wanted body-belts, Warleigh leggings, gas masks, pneumonia jackets and operation shirts. Sally hated to knit and so did Mary. Rosalind enjoyed it.

'Take care you don't show any light,' she said mildly, for the penalty of failing to conform was actually One Hundred Pounds or six months' imprisonment. People were making blinds from old curtains and women's skirts.

'Oh, that's all right!' Sally came back to the table. 'I suppose I must do my beastly algebra. Oh dear, there's never any peace these days!'

At first the War had been fun, then it had been a bore, now it was rather terrible. Many girls at school had lost their fathers and brothers, and when it came to your best friend (whose name was Charlotte Greene) having to leave because her father was killed and there was no money in the family any more – why, then you positively realized it. Tom had been home on leave twice, and last time he had been pale-faced, nervous and oddly silent. But the worst was Maurice, Alfred's son, who, two nights before he went back, alone with Sally in his father's dining-room had, quite unexpectedly, burst into tears. He had been joking but a moment before.

'I don't want to go back! I don't want to go back!' he had cried.

Sally had plenty of common sense. She never lost her head, but if at that moment it had been suggested that she should return to

France instead of Maurice, she would at once have agreed to go.

She stood by the table thinking of her father (so far away in Russia, with only his one arm), of Tom who wrote such splendid letters, of poor Maurice and of Gordon Newmark, who did not seem to mind a bit and had won the DSO. Standing there, thinking, it seemed to Sally as though, across a dark stretch of water, there was a black marshy land and down its length spread a vast scaly dragon, flame issuing from its jaws.

'You funny little thing!' said Mary, who, drawn to her full height, was looking very beautiful in front of the blind. 'What are you thinking about?'

But Sally pushed past her and, on the other side of the blind, stared into the dark. Even as she looked a flame of light shot up into the sky.

'*That* was a flash!' said Maurice Herries.

This was from one of the gas-projectors from the hill behind them. They were hurling opened cylinders of gas on to the enemy position some thousand yards away. Maurice shivered. Time was short. He ordered the morning rum issue to be taken round the platoons. Then suddenly there began a procession of 'whizz-bangs'.

Maurice stood there wishing that he might 'stop one' before he had to go over the top. It was that cold, terrifying moment half an hour before the dawn when everything is clear and un-mistakable like hell. 'In another forty minutes I may be dead. In another forty minutes I may be sticking my bayonet into a Boche's belly, deep, deep, as though into butter. In forty minutes I may be mad with pain, my sight gone, my body crippled for life . . .'

Many men did not think of those things. Maurice was a poet. He thought Shakespeare, Blake and Gerard Manley Hopkins the three greatest men in the world. He loathed the mud and the filth and the smells and Berkley Cannon, his best friend, dying in his arms, and he loved the comradeship, the good humour, the courage and friendly simplicity of common men, the moments of ecstasy . . . and he hated this pause before action, hated it as he had never hated anything in his life before.

He wondered whether a Boche attack had forestalled their own. 'Perhaps they have learned our plans and will shatter our huddled groups before we leave our lines.'

Then the flame! It stabbed the sky. First the roar was one blow as on a great sheet of iron, then after a pause another, then a pause again and another. Then one continuous throbbing thunder. The shells screamed and a pillar of fire leaned up the wall of the dim uncertain sky. 'Our barrage,' Maurice thought. 'Zero hour.'

Maurice shouted to his little group, they jumped out of the trench and stumbled forward. Now came the moment that he always dreaded, when the group broke and one straggled forward singly, one little mannikin in a world of malignant danger. Through the noise as of cannon-balls rolling down sheets of iron, there was the phut! phut! of rifle bullets. And there to the right are heads of Boches in a shell hole shooting. Trotter, a giant of a man, one of the jolliest, most carefree and kindest, staggers, seems to leap on his feet, crashes down. 'No, there is no chance for us tumbling through this mud with these fellows shooting at us,' and he and Conklin, Bush and two others have slithered down into a shell hole and are firing over the top of it. Conklin's face is smashed in. We have got two of the Boches but more are running up. The sky is lightening, and the roar of the guns, and now the German guns, thunders on – but by this time it is familiar, belonging to a world that one knows, that is part of one, that is almost friendly.

Then Maurice 'stopped one'. There was an impact on his right shoulder as though a big stone had hit him. No pain. He slipped down into the bottom of the shell hole and, staring upwards, was aware now that the sky was much lighter and, to his great surprise, that he was alone there except for Conklin who, his smashed face in the mud, huddled at his feet. His shoulder, his arm, his hand were soaking wet, but still there was no pain. He did not want to move. He was quite happy. A faint, a very faint blue was stealing into the sky, and some small clouds, like rosy petals, seemed to his eye to be dancing, gently and carefully, against the blue.

The thundering noise withdrew, and in front of his eyes, which he soon must close, a small and delicate flame wavered. The flame of the candle that Sally had lit! He smiled. He would write a poem about it, this small candleflame that neither the wind of the great guns nor the delicate fleeciness of the morning clouds could put out. Pity that his father hated him to write poetry, thought all books a mistake, wanted him to add up sums in the City. He would never add up sums, but he would write poems to the glory of England as Rupert Brooke had done, or about old ships like Flecker ... He would carry on the glory of the Family, would go and live in Cumberland, near the sea, in the valleys of which old Benjie Herries had told him. A face bent close to his. Someone moved him and a flame of pain licked his heart. He cried out and the flame moved up, spreading, glorious, golden, blotting out, with its light, the whole world. There were two flames . . .

The two flames burnt steadily, illuminating the mirror, lighting the dressing-table, the pictures on the walls, of 'Queen Victoria receiving the News of her Accession' and 'Dignity and Impudence', the narrow bed and the small shining table beside it.

'The electric light's fused,' said Gordon Newmark, looking in at the door.

'I know,' said Tom. 'I've found some candles.' He sat in front of the mirror, brushing his hair with his two old battered silver brushes.

'Hurry up, you blighter,' Gordon said.

'All right. I won't be a minute.'

Gordon Newmark was broad and tall and the pink of self-confidence. Tom seemed gentle, small, submissive beside him. Tom was thirty-two and Gordon twenty-one, but Gordon had won the DSO, loved the War – 'best time I'm ever likely to have, old boy' – and was home now on leave as a kind of conqueror, patronizing, in a jolly friendly way, all the family, especially his old father and mother and his sister Ada, who all adored him. He was, if he had known it, the recurrent Herries type, the type of old Pomfret, of Prosper – Jennifer's father, of Rodney – Cynthia's grandfather, and especially of Walter – Tom's great-grandfather. But he didn't know it. He didn't care. He was the triumphant, riding, roughshod, bullying Herries. But the type had softened, emasculated a bit. He thought old Benjie a dissolute old rogue and Tom a 'soft 'un' and Maurice Herries 'a decent sort of ass who writes poems'; his type was as far from the other as ever, in the family history, it had been, but the two did not quarrel any more. Life was beginning to move too swiftly: you had too much to do to bother about quarrels. The Herries didn't fight any more. But Gordon felt, all the same, a sort of friendly scorn as he saw Tom struggling into his clothes. Under the light of the candles Tom's face was serious, careworn, too kindly to be aggressive. 'That's all he'll ever be,' Gordon thought, 'a sort of second-rate journalist. Thinks too much about other people. Almost a woman – about his old father, his kid sister, his father's mistress who died. I'd worry!' thought Gordon, who hoped that night to pick up a pretty girl somewhere . . . you

needn't be too particular these days when you'd be returning in a
week's time to be killed maybe ... But Tom didn't want a girl.
He was sweet on Mary Worcester. Poor old Tom! He hadn't a
dog's chance with that beautiful swollen-headed female!

Tom blew out the candles. They groped their way down the
dark staircase. Tom still stuck to the rooms in Tite Street. In the
dark King's Road they found a taxi, and through a town of pitch
they plunged until the friendly arms of the Carlton Grill received
them. Then they went to the Alhambra to see *The Bing Boys* for
the twentieth time, sang *If you were the only girl in the world*
with other of their slightly intoxicated fellows and roared at
George Robey whenever he lifted his eyebrows.

Afterwards they found a dingy door in Soho and behind it a
yet dingier nightclub known as 'The Five Pennies'. Tom had not
wanted to go. 'Leave' was offering no attractions. He wanted to
be back in France, although he didn't like that either. Mary
tortured him. She liked him, he thought. Sometimes he fancied
that she more than liked him, but he knew in his heart that he
had no chance with her, and knowing it loved her only the more
desperately. He had loved her always. He was chaste, having had
no sexual experience whatever, and this chastity seemed, just
now, to separate him from everybody. Men, all men, seemed to be
caught into a passionate longing for sexual intercourse – any
intercourse with anyone ... It was a hunger, the only solace for
the filth, the fear, the cold, the wounds, the long drawn-out
tension of this fantastic trial. And he? He thought always of
Vanessa and of Mary. Of his father and Sally and his friends as
well, but Vanessa and Mary were always with him, one of the
kindest, gentlest, most understanding of mothers, the other the
loveliest, divinest of goddesses. And he could touch neither: one
was a ghost, the other a dream ...

As he sat in the small, fearfully hot and indecently smelling
room of 'The Five Pennies' he screwed his courage to the sticking point. His life seemed just now to be running on hard lines,
but it was worse for others. Worse for poor Maurice, for instance, who had lost his arm, worse for hundreds, for thousands
of fine men. He would stick it, but he wished that he had
Gordon's hardy indifference – Gordon who was, at this moment,
talking to two women with a carefree gaiety that made him seem
the only really happy person in the room. A girl came and sat
beside Tom. He ordered her a drink; drink was being served in
coffee cups. He watched Gordon a little anxiously. He knew that

these places just now were haunted by 'crows', women who made their men friends drunk, took them on somewhere and robbed them of everything they had. But Gordon was no fool. He knew a thing or two.

The girl at Tom's table was tired. She complained, through the raucous jazz music, in a weary little voice, of the violence and callousness of men. Men didn't seem to care. They weren't kind any more. Generous, yes, but not kind. Life wasn't really gay although everyone pretended that it was. Food was awful. Why, fancy, eggs were a luxury food. Fancy eggs being a luxury! Butter was half a crown a pound and a chicken cost thirteen bob! Why, fancy a chicken costing ... So she went on, repeating everything twice.

Suddenly, into the middle of the jazz, the laughter, the movement of the dancers, a voice broke. A tall swaying officer had pushed into the middle of the floor, he was brushing the dancers aside. He was drunk, of course. And he cried out in a shrill scream:

'Blast this bloody war! To hell with it! Blast this bloody war! To hell with the bloody war! To hell ...'

Two waiters caught hold of him and led him away. People laughed.

'You see,' said the girl. 'That's just what I say. What I mean to say is that nobody really enjoys things much. And they aren't kind any more. If you were a woman you'd agree with me. And the women aren't kind either. What I mean to say is, it's affected everybody, and how we're ever to get back to the way we were—'

'We'll never get back,' said Tom.

He was watching a man near him who held up, with a rather unsteady hand, a lighter. He pushed at his cigarette with it. The little flame burnt bravely, with a fine uprightness. Then it went out.

KALEIDOSCOPE

II

TRIUMPHAL ARCH

IN the early days of 1917 Sally Herries had a strange experience. It was at Cynthia's house in Eaton Place.

Altogether life was strange at this time, strange and yet familiar. Sally was over thirteen years of age, went to school every day, did on the whole what she was told, was calm and quiet and collected, but suffered, at unexpected moments, extraordinary and poignant longings for her mother – also, but less poignantly, for her father and for Tom.

She had only a few friends, but in this dark uncertain world that now surrounded everyone friendships were not important. Some of the girls at school she liked, but they had all now their own especial interests – the ways in which they were helping the War, brothers, fathers at the Front, food that had become important because it was rationed, the personal experiences of air raids or the second-hand experiences of emotionalists, rumour and story and gossip; it seemed that all these things kept one apart from the ordinary relationships of ordinary life. Sally did not care. At Eaton Place she was quite alone. Mary and Rosalind were too old, Peile a silly (but kindly) old man, Cynthia infinitely distant.

But *how* fantastic a world it was! That moment after dusk when all the world was dark, the first experience of an air raid with the alarm, the silence, the distant firing, the expectancy (not at all frightening – pleasurable, like being at the theatre just before the curtain went up), the rumours, the stories that people told, the anxieties about Tom, about Gordon, the many women wearing black, the tales that reached even her ears of the funny ways that soldiers and their girlfriends had in places like Trafalgar Square after dark . . .

She was aware that her family were behaving very finely. She herself caught some of the family pride. It was really true, she felt, that but for her family England and the War would be lost. When she went to other people's houses – the houses of the parents of her friends – she heard many very despairing remarks. It would make no difference, they said, that America had severed diplomatic relations with Germany. America would not be able to be in time, we would all be defeated before America could do anything. Someone told a story about going into a tear-shell factory and weeping tears enough to fill a jug. People recounted horrible details of wounds and suffering and lonely agonies. Sally tried not to listen but she *had* to . . . Her imagination was vivid. She saw these dreadful things as though they were happening in front of her. She grew older very quickly. People said that we were bound to be beaten. All the glory was gone. We were led by idiotic Generals, our politicians were impossible fools. People

said that it would be better if we made terms with the Germans.
Let *them* have the glory!

'Oh no!' Sally cried out in the house of kind Mrs Mickleham,
the mother of Connie Mickleham who was so clever at algebra.
'That would be wicked!' And for once she burst into tears and
ran from the room.

But *inside* the family it was *all* quite different. No one dreamt
of anything but complete victory. We would go on for ever and
ever but victory must certainly be ours.

It was now that the Herries were seen at their very best. Their
normality, their common sense, the absence of *grab* in their
natures, their non-property qualities, so to speak, their courage,
their indifference to facts that they refused to realize, enabled
them to become completely patriotic. They loved their country
because their country depended on them and while *they* were
there all must be well.

Maurice came home without an arm and sat, with a white face,
staring into distance. They were sorry for him but disregarded
him. Gordon came home, filled with the War. It was glorious.
When the Americans came in we would soon sweep the dirty
Boche back to Berlin. He had extraordinary stories about the
dirtiness of the Boche, his meanness, cruelty, cowardice and sav-
agery. The Herries on one side, the Germans on the other. Who
could doubt of the result?

It was on one March evening that Sally had her funny little
adventure.

She had been doing her schoolwork in her cold little room at
the top of the house and remembered that her geography book
was in the dining-room. She came downstairs for it. The house
was still and plunged into that eerie dusk that seemed now to be
always the atmosphere of rooms and passages. She reached the
hall that had only a light at the farthest end, near the kitchen
stairs. She walked forward to the dining-room door and saw that
a man was hiding, close up against the wall, behind the umbrella
stand. He was a little man with spectacles, a rather dirty face, and
he was in uniform. As she saw him he whispered, but without
moving from the wall to which he seemed to be fastened, 'If yer
say a word I'll throttle yer.'

It was all part of the general strangeness, the half-light, the
silent streets, the sense of the War, prowling like a large cat
almost at one's very door, of Benjie somewhere in Russia, of Tom
underground in France eating plum and apple jam to the light of

a single candle, of that man weeping a bucket of tears in the factory, of Maurice without an arm, that this little man should be pinned against the wall of the house in Eaton Place.

She saw that he was very frightened and she wanted to give him something. She gave him half a crown that she was saving to buy something for Tom with.

He said 'Gawd bless yer, miss', and in another moment had opened the hall door and slipped away, letting into the house a blast of cold biting air before the door closed. She stood there wondering. What had he wanted? Had he come to steal? He looked very unhappy. He was a piece of the War. She had encountered the War. She continued quickly to grow up.

Her father, crossing a small snow-covered square in Petrograd, heard a strange sound. He was walking with a little black-bearded Jew, Konrad Mathias. Mathias had just said: 'It is between personality and non-personality. Everything comes down to that. Am I, Konrad Mathias, an individual with a history, an important history like no one else's, or am I a little gas, a little acid, a little water, dissipated at the prick of a pin? ... Do you see? Am I Konrad Mathias? Am I? Am I?'

'I should think you probably are,' Benjie had said, looking at a church dome, a brilliant green against the burning blue of the sky. The snow sparkled at his feet. 'I like this,' he said. 'The green, the blue, the sparkling snow. It stirs me – not the acid and water in me, I think. Or is it?'

'No, no!' Little Mathias, in his black woolly fur cap, jumped on the snow.

'Well, I don't know,' Benjie said. 'The individual can't be very important. If the world goes topsy-turvy the individual starves and is very quickly gas and water again. There's a revolution in South America and Mr Smith in London loses his job. His child dies because it hasn't enough nourishment. It's the revolution that matters. Certainly not Mr Smith.'

'Oh, you're wrong,' Mathias cried. 'What if he does lose his job? He's losing it or gaining it all the time. Everyone in a lifetime meets his personal crisis whether there's a revolution or not. Birth, love, death, economic struggle, falling out of love with one's wife, seeing a pretty girl round the corner, having a suspicion there's a God, then deciding there isn't. Always the same crisis turning up for everybody. The hoops of the circus – you must jump through them. That's fate. The way you jump. That's free will and is the only thing that matters. It's the individual who is always different. How will you meet this? A toothache, syphilis, cancer, a sudden bit of success. That's history.'

'Then you believe in God?'

'Of course I do. Only He doesn't interfere. He sets the scene. You play your part. I've been about the world a lot. It's everywhere the same. Are you a realist or a romantic? If you're the first it will be the dates, the scientific facts, the large movements, the cold truth that will seem to you to be important. If you're the second it will be the things behind the facts – what each man does with his soul.'

'You think man has a soul?'

'A spiritual life? Of course. It's the only thing that squares the facts.'

'Is there a life after death, do you think?' Benjie asked more eagerly than he had intended.

'Life? Death? There's always death. Every man is living and dying all the time. But *physical* death – that's not important. Men are so thoughtless. And they worry about the wrong things.'

'So you think the old world is finished?'

'Of course it is. And the new one will take a long while settling itself. But that doesn't matter. Men will have their personal histories just the same. Why, take myself! I'm fifty-five – a Jew of no importance whatever. But I was afraid for years, afraid of everything and everyone. Thought people despised me. And I was greedy too. Now I'm not often afraid and not greedy. That's more important than a revolution. Not because I am important, mind you – no more and no less than the next man – but it's important to God that I should get a move on. More important than that Napoleon should win Austerlitz or Rasputin be murdered.'

'But Rasputin's death has affected millions.'

'No. Only provided situations for men to meet. They'd meet them in one fashion or another in any case.'

It was then that Benjie heard the noise. It was like the sharp cracking of twigs. The scene was very peaceful. At the end of the square was the canal and along the side of it a cab was slowly crawling, the *isvostchik*, in his fat clothes, bunched up on the seat. Some birds flew slowly across the blue. Some church bells were ringing. It was about three in the afternoon.

A moment later it was as though the blue sky had burst and

poured confusion on to the earth. Down the path by the canal a mob of people, shouting, crying, came pouring, and on to the square from the other end rolled a lorry, piled high with soldiers, bristling with rifles. The lorry stayed still. A man came running from the canal. He ran a little way into the square, outlined very sharply against the snow. He stopped and looked back at the people. Then from the lorry there came a noise like the clearing of a throat, and the man ran a step, stood, crumpled at the knees, fell, raised himself, fell flat, wriggled like a worm and lay still.

Benjie had known many bad moments in his life but none so bad as this one – for there he was, isolated, alone in all that gleaming, glittering colour. He must run for miles, it seemed, before he could reach security. But Mathias was already running. An absurd notion came to Benjie that it would be undignified to run. He walked slowly, his hand in his pocket. But now many people were running into the square, and as they did so a red light rose like a fan above the houses and spread into the blue.

He walked slowly and as he went repeated to himself like a man in a dream, aloud: 'This is Revolution. This is Revolution.' Then he saw the square flooded with people. They were shouting: 'To the Nevski!' 'No, no, to the Duma!'

He was carried with the crowd . . .

And it was now September. Tom on leave, walking down Piccadilly, heard the air-raid warning. Instinctively he hurried his step and then slowed down again. For what did it matter?

He had come from half an hour with the lovely Mary. On his way there he had thought: 'Well, now, tonight I'll ask her. She will be sorry for me, perhaps, moved because next week I return to France. She will think "Oh, poor boy". And she will be kind.' As he had walked towards Eaton Place his love – that had been part of him for so long now, that had gained so terribly in intensity out there where every homeward vision shone with a mystical light – his love had dried and constricted his heart so that it was a shrivelling little ball in his body. Away, beyond the houses, not far distant, somewhere hanging in the pale September sky was his hope. He would say:

'Mary, I have loved you so long. Let me go back with just this to remember! I may not return. Be kind to me.' A weak, cowardly sort of prayer, but he was beyond all pride now. He wanted her so. His thoughts were lascivious and pure, of the body and the soul, all things together. Oh! if she would only be kind!

And she had been kind – kind and abstracted. Her eyes had rested on him without seeing him, and then she had been suddenly aware that she must do something about this poor man who had loved her since she was a child and was so good and patient and so tiresome. And next week he would return to France and would suffer horrors, perhaps, would be frightened and tired and lonely.

Comprehension came into her eyes. She saw Tom. She wanted to be good to him. She asked him questions about the Front.

But he knew that it was only kindness. He refused a second cup of tea and went.

So he did not mind now if there were an air raid. The omnibuses seemed to hasten, and soon, as he neared the Circus, the streets were quite empty. This was the week when there were almost daily air raids. They said that people's nerves were beginning to go, and Tom remembered how a friend had told him that, two nights ago, he had walked down a street in Pimlico during a raid and that it had been naked, empty, shining, but that behind every window people were playing pianos.

No pianos here. Nothing but the Circus, bare as though set for a scene in a theatre. The firing came nearer and flashes lit the sky. Light hit the Circus and sprang away. But nothing happened. The all-clear sounded. He went on a bus back to Chelsea.

During the remaining days of his leave he found that he could endure no one but Sally. For the first time he was afraid that his nerve was breaking. He was so *tired* of it – sick to death of it all, he was. And worst was the chatter. He lunched with Alfred and listened to Gordon. He lunched with Cynthia and listened to poor old Peile. He heard that Sir Henry Wilson was sold to the French, that £100,000,000 had been spent on gas, that German cruisers were lying off Harwich, that . . . Oh, what did it matter? Everything was unreal now. Life itself was unreal, the physical processes of the body, the putting on of a collar, brushing one's teeth . . .

He went to entertainments, heard Beecham conduct *Figaro,* saw a farce, was made miserable by a musical comedy. All these were unreal.

But Sally was real. He had always loved her with that patient, unchanging, unfaltering devotion that was so especially his. He delighted in the growth that he saw in her. Although she was so young she had great common sense, courage and much humour. And, in one way or another, she constantly reminded him of Vanessa. She had Vanessa's integrity.

On the last evening before his return they talked.

'I wish I was going with you, Tom,' Sally said.

'Do you?' he laughed. 'You wouldn't like it.'

'No, of course I shouldn't. The girls at school all wanted to go once, were dying for the time when they'd be grown up enough to be nurses or something, but now they're not so keen. I don't want to go for any adventurous reason. Only to help.'

'You do help,' he said, 'by staying quietly here and being good-humoured and patient.'

'How long do you think it will last, Tom?'

'Oh, I don't know.' He was holding her small but strong hand in his. 'I've given up prophesying.'

'Do you think that after all we may be beaten?' Her voice sank into an awed whisper.

'No. The Germans won't last as long as we will – not now the Americans have come in.'

'Yes – but the Russians won't fight any more now, will they?' She seemed to be looking into great distances. 'I wonder how Daddy is?'

'Oh, he'll be all right wherever he is,' said Tom.

'When I grow up I hope I shan't forget all I feel now. Don't you, Tom? It would be awful if when we're older we all forgot how horrid it all is and let there be another war.'

She sat on the edge of his chair and put her arms round his neck.

She produced a present, a scarf that she had knitted.

'It isn't very good. I'm not clever with my fingers and, to tell you the truth, I'd have hated the bother if it had been for anyone else.'

So he went back again, trying not to think of Mary. But he didn't think of anyone much. He was terribly tired, not in the body but in the head. And he dreaded the noise. It would be almost better to be dead, because then at least there would be quiet.

And Maurice, the son of Alfred, the son of Amery (thin-legged, dyspeptic, high-stocked, over-large Adam's apple), the son of Durward (of Rocklington Hall; stout, plethoric, fine calves), the son of Pelham (stubborn, hot-tempered), the son of Grandison (exceedingly stout, dewlapped like a bull, intimate with St John), son of Robert (stout, good-natured sot, gambler and humorist, a friend of Charles II), son of Robert who first brought distinction on the family by breeding bullocks in Wiltshire and marrying a Scottish heiress – (he was son of the Herries who came to watch

German miners in Borrowdale in his Queen's service, that cross-grained bitter fellow whose portrait hung in the Herries house in Rosthwaite and later at the Fortress) – well, what of Maurice?

Not very much. 'A poor reward for all the trouble I've taken,' his father would think, looking at him. 'What if he *has* lost an arm? So have lots of other fellows, and worse, blinded, tubes in their stomach, mice in the brain – and there he sits, doing nothing but stare or read or listen to high-class music on the gramophone. Can hardly believe he's my son. Rotten pessimist too. No patriotism. I believe he likes the Germans better than the English.'

So Alfred told him one day at lunch:

'My God, Maurice, I believe you'd rather be a German than an Englishman.'

Maurice gave him a queer look.

'I'd rather be anything than a Herries,' he said.

For by this time in the spring of 1918 he was very, very tired of his family. It was May and the Billing-Maud Allan case was amusing everyone at the Courts. That the case was poisonously hysterical startled nobody. The Family – Alfred, Gordon, Cynthia – alluded darkly to perversion. 'We must sweep these abnormalities from our national life,' wheezed old Horace. 'It's a splendid thing for England that this cancer should be revealed.' But he confided privately to Maurice: 'I know what you're feeling, my boy. To tell you the truth, I'm not as optimistic as I used to be. But one has to put a brave face on things.'

'Why?' asked Maurice.

Horace didn't exactly know. He supposed that he had always been determined to see the bright side of things. All his life it had been the same. After all it wasn't life that was important but the way that you dealt with it. Some writer had said that somewhere, and he thought that it was very true. He wheezed in his chair (his heart was bad) and looked bravely, through rheumy eyes, into Maurice's face.

'I've been laughed at all my life,' he said. 'I've wanted people to like me and they've only laughed at me. I've thought I've done my best, but I can see now that I've failed. My sister went on the streets and died there, and everyone's found me a bore.' He sat there; a thick heavy tear trickled on to his fat cheek and stayed there. He brushed it away.

'All the same,' he said, 'even if I've made a mess of things, what I say is true all the same. It's better to be cheerful and it needs a lot of obstinacy. Cheer up, Maurice. You might have lost both your legs, you know.'

But Maurice couldn't cheer up. His father, his sister, all the Herries save little Sally, drove him mad. He thought perhaps that he was going mad. There were times when the guns sounded so loudly in his ears that he could hear nothing else. He would sit in his bedroom and try to read Joyce or T. S. Eliot or D. H. Lawrence. Beautiful, wonderful things their books had in them. They told the truth at last. For centuries writers had been lying about life, but now no honest writer need ever deceive again. Lawrence seemed to him a kind of young god, fighting all the hypocrisies, the prejudices, the falsities of mankind, and fighting all alone, his back to the wall. He had been persecuted by the damned interfering authorities simply because he protested against this bloody war. And then, when Maurice thought of the authorities (he saw them as a fat, red-tabbed crimson-faced officer screaming at some trembling private . . .), he would get up and walk about his room, and the stump of his arm would ache and the guns would sound in his ears and strange fierce lights would flash over the dressing-table and crimson the eiderdown on his bed.

There came a night when he thought that he would end it. He woke at an early hour of grey dawn and a voice said, quite clearly, in his ear: 'Come on. Put an end to this. You've had enough of it. You're never going to be any good at anything. Never. Life is endless.'

So, as though obedient to a command, he got out of bed and wondered what he would do. Should he go down to the kitchen and turn on the gas? That seemed a long business and would need a lot of arranging. He had a penknife. Should he cut an artery? A messy affair. Should he throw himself from his bedroom window? That might not finish him. He walked up and down, followed, it seemed to him, by this persuasive voice.

'Go on, you're no good. You're spoilt and finished. Better get out of it . . .'

At last he sat down in the chair by the ash-strewn fire and burst into tears. He cried and cried as though he never would stop. Then he fell asleep in the chair where he was.

A poor affair. Nothing fine about it anywhere. He had a job those last months in the Ministry of Information and so he walked, alone and unattended save by his private demon, from one place to another . . .

*   *   *

About half past ten on Monday morning, November 11th, Benjie went into Hatchard's bookshop. While waiting there he was accosted by a stout pale-faced gentleman who said to him: 'I say – the Armistice is signed.'

'Oh, is it?' said Benjie, bought his book and walked into Piccadilly. There was no sign anywhere of excitement – the buses rolled along, people passed on their business, a young man stood with his eyes seriously fixed on Mr Jackson's appetizing window.

Benjie had moved from Chelsea after his return from Russia and had rooms now in Ryder Street. As he was about to turn into Jermyn Street he spoke to an old man with newspapers.

'Is it true,' he asked, 'that the Armistice is signed?'

'Can't say, sir, I'm sure,' the old man answered, rubbing his nose with the back of his hand.

'Very strange,' Benjie thought. 'This is the moment for which we have all been passionately waiting and no one cares, no one cares at all.'

Entering his flat he saw Sally and Tom sitting together on the sofa.

'Hullo!' he said. 'What are you two doing here?'

'Tom found me in Piccadilly,' Sally explained.

'Why aren't you at school?'

'There's mumps. We were all sent off this morning.' Then she added: 'Tom says the Armistice is signed.'

The valet of the flats came out of Benjie's bedroom with a suit over his arm.

'Bailey,' Benjie said, 'the Armistice is signed.'

'Indeed, sir,' said Bailey. 'I'm very glad, I'm sure. A great relief to everyone. Will you be in to luncheon?'

'Yes – no. Look here, we'll go and celebrate somewhere.'

He looked at both of them.

'Are you sure it's true?' he asked Tom.

'Oh yes – quite sure. The paper had it in an hour ago.'

'This is all wrong,' Benjie thought. He went to the window and glanced down into Ryder Street. No one was stirring.

He looked back at them. 'One day in Russia,' he said, 'about a week after the March Revolution, I got caught in the crowd. We all marched singing through the streets. Everybody was singing. It was the most marvellous thing ... Well, why aren't we singing? The greatest and most horrible war in history is over.'

'I suppose we can't realize it,' said Tom. 'And we're all rather tired.'

'Yes, we're all rather tired,' Benjie thought, 'and we're going to be tired for years and years. Perhaps nobody will have the energy to sing again.'

'All the same,' he added aloud, 'it's something that men aren't going to be killed any more. That's something.'

At that moment they heard the maroons going off and the silver clock on the mantelpiece struck in its thin surprised tone eleven o'clock. They all went to the window and saw people pouring into the street. From every door they seemed to be coming. Men, without hats, rushed out, waving their arms. Flinging the window open, Benjie could hear distant shouting.

'Come on,' he said. 'Let's go out and see the sights.'

After that they were part of a vast, wild, cheering and yet oddly unexcited crowd. That at least was what Benjie felt, as though all these people said to him with one voice (not a loud voice – almost a whisper): 'It is right for us to be excited. We've won a great war, but life is changed. We can never be quite so light-hearted and careless again. Once, not so very long ago, on Mafeking night, we all went mad. But we shan't go mad now. We have to behave as though we were gloriously happy. But we are not. By tonight we may be drunk a little and make a noise, but it doesn't mean anything.'

Nevertheless, with Sally close at his side, he could not but feel that something was accomplished. Another phase of history, another phase of his own life, was closed. His adventurous days were over and so too, maybe, were the adventurous days of the world. It would be all cold mechanism now – mechanism, science, a remorseless progress.

He had a sudden longing for Vanessa and at that same moment Sally said: 'How I wish that Mother was here!' He pressed her arm close to him. So long as Sally was alive things would not be mechanical. She was too individual for that.

They had pushed their way to Trafalgar Square, but here they were brought to a standstill. A thick unbroken mass of humanity. Men were shouting and singing, girls waving. But Benjie felt that everyone was waiting for something. That moment of singing in Petrograd would not be recovered here. It would never be recovered. It had been a moment of extravagant idealistic hope.

'There should be a Triumphal Arch,' he thought. 'Here in front of the lions. And everyone should march away under it, swearing as they passed beneath it that never again would men hate, plunder, be greedy ... Never again!' He smiled. Not bad

nonsense for an old cynic like himself. That was the sort of thing
that old Horace would say. Alfred and Gordon and the others
would have a fine time tonight. They at least would be happy, for
they had won the War and were Lords of the Earth.

But not perhaps for long. The battle was not over yet between
the Maurices and the Gordons, the Cynthias and the Vanessas.

'Come on,' he said. 'We'll go to the Berkeley and have a
feed.'

A thin rain had begun to fall. There was no Triumphal Arch.
As they pushed their way slowly Benjie saw a soldier, motionless,
staring, unshifted by the crowd. 'Perhaps he's thinking that now
he won't be killed. He won't have to go back to that hell. That's
something anyway.'

He thought constantly of Vanessa. If she were here how happy
she would be that he was safe now, and that Tom was safe. She
would be happy for all the women all over the world.

All the women! Yes, that was something.

But there was no Triumphal Arch.

SALLY AND TOM

CYNTHIA gave Gordon Newmark a theatre party on his
thirtieth birthday (he was thirty on February 4th, 1925) and
Sally and old Horace Ormerod and Rosalind and Adrian came
too. Cynthia (who was now over sixty, although you would never
think it unless you looked at her neck), had a weakness for
Gordon and hoped that, with judicious management, he might
be induced to marry her daughter Rosalind. Rosalind was a good
girl, had the best character in the world, and, although she was
on the plain side and was now over thirty, would make a good
wife for Gordon. Gordon once might have married her, for he
was just the kind of man to appreciate good solid wearing qualities in a wife, but after the deaths of old Sidney and Mary
Newmark (they died within a week or two of one another) it was
discovered that their children, Gordon and Ada, would have
large fortunes. Gordon was, of course, in his grandfather's
business but made his headquarters in London. He was of
another generation from old Horace Newmark, who thought that
there was no city in the world to equal Manchester. Gordon was

good-looking, with clear-cut features (a little too clear-cut perhaps) and that fashion that cropped up again and again in Herries businessmen of wearing clothes that looked too immaculate to be human. He was an agreeable well-mannered fellow, proud of his own looks, his D S O, his business ability, his family and his 'I like a man with no nonsense about him' – one of his favourite sayings. He intended a little later to go into politics and he would have a peerage before he finished. But first he must marry, and Cynthia hoped that in spite of his money, his profile and his self-confidence he might marry Rosalind.

For alas, neither Mary nor Rosalind was yet married. It was too extraordinary! Mary was still lovely, but for some reason young men didn't propose to her. They came up to her, looked at her with wonder in their eyes and went away again. The fact was that, thirty years earlier, when Vanessa ruled Hill Street, Mary would have been exactly what everyone wanted – beautiful, dignified, graceful, and not too clever. Now the young men (who after all had served their country) wanted something more lively.

So Cynthia had her troubles. Peile was aged and, although his figure was still good, this new post-War world appeared to have struck him dumb with amazement. It had been, at one time, the middle classes that had seemed to him astonishing. He had appealed to his Herries relations to save the country. But the job had been, it seemed, altogether too much for his relatives. So now, standing on his thin aristocratic legs, looking at the Income Tax and the closing of the great houses of England and the young women who looked like boys and the young men who looked like girls, he could only stare and stutter and gasp.

So he was not of very much use to Cynthia, who, from the house in Eaton Place, did what she could, looking now like a rather pretty little pig, with her hair a little too yellow, her cheeks a little too pink, her skirts a little too short, and her neck (in spite of all she could do) a little too wrinkled.

She had invited Sally to the theatre party because she had invited old Horace. She had had no intention of asking Horace, but one afternoon when he had called on her and had sat there looking so old and pathetic, her heart (which was still kindly when she gave it an opportunity) was moved to say: 'Well, Horace, you must come to the theatre with us. Come next week. We are going to that play that everyone is talking about – by a new young man whose name I forget. They say he's extraordinarily clever and only left school last year.' Horace, who was now nearing seventy, had purple streaks on either side of his nose, an unwieldy stomach, and a cheery smile that was habit rather than intention (and so seemed to Cynthia terribly pathetic), said eagerly that he'd love to come. He was free practically any night next week.

('What a bore!' thought Cynthia. 'Whatever did I ask him for?')

Having done so she must also invite Sally, for the strange thing was (one of the many strange things about Sally) that she was attached to Horace; she was kind to him and never showed him that sharp tongue and penetrating criticism only too apparent with others. Sally would look after Horace. It was a pity that Gordon did not like Sally. That, however, would throw Gordon all the more into Rosalind's company, and she, Cynthia, could be amused by Adrian, who was elegant, witty, drily cynical, and knew the private behaviour of everyone.

So they went to *The Vortex*. They met at the theatre because the play began early, and instead of dinner before they would have supper at the Savoy Grill afterwards. Sally was the first to arrive and Gordon the second. Each was annoyed at seeing the other.

'Who else is coming?' asked Gordon.

'Horace.'

'Horace? Oh Lord, what a bore!'

'Why?' said Sally.

'Oh, well, he's a bit comic,' said Gordon.

'Comic?' said Sally. 'So's everyone. I am – you are.'

Gordon said nothing but he was greatly annoyed. *He* comic? You might call him anything you like – everyone with personality has detractors – but comic? He looked at Sally with great distaste. Her hair, which had now lost its carroty shade and was a plain dark brown, was bobbed in the new fashion. With a few more inches and a little more colour she would not have been so bad. She was slim, her eyes and mouth were bright, alive – too alive, perhaps, for he hated young girls to look sarcastic. She was unlike other girls and that he also disliked. The height of good form, he thought, was that you should not attract attention in a crowd. Of course if you were a *beautiful* woman, that was another matter. No one could call Sally Herries beautiful, and there she was, thinking no end of herself, secretary to some old Jew (she worked because she liked it, not because she had to), living in the most independent manner with another girl, illegitimate (although of course in these days no one minded that) and, worst of all, Benjie Herries' daughter. Now that Gordon considered himself the head of the Herries family and responsible for its good behaviour, he greatly regretted Benjie, who, in spite of his being seventy and having only one arm, often behaved outrageously and had some dreadful friends.

So Gordon ('Who *is* that handsome man?' someone, standing near him in the foyer, asked her companion. 'What splendid features! He looks like an actor.') and Sally stood there disliking one another exceedingly. The others arrived and they all went in. Soon the curtain went up, and the young author of the play, himself playing the lead, began to tell the other characters exactly what he thought of them.

Cynthia, as she listened, became more and more uncomfortable. What a *very* queer collection of people! The mother, with her cropped hair, her painted face, her passion for cigarettes and cocktails, was of course nothing like Cynthia, and it made it all the queerer that the part should be acted by nice Miss Lilian Braithwaite, whom Cynthia knew well, a charming woman with nothing very modern about her. No, the mother on the stage was nothing like Cynthia, who was received everywhere, and by the young people especially, with the greatest warmth. She so often said: 'I don't feel a day more than thirty', and it was true, she did not, unless her neuritis bothered, or chance had forced upon her a succession of late nights. No, she did not resemble this woman in any way nor did any of the friends of Mary or Rosalind resemble the girl with the Eton crop, played by Miss Molly Kerr, or the dreadful young man whom Noel Coward presented so vigorously. When the curtain went down she turned to Adrian.

'Well I never – what an extraordinary lot of people!'

Adrian, whose eyelids were always a little weary like Mr Pater's Monna Lisa's, said: 'Oh, do you think so? There are lots like them nowadays!'

'Surely not!'

He waited a little. Then he said:

'When I see this sort of thing, I think of Vanessa. I never forget her as I saw her first at a ball. She was dressed in white, with her dark hair piled on the top of her head. I have never seen anything so beautiful before or since.'

'Poor Vanessa!' said Cynthia. 'How terrible she would think all of this!'

'Not at all,' Adrian said sharply. 'She was too simple to be frightened off by external differences. She would be shy, of course, and think that she was being stupid, but she would make friends with that boy and girl in no time. There's been nobody like her since she died.'

'Oh, do you think so? Well, if you come to that, nobody's like anybody, are they? But I can't agree with you, Adrian. Vanessa would be miserable in a world like this. She wouldn't know how to adapt herself.'

'She wouldn't try to,' said Adrian rather crossly. 'She'd just be natural. Of course some people would find her dull. Some people always did. But others – she'd be just what they are always look-ing for now and can't find.'

('Adrian's getting a bore,' Cynthia thought. 'And old – a fussy old Foreign Office bachelor.')

Sally took Horace for a stroll.

'Are you enjoying yourself, Horace dear?' she asked him.

'Oh, I should just think I am!' he answered her in his full philanthropic voice. 'I enjoy everything. When you get to my age, my dear, you'll realize how true it is what Stevenson once said: "We all ought to be as happy as kings." '

'Your tie's up at the back of your collar,' Sally said critically. 'What a whacking lie if Stevenson ever did say that. And you know you don't mean it, Horace. Even though you've been pre-tending to be jolly all your life you needn't pretend it now with me.'

'But I *am* enjoying the play,' he said a little sheepishly. 'I don't go so often to the theatre nowadays, you know. I like a jaunt. I'm a lonely old widower and a bit of fun does me good.'

Behind his red cheeks and large round glasses and protruding chin there was fear: fear of illness, fear of being laughed at, fear of solitude at the last and, above all, fear of being left behind. Sally knew that it was true, that the world found Horace a dread-ful bore, that men at the Club slipped away as he approached, that young men laughed at him and that all his relations despised him. She was fond of him because she knew all these things.

'Lonely! Of course you're not!' she said cheerfully. 'Look here, come and have tea with Margaret and me tomorrow afternoon. I've got an afternoon off. My old Jew's going down to Brighton.'

'Oh, thank you, my dear.' Horace's glasses beamed. 'I should enjoy it immensely. I like your friend Margaret.'

'Margaret's a pet,' said Sally.

'And when is your father returning from South Africa?'

'Oh, any day now.'

'And Tom – how's Tom getting on?'

'Very well indeed. He writes some of the leaders now.'

'That's fine,' said Horace, looking proudly about him. Here he was with a splendid girl – a true representative of the young generation – and she had asked him to tea, and Cynthia, one of the smartest women in London, had invited him to the theatre, and he belonged to one of the most prominent families in England. He forgot, in his sudden exuberance, the faded gloom of his rooms in Jermyn Street, the surly indifference of his man-servant, and the rude manner with which Alfred had turned his back on him a few days ago.

He had always said: 'I don't know what it is, but there's a sort of inner happiness in me which nothing can destroy.' It wasn't quite true any longer and he had never realized that his consciousness of it had been, in the past, one of the principal reasons for his unpopularity, but it was true enough at the moment for him to look at all the men near him with a certain kindly condescension as though they had all just fallen into the water and he was there, with a strong manly hand, ready to pull them out again.

Cynthia and Adrian joined them.

('Why is it,' Sally had once asked Tom, 'that all the members of our family move about as though they had just opened public buildings?')

'I think the play's absurd,' said Cynthia. 'I never saw such people!'

'Oh, do you?' said Sally. 'There are lots of them about. I'm rather like it myself.'

She wasn't and she knew that she wasn't, but it pleased her to irritate Cynthia.

At that moment Adrian brought up a man. 'Cynthia, this is a friend of mine at the Foreign Office – Arnold Young.'

The man was perhaps about five-and-twenty, slim, tall, fair-haired. He had a weak chin, a mouth with humour and bright blue eyes. He looked weak and amiable, as though he needed caring for and would be charming if you cared for him.

Sally looked at him and her heart was moved. He instantly smiled. 'You were rather like a choir boy,' he told her afterwards, 'who was bored to death with the sermon.'

The bell rang and they turned into the passage.

'Do you like this play?' the young man asked Sally.

'Oh, frightfully!'

'Isn't Noel Coward marvellous?'

'Simply marvellous.'

And just as they reached the stalls he said to her:

'I say – I hope we meet again somewhere.'

They must have met somewhere again very shortly after this, because, about a week later, Sally had this conversation with Tom.

Tom, who was a concrete Conservative, still inhabited the rooms in Tite Street.

Tom was now forty-one years of age. He was heavily built but not stout, short and square-shouldered, with a pale, anxious, extremely kindly face. Many years of journalism had not changed him. He was dressed in a black coat, black tie, striped dark trousers always. He played golf a little, and in the summer tennis a little. He liked his work but was not enthusiastic about it. He had only two passions – Cumberland and the few people he loved – Vanessa, his father, Mary and Sally. Over these four (Vanessa's ghost was certainly one of them) he watched and worried until they would sometimes scream with annoyance. He knew this and now did all he could to hide his care for them. He pretended to be quite indifferent as to whether they came or went. He was even a little afraid of letting Vanessa's ghost know how often he thought of her! Because he cared for his father less than for the others he irritated him the least. Besides, in these days, Benjie was often abroad. But Mary and Sally were simply his whole world. When they snapped at him, as they frequently did, he would slowly flush and blame himself for being so tiresome. Curiously, in relation to the rest of the world he was rather indifferent. Men in Fleet Street both respected and liked him. He was not clever enough to rouse their jealousy and he was always ready to do someone a turn, not from sentiment but simply because he was good-natured.

But that world hardly existed for him. He would have been a better journalist if it had. When he could snatch a night or two he would hurry up to Cumberland. There was a farm between Grange and Cat Bells where he always had a bedroom. Then he would walk, generally alone. He knew the Tops like his London bedroom wallpaper.

Sally loved him and bullied him. It exasperated her that year after year he should long for Mary Worcester who would never marry him. With glee she told him one day that people said that she was going to marry the young Duke of Wrexe.

'Funny, isn't it? History repeats itself. Our great-grandmother was engaged for a while to the Duke of Wrexe of her day. The lovely Jennifer – lovely and stupid like Mary.'

However, the young Duke of Wrexe married an American girl.

'Why do you tease me about Mary, Sally?' Tom asked her once. 'I never mention her.'

'Why do you go on year after year when it's hopeless! I want you to marry a nice good girl and make me an aunt.'

'You wouldn't like it if I did,' he said truthfully.

On this particular day when Sally had tea with him in Tite Street she did not tease him. She was very affectionate. He loved her dearly when she was kind. All the best in her came out. Her eternal qualities of courage and honesty were transmuted when she was kind into a true nobility. When she was not kind she seemed sometimes hard and selfish.

But today she looked at him with eyes of love. She sat on the edge of his armchair, swinging her legs, his arm round her.

'When's Father coming home?'

'Any time now.'

'I wonder what he's been doing in South Africa. I hope he's been behaving himself. Every year I think he's getting too old to misbehave any more, but he doesn't. Vanessa managed him, but no one else ever has.' She waved her arms. 'I love him! He's such a pet with his little ruddy face and his sharp eyes and his one arm and his eagerness to fall into any scrap that's coming! He'll startle us all yet and shock the family once again before he's done.'

She looked at Tom meditatively.

'Tom, I'm going to tell you something. You'll probably hate it. I'm in love – for the first time in my life.'

His arm clutched her a little more tightly. His heart began to hammer and he told himself: 'Now be careful. Don't show her that you mind. Don't show her that you're anxious. She's a modern girl. She won't stand being warned or advised.' He was able to say very quietly:

'Who with, Sally darling?'

She stroked his head.

'That's right, my pet. You're taking it well. He's a man in the Foreign Office. He's a friend of Adrian's and his name is Arnold Young.'

'Oh yes? I don't think I've met him.'

(Inside he was saying to himself: 'Now I shall have to protect Sally without her knowing it and see that he treats her right. She thinks she knows everything about life, like all girls now, but she doesn't.')

'No, you wouldn't have. Well, he's tall and got a lovely figure and he's very fair with blue eyes. On the other hand, he has no chin and wants looking after. He has a mother who plays bridge, morning, noon and night.'

'Does he know you're in love with him? Where did you meet him?'

'I met him when I went to *The Vortex* with Cynthia. I don't think he knows I'm in love with him. We've only met twice. I'm very rude to him. I've never been in love before and it's a funny feeling.'

'Would you like to marry him?'

'Yes, I think so – if he asked me. Of course all Margaret's friends think marriage is rot nowadays. As long as you don't have a baby there's no point about marriage, they say. But I don't quite agree. It's all very well going away with a man for a weekend, but I think it would be nice to *look after* Arnold, run his home for him and everything. I expect I'm old-fashioned. Margaret says I am.'

'Is he a decent fellow?' Tom asked. 'I mean has he got a mistress somewhere or anything like that?'

'Oh no,' said Sally. 'He doesn't seem to care for girls. He's terribly under his mother's influence. That's the worst thing about him. But he isn't one of those, you know, or anything like that. Not a bit nancy. I don't say he's very fine or grand or wonderful. I'm just in love with him, that's all – here in the pit of the stomach!'

Then to Tom's astonishment she put her arms round his neck, kissed him and laid her cheek against his. She hardly ever kissed him.

'Do you know,' she said, 'we're all by ourselves – Vanessa, Father, you and I. Misfits. Still, we don't have a bad time.'

She began to roam round the room. Looking up, on a shelf above her head she saw an old green book. She stood on her toes and brought it down. She looked into it. It was a large fat book filled with rather faded writing in an old-fashioned female hand.

'What's this?' she asked.

'Oh, don't you know? That's some recollections Judith Paris

wrote when she was an old lady – or rather she dictated them.'

'How marvellous! May I read them?'

'You'd better not take them away. Father asked me to take care of them for him.'

'Why – are they shocking?'

'Not in the least. But Judith gave them to Adam, Vanessa's father, and Vanessa gave them to Father.'

'Oh, but listen, Tom! They go back ever so far – almost to the beginning of the eighteenth century.'

'Yes; Judith lived to be a hundred, you know.'

'Oh, let me take them! I'll be frightfully careful.'

He hesitated. 'Well, if you're *fearfully* careful—'

'Of course I will. I must go now.' She came to him and kissed him. 'Dear old Tom. I don't want to be sloppy, but you *are* a darling.'

He held her with his hand on her arm.

'Sally. Look here. I know you hate my being serious, but – well, what I mean is you haven't got anyone but me, in a way. Father isn't here and he wouldn't be much use. Vanessa told me to look after you.'

She smiled.

'Well – what is it?'

'You will be careful, won't you? I know girls know everything these days. Since the War they don't care *what* they do. But – you'll be careful, won't you? Tell me if you want any help about anything. Are you sure he's a decent fellow?'

'Of course he is. I can look after myself.'

After she was gone Tom walked about the room sighing. She looked such a baby. She was such a good sort. He loved her so dearly. But there you were. It wasn't the thing now to show your feelings. He had such a lot. Had he only been able to write! He sat down and soon was lost in a book of Santayana's. Now *there* was a writer!

On a day in April Adrian gave a luncheon party at his rooms in Lincoln's Inn. He invited Sally, Maurice, Maurice's young woman, Arnold Young, Miss Culloden, the well-known novelist, and her friend Miss James.

Sally hadn't known that Arnold was to be there. She had not seen him for three weeks. Adrian had asked her very casually and she had thought that very possibly she would be the only guest besides Maurice and Emily Tempest, to whom he was engaged.

When she saw Miss Culloden she was afflicted with the shyness
that she inherited from her mother. She was always sorry when
she was shy, because shyness made her rude and abrupt in self-
defence. Sally had read none of Miss Culloden's books. She read
very little and for the most part the authors whom her friend
Margaret admired – Lawrence and Aldous Huxley. She had attempted *Women in Love* and *Ulysses* and found them very tiresome. Then one evening she had found an old faded copy of
Rider Haggard's *She* tucked away on a shelf. Scornfully she had
begun it, and Margaret, coming in at one in the morning, had
found her, curled up in a corner of the sofa, entranced.

'Whatever are you reading?' said Margaret. And then, when
she saw, all she said was: 'My God!'

So Sally did not know what her real taste in books was. But she
did know that she had read nothing by Miss Culloden.

Miss Culloden was a large cheerful friendly woman who reminded Sally of one of those broad-backed white horses at the
circus, who go patiently round and round while ladies spring on
to them and off them again. Miss James was her little friend who
went with her everywhere and 'brought her out' on the subject of
her works. Sally could not conceive why Adrian had invited her,
for Adrian's taste in the Arts was severe, but it afterwards appeared that Miss Culloden had met him somewhere and had
insisted on being invited. That was why the party today was
mainly 'Family'. No celebrated persons. Miss Culloden was the
life and soul. She was one of those fortunate writers (very rare)
who are completely satisfied with everything – their own works,
their publishers, their public and everything concerning them.

'You remember, Molly,' said Miss James, 'there was that chapter about Venice in *Grapes and Thistles* – one of your best bits, I
always thought.'

Adrian changed the conversation to Sargent, who was recently
dead.

'Everyone said at the time,' said Miss James 'that the artist in
Models for Sale was intended for Sargent.'

'Well, he wasn't,' said Miss Culloden very firmly. 'He was a
composite portrait.'

'I remember you were very anxious at the time,' said Miss
James.

'Well, I'd have hated Sargent's feelings to be hurt. People are
terribly sensitive. They're hurt if they think they're *in* a book and
they're hurt if they're not.'

After a while Miss Culloden surveyed the table. 'You're quite a family party, aren't you? Netta and I feel honoured at being made one of you like this. Oh yes, I know what I wanted to say. I was hearing about a marvellous member of your family the other day, an old lady who lived to be a hundred. And she'd actually seen Napoleon just before Waterloo, and knew Disraeli and all sorts of famous people. Wouldn't she be wonderful for a novel? I wonder if you'd all mind if I wrote a book about her one day?'

'I don't think she actually *saw* Napoleon,' Adrian said. 'She was Sally's great-grandmother—'

'Was she *really?*' Miss Culloden beamed upon Sally. 'Oh, how splendid! Now do tell me!'

'If you ever *dare* to put her in a book,' Sally said, her voice trembling, 'I'll bring an action.'

Everyone was uncomfortable. That was just like the girl, Adrian thought, to take the old fool seriously. You never knew what she *would* be serious over! But of course with Benjie for a father . . .

However, Miss Culloden didn't mind in the least, but thought: 'What a strange, unusual little girl! I'll see more of her.'

Adrian changed the conversation yet once again and asked Miss Culloden whether she had been to the theatre. Had she seen *No, No, Nanette?*

'Yes, indeed – and it's simply splendid—' she began.

But Sally was miserable. There she was, making a fool of herself before Arnold. She could remember when she was seven or six or some absurd age that Vanessa had warned her about her tempers. She could see Vanessa standing by the window in the room at Hill Street, the room with the two yellow globes and the picture with 'Miss Muffet and the Spider'. Yes, Vanessa was there, wanting not to laugh, wanting to be stern and severe, but Sally had made a face and Vanessa had laughed . . .

'—and if Miss Herries *ever* forgives me,' Miss Culloden was saying, 'I shall ask her one day—'

Everyone was looking at Sally as though they expected her to do something, so she smiled at Miss Culloden, hating herself, one of those horrible smiles that you fastened on to your mouth as a dentist fastens on a gag.

And not only was Vanessa standing there, but now also Judith Paris, for, in the last few weeks, Sally had absorbed that old green book into her very blood and bones. She knew it almost by heart and it was agony to her when it stopped, stopped at one of its most thrilling moments when Judith was remembering the terrible quarrel about the fan at Christabel's Ball. Why, conceive it! Here was Sally and there at her very elbow was Judith who, going on a jaunt with her French husband to the 'Elephant and Castle', had worn a dress – 'a jaquette of pale silver-coloured silk and the bodice and underdress were of dark wine colour: I wore a hat of light straw and my shoes had silver buckles'. There was Judith in her old age dictating to her great-great-niece Jane Bellairs, who, a sweet old maiden lady with ringlets, had died as recently as 1905, and here was she, Sally, in 1925, feeling that Judith was in the very room with her, the hat of light straw perched on her red hair . . .

'I'm sure you are wrong, dear,' Miss James was saying in her firm even voice that was like a ruler drawing lines on a piece of white paper. 'It wasn't until *Love in a Garret* that America really took you to its heart. I remember so well your telling me that the Americans were fickle and that you were not going to allow yourself to be persuaded by the success of one book into thinking that it would last. You told me, I remember, that Sir Philip Gibbs said—'

'Oh, God! this is awful!' Adrian thought. He looked at Maurice, who was one of the discontented members of the family. 'A legacy of the War' Cynthia called Maurice, and it was certainly true that he had lost an arm and written a little book about Blake and got himself engaged, when he had no money at all, to a young woman who painted ladies with green hair and the oddest legs, all things – in the opinion of Cynthia and Alfred and Gordon – that might be classed together as a 'pity'.

'Oh, these awful women!' thought Adrian. 'What *can* Maurice be thinking of them?'

He had a high opinion of Maurice, who had bought a Matisse in Paris very cheap, and had had tea with James Joyce. But he was wrong about Maurice, who liked Miss Culloden very much. She reassured him. Obviously to her the world was not a bloody, menacing place in which everything and everybody was going to hell. He liked her, whereas he loathed Gordon, who also believed in life. But then Gordon believed in life because Gordon was such a wonderful fellow, and Miss Culloden believed in life because she was naturally happy, like a lark in the sky . . .

When the party was breaking up, Arnold said to Sally: 'Can I take you anywhere? I've got a car.'

Sally's heart leapt for joy.

'Yes, you can,' she said. 'Anywhere you like. I haven't got to be at the office till four.' She was so happy that, on bidding farewell, she looked up at Miss Culloden and said, smiling (this time with real if rather childlike sincerity):

'Please forgive me if I was rude.'

'Rude, my dear!' cried Miss Culloden. 'Why, you're too sweet for anything! Now you must come and have lunch with me, you really must – and I promise not to say a word about your great-aunt or whatever she was. Now what day can you come?' She produced a small silver-edged notebook. 'I'm talking to the Soroptimists on Tuesday and there's Marie Lowndes on Wednesday. Thursday I'm going out to Surbiton. Now what about Friday? Friday's quite all right. There's only the Tallboys Club Committee in the afternoon ... Now *what* about Friday?'

So Sally was engaged for Friday.

In the little car (which was bright red in colour and *very* smart) Sally said: 'Where are we going?'

'Anywhere you like.'

'Haven't you any work or anything?'

'Oh yes, but I *must* talk to you.'

'Well, let's go to the National Gallery and look at the Sargents.'

Side by side on a settee alone in the room, looking at one lovely woman after another, Sally said:

'I like Mrs Charles Hunter's hat.' Then she added: 'They're all quite unreal, aren't they?'

'Yes,' said Arnold. 'He despised women. The only thing he admired about them was their clothes. You can see how he hated his sitters. His hatred is real in the pictures even if nothing else is.'

'Yes,' said Sally, who, sitting there very meekly, wishing that her legs were a little longer and that altogether she was built on a larger scale, was nevertheless a great deal happier than any girl of her generation thought it fitting to be.

'Will you marry me?' Arnold said suddenly.

'Yes,' Sally said. 'I'd love to.'

'I'm terribly glad,' Arnold said. 'I loved you from the first moment I saw you.'

As he said this Sally thought that he'd never wanted looking after so badly as now. She longed to put her arm round him. All she said was:

'You know I'm illegitimate.'

'What on earth does that matter?'

'Have you any money, Arnold darling?'

'Well, not a lot. There's what I get in the Foreign Office and my mother makes me an allowance.'

'Your mother doesn't like me,' Sally said quickly.

'She will when she knows you, darling.'

'No, she never will. She thinks I'm Bohemian and she's heard things about Father. She knows Father and Mother weren't married. These things matter to *her* and always will.'

A shadow seemed to pass very swiftly over Arnold's face. (Poor dear! he certainly *did* need looking after!)

'She wants you to marry a fine girl of a noble family. Her generation are *like* that.'

'Well, your family's all right. It's one of the best in England.'

'I know, dear – but don't let's be snobbish. The point about our family is that there are the right ones and the wrong ones. There always have been. Cynthia Worcester and Alfred and Gordon are the right ones – but my father and I are the wrong ones, I'm afraid.'

'What nonsense you're talking, Sally darling. You're splendid! You're wonderful! And my mother isn't going to say whom I'm going to marry! It's my life, not hers!' It was the bravest thing Arnold had ever said.

'Well, you go and talk to her,' Sally said, laying her hand for a moment on his. 'I won't be engaged until you've talked to her, but I do love you frightfully and I think I always will.'

There, in that public room, in front of all the Sargent ladies, they kissed, and as he felt Sally's small body tremble against his he swore to himself that he would defy a thousand mothers . . .

'Oh, of course,' young Mr Elton was saying, 'if you prefer to read people like Galsworthy and Barrie—'

'Why shouldn't I?' said Mary Worcester. 'I don't, if you want to know. But why shouldn't I?'

'Because they're false as hell,' said young Mr Elton. Then he saw that his audience was despicable, made his adieus and departed.

'I suppose I'd better be going too,' said Tom.

'I don't think Mother will be in now. She's playing bridge and *said* she'd be back, but with bridge you never know . . .'

Tom stood in the middle of the charming little drawing-room, which in the fashion of the moment had only one French picture on its walls – a late and not-at-all-good Utrillo – a bronze by Dobson on the mantelpiece, and very little else.

Then, hiding his fear, he spoke the words that, for almost all his life, had been trembling on his lips. Why now? Was it less hopeless than ever? Certainly not. Mary, who in these days was often depressed, was very depressed indeed at the moment. An extremely agreeable handsome young man, who would have been an excellent escort to all kinds of places, had found her, like all the other agreeable young men, most appallingly dull. She didn't *want* to be dull. She was ready to admire their painters, their poets, their morals, their cynicism, their atheism, although in her heart she found all these things unpleasant, but it was of no use. They found her a bore and practically said so. She was thirty-two. Life was ghastly.

Nevertheless the words came pouring from Tom's lips.

'Mary, I can't help it. I've wanted to say this so often. You know I have. Won't you marry me? I've loved you all my life. It mightn't turn out so badly. I've got a rise. I'm doing leaders on the paper now, and there are articles too I write for the weeklies. It isn't such a bad income and, if you married me, I believe I could do ever so much better still. I would look after you – I would care for you—'

He stopped because the words choked him. He looked away from her at the Dobson bronze, a figure with thighs so enormous and a head so small that it filled him, at this moment, with terror.

Mary looked at him with great kindness. She patted the grey sofa with her hand.

'Tom, come and sit down.' He came and sat down. 'You know I can't.'

'Why not? No one has loved you so long nor so faithfully—'

'Yes, I know. But there are other things beside fidelity. One thing is that I don't love you. You know that I don't. That isn't my fault or yours. Another is that I'm frightfully stupid. If I lived with you I'd bore you terribly. Another is that I must marry someone with money. And another – perhaps the most important – is that I never would marry any member of our family.'

He came closer to her and she allowed him to take her hand.

'Then there's another. You're *too* good, you're *too* faithful. I couldn't bear anyone who loved me as you do. I know I'm not worth it, but it isn't that. No one's worth it. But I like people who are independent of me, who don't give a damn whether I'm nice to them or no. If I snap at you it's as though I struck you. You wince. But I *do* like you. I don't mean that. Only to live with you – never, dear Tom.'

She hesitated, then went on:

'You see, you're old-fashioned. You believe in God and kindness and charity and all the old things. How you can, I can't think! It's a rotten world run by stupid people. It may come right again one day, although not in our time, I expect. You're like old Horace in that, except that you really *do* believe in the things you say. You're like Vanessa, who was, I'm sure, the finest woman who ever lived, but she simply doesn't *belong* to our time.'

'You're not to say a word—' began Tom.

'There you are, you see? You won't face the facts. You never do. I didn't know Vanessa very well, but I *do* think she was splendid – much finer than any of us are! But she seems old-fashioned now – she was Victorian – and you're a bit Victorian too.'

There was a long pause. Then he said:

'What do you mean – you wouldn't marry one of the family?'

'Just what I say! I hate and loathe our family! Either we're prigs or we're mad. We are so damnably English whatever we are. Mother's all right, I suppose, but look at Father and Rosalind and Alfred and Gordon – and poor Maurice who's as cracked as can be; and there was Ellis who was mad for years; and Rose, Horace's sister, who died in the gutter. And if you go back it's just the same. Your grandfather was murdered by your great-uncle, and before that there was a Herries shot himself in London, and there was the crazy Herries in the eighteenth century. And in between the others have all been dull and self-satisfied and self-righteous. I shall marry someone or other just to get away. But I won't marry to stay.'

Tom answered slowly: 'You're wrong, Mary. Whether we've been mad or sane we've been alive. You may laugh at England, but it's the finest— Oh, don't let's talk about the family! What does it matter? I'm only half Herries! The family can't make any difference! And I won't fuss over you, Mary, really I won't. You shall have your own life. You shan't see more of me than you want to! We get on together. We have for years. You like being with me. If you married me—'

She sighed. 'It's a shame,' she said at last. 'I'm glad you've told me, though, because – now that you see that it's hopeless perhaps you'll find someone else. I've wanted for years to tell you how

hopeless it is. Of course I like you and like being with you –
sometimes. But I'm not worth it – not worth your kind of devotion, Tom. And you'd regret it like anything. I shall get fat and
plain and peevish. I haven't an idea in my head, only scraps of
other people's ideas. And I want money. It's the only thing that
can save me. With money I can make things do, perhaps. Without it—'

'If you loved me,' he said at last, 'would any of these other
things have mattered?'

'Once they wouldn't. But now – it isn't love I want but money
and comfort and safety.'

He got up. She liked him at that moment very much. She got
up and held out her hand.

'Goodbye, Tom dear,' she said.

'Goodbye,' he answered and left her.

He went back to Tite Street, sat in his room, his head between
his hands, thinking. This was awful. Mary's refusal had made no
difference to his love for her. How could it when it was part of
his vrey being? But now he had got to make terms with it, he
thought. He must manage his life henceforth so that this dead
hope did not spread like a cancer into all his energies. For, until
today, there had always been a hope – for years and years that
hope had been a light in his room. Now he must manage without
it.

He was so desperately tired that he slept in his chair, his head
forward on his breast.

He woke to find that the light had been switched on and his
father was standing there. He rubbed his eyes, for he was only
half awake, and Benjie was like a figure in a dream, standing in a
rough heather-coloured overcoat and holding on a chain a very
alert, eye-shining, panting rough-haired terrier.

'Good God!' Tom cried, jumping up.

'Yes,' said Benjie smiling. 'Here I am.'

'Why didn't you send a wire?'

'Well, you see, Tom, I didn't know when I'd arrive. As it is
I've been in the New Forest a whole week wandering about.
That's where I bought this.'

The dog, its tongue out and its brilliant deep brown eyes
almost jumping from its head, strained at the hold. The colour of
its coat was black and tan, with a fine rough white patch across
the neck.

'Why didn't you write from the New Forest?' asked Tom.

'Oh Lord, I don't know! Don't badger me. My bags are in the

other room. Isn't this a nice overcoat? I won it in a bet on the boat. Luckily the other fellow was just my size. Heavens! but I'm tired!'

He took his coat off. He was thinner and browner than ever, thought Tom, and his eyes had the same desperate brightness as the dog's. He went and poured himself out a whisky and soda. He sat on the edge of the deal table, swinging his thin legs, his little animal-like face cocked a bit over his glass. Tom had noticed that the very first thing he had looked at across the room was a large photograph of Vanessa.

'Any news?'

'Sally's engaged.'

'What!' Benjie sprang off the table. 'Sally! My little Sally! Heavens! Who to?'

'A fellow called Young – Arnold Young. He's in the Foreign Office.'

Benjie was excited. He came over to Tom, holding up his glass with his one hand.

'What's he like?'

'Oh, he's all right, I suppose. Sally thinks so. But he's just the sort of chap Sally would pick up – a bit weak, I should think, and wants looking after.'

'Any money?'

'Got a rich mother, and I should think she's bloody from what Sally says. Nor does she like Sally. She goes about everywhere, I believe, saying that there's no engagement and it's preposterous and so on.'

'Why, what has she got against my Sally?'

'Oh, I don't know.'

'Born out of wedlock, scamp of a father – that sort of thing?'

'I don't know. I haven't seen her.'

Then, very like Benjie, he drove the thing right out of his mind. He had released the dog, who now bounded all over the room, sometimes prancing on four legs at once like a young lamb, and examining everything.

'What's it's name?'

'Sam.'

'It's a shame to keep a dog like that in London.'

'I shan't keep it in London. I'm going up to Cumberland.'

'Oh, I say, are you really!' Tom's eyes shone.

Benjie put his glass down and rested his hand on Tom's shoulder.

'Like to come too?'

'Wouldn't I, though!'

'Could you get off?'

'Yes, for a bit, I think.'

Benjie looked at him critically, then drew him closer until shoulder touched shoulder.

'You're not looking any too fine.'

'Oh, I'm all right.'

Father and son gave one another a glance and each smiled.

'What's the matter? Mary turned you down?'

'Yes. How did you know?'

'Oh, I guessed. I'm a bit lonely too. South Africa was all right – interesting seeing it again after all these years. But it would have been better if Vanessa had been there.' Then he added cheerfully: 'I say – Mary's damned dull, you know.'

Tom shook his head.

'You don't understand how it is.'

'Oh, don't I?' He laughed. 'You bet I do! I've been in love with the same woman fifty years. How about that?' For a brief moment he held Tom closely to him.

'Come on and eat.'

'What about the dog?' asked Tom.

'Oh, he'll come too. I know a place where they don't mind dogs.'

Meanwhile on that same evening another member of the family was carrying on the Herries history a further stage. Arnold had taken Sally out to the theatre – to Mr Lonsdale's play *Spring Cleaning*. Sally enjoyed the play, although she thought it old-fashioned. They were having supper at 'The Gargoyle', they were dancing a little, talking a little. They were, both of them, terribly in love.

'Yes,' said Sally. 'I think all these plays about how wicked we are seem very Victorian – *East Lynne*, you know. There's *The Vortex* and *Fallen Angels* and the one tonight. All the young men are – well, you know, and the young women have monocles and Eton crops. Everyone drinks and they go to bed with one another in the bathroom. Just as they did in Mrs Henry Wood's day—'

'Well, aren't we all like that just now? Look round you, my pet, and observe.'

'There are just about forty million people,' said Sally, 'who've never heard of "The Gargoyle" or Noel Coward. They don't sleep together in the bathroom nor do their young men powder their faces.'

'What do they do then?' asked Arnold.

'They go to football matches, read the *News of the World* and sleep cosily with their wives and husbands.'

He drove her to her door. Then he asked her whether he might come in for a moment. She hesitated, for Margaret was away. But then she nodded. The sitting-room that she shared with Margaret had a very comfortable sofa, a long well-filled bookcase, a gas stove, and posters by Mr McKnight Kauffer pinned to the walls. Over the mantelpiece there was a watercolour by Charles Holmes of a black hill with a shaft of sunlight breaking on it and illuminating a field that shone with the brilliance of a missal.

'That's nice,' said Arnold. 'Where is it?'

'It's Stonethwaite Valley in Cumberland.'

There was also an old photograph of Vanessa. She was standing, her hand on a chair; her dress had the puffed sleeves and the small waist of the period. But she did not look absurd. She looked very charming indeed.

'Who's that?' Arnold asked.

'That's my mother.'

'By Jove, she was a beauty.'

'Yes, wasn't she?'

On the sofa she gathered him into her thin childish arms.

'Oh, Arnold,' she said. 'I want you to be happy!'

(She was not aware that more than a hundred years before in a ragged deserted house in Borrowdale, Judith Paris had said the same words. But Judith had not loved Vanessa's grandfather.)

He strained up to her, putting his arm up to hold her round boyish head as in a cup.

'And so do I you.' He kissed her, holding her so closely to him that their two hearts seemed to beat as one.

'Well, you can make me happy – frightfully happy—'

'Yes, darling?' Sally said, stroking his hair.

'Let me stay here tonight.'

She drew away from him, placing her hand firmly on his arm. She sat back against the corner of the sofa and looked at him.

'Well, really, Arnold!' She was suddenly frightened, frightened in a way that a modern girl with all her knowledge of life should never be.

He began to speak eagerly.

'See here, Sally. There's nothing so very dreadful. I know how to look after you. Why shouldn't we have a good time? Everyone else does. You don't believe in God or hell-fire or any of that old junk, do you?' He laughed rather nervously. He was not a practised seducer. He had never seduced anyone before. He did not feel that he was trying to seduce Sally. He simply, he thought, loved her so madly that he wanted to be as close to her as possible.

'I don't believe in hell-fire,' she said slowly. 'But I'm not sure about God. My mother believed in God.'

'Of course. So does mine. All their generation did, but ours doesn't. We're simply some sort of chemical mixture. There's no future or past or anything, so why shouldn't we enjoy ourselves? We'll only be young once, and perhaps before we're much older there'll be another war like the last and we'll all be blown to bits.'

'I think it would be nicer,' Sally said slowly, 'to wait till we're married. If we have everything now there won't be anything new to experience later on.'

'Yes, but don't you see, Sally? As we are going to be married it doesn't matter anticipating it a bit, does it?'

She knelt on the sofa, turning her little body towards him, holding his head between her hands, looking at him very seriously.

'Arnold – we *are* going to be married, aren't we?'

'But of course we are!' He moved his soft cheek against her hand.

'Yes, but what if your mother goes on hating me?'

'She doesn't hate you. She doesn't know you.'

'No, she *won't* know me! Now tell me – it's true, isn't it? – she told you that our engagement is absurd, that I'm no good and my father's no good and that she won't have her darling wee pet of an Arnold marrying a little bastard.'

'No, of course not, darling. How absurd you are!'

She jumped back from him, sprang to her feet. She stood there, small, pale-faced, but dominating.

'Now listen, Arnold! She *does* say that. You know it and I know it! And I'll tell you something – I'm as good as anyone in England, as proud, as independent. I had the grandest mother anyone ever had. There never has been, and there never will be again, anyone as fine as Vanessa. And I don't want your damned charity. And your mother can be as superior as she likes, I'm not going on to my knees and imploring, but her—'

He was in a dreadful state. He had never loved her so much as at that moment. He had in fact (and this was true) never loved anyone before.

'Sally, my sweet, my pet. We'll be married when you like. Tomorrow if you wish. Anything you say—' He caught her with his arms, carried her back to the sofa, and they lay there, close together, saying nothing, he kissing her mouth, her eyes, her hair.

And she thought: 'How terribly I love him. I'd give him any-thing. Why not be kind while one may?' As his body trembled in her arms she was infinitely touched. Oh, darling Arnold, darling, darling Arnold! Judith had loved a man outside marriage, and her own mother ... She was herself illegitimate ... and in these days, when everyone was free ... He was right ... Who knew how long their happiness might last?

Why should she not be kind? Why should she not give any-thing she could that would make him happy? She sighed, touched his cheek.

'All right, Arnold darling,' she said. 'You can stay.'

MEN AT WAR

On this evening of May 3rd, 1926, Benjie took the dog Sam out for a little exercise. He had, only the day before, returned from Morocco and found that he was plunged into a world of turmoil. Tom, who was pale and tired and plainly overworked, said that by next morning we might find ourselves plunged into Revo-lution. 'Revolution,' said Benjie; 'how absurd!' But to himself, perhaps, more than to anyone else in London it did not seem absurd, for he carried, always present with him, that picture of a ragged mob crossing a bridge, of the skaters vanishing, of a sudden rifle shot, of a square frozen and bare under a shining sun but quivering with danger, and, most tremendous of all, a multi-tude of people singing as though Paradise had come. And had Paradise come? Not at all. Murder, destruction, and the slow agonizing beginning of a new world ... So here it might be also.

But what, he inquired, had been happening? Tom entered into a slow and tortuous explanation. The Secretary of the Miners' Federation, Arthur Cook, had made the trouble. After the

Samuel Commission had recommended reduction in pay, Arthur
Cook had replied: 'Not a cent off the pay, not a minute on the
day', and all the miners of England had repeated his words with
emphasis. The Government had announced the withdrawal of
the subsidy, and on April 23rd the owners had delivered an ultimatum. Cook had not liked the terms of the ultimatum, his men
had appealed for help to the Trades Union Congress, and that
body, in its turn, had put the question of a General Strike to a
ballot of its unions.

No one supposed that the Trades Union Congress really
wanted a General Strike – of course they didn't – but they
thought that mild Mr Baldwin would capitulate. However, mild
Mr Baldwin gave a puff or two at his pipe and *didn't* capitulate.
(It happened that the Government had been making their preparations ever since 1925.) Well, then, on this very Monday,
members of the Association of Printers' Assistants working for
the *Daily Mail* had demanded the withdrawal of a leading article
entitled 'For King and Country', and the men on the *Daily
Mirror* had objected to a news article directing anti-strike volunteers to recruiting stations in the London area. The General
Council Committee thought that they would go and have a talk
with Mr Baldwin, but when they went to see him he was not
there. They were greatly surprised.

At midnight the General Strike was to begin. On the evening
of the Monday, Benjie took Sam for a little walk. It was a fine
night, and he went to Hyde Park, thinking that it would be a good
occasion for himself and Sam (who was in excellent spirits) to
listen to the Marble Arch orators. They would surely be at their
best at such a crisis and most amusingly violent. But the gates at
Hyde Park Corner were closed. A cordon of police was stationed
there, and the policemen said, quietly and coldly as though they
were thinking of something else: 'Move on there, please!'

He joined the crowd pressed against the railings, and in this
crowd no one spoke – only they gazed. Very odd, thought Benjie,
on this fine May evening, and the strike not yet declared, to
see Hyde Park a camp. Inside the railings there were fleets of
lorries and huts and tents rising. No one spoke: only Sam barked
at a chow tethered by a blue cord to the arm of a lady. Benjie
looked at the lady and saw that she was fair. Her figure was as
slim as fashion dictated figures should be (to Benjie's constant
chagrin, for he liked figures to be plump). She was wearing a
little blue hat, her hair was pale gold, and she had the face of an

innocent, rather bewildered child. Her chow was aloof and dignified. Sam, at the end of his lead, strained towards it. Benjie raised his hat.

'The Government seems to have got in first,' he said.

'Oh yes,' she answered in a voice that was all music. 'Isn't it splendid of them?'

It had been difficult, with his one arm, to raise his hat and control Sam at the same time. His movement had for a moment jerked Sam on to his hind feet. She smiled at that. After all he was seventy-one, but no one would know it. He was spare and tough as he had been at forty.

'What is going to happen, do you think?' she asked him.

They walked away together. Half an hour later she had given him her address. She had rooms, it appeared, on the Chelsea Embankment. Her name, it seemed, was Miss Grace Mortimer.

He took her, that same evening, out to supper.

When he reached his own place at three or four o'clock the following morning he was aware of a deep and bitter unhappiness. He sat on his bed in his shirt, staring at his own abasement. He was not abased because he had been friendly to Miss Mortimer. He had done no harm to the pretty lady, to whom sudden meetings with strange gentlemen were no novel affair. She had been charming, had talked of her father, a General, now deceased, had shrugged her bare shoulders at the way the world was going, had thanked him for his generous gift, had begged him to come and have tea with her on the following afternoon. He had not told her that he was over seventy, and he was certain that she had not supposed him a day more than fifty. He had been ashamed of nothing that he had done, and yet he was most utterly ashamed.

At that hour of the morning with the chilly room hostile and the town preparing in a ghastly silence for the coming day's warfare, he was as lonely an old man as the world contained. Sam was sleeping in his basket near the window, comfortable and indifferent.

'Vanessa! Vanessa! I want you, I want you! Where are you? Why aren't you here to keep me company in this damnable world?'

Then he got off to bed, pulled his shirt over his head, did his exercises. Afterwards he lay sleepless, seeing the lorry, projecting rifles like a hedgehog, hearing the wild shouts beneath the window, starting at that sudden flame on the horizon of a burning building ... He had never loved London so dearly as in those hours.

When daylight came he was still ashamed and abashed. He was saying to himself, as he had said so often before, that he was finished with women, but that statement did not lessen his abasement. He lay in bed, his head resting on his arm, wondering what was happening to the world and hating and despising himself. Here was the country tumbling into ruin and he doing nothing about it, but worse than that, here was he himself a hale and hearty old man who did nothing but wander about the world, sigh for a woman long dead, and appease his appetites in any selfish easy way that appeared to him. He was not convicted of sin. He did not feel a sinner who must hurry to repentance; but he *was* convicted of waste, of sterility.

He had achieved some kind of relation with his son, it was true, but in spite of their greater friendliness Tom still bored him. Tom wanted to mother him, and oh, God! he hated to be mothered!

And then there was Sally. Before he had left for Morocco he had taken Sally to the theatre. He could see that she was unhappy, but she wouldn't tell him anything. Just like these modern children; got no confidence in their parents. There was a gulf fixed between his generation and theirs. She was unhappy This young man of hers was no good. Benjie didn't like him, a weak backboneless kind of fellow, the sort of man women wanted to help. He was making Sally miserable, and Benjie's heart ached for her. He wanted, in fact, to be allowed to love someone – yes, although he was past seventy. He was damnably lonely and no use to anyone. Perhaps after all there was something in what Vanessa said. There was somewhere another, a secret life, and if you didn't find it you were 'left' when you were old. Oh, but he was not going to whine! He didn't care if he *was* alone. Everyone was alone if it came to that. He had better be up and doing, see what was happening to this crazy world.

While he was dressing Tom came in.

'Look here,' said Benjie. 'How can I make myself useful?'

'Oh, easily. They want volunteers for every kind of thing. You can take that car of yours and drive people to their offices. Everyone's walking. It's a sight, I can tell you. Outside the Foreign Office it's packed with people waiting to enrol. They've enlisted a hundred thousand in the Volunteer Service Corps already.

They're going to supply two million gallons of milk a day from Hyde Park. It's marvellous! England's middle class counts for something in a crisis.'

'Yes, that's what Russia hadn't got,' said Benjie. He added, smiling: 'Our family will be pleased. I bet they're all busy serving the country. Any fighting yet?' Benjie asked.

'No, I don't think so. But I dare say there will be. I've got to go down to Limehouse.'

Benjie looked out of the window. Not a soul was to be seen. He went out. Everyone was walking. He came to Birdcage Walk and found it packed with cars, crawling along four abreast. He discovered that the gates of Charing Cross railway station were locked. No one seemed to know quite what to do. It was a new world, a new life, but beneath the uncertainty he was aware of a strong united determination. He seemed to feel it in the very stones of the street. 'The Strike hasn't got a chance,' he thought. He decided that he would get his car from the garage and be of some use. He climbed on to a pirate omnibus driven by a very bright but determined young man in knickerbockers. Two young men standing beside him were going down to Dover to assist in the unloading of ships. He thought that he would offer to go with them, but an unwonted shyness stopped him. He saw an omnibus that had been in the wars, standing derelict surrounded by a large, gazing, meditative crowd. He noticed a big advertisement on its boards: 'Maurice Moscovitch: The Great Lover.'

The great lover! Well, he was done with women and all the silly, sterile, messy things in his life, and then he saw a girl near to him, swaying uncomfortably as the bus moved. A pretty girl looking defenceless and a little frightened. He wondered whether she would not like his assistance. A fat, rather breathless man near him said: 'This bloody Strike's being helped by the bloody Germans. Give you my word! Syndicate of German financiers. I happen to know. They're landing bullion on the East Coast from a small ship.'

Instantly Benjie's temper, which was easily moved, was up. Silly damned liar! He'd like to tell him so. He nearly did, but got off at the top of Knightsbridge instead. Yes, he got off and walked straight into Gordon Newmark.

'Hullo!' said Gordon. 'Why, it's Benjie!'

'Yes,' said Benjie. 'It is!'

'Isn't this splendid!' said Gordon. 'We'll show them, the dirty tykes. No one knew what England was capable of until now.'

He was swelled with elation, triumph, pride and satisfaction. His handsome face (Benjie always thought that he looked like a horse that was one of the best and smartest performers in the most famous of circuses) was carved into a proper model of all that the English ruling classes should be.

'Here!' cried Gordon. 'What are you doing to help?'

'What ought I to do?' Benjie asked modestly.

'Go down to the Mansion House. They'll soon enrol you there and tell you what to do.'

'I will,' said Benjie. 'Thanks very much.'

At the same moment his daughter Sally was saying to her employer, Mr Bimberg:

'No, thank you, Mr Bimberg. I can get home quite all right this afternoon.'

Mr Bimberg was plump, bald and very neatly dressed. She had been quite comfortable with him for a long time now, but of late – within the last few months – he had taken, it seemed, a new interest in her. He put his soft round hand on her arm, he patted her shoulder. A pity, because the job suited her.

But this morning she was too deeply involved in her own private history to consider the outside world very deeply. She was fighting with all the strength that she had to keep dreadful terror at bay. As she sat taking down Mr Bimberg's letters her thoughts were wild. Arnold had not kept his appointment last night. She had waited and waited. He had arranged to take her to *The Best People* that they might together admire the fine art of Miss Olga Lindo. She had sat in her evening frock (she had worn it only twice before) for a whole hour. How horrible that hour had been! Sally was tutored to conceal her emotions, but after that agony of suspense she had burst into tears, torn off her frock and lain on her bed. He might come. Something had kept him. Ten. Eleven. Midnight. But why had he not telephoned? In the morning there would be a letter. But there was no letter. Choking her independence, she had telephoned. He had left the house half an hour before. So, her head up, looking gravely at Mr Bimberg, she had taken down his letters.

At lunchtime, alone in the room, she had telephoned again. Arnold answered her. Her heart hammering, her voice a little breathless in spite of herself, she said:

'Arnold, whatever happened last night?' (She would forgive him whatever his excuse might be.)

'Oh, my dear, I'm too frightfully sorry.'

'No – but whatever was it? I waited and waited.'

She knew that he hesitated.

'Darling, I'll explain everything. It wasn't my fault. Really it wasn't.'

'But what *was* it?' Her knees were trembling. She steadied herself with her hand on a chair.

'I can't explain here.'

'But why didn't you telephone?'

'I couldn't. It was impossible where I was.'

'But where were you?'

'Don't be so difficult, sweet. You know how difficult it is on a telephone.'

'But we can't leave it like this. I waited and waited. It was awful. How soon can I see you?'

Again he hesitated. Then he said:

'All right. I'll come along to your place about six.'

'You *will* come?'

'Of course I will.'

A little reassured she sat there, thinking. She did not go out to lunch, but stayed there without moving. She ought not to have told him that she cared. It was the doctrine of her friends that a girl never showed that she cared for a man. She could hear Margaret saying: 'So of course I told him that if he wanted to go he could. *I* didn't mind. So off he went, and I rang up Archie and we had a grand time at Ciro's. *Of course* he came round the next day . . .'

But she wasn't quite like that. She had been Arnold's mistress for nearly a year and that did make a difference, didn't it? It made a difference in every kind of way, because Arnold now had everything he wanted while she . . . she wanted more and more. Not physical things, but for him to *want* her and to need her, to depend on her . . . The physical thing was nothing, and yet it was everything because, after it happened, Sally was his mother, his sister, his friend, his companion, while Arnold was still only Sally's lover and that not so warmly as once he had been. He should have married her. It was not perhaps very fine of him to fear so abjectly his mother, and yet Sally understood that too. *She* was not afraid of his mother, but it was natural that Arnold should be. For he was afraid of a great many things, which was partly the reason of Sally's love for him because she wanted to shelter and protect him.

As the afternoon went on her fears grew again. *Why* had he not come?

'Yes,' said Mr Bimberg. 'You had really better let me drive you home.'

'Oh no, thank you, Mr Bimberg.'

'You'll have to walk all the way, you know.'

'I'm not going very far.' (Which was untrue.)

He looked at her with his round eyes like rather damp marbles. She thought that he was going to touch her. She stood her ground. But he did not. He sighed and ambled away.

The streets were very strange. Crowds of people were walking, all rather quickly and rather silently. Was this Revolution, the kind of thing that had happened in Russia? She did not care in the least if it were. She only cared about Arnold. They all walked together like an army obeying orders. She began to be conscious of something corporate in this movement. She saw an omnibus, ran for it, stood packed in a confusion of legs and bodies, had her penny collected by a very pleasant red-faced man in a brown suit, jumped off again, stood in a side street listening to the sudden silence as though she expected to hear a gun fired or to see a flare of light against the sky. *Was* this Revolution? Would there be fighting and barricades? Perhaps Arnold would need her more if there was fighting – and she had a curious quick picture of herself as a small child, looking up from her book in the Hill Street house, seeing Ellis in the doorway and hearing him say: 'Sally, do come and play soldiers . . .' She looked at her wristwatch and hurried on.

'I mustn't show him that I care,' she thought. 'I must be quite indifferent. I *know* that he wants me. He *can't* do without me.'

When she reached the flat Arnold was already there, standing in front of the fireplace. When she saw him she loved him so dreadfully that it was all she could do not to hurry into his arms. But she did not. She went into her room, took off her small brown hat, gave her cropped hair a shake, waited for a moment staring at, but not seeing, the photograph of her mother on the mantelpiece. Then she came in, sat down, lit a cigarette and said:

'Well, you're a beauty, Arnold. Whatever did you let me down for like that last night?'

He did not move towards her, and there was a constricted movement at her heart as though a cold finger had touched it. But she looked at him quietly, noticed his tie of blue and red stripes, his pale long hands, his eager, easily startled eyes. Yes, she knew him so very well.

'Look here, darling,' he began. 'I'm most awfully sorry about last night.'

'No – but what *was* it? Of course I'd have understood if something had kept you, but even then you should have phoned, shouldn't you?'

She knew that her voice slipped into a sharper pitch, not from anger but from fear.

'Oh yes, I should. I meant to. But you see I was at home—'

'Well, you've *got* a telephone in your house, haven't you?'

'Yes. Of course. Don't be facetious, Sally . . .' He came forward a few steps, hesitated, then plunged.

('Why,' thought Sally to herself, 'he's just like a piece of seaweed, yellow, and if you pressed any part of him with your finger it would go "pop".' At the same time she wanted to take him and smooth his hair, calm his fears, give him a present, offer him a drink, lie down on the outside of the bed with him, draw his head to her breast and listen to a catalogue of his troubles. At the same time she also wanted to throw the book on the table – she even saw the title, *Jacob's Room* – at his head and stamp on his toes. She always said that he wore shoes with too shiny a toe.)

These things passed through her mind and like odds and ends caught up with a shower were drowned in the one and only insistent drumming consciousness:

'He's come to tell me something. He's not going to see me any more.'

'The fact is, Sally, I had an awful row with my mother last night.'

'Oh, did you? What about?' (But she knew quite well what about.)

'About you. She says that I have to choose.'

'Choose?'

'Yes. Between you and her.'

Sally stared at him and saw the seaweed, gold with dark brown fronds swaying in a sea pool, swaying indeterminately while the breeze ruffled the water of the pool into little angry protests.

'Oh, I see. She's told you that before.'

He went back to the fireplace, hanging his head at the gritty little fire and kicking the fender with his shoe.

'Yes, I know.' He turned round and faced her. 'Look here, Sally. I'm no good. You've got to give me up. I can't stand it. I've had more than a year of it, facing Mother. It's more than my being afraid of her. It's like being afraid of oneself. Oh! I can't explain these things, but I'm sort of inside her. Part of me thinks just as she does – I've loved you frightfully, I do love you frightfully now, but all the time I'm wanting to be right with Mother again. I thought, perhaps, she'd get over it. I thought she'd get used to the idea. But she doesn't. She hates it more and more.'

'*Why* does she hate me?' Sally asked in a small sharp voice.

'Oh, it isn't *you* that she hates! I think she'd make a fuss about my marrying anyone. She doesn't want to lose me. Of course that's all wrong and very selfish, but in a way I understand it. I don't really want to lose her either. All the same she'd get over that – because she's really an awfully good sort – if you ... if you—' He hesitated. 'You see, Sally, she's heard a lot about your father and she says that there's one side of your family that's mad and it always has been. Of course that's all rot—'

'It isn't all rot at all,' Sally interrupted. 'If you look at it from one point of view it's true, I suppose.'

'Mother isn't conventional exactly, but—'

'Does she know,' Sally interrupted, 'that I'm your mistress?'

'No, she doesn't.' He squared his shoulders. His face was so white and miserable that something in Sally cried: 'I hate both these women who are making you so unhappy. Pay no attention to either of them.' And something else in her cried: 'You're a wretched weak creature and I'm a fool to have bothered over you for a single moment.'

'To tell you the truth, Sally, I'd be afraid for her to know. She's old-fashioned about those things. And it wouldn't make it better if she did know.'

'She'd see me as the designing siren, I suppose,' Sally said. 'Well, perhaps I have been.' Then, after a pause, she asked: 'What exactly did happen last night?'

'I was dressed and just going out to you when she came into my room. She asked me where I was going and I told her. She made a most awful scene. Oh, it went on for hours! She cried. She wouldn't let me telephone or anything.'

'I see,' said Sally. 'And then?'

'Oh, then – at last—'

'You promised to give me up?'

He nodded his head.

He began a torrent of explanation. She cut him short.

'All right, Arnold. I understand perfectly.'

She went up to him, kissed him gently on the forehead, held out her hand.

'Goodbye, my dear.'

'No, but Sally—' He tried to catch her in his arms. Quietly she moved away from him, stood looking at him for a moment, then said:

'Now cut along. We've had a lovely time and I don't blame you a little bit.'

He was going to speak again but, looking at her, decided not to. He picked up his hat and coat and went out.

Into his small room at the Mansion House, Benjie was aware just as the clock struck seven of the intrusion of panic. A stout General with very bright red tabs on his shoulders was shouting down the telephone: 'Oh, but, look here, the thing's absurd! Give the feller a kick in the pants and tell him to clear out. What do you say? I can't hear ... very bad at Camden Town? Well, tell Ritchie to cut along ... Hullo! hullo! are you there, Ward? Well, why couldn't you say so? Can you hear me? Hullo! hullo!'

Benjie, his gaze idly fixed on the General's large posterior, wondered for the first time whether after all the Herries would manage to hold the fort. Everyone seemed to him to be Herries down here, and he himself, in these few days, had become civilized Herries too. He had enrolled countless men and women, urging them to do their utmost for King and Country, and as, with serious and patient faces, they had promised him to do so, he had thought: 'By God, this country is all right. The heart of this old country is sound', almost as though he had been Cynthia or Alfred or Gordon or Adrian or even old Horace, who, the night before at Cynthia's, had beamed sentimentally through his glasses and, like a bishop pronouncing the blessing, had said: 'This will go down in history. England has proved herself.' It *would* go down in history, but he was not sure whether it would be quite in the fashion that his family had desired. What was happening beyond this quiet and dignified room?

The Government in its *British Gazette* proclaimed that it was maintaining with complete success all the vital services of supply – light, food and power. Communications were improving every day. On the other hand, fifty London General omnibuses had not returned to their depot last night; at Middlesbrough some women and boys had held up a train; a motor-bus had been set on fire in East London; shops were being looted in Edinburgh; and Mr Saklatvala had been sentenced to two months' imprisonment. On this very morning the *British Gazette* announced that they had discovered that the General Council had issued a new order to 'paralyse and break down the supply of food and the necessaries of life'. How far would this spread? Every day increased the danger. He did not know that at any moment returning through Piccadilly he might not see the appearance of the lorry bristling like a hedgehog, the pieces of red cloth tied to the rifles, the windows of the Ritz smashed with machine-gun fire. 'They don't know. They haven't had the experience, any of them. They are blind to everything. Their whole social order has crumbled to pieces under their very eyes and they are not aware of it. This machinery – the machinery they've been used to so long – may vanish in a moment's temper ... They don't know it. They haven't seen it ...'

'By God!' the General was shouting into the telephone, 'tell them they've *got* to or it will be worse for them. This isn't Russia, you know.'

No, it wasn't Russia. The Herries were here. There had been no Herries in Russia. All the same ...

'Coming along, Herries?' the General said, his face beaming. 'I told the bastards where *they* got off. Coming my way? I'll drive you.'

So he sat in the back of the car with the General and discovered as, with throngs of pedestrians on every side of them, they pushed their way towards Trafalgar Square, that this fine stout kindly officer was happier than ever he had been in his life before.

'This is what I've been wanting, Herries. Teach the blighters a lesson. I'll be damned glad myself if it does come to real trouble. Give us an excuse to be rid of a few of them. That feller Saklatvala – I'd string him up on a lamp-post if I had *my* way. By God, I've never been so proud of my country as I am tonight.'

So the Herries were saying. They'd all like to string Saklatvala up on a lamp-post. Old Judith Paris, he remembered, had written in her book somewhere of seeing a boy hanged outside a butcher's shop. She hadn't liked it. But then she'd always been a queer one. And the Herries were right. Civilization had got to be kept on its feet. But suppose the old world was gone. Gone for ever and ever? Suppose on that evening when the whole world had burst out singing (he had sung like the others) they had sung the old world out of existence? Why, then *where* would the Herries be?

The town seemed to him sinister tonight. It had started to rain and soon it was a downpour. Through the rain the town was walking home. In the heart of the crowd the motor-cars, loaded with people – shopgirls, secretaries, elderly women, old men like himself – ploughed the way. The lights flared and the darkness stifled the lights. The whole town seemed on the move as though the order had been given to abandon it, and everyone was fleeing for safety. And yet they were not fleeing. That was the very last thing that they were doing. These people were defending the town, nobly, gallantly, without a thought for themselves. But what about the enemy? *He* knew how silent a thin street could be, and behind every window a concealed rifle. *He* knew how men could gather, in secret, in silence, and then, at a spoken word, the familiar places – so old, so safe, so complacent – would be filled with death. This was no melodrama. Efficient, historical fact. One machine gun at the Oxford Circus end of Regent Street, where they now were, and that crowd would turn in upon itself, would scream, cry aloud, bodies crushed into the mud, and the rain pouring down ... Oh, he was an old man! What had happened to his nerve?

'And that, my dear feller,' the General was saying, 'is the way *I'd* deal with them!'

At the top of Portland Place, where several roads meet, there was a complete confusion. Under torrential rain a mass of cars, coming from different directions, faced one another like angry herds of cattle. Horns hooted, men shouted, nothing could move. A policeman, his black cape shining in the rain, appeared as it seemed from the bowels of the earth, waving his hand. He came right up to the General's car, placing his hand on the bonnet, and Benjie saw his face, his blue eyes, his cheeks wet with the rain, and a clear, unflinching, unhesitating power of direction and order in his every movement. He seemed a giant from some other planet, impersonal and inhuman. He called out, waved his hand, and at once the disorder was composed into order: the cars separated and divided. Benjie was reassured. 'That man wasn't in Russia,' he thought. But just before his own car moved on he saw a girl, almost slipping, recovering, placing her hand for an instant against the window. It was Sally.

'Here. Let me out. Goodnight, General. See you tomorrow.'

A moment later he had caught his girl's arm.

'Hi! Sally! What are you doing here?'

The rain was driving in their faces, and the collar of her waterproof was drawn up. He held on to her arm, but he could feel that she was resisting him. They had moved away from the roar and confusion and stopped under a lamp. She looked up at him.

'Hullo, Father!' she said. 'What a coincidence!'

'The lamplight,' he thought, 'is making her look like this, and the rain. By God! something has happened to her, though. She's as though she were walking in her sleep.' Then she woke up. He felt her arm tremble under his hand, and her small pale face under the light little hat from which the rain was dripping hardened into that look of angry determination that was often exactly his own.

'I must get on,' she said. 'I'm late.'

'Where are you going?'

'Oh – I've got an engagement with a friend.'

Then her lower lip began to tremble. He saw that she was on the edge of tears. He put his arm round her.

'You haven't any engagement, my dear,' he said. 'Nor have I. I'll take you home.'

She had ceased to resist.

'All right,' she said. 'I don't care.'

They walked back to Oxford Street and not a word was spoken. Then they found an omnibus that was driven by quite an elderly party with a white moustache and was crowded with rowdy young men who were going off on some job.

'They say there's been terrible fighting in Camberwell tonight,' an elderly lady said.

'We'll protect you, ma'am,' the young men shouted. 'Lenin shan't get you.'

When they were in Sally's room and had taken off their wet things they sat opposite one another on either side of the fire.

'Margaret coming in?' Benjie asked.

'No, I don't think so,' Sally said. Then she added: 'I've nothing to give you to eat, Father. There isn't a scrap in the place.'

'That doesn't matter.' He pulled out his pipe, crossed his thin legs, leaned back. He was weary. This was a life, when all was said and done, for an old man of seventy-one, and, fit though he was, his back ached and his legs told him that they had done enough for one day.

'Look here, Sally – that was all my eye about your going anywhere. You didn't know where you were going.'

She didn't answer him.

'What's the matter?'

Still she didn't answer him, but sat up straight in her chair, her hands crossed over her knees.

'Why don't you let me take you out and give you a meal?'

'Oh, it's all right, thanks.'

He said at last: 'I wish to God Vanessa was here.' He went on to cover the silence:

'You know, Sally, we ought to see more of one another. I've been a bit shy, I dare say, but it's been my fault that I've never, in all my life, been able to get on any very sound terms with anyone except your mother. Light come and light go. And now I'm paying for it. All the same,' he said, 'you and I and Tom – we've only got one another now. You've got your young man, I suppose.'

'He's gone,' she said.

'What do you mean – he's gone?'

'Oh, he left me three or four days ago. His mother didn't like me.'

'Oh, so that's it,' said Benjie softly.

There was a long silence.

'Well, my dear,' Benjie said at last, 'I shouldn't worry about him too much. You'll find someone much better.'

'Oh, I dare say,' said Sally.

'He was frightened of his mother, wasn't he?'

'He was very fond of her. He hoped for a long time that she would get used to me. But she didn't.'

'Was it partly,' Benjie asked, 'because you had a bad lot for a father?'

'It was all of us. You and I and Vanessa and Judith Paris and your father being shot. Right away back. She seemed to know all about us. Now if I had been Rosalind or Mary it would have been all right.'

'I see,' said Benjie. 'Sins of the fathers. Very unfair, I always think.'

'She didn't know I was sleeping with Arnold,' said Sally in a dull toneless voice. 'That would only have made it worse.'

'He was a bit of a cad, I should say,' Benjie remarked. 'All the same I'm glad he didn't marry you.'

'No, he wasn't a cad at all. I understand him perfectly.'

'You'll get over it, my dear. One gets over everything. (All the same, he thought, I've never got over being without Vanessa.) I've come to the conclusion there's a lot to be said for marriage. Oh, I know, your generation don't think so, and I know that Vanessa had the hell of a time with Ellis. All the same I can see now that it would have been very pleasant if your mother and I had been married. It's the best arrangement society's discovered yet.'

'I didn't care,' Sally said, 'whether I was married to Arnold or not. I wanted to look after him. I wanted – I wanted—'

Her voice broke. She tried to recover herself, beating her hand against her knee. Her mouth moved and quivered and shook. Then she began to cry.

Benjie went over to her.

'Here, Sally – don't cry. It's all right. You've got your life in front of you. Darling – Sally darling.'

He knelt down beside her, putting his arm round her.

'These days – I didn't know anything could be so bad ... I didn't know I could miss anyone so much. I thought I knew enough not to be hurt by anything. He was so sweet ... He loved me ... he did really ...'

'There, Sally, it will be all right. Really it will. It's been my fault. I haven't been with you as I ought to be. We'll stick together now. You can tell me anything. I've been very lonely too ... Hellish ...'

He drew her with him to the other chair, a big roomy one. He sat back and, with his arm around her, wrapped her into his embrace. She was folded up in his arm like a child. She was so small that he could hold her easily. Her hand was clenched inside his. She dried her eyes and with little convulsive sobs told him everything: how Arnold had not taken her to the theatre, of their last meeting, of how, next day, she had not known what she was doing, had wandered about in the crowds, had worked for Bimberg mechanically, had not slept at all for three nights – and tonight she had not known, she had thought that perhaps now that everything was over it would be better ...

He held her more tightly, feeling her quiver against his heart.

'I know. We all go through it. It doesn't matter what generation we belong to, how much we think we know. It doesn't make any difference ...'

He thought of that last talk with Vanessa in his room, the agony and distress of letting her go. He was ashamed of his casual life, his neglect of his promise – 'I swear, Vanessa, I'll never let her go again.'

A long time after, Sally got up from her chair, went into her room and washed her face and hands.

She stood looking at him, and smiled.

'You're rather a pet,' she said. 'You've been awfully nice to me.'

'What shall we do?' he asked. 'Go out and have a meal?'

'Oh no. I don't think I could eat anything.'

'Let's see how the Strike's going.' He went to the wireless and turned it on. Someone was speaking. 'Why, it's old Baldwin!' Benjie said.

Mr Baldwin was saying:

'The Government is not fighting to lower the standard of living of the miners. That suggestion is being spread abroad. It is not true. No honest person can doubt that my whole desire is to maintain the standard of living of every worker.'

Then after a while there were the sonorous tones of Lord Oxford:

'The real victims of a general strike are what is called the common people. We should have lost all self-respect if we were to allow any section of the community, at its own will and for whatever motives, to bring to a standstill the industrial and social life of the nation. That would be to acquiesce in the substitution for Free Government of a Dictatorship. This the British People will never do.'

The voice died away. Sally's eyes were closing.

'Go on. Go to bed,' said Benjie.

He went with her into her bedroom and, with a little sigh, without taking off even her slippers, she lay down on the bed. He lay down beside her, taking her in his arm again. In a moment, her head against his waistcoat, she was asleep, and he lay there, looking with his sharp, ironical eyes at the ceiling, happier than he had been for many a year.

BELOVED MOUNTAIN

'AND now,' said Tom, 'as we cross the bridge you'll see how beautiful it is!'

'And I hope to God she will,' he thought, for he was convinced now that the visit, the visit to which he had looked forward with such eagerness, would prove a terrible failure. Sally had invited herself: he would never have dared, of himself, to ask her. He had taken his three weeks' holiday late this year – it was now early in November 1928 – and, as always, had come up to Cumberland. He wanted to be nowhere else. It was lovelier with every visit. He had taken rooms in a house, Bella Vista, on the road from Grange to Manesty, and settled in there, very happy with Mrs Zanazzi, his hostess, and Miss Zanazzi her daughter, and his books, walking every day, sometimes a long tramp, when he would be away in Eskdale, or by Esthwaite, or Patterdale for the night. He was forty-four now and used to being alone. His father was in Spain. He had friends in London, but no one whom he wished to have with him.

And then Sally had written, saying that she would come and stay with him for a week, Sally who had been so strange and hard for so long, who had scarcely seen him, who had had nothing to say to him when they were together.

He had been terribly excited. Mrs Zanazzi had arranged that Sally should have the best bedroom in the house, the room with the view out over the shelving fields to Skiddaw and the Lake.

They would have a glorious week. He and Sally would recover one another again. He knew how unhappy she was and, if he were very careful and did not show her in any way that he wanted to help her, he might give her something that she needed. Oh yes! how *very* careful he would be!

So he had gone to the station full of eager expectation. She wouldn't think much of his small Austin, but he would explain to her that it was better to have a small car in this country; so often the bridges were narrow and the roads little more than lanes . . .

When he saw her come from the train he had gone eagerly forward.

'Hullo, Tom!' she had said, and, at once (so sensitive he was) he had known that there was no change, that she was hundreds of miles away from him, that she didn't care for him, that she didn't know why she had come.

And the drive in the Austin had been terrible. She had shown no interest in anything. When he had asked her about London and had she been to parties and how was old Bimberg and Cynthia and Maurice and Margaret, she had assured him, 'Oh yes' and 'Oh no' and 'Everything's just the same'.

'And now,' he said, 'as we cross the bridge you'll see how beautiful it is!'

To himself it was exquisite. The brilliant autumn colouring was gone. Everything was silver-grey. There had been much rain and the Lake had flooded; the stream ran under the bridge in tumbling curves and circles, watched gravely by the dark hills while the last pale leaves clung to the trees; the fields were faintly green, floating in the last light of the autumn day towards the Lake like green smoke gently stirred by the wind.

He did not know that as Sally looked out she was caught by a quick apprehension. 'Something awful is going to happen. Why did I come? Whatever made me write and ask to come?' Tom's kind and serious face, his short heavy body bent a little forward at the wheel, his eagerness to make her happy . . . Oh, why was Tom always the same, why was he not some heavenly messenger who had swung down in a silver aeroplane and whispered to her: 'You have had enough of this. You have had more than two years of it. I will catch you up and we will fly, like the golden Eagle, into coloured clouds and a foaming brilliant sea'? But Tom was no heavenly messenger, and like green smoke those sleepy fields rolled into the Lake.

A pale ivory twilight lay over the landscape when Sally looked from her window. She could distinguish no detail, only overhead, above the dark shadows of clustering trees, the sky broke into spaces of dim ghostly light as though a moon were somewhere hiding. When she heard running water something caught at her heart. Since her babyhood she had never been in this country, but now it was as though something familiar were returning to her; the smell of wet leaves, the sky that revealed nothing and yet seemed a world of motion and movement, the queer windy whisper in the air, dark shapes on the horizon that were, she knew, the mountains, these things were all familiar to her and unique. No country of hill and field where she had been was like this one, and yet she could see nothing but shadow and, when a dog barked, it was a voice welcoming her, reproaching her for being so long away.

After supper when she sat opposite Tom in the sitting-room she smiled.

'I like being here, Tom,' she said. 'It's as though I'd been here before.'

'Well you have. You were born not far away from here.'

'I know. In a farm, in a storm. Mother nearly died getting to the farm. She often told me.'

'The funny thing is,' Tom said, 'that we came into this country two hundred years ago – old Rogue Herries riding a horse with his small son in front of him. Then we grew and multiplied like the Israelites. We covered the country. And now we've died away again. There are none of us here any more. But it's caught one after another of us, set its seal on us, made us influence others. Perhaps, although we haven't any of us been important, we've altered England's history by coming here.

That's what a small piece of country can do.'

'You ought to write about it, Tom,' she said, laughing and thinking that he was nicer here, sitting back, smoking his pipe, than he was anywhere else.

'I can't. That's what's so damnable.' He picked up an orange-covered book on a table near him. 'Listen to this, Sally.'

He read:

'So she let her book lie unburied and dishevelled on the ground, and watched the vast view, varied like an ocean floor this evening with the sun lightening it and the shadows darkening it. There was a village with a church tower among elm trees; a grey domed manor house in a park; a spark of light burning on some glasshouse; a farmyard with yellow corn stacks. The fields were marked with black tree clumps and beyond the fields stretched long woodlands, and there was the gleam of a river, and then hills again. In the far distance Snowdon's crags broke white among the clouds; she saw the far Scottish hills and the wild tides that swirl about the Hebrides. She listened for the sound of gun-firing out at sea. No – only the wind blew. There was no war today. Drake had gone; Nelson had gone. "And there," she thought, letting her eyes, which had been looking at these far distances, drop once more to the land beneath her, "was my land once; that Castle between the downs was mine; and all that moor running to the sea was mine". Here the landscape (it must have been some trick of the fading light) shook itself, heaped itself, let all this encumbrance of houses, castles, and woods slide off its tent-shaped sides. The bare mountains of Turkey were before her. It was blazing noon. She looked straight at the baked hillside. Goats cropped the sandy tufts at her feet. An eagle soared above her. The raucous voice of old Rustum, the gipsy, croaked in her ears, "What is your antiquity and your race, and your possessions compared with this? What do you need with four hundred bedrooms and silver lids on your dishes, and housemaids dusting?"'

'Whatever's that?' asked Sally.

'It's *Orlando,* by Virginia Woolf. Just out.'

'I don't understand a word of it. What's it mean?'

'It means what it says. You must forget things like space and time.'

'How can you?'

'You can if you like to go far enough. Do you remember in Judith's book, little Harcourt Herries reciting Pope to Francis and David at Ravenglass? Well, he's still reciting it. He's still moved by the beauty of it as I'm moved now by the beauty of this.'

'That's nonsense,' said Sally.

'Yes, if you like to think so.'

They sat in silence, quite happy, coming closer to one another with every tick of the clock.

'I'm beginning,' said Tom, 'to see why we are all so restless and unhappy. It's an awful time really. No one seems to be sure of anything any more – religion, economics, politics. So many people out of jobs. Why, look at you and me and Father. I lost Mary, you lost Arnold, Father lost Vanessa. And so in a way everyone we know seems to have lost something. But then, as the gipsy says in *Orlando*, "What do you need with four hundred bedrooms and silver lids on your dishes?" You don't need them if you discover the other world. Do you think I'm talking rot?'

'I don't understand a word that you're saying.'

'Well, I'm a failure, a complete and absolute failure. I wanted to be a good writer. I wanted to marry Mary. I adored Vanessa and she died. I wanted you and Father to need me – and you don't. Nobody needs me. So I'm a good example of times like these. I've been unhappy and restless for years. But lately I've been finding out that there's a world that has nothing to do with my needs, nothing to do with space and time, a world that has been showing me points of light for years like the sun flashing on a window, but I haven't seen ... If I could *live* in that world, Sally, it wouldn't matter how much a failure I myself was because it's so beautiful, so timeless and so alive that personal failure is of no importance at all.'

'It all sounds very vague to me,' said Sally, but looking at him with curiosity. It was so odd to see Tom with his heavy body, thick shoulders, quiet ways, bursting like this into fantasy.

'But I too can be fantastic,' she thought, realizing suddenly why it was that, through all these years, she had never been really intimate with Margaret. 'I too can be fantastic,' and, looking into the fire, she let her mind wander back over the past year, which had, in truth, been as nasty and spiteful a year as she had ever known. Later, lying in bed, unable to sleep, she reviewed it and discovered that it had already altered its colours under the

influence of this place. Like the families in Genesis, Margaret led
to Olive Stane and Olive Stane to Miss Bourchier and Miss
Bourchier to Freddie Tallent and Freddie to Freda and Freda to
William Blake and William Blake (so *very* unlike the poet!) to
Mrs Carslake-King and Mrs Carslake-King to stout, solid and
feminist Mrs Brent. At the stopping place of Mrs Brent, Sally
considered herself as a feminist. She had not been a very good
one. Why? It had seemed, after the tragedy of Arnold, the natural thing to consider men feeble and conceited and exasperating
creatures. There was, if you were to believe them, a regular war of
the sexes. All the men stood up for one another and were most
unfair about it, and all the women stood up for one another and
were not unfair about it. Some of the women were grand – Olive
Stane and Miss Bourchier for instance. They had wit, humour,
generosity, courage. What did they lack? They lacked nothing
perhaps, but spent their time altogether too much in London
literary sets, never really meeting anyone but one another, although they thought they did.

And so, not one of them reached the first class. As writers they
were clever and no more, as politicians they were not effective, as
women they left men cold and frightened.

So Sally, who had never really been at home with them because
she was not clever enough, admired them and left them. She
went for a while to parties, but this life she soon abandoned. She
disliked to be made love to in an absent-minded way, which was
what the young men did; she disliked to be drunk; she disliked
not to know the name of the hostess who was entertaining her.
She disliked to drink gin dressed (for it was, that night, an Infant
Party) as a babe-in-arms. She disliked people to take it for
granted that unless she was Lesbian she was uninteresting.
Nevertheless she did not make the mistake of supposing that the
whole of her generation were worthless. On the contrary, she
found among them enough courage, honesty and common sense
to save Europe were someone really worthwhile to get hold of it.
Only there was not, it appeared, anyone worthwhile. Lenin was
dead and Mussolini was in Italy.

So, unable to be intellectual, and weary of parties, she fell back
on the Family. There were not many just now, of her own gener-
ation. There were two distant cousins, Phyllis and Anstey
Veasey. Their great-grandfather had been the younger brother of
Anna Veasey, who had married Warren, Adam Paris' father.
Their own father was a Judge and they lived, in considerable

splendour, in Connaught Place. They were amusing, full of vitality and very sure of themselves. Then there were two girls,
Mabel and Jessie Rossiter, relations of Adrian's, who lived with a
widowed mother in Chelsea. They were nice girls but extremely
serious, believing in Bertrand Russell and determining, as soon as
they had children, to encourage them in complete freedom of
expression.

No, so far as Sally was concerned, her only friends in the
Family were poor old Horace and Maurice.

Maurice's marriage was unhappy, but just now everything
about him was unhappy. He could not forget the War. He could
not translate his experience of it into indifference and a kind of
shoulder-shrugging tolerance as did so many of his contemporaries. Sally did what she could for him and he loved
her.

No, she decided, turning over restlessly on her bed (which was
comfortable because Mrs Zanazzi knew how to please her guests),
everything for ages had been awful except her father. There the
relationship begun on the week of the Strike had bloomed. They
were friends now and always would be. They enjoyed their times
together, they understood one another, they cared for one
another. And it was Benjie who, just before he had gone away to
Spain, had suggested that she should go up to Cumberland and
stay with Tom.

'You'll find it's like going home,' he had said.

Two things still troubled her, though. One was that she could
not forget Arnold. He had married a Miss Thurston. Their pictures had been in the papers. That was all that Sally knew. But
surely by now she, a sensible modern girl who would stand no
nonsense, would have rid herself of his presence. But she could
not. He still haunted her at every turn. Little things that he had
said, done, looked, been . . .

And the other ghost was Vanessa. It was, she supposed, because she had been so unhappy that she had thought of her
mother so constantly. But it had been more than thought. In
London she had been constantly expecting that her mother
would appear. She had even at times run up the long dark staircase to her rooms, thinking – in spite of all common sense and
practical wisdom – that Vanessa would be there, waiting for her.
This was a ghost that had no sense in it at all.

So, lying restlessly on her comfortable bed, she decided that
things in general had been altogether rotten. Was there something

in what Tom had said that evening about finding another world? Was that what everyone was wanting? Was this other world ... and, so wondering, she fell asleep.

In the days that followed, the country opened up on every side of her. Miss Zanazzi was a great walker and climber. What she said was: 'There's no end to all of this, Miss Herries. You can go to the same spot every day for a year and it's always different. The changing clouds and the light, I suppose.' She explained to her that every part of the country had its own personality: Wastwater and Wasdale were savage, Windermere polite, Ullswater a fortress, Buttermere a fairytale, and every hill a separate character. Of course Scotland was bigger and finer, but the charm of this country was that it was so close together. With every step the view changed and the colours altered. 'It's mysterious, Miss Herries. You'll never come to the end of it.'

She went with Tom to Rosthwaite and saw the little hill where old Rogue Herries' house had been. There was a sturdy little stone house there now. They went to Uldale and saw the green field, on the edge of the moor, next to the church (that had not been there in the old days) where David's house had been, where Judith had grown up, where Adam had died. They climbed Ireby hill and looked over the wall at the Fortress and saw an old lady come to the dining-room window and stare at them.

'Uhland still walks there. I'm sure he does,' said Tom.

They walked up the road from Bella Vista and looked at the cottage on Cat Bells.

'Who lives there now?' Sally asked, and Tom told her that it was a novelist, none of whose books Sally had ever read.

'What a shame!' said Sally.

'Oh, I don't know,' said Tom. 'If he's happy – only I wish he hadn't painted his garage door blue.'

So everything was gone and yet everything remained. They went up from Rosthwaite to Watendlath and visited John Green's House where Judith had lived with her French husband. The sun was shining on a birch tree, and they noticed, as Dorothy Wordsworth once had noticed before them, how '*it glanced in the wind like a flying sunshiny shower*'. Tom found the place in the *Journal* that evening and read from it:

'*It was yielding to the gusty wind with all its tender twigs. The sun shone upon it, and it glanced in the wind like a flying sunshiny shower. It was a tree in shape, with stem and*

*branches, but it was like a Spirit of water. The sun went in,
and it resumed its purplish appearance, the twigs still yielding
to the wind. The other birch trees that were near it looked
bright and cheerful, but it was a creature by its own self among
them ... We went through the wood. It became fair. There
was a rainbow which spanned the lake from the island-house
to the foot of Bainriggs. The village looked populous and
beautiful. Catkins are coming out; palm trees budding; the
alder, with its plum-coloured buds.*

'Now isn't that lovely?' said Tom. 'As fine as any poem by her
brother. But how does she do it? There's hardly a word of more
than two syllables. I suppose it's partly that she was so honest –
no humbug – and partly that she found everything beautiful
from the village to the smallest twig of the birch.'

But Sally was thinking of Judith in Watendlath:

'Do you remember how she saw her husband coming down the
path, after he had been away so long, with the bright bird in the
cage? It's as though it happened while we were there.'

'Do you see?' said Tom triumphantly. 'I told you that Time's a
fallacy. Live here long enough and you'll see that that's true.'

She felt that the process going on within her was mysterious. It
was, as Benjie had told her, that she felt as though she had come
home. 'I belong here. All my friends are here – and Tom is really
a darling.' For the first time she began to forget Arnold.

But the days were passing and soon she must return to Mr
Bimberg. They decided that they would do one grand expedition
before she returned to London. But it was late in the year for
grand expeditions, and Miss Zanazzi warned them: 'The weather
can be funny this time of year. Mists, you know, and there might
even be some snow. It's turning colder.'

It was. One night there was a furious gale and the wind tore up
the valley, whipping the trees on the right of the house, lashing
the windows with rain, screaming with an exultation that Sally
found splendid as it galloped up the mountainside.

The streams began to beat like drums and, behind the uproar,
it seemed to Sally that men were shouting, calling, crying aloud.
Yet, next morning, a shining and placid peace lay over the
country. A frost glittered on the chrysanthemums and a long
stretch of purple lay above the faint browns and greens, staining
the bare trees and spreading on the hillsides in a thin grape-
coloured cloud.

'How lovely!' Sally thought. 'It is as still as a dream.'

So they decided to make their expedition next day. Tom would drive the Austin to Seathwaite, leave it there, and then they would go up Stye Head, climb Scafell and be back for supper.

Next morning the sky was flurried with little white clouds and the air was sharply cold. Miss Zanazzi told them that the glass was going down, but she thought that they would be safe for the day. They started out in splendid spirits.

As they began to walk from Seathwaite, Tom said:

'You know, Sally, I think this has been the happiest week of my life.'

Sally, who disliked very much to express her feelings, said:

'Well, that's all right.' But she added, because she could not help herself: 'We'll come up here together again, won't we? — just the two of us. And perhaps Father.'

'Oh, Father knows every inch of it. He loves it more than I do.'

Tom chattered away. He wasn't tiresome any more and Sally realized that people who need affection are natural and easy once they have got it. They are embarrassing only because they are starved. 'I don't believe I'll ever be annoyed by him again,' she thought.

They crossed the little Stockley Bridge. They had been hemmed in by Glaramara on the left and Base Brown on the right, and now the sharp precipices of Great End filled up the valley in front. It was here that Sally had the first perception that she was moving into an uncertain world.

'You'd think,' Tom said, 'that you're looking at the same hill all the time, Great End. Well, you're not — halfway between Seathwaite and Seatoller it's Lingmell you've been looking at.'

The tops did indeed appear to be different with every step, and soon after leaving Seathwaite all the civilized state of man dropped out of existence. Sour Milk Gill was a raging torrent, and the wind that blew in between crevices of rock and boulder frothed it to a spume. They were shut in by a barricade of hills, Glaramara on the left and Base Brown on the right.

'Base Brown,' Sally said. 'What a horrid name!' She was conscious of a return of the apprehension that she had felt on her drive from the station the first day. It was as though a wall of grey menacing stone rose in front of her and on the other side of it was Margaret throwing a book on to the sofa and crying: 'Well, of all the tosh!' and Humphrey Bell, the novelist, who could not

forget that the War had personally insulted him and was therefore most blameworthy (as though the War were an absconding
solicitor!) ... and the wooden barricades in Piccadilly Circus,
and Olive Stane saying: 'Oh, I'll make it a Gin and It', and poor
old Horace leading her so proudly in to dinner at the Piccadilly
Grill, and the shimmering rug with purple trees and dark green
birds on Cynthia's dining-room floor, and Adrian giving her tea
in his lovely flat with the Duncan Grant landscape that had a
barn in it of so deep an amber-red, and the green Elk of Carl
Milles, and Unamuno's *Quixote* open on the table, and the old
blind man in Piccadilly with the cup and his fat body and
patient, patient face.

'And now we climb,' said Tom. 'Not much of one. That's
Taylor Gill on the right. I've never seen it so fierce.'

She was both frightened and exhilarated. Everything seemed
fierce and angry. The wind rose as they rose. In an incredibly
short time the Borrowdale valley was far below, and at the far
end of it over Skiddaw and Blencathra a grim wall of grey cloud
was mounting but, miraculously, from some unseen place, a
tongue of sunlight struck the valley, quivering across it like a
searchlight.

At the top they were on a long boggy flat through which a
stream ran. Lingmell was in front of them and Scafell Pike to the
left of it.

Now they were truly in no-man's-land. A bird flew slowly,
mournfully over their heads, but otherwise there was no sign of
life at all. Sally saw that Tom was now completely happy, and in
his happiness he had a strong family likeness to Benjie and Vanessa when *they* were happy. The true Tom appeared as he never
appeared in London. His body did not seem thick and clumsy
now. Sally was surprised at the easy agility with which he moved.
In London, when he was in a room, you always watched with
anxiety lest he should knock something over. Every teacup was in
peril from him, but now you felt that he could shoulder a mountain with safety. He began to sing slightly out of tune, and soon
Sally began to sing too. Really this was a splendid day.

They reached Stye Head Tarn and, as they did so, a pale sun,
dim and veiled, burst the grey paper tissue of the clouds and
shivered with a queer iridescent shimmer on the black surface of
the little Tarn.

It was very cold, but they found shelter behind a rock on the
slope of Green Gable, looked down to the Tarn across the flat,

and ate their luncheon. This was the very wildest scenery that Sally had ever beheld. There were of course many places of far greater splendour and terror in the world, but the intimacy and closeness of this place made it personal, as though it had a quality of fairy tale – one of the old stories when the hero reaches at last his perilous destiny, and from the dark rock, the shaggy tree, the awful enemy emerges. And yet, with this peril there was also friendliness. Gable with its great rounded top is the least hostile of all mountains, and the whole plateau with its stream and tarn is kind because it has been there for so long and is so sure of its passive power.

'It was just above here,' Tom said, 'by the other tarn that David fought his duel.' As he spoke a ripple of light ran across the Tarn. Everything sprang to life as though it answered him, then fell into a waiting silence again.

It was too cold to remain long where they were and, after they had eaten, they walked slowly up the slope to Esk House. Here, when Sally looked down into Eskdale, she gave a cry. The valley was sombre today and for many an observer would have seemed little more than a tumble of rock and rough grass falling away to the sea, but at that moment, more than any other, Sally felt that she had come home. On every side of her the hills rose darkly to a dark sky and there was a strength in all those uncouth forms, a strength and patience, a wildness controlled, that seemed to her lovelier than anything that she had ever known. She caught Tom's arm and held it. 'I feel as though I could never be unhappy again,' she said.

Then they started slowly to climb the Scafell Pike track. The wind was rising, murmuring from top to top, and the faint illumination of the pale sun vanished suddenly as though at a word of command. The heavy sky seemed to move down in a lower band above their heads.

'I thought I felt a flake of snow on my cheek,' Sally said.

'Oh, that's all right. It won't come to anything. Not at this time of year,' Tom answered. 'We'll soon be at the top.'

They turned slightly to the right up a green slope which was not difficult, although beyond them the eastern buttress of the Pike had a grim look.

Tom glanced at his wristwatch. It was later than he had supposed; you grew, through the summer, accustomed to Summer Time and fancied that the light would last for ever. There should, for a long while yet, be enough, but it was a dark day and, in the last half-hour, had grown very swiftly darker.

Instinctively he hurried his steps and Sally called out: 'It's all right, isn't it? We've got plenty of time, haven't we?' She had to shout, for the wind whistled in the air.

'Quite all right,' Tom called cheerfully.

She wondered whether she should suggest that they should turn back. Something would have frightened her had she not been determined against any sort of fright. Where Tom could go she could, and she knew that these were little hills and that, in summer, the slopes of Scafell were like a picnic party. Nevertheless she had spent her life in the town; this was the first day she had ever had on the Tops and her feet ached: if she stopped for a moment the wind cut her with its cold, and again she felt some lingering flakes of snow against her cheek. But more than these things it was the changed aspect of the scene that alarmed her. The hills appeared to have doubled their size, and instead of that entire intimacy they had drawn apart, lifting black shoulders and ragged edges against a sky that seemed now to be alive with dark motion, piles of cloud with the dead whiteness of dried bones running before grey unsubstantial vapour. Still, where Tom could go she could.

He stopped for her and held out his hand.

'We'll go back if you like,' he said.

'Oh no – we're near the top, aren't we?'

'Very near – and then we can run down in five minutes.'

When the Pillar and Steeple came into view Tom, who had often climbed this before, although always in fine weather, knew that the rest of the way would be rough.

'Look here, Sally. Perhaps we'd better go back.'

'Oh no. Let's do it now we're here.'

The path now was a confusion of rough stones and the wind seemed to meet them from every quarter. A scurry came up from the valley and with it a whirl of light wet snow.

Then, a moment later, from no quarter at all as it seemed, a blinding storm came upon them. There was snow in it and a wet mist, and it appeared to Tom that from below them, on either side, a boiling vapour of mist rushed, edging up.

They were near the top, he supposed, but he could see nothing. He caught Sally close to him. It was as though they both of them stood on air. If there was ground it rocked under their feet, and the gale lashed their faces like the sharp whip of stinging twigs.

With his arm round her he shouted: 'I say, this is awful. We must find shelter somewhere. This will soon be over.'

The trouble was that it had become suddenly unknown country. He knew that on the one side of the Pike it was easy descent but on the other it was rock and precipice. They moved forward together, step by step, stumbling over the stones. The wind was ferocious, and the sleet came in waves as though it were timed and obeyed a certain rhythm.

Sally stumbled, she caught his arm, then put her hand up to his wet cheek.

'I wanted to be sure you were there. It's the cold – it takes your breath.'

He must shelter her somewhere until this gust was over, but he feared the whirling dusk that was now so thick and clinging that he was like a blind man who, sightless, yet knows his room is turning about him. He felt that all round them was a world of rock; stones that would seem minute enough in daylight now were gigantic. It was as though one single rock moved with them, maliciously keeping them company.

'Look here, Sally,' he said. 'What do you think we had best do? I don't know where we're going. If I could tell which way the wind's blowing, but it seems to be coming in every direction at once. If we could touch grass we'd be all right, but the fact is I'm afraid of striking the rocks on the other side.'

She scarcely heard him. She was ready for anything, but this icy wind was beyond any experience that she had ever had. The cold seemed to grip and shake her; she had never known before what it was to lose faith in her own power of resistance, but her knees were cut with the cold, her head was buffeted and her hands were gone.

She realized that they were beginning to descend, and the wind now leapt up from below, tugging at their feet.

They turned the edge of a rock and the gale fell. Bending down Tom saw that the rock was arched. He groped round it and found that within the curve there was shelter.

He manoeuvred her into its hollow. 'Look here. Rest your back against the rock here. Now bend your knees up. You can't feel the wind now.'

The relief was blessed, for the roar had died, her face was no longer torn with the cold, and she could feel her hands again. He knelt in front of her.

'Thank God. You'll be all right there till the storm's over. I don't suppose it will last long. It doesn't as a rule when it gets up as suddenly as that.'

She pulled at his arm.

'Come in too.'

'No. There isn't room. I'll stay here for a moment. Any second the mist can blow away and I'll see where we are.'

She held on to his arm.

'Tom, you're grand – as though you'd been in storms all your life. You are a brick to look after me.'

She'd never before praised him for looking after her. Well, that was something. He had his back to the gale and it was as though a thudding door of ice beat upon it. He turned sideways, lying up partly against her. So they waited, her hand on his knee.

He thought: 'Now I can do something. I'll see that she's all right. We'll be laughing at this in half an hour.'

Then the sleet changed to snow. There was a thin bright whiteness in the air; in spite of its thinness the general scene was no clearer. Nothing was more visible, but now the touch of the storm was soft and clinging while the wind moaned through the web with a singing, whining cry.

They waited. Time passed.

A long time later Tom put his hand on Sally's. It was icily cold. He bent forward and touched her cheek. She whispered, in a voice strangely unlike hers: 'It's fearfully cold, Tom.'

He took off his waterproof and his coat, then his thick woollen jersey.

'Look here. You've got to put this on.'

She acquiesced, and he knew at once that she was already sleepy with the cold, for, in her own self, she would have eagerly resisted.

But, as he held her against himself, he felt her whole body slacken. He pulled the jersey over her head, then laid his coat over her, thrusting her hands into its pockets. Lastly he took the waterproof and wrapped it round her legs. He saw that she was curled up well within the shelter of the rock. Her head fell forward and he knew that she was asleep ...

He waited. His eyes stared into the dancing thickness that now had, it seemed, a rosy light at its heart. Then the cold bit him; he felt its teeth at his breast and a warm breath against his nostrils as though out of the storm an animal had crept to him for shelter ...

Circles, crimson at the edge with centres of dazzling white, floated, hung, fell slowly and rose like telephone wires seen from a train. With a terrific effort he rose to his feet, tottered, balanced himself against the rock.

'Sally!' he whispered. 'Are you all right, Sally?' But of course she was all right. He smiled. Then he moved. He must move or he would sleep.

He stumbled into the light. For now the world broke into a dazzling brightness. He stepped forward to greet it. Soft hands caressed his cheeks and someone stroked his eyes.

Oh! Beloved Mountain! This place of light and splendour for which all his life long he had been waiting. Beloved Mountain that took him now with the warm strong caressing grasp of a friend.

Everywhere about him, from the height and the depth, voices greeted him. A light, more splendid than any that he had ever known, dazzled his closing eyes. He ran forward and fell.

Later a shepherd, looking for his sheep, found Sally sleeping under the rock.

FAMILY DINNER

Two events of the first importance occurred during the spring of 1930 in the Herries family: one was the marriage on April 3rd at St Margaret's, Westminster, of Miss Mary Worcester to the Marquis of Paignton, the other was Alfred's removal to a very fine and spacious house in Hampstead. The two events were celebrated by the dinner that Alfred gave in the second week of May.

Lord Paignton was thirty-eight years of age when he invited Mary to be his Machioness, and Mary was thirty-seven, so there was, as Adrian said, 'nothing of the virginal about it'. All the same Paignton was a very 'virginal' man. He had proposed to other ladies on other occasions and had twice been engaged, but none of these young women had been serious enough for him. He was himself intensely serious-minded as was right and proper in the future Duke of Wendover. He was famous for his conversational opening gambit: 'If you are at all interested in my opinion of the matter ...' He had excellent views on Tariffs, Russia, Unemployment, the Pound Sterling, Agriculture, and Why Our Churches are Empty Today. But the interesting thing about him, Adrian thought, was that he was marrying Mary for her brains rather than her looks.

She still *had* looks of a statuary, marble kind and he would, Adrian thought, be just the man to admire her poise, her immobility and air of watching repose. But no, her brain was the lure. 'I'm marrying the most intelligent woman in England,' he told his friends at the Bendish, a little club in St James's Street where gatherings were held of so solemn a character that it was said that a waiter there hung himself because he hadn't seen anyone smile for five years.

'Does he think her clever because she never says anything?' Adrian wondered. But it did not matter. The Herries were pleased, although by this time they were so firmly the backbone of England that nothing either here or there could make any difference. Cynthia was now entirely swallowed up in the waters of bridge, and was so weary with her long, long efforts to find a husband for Mary that, when at last Mary found a husband for herself, she had very little to say about it.

Rosalind had married a Major Brigstock, a good fellow who luckily believed the Herries the finest family in the world, and Peile had died two years ago from influenza, so Cynthia thought now of nothing at all but Contract, her two Pekinese – Tang and Ming – and her figure, which was by this time as thin and sharp as a needle.

Alfred bought the house in Hampstead because money was very uncertain and he thought it not a bad thing to have it in property. He also saw quite clearly that very soon now the West End would be nothing but shops, and anyone who had to live in London would be ashamed to be seen south of St John's Wood. He had also a very charming house near Sunningdale and, although he was sixty-eight this year, played a good game of golf every weekend. He was a dry self-satisfied old man with supreme confidence in himself and a contempt for anyone who was not practical. But he could be generous and, when his liver was in good order, could tell a funny story. He was now deeply disappointed with his son, Maurice, who settled down to nothing, thought that he could write poetry, and led a cat-and-dog life with his wife. On the other hand his girl, Clara, had married a rich American, Borden Wadsworth, and entertained regally in Chicago.

His only trouble had been that he liked women around him. Men as companions were only useful for golf and an exchange of opinions about the money market. Quite recently this lack in his life had been strangely supplied. A woman called Abigail Hill, a single lady of forty or so, occupied the position of his best friend. The true story of Abigail Hill was a most interesting one and her influence on the whole Herries family already promised to be remarkable. She was a tall, gaunt, extremely fashionable woman who had lived, it appeared, for many years at Eastbourne with an old invalid father. He, dying, had left her a large sum of money. She had come to London and had taken a large flat at the Marble Arch end of Park Lane. Here she entertained, and with excellent taste. She was, apparently, cynical and plain-spoken. She won a reputation for her caustic remarks. But, cynical or no, she became attached to old Alfred and he to her.

No one suggested for a moment that there was anything lyrical in their association. They were quite simply good friends and, whenever he gave a dinner party, it became natural to find her there as hostess. She furnished the Hampstead house for him and did it magnificently. She was modern and not too modern. This was a good time, because of the growing distress in Europe and America, for 'picking up' things cheaply, and Alfred's pictures and furniture were worth seeing. He, like the other Herries before him, cared little or nothing for property as such. It was beneath a Herries' dignity to think that he or she was valuable because of possessions. All Alfred wanted was that he should be suitably surrounded. Abigail Hill saw that it was so.

In a short time she had made her mark on every member of the family. She played bridge with Cynthia, talking cynically with Adrian, flattered Gordon, soothed Maurice and even bothered to have tea with poor old Horace. The only members of the family with whom she could do nothing at all were Benjie and Sally. She complained of them to Alfred.

'They're too sentimental for anything. They don't seem like your relations.'

'Benjie's always been a bad lot,' Alfred said, 'and his daughter takes after him.'

Nevertheless they were invited to the dinner party because Abigail said that what was needed was a little variety. 'You're all a little monotonous in the lump,' she said, 'and as a matter of fact I rather like Benjie even though he detests me.'

Adrian was engaged and therefore a young Frenchman and his sister, children of a French financier of importance to Alfred, were invited. They were the only two present who were not of the family circle, and only at the last moment was it discovered that the Frenchman, Raymond Herriot, was blind – blinded in the War.

'That's uncomfortable,' Alfred said. 'I wish we hadn't asked them.'

'I believe he's no trouble at all,' Abigail answered. 'He goes about quite a lot.'

The dinner party consisted of Alfred, Miss Hill, Gordon, Maurice and his wife, Tim Bellairs the painter, now living in London, Phyllis and Anstey Veasey, Mary and Lord Paignton, Cynthia, Rosalind (her husband the Major was away in Ireland), Raymond and Mlle Herriot, Sally and Benjie.

Yes, quite a party.

Sally had given up her rooms and lived with her father ever since Tom's death. They got on splendidly. Now as she drove him up to Hampstead in her small bright-red Midget he thought of her with most loving affection. Tom's death had wrought a deep change in her. It was strange, when you thought of it, that Tom had longed all his life to do something for those he loved, and in his death, which had seemed accidental, gratuitous, he had at last won his desire. Well, perhaps nothing was gratuitous, accidental . . .

But with Sally it was the three great unhappinesses of her life – her mother's death, her misadventure with Arnold, and Tom's death – that made her what she now was, and Benjie, looking at her, knowing her courage, common sense, humour and kindness, wondered whether ever in England before there had been created a generation so fine and intelligent as this one of Sally's. 'Only we can't tell yet. We can't tell for another twenty years.'

Assembled in Alfred's grand drawing-room, panelled, the splendid possessor of three lovely Canalettos, they found that they were the last of the party.

'Yes, this is the Family!' Benjie thought, sarcastically, for whenever he encountered them en masse he disliked them, felt that they disliked him and would be relieved if he left them for ever. He could never be with the Family without, at the same time, feeling rather ashamed of himself, and that made him both shy and angry. For they had succeeded. As a family (for they had only the slenderest connexion with the Scottish Herries) in 1730 they had been nothing, in 1780 a little something, in 1820 people were aware of them, in 1850 they counted, in 1900 they were prominent, and now in 1930 they were everywhere . . . And yet for him now as he looked at them, the romantic period of their history was closing. They no longer fought, struggled, were

jealous, cruel ... Cynthia, Alfred, Mary, Gordon, Rosalind ...
They had become part of England, and future history would be
made of struggles elsewhere and of another kind.

'We've been interesting for just two hundred years,' he
thought. 'Sally and Maurice and the Veasey children may make
history, but it will be a new chapter.'

For he was old enough now to be a philosopher and have a
perspective. And, physically, he was in splendid condition for an
old boy who had led a life, had only one arm and was seventy-five
years of age.

They marched into the dining-room. The long shining table
was lit by tall candles in high silver candlesticks. Over the mantelpiece was a fine picture by John of a peasant in a blue cloak
standing against a background of dark hills.

Benjie threw his eye around him. He was himself sitting between Phyllis Veasey and a grave dark girl with charming intelligent eyes whose name he did not know.

'Who is it on the other side of me?' he asked Phyllis under
cover of the opening babble of conversation.

'French,' said Phyllis. 'A Mademoiselle Herriot. That's her
brother over there next to Sally. He's blind.'

He looked across and saw, next to Abigail Hill, a young man
with black hair and a strong watchful face. He was watchful
because he was blind. His brown eyes gazed with a steady absorbed look in front of him and, instead of appearing sightless,
had a penetration that seemed to go beyond all things physical, to
rest calmly on a world where everything was quiet, profound and
real ...

'Vanessa's world,' Benjie thought.

Phyllis Veasey began at once to talk. She found it difficult to
keep still. She was gay, bright, like a coloured bird who had just
risen from the water and must shake the sparkling drops from its
wings.

She had been reading a very long book called *Kristin Lavransdatter*.

'I'm afraid you don't read much, Cousin Benjie.'

'No, not very much. I never have. I'm an old man and want to
see everything I can before my time's up. I like a man called
Hudson who writes about birds.'

'Well, *Kirstin Lavransdatter*'s miles long. I like long books,
don't you? You go on and on and on. I got this one from the
Book Society.

'What's the Book Society?'

'Oh, five writers tell you what to read.'

'Why five?'

'Oh, I don't know. Five's better than one. Not so prejudiced.'

'I should have thought five times as prejudiced. Anyway, what do you want anyone to tell you what to read for? Why don't you decide for yourself?'

'Oh, there isn't any time and one wants to read what other people are reading.'

'The girl's an idiot,' thought Benjie crossly. He found that his temper rose just as quickly as ever it had done in spite of his seventy-five years. So he turned to Mlle Herriot and found, to his relief, that she talked perfect English. For his own French was nothing to be proud of.

'Don't we seem odd to you,' he asked her; 'an English family all dining together inside the security of one's own fortress?'

'In what way – odd?' She had a most charming smile, gay and gentle. And, at that same moment, he realized that young Herriot, turning to Sally, had the same smile.

'Well, the French and English never really understand one another, do they? And never will. You are so realistic. We so sentimental. Now we don't look sentimental, all of us in this room. But I assure that we are. We believe devoutly in our fairy stories – the splendour of England, that hearts are more than coronets, although we are the most snobbish people on earth, and that the Herries family is unique in the world for its qualities of good sense, patriotism and fine breeding.'

'But I think England *is* splendid – and France too. You see, I also am romantic. I think, too, that England has her faults, her stupidities, and France too. Now is not that a safe answer?'

'Very safe,' he said, smiling. 'That is your brother – on the other side to the left, sitting next to my daughter?'

'Yes. Oh, is that your daughter? What an amusing face she has! And how intelligent! She is more alive than anyone else here.' Then she hurried on lest he should think that she was paying obvious compliments. 'My brother, Raymond, was blinded in the War. He is the most splendid man I know. His blindness hardly handicaps him at all. He lives in Berlin. He is working with a group of other young men for international understanding.'

'Not an easy job,' said Benjie.

'No,' Mlle Herriot said eagerly. 'But most interesting. He gets on with the Germans splendidly. His blindness seems to help him. He says that people accept from him, because he is blind, more than they would from others.'

'Perhaps it would be better if some more of us were blind. We might see farther.'

Just then he caught Sally's eyes and they smiled at one another. He could see that she was very happy. She was. She had not looked forward with great pleasure to this party. Big dinners were out of fashion now, family groups were out of fashion, and old Alfred and Abigail were not, in Sally's view, an interesting pair.

She had left Bimberg long ago, and now (because work she must) was helping the famous Lady Connington in an effort to rouse the people of England to an interest in the League of Nations. Benjie was not rich, nor had she inherited anything from Ellis who, in a will written shortly after Vanessa's flight, had left his wealth first to the Miss Trents, and at their death to charities. Lady Connington was a fool, and the League was not, at times, very encouraging. It attracted so many half-baked nitwits. Nevertheless, Sally was staunch to it. It was, Mr Rack-Bunden told her, 'the only thing there is. Without it our civilization is ruined. We go tottering into the abyss.' So Sally held on to the League, went about the country in her MG speaking for it, and explained to Sheffield and Newark and Doncaster what Gandhi's theory was and what was happening in China . . .

She had felt, in fact, after Tom's death that she must try and do some good somewhere. Do something for him in return, as it were. She had long ago understood that among her friends the worst thing that anyone could say about anyone else was that he or she was trying to do good. It was simply too 'shy-making', in the phrase of the moment. At the same time she realized that many of them did a great deal of good in a humorous, cynical, and 'Don't you dare to remind me of it' manner. She hid her motives; she tried to pretend that Lady Connington and the League satisfied her. She was exceedingly lonely. Here she was, twenty-six years of age, and she had achieved nothing whatever except to be considered, by a stupid, ignorant woman, not good enough for a weak, helpless young man. She had lost her mother, her lover and her brother. She was beginning to wonder, in spite of her twentieth-century materialism, whether there was not a curse on her father and herself. They were, both of them, so plainly isolated, by themselves, not wanted.

So she had not looked forward to the dinner. Abigail Hill did not like her; Alfred thought that she encouraged Maurice in his discontents; Gordon disliked her; the Veaseys were afraid of her.

And then, when, after five minutes, a few words with Gordon, her neighbour on her left, had convinced her that their hatred of one another was entirely mutual, she turned to her other companion. He turned also with eyes that seemed to stare with a gentle, almost indecent obstinacy into her heart. They did, indeed, make her heart suddenly beat with a confusing rapidity. She did not know him. She had never seen him before. Why did he stare at her so? And then she saw that his hands moved round his plate, touched, very quickly, the knives and forks. Then that his duck had been cut into small pieces before it was brought to him. She knew now why his eyes so unwinkingly stared.

'You must forgive me,' she heard him say (his English was good, but it had a pleasing accent). 'I am blind, and so am unable to be sure whether you want to talk with me or not. I don't even know whether you are looking my way.'

She touched his sleeve with her hand.

'I am looking your way and I want to talk.'

'*Bien.* Thank you very much. I don't often go to dinner parties because I'm afraid of being tiresome. Or, rather, I did not. But now my life in Berlin includes a good deal of – what do you say? – sociability, so I am getting over my shyness.'

'Oh, do you live in Berlin?' asked Sally.

'Yes. I was blinded in the War. At Verdun. I was in hospital for two years and did not know what to do with myself. And then in '25 a very brilliant man, a Swiss, a Monsieur Holthois, formed an International Group with members in all the principal cities in Europe – also in America. His purpose was no more than for internationally-minded people of every country to be in constant communication – see each other often, you know. We are all patriots, but internationalists as well – not so difficult as you suppose. Our only rules are that we deliberately discuss everything – are not afraid to – and that we see one another's point of view and that we allow no difference of opinion to separate us. We are growing very fast, and I am the principal French representative in Berlin. But, dear me, I talk only of myself. Tell me about *you*. What are you called? Who are you? Married or single? What do you look like? You see, you must help me.'

'Yes,' said Sally, rather breathlessly. 'I want to. My name is Sally Herries. I'm twenty-six years of age and not married. I help

Lady Connington about the League of Nations, or try to, but I'm not much use, I'm afraid. My father is sitting on the other side of the table. He and I live together. My mother died when I was only nine, but I've never forgotten her. She was the finest person I've ever known. Then my only brother was killed in Cumberland in 1928 – we were caught in a storm on a mountain, and he kept me warm by wrapping his clothes round me, and he fell over a rock and was stunned and died of the cold.'

'I'm very sorry,' said Raymond Herriot.

'Yes, so you see there's nothing very special about *me*.'

'Would you please tell me,' he asked, dropping his voice a little, 'if you do not think it impertinent, what you look like?'

'Of course.' She laughed. 'Shall I be honest? I'd better be, because other people would tell you the truth if I didn't. I'm short and small. I've got dark-brown hair – short, you know – a sallow complexion which I try to brighten up a bit, a snub nose and not a very pretty mouth. On the other hand, my eyes are nice. I've quite good hands and very small feet – only my legs are too short.'

'Thank you,' he said.

She did not know whether she had been impertinent and too familiar or too hasty. She had never had an experience like this before. She felt that she would tell him anything.

'One thing you have not said. You have a beautiful voice.'

'My voice isn't bad,' she answered recklessly, 'when I'm in a good mood. I have an awful temper. I get that from Father, and then, when I lose it, my temper I mean, my voice has a nasty edge to it.' She added, thinking that it was time to get away from the personal: 'What a wonderful thing to do! To work like that in Berlin! I do envy you.'

'Come and work there too,' he said earnestly.

'Oh, do you think I could?'

'Why not?' Then he added: 'I feel as though we were meant to meet tonight. Please let this not be our last meeting.'

'Oh no!' Sally said. 'Oh no! We'll meet as often as you like!'

It was after that that her eyes met Benjie's and they smiled.

By this time everyone was very gay. Alfred's wines were excellent, and that spirit of self-confidence that always developed when members of the family were for a time together was now most happily universal.

Dessert came and Alfred made a little speech (he liked to make speeches).

'I welcome you all to my new house and I hope you will be

very often here. It may seem ostentatious for an old man like me to have a new house, but it is intended for the Family as much as for myself. I don't know whether some of you remember,' he went on. 'It is a long time ago but it is very vivid to myself. At the beginning of the War, before Gordon and Maurice went to the Front, some of you had dinner with me, and Sally here, who was only a child then, lit a candle which we passed from one to another. I must say that I think there has been something that has held us all together through all the hard times, and will, I am convinced, hold us together still.

'I would like to say how pleased I am that on this occasion we should have with us two friends from that splendid country so grandly our ally then and now. I drink to the health of glorious France.'

Everyone stood up and drank.

Then young Herriot replied. He said only a few words:

'I must thank you very much on behalf of my country and my sister and myself. We are all proud of the countries to which we belong: it is, I think, that pride, one of the finest things in human nature – but with it there must go something as fine – pride in the whole world, a desire to see the whole world one, so that so dreadful a thing as war can never return to the world again.'

Then there was a very regrettable episode – one of those episodes for ever recurring in the Herries history. Young Anstey Veasey had been drinking. He was a nice young fellow. Everyone agreed about that afterwards. What he did any one of his generation might have done. Luckily the little affair was very soon over. Fifty years ago there would have been more lasting consequences; a hundred years ago perhaps a family feud as in the famous ancient story of poor Christabel and the fan. But now – well, now in the twentieth century the Herries temper had mellowed, the hysterical element in it had been taught discipline.

What occurred was that young Veasey cried out:

'It's all very well for you fellows who had all the fun to say that there's to be no war – but what about us? Are we never to have any adventure again? Oh, I know what all you older people say – that the last war was horrible and the next one will be worse. But how do we know? You had some pretty good times in the War. I've heard lots of fellows say it was the best time in their lives. Of course men were killed and wounded, but we've all got to die some time, and after all it's the greatest adventure can happen to anybody. I don't think another war would be such a bad thing when all's said and done. It would clear up some of the mess the world's in anyway. After all, you can't stop men fighting. It's their nature to fight, and I think a jolly old scrap with the Russians or someone would do a lot of good.'

He was, of course, only a boy who had had too much to drink, and his silly nonsense should have passed unnoticed.

But what happened was that before anyone else could speak Maurice had sprung to his feet.

'It's a damnable lie!' he cried out. He stood there, white-faced, his thin nervous body trembling, his voice pitched high. 'I say it's a lie! My God, is this what we went through all that hell for? Only a few years and already there are fools daring to talk that blasphemy. We suffered – we suffered, millions of us, men, women and children suffered. We went through hell day after day, month after month, year after year. Our lives have been wrecked. We've lost everything, friends, faith, belief in God ... We've been ruined, been damned ... The only hope we've ever had is that at least what we suffered has made it impossible for anyone to suffer that way again. And now, now – already – it's coming back, and men dare to say they want it back – and all we've been through has been no good. Anyone, anyone – who helps another war is damned. They're enemies of their fellow-men – the cruellest—'

He stopped short and, to everyone's horror, burst into tears. He stood there, his hand in front of his face, sobbing. Then, with a gesture of his hand, his head down, he turned and hurried from the room.

There was a moment's silence then. Rosalind got up and went after him.

'I say,' said young Anstey, 'I'm most awfully sorry—'

Paignton broke in: 'If anyone cares to hear what I think—'

Conversation became general. It was very unpleasant, of course, and especially because there were those present who were not English and because Maurice was Alfred's son.

But all the concentrated common sense of the Family rose like a calming breeze. They knew nowadays – Alfred and Cynthia and Gordon and Mary – how to deal with that sort of hysteria. Poor Maurice! It was natural enough that he should feel as he did, but at his age he should really have learnt to control his emotions – one of the first and most important lessons.

Soon everyone was easy again. Rosalind returned and said that Maurice had gone.

'He's been having his headaches,' she explained.

'Poor boy!' Alfred said. 'You'd think that after all these years his nerves would be in better control. I think of sending him to Vienna. There's a doctor there . . .'

Later, in a corner of the drawing-room under the enchanting Canaletto that showed the gondolas like butterflies, the figures of rose and silver in their masks crossing the bridge, Sally had some last words with Raymond Herriot. His sister was saying her farewells to Alfred.

They were partly concealed from the others by the folds of a curtain of dark shadowed gold. He put out his hand and touched her sleeve. Then his hand rested firmly on her arm.

'It is,' he said, 'how do you say? – up to you, our next meeting.'

'I will meet you whenever and wherever you like,' she answered.

'Well, then – why not tomorrow? Would you come and have tea, perhaps, with my sister and me? We are at Brown's Hotel.'

'Yes. Of course I will.'

'*Bien*. And then one day perhaps you will come to Berlin?'

'Yes, if you would like me to.'

'Yes, I would like you to.' His face broke into a beautiful smile. 'I have a perfect picture of you in my mind – already.'

'You must ask your sister,' Sally answered.

'I don't need to ask anyone.' Then very abruptly he said: 'Now, how old do you suppose I am?'

'Oh—' She moved a little closer to him. 'I should say – thirty-five.'

'Yes – thirty-six. And still a bachelor. Strange, is it not?'

'I don't know. I'm not married either.'

'Yes, that is very strange. But you are ten years younger.'

She said nothing.

With that quiet gentle voice that she found extremely charming he asked her: 'That is not too great a difference in years – between us?'

'No. Of course not.'

She could not help herself. She put out her hand and caught his. He held hers and then, raising it, kissed it.

She sat beside her father, driving the car, staring in front of her.

'Did you enjoy it?' he asked her.

'Yes, Father – most awfully.'

'Pity Maurice had that outburst. I hate to see a man cry. Poor chap. If I had my way, I'd give young Anstey a good leathering. Rotten manners with Herriot there!'

'Lots of his generation think like that.'

'Do they? More fools they.' He looked at her. 'You seemed to get on well with that young Frenchman.'

'Yes. I'm going to tea with him and his sister tomorrow.'

Then she added:

'He thinks I might help him in their work in Berlin.'

'Oh, does he? Would you like to?'

'Yes, I think I would.'

He sighed, but so gently that Sally did not hear him. So that was Sally's destiny. Just what she wanted, someone with her own notions, someone for her to look after. But blind? And a Frenchman?

Sally would manage it. She'd found what she wanted. And so the last link was broken. He would be alone now – the last of the bad Herries. They were all good now . . .

Cumberland.

It was as though the Derwent suddenly broke in a torrent across Piccadilly and Glaramara rose towering above the Ritz.

He put his hand on Sally's knee.

'He looks a fine fellow,' he said, 'if you want to know what I think about it. And when you're married I shall take the next train for Keswick.'

Sally laughed.

'Father, how ridiculous! I don't know that he even likes me.'

'No, but I do. Look out! You nearly had that taxi.'

When later she kissed him goodnight she was quite especially affectionate, and, after she had gone to bed, he sat for a long while looking at Vanessa's photograph.

'Sentimental,' he said, knocking his pipe out on the fender. 'That's what I've become! All the same – Vanessa would have approved of that man. He's her sort.'

COUNTRY FAIR

SALLY HERRIES was engaged to Raymond Herriot just
before Christmas 1930. They were married in London at a regis-
ter office on the 14th of November, 1931.

In February 1932 Benjie paid them a visit in Berlin. He stayed
with them for a fortnight and had a grand time. The more he saw
of young Herriot the better he liked him, and Sally's happiness
was founded on excellent reason. The only thing that distressed
him was that she might become *too* international. She had, in a
few weeks, the troubles of Germany at her fingertips. She knew
what Schleicher wanted, what Hitler said, and what the German
Princes were doing. She also knew why the middle-class German
was starving. At the same time she understood to a marvel what
were the difficulties of M. Herriot (no relation at all of her husband's). She understood the ambitions of Mussolini, the restlessness of the Japanese, the confusion of the Chinese, why America
would be Democratic before the end of the year and just how far
the Five Year Plan had collapsed.

'You know,' said Benjie when he had listened to a great deal of
discussion, 'I'm so old now that none of these things seem to me
of the least importance.' He patted Sally on the shoulder. 'When
you are busy making the new world don't forget there's such a
place as Cumberland.'

'There you are, you see,' Sally said. 'How can you say that the
state of the world isn't important? How can Cumberland be
happy if there isn't enough to eat?'

'Temporary questions, temporary questions,' Benjie murmured. 'There's something more important.'

'What is?' She put her arm around his neck. He was such a
fine old man, so sturdy on his legs, so irascible and jolly and
indignant and easily placated, so strong and healthy for his
years.

'I don't know – and I don't care, as long as I know that something is—'

He kissed her. They were saying farewell. It was in the
Kurfürstendamm on a Sunday evening. They had been seeing
Jannings' new film *Tempest* with the new actress Anna Sten. She
had excited Benjie and he would have given anything to be able

to kiss her adorable and most mysterious almond eyes. 'But I don't kiss women any more,' he told Sally. 'Or hardly ever. Old men of my age should look and not touch.'

He was catching the night train to the Hook, and in the train he felt for a while very melancholy. The last link was gone. Not only was he alone now, but the romantic history of the Herries family was closed and finished. He would go back to Cumberland and never leave it till he died. He hated to feel lonely, so he thought of Vanessa. He opened a novel that he had been told was good – *The Fountain*, by Charles Morgan. He was very quickly interested in it although he seldom read novels. 'Sort of book Vanessa would like,' he thought.

In the summer he did a ridiculous thing. He bought a caravan. He had been staying for some days near Canterbury and he saw this thing. It looked very handsome, for it was painted a deep crimson and the curtains of the little windows were pink and white. It contained, he discovered, every possible requirement and was remarkably cheap because its owner had just been declared bankrupt. He found that his motor-car could be attached to it very comfortably. He bought it there and then. Afterwards he had the difficult task of explaining its advantages to John Holly. Holly was his man, chauffeur, cook, bottle-washer, general factotum, friend and perpetual grumbler, who had been with him now for several years. He was a small spindle-shanked man whose appearance was never as smart as Benjie wished. He had a passion for engines, dogs and women. He was sober and industrious, but an abominable gossip and a Bolshevik in politics. He was no respecter of persons.

'Gor blimey! What do you want a bloody caravan for?'

'To live in.'

'To live in? You can't live in a caravan in London.'

'We aren't going to live in London any more, John. We shall probably never see it again. We are going up to Cumberland to stay.'

'Oh, well, you can take my notice. I'm not going to live in the country.'

'All right. You can go as soon as you like.'

'I damned well would go it if weren't for the dog.'

'There you are, you see. It's much better for Sam to live in the country. You're always saying he doesn't get enough exercise.'

Sam, although he was no longer young, behaved like a puppy still. Holly adored him.

'A caravan! My God! We *will* look a couple of pretties!'

Before his departure for Cumberland, Benjie went round and said goodbye to the Family. They were none of them sorry to see him go, as he very well knew. Only Horace perhaps regretted him, which was ironic, because Benjie had for so long detested Horace. However, Sally had cared for him, and now at the age of seventy-four he put up, on the whole, a very brave show.

He was as optimistic as ever and even quoted 'God's in His heaven: All's right with the world'.

'Everything possible is wrong with it,' said Benjie, 'and we're two old derelicts who ought to have been dead long ago.'

'I'm remarkably well,' Horace said, 'except for a twinge of rheumatism. I'll come up and visit you in Cumberland one day.'

'I'm damned if you will,' thought Benjie. However, he shook him warmly by the hand.

Cynthia's Pekinese barked at him until he was deafened (he detested toy dogs), Alfred showed him round the Hampstead garden, Gordon slapped him on the back, Adrian, who was now a weary dyspeptic pessimist, said to him:

'I'll be sorry not to see you about, Benjie. I've always admired you, you know.'

'Admired me? Good God – why?'

'You've always gone your way. I might have done once. And then you make me think of Vanessa, the only woman I ever really loved.'

They weren't so bad, he thought, when he'd said goodbye to all of them. He had fought them all his life and was glad to be rid of them, but he saw quite clearly their integrity, their wholesome common sense, their loyalty to their own beliefs.

'There have to be the imaginative and the unimaginative, but they'll never understand one another. And that's that.'

August this year was luckily a dry fine month. Everyone was astonished – as everyone in England always is when holidays are fine – astonished and a little indignant, as though England were posing slightly. The caravan was most amusing. Benjie, Holly, and Sam all slept in the little cupboard behind the general living-room unless the nights were dry, when Holly and Sam slept out of doors. But they got on very well. They were all quiet and unemotional sleepers.

There was a great deal of traffic and general holiday rejoicing. Holly, as was the way of his kind, was extremely proud of the caravan in the presence of strangers and very indignant about it to Benjie.

'Blasted old inculus' (he meant 'incubus'). 'It wobbles like an old fat woman.' But he talked to everyone – farmers, hotel girls, motor-cyclists and the AA officials.

'Ought to have one,' Benjie heard him say. 'Everyone will be having them soon. They say we all got to economize. Well, what about it? Most economic thing going.'

When they were north of Doncaster, Benjie's spirits rose higher and higher. For one thing, he'd never felt better in his life.

'What do you think of me for seventy-seven?' he would ask John. He would be doing his exercises, half stripped on a sunny morning outside the caravan, while Sam sniffed for rabbits under the hedge.

'Take care you don't catch no cold,' John would say. 'And another thing. Don't let no women see you. They'll think we're nudists.' Then, with a reluctant and cynical smile he would add: 'You've got a fine brown skin – like the gipsies. I'm a gipsy now myself, I reckon, but I can't get that brown colour. Lived too much in towns.'

On the whole they found that farmers, proprietors of fields, publicans and sinners were all very agreeable to them. A very good thing, for Benjie's temper was up in a minute.

'I give what I get – always have. Give me sauce and you'll know it.'

Then, when they came to Kendal, it was just like going home. There's a brow of the hill between Kendal and Windermere when the waters of the Lake are suddenly revealed. It is as though a door were unlocked. Benjie caught Holly's shoulder. 'Look at that, John, and thank your Maker.'

'Here, look out – I'll be driving into the hedge.'

'Well, stop the damned thing.'

All three of them got out and looked at the Promised Land.

'The only woman I ever loved lived with me there. I was born there. My children were born there.'

'What!' said Holly, astonished, 'Only loved one woman in your life? A gay old man like you? Glad I can't say the same.'

But Benjie didn't answer.

They came into Keswick on a fine summer's afternoon and attracted a good deal of attention, but they didn't stop there. They found that on the following day, September 3rd, were the Braithwaite Games, so Benjie said that they should pitch their caravan in a field nearby. They found a nice green one under the beneficent shadow of Grisedale and Grasmoor. They found a farmer too, a little bouncing man with a red face.

At first he was very angry and then he was very friendly. He told them to clear out and Benjie spoke his mind. Holly, watching them, found it amusing to see two little men so furious.

'What I want to know,' Benjie remarked, 'is why you can't keep a civil tongue in your head. We aren't doing any harm to your blasted field. I'll pay you properly, if that's your trouble.'

'Aye,' said the farmer, 'but I don't want your money or your company either.'

Then he smiled. Benjie was standing, with his hat off, his blue eyes fiery as though he wanted nothing better than a hand-to-hand encounter.

'It's a nice day,' the farmer said. 'You can stay if you like – and I don't want your money either.'

They shook hands and finally sat down on the steps of the caravan and had a chat.

And next morning it came down a regular posh. Not only did it pour, but the wind blew, and not only did the wind blow, but it blew from every possible direction. The whole world was a turmoil of wind and water. But Braithwaite people are not easily discouraged. Have they not the finest village hall for entertainments in the County? No, they are not the people to be defeated. Benjie in a mackintosh and Sam with his stiff short hair blown sideways and one ear over one eye (all the work of the wind) went along to see how things were progressing. They discovered that the tea tent had just been blown down for the third time. Everyone was in a state of mind. As the *Mid-Cumberland Herald* afterwards neatly put it: '*All morning wind and rain conspired to make conditions as unpleasant as possible. While the caterers were manfully struggling to erect a marquee in which to feed the spectators, and had to give up after the third attempt, the would-be spectators were debating in their own minds whether to attend or not. The secretary and committee were wondering what the patrons would do.*'

Benjie and Sam assisted for a while and then, feeling that they were wet enough for anything, went back to the caravan. Here, for the rest of the morning, while the rain beat and the wind blew, Benjie wrote to Sally and entertained Sam.

Sam had never grown up. He had not changed in the slightest since Benjie first had him; the white and brown curls of his coat were as charming as ever, his brown eyes as alive and his body as packed with quivering and alert eagerness. A small rubber ball was everything that he needed to turn life from a dull sombre business into a matter of quicksilver daring and adventure.

The caravan apartment was small and loaded with cooking things, clothes, a rifle, a broken-down armchair, a radio and a number of books. In and out of this confusion Benjie and Sam enjoyed an entertainment that had surprise for motive and confusion for its atmosphere. As the ball bounced man and dog rushed for it together. Benjie was, after many years of practice, up to every kind of guile, but Sam knew all the tricks. He stood, the stump of his tail erect and quivering, his eyes on fire, his nose twitching, his right forleg trembling! Had you shouted in his ear that the Last Trumpet was at hand it would have been no matter. Benjie, his arm raised, held the ball: he feinted towards the cooking stove and Sam's body swung in that direction but his eyes did not shift. He knew, too, of that. When the ball bounced his teeth snapped, he sprang and Benjie grabbed. Books fell, tins rattled, clothes swung in mid-air. Benjie was on his belly groping under the chair while Sam, in no way deceived in this manoeuvre, knowing well that Benjie had the ball set in his hand, stayed, his legs parted, his eyes burning, his complete soul (for he had one) concentrated . . .

Meanwhile the rain lashed the caravan, sweeping across the field in sheeted splendour.

'Not bad for seventy-seven!' Benjie cried to Holly, who, standing disdainful in his yellow ulster, saw his master with his shirt open, on his knees, and dust on his cheeks.

'Gawd, what weather!' Holly said.

Nevertheless in the afternoon they ventured and had their reward. Cumberland people are not to be shaken by the weather and there was a good crowd. The weather in fact shook its head and decided to improve. The rain when it did come was a deluge, but in between the sun shone and the colours came out like a picture show. The clouds rushed like mad things across the sky. The sun fell, as though the light had been spilled from a bucket, on to Skiddaw and at once the purple glow of the heather on its flanks spread like a living shadow from shoulder to shoulder while above and below it the green turf almost hurt the eye with its brightness. Then, on the other side of the valley you might see (if you had time to notice) the dark clouds piling up over the tops and swinging through Coledale Pass like an army. On the clouds came and a minute later the rain poured down. The army marched on to invade Keswick and out the sun came again. If you cared to watch you could time the showers and run for shelter.

In the heavens it was all life and movement and on the ground the same stir and constant change.

Benjie drew a deep breath of satisfaction. When he saw Mr Bowe, the secretary, who for weeks past had been saying to all and sundry, 'Now, whatever you do you mustn't miss Braithwaite', hastening hither and thither to see that everything was up to time, his own excitement was intense. He was home again; he was among friends again; he was breathing the air that was, by right of birth, his own. He knew exactly what they were all feeling and wanting and hoping, and he felt and wanted and hoped with them. The clouds were his and the grass was his and the surrounding watching hills.

In a noisy crowd the bookies shouted their odds. In spite of the rain the booths with sweets and apples and ginger-beer drove their trade. Dogs were everywhere, and children and anxious parents, farmers and Keswick citizens and men from Cockermouth and Bassenthwaite, from Under Skiddaw and Threlkeld and Grange and Portinscale.

Soon everything was in motion. In the centre of the field were the wrestlers, the twelve-stoners and the ten-stoners, moving slowly round and round one another with a heavy foot-treading solemnity. Round and round they would go, arms out, broad backs straining; they would seem thus like nothing so much as dreamers who find that meditation on the Deity, the character of the soil they tread, the end of their mysterious destinies, can be obtained best by this slow motion and steady contemplation. Western mystics with their proper sacred ceremonies – and then suddenly there is a start, a jerk, they are locked in one another's arms like lovers, a face stares to the sky, a vast leg stiffens, there is a fall.

'Aye, it will be Blakeney's for sartain,' a farmer beside Benjie prophesied to him gravely.

'Why Blakeney?'

'Didn't ye know? Three times nine and a half stone world champion – aye. He's a lad . . .'

Round the circle of the field the flat-racers were already arranging themselves.

But it was the Puppy Trail that made Benjie's heart beat. In his excitement he dragged Holly by the arm, for that man of a mechanical world was gazing about him with an urban civilized scorn for these poor countrymen who knew nothing better than, on a wet day, to strip almost to the buff and circle slowly round and round on a sodden field.

Benjie might be seventy-seven, but he ran as well as anyone, climbed the low wall and hurried into the next field to see the start of the Trail. At the sight of the men holding the hounds in leash, at the sight of those same hounds straining, yelping, pulling, he sniffed the air as though he were an old hound himself. The last hound trail he had seen he had been with Vanessa over Loweswater way. It had been a glorious day, he remembered, so hot that they had sheltered together under a thick tree for the cool. Afterwards they had had their tea there, and the shadows, moving to the sound of the running beck at their side, had slowly covered the slope of the hill. Then the first stars had come out and, as they had walked together to the road, they had heard from the tent the softened buzzing of the band . . .

Now, as he waited, the sun flashed between the showers, the two trail runners with their 'pads' of old stockings and their aniseed bottles came running in, someone dashed down the flag and the hounds were off. Up the hill, over the wall, across the field and they were lost to view.

After they were gone there was a strange silence, a vacuum, a sense of 'How shall we fill in the time until they're back again?' Some with field glasses climbed the slope, others stood in clusters discussing results – was it to be Starlight or Saturn or Meg?

They turned back for a brief while to watch the wrestling. As Benjie stopped before the wall he felt his shoulder gripped. Against him, at his shoulder, was a strong old man roughly dressed in corduroys, black-haired, bent a little in the back. It was George Endicott.

Benjie stared, feeling that now at this very moment he was wrestling with George on that parlour floor while on the staircase above the woman stood with the candle, waiting, listening . . . that moment that had twisted wrongly his whole life. He had not seen Endicott for ten years.

'George!'

'Funny to see you here. Thought you were dead.'

'And you.'

'Come and have a drink.' It was as though they had never parted. It was his last struggle. He was old and Endicott was old, but there was time yet, old though they were, for the ancient shabbiness, wildness, waste, to return. George had still his black

eyes, his loose mouth, that animal lurch of his shoulders. Benjie
had never gone away with George yet but that one thing had led
to another and so, step by step, into a craziness that ended in
darkness. Odd how, at the sight of George, that other world
crowded in, all the women he had kissed, the silly toasts he had
drunk, the fights he had fought, yes, and further back through
that, striking back to some old scene when a woman had been
sold in a tent and on a starlit night swords had flashed, and on
the Carlisle wall, befogged, he had seen the Devil . . . Had he or
had he not? Was this the last touch of that wild hand on his
shoulder?

It seemed that it was, for, smiling he said:

'No, George, thank you.'

'What?' said George. 'Too old for drinking?'

'Oh, I'll drink with you some time, but I'm waiting for the
hounds to come back.'

George's dark eyes covered him. They studied him from head
to toe.

'You look fit.'

'Yes, very fit, thanks. Only a stiffness in my right leg once and
again. Are you staying round here?'

'No. I'm moving on to Carlisle tonight. Like to come?'

'What are you doing there?'

'Eh, I don't know. Meeting a man about a dog, you know.'

There flamed up in him one final tempting impulse. He was
lonely. He had thought, this morning, that it was happiness
enough wandering the country with John and Sam. But he
didn't know . . . It would be good to be with George again, to
move, ancient though he was, into that old world without law,
without order, without discipline.

Then he shook his head.

'Afraid I can't.'

'Sure?'

'Yes. Can't get away.'

'So long then. See you some time.'

George vanished and Benjie turned back to see where Holly
was, almost as though he needed protection.

He felt an intense relief as though a weight that had hampered
him for years past were gone. A relief – and a loneliness – for he
was old and, in the final stage of life, with every added year our
fellows recede from us further.

He waited on the edge of the hill, watching for the first sight of the hounds. To John at his side he explained the mysteries. 'You must be careful laying your trail. You've got to watch out that it isn't too dangerous for the hounds, loose scree or falling boulders, and your curve mustn't have too small a radius because a clever hound will pick up the scent on the far side and cut off a troublesome corner. There are hounds who'll be half a mile ahead of the others again and again simply by cutting off corners. And you've got to watch out for men stopping them on the course, giving them meat or something. Once you have betting, men will do anything. All the same it's the prettiest thing in the world, this and sheepdog trials. You've come to the right country, John.'

'Well – so you say—'

Then, suddenly, there was a shout. Over the top of Barrow the hounds had been sighted. Against the dark green slopes you could see the light-coloured bodies moving now in spots of colour, hidden by trees and then, in a moment, all in a line along the fell path.

'There they are!' 'I can see Starlight!' 'Meg's in front.' 'Nay, that's Saturn!'

Now they had all vanished behind a knoll. There was a breathless pause and then a great shout as two hounds appeared abreast.

' 'Tis Starlight!'

'Nay – Saturn! Saturn! Saturn!'

'Yes, 'tis Starlight all right!'

Then down, down the hill they came all together over the hedge on to the roadway. At the last fence Saturn was over first, Starlight just behind him.

'By God! a grand finish!' someone shouted.

But the hullabaloo was now fearful, for all the trainers, with signals perfectly understood by their hounds, let them know, with plenty of time to spare, where the finishing point may be. The shrieks, yells, howls, whistles can be heard a mile away, and some farmer driving his cart up a country lane catches the din on the breeze and will say:

'Yes. Yon's t'hound trail at Braithwaite.'

Starlight and Saturn were up the field together, and had either slackened victory would have been to the other. Did they slacken? Not they. It was one of the best finishes for years – and Saturn has it, two lengths ahead of Starlight, and Granite close behind him.

The rain came, the rain cleared. A lovely mellow light covered the earth. It was the final of the twelve-stone wrestling – Bob Greatouse of Arradfoot had been beaten in the final of the twelve-stone by Blakeney the champion, but the other Greatouse of Arradfoot was in the final of the ten-stone. He was wrestling Pickthall of Cleator Moor. All men held their breath. The two figures went round and round. There was a clinch. Everyone said 'Ah!' Pickthall was thrown with a back-heel ... Round and round again. Another 'Ah!' Pickthall was thrown again, this time with a twist off the breast and a back-heel. Arradfoot could be proud that night.

Benjie was talking, he did not know to whom. Everyone was friendly. Someone asked him whence he had come.

'Oh, from the South.'

And where would he be going to?

'I'm going nowhere. I'm staying here.'

'Aye. Nowt t'matter wi' Coomberland.'

He turned back and looked up to Barrow.

Yes, he was staying. He'd come home.

THE EAGLE

DURING the following weeks Benjie made a number of friends. He was of course quickly recognized, the wild young Herries who had grown up with his mother at Ireby, married beneath him, disappeared and then returned with a woman not his wife, shut himself up for years in Newlands.

In the old days you might have disapproved or not disapproved according to your own uprightness of character. But now he was no longer a danger. They called him 'an old rascal' but his teeth were drawn now. He was a character with his one arm, his short-cropped grey curly hair, face like a russet apple, bright blue eyes. And he liked to wear blue shirts and dark-red ties. So he went about the district with his caravan and his man and his dog.

'Yes, he's a rascal,' they'd say, but he never did any harm to anyone. He had a fiery temper and knocked a man down in Cockermouth in spite of his seventy-seven years, but for the most part he was ready to be friendly.

Moreover he was a Herries, and the Herries, although they'd been queer, had been fond of the district for two hundred years.

And Judith Paris was still remembered everywhere – Madame with her white hair and grand manner and walking stick.

'Glad you've come back,' they said to Benjie, and they were.

There came a day in October at last when he thought he would pitch his caravan in a field by Rosthwaite. He had avoided this for weeks: some superstitious feeling had kept him away, as though that ride from Keswick to Rosthwaite and his sitting down there at the spot where the Herries house had once been under the shadow of Watendlath, had some kind of deep spiritual significance for him. He didn't believe much in deep spiritual significances, but there came times when a man stopped, like Balaam's ass, at a shadow on the path. He had been everywhere else – Uldale and Ireby and Cat Bells and Newlands and Seascale and Gosforth and Ravensglass – all the places that kept anything of Vanessa in their atmosphere – but he had held back from Rosthwaite.

'When I get there I'm closing the chapter.' He didn't know, but he thought it likely that he would end his days in Borrowdale. 'And then that's the finish. No Herries here any more.'

But at last, on a lovely October day, he decided to move on to Rosthwaite. First he had luncheon at the Keswick Hotel, by invitation, with two Keswick residents – Mr Glossop and Mr Blane. Mr Glossop was a bachelor, a large stout cheery man in very baggy knickerbockers. He lived in St John's in the Vale and was reputed to be wealthy. Mr Blane was married, had three children and a small income. He had been a Civil Servant in India, had retired, and suffered from a very uncertain digestion. It was natural that Glossop should be an optimist and Blane a pessimist, but Benjie was interested to realize, as luncheon continued, how very much less certain he was of his opinions than were these two much younger men. He neither knew so certainly nor cared so deeply.

As they walked into the hotel Glossop was waving his arms and crying out cheerily: 'What a day! What a grand day! How are you, Mrs Wivell? Pretty good? That's right ... No, Herries, as I was saying, this Government seems to be doing wonderfully well. Of course we know that people complain about the Means Test, but what I say is this ...'

Later at luncheon Mr Blane looked at Mr Glossop with his rather dim yellow-shadowed eyes and remarked, nervously crumbling his bread:

'Really, Glossop, how you dare! Why, we're on the edge of the pit, the whole lot of us. Hasn't sterling gone down eight points this very week? Isn't France at her wits' end to balance her budget? Haven't those poor fellows from all parts of the country been marching through the rain all this week on London? Isn't Germany making ready to fight Poland and shan't we be compelled because of Locarno to join in? Really, Glossop, I'd be surprised if I didn't know you. Don't be taken in by him, Mr Herries. His spirits go down to zero the minute he has the toothache—'

'Ha! Bah!' said Glossop. 'You're a defeatist, Blane, that's what you are! One would think that a little bit of discomfort means the ruin of the universe! Why, after the Napoleonic Wars they had thirty years of distress and a much worse distress than anything we're experiencing. You just wait until after the American election. You'll be surprised how quickly things settle themselves and trade's booming again! Why, Davis from America is over here consulting with MacDonald this very week, and I see that today's *Express* says ...'

So it went on and Benjie's mind wandered. He pulled himself together to say once:

'I've got a girl in Berlin working on international affairs.'

'And what does she tell you?' said Glossop, beaming.

'Well, she doesn't tell me anything.'

And then a little later he remarked:

'Of course if they can teach Doyle to defend himself he'll make some of those Americans look silly. He's a natural fighter.'

But he couldn't really attend. Mr Blane cried:

'Well, I simply can't understand you, Glossop. There you are, fiddling while Rome is burning.' He added, 'We're bewildered, that's what we all are. Don't feel safe any more.'

And Benjie thought: 'That's his generation – afraid. Sally's isn't.'

He remarked: 'Sam had a great fight yesterday in Penrith. One of those nasty Aberdeens some fat woman was carrying round with her. He just about bit its ear off.'

And after luncheon he could not fix his mind on serious matters. It was as though this going out to Rosthwaite were all-absorbing. They went with him through the town to where his caravan was pitched between the Art School and Crosthwaite Church. All the way along Mr Glossop was heartily greeting his friends.

'How are you, Mrs Fox?' and then in parenthesis, 'Mrs Fox of

Fawe Park – American – charming woman', or 'Fine day, Mrs Johnson. How's the boy getting on at Cambridge?' or 'How do, Todd', or 'How are you, Lewin?' as a clergyman passed them on a bicycle. While on the other hand Mr Blane recognized no one, nor did he see the charm of the old tower nor the break between the houses which showed the sunlit hills rolling through the mortar and brick, nor the white cloud like a gigantic bird's nest perched between the breasts of Skiddaw. He saw nothing, for, defeated once again by the malignant obstinacy of his greed, he had eaten Cumberland ham at luncheon, the richest ham in the world and for him the most destructive. Already he saw pain and discomfort approaching him down the road . . .

Before Benjie sat with Holly in the front of the motor that pulled the caravan (and Sam on his knee) he shouted to Mr Blane:

'Try five-minute exercises with your colon like that fellow I read about in a book the other day. Nothing like it for the digestion.' But Mr Blane didn't think that funny. He assumed a rather sinister air.

As they sputtered off along Main Street, Benjie was cross.

'Having a joke with some men about their digestion is as serious as joking about their religion.'

'That's all right,' said Holly, 'if your stomach's behaving proper. You've got a stomach like an ostrich. I've always said so.'

As usual, they were a sensation in the town, and today, under the blue sky, the red caravan with all the handles to the doors highly polished was a fine sight. Benjie, his hat cocked on one side, a late rosebud in his buttonhole, was a throw-back, as he himself had observed, to Britannia seated on her throne in the old circus processions.

'You know, Holly,' he said, 'two hundred years ago on a dark night a very wicked ancestor of mine rode out into Borrowdale just as we're doing.'

He was thinking a lot about Francis Herries just then, for a fortnight ago he had read Judith's book once again right through. Times weren't so good, with investments down as they were. It was true that now that Sally was settled his needs were small, but he had wondered whether, after all, Judith's book mightn't be worth publishing. After reading it he decided that it would be sacrilege. But the whole world of that book was very present to him. When you were as old as he was time vanished and had no meaning.

Holly had no interest whatever in the Herries family, but he
was interested in scandal.

'What way was he wicked?' he asked.

'Oh, the usual way.'

'Wine, women and song! Oh, boy!' said Holly.

'There's no need to be American, John,' Benjie remarked.
'They're fine people and their own language suits them, but
you're English.'

'You bet,' Holly said. 'No damned foreigners for me.'

When they reached the Ashness gate Benjie made him pull up.
He got out and looked across the Lake. There was not a ripple on
the water, which was coloured so faintly blue that it was almost
white, to the Manesty bank. Here the trees, the chesnuts, the
maples, the larches flamed on the water's edge. They seemed in
actual fact to be burning. You might fancy that, across the still
water, you heard the branches crackle in the blaze. From the
darkest crimson, through amber, orange, the rich yellow of a
canary's wing, to the faint gold pallor of Chinese lacquer, they
were massed against the red cloud of bracken that covered the
fell. To the right the cloud that had been a bird's nest on Skiddaw had grown until it enveloped the peaks in a tumbled mass
that glittered like frozen snow. There was no sound nor breath of
stirring.

'It's a fine day,' he said, climbing back beside Holly.

'And it'll rain tomorrow, I bet you,' said Holly.

With every yard of ground – past the Lodore Hotel, the Borrowdale, Grange Bridge, the Bowder Stone, down the hill into
the valley – Benjie's spirits rose. The outer world slipped behind
them. The old valley was still shut in even as in ancient days,
when its citizens had, as the legend went, tried to build a wall to
enclose the cuckoo. Glaramara and Grey Knotts and Brandreth
were the advance guard; Gable, Scafell, Great End, Bowfell were
still guardians at the close, as for so many hundreds of years they
had been. The valley was as still as the Lake had been, and above
the green fields, to the right at the side of the streams, the leaves
in orange and crimson lifted their glory to the blue.

'Where are we going?' asked Holly. 'Does this valley lead to
anywhere?'

'No. It does not. We're stopping for the night near the place
where that same ancestor of mine built a house.'

'Kind of lost sort of place, this valley,' said Holly.

Where the path leads off the high road up to Watendlath they halted. Here there was a little stone bridge that crossed a stream flecked now with the blue of the sky, and just above it was a solid little stone house.

'Is that the place your ancestor built?'

'No. That's not the house, but it's the spot. Two ladies lived there, but now it's sold. There's nobody in it, I fancy, just now.'

After some trouble they found a spot on the level below the house where the caravan could remain.

When they were settled Benjie lit a pipe, and taking with him that day's *Times* which he had procured in Keswick, Judith's book at which he thought he would have another look, and Casson's *Wise Kings of Borrowdale* (an old friend of his that he had not seen for many a year but had found today in Chaplin's shop), he seated himself comfortably on the step of the caravan while Sam pursued idyllic scents on the border of the stream.

He had only to raise his eyes, he reflected, and there was old Rogue Herries riding up the path with the little boy in his arms ... The boy runs forward and flings open the door ...

He opened Judith's book at the beginning and read:

'I, Judith Paris, was born at Rosthwaite in the valley of Borrowdale, Cumberland, on the 28th of November in the Year of Our Lord 1774 ...' He skipped a little, but old Aunt Jane's feminine mid-Victorian hand was wonderfully clear. 'I have heard very much of what happened in those long-ago times from my half-brother David Herries. David Herries was my father's son by his first wife, and he was fifty-five when I was born, so that I could have been his granddaughter ... He told me that he remembered exactly the night that he first arrived in Keswick. He could remember every detail, and so do I, even at this distance of time. How he was in the inn at Keswick in a big canopied bed with his sisters Mary and Deborah. The canopy that ran round the top of the bed was a faded green and had a gold thread in it. There were fire-dogs by the fire with mouths like grinning dragons. And he remembered that a woman was sitting warming herself in front of the fire, a woman he hated. Then his father came in and thought he was sleeping. He remembered that his father was wearing a beautiful coat of claret colour and a chestnut wig, and there were red roses on his grey silk waistcoat ...'

Benjie skipped a page or two. He came to the ride through Borrowdale. 'David was wide awake now and knew that his father was happily drunk. He sang a song that was popular with children then. David had played it as a game:

'*Lady Queen Anne who sits in her stand,*
And a pair of green gloves upon her hand.
As white as a lily, as fair as a swan,
The fairest lady in a' the land.

'They rode on and suddenly the clouds broke and a moon sailed out and the sky was covered with stars. Then they moved up the little hill and it was all very quiet. It all seemed very wonderful to David, who had never seen mountains before, and of course they were very large in the moonlight.

'Then they stopped and someone said:

' "That is the house on the left of us."

'They went on through a thick group of trees and now they were outside a rough stone wall guarding a courtyard where grass was growing. David remembered that he was sadly disappointed in his first view of the house, for it looked so small under the hill. Then some dogs ran out, barking, and his father put him to the ground and he ran forward and was first into the house. In the hall, which through the open door was moonlit, he saw two shining suits of armour . . .'

'It's all very vivid,' thought Benjie; 'if I try hard enough I can see it just as it was and the boy running across the courtyard.' The air was so still that it was not difficult to fancy that there were figures standing listening, and that the old house was still there with the moon shining in on the suits of armour.

The fresh air made him feel sleepy. The past was so much more real to him than the present, as it is perhaps to all old people. The things that the two men had discussed at luncheon were dim and shadowy.

'It may be,' he thought, 'that it is only when you are old that you see things in their true perspective. The world seems to be crumbling but it has crumbled so often before, changing into a new shape that will appear as solid to another generation as its earlier form seemed to the older people. But I'm no philosopher. I've been better at doing things than thinking them.' And his life crowded up into his consciousness, all of it moving at the same time. He was with Barney and Ellis at the music hall and a lady gave him a white rose, he asked Vanessa to marry him in the moonlight in the Fortress garden, he wrestled with Endicott; once again, misery at his heart, he told Vanessa that he was married, and once again he stood by the Chinese clock while Ellis shouted at them from below; he was in Newlands and there came the most wonderful moment of his life when Vanessa, brushing her hair, turned and looked at him . . .

He would go no further. But how strange that all these things should be still so alive and other things that had nothing to do with his heart – Africa and Spain and (the greatest moment in his life apart from Vanessa) the sunlit day in Petrograd when they had marched, singing, into the new world. Why, he thought, were the only things that counted in a man's life, when you looked back, the things that touched his spirit – if he had one?

Was it true, as Vanessa believed, that there was a secret life, progressive, unceasing, all-important?

Holly had come to the caravan door, a frying-pan in his hand. 'John, do you think there's a secret life?'

'Will you have your eggs scrambled or fried?' John asked, disregarding, as he so often did, Benjie's mad way of asking questions that meant nothing.

Benjie turned back to the scene. It was growing cold. As fire dies into ash so the sky was fading into grey. He was very happy. His memories and this country made him so.

He opened Casson's thin green book, but could scarcely see to read.

> *I bid ye mourn not for the death of beauty.*
> *For, though the Springtide fades from Cumberland,*
> *Her streams and tarns, there is eternal spring*
> *In heaven. And, on my island where I live,*
> *I dream that heaven is very like this land,*
> *Mountains and lakes and rivers undecaying,*
> *And simple woodlands and wild cherry flowers.*
> *At least I know no better. But weep not.*
> *For, though this land is but the shadow of heaven,*
> *It yet is heaven's shadow.*

He was almost asleep. His pipe fell from his hand. It was so small a country – this green valley, up the Pass into the hollow guarded by Gable, and the Scafells with dark Wastwater to one side, lonely Ennerdale to another, Eskdale, and, to the south the Pikes and Langdale, Esthwaite and Windermere and Coniston. One turn of the hand to the north, and in close company Grasmere and Rydal, Ullswater, and so, towards the Border, Derwentwater, Buttermere, Crummock . . . a land that the sweep of a bird might in a flash of the sun cover with its shadow. England itself, from these little hills and lakes, through the dark space of the Midlands, in a moment of time, over field and stream and sloping hill to the sea ...

The Eagle's wing embraced it. The White Horse, striking upward from the dark water, climbed the icy hill. The Eagle free, the White Horse triumphant, the same Eagle, the same Horse as in captivity, now lost themselves in a larger liberty, in a purpose far grander than their individual struggle ...

Was he asleep? He thought he heard Holly's voice:

'You'll get cold out there. Supper's nearly ready.'

But he rested his head against the upper step. He sighed with happiness because all the struggle was over. No one was afraid any longer. Vanessa was all right. Tom was all right. Sally, who knew no fear, was building the new world. And he himself was at home where he had always wanted to be.

He turned his head, smiling, and sleepily murmured, as in the past he had so often done:

'Goodnight, Vanessa.'

Over this country, when the giant Eagle flings the shadow of his wing, the land is darkened. So compact is it that the wing covers all its extent in one pause of the flight. The sea breaks on the pale line of the shore; to the Eagle's proud glance waves run in to the foot of the hills that are like rocks planted in green water.

From Whinlatter to Black Combe the clouds are never still. The Tarns like black unwinking eyes watch their chase, and the colours are laid out in patterns on the rocks and are continually changed. The Eagle can see the shadows rise from their knees at the base of Scafell and Gable, he can see the black precipitous flanks of the Screes washed with rain and the dark purple hummocks of Borrowdale crags flash suddenly with gold.

So small is the extent of this country that the sweep of the Eagle's wing caresses all of it, but there is no ground in the world more mysterious, no land at once so bare in its nakedness and so rich in its luxury, so warm with sun and so cold in pitiless rain, so gentle and pastoral, so wild and lonely; with sea and lake and river there is always the sound of moving water, and its strong people have their feet in the soil and are independent of all men.

During the flight of the Eagle two hundred years are but as a day – and the life of a man, as against all odds he pushes towards immortality, is eternal ...